Brides of Bonneterre Trilogy

BRIDES OF BONNETERRE TRILOGY

KAYE DACUS

ISBN 978-1-61626-220-4

Published by Barbour Publishing, Inc., P.O. Box 719, Uhrichsville, Ohio 44683, www.barbourbooks.com

Our mission is to publish and distribute inspirational products offering exceptional value and biblical encouragement to the masses.

Printed in the United States of America.

Stand-In Groom

Dedication

To my two most loyal readers, Mom and Mamie; and my hero, Daddy. Thanks for believing in me even when I didn't believe in myself.

Acknowledgments

This book is the product of more than four years of work, and it would be impossible to acknowledge everyone who's had a hand in it. Special recognition goes to my two grad school mentors, Leslie Davis Guccione and Barbara Miller, who shaped my writing and guided me through the revision process; and to my agent, Chip MacGregor, for working so hard and patiently to help me get it published.

Chapter 1

Nothing like running late to make a wonderful first impression.

Anne Hawthorne left a voice-mail message for her blind date, explaining her tardiness, then crossed her office to the gilt-framed mirror that reflected the view of Town Square through the front windows. At a buzzing jolt against her waist, she flinched, smearing her lipstick.

Great.

The vibrating cell phone chimed out a wedding march. A client. She reached for a tissue to repair her mouth while flipping the phone open with her left hand. "Happy Endings, Inc. This is Anne Hawthorne."

"I can't do it! I can't marry him!" Third call today.

Why had she agreed to be set up on a date the Thursday of a wedding week? If it were just the regular weekly dinner with her cousins, she could skip out and get some work done. "Calm down," she said to her client. "Take a deep breath. And another. Let it out slowly. Now, tell me what happened."

Fifteen minutes later, still on the phone, she pulled her dark green Chrysler Sebring convertible into a parking space in front of Palermo's Italian Grill. She sat in the car a few minutes—air conditioner running full blast—and listened to the rest of her client's story.

When the girl paused to breathe, Anne leaped at her chance. "I completely understand your concern. But sweetie, you have to remember most men aren't interested in the minute details of a wedding. Just because he doesn't care if the roses are white variegated with pink or solid pink, don't take that to mean he doesn't love you anymore. Which ones do you like the best?"

"The variegated roses," the bride-to-be sniffled into the phone.

Anne turned off the engine and got out of the car. The heat and humidity typical for the first day of June in central Louisiana wrapped her in a sweaty embrace. "Then get the flowers you like. He will be happy because you're happy. Do you want me to call the florist in the morning?" One more change the day before the wedding. Saturday couldn't come fast enough.

"Do you mind?"

"That's what I'm here for." She opened her planner and made a note at the top of the two-page spread for tomorrow. "Feeling better?"

"Yeah. Thanks, Miss Anne. I've got to call Jared and apologize."

"See y'all tomorrow." Anne made sure her phone was set to vibrate-only mode and entered the most popular new restaurant in Bonneterre. Maybe she should have left the planner in the car, but she would have felt naked, incomplete, without it.

The heavenly aroma of garlic, basil, and oregano mixed with the unmistakable yeasty scent of fresh bread and wafted on the cool air that blew in her face when she opened the door. Her salivary glands kicked into overdrive, and her stomach growled. She really needed to stop skipping lunch.

Winding through the crowd of patrons awaiting tables, Anne scanned faces for the man her cousin Jenn had been *absolutely dying* to set her up with for months. She'd made a point of watching the local news broadcast on Channel Six last night so she'd know what he looked like. Her right heel skidded on the slatelike tile and she wobbled, her foot sliding half out of the black mule. Anne hated shoes that didn't stay on her feet of their own accord, but they were fashionable. She righted herself and arrived without further incident at the hostess station.

"Miss Anne!" A young woman in a white tuxedo shirt and black slacks came out from behind the high, dark wood stand and threw her arms around Anne's waist.

She recognized the girl as a bridesmaid in a wedding she'd coordinated just a month or so ago. What was her name? "Hey, sweetie! It's so good to see you. How are you?"

The bubbly brunette stepped back. "I'm great. I'll be getting my degree in August, and I already have job offers from advertising agencies in Baton Rouge and Houston."

Anne smiled, remembering the girl in a pewter, floor-length straight skirt with a corset-style bodice. The bride had let each of the girls choose which style top they were most comfortable in. Gray bridesmaids' dresses. Purple and lavender florals and bunting. The Garrity-LaTrobe wedding. Six female attendants. Of course! "How exciting. Congratulations, Carrie."

"Thanks. Are you meeting someone here?"

"I am, but I don't see him. The reservation was for seven fifteen under my name."

The girl ran her french-manicured acrylic nails down the waiting list and stopped at a crossed-out line. "Here you are. They were getting ready to reassign your table, so you got here just in time. Follow me, please."

Walking through the packed restaurant behind the slender, petite young woman, Anne tried not to feel self-conscious. At nearly six feet tall and doing well to keep herself fitting into a size eighteen, she hated to imagine what others thought when they compared her to someone like this little hostess—five foot fourish with a waist so small she could probably wear Anne's gold filigree anklet as a belt. When working, Anne rarely thought about her stature or size. In public, though, all the comments and teasing she'd received when she'd reached her full height at age thirteen rushed back into her memory. If only she'd had some athletic ability, she might have been popular and not fallen for a man who'd strung her along until he didn't need her anymore.

"Here we are." Carrie gave a bedimpled grin and bounced away.

"Thank you." Anne chose the chair facing the entry and set her purse on the floor and her planner on the table. She glanced at her watch again. Seven thirty on the nose. Surely her date wouldn't have given up waiting on her after only fifteen minutes.

"Still waiting on someone?" The young waiter—probably a student at the Bonneterre branch of the University of Louisiana—handed her a thick, faux leather–bound menu.

Not that I want to be. "Yes. He's probably just running a little late."

"Can I go ahead and get you something to drink while you wait?"

"Sprite with a cherry and twist of lime, please. Are Mr. and Mrs. Palermo here tonight?"

"Yes, ma'am, I believe the owners are here. Is anything wrong?" Worry etched the young face.

She gave him the reassuring smile she'd perfected over the years of working with nervous brides and frantic mothers of the bride. "No. I'd like to discuss planning a few events with them. But only if they have time. If they're busy, I can come back early next week."

His relief obvious, he grinned and nodded. "Yes, ma'am. And I'll be right back with your cherry-lime Sprite."

She turned her attention to the menu, pleased to see the broad range of selections.

The waiter returned with her soda. "Here you are. Can I get you an appetizer while you wait?"

She probably shouldn't, but—"I'd like the fried calamari and crawfish tails, please, with the cayenne-Parmesan dipping sauce."

"Excellent choice. My favorite."

She listened to the specials, making a mental note of the eggplant roulade—"Fried or grilled rounds of eggplant smothered in a spicy cream sauce with crawfish, bacon, and fresh spinach"—and the jambalaya alfredo—"With chicken, andouille, and traditional Cajun seasonings in the cream sauce."

"I'll be back with your appetizer in a little bit." He glanced at the still-empty chair across from her but didn't comment before walking away.

Anne set the menu aside and zipped open her camel-colored leather planner. Taking out a legal pad and pen, she reviewed her notes all over the two-page spread for today and the notes for tomorrow, then wrote out a to-do list of what she still needed to accomplish before her eight o'clock meeting with the bride, groom, and minister in the morning.

"Anne Hawthorne?"

She looked up at the voice and stood to hug former clients. She chatted with the couple for a few minutes before they continued on to their table.

Anne had just regained her seat when another former client came over. Anne hugged the young woman around the bulge of her pregnancy as she asked Anne to plan her baby shower. They looked at Anne's calendar and set an appointment to discuss ideas and dates.

The waiter returned with the calamari and crawfish tails and eyed the empty place as he set the dish on the table. "Do you want to wait until your companion arrives before you order?"

Maybe she should call to see what was going on. "Give me a few minutes?"

He nodded. "Enjoy the calamari."

"Thanks."

"Sure."

Grabbing her purse but leaving the planner on the table, Anne crossed the restaurant to the quieter lobby area outside the restrooms. She dialed and pressed the small cell phone to her ear.

Without ringing once, his voice mail picked up. His outgoing message gave his office phone number, which she repeated in her head while waiting for the tone. "Hi, this is Anne Hawthorne. It's. . . a little after eight, and I've been at the restaurant for a while and just wanted to see when you think you might be getting here." She left her number and disconnected, then called his office phone, which rolled into voice mail after three rings. Rather than leave another message, when given the option, she hit the number 0. After a couple of clicks and an ad for the TV station, someone picked up.

"KCAN newsroom. How may I help you?"

"Hi, I'm trying to get in touch with Danny Mendoza."

"Is this Anne Hawthorne?" the female on the other end asked.

Frowning, Anne started to pace. "Yes."

"I'm so sorry I didn't have time to call you before now. Danny got called in on a breaking news assignment and will be out in the field for the rest of the evening. He asked me to let you know he wouldn't be able to meet you but that he would call you tomorrow."

She squeezed her eyes closed and rubbed her forehead. "Thanks for letting me know. If you talk to him again this evening, tell him—" What? *Thanks for standing me up?* "Never mind. I'll just leave a message on his cell phone."

"Okay. Listen, I'm really sorry I didn't have time to call you."

"Don't worry about it." Anne ended the call, hooked the phone back on her waistband, and returned to her table. The aroma from the fried squid and crawfish on the plate in front of her tantalized her taste buds.

"Any word?" The waiter returned and tipped his head at the empty chair.

"Yes. He got called in to work so won't be coming."

"Oh. I'm sorry. Do you want me to box this up for you?"

"If you could bring me a box, that would be great, because I'll never be able to eat all this and a meal, too."

"You mean—you're going to stay?"

Anne tried not to laugh at his surprised expression. "Of course. I've been waiting to eat here for a month. I'm going to have the eggplant roulade—with the eggplant grilled instead of fried."

"Yes, ma'am. I'll go place your order now and bring you another drink."

"Don't forget the box for this." Anne served a few pieces of crawfish and calamari onto the small appetizer plate. Jenn always liked Anne to bring home leftovers after dining out, to see what other restaurants were doing.

At the thought of her restaurateur cousin, Anne shook her head. This was the third time Jenn had set Anne up on a blind date and the third time it hadn't worked out. Jenn had a habit of setting Anne up with men of Jenn's taste rather than Anne's type. At five foot six, Jenn didn't have to worry about towering over her dates. Five inches taller, however, Anne wanted to date someone who was at least six feet tall so she didn't feel like quite such an Amazon beside him. But it seemed as though *tall*, single Christian men over the age of thirty were hard to come by.

Of course, every man Anne had gone out with in the past who had matched her ideal of the Perfect Man had ended up being Perfectly Wrong for her. Maybe she needed to stop focusing on the physical type and just get out and have fun meeting new people.

She spent her life making others' dreams come true. Well, it was time for Anne Hawthorne, wedding and event planner extraordinaire, to start creating her own happy ending.

George Laurence perused the menu, surprised to find the wide variety of dishes listed. His experience with Italian restaurants in midsized American cities primed him to expect spaghetti, lasagna, and fettuccini. So far, Palermo's Italian Grill in Bonneterre, Louisiana, appeared promising.

"So, George, where do you hail from in England?" Across the table, his employer's local lawyer shook out the folded fabric napkin and laid it in his lap.

George closed the menu. "I spent my childhood in London. My late teens and early twenties in Edinburgh."

"University of Edinburgh, huh? Heard that's a great school." Forbes Guidry handed his menu to the waitress and placed his order.

George considered his response as he ordered crawfish-stuffed manicotti. He'd wanted to live in America because he'd always heard that people weren't judged by their family background, wealth, or education. After five years of working for one of the wealthiest people in the country, he'd learned otherwise. The social prejudices in England and America differed but still existed. When most Americans found out he'd never attended college, they made assumptions about his intelligence and ranked him lower in their estimation.

He handed his menu to the server and returned his attention to the lawyer. "I wouldn't know about the university. I never had the opportunity to attend. I started working when I was sixteen." First, there would be an awkward silence, then a mumbled apology—

"I'm impressed." Forbes took a sip of his water, seeming unflustered. "Just from talking on the phone this afternoon, I would have guessed you had at least a master's degree if not a PhD."

George opened his mouth, but nothing came out. No one had ever given him such a compliment. Although, he had heard lawyers in Louisiana weren't to be trusted. Was this man, with his tailored suit, expensive haircut and manicure, and impeccable manners, just one of those Artful Dodgers who could charm his way out of any situation? Or was he as genuine as his Southern accent and friendly demeanor indicated? George hoped for the latter. He'd never pretended to be someone else before and needed an ally, someone who knew his true purpose and identity.

"Thank you." No other response came to mind. Instead of putting on false modesty or being arrogant by focusing on his own merits, George returned to a previous conversation. "You said a housekeeper has been hired?"

"Yes, but since no one's been in residence, she just goes by every so often to dust and let the exterminators in, that kind of thing. The house was built like a typical English manor, or so I'm told. There are two bedroom suites in the basement beside the service kitchen. I figured you'd take one and Mrs. Agee would take the other. Now, to business." Forbes reached under the table and retrieved a document from his briefcase.

The document. The addendum to George's work contract—the contract he'd never wanted to sign in the first place. The rules by which he would have to live his life while in this quaint Southern city. He clenched his fists under the table. If keeping his work visa didn't depend on this. . .

"I assume your employer discussed the details of the addendum with you." Forbes handed the contract across the table.

George nodded, guilt clenching his gut. "Yes."

"As his legal representative, it is my responsibility to remind you of the confidentiality clause. Should you reveal to anyone, including the wedding planner, the identity of your employer or that you are not Courtney Landry's fiancé, your employment will be terminated. As you know, if you lose your job, you will be in violation of your work visa and must return to England."

The only reason why George had agreed to this charade. "Yes, I understand."

"Take it with you and read over it tonight. Any questions you have can be discussed when we meet tomorrow at ten."

George tucked the document into his own attaché case. "Very good."

"Whew. Now that that's over, we can enjoy our dinner."

"Yes, indeed." George needed a neutral topic to have time to take his mind off the fact that he was about to spend the next five weeks living a falsehood. He still hadn't figured out how to do it and maintain his Christian values. "Have you lived in Bonneterre all your life, Forbes?"

Over the salad course, the lawyer talked about Bonneterre as it had been during his childhood. George consciously made eye contact every fifteen or twenty seconds while also looking around the restaurant decorated to resemble a Tuscan villa.

Movement at a nearby table caught his attention. A waiter stopped, two fancy desserts perched precariously on his tray. With great ceremony and flourish, he placed the sweet delights on the table.

What was it about the patron that made him stand out? The fork in the young man's hand trembled, and he never took his gaze off his pretty companion. Neither could be much older than twenty. The lass took a couple of bites of the chocolate confection, but her fork stopped when she went for the third. She frowned, then dug something out. A small box. A few moments later, she let out a high-pitched gasp and threw her arms around her beau's neck. The lad dropped to one knee, and the crowd broke into applause.

George hoped the two young people had given this decision prayerful consideration. He hadn't been much older than the newly engaged couple when he'd prepared to propose to his first love. Praise God he'd learned her true nature before making a complete fool of himself.

Forbes clapped with enthusiasm. "Good for them."

"Are you married, Forbes?"

The lawyer held up his left hand and wiggled the empty third finger. "No. Don't know if I ever will be, either."

George sat back, surprised.

Forbes laughed. "Now, before you go getting the wrong idea about me, let me explain. I don't know if I'll ever find a woman my sisters and mother will find suitable for me. They've been trying for years. But the ones they like, I can't stand."

"And the ones you like?" George raised his brows.

"Humph. That's the problem. I can't even find one to bring home for them not to like." He sighed. "I suppose when God's ready for me to fall in love, He'll throw the right woman into my path."

"Hopefully you won't be driving at the time." George kept his expression serious.

Forbes blinked, then threw his head back in laughter, drawing the admiring gazes of several nearby female diners.

The waitress arrived with their meals. George glanced at the proposal-couple's table. A woman in an aubergine suit knelt between the two, listening to the animated young woman, her focus earnest and interested. Her blond hair was caught up in a french twist, and even from this distance, he could see a sparkle in her electric blue eyes. Everything about her—from her smile to the way she put herself below the level of the young couple—bespoke someone who put others before herself. The kind of woman he'd always dreamed of finding.

"George?" A frown etched Forbes's celebrity-caliber face.

George nodded his head toward the beautiful woman still kneeling beside the other table. "Who do you suppose that is?"

"Well, well, well. I knew she had other plans tonight; I just never imagined. . ." Forbes's smile took on a warmth usually reserved for a man's mother, wife, or sisters—or sweetheart. "She's a professional wedding planner. Right now, she's listening to all the young woman's childhood dreams of what her wedding should be like. When she meets with them in her office sometime next week—and don't worry, they'll be there—she'll already have a preliminary budget worked out."

George's heart sank at the woman's title. "Wedding planner? Is she—?"

"She is. She's going back to her table now." Forbes leaned to his left to watch her progress over George's shoulder. "If I can catch her before she leaves, I'll introduce you."

George nodded, keeping his turmoil under tight control. This would have been a lot easier if she'd turned out to be some old, grandmotherly type. How would he ever convince this wedding planner he was the bridegroom when he found her so utterly attractive? *God, what have I gotten myself into?*

Chapter 2

As soon as she returned to her table, Anne wrote down all the details of her conversation with the potential new clients. Of course, if they really wanted to get married in three or four months, she might not be able to take them on. Her schedule was so full now she rarely got more than four or five hours of sleep every night of the week. Just about the only remnants of her personal life she hadn't given up were church, Sunday dinners with the entire extended family, and Thursday night dinners out at Jenn's restaurant with the cousins.

In five years, her business had gone from operating out of the second bedroom of her apartment to allowing her to lease a storefront on Town Square. Six months ago, she'd purchased the Victorian-turned-triplex, where she'd lived in the second-floor apartment for nearly five years. Never in her wildest dreams had she imagined she'd be so successful. Of course, the article about her in *Southern Bride* back in January had helped.

Satisfied vindication filled her. Her ex-fiancé might have taken her for all she was worth ten years ago, but she'd still been able to get out of debt and make something of herself.

Good grief. Why did she still feel she had something to prove to *him*? Just because she'd supported him until he'd become a mega-movie star whose photo graced the front cover of every gossip magazine and tabloid known to man. Just because she'd dropped out of graduate school to go to work full-time to be able to send him rent money out in Los Angeles—

"Here you go."

She jumped at the sound of the waiter's voice and quickly closed her planner and put it on the floor. "Thank you. It looks wonderful."

"Enjoy."

Pushing aside the memories of her first and worst relationship, Anne determined to enjoy her meal and not let the past interfere with the present. The only thing she could do was make sure she never let another man use her and dump her again. She deserved better.

As she savored each bite of the eggplant roulade, she let her gaze wander across the restaurant to make sure she didn't miss seeing or speaking to anyone else she knew. Casual conversations with acquaintances could turn into referrals. At the sight of her cousin Forbes, with his dark good looks, halfway across the room, she paused. Women young and old turned to cast admiring glances in his direction.

Who was he with? Seated, the other man appeared to be about the same height as Forbes with a more slender but still athletic build, while his slightly too-large nose and sharp chin gave him a distinct profile.

Something stirred inside Anne that she hadn't felt in a long time—interest. He wasn't conventionally handsome—nothing compared to her cousin—but the way his sharp features softened when he smiled at the waitress created a tingling sensation in her stomach that she hadn't felt since high school. He had medium-brown hair but looked like he was graying a bit at the temples, adding a distinguished air. She should go over and speak to Forbes so she could meet this handsome stranger. But if they hadn't tried setting her up with him, he might be married—

"Is everything okay with your dinner?" The waiter replaced her half-full glass of soda with a fresh one.

"It's lovely, thank you. My compliments to the chef. There's just no way I can eat such a generous serving in one sitting."

"I understand. Can I get you another box?"

"Yes, please. And if you can go ahead and bring my check, I'd appreciate it."

"Yes, ma'am. Can I interest you in a dessert to go? Tiramisu, maybe?"

She smiled and shook her head. "I'll have to pass."

In a few minutes, she boxed up the remaining half of her meal, all the while keeping tabs on Forbes's table to make sure they didn't leave before she managed to get over there or catch his eye. She left enough cash in the black folder with the receipt to cover a generous tip and picked up her purse, planner, and to-go boxes.

She crossed the room, stopping twice to speak to acquaintances and see baby pictures or leave a few business cards for any newly engaged couples they might know. Keeping her attention anywhere but on the handsome stranger proved difficult. She must learn his identity.

When she drew near, Forbes glanced in her direction. "Here's someone you should meet," he said to his dinner companion. Forbes stood to draw her into a hug, his grin creasing the corners of his grayish blue eyes.

"Hey. I didn't want to interrupt, but I couldn't just leave without stopping to speak to you." She turned and smiled at the stranger, who'd also stood. He was a couple of inches taller than she, but more slender than the men she usually found attractive. She gazed into eyes the color of light-roast cinnamon hazelnut coffee, and her heart fluttered. Fluttered! Like some addlepated schoolgirl.

She regained control of her senses and extended her right hand. "Good evening. I'm Anne Hawthorne."

His grasp was firm, his skin soft. He worked indoors, probably at the law firm with Forbes. Then why hadn't she met him at the office Christmas party?

"George Laurence, ma'am, at your service."

Tingles danced up and down her spine. A British accent! She'd always dreamed of marrying a man with a British accent.

Get ahold of yourself, girl! You're thirty-five years old, not some starry-eyed teenager. "It's very nice to meet you, Mr. Laurence. So how do you know Forbes?"

The Englishman cleared his throat and looked at her cousin. She frowned.

Forbes rested his hand on her shoulder. "George. . .represents someone I work with."

Hopefully he wasn't in town briefly for a trial or something like that. "So you're a lawyer, too, Mr. Laurence?"

"Not exactly." Had he grimaced? Frowned? Grinned? The expression was there and gone before she could be certain.

"It's complicated, Anne." Forbes squeezed her shoulder. "I thought you were waiting on someone, or we would have asked you to join us. How was your dinner, by the way?"

Okay, obviously this guy was working on some case that was so confidential they couldn't even discuss it in front of her. "The food was great. I hadn't planned on eating alone tonight, but you know, 'the best-laid plans. . .' " Her cheeks burned as she was conscious of George Laurence standing next to her. Time to try to make a graceful exit. "Well, I'd best be going. As I said, I didn't want to interrupt."

"George, if you'll excuse me for a minute, I'd like to walk Anne out to her car." Forbes herded her toward the front door, stopping with alacrity, although only for a moment, when a family acquaintance recognized them. On the way past the hostess stand, Anne took one more peek at George Laurence, now sitting by himself at the table. Handsome, British, and at least six foot two.

She bit her bottom lip to contain her grin and braced herself for the heat as the air-conditioning chased them out the door. "Why haven't I ever met him before?"

"Because he just arrived in town today." Forbes tucked her left hand under the crook of his elbow, then took her food boxes and planner. "All kidding aside, what happened with your date, Annie?"

"I don't know. I was running a few minutes late, and when I arrived, he wasn't here. After I'd been here awhile, I called to check to see when he was coming, and some gal at his office told me he'd gotten called in for a breaking news story. So I had dinner by myself—" Her left heel caught in a crack in the cement parking lot and the shoe twisted out from under her. Thank goodness for Forbes's supporting arm, or she would have fallen face-first onto the pavement—which would have been a fitting end to a night like this.

"Maybe it just wasn't meant to be."

"He left word that he'd call me tomorrow." She stopped at her car, pressing the unlock button on her key-fob remote, and took her food and planner from her cousin. Forbes opened the door for her, and she ducked in to set her things atop a stack of files on the passenger seat. She narrowly missed hitting her head on the door frame as she stood. "Of course, I can't imagine why he'd rather go out with me and not with Jenn."

Forbes placed his hands on her cheeks and pulled her close to kiss her forehead. "Because you are a beautiful and interesting woman, Anne. Any man would be lucky to have you. If we weren't related—" He waggled his well-groomed eyebrows.

She groaned. "Forbes! I really wish you'd stop saying that. It's bad enough that half your coworkers think I'm your wife because you take me to every office party." If they weren't related, he'd never have given her a second glance. Not someone as good looking and popular as he'd always been. Of course, she had somehow been noticed by—

No. She'd already determined not to think about that tonight. That part of her life was long over and done with. "Tell me about this George guy."

"He's not for you, Anne."

"I didn't notice a wedding ring."

"No." Forbes ran his fingers through his short, dark auburn hair.

She narrowed her eyes and crossed her arms. Forbes never

touched his hair for fear of messing it up.

"Just take my word for it. He's—not available."

"Oh, so he's—" She stopped when he pressed his fingers to her lips.

"Not available. Leave it at that, please?" He kissed her forehead again. "Now, go home and get some rest. I'm sure you have a very busy day tomorrow."

"Rest?" She kept from snorting as a rueful laugh escaped, but just barely. "Do you see the stack of file folders on the passenger seat? It's a wedding weekend, honey. I wouldn't have taken the time to do more than pick something up at Rotier's on my way home tonight if Jenn hadn't insisted I go out with—" She snapped her fingers, her mind drawing a blank on her no-show date's name.

"Danny?" Forbes prompted.

"Yes. With Danny." She opened the car door. "Oh, and Forbes?"

"Yes?"

"Should your friend George ever become not *not available*, you'll let me know, right?"

"You'll definitely be the first person I'll tell. Good night, Anne."

She waved as he walked away, then got in the car and put the top down to enjoy the evening air.

Whatever Forbes meant by "not available," God hadn't let her cross paths with George Laurence for no reason. For the first time in her life, she wasn't just going to take Forbes's word.

George sipped his water. *Anne Hawthorne*. Something about her just wouldn't let him be. She was pretty, yes. Tall for a woman, with a striking figure as well. But he'd met hundreds, perhaps thousands of beautiful women in his life. No, it was something in the expression of her eyes—something real that he wasn't used to seeing.

Setting his goblet back on the table, he took a deep breath and blew it out. *Lord, how did I get rooked into this scheme? I only signed the first contract five years ago because it ensured me a work visa and job security. This is the first time since then I've truly resented anything my employer has asked me to do. How can I live a life pleasing to You if I'm practicing deception? Yet how can I refuse when it means going back to England? If You can just get me through the next seventeen months until I can apply for citizenship—*

The chair across the table scraped against the ceramic tiles. George conjured a smile for Forbes. How did this man know Anne Hawthorne?

"Sorry about that. Dessert?"

George declined. "You know the wedding planner well, then?"

"The—Anne? Yes, I've known her all my life. She's my cousin."

His cousin. George kept his grin in check. Whether she was his cousin or his sweetheart shouldn't matter. She was still beyond his reach. The contract addendum litigated that. Maybe once his employer revealed the truth at the engagement party. . .

But by then, George would have been lying to this woman for more than a month. She would hate him, and her hatred would be well deserved. By then, he would probably hate himself as well.

To keep from dwelling on such thoughts, he turned his attention to his dinner companion. "When will the plumbing be repaired so Mrs. Agee and I can move into the house?"

"A few days more—probably next Monday or Tuesday. When does Miss Landry arrive?"

"Sunday evening. She has planned to lodge with a childhood friend while in town."

"Good." Forbes folded his napkin and laid it beside his empty plate. "Although it's not generally known who owns the house, it's better if she is seen only with and around people she's known all her life. Less suspicion will be raised that way."

"Would it be better if I stayed elsewhere?" Although he loathed the idea of spending the next five weeks in a hotel, better that than reveal his employer's secret before the time of his employer's choosing.

"No. I think you'll be fine staying out there. The rumor around town is that the property was purchased by a wealthy out-of-towner, and you'll serve as the mysterious, eccentric new owner for the time being."

"Does Mrs. Agee know—?"

"Who her real employer is? No. She signed a contract with a confidentiality clause, but we felt at this time she didn't have a need to know. When the time is right, she'll be informed."

George nodded at the waitress to take his dinner plate and waved off the dessert menu. "And Ms. Hawthorne? If she were to sign a confidentiality agreement?"

"No." Forbes's expression became courtroom-caliber serious. "She is not to be told until the day of the engagement party. I don't—she doesn't need to know you aren't Courtney Landry's fiancé. Of course, that means you will have to handle some details yourself."

Some details? George nearly laughed at the understatement. How was Anne Hawthorne supposed to pull together an engagement party when seeing the invite list might tip her off as to the true identity of her client? And what about the invitation itself? It couldn't have the name George Laurence on it. He'd have to do that, too. The more he thought about the event, the more tasks he discovered would fall to him to accomplish.

At least the next few weeks wouldn't be boring.

As she climbed the back stairs to her apartment, Anne juggled her duffel bag, attaché case, purse, stack of files, and the cup of gourmet coffee she'd stopped for on the way home. As soon as she dropped everything but the coffee cup on the kitchen table, she realized she'd left the food in the car.

She jogged back downstairs, retrieved it, and went up to the apartment on the third floor where, as she expected, the door was unlocked. In the dark kitchen, she found a grease pencil in a junk drawer, wrote a note on the lid of the top Styrofoam box, and put them both in Jenn's refrigerator.

Back in her own apartment, she turned on the computer in the guest bedroom, started the music media software, and filled the apartment with the dulcet tones of crooners such as Frank Sinatra, Ella Fitzgerald, Bing Crosby, Kay Starr, and her favorite of all, Dean Martin.

Singing along with Dean's "Ain't That a Kick in the Head," she returned to the kitchen and retrieved her mail from the floor where Jenn or Meredith had slid it under her back door.

She'd be surprised if George Laurence was any younger than forty.

Astonished by the wayward thought, warmth washed over her at the memory of the intensity of his gaze earlier.

Since her broken engagement ten years ago, every time she'd felt the least attracted to a man, her internal alarms had gone off. She trusted the instincts born of experience to keep her from being hurt again. But the entire time she'd stood there talking to George Laurence, all she'd felt was a profound sense of interest in getting to know him better.

God, what are You trying to tell me? Is he the one? Is this finally the answer to my prayer for a husband?

No answer came to her over the soft warbling of Frank Sinatra crooning "The Coffee Song." The fact that her mind had instantly jumped to wondering if George Laurence was her future husband did bother her a bit. After everything she'd been through, the desire to maintain her independence—as a person and as a professional—kept her working eighteen to twenty hours nearly every day. Yet deep down, she just wanted to fall in love with someone and experience his falling in love with her in return. Not wanting anything from her, just loving her.

George Laurence seemed like the kind of man who had everything together. His expensive suit and shoes, grooming, and impeccable manners stood as proof of an established man comfortable with himself and those around him. So many of the men she'd gone out with at her cousins' behest were still trying to "find" themselves, even into their late thirties or early forties, and wanted to be with a woman who would have a stabilizing influence on them.

Anne, however, didn't want that kind of turmoil in her life. She wanted a man who knew what he wanted out of life, a man comfortable with himself, and with simple tastes—classic music and movies, dining out—who didn't mind the hours she put into her business.

Her phone chirped the *Pink Panther* theme. She unclipped it, flipped it open, and pressed it to her ear. "I wondered when you were going to call."

Meredith laughed. "I didn't figure you'd be home any earlier than now, but if you were still on your date and having a good time, you wouldn't answer. So?"

She filled her cousin in on the evening, and by the time she got to seeing Forbes, she heard Meredith's SUV pull up the driveway. Although she trusted her completely, something kept Anne from telling her about how she felt when she met George Laurence. Anne wasn't sure herself what her feelings meant. She needed time to pray. . .and time to get to know him better.

"Do you want to come up for a few minutes?" Anne asked, crossing to the kitchen window that overlooked the carport.

"You working tonight?"

"Yeah."

"Just for a minute, then—Jenn sent some peach cobbler for you."

Anne opened the door and closed the phone. Meredith Guidry's strawberry blond head came into sight in the dim stairwell. Anne met her on the landing and accepted a plastic tub of the still-warm dessert while leaning forward to kiss Meredith's cheek.

"Did y'all have fun tonight?" She ushered Meredith into the kitchen.

"Turned out to be just Jenn, Jason, Rafe, and me. Seems it was a big night to have other plans. How much work do you have left to do tonight?"

"A few hours. What was Rafe's big announcement?" Anne closed the door and leaned against the kitchen cabinet. Meredith, Forbes, and Jenn's younger brother piloted the private jets owned by their parents' commercial real estate and investment corporation.

"He took a job with Charter Air as a senior pilot or something like that. He said he wanted to do more flying and less paperwork—Daddy had him working in the capital ventures office when he wasn't flying. Since Mama and Daddy aren't traveling as much, they decided to sell off the two company jets and sign a contract with this charter service."

Anne's stomach churned at the thought of flying.

"Of course, that means Rafe will be gone a lot more now," Meredith continued. "Most of his flights will be single-day round-trips, but occasionally he'll be gone overnight. He's going to get to fly bigger planes, too. Not the big commercial planes, but the kind that carry about thirty passengers—"

Bile rose in the back of Anne's throat, and clamminess spread over her skin. That was the same size plane. . .

"Oh, Annie, I'm so sorry. I didn't mean to remind you of—here." Meredith pulled over one of the tall, ladder-back chairs from the table. "Sit down and put your head between your knees."

Anne sank into the chair, drew a few deep breaths, and tried to smile. "I'm okay. It's been a long time since I've had that kind of reaction just from someone talking about planes."

"You sure you're okay?" Meredith crossed the kitchen, took a glass out of the cabinet, filled it with water from the refrigerator door, and handed it to Anne.

Anne sipped it and pressed the cold glass to her forehead. "I guess I'm just tired. You'd think after twenty-seven years and thousands of hours of therapy, I'd be over the fear."

Meredith gave her a sympathetic smile and rested her hand on Anne's shoulder. "I'm so sorry."

Patting Meredith's hand, Anne set the glass on the table and rose, her knees not too weak to support her. "I know you are. If you talk to Rafe before Sunday, tell him congrats from me."

"I will. Good night, Anne."

"Sweet dreams, Mere."

Shutting the door behind her cousin, Anne took a few more deep breaths and tried to put the images and sensations from a lifetime ago out of her head. The best way was to concentrate on something else.

Work.

For the next two hours, she focused on entering data into the software her cousin Jason had written for her to help with organizing seating arrangements at events, then moved on to making lists of everything that needed to happen in the next forty-eight hours—not just for the wedding on Saturday, but for weddings coming up in the next few weeks as well.

Why was George Laurence in town, and why was Forbes being so secretive about it?

She shook her head and returned her attention to the half-finished checklist on her computer screen—and saw she'd typed George Laurence's name. She deleted it and continued working, only to have the memory of their brief encounter pop up when least expected.

At 2:00 a.m., she finished the last list, saved everything, e-mailed the files to herself at work, and shut down her computer. When she finally climbed into bed, she grabbed her burgundy fabric- covered prayer journal and fountain pen filled with purple ink from the nightstand:

> *June 1—Lord, I know there's a reason why You had me meet George Laurence tonight. I've never felt this way about any other man I've only just met. Could he be the one You've had me waiting on for so long? I don't know what Forbes meant by "not available," but I do intend to find out. You showed me tonight that I need to take that first step on my road to my own happy ending. Thank You, Lord, for the confirmation I've made the right decision.*

She set the journal aside and pulled out her worn, black leather Bible, flipping it open to where the ribbon held her place from this morning. She'd read the twenty-seventh Psalm many times in her life, but this night, the last two verses stuck in her mind: *I would have despaired unless I had believed that I would see the goodness of the Lord in the land of the living. Wait for the Lord; be strong and let your heart take courage; yes, wait for the Lord.*

She closed her eyes and cleared her mind. "Lord, I've been waiting for a very long time. Please let this be the answer to my prayer. Let George Laurence be the one."

Chapter 3

The bell on the front door of Anne's office jingled at 9:50 Monday morning. She looked up from Saturday night's invoices, which she'd been entering into her expenses spreadsheet. Her heart thudded. Dressed in a dark gray suit, a white button-down, and a colorful tie, George Laurence cut a dashing figure. More slender than she'd remembered from last Thursday, but with broad shoulders that suggested he worked out.

She saved the Excel document and went around the desk to greet him. What was he doing here? Had he gotten her office address from Forbes? Had his "not available" status changed over the weekend? And who was the young woman—"Courtney? Courtney Landry?"

The beautiful brunette stepped forward and extended both hands. "Miss Anne! I was so afraid you wouldn't recognize me."

Anne clasped the girl's hands, and they exchanged kisses on the cheek. "How could I not? Your sister Brittany's wedding was only last summer. You'd just graduated from high school, if I remember. Did you enjoy your first year of college? UCLA, right?"

Courtney's perfect, homecoming-queen features glowed. "Right. It was *awesome*. I loved it. It seems like a long time since you used to come over and babysit and tutor me in—well, everything." She squeezed Anne's hands. "I set up the appointment for today because I want you to plan my wedding. There isn't anyone else in the world I trust more than you to pull it together exactly the way I imagine—like, even better, I'm sure."

"Your—" Anne's heart dropped into her left big toe. She glanced over Courtney's shoulder at George Laurence, who stood in profile looking at photos of previous events on her wall. The name Landry was all that had downloaded from the request form on her Web site for ten o'clock Monday morning—now. "Wait a minute. Are you telling me that you—that you and he—" She swallowed hard. "Congratulations, Courtney. Why don't we sit down and discuss your ideas."

She couldn't meet George Laurence's gaze as she waited for him and Courtney to be seated on the Chippendale-style sofa under the picture window. "Can I get anything for either of you? Coffee? Tea? Water?"

Courtney shook her head as she sat. George also declined. He lowered himself onto the love seat a good six inches from Courtney.

Odd. Without exception, every couple who'd sat across from her in their initial consultation couldn't keep from touching each other—holding hands, his arm around her, her hand on his knee, some kind of contact. George Laurence, however, was as stiff as Courtney was animated when she started talking about her ideas for a grand outdoor wedding at a plantation home down on River Road. Could be a cultural difference. She'd never had a British client before.

Thursday night, she'd been so sure he was "the one." How could God have put that attraction in her if He hadn't meant for her to be with this man? She had to stop thinking about him. Focus on the wedding. His wedding. She swallowed hard and realized the girl had stopped talking. "That sounds lovely. Have you determined a budget yet?"

Courtney cast a furtive glance at George, her cheeks turning a becoming shade of pink. "Um, there really isn't, like, a set limit on what we can spend."

Anne frowned. "I'm not certain I understand what you mean." She looked at George, but his bland expression betrayed nothing.

"I mean, Cl—" Courtney broke into a coughing fit, bringing a delicate hand up to cover her mouth.

Anne leaped up and went around to the small refrigerator hidden in the base of one of her built-in cabinets. She took two bottles of water back with her and handed one to Courtney. George waved off the one she offered him as he pressed the blue silk handkerchief from his coat pocket into Courtney's hand. The expression on his face showed more fatherly concern than romantic interest.

Yes, that was part of it. Part of what bothered her. The age difference. George Laurence had to be older than Anne herself, while Courtney wasn't quite twenty. What was he thinking, marrying a girl half his age?

"I'm so sorry," Courtney said after taking a swig of the water. "Must be allergies or something." She looked at George before taking a deep breath and continuing. "Anyway, what I was saying is that my fiancé, well, I don't even know how to say this without sounding, like, stuck up, but he has, y'know, a lot of money."

Anne couldn't look at him. Why was he leaving this all up to Courtney? Why couldn't he come out and say it himself?

"He told me I could have anything I wanted, no matter what the cost." Courtney's eyes took on a dreamy quality. "Miss Anne, do you think it would be wrong of me to get married in a pink dress? I saw a picture in one of the magazines—I should have brought it with me—some actress or singer who just got married wore a green dress because green is, like, her favorite color. My favorite color is pink, and I've always dreamed of getting married in a pink dress like the one Princess Aurora wore at the end of *Sleeping Beauty*, y'know?"

Pink? Anne still tried to fathom the idea of a budgetless wedding. "I'm positive we can find the perfect dress for you." She turned to George, sitting so erect his back hardly touched the sofa cushion, hands clasped in his lap. "I realize you've told Courtney she can have whatever she wants no matter the cost, but can you give me a ballpark figure so I can start working up a plan of action?"

"I've—it's just as she said: whatever she wants, no matter the cost."

Really? Anne bit the inside of her cheek to keep her grin intact. Going to play that way, huh? Well, his "no matter the cost" would be put to the test as soon as she could sit down at the computer and start working up a plan based on everything Courtney said she wanted. No calling in favors from childhood friends on this wedding. If he really meant what he said, all of her vendors—*all* of them—would be rewarded for every discount, freebie, or no-charge delivery they'd ever given her. And for the first time, she might actually get her full fee, on time.

She picked up her planner. "Let's talk dates."

"Third Saturday in October," Courtney said. "That's the date we've chosen. Oh, but we want to have an engagement party the Friday after the Fourth of July."

Five weeks for the engagement party and four and a half months for the wedding. If she truly had unlimited financial resources, no problem. Anne had planned to take the weekend after the Fourth off, but for a commission this size. . .

"Let's see. That would be Friday, July seventh. . . ." She marked the date in July, then flipped to October. Nothing else on her calendar for that week. "Both dates look good." She closed the planner. "Now here's what we do next: I'll work up a proposal, complete with a budget, based on what you've told me, as well as a contract. If I can get an e-mail address, I can send both to you for review before our next meeting. Can you come in at three o'clock Thursday?"

George pulled out a touch-screen PDA and tapped away at the surface with a stylus. "Thursday afternoon looks clear." He clipped the thing onto his belt and reached into his shirt pocket, withdrawing a business card.

Anne took the card, hoping to get some idea of who this guy was. Against a plain white background, all she saw was George F. Laurence in the middle with his mobile number—a New York area code—at the bottom left and an e-mail address at his own dot-com on the right. Aha. If he had his own Web site, she could look it up and find out more about him.

Standing, she gave each of them one of her cards. "If you think of anything else you'd like me to figure into the plan, please call."

Courtney came around the coffee table to hug her again. "Thank you, Miss Anne. I know I'm going to have so much fun working with you."

"I'm delighted to have the opportunity." She walked arm in arm with Courtney to the door. "I'm serious. Call me if you think of anything. I'm available all hours, not just when I'm in the office."

"Thanks." Courtney grinned.

Anne turned and extended her hand to George. "Mr. Laurence, it was nice to see you again."

He shook hands with firm brevity. "Ms. Hawthorne." He bowed his head slightly and opened the door for Courtney.

She kept her smile pasted on until they were past her front windows, then spun on her not-too-high heels and crossed to her computer. If he had his own dot-com e-mail address, he must have a Web site. She opened a new Internet window and entered the address. The high-speed cable connection paused for a moment; then an error message popped up on the screen: WARNING! YOU DO NOT HAVE PERMISSION TO ACCESS THIS PAGE. She tried refreshing the page, but the same warning came up. So she did a Google search for his name. Lots of genealogy sites with George Laurences listed, but nothing that seemed to point toward the man who'd just shattered her girlish hopes and dreams of the past several days.

She slumped forward until her forehead touched the screen. "God, why are You doing this to me? Why did he have to turn out to be some kind of eccentric millionaire who's into much younger women? Why couldn't he have turned out to be a nice, simple British guy who likes old movies and Dean Martin?"

"I don't think this plan is going to work." George turned down the volume of the Rat Pack & Friends satellite radio station and adjusted the hands-free earpiece of his mobile phone.

"What happened?" Digital static crackled through Forbes Guidry's voice.

"She thinks I'm some sort of debaucher of young women."

"What?"

George had to smile at the astonishment in Forbes's voice. "She didn't say it in so many words, but I could tell from her expression when she first realized why we were there."

"From Anne's expression? She's usually so good at hiding what she's thinking, even from those of us who know her best."

"I think Ms. Hawthorne is suspicious of the nature of my relationship with Miss Landry. And with every right to be so. Why would a man forty-one years old be marrying a girl half his age—less than half his age?" *Especially a man like me at whom no woman would ever look twice?* George shook off the negative thought and turned the leased Mercedes Roadster convertible into the driveway that should lead to his employer's nineteenth-century home.

"Anne's pretty open-minded. I mean, she does have high morals, but when she takes on clients, she doesn't let things like age differences in the couple interfere with her job."

Enormous oak trees lined the narrow road, creating a canopy overhead that allowed no sunlight through. George removed his sunglasses and slowed the car. After five nights in a hotel, he hoped all the plumbing repairs were indeed completed. He didn't want to wake up in the middle of the night with water dripping on his head, as Forbes told him the leak had been over the basement service quarters.

Anne might be open-minded, but he'd seen the look of pure astonishment in her eyes for a split second before she'd slipped into her professional persona. "Look, mate, she's your cousin, and you know her better than I do. I just don't want to see anyone get hurt because of this."

The tree-shaded drive rounded a corner to reveal a magnificent mansion, just like the kind used in movies about the American Civil War. "Love a duck," George breathed, stopping the car to drink in the view.

"I beg your pardon?" Humor laced Forbes's baritone voice.

"Oh, sorry. I've just seen the house."

"Pretty amazing, isn't it?"

"I'll say." Red brick with a white-pillared porch dominating the front, the manse loomed ever larger as he drove closer.

"Listen, you focus on getting settled in and don't worry about Anne. If she has a problem with you or the situation, believe me, you'll know about it. With Anne, you don't have to guess."

George bade the lawyer farewell, ended the call, and followed the paved carriageway to the separate garage building in the back. The land sloped down toward a large pond, exposing the basement level of the house. Mrs. Agee, the housekeeper, had moved in yesterday, but when George tried the main service entrance, it was locked. He punched in the security code Forbes had given him on the panel beside the door and entered.

"Hello?" His voice echoed through the shadowy interior of a cavernous kitchen fitted out with enormous commercial-grade appliances set in redwood cabinetry with gray granite countertops.

"Someone there?" A woman's voice came from a hall to his right, and bright lights blazed, momentarily blinding George.

"Mrs. Agee?"

An African-American woman entered the kitchen—tall, softly built, her gray hair kept back from her angelic face with a flowery scarf. "I've been expectin' you for a couple of hours now." She crossed the room, right hand extended. "I'm Keturah Agee, but you can just call me Mama Ketty."

Now he was almost certain he'd stepped out of real life and onto a movie set. He shook her hand. "George Laurence."

"Let's get you settled in, baby, and then we can discuss business matters."

He followed her through the stone-arch doorway into a hall with gleaming wood floors. The corridor extended the same short distance to the left and right of the doorway.

"I've taken up residence in the suite on the left." She pulled a key out of the pocket of her khaki pants.

The antique brass key was heavy in his hand. "Is locking the doors necessary inside the house?"

"It will be if there's ever a party here and this lower level is swarming with caterers and day-hires." She looked at the gold pendant watch hanging from a long chain around her neck. "It's nearly three. Can I make you some tea?"

Teatime really wasn't until four. "I'd love some."

She smiled, showing a full set of straight, white teeth and dimples in both cheeks. "I'll put the water on while you get yourself settled in."

By the time he'd gotten his two suitcases and hanging bag out of the car, the teakettle whistled, drowning out Mama Ketty's humming. She winked at him as he wheeled the luggage through the kitchen. He paused at the door to his room, hoping it was large enough that he wouldn't be tripping over the end of the bed, as in his room in the New York town house.

The door swung open on silent hinges. The dark wood flooring continued into a long but very narrow room. Well, if he was going to have to stay in the tiny space, at least it had a large window overlooking the back lawn and the pond. He opened the door to his left, expecting an equally small bath, and entered a second, much larger room.

In relief, he sank onto the queen-size bed that sat on a plain metal frame under another large window. Dark wainscoting gave way at waist height to walls painted hunter green. Two more doors revealed a walk-in closet and a large private bath.

He'd have to go furniture shopping, but the size of the suite more than made up for being sent into exile for nearly five months.

The sweet aroma of cinnamon and vanilla drew him back out into the kitchen. He sat in one of the tall chairs at the bar on the back side of the island. Mama Ketty set a white cup and saucer in front of him along with a dessert plate piled with sweets and pastries.

He'd just bitten into an oatmeal cookie when a chime reverberated through the room.

Mama Ketty looked perplexed. "Someone's at the front door."

"I'd best go see who it is." He stood, then looked around. He didn't know how to access the main portion of the house.

"Beyond the pantry." Mama Ketty indicated the opposite side of the kitchen from their suites. "Enter the security code before you open the door at the top. The upstairs is on a different zone than down here."

He jogged up the enclosed wooden staircase and found himself in another kitchen—smaller but still well appointed. He crossed to the swinging white door and exited into a wide foyer. The hall ran the length of the house, the front door on the opposite end. Two figures stood on the other side of the etched oval glass; he entered the security code and slid the dead bolt lock open.

"Miss—"

"George!" Courtney stepped forward and hugged him. "Mama had to come by and see the house." She gazed at him with wide eyes begging him to maintain his fictitious identity.

Forcing a smile, he stepped back and motioned the two women in. The only similarity between daughter and mother was their chestnut hair. Courtney, about average height, possessed a natural grace and a dancer's figure. Her mother, however. . .

The cloying odor of an entire flower garden preceded the woman into the house. Dressed in a bright pink sateen jogging suit, she sported overly large sunglasses, which she pulled down to the tip of her nose with claws painted to match her outfit.

"Mrs. Landry." He took her proffered hand, hoping her nails wouldn't impale him. "It is nice to finally meet you."

She looked him over from head to toe and raised her painted-on eyebrows. "So you're the cause of this. To think, my own daughter springing a surprise like this on me. She used to tell me everything, you know. Humph. I expected you'd be—"

Younger. So had Anne Hawthorne.

"Taller." Mrs. Landry brushed past him.

Courtney shrugged and cocked her head to the side in an apologetic gesture. He followed along behind as Courtney explored the house with her mother. He'd served in some of the largest estates in Britain yet was impressed by the obvious care taken in the restoration of this property.

"Oh, I have the perfect pink faux-fur rug for this room. It would make such a cute nursery." Mrs. Landry gave George a significant look over her shoulder from the doorway of the last room on the third floor.

He shuddered internally as he inclined his head toward the woman who fit the stereotype of nouveaux riches every person in the service industry feared working for.

Courtney checked her watch. "Oh, Mama, we need to go if you're going to have time to get ready for the homeowners' association meeting tonight."

He stepped out on the front porch with them, astonished to see a Rolls-Royce in the driveway. The chauffeur scrambled out and opened the back door.

"Mama, you go on. I need to speak with George for a moment." Courtney watched her mother climb into the car. As soon as the door closed, she turned back to look up at George. "I'm so sorry I sprung that on you without any warning. My friend I thought I was going to stay with ended up going to Australia for the summer, so I'm having to stay with Mama instead."

"And she didn't know you were engaged?"

"Not until I told her at breakfast this morning right before you and me went to meet Miss Anne. Mama wanted me to go to the beauty salon with her and was like, 'Where are you going?' And I was all, 'I have plans.' But she was like, 'You just got here—how can you have plans?' and got all up in my face until I blurted out where we were going. It wasn't exactly how I wanted to tell her—I wanted her to find out when everyone else does at the engagement party." She grabbed his hands and stood on tiptoe to kiss his cheek.

"Thanks for playing along."

Mentally, George added elocution lessons to the etiquette he planned to teach Courtney between now and the engagement party. "That's what I'm here for."

"Come to dinner with us tonight?"

"Of course."

She gave him directions to the restaurant, although he'd MapQuest it as soon as he got inside. He waited on the porch until the car disappeared between the tree rows, then leaned against the front door after closing it and resetting the alarm. The deception had just gotten a little bigger. Now Courtney's mother believed he was the fiancé. But concealing the truth of his identity from the wedding planner had felt much worse than this.

The wedding planner.

He cut off all the lights and descended toward the service level.

Anne Hawthorne.

When he'd seen her at the restaurant, he'd immediately wanted to get to know her better. No one had affected him like that in a very long time. And he must lie to her to protect his employer's identity and keep his job.

He shook his head as he regained his seat at the island. The next five weeks were going to be, *like*, the longest of his life.

Chapter 4

"What in the world is wrong with you, Grumpy McGrouch?"

Sitting at the large table in the back room of her cousin Jenn's rustic seafood restaurant Monday evening, Anne thought she was doing a good job of hiding her emotions. But Jenn was right: Anne had been in a bad mood ever since Courtney and her fiancé had left her office that morning. *Not available*. Just wait until Forbes got here!

"No joke," chimed in Meredith. "All you've done since you walked in is shred every napkin on the table. Was the wedding this weekend really that bad?"

Anne glanced around at the blizzard of white paper on the table. "I'm sorry, y'all. I asked for us to have dinner tonight instead of Thursday, and here I am being completely unsociable. It's just been—a stressful day."

Meredith squeezed Anne's shoulder. "No, we're sorry for teasing you."

Jenn flopped into the chair on her other side. "Hey, you were going to tell us about that guy you saw. The one having dinner with Forbes the other night. Forbes is running late. So tell us."

Anne snorted. "Well, when I first saw him, I thought he was handsome—and I seriously felt like maybe God had finally answered my prayers." She crossed her arms and slouched down in the plush red chair.

"But something changed?" Meredith prompted, pushing back a piece of hair back from Anne's face and letting her hand rest on Anne's shoulder.

"He's *engaged.* He and his fiancée were my ten o'clock consultation this morning."

"Oh, Annie." Jenn vigorously rubbed Anne's other shoulder.

"That's not the worst part. The worst part is that his fiancée is Courtney Landry."

Meredith cocked her head. "Courtney. . .which one is she?"

"The baby. The one who's barely nineteen years old. I mean, this guy has to be at least forty. You'd think Forbes—"

"Did I hear my name?"

"Speak of the devil." Jenn stood to allow her oldest brother to take the chair on Anne's left.

"Devil indeed." Anne punched him in the arm as soon as he sat down. *"Not available?"*

"Ouch! Wha—?"

"George Laurence! I felt like such an idiot this morning when he and his fiancée walked into my office. The least you could've done was tell me he's engaged. Then I wouldn't have—" Oops, she'd almost said too much.

Forbes stood and shrugged out of his suit jacket. "Wouldn't have what?"

She scrambled for something believable. "Wouldn't have acted so surprised when they walked in."

"You didn't have their names written down in your calendar?" Forbes sat and shoved the pile of shredded napkins to the middle of the large round table. "Really, Anne, you're usually so much more organized than that."

That little half grin, dimple, and sparkle in his blue eyes weren't going to work this time. "When the information downloaded from the Web site, all it had was her last name, which is pretty common in this state, if you haven't noticed. I arranged the appointment by e-mail, and she never signed her name to any of the correspondence."

“But it’s going to be worth it, huh?” He nudged her with his elbow.

“Hrrrrr.” She groaned, smiled, and shook her head. “Yeah, it’s going to be more than worth it—if they’re telling me the truth.”

Forbes’s left eyebrow shot up. “What leads you to believe they’re not telling you the truth?”

“No limits to what can be spent? Come on. Everyone has their limits.”

“Oh.” He loosened his tie and turned to look over his left shoulder. “Hey, Jenn?” he called across the room to his sister.

She waved at him but didn’t turn from her conversation with two of her servers. When she was finished, she rejoined them. “What’s up?”

“That new music come in yet?”

“Yep—even those tracks Annie wanted me to order.” Jenn poked Anne’s shoulder. “And I just want you to know, those were hard to come by, too.”

“Thanks. I’ve got to expose y’all to the classics. All this new music—”

“Good grief!” Jason, a younger cousin to all of them, flopped into the chair beside Meredith. “Karaoke hasn’t even started, and she’s already griping about modern music.”

Anne laughed along with them. She’d save the lecture for the next couple choosing their reception music. Once the other cousins arrived and the food was served, they cajoled Jenn into opening up the microphone an hour early.

“You’ll have to get up and do a couple of those songs you want us all to hear so much,” Forbes said.

Anne shook her head, and her stomach flip-flopped. “No. You know I can’t sing in front of a crowd.”

“Once you’re up there with the spotlight on you, you can’t see anyone. Just concentrate on the words going across the TV screen, and you won’t think about anyone else being here.” Jenn jogged across the restaurant to the stage.

The rest of her cousins caught on to Forbes's suggestion and started chanting Anne's name. A bit of feedback quieted the now-packed restaurant. Anne angled her chair to see the stage better.

"Welcome to the Fishin' Shack, where every night is family-friendly karaoke." Jenn's announcement and following dialogue with her patrons got the crowd riled up. "Now I see the sign-up list is already pretty full." She pointed at the small whiteboard beside the stage. "And I usually open it up to the first person on the list. But tonight, we have a special request from the large party in the back." She cupped her hand around her mouth and whispered, "That would be my crazy family."

The men at the table stood and cheered as if their football team had just scored a touchdown.

Jenn's eye-roll was easy to see from across the room. "Anyway, if you've looked at the new music list tonight, you may have noticed some strange titles. Anne—why don't you come up here and entertain us with one of them?"

Anne's cheeks burned. She hated being put on the spot—especially when it meant public humiliation. The cousins started chanting her name again. She narrowed her eyes and grimaced at them before rising and crossing the dining room. She took the list from Jenn and picked out the first song title she recognized, pointing out the number to the sound guy.

Jenn hadn't been lying. Once she stood on the platform, she couldn't see anything but dark shadows beyond the bright spotlight.

The trumpet blast that started Dean Martin's "Ain't That a Kick in the Head" drew whoops and cheers from the crowd. She smiled and started singing—nervous at first, then with growing confidence as she lost herself in one of her favorite singer's signature songs.

She didn't do it justice, but she did have fun. The audience cheered and clapped when the music ended. The next person, an older gentleman, took the microphone from her but stopped her with a hand on her arm. "I haven't heard that song since the last time I saw the Rat Pack on stage in Vegas. Good choice."

Several people stopped her on her way back to the table to let her know how much they'd enjoyed the song.

"And we ought to see if that Elvis impersonator Sara had at her reception is available. You don't want your uncle Billy Joe doing it once he gets into the beer."

George coughed and reached for his water glass. Since sitting down for dinner at the upscale restaurant, one absurd comment after another had spewed forth from Mrs. Landry's mouth, nearly bringing the half-chewed food back out as well.

If Courtney's shoulders drooped any lower, she'd be under the table. His heart twisted with compassion for the young woman. To be so browbeaten by a woman with such poor taste. He steeled himself to do what he'd been dreading all evening—living up to his namesake and facing the dragon.

He drew in a deep breath, wiped his mouth on the white cloth napkin, and laid it beside his plate. "Mrs. Landry, while I thank you for making suggestions for the wedding, I would ask that you cease now. Your daughter has hired a professional wedding planner to take care of all those details."

Mrs. Landry's mouth hung open, exhibiting the remains of the pasta she'd been chewing. "I beg your pardon!" She slammed her fork down hard enough to make the glassware on the table tremble and clink together. "Courtney, are you going to sit there and let him talk to me like that?"

Tears brimmed in the girl's eyes. "Mama, please. You're making a scene."

"He started it." Mrs. Landry pointed across the table at George.

How had Courtney turned out to be so delightful? He had to get her away from the harpy before Mrs. Landry ruined this experience for her. He dropped a hundred-dollar bill on the table, then stood and offered his hand to Courtney. She folded her napkin beside her plate and rose, not looking at her mother.

"Mrs. Landry, dinner was—enlightening. I will take Courtney home." He gave the sputtering older woman a curt nod and led Courtney out of the restaurant.

Outside, Courtney threw her arms around his waist. Taken aback, he froze, hands hovering away from his sides.

"Thank you so much. I've been wanting to tell her all afternoon to shut up. She offered to pay for part of the wedding, but probably only so she can have some say in what happens."

He patted her back. "Do you want her involved in the planning process?"

"No!" She released him. "I don't even want her *at* the wedding, much less having any say about it."

"Now, miss, she is your mother."

Once again, tears threatened to overflow the innocent brown eyes. "That's just it. She is my mother, and she knows exactly how to get under my skin. I don't know how I'm going to last four months in her house."

"You don't have to." The valet arrived with the car. George held the door for her, then went around and climbed in. "You're going to direct me to her house, and you are going to pack your bags and move into your fiancé's home."

Her full lips started to form into a smile. "Mama will flip when she finds out."

They'd been at the house nearly twenty minutes, and Courtney was halfway through moving her clothes from the bureau to a suitcase, when her mother stormed into the room. "Just what do you think you're doing?"

"Packing, Mama." Courtney continued arranging the folded T-shirts in a layer on top of the blue jeans.

George moved in between them as Mrs. Landry reached out to grab Courtney's arm. He intercepted her hand. "Kindly allow Miss Courtney to continue what she's doing."

Mrs. Landry gasped and jerked away. "How dare you come between me and my daughter!" Her voice rose to a pitch that would soon have all the dogs in the gated, exclusive subdivision barking. "Where do you think you're going to go? To live in *sin* with *him*?" She practically shrieked the accusatory words.

"Mama!"

"Mrs. Landry, that is quite enough." George used every ounce of training and past experience to keep his voice even and low. "Courtney is going to move into one of the third-floor bedrooms. I will be staying in a room in the basement—beside the housekeeper's room. Nothing untoward will happen."

"If you're not—then why—?"

"Because it's obvious she cannot stay here one moment longer."

"Well, I never!" Mrs. Landry folded her arms across her ample—and most likely not natural—chest. From the way her face screwed up, she seemed to be trying to conjure some tears. "I can't believe you're going to choose him over me! Is that what you really want? Because if you leave here, that's what you're doing. I'll. . .I'll never speak to you again."

Courtney kept packing; but her hands shook, and she tossed items in the suitcase haphazardly. George mirrored Mrs. Landry's movements to stay between them.

"Court?" Mrs. Landry glared at him when her daughter didn't answer. She planted her fists on her hips. "Fine. But you'll come back here begging my forgiveness before too long." She turned and flounced out of the room.

"I'm through here." Courtney slapped the lid of the suitcase down and zipped it closed. "If I've left anything behind, we can come back for it tomorrow when she's at the tanning salon."

Although happy to be leaving, George dreaded going downstairs and walking through the house again. Gold-plated cherubs and low-quality reproduction Greek and Roman statuary crowded every inch of space possible.

The wheels of the suitcase caught on the faux tiger-skin rug—at least he *hoped* it was fake—that covered Italian ceramic tile in the front foyer. He heaved the bag up and carried it to the door.

Her baggage barely fit into the car trunk.

"I'm so sorry about my mom." Courtney rested her elbow on the windowsill but leaned toward him as the cabriolet ragtop closed. He didn't want to take any chances with the thunder growling in the distance. "She always wanted to be rich—I remember she and Daddy used to argue all the time about how she wasted money on junk. Then after he died. . ."

He started the car and left with all due haste. "How long ago did your father pass away?"

"Ten years ago in April—an accident at work. Mama got a lawyer, and the chemical plant settled out of court for millions of dollars. Mama finally had more money than she could spend on all of the chintzy junk she'd always wanted. Lucky for me, she decided to send me to a private prep school, where I lived on campus nine months out of the year."

That explained how she'd escaped unspoiled. "I've seen enough people like her in my time. You don't have to apologize for her actions or words."

Thank God his employer's home lay on the other side of the city from her mother. Unfortunately, Mrs. Landry had been to the house and could probably find her way back should the fancy strike her. His stomach churned—although it could have just been hunger pains since he'd only eaten a few bites of his dinner before making the grand exit with Courtney in tow. "You don't think your mother will show up on the doorstep, do you?"

"Nope. There's no way she could find it again. She didn't pay attention on the way over, and she fired that driver this afternoon because he didn't change lanes when she told him to."

At the front door, he taught Courtney the security code to get in. She insisted on carrying two of the smaller suitcases, while he managed the large one and the hanging bag. Why had he decided to put her on the third floor? The second floor would have been much easier on his knees than climbing all these stairs.

Courtney chose the room at the end of the hall—the one that would make a "perfect nursery," and one of the few that had a full set of furniture. Pale pink walls and white and pink linens hugged the room in femininity. Perfect for the very feminine creature who stood beside him—whose stomach emitted a roaring growl.

She rubbed her tummy and grinned at him. "I'm kinda hungry. Think we can raid the kitchen?"

He returned the smile, his own stomach feeling grumbly. "I'd like to introduce you to Mama Ketty, the housekeeper and, for now, cook."

As he'd hoped, Mama Ketty cooed over Courtney and insisted on cooking dinner for her, even given the late hour of nine o'clock—Mama Ketty's normal bedtime. Mrs. Agee bustled around the kitchen in her bathrobe and slippers, silver hair mounted on enormous curlers and covered with another colorful scarf.

"Show me your room, George." Courtney slid off the barstool.

"There isn't much to show." He ushered her down the hall, opened the door, and motioned for her to enter.

"This can't be your bedroom. No, you'll have to move into one of the upstairs bedrooms."

He laughed. "No, this is just the antechamber."

She opened the second door and looked around. "Well. It's big enough." She disappeared through another door. "And the bathroom is great—better than mine at Mama's house." Coming back out, she pinned him with an amused gaze. "Tomorrow we go furniture shopping. I know you have a budget to furnish your room—I heard that part of the conversation at least. I know all the best places where you can get nice stuff cheap."

Furniture shopping with Courtney would help seal his assumed identity. He pushed aside the guilt that threatened every time he thought about the untenable situation he'd allowed himself to become entangled in. How was this going to reflect on his witness as a Christian when the truth finally came out?

"Now, George, it won't be as bad as what you're thinking—no, I can tell by your expression you don't like shopping. But it'll be fun; I promise."

He immediately composed his expression and bowed his head toward her. "As long as I don't end up with a pink faux-fur rug, I would appreciate your help."

Laughing, she tapped his arm with her fist. "Not funny."

"You two 'bout ready to eat?" Mama Ketty stood in the doorway, arms folded.

They followed her back out into the kitchen and sat at the bar, where she'd put plates piled high with scrambled eggs, bacon, sausage, and hash browns. Beside the main dish sat smaller plates with a stack of pancakes dripping with butter and syrup.

"Breakfast food's my specialty. Coffee's on—decaf—and I"—she paused to kiss Courtney on the cheek—"am going"—she kissed George's cheek—"to bed."

"Good night, Mama Ketty."

"Thank you so much, Mama Ketty," Courtney said around a bite of pancakes.

George poured coffee while Courtney wolfed down the food. She was halfway through when her cell phone sounded a familiar tune. Her eyes lit up, and her countenance glowed. To give her some privacy, he took his plate and coffee into the staff dining room—an octagonal chamber with a round, eight-person table as the centerpiece.

He'd no more than sat down when Courtney squealed with excitement and rushed into the room, phone still pressed to her ear. "Can you take me to the airport tomorrow? Charter terminal?"

He frowned but nodded. "Of course."

She jumped up and down a little bit and returned to the kitchen.

He ate slowly, enjoying the disparate flavors of the foods—the briny crisp bacon, spicy link sausage, eggs oozing with cheddar cheese, all washed down with rich, dark-roast coffee.

"I'm going to New York—and then he's taking me to Paris to

buy me my trousseau." Courtney leaned over him from behind, hugging him around the neck.

She'd needed something to take her mind off the scene at her mother's home. "I know you'll enjoy that."

"He also said something about apartments for me, and you could give me the addresses?"

"Of course." Three months ago George had signed leases on town houses in both cities when his employer decided to propose but wanted to keep the relationship a secret. Besides, she wouldn't have stayed in his apartment with him anyway. She wouldn't risk her reputation that way. "When do you expect to return?"

"In about three weeks."

"Three—" His mouth went dry.

"Yeah. Sorry to leave at such a crucial point in the planning, but this is the only time his schedule will allow—probably the only time we'll be able to see each other much before the wedding." She kissed his cheek. "Well, I'm off to bed. I rinsed my plates and cup and put them on the counter by the sink."

"That's fine." His mind reeled. Three weeks. The three most critical weeks for planning the engagement party—scouting out a location, securing a band, selecting invitations, creating the list. . .

And he'd have to do it alone with the most attractive woman he'd ever met.

Chapter 5

Left on his own after Courtney's departure, George found getting out and about in Bonneterre eye-opening. The mental image he'd created of a midsized city in central Louisiana had been built solely on anecdotes of his employer's childhood and a few films he'd seen supposedly set in the area.

He hadn't quite believed he'd hear Cajun-French spoken in the stores and zydeco music on the radio or see alligators swimming around in swamps, but he also hadn't expected a teeming, modern minimetropolis, either.

Using his need for furniture as an excuse for leaving the house early each morning and not returning until late in the evening, he explored the city on his own. Although Mama Ketty fed him well, he discovered Beignets S'il Vous Plait, a chain of cafés around town that only served the powdered sugar–dusted, fried french puff pastries and the best coffee he'd ever tasted. The last three mornings, he'd started out his jaunt with a tall chicory coffee and a plate of three beignets.

He really wanted to explore Old Towne, Town Square, and the Riverwalk, but being in the vicinity of Anne Hawthorne's office with the possibility of running into her stopped him.

Slipping into the café's men's room, he washed the stickiness from his hands and checked his shirt for any signs of white dust from his morning snack. He'd have to go back to the house and change clothes before meeting with Anne this afternoon. Khaki pants and a navy polo shirt weren't his idea of a professional appearance.

He turned the air conditioner up to high when he got back in the car. Ten in the morning, and the Mercedes' external temperature gauge registered eighty-eight degrees. If only Bonneterre were located farther north—*much* farther north—he could call it ideal.

His cell phone began to play Nat King Cole's "Mona Lisa." Smiling, he turned down the radio to answer the call.

"Good morning, Miss Landry. How may I assist you?"

"George, I just got off the phone with Anne. She's going to make some changes to the contract and have you sign it. Can you pull together the address book so we can get a mailing list to her for the engagement party?"

"I believe it would be better if I handled the invitations. Since Miss Hawthorne is supposed to believe I am your fiancé, she would find it rather odd when my name isn't on the announcement, wouldn't she?"

Courtney giggled. He'd come to enjoy that sound so much. "Okay. Well, can you tell her that when you see her?"

"Yes, miss." She never demanded. She always requested. "Have you settled into the apartment?"

"Oh, it's so cool—I have the best view of Central Park from my window. And I'm in walking distance of all of the fabulous designer stores in Manhattan." She giggled again. "Oh, and George, thank you."

Heat rose in his cheeks. "What for?"

"For the pink and the lace and the ribbons. I know you had to be the one who had my room decorated for me."

"You're welcome, Miss Courtney."

"Speaking of decorating—how is your furniture shopping going?"

"The stores you recommended were wonderful. I think you'll approve when you return."

"I can't wait to see it. Oh, the car's here. Gotta run."

"Good-bye, miss."

"G'bye, George."

After losing track of time exploring a few shopping centers near the large enclosed mall, George returned to the house, stomach growling. He parked in back and headed for his room to shower and rid himself of the sticky feeling from running in and out of stores in the heat and humidity. He was going to have to rush to be on time for the three o'clock appointment with Anne.

The cell phone rang again while he stood in the closet, peeling off the sweaty clothes. "Hello, George Laurence here."

"Mr. Laurence, this is Anne Hawthorne. I wondered if we might push our appointment back to three thirty. I've had to take care of an issue with a vendor and will be late returning to my office."

The longer he could put it off, the better. "Three thirty will be fine."

"Thank you so much."

George ended the call and jumped in the shower. Then, although he hated to do it because of the heat, he dressed in black summer-weight wool trousers, a long-sleeved shirt, and a tie.

His phone beeped. A message from his employer. He grimaced at his reflection as he straightened his tie. Oh, to be able to turn off his cell phone and not have to jump to do someone else's bidding at any time of the day or night. Whoever had invented the mobile phone should be publicly executed.

He listened to the message and made notes on tasks he needed to do, e-mails he needed to send, and plans he needed to make on his employer's behalf. All of it could wait until later.

The luxury convertible twinkled at George in the shimmering sunlight as he approached it. Too bad he couldn't keep this indulgence. When his employer arrived, George would have to hand over the keys of this beauty and find something more in keeping with his own income.

Crosstown traffic was heavy for midday. He thought he noticed a group of women seated at alfresco tables outside of a coffeehouse admiring him, but he didn't want to turn around and look. He never ceased to be amazed at how the appearance of money could make women pretend to find him attractive.

He'd never had any delusions about his physical appearance. He'd been a slight lad growing up—a slight lad with an angular face, big nose, and unevenly spaced teeth. Although his teeth had straightened out somewhat as he grew up, he still tried to keep them hidden as much as he could. His nose, large to begin with, had been broken in a school rugby game when he was fourteen, so was a bit asymmetrical, too. His shoulders were broad, and he was tall; but if he didn't work out with weights at least four times a week, he could hide behind a lamppost just by turning sideways. He kept his light brown hair short, and several years ago, he'd started to develop wrinkles around his eyes.

Put him in an expensive Mercedes, and the women would look. Stand him beside someone like his employer or Forbes Guidry, and no one saw George Laurence.

"Lord, I know this has been a recurring theme in my prayers, but You know how much I would like to marry and have a family. I cannot ask a woman to live with the kind of schedule I must keep for my current employment. Please show me a way to do something else and still remain in this country." George looked around to make sure no one saw him talking aloud in an otherwise empty car. What did it matter? It wasn't as if he were talking to himself. He was talking to Someone more important.

He pulled into a car park just off Town Square. When he stepped out, the air wrapped around him like a sweaty gym sock. Why anyone would choose to live in these conditions baffled him. He'd take the clammy weather of northern England any day.

Following the sidewalk into the traffic-free square, he admired the original late-Victorian architecture. The row houses facing the large central commons had long ago ceased to be residences and were now stores, restaurants, and other businesses. The obvious attention to historic preservation made the commercial area feel more like a small English village and less like the large American city it really was.

Just before he reached Anne's office, he paused and drew in a deep breath. *Lord, again I ask, please help me to keep my word to my employer without having to lie to this woman. And please help me to overcome the growing attraction I feel for her.*

Anne's skin tingled when George Laurence—and only George Laurence—entered her office. *He's engaged, he's engaged, he's engaged. . . .* "Good afternoon, Mr. Laurence."

"Good afternoon, Ms. Hawthorne." Today he wore a light blue button-down with black dress pants. The multicolored tie looked expensive.

"Is Courtney running late?"

"She is in New York. Shopping. She asked me to come in her stead and begin work on the events with you."

She swallowed hard. Working alone with George Laurence. *God, what have I done so terribly wrong that You're punishing me like this?*

Sharp pain shot through Anne's left temple as she looked down at the paperwork on her desk. She knew better than to skip meals, but she'd been so busy this afternoon that lunchtime had completely passed her by.

She motioned for George to have a seat at the small round conference table beyond the sofa and wing chairs, biting back a smile when he waited until she sat before he did. She moved the vase of purple tulips aside and placed the file on the table facing him. "Here's the adjusted contract. Negotiated items are printed in blue ink. Items that incur an additional consultant fee are in green."

He read through the detailed list of services to be provided. "You label and stuff the invitations yourself?" He looked up at her without raising his head.

Bedroom eyes, grandmother would have called the cinnamon-colored orbs burning holes into Anne's self-consciousness. He was quite a handsome man, in spite of his being *engaged*.

"Yes. I'm also the copywriter, and I will design the programs for the ceremony, as well as other services."

"We can strike the invitations for the engagement party from the list. I will take care of those myself." He pulled a black metallic pen out of his shirt pocket and crossed through the line item.

He would do it himself? Was the budget monster rearing its head? "I'll remove that from the final version, then." Her stomach churned, and her head throbbed. She knew if she didn't get something to eat soon, she'd be in serious danger of passing out.

Before she could stop herself, she asked, "I know this will sound like an odd question, seeing that it's after three thirty, but have you had lunch yet?"

An audible rumble answered her question before he could speak. "No, I have not had lunch yet."

She couldn't be certain, but she thought he might have actually blushed. She suppressed her smile. "Would you be interested in walking over to The Wharf with me? I need to talk to the owners about the date for the rehearsal dinner, as it was one of the restaurants on the list Miss Landry e-mailed me yesterday. While we're there, you and I can discuss the contract and some other paperwork I'll need you to fill out."

As they walked across the park in the middle of Town Square, she found herself glad George was just a bit taller than she. Being full-figured was bad enough, but towering over men made her even more uncomfortable. She hadn't met a man who didn't find her height intimidating until she'd met Cliff Ballantine in eleventh grade. . . .

No. She wasn't going to go down that road right now. She was trying to stay positive. "How long have you lived in the United States, Mr. Laurence?"

"Five years."

"And do you like it?"

"I'm not overly fond of Los Angeles or New York. Montana is very nice, as is New Mexico. Alaska was beautiful. Las Vegas is garish and noisy. And I find your city charming. I've been to many other places. Each was unique in its own way."

His response was the most words Anne had heard him string together since meeting him. She watched him from the corner of her eye as they crossed the cobblestone street. He carried himself regally, broad shoulders high and proud, chin parallel with the ground, eyes forward. He wasn't a lawyer. He "represented" a client of Forbes's. Some kind of an agent, maybe?

"You've seen a lot more places than I have," she admitted with a sigh.

"It's part and parcel of the job. I go where my employer needs me. Since my current employer roams the earth, I must make sure he lands in the correct spot." He opened the front door of the restaurant and motioned for her to enter ahead of him.

The hostess hugged Anne. "Hey, Miss Anne. You haven't been in for a couple of weeks. We've been worried about you."

"Hi, Sarah. It's June—you know, the busiest month for weddings."

The college student giggled. "I know." Sarah looked over Anne's shoulder, and her eyes widened when she saw only George standing there. "Table for *two*?" the college student asked with a grin.

Anne shook her head, exasperated, but smiled. "Yes, please. By the back windows if there's anything available."

"Right this way."

From the expression on the girl's face, Anne knew that before the server came around, the news that Anne Hawthorne, the spinster who planned everyone else's weddings, had come in with a man would have gotten back to the dishwashers. She fully expected a slow but steady progression of employees past the table in the next fifteen or twenty minutes. Never before had she come in with only a man. Usually she came in alone to eat and meet with one or both of the owners to discuss events. Sometimes she would bring in clients who weren't familiar with the restaurant. Speculation would run wild.

"Sarah, can you let Samuel or Paul know that I'll need to talk to them after we have lunch?"

"I'll do it, Miss Anne." The hostess's blond hair bounced as she made her way to the kitchen.

By the time Anne and George placed their meal orders, four different people had come to the table to make sure they were being served. Anne could barely contain her laughter. She hated to think how many it would have been if they'd come in after the five-thirty dinner shift came on duty.

"Now that we have a few minutes," she said, taking a fresh yeast roll from the basket George offered, "I'd like to go over a few of these forms I'll need you to fill out." It was all she could do to be polite and cut the roll open, spread butter slowly onto it, and leave it sitting on the bread plate rather than stuffing the whole thing in her mouth.

George anointed the steaming roll with cold butter. His stomach rumbled at the yeasty aroma as he tore off a bite-sized piece and brought it to his mouth. The saltiness of the butter mingled with the sweetness of the bread and melted on his tongue. He had to stop himself from sighing in contentment.

The shuffling of papers across the table drew his attention back to Anne.

"Now that the terms of the contract have been agreed upon, there are a few fact-finding forms I need filled out." She handed him a packet of several pages stapled together. "This is the registration form."

He glanced over the first page. Bride's full name, groom's full name, maid of honor's name, best man's name, number of bridesmaids, number of groomsmen. . . . Guilt robbed him of his appetite. *Lord, how am I going to keep up this charade?*

"Some of the items on this list are going to be very important to me as I work on the final budget next week. I would appreciate it if you could get the information back to me by Monday morning."

Another server stopped at the table and asked if they needed refills of their mostly untouched beverages. George didn't quite understand the smile on Anne's face when she declined the offer. He found the constant interruptions somewhat annoying.

As they ate their meals, he unobtrusively but carefully watched the wedding planner. Her manners were impeccable—better than those of most of the aristocracy he'd served over the years. She took small bites, laid down her fork between them, kept her left hand in her lap, and maintained a straight posture without looking stiff. She might be able to help him give Courtney a few lessons before the formal parties, just to keep Courtney from being so nervous about her social skills.

The waitress was just clearing their plates when an older man with dark hair approached the table.

Anne stood and received a kiss on each cheek. George stood as well, laying his napkin beside the silverware.

"Sarah mentioned you were here." The man's decidedly Irish accent surprised George, though he didn't show it. "You fell into a bit o' luck, darlin', as I didn't know myself that I would be here today."

"I have a new event I'm planning, and I hoped to check some dates with you."

"Aye, I knew you were here for more than just our fine food." The restaurateur turned his attention expectantly toward George.

"Samuel Maguire, this is my client George Laurence."

George shook hands with the Irishman. "It's a pleasure to meet you, sir."

Pulling a chair over from another table, Maguire joined them. He put a black, leather-bound planner on the table, winked at Anne, and then turned to George. "Our little *cailín* here is the best businesswoman in town. If I'd known her ten years ago, I'd have retired from being a surgeon then and started my restaurant with her as my partner."

George gave the man the smile he knew was expected but didn't say anything. As he watched her interact with the restaurant owner, he was impressed by her ability to make the negotiation sound like casual, friendly conversation. From the obvious shorthand between them, they had a long-standing relationship, and George got the feeling the restaurateur would do anything within his power to accommodate whatever she requested.

The date Courtney wanted the restaurant for the rehearsal dinner had been booked for months. Anne showed no outward sign that this bothered her at all.

"If they happen to cancel, call me; but for now, let's go ahead and reserve it for that Friday night instead, and I'll discuss the date change with the bride." Anne made a notation in her file. "When can you meet to discuss a menu?"

Maguire consulted his calendar. "How about. . .next Tuesday afternoon?"

Anne looked across the table at George. "Mr. Laurence, are you available next Tuesday afternoon?"

George knew he would be, but pulled out his PDA just to put the appointment in his schedule. "What time?"

"Is three o'clock all right?" The Irishman looked from George to Anne and back.

"That should work well in my schedule." George notated the appointment.

The waitress returned to the table with the check for the meal. Maguire whisked it from her hand before Anne could take it. He stood, leaned over, and kissed her on the cheek. "It's on me, darlin'."

"Thank you, Samuel."

"My pleasure, Anne." He extended his hand to George. "Mr. Laurence."

George stood to shake hands. "Mr. Maguire. Thank you for your hospitality."

The owner escorted them to the front door of the establishment. "We'll be seein' you next week, then."

Outside the restaurant, Anne handed George the second file folder she had with her. "These are all of the forms I'll need back by next Monday. Can we meet around ten?"

"Ten on Monday morning will be fine."

"Very well."

He thought he could sense a stiffness in her body language but couldn't be sure. One thing about this woman that continued to impress him was that she could mask her feelings as well as or better than he could.

As she walked back toward her office, he couldn't help but admire her shapely figure. That combined with his growing admiration for her could be dangerous. Very dangerous.

Chapter 6

George stared at the form he'd been trying to fill out for two days, then tossed the pen on the desk and stood to pace the tiny antechamber. How had he gotten into this position? He had signed a contract agreeing to lie about his identity. Every scripture he'd ever read about the evils of lying jumbled in his head.

His gaze fell once again to the paperwork littering the desk. He couldn't face it any longer. Besides, why was he sitting alone in the house wasting this beautiful Saturday morning by becoming more and more frustrated with his job?

Tucking his keys and cell phone in the pocket of his jeans, George grabbed his sunglasses on his way out the door. He hadn't attended church last weekend and had a sudden need to find one to attend tomorrow morning. He consulted his city map and set out toward the shopping district, where he'd seen several churches.

After a quarter hour, he passed the large stone arch marking the entrance to the University of Louisiana. He could picture Anne Hawthorne as she must have been years ago as a student here—sitting on a stone bench in the shade, chatting with chums. . . .

The random thought surprised George. He couldn't let his fancy get the better of him. He had a professional role to maintain.

How gutted would she be when she learned the truth? He hoped she would be happy for the opportunity rather than upset, but the more he got to know her, the more he worried about her reaction.

"Father, give me strength. I do not want to hurt Anne Hawthorne. Not when I'm coming to care for her—" He let his prayer stop when he spied a large structure on his right. The pictorial stained-glass windows reminded him of St. John's Cathedral, and the architecture seemed to be based on Middle English design. How long had it been since he'd been home?

The name on the sign near the street was incongruous with the size of the building. Judging from the sprawling wings of the structure, Bonneterre Chapel was larger than any church he'd attended in California or New York.

He pulled up beside a few cars parked near a side entrance, hoping to slip in and take a quick look around. A florist truck pulled up halfway on the sidewalk near the door. George waited until the three men from April's Flowers entered the church, then followed them.

Inside, he removed his sunglasses and discovered he'd entered a room that reminded him of the lobby of a small but expensive hotel; for all that the exterior of the building recalled a long-past era, the interior was anything but old.

The mossy green carpet of the foyer gave way to rich dark blue in the sanctuary. He drew a deep breath, and the muscles in his shoulders relaxed. The bright sunlight from outside filtered in through the multicolored glass windows and the Bible-story images glowed in rainbow hues.

He started when a female voice broke the reverent silence of the worship center.

"Let's place the candelabra here. . .here. . .here. . .and here."

His gaze snapped to the altar at the front of the room. Although distorted by echoing throughout the cavernous space, Anne Hawthorne's voice was unmistakable.

As before, her blond hair was pulled away from her face into a clip at the back of her head. She had an open notebook cradled in her left arm, a pen or pencil in her right hand, and a roll of masking tape around her wrist.

Unlike their previous encounters, when she'd been dressed in conservative business suits, she wore khaki shorts and a sleeveless denim shirt. Even though she was slightly larger than what most men would consider to be beautiful, George admired her athletic hourglass figure.

Only the lights over the altar were on; George stayed concealed in the shadows under the overhanging balcony. He slipped into the end of the rear pew nearest him and sat, wanting nothing more than to watch her.

As she directed the three men from the florist shop on the exact placement of the arrangements on the stage and around the chancel, she also instructed two others on the placement of tall candlesticks at the ends of the pews that flanked the central aisle.

"I'll need you to start lighting those at two fifteen," she said. The two young men, probably university students, followed her like trained Labradors. "All of the candles should be burning with the hurricane glass in place by the time we start seating guests at two thirty." Her gentle voice resonated with authority. "I'll let y'all get started on those. I need to make a few phone calls."

"No prob, Anne," one of the men said with a mock salute.

Not wanting to be seen, George was about to stand and slip out of the room, but Anne headed toward him, making flight impossible.

Before he could prepare an explanation for his presence, she moved into a pew in the middle of the room and sat down. With her back turned to him, he could barely hear her, but from what he could make out, she called the bride, the groom, the maid of honor, and the best man to ensure everyone was on schedule. She then called the caterer, the bakery, and someone at the venue where the reception was to be held to check that everything would be ready at the right time.

Her voice was pleasant, and her laugh melodious. He could tell just by the number of calls she made that her workload today was stressful, although she didn't let stress manifest itself in her interactions with clients and vendors. He was impressed.

She was on the phone with what sounded like the limousine company when George heard her say, "Manuel, I hate to interrupt you, but I have another call coming in. Do you mind holding? Thank you." She took the phone away from her ear for a moment, pressed a button, and then put it to her ear again. "Happy Endings, Inc., this is Anne Hawthorne."

A moment's pause grew into a long silence. Anne's posture changed from relaxed to so stiff he could almost hear the bones in her spine protest. He wondered who could be on the other end of the connection and what that person was telling Anne to cause such a reaction.

After several long moments, he heard her say, "Yes, Miss Graves, I understand. However—"

He leaned forward and rested his forearms on the pew in front of him. Although her body language bespoke strain, her voice didn't betray it. He listened, fascinated.

"Yes, I have written it down. . .two hundred for the ceremony, four hundred for the reception. . .formal evening wear, black tie required. . . Yes, of course. . . . I will look into that for you. . . . Right now? Your wedding isn't for nearly a year. I haven't booked anything yet, but—" Anne paused. "I will let you know as soon as I do. Yes. . . I will call you first thing Monday morning."

Her shoulders raised and lowered as she took a few deep breaths. She listened to her client a little longer, then raised her left arm up to catch a beam of light on the face of her watch. "I will be finished here today around midnight. I won't be able to get back to my office until then, but I have the information you requested. I can e-mail it to you tonight so that you have it first thing in the morning."

She was willing to do that for a client? Go back to her office at midnight after working all day on someone else's wedding? He remembered his own complaints to God about his employer sending him here and felt lower than the belly of a duck.

Anne pulled out her well-worn tan leather planner. "Yes, Miss Graves. I can meet you tomorrow after church—"

Would she be willing to give up church for a client? How many Sundays had George had to leave services early or give them up entirely to attend to his employers' wishes?

"I'm sorry, Miss Graves, but I cannot meet you before twelve thirty. . . . Yes, that's fine. I will meet you at Beignets S'il Vous Plait on Spring Street at twelve thirty tomorrow." Anne closed her phone and remained still and quiet for a long time.

What could be going through her mind right now? George longed to join her and ask her more about her job, about why she was willing to give up so much time for other people, about how she found the strength to keep giving of herself and receiving nothing in return.

She jumped when her phone beeped and quickly looked at the display screen, and a noise escaped from her throat before she put the phone back to her ear. "I'm sorry to keep you on hold for so long, Manuel. . . ."

As quietly as he could, George exited the church and climbed back into the car. He'd left his PDA in the car to charge and the screen flashed, indicating he had voice mail. The display showed that Courtney had tried to ring him up three times while he'd been inside.

He gripped the steering wheel hard. He was supposed to be back at the house filling out the paperwork for Anne, not spying on her as she set up someone else's wedding. Over the past week, he'd indulged himself with his daily jaunts into town, putting off work he needed to do for his employer—hiring a few more house staff, creating the engagement party invitation for when Courtney sent the revised mailing list back to him. . . .

He could take lessons on professional demeanor from Anne Hawthorne. She worked harder to ensure her clients' happiness than any butler, valet, or majordomo he'd seen in the entirety of Britain, including his father.

Needing someone to talk with about the security concerns for when the party guests arrived, he called Forbes Guidry. He couldn't remember when he'd had time to build a friendship with another man. The lawyer had come to mind each time George prayed God would bring new friendships into his life. He liked the Southern gentleman, who was his best resource in town. Aside from professional considerations, though, he had to find out all he could about Anne. Because once he no longer had to carry on this charade, George planned to get to know her better, too.

Chapter 7

Multicolored folders littered the top of Anne's desk Monday morning, each containing pieces of someone's dream. Dreams she shared but knew would never come true for her.

With a sigh, she rummaged for the red folder containing the list of vendors for her friend Amanda's wedding. She found it, stacked the rest, and pulled out a green ballpoint pen. Her gaze darted to the clock as she lifted the phone receiver and dialed. Fifteen more minutes and *he* would be here. Her heart beat a little faster as George Laurence's image formed in her mind. She shook her head and turned her attention to the phone as someone answered.

"Bonneterre Rentals."

"Hi, Joe, it's Anne."

"Hey, gal. How's it going?"

She chatted with Joe Delacroix for a few minutes. "I'm just calling to confirm delivery time of the tent, tables, and chairs for the Boutte wedding on Saturday."

"Amanda Boutte who went to high school with us?"

"Yep. She's finally giving up on the single life."

"Good for her."

Papers rustled on the other end as he looked up the information for her. She glanced at the clock again. Thirteen more minutes until George Laurence arrived. His milk chocolate eyes burned in her memory, as did his baritone voice and the accent that sent shivers up her spine every time he spoke.

What had he been doing at the church Saturday morning? She hadn't noticed him until after the phone call from Brittney Graves. She'd stood and turned to run down to the fellowship hall to get a bottle of water out of the vending machine. The retreating figure exiting through the wide-open doors had startled her at first. . .until she recognized the sharp yet enticing profile of her newest client.

Had he been checking up on her? Did he not trust her ability to handle a wedding as large as his? Dared she ask him? Her heart fluttered. Why did he have to be so handsome, so charming?

"Saturday at 10:00 a.m."

What was happening Saturday at 10:00 a.m.? "What's that?"

"Delivery of your rentals, goose. Isn't that why you called?"

Anne banged her forehead with the heel of her right hand. "Of course. Sorry, hon'. I just got distracted." She wrote the time on her list. "I'll see you then."

"All right. Look, don't work too hard, okay?"

She let out a rueful laugh. "I'll try, but that's the best I can promise. Talk to you later."

"Bye, Anne-girl."

She grinned at the nickname Amanda had started everyone using for her when they were teenagers. "Bye, Joey."

Hanging up the phone, she closed her eyes and took a deep breath. "Pull yourself together, woman!"

She shook her head and returned her attention to the file in front of her. Four vendors left to call and only ten—no, nine minutes in which to do it.

Aunt Maggie, catering Amanda's reception at cost, was filling Anne in on the latest family news when the bell above the front door chimed and George Laurence entered.

"I'll have to call you back later about Amanda's cake. B'bye." Anne hung up, stood, and extended her right hand across the desk, proud it didn't tremble. "Mr. Laurence, thank you for coming in today."

"My pleasure, Miss Hawthorne." He nodded, returned her firm grip, and then sat in the chair she indicated. "At this juncture of our work relationship, I see no need for us to be so formal as to use titles and surnames. I'd be pleased if you'd consider calling me George."

Tingles climbed up the back of her neck to her scalp at the sound of his voice. "Thank you, George. I agree." She closed the red folder and swapped it for a blue one. "Why don't we begin with the registration form?"

Why now, Lord? Did You bring him into my life just to taunt me? Why do I feel so attracted to someone I can never have? She swallowed hard as the prayer she'd repeated fifty times in the last two days ran through her mind.

She took the six-page questionnaire from him, surprised by how little he'd filled in.

"I know you were hoping for more information," George said, "but my. . .there are reasons I cannot discuss for withholding some data. I have included a preliminary head count for the ceremony and the reception. I have detailed Courtney's desires."

Anne flipped to the third page. "A formal, late-afternoon wedding with one hundred fifty guests, and a black-tie, invitation-only reception for seven hundred." She removed her reading glasses as she looked at him. "Are these solid numbers that I can use in my budget?"

He nodded—a quick, crisp movement, almost as if he were saluting her. "Yes, with a margin of error of no more than ten for the wedding and fifty for the reception."

Anne made a notation on the form. "I notice there are two names written down for Miss Landry's honor attendant. Does she plan on having two maids of honor?"

A slow smile spread over his face, bringing an indulgent twinkle into the Englishman's light brown eyes. "She. . .decided she couldn't do without both ladies in her bridal party. Is that problematic?"

"No, I've planned a few weddings with two honor attendants."

She looked down at the form and turned to the fourth page. Indulgent. . .again, more like a father than a fiancé.

She choked when she saw the dollar amount written on the estimated budget line. Her eyes teared up as she wheezed and reached for her bottle of water. Surely he'd scrawled at least one too many zeros. He'd doubled her original estimate, and she hadn't counted on that number being true.

She cleared her throat and took another sip of water. She could work around her attraction to the Englishman. With what he was willing to pay for his wedding, her business's future was assured. And her business was the only future she could count on.

George leaned forward in concern as Anne took another sip of water. "Are you all right?" Her cheeks were flushed, and her eyes watered from the vehemence of her coughing.

She held up her hand in front of her and nodded. After another sip of bottled water, she took a deep breath and cleared her throat. "Just got a tickle," she said in a hoarse whisper.

Her azure eyes glittered as she returned her gaze to the paperwork in front of her. He felt like a schoolboy who had failed an examination, dissatisfied he couldn't give her complete information. He'd spent hours on the phone with Courtney yesterday trying to get her to make up her mind about the major details.

"Ten attendants each. Does that number include the honor attendants?" She looked at him, her fine brows arched high.

George's heart thumped. Her gaze could pierce a man's heart with its intensity. "Yes, that number includes the honorables."

She looked down, but not fast enough to keep him from seeing the corners of her mouth turn up in an amused smile. His face burned at the realization he'd gotten the terminology wrong.

"What's this list?" she asked when she got to the back page—his addendum.

"Those are restaurants in New York and Los Angeles my—we

would like for you to contact regarding specific food items for both the engagement party and the reception. I have not yet had time to research them to find the phone numbers and contact names for you, but listed under each is the item my—we would like shipped in."

She looked down the page. "Oh. I see."

Uneasiness settled in George's mind. He had to get over this attraction to the beautiful woman sitting opposite him. Twice he'd nearly slipped up and said "my employer." If he wasn't careful, his employer's name could pop out of his mouth before he could stop himself. Fear of losing his job if he slipped up and revealed too much made him sit straighter and try to reconstruct the barrier around his heart to keep Anne Hawthorne's big blue eyes from getting under his defenses.

He watched Anne carefully as she read through the details Courtney had given him over the phone. Most of the outlandish requests—such as having caviar flown in from an importer in San Francisco for the engagement party—were from his employer, not Courtney. Over the years, George had heard all about the extravagances other wealthy American couples had included in their weddings.

But while his employer wanted to best them all, he'd left the task of hiring a wedding planner in Courtney's hands. As much as George respected Anne Hawthorne's abilities, she might not be the correct person to pull it off. Although the article Courtney had shown him boasted of the number of weddings Anne Hawthorne had planned in her career, was she capable of organizing and executing an event of this magnitude?

She reached for her Rolodex and flipped through several of the sections before she stopped and pulled out a card. "I've worked with Delmonico's in New York before." She flipped through a few more sections. "And I know someone at Pskow Caviar Importers, too." She clipped both cards to the page.

His skepticism decreased a notch. "At the bottom are several local restaurants. Courtney wants some regional dishes included as well."

She continued to read, then opened her top drawer and withdrew a red pen, which she used to cross through one of the names on the list. "Pellatier's closed down six months ago."

"I will inform my. . .Courtney next time I speak with her."

"Thank you." She set the questionnaire aside. "This will allow me to work on a revised budget in the next few days. I may need to call you if I have questions on some of the items we did not discuss today, however." Her expression asked his permission.

"Please, call me anytime you need to."

Her responding smile was beautiful, but tight and forced.

She didn't trust him. The truth stung, but he didn't really blame her. He was being dishonest with her, after all. More than anything, he wanted to earn this woman's trust and respect to ensure she wouldn't hate him when the truth was made known.

Father God, after all this is over, how will I ever deserve forgiveness from either You or Anne?

He kept his tone light, positive, and helpful as they reviewed the remaining paperwork he'd labored over all weekend. To his relief, she had only a few questions, which he was able to answer.

The clock on the credenza behind Anne chimed ten thirty, and she set the paperwork aside. "Are you ready to go see some possible sites for the engagement party?"

He stood. "At your service, ma'am."

She smiled and crossed to the front door, yet did not exit. Instead, she locked it and turned over the sign hanging in the window to let passersby know the office was closed. She led him through the arched doorway at the rear of the office down a hall lined with boxes spilling their contents onto the hardwood floor. Silk flowers, fabrics, glassware, candelabra, and other decorative items glinted in the soft incandescent light.

"Most of this is for the wedding I have this coming weekend." Anne folded back a tablecloth dangling over the edge of a box.

He nodded, distracted by the lock of golden hair that had escaped her conservative french twist and skimmed the curve of her neck. He wanted to reach out and remove the Spanish-style comb holding her hair back. She was beautiful with it up, but he was sure when she had it down—

No. He clasped his hands behind his back as he followed her through a small kitchen and out the back door to the alley where her car was parked. He had to stay professional, at least as long as she thought he was the groom.

She used a remote to unlock the doors of a midsize American-made convertible.

Without thinking, he crossed to the car and opened the driver's door. She paused a moment, surprise flickering across her face. Although the expression disappeared in a split second, her cheeks remained a bit more pink than normal.

His own face flared with heat. "I beg your indulgence, ma'am, but in England, one always holds open a door for a lady."

She smiled. "No need to apologize. It's still a common practice here in the South, too. Thank you." She climbed in, and he secured the door.

As he went around to the other side, she started the engine and closed the roof. After he was situated inside, she handed him several packets of collated pages.

"Here is information on each of the sites we'll be visiting today. I thought you might like to know a little about each place before we arrive."

He regarded her from the corner of his eye as she reached behind her to put her case on the backseat, fastened her seat belt, slid on a pair of stylish sunglasses, and shifted the car into reverse.

Glancing through the brochures, he looked for the best aspects of each locale. He didn't want Anne to think he was focusing only on the negatives, but with the list of requirements Courtney had passed along to him this morning, he wondered if they'd be able to find a place.

By the time they left the third site, Anne was annoyed with him. He tried to be positive, but none of the three would be suitable.

The first, a privately owned park, was too close to the motorway and the airport. While they looked at the beautiful open pavilion, the owner's description of the amenities was drowned out by a jet coming in for a landing.

The second site, a converted nineteenth-century sugar refinery, had an impressive view of downtown Bonneterre, but the narrow, winding carriageway wasn't paved and wasn't conducive to the limousines or luxury cars the guests would be arriving in.

The third site, the courtyard of the university's horticultural gardens, was fine until the groundskeeper mentioned the building would be undergoing internal restoration beginning next week and would be inaccessible to the guests, necessitating portaloos—not acceptable.

Anne drove across the campus toward the fourth property, and George's hopes rose. The driveway was wide and well paved. The crepe myrtles that lined the drive were covered in bright pink blossoms—Courtney's favorite color.

"How long do the trees bloom?"

"All summer. Since it stays so warm here, they don't usually lose their color until October."

The building they approached resembled his employer's antebellum mansion, except on a grander scale, and sat on a bluff overlooking a small lake to the west and the college campus to the east, which should appeal to his employer's sense of the dramatic.

Anne parked near the building under one of the enormous shade trees that encircled the lot. A young woman—pretty with ginger hair—met them on the wide porch that wrapped all the way around the building.

When the two women exchanged a kiss on the cheek, George was struck by how much they favored each other.

Anne turned and motioned toward him. "George Laurence, this is Meredith Guidry, executive director of events and facilities for Boudreaux-Guidry Enterprises."

Mededith was slimmer and several inches shorter than Anne,

but her handshake was surprisingly strong. "Welcome to Lafitte's Landing, Mr. Laurence."

"Guidry. . . ?" He glanced from Meredith to Anne and back. "Are you related, by chance, to Forbes Guidry?"

Meredith smiled. "He's my brother."

"Which makes you two. . ." He pointed from one to the other.

"Cousins." Anne nodded.

Meredith swept her arm out to the left. "Why don't we walk around the building so you can get a feel for the views this site offers?"

George walked beside Meredith and tried to concentrate as she launched into the history of the building, which had originally been a plantation house, including what year it had been built and the subsequent fires, reconstructions, and expansions. When they'd made a full circuit of the building, she pointed out the magnificent vista of the lake.

The view was breathtaking. He couldn't find a fault with this site. . .so far. As a bead of sweat trickled between his shoulder blades, George reached up to loosen his tie but stopped and returned his hand to his side. Everything his father had taught him about maintaining a professional appearance no matter the weather rang through his memory.

"Would you like to see inside?" Meredith asked him, moving to open the double doors before he could do it for her.

Cool air poured out onto the porch, and George stepped in across the raised threshold. The interior of the building featured decor appropriate for the 1840s, the period in which it had been built, according to Meredith. The wood floors gleamed, the crystal chandelier in the wide entry foyer sparkled and threw rainbows around the room, and the enormous ballroom at the center would be large enough to hold the two hundred invited guests—with dining tables and a separate dance floor area. The cavernous, three-story-high room had wood wainscoting up to the windowsills and rough white plaster above. Tall windows let in plenty of light and all of the views surrounding the building.

As he turned to tell Anne he thought they should move this property to the top of the list, her cell phone rang.

"Please excuse me. I must take this call." She stepped back into the entry hall.

To fill the time while Anne was on the phone, Meredith recounted a few events the venue had hosted over the years.

Even though Anne had stepped into the entryway, George could still hear her voice and see her from where he stood near the entrance of the ballroom.

"Hello, Amanda. How is the bride-to-be? Only four and a half days left." Her posture and cheerful expression changed as she said, "Oh, honey, that's just prewedding jitters. I'm sure he'll—"

The caller interrupted her, and Anne's shoulders slumped as she raised her right hand to rub her forehead. She squeezed her eyes closed and grimaced as she listened to her client. Her voice was low and soothing when she continued. "Sweetie, I understand you feel like you're never going to be able to work this out, but I know David really loves you. Let's not cancel anything until we have a chance to sit down and talk about it. What time does he get off work? Six? All right. I'll tell you what. I'll call him at work. I want both of you to come over to the office this evening, and we'll sit down and discuss this. Okay, honey? You're very emotional right now, and I don't want you to make a decision you'll end up regretting. I'll see you tonight, sweetie."

George was so focused on Anne that he started when Meredith cleared her throat. "She is very good at her job."

"Yes, she is brilliant at her job."

As he listened to Anne on the phone with the disgruntled groom, he realized that not only was she a wedding planner, but she was as close to a marriage counselor as some couples would ever have. Her caring came from having genuine feelings for the people she worked for, not just a concern for her business's bottom line. He suspected that if she felt it would be in the clients' best interest to call off the wedding, she'd be the first one to tell them so.

He asked God to forgive him for ever doubting Anne's ability to plan this wedding. He just hoped when the time came and his true role was revealed, Anne would be able to forgive him, too.

Chapter 8

From the expression of pitying concern on George's face, Anne knew he'd overheard her phone conversations. She should have walked farther away. Following George and Meredith out of Lafitte's, she felt turmoil built up inside. If he had been checking up on her Saturday because he didn't trust her ability to plan his wedding, she needed to know. She'd prove to him she could do this as well as or better than anyone else.

Her thoughts returned to her more pressing situation as George took pictures of Lafitte's Landing with the digital camera in his PDA. She and Amanda had grown up together but had never really been friends until just a few years ago when they had run into each other at church. She'd been surprised when Amanda asked her to plan her wedding, knowing how tight finances were for the couple, as they were also purchasing a house.

What Amanda and David didn't know was that for their wedding gift, Anne was providing her services for free. Through her connections in town, she'd gotten deep discounts on nearly everything for the rehearsal dinner, ceremony, and reception. She hadn't asked them for a deposit check, and she was scheduled to have the final meeting with them tomorrow, when she planned on handing them her bill, marked Paid in Full.

Now she had to try to put all the pieces back together before her friends made a huge mistake by calling off their wedding. She wasn't worried about the logistics of canceling an event with such short notice—she'd done it several times before. But she knew deep down that these two people were supposed to be married. She just had to get them to see that.

She nearly bumped into George when she walked out the front door.

"Thank you for your hospitality." George shook hands with Meredith again. "I will speak with the bride by telephone tonight and hope to speak with you again tomorrow."

"Thank you, Mr. Laurence. I hope your fiancée likes Lafitte's Landing as much as you do." Meredith turned to Anne. "I'll see you later."

Anne hugged her cousin. "Thanks for meeting us up here, Mere. I'll talk to you soon."

"I'm sure you will."

Anne ignored the saucy gleam in Meredith's eyes and followed George to the car.

A slight breeze rustled the top of the canopy of trees. The buzz of cicadas resonated in harmony with the sound of the lake in the background and the birds chirping overhead. Lafitte's Landing was one of Anne's favorite places, and she recommended it to nearly every client with a large guest list. The fact that it was owned by B-G Enterprises and she could count on Meredith's help, as well as B-G's executive chef, Major O'Hara, helped a lot.

In the car, she turned up the air conditioner and looked at her day planner. They had appointments to visit two additional sites down in the nearby town of Comeaux but weren't scheduled to see the next one for nearly two more hours.

She fastened her seat belt and pulled out of the small parking lot. Her stomach clenched, reminding her that breakfast five hours ago had consisted of a banana and a small bowl of dry cereal, as she'd been out of milk.

Mr. Laurence—George—deserved to be able to stop for lunch, too. Just because she usually worked through lunch didn't mean she had to force him to do the same.

"Do you like seafood, George?" She stopped at the end of Lafitte's Landing's long driveway. She waited for his answer, since it would determine which direction she turned.

"Yes. And I have heard that the seafood in Louisiana is incomparable."

"Well, I think it's pretty wonderful, but I don't have much to compare it to." She turned right and headed south instead of back toward her office.

After a few moments of silence, George asked, "Is planning an outdoor event more difficult than indoor?"

"Somewhat. There are more variables—more things that can go wrong, more safeguards and alternatives that need to be planned. It's almost like planning two events in one." She glanced at him from the corner of her eye. Even though his posture was erect, his body language was relaxed, comfortable. She narrowed her eyes a little as she returned her focus to the road. She wanted to ask him why he'd been watching her Saturday morning, but the words wouldn't leave her mouth.

"I'm very pleased with Lafitte's Landing. I believe we've just secured the location for the engagement party. I'll send my. . . Courtney a message."

She glanced at him again and saw he was reviewing the digital pictures he'd taken of the location on the screen of his PDA. Whenever he spoke of Courtney, he tripped over her name. He never personalized the relationship—and if he ever did say "my," he always stopped himself as if not wanting to commit to saying "my fiancée."

Silence descended on them as she navigated lunch-hour traffic in midtown. Without thinking, she powered on the stereo.

Beside her, George started visibly when Dean Martin singing "That's Amore" blasted through the speakers. Embarrassed, she fumbled with the buttons and turned it off again.

"No, don't turn it off." George reached over and turned it on again but adjusted the volume lower. "Not many people listen to Dean Martin these days."

Her cheeks burned. Yet another example of how backward she was—she didn't even listen to contemporary music.

"They just don't make music like this anymore. It's a shame, really."

Was he serious or patronizing her? He'd leaned his head back against the headrest, and he looked fully relaxed. The CD moved to the next track, and he started to hum, then sing along with "Memories Are Made of This." Same taste in music to add to the ever-growing list of his attractions. He probably liked old movies, too.

Twenty minutes later, after being treated to George's perfect imitation of Dean Martin through several of her favorite songs, she slowed and passed an old-fashioned general store and gas station. "This is the town of Comeaux."

George craned his neck to take in the sights. "How far outside of Bonneterre have we come?"

"We're only about twenty miles from Town Square—about ten miles from the city limits. I know it feels like we're out in the middle of nowhere."

"How beautiful."

Anne glanced past George at the enormous, gingerbread Victorian house. "That's the Plantation Inn Bed and Breakfast. Some of my clients who can't afford big expensive trips for their honeymoons come down here. I've stayed here a couple of times, too, when I just needed to get away."

A few blocks down, she pulled into the gravel parking lot in front of a building sided with rough wood planks that featured fishing gear hanging from rusted iron nails as decorations.

The interior of the Fishin' Shack was dim and cool compared to the sultry sunshine of a June day in Louisiana. The aroma of sweet seafood and spicy Cajun seasonings hit her full force as she entered. Her stomach growled loudly.

"Anne, what are you doing here?" Jenn stepped away from a

table and met her at the door.

Anne hugged her cousin. "I'm in the area looking at venues and had to stop somewhere for lunch." She stepped out of her cousin's embrace before the younger woman spilled the iced-tea pitcher she held.

Jenn looked behind Anne, and her eyes widened when she saw George.

"Jennifer Guidry, this is George Laurence, my client." Anne stepped back to include George. "Jenn is the owner of this place."

"My pleasure, Miss Guidry." He paused, her hand still clasped in his. "Guidry. . .let me guess—another one of Anne's cousins."

"Yep, and proud of it." Jenn led them to a table away from the moderate-sized lunch crowd and placed the large laminated menus on the table as Anne slid into the booth. Jenn turned to George. "Since you've never been here, I'll let you know that our Cajun dishes are very spicy, but we can tone that down if you like. If you don't see anything on the menu that you like, just let me know, and I'll talk to the chef." She winked at him.

Anne held in her laugh as her cousin turned on all of her Southern charm for the handsome Englishman. When Jenn returned with their beverages, George ordered the traditional fish 'n' chips basket, while Anne ordered her favorite Cajun grilled shrimp Caesar salad.

As they waited for their meals, she struggled to think of a neutral topic of conversation but was saved from having to come up with appropriate small talk when George remarked, "Hawthorne isn't a name one would typically associate with Louisiana."

He wasn't the first person who'd pointed that out to her. "No. My father was from Boston but came here for college, where he met my mother." She'd explained this so many times over the years it was hard to keep it from sounding rehearsed.

"I've been to Boston. It's a very interesting city."

"So I've heard." Anne traced the ring of moisture her glass of tea left on the table as she took a sip.

"You've never gone there yourself? Not even to visit family?"

"I. . .don't fly." Anne swallowed hard and raised her left hand to make sure her shirt collar covered the twenty-seven-year-old scar on the side of her neck.

"Why ever not?" As soon as the words were out of his mouth, he held up his hand in front of him. "No, wait. I apologize. That question is presumptuous. Please do not feel you have to answer it."

"It's all right." She took a fortifying breath. "You see, when I was eight—"

"Here's your lunch!" Jenn called cheerily as she swooped down upon them. She gave Anne a wink and floated away to visit with other patrons.

"You were about to tell me why you don't fly," he reminded her.

Anne lifted her napkin to dab the corners of her mouth and cleared her throat. "The only time I was ever on a plane was with my parents when I was eight. It was a commuter plane that held thirty people. The pilot tried to take off in the middle of a thunderstorm, but. . ." She took a deep breath to calm her voice and try to settle her stomach. "We crashed, and I was one of only five people who survived."

Silence settled over the table. He swallowed a couple of times. "I'm sorry."

She shook her head. "Don't be. It was a very long time ago. I tried to get on a plane when I was fifteen and had such a bad panic attack that they had to take me to the emergency room." She hadn't meant to reveal that to him. No one outside of her family—except for the airline and emergency room staff who'd helped—knew about it.

He nodded slowly, taking a moment to push a morsel of fish onto the back of his fork with his knife. Before putting the bite in his mouth, he asked, "Where would you have gone had you gotten on that plane?"

"New York with my grandparents and aunt and uncle." She pushed her half-finished salad toward the end of the table to let Jenn or the other servers milling around know they could take it away. She'd felt half-starved when they sat down, yet talking about her aversion to flying spoiled her appetite.

"And have you never tried to board a plane since then?"

Why had he decided to take such an interest in this topic? She leaned back against the padded booth seat and crossed her arms. "No. I'd love to see Europe, but I don't want to go through another panic attack."

"Hmm." It was a short sound from the back of his throat. "Have you ever considered taking a ship over?"

He was as tenacious as a coonhound that had treed its prey. Why wouldn't he just let it drop? "I've looked into it, but being self-employed, I can't be gone for that long. How often do you go back to England?" Hopefully he'd take the hint and let her change the subject.

"I've traveled to England several times in the past few years in the capacity of my job." He wiped his mouth with his napkin, then laid it beside his plate. "Do you mind if I ask, how did you come to the decision to pursue a career as a wedding planner?"

Not really the topic she wanted to discuss, but much better than talking about planes and flying. "When I left graduate school, I went to work as the event planner for B-G—yes, the job Meredith has now. After several years, I realized I enjoyed planning weddings the most and felt like God was leading me to start my own business."

A light Anne hadn't seen before sparked to life in George's eyes. "You felt *God* was leading you? I've always admired people who listen for God's voice and take the leaps of faith He sometimes asks of them."

Was George a believer? She wanted to ask but didn't want to embarrass him. "Faith is something I've struggled with my whole life. But I knew I just had to do it."

"What a blessing. . .to know what you're doing is God's plan." His voice sounded almost sad. "And you are good at it. I. . .I happened by the Bonneterre Chapel Saturday morning and watched you work. I should have made my presence known, but you were busy, and I didn't want to interrupt."

His admitting he'd been there was a surprise, but the words of affirmation floored her. "Thank you. What brought you by the church?"

"I was out for a drive and was drawn to it. I would like to find a congregation to attend regularly, since I will be living here until October. I noticed the door was open and let myself in. It's a beautiful church."

"Yes. It's a very easy place to hold a wedding. Not much in the way of decoration is needed, and the colors are neutral enough that they go with anything a bride could choose. Plus, I know practically everyone on staff—that's the church I grew up in."

"And do you still attend there?" Interest in the subject lent a new warmth to George's handsome features.

Anne's heart skipped a beat when his brown eyes twinkled. "I do, although sometimes it's hard to make it to Sunday morning service when I have a late evening wedding the day before. Are you—did you grow up going to church as well?"

He shook his head. "No, I prayed to receive Christ as my Savior about twenty years ago. The head of staff at my first professional position was a Christian. We read the Bible and prayed together every day before we started work."

"Do you still keep in touch with him?" She smiled up at the waiter who came by to clear their plates, then returned her focus to George.

"He passed away five years ago, just after I came to the States to work." George's eyes softened as he spoke of his mentor. "I couldn't attend his funeral, and while I do miss being able to speak with him, I know I'll see him again."

His openness made Anne even more uncomfortable. Every detail she learned about him served to reinforce her attraction to him. She couldn't allow herself to feel this way about a client. She wasn't sure what to say, and silence once again settled between them.

They were saved from a moment of awkwardness when Jenn

returned to the table. "How were your meals?"

"Very good, as usual," Anne told her cousin, but Jenn wasn't looking at her.

"The fish and chips reminded me of a pub in London we frequented when I was a boy." George smiled politely.

Even though she hadn't known him long, just from watching him carefully today and in their past few meetings, Anne was starting to be able to read his facial expressions. He was better at controlling his reactions and schooling his features than she, but his eyes gave him away. His beautiful eyes that were the color of sun-brewed iced tea. . . the very same eyes that were now looking at her askance.

"Anne?" Jenn nudged her. "Are you all right?"

"I'm fine. I just zoned out there for a second." Heat crawled up her cheeks.

Jenn removed the cap of her pen with her teeth to write something on her order pad. Speaking around the cap, she said, "I asked what site y'all are going to visit next."

"Oh. Comeaux Town Center. Then Benoit Hall."

"Lafitte's Landing has those two beaten, hands down." Jenn tore off the sheet she'd written on and put it facedown on the table in front of Anne. "George, great to meet you. Hopefully I'll see you around again soon."

He nodded noncommittally.

Jenn leaned over and kissed Anne's cheek. "Annie, I'll see you back here for dinner Thursday night."

"I should be here, but don't be surprised if I'm late." Anne picked up the ticket and slid out of the booth.

"I'll save you a seat."

"Thanks." She gave her cousin a quick hug. As soon as Jenn walked away, Anne reached into her small purse and pulled out a twenty-dollar bill, which she left on the table.

George reached for his wallet, but Anne stopped him. "I never make a client pay for a meal. Company policy."

He looked uncomfortable but didn't argue with her.

Anne looked down at the check. Rather than a receipt for their lunch, it was a note in her cousin's chunky, loopy script. She read it as she walked toward the door.

He's hot. Find out if he has a brother and let me know.

—J

Anne smiled and shook her head. When would her cousin figure out that she was a wedding planner, not a matchmaker?

Chapter 9

At eight o'clock Tuesday evening, fourteen hours since the beginning of her workday, Anne locked the front door of her office and turned off all the lights. But after two hours of draining mediation, Amanda and David's wedding was a go for Saturday.

Her back ached between her shoulders, and she rolled her neck to try to work out the stiffness. Next stop: home, where she would fill the spa tub with hot water and her favorite tea-therapy essential oils and try to release some of this stress. Her stomach rumbled, and she adjusted her plans to include running by Rotier's on the way to get her favorite grilled chicken club sandwich.

The sandwich never made it out of the car. In the ten minutes from the restaurant to the converted Victorian triplex, she'd wolfed down the club and most of the large order of french fries. Her eyelids drooped as she parked between Jennifer's red classic Mustang and Meredith's white, late-model Volvo SUV.

She'd rather hoped the girls would have gone out tonight so she could be sure of some private time to unwind. Even though each had her own apartment—Meredith on the ground floor, Jennifer on the third, and Anne in the middle—they rarely, if ever, hesitated to drop in on each other if the mood struck. Especially Jenn, who couldn't seem to comprehend why anyone would ever want to be alone.

Anne waved bugs out of her face as she fumbled to find the

key to the back door. Maybe they should replace the incandescent porch light with a bug zapper.

She smiled and crossed the threshold. With the deposit for the Landry-Laurence wedding safely tucked away in the bank, she could get an architect out to start redesigning this place back into a grand single-family home. She hadn't told the girls yet, just in case something fell through. But it was time for all of them to move on, live by themselves.

Thursday night at the family singles' dinner would be the perfect time. That way she wouldn't get fussed at for leaving someone out of the telling.

The wooden stairs creaked, and she winced, hoping neither of the girls would notice. The rear entrance opened into her kitchen. She snapped on the lights. . .and groaned. A couple of cabinet doors stood ajar, and half of her mixing and serving bowls sat on the previously empty countertop.

"Hey, Anne—" Meredith stopped in the doorway.

Anne dropped her bags on the kitchen table, shrugged out of her suit jacket, and waved toward the mess. "Jenn?"

Meredith nodded, stepped back out into the hall, and bellowed her sister's name. "She came down a couple of hours ago to 'borrow' some flour—and sugar and eggs and baking soda. I didn't realize she needed something to mix it all up in, too."

Anne leaned over to replace the stack of bowls in the cabinet under the sink. "Looks like she needed the mixer, too. How a woman who has her own business—"

"You rang?" Jennifer bounced into the room. "Oh, sorry. I was about to come down and put all that away, Anne."

Meredith sat at the table, and Jennifer hopped up to sit on the counter beside the refrigerator. So much for a quiet evening and a long, hot bath.

"So—are you going out with him?"

"Going out with—no, he's engaged!" Why in the world would Jenn ask that when she knew George Laurence was a client?

Jenn's pixie-esque face crumpled into a frown. "Danny Mendoza's engaged? Then what's he doing sending you flowers?"

"What are you—?" Anne turned and for the first time noticed an enormous floral arrangement in the middle of the table. She must be more tired than she thought to have missed it. Meredith plucked the card off its stick and handed it to her. The flap on the tiny envelope hadn't been sealed, thus explaining how Jenn already knew who'd sent them. Anne opened it and read the note:

Anne—

Sorry I've missed you the last few times I've called. I hope to talk to you soon and look forward to getting to know you better.

Danny Mendoza

What was wrong with him? He'd stood her up a week and a half ago, and she'd been avoiding his calls since then. Why wasn't he getting the hint?

"Obviously he cares enough to drop a wad of money on flowers." Jenn cupped a stargazer lily and inhaled its spicy fragrance. "Are you going out with him again?"

"What *again*? I haven't been out with him *yet*." Anne concentrated on putting the card back into its sleeve. She worked with April's Flowers enough to know Danny had indeed "dropped a wad of money," as Jenn so eloquently put it. Over two feet tall and about as wide, the bouquet featured not only the dark pink and white lilies, but also deep red roses, purple delphiniums, pink gerbera daisies, blue phlox, violet veronicas, lilac blossoms, and white hydrangeas.

"How could you not see them when you came in?" Meredith fingered a velvety rose.

"Have you seen the two arrangements in my living room? I have two others at my office, in addition to the purple tulips I get from April's Flowers every time they get some in stock. The florist shops around here like me to keep them in mind when making recommendations to clients, so I get at least two or three deliveries every couple of weeks." She turned the vase so the large purple bow faced forward. "I don't think that going out with someone whose schedule is as hectic as mine is a good idea. When I meet the right man, I'll know it."

The image of George Laurence flooded her mind's eye. Why did he have to be engaged? She tried to stop the flutter in her heart, but the memory of their conversation over lunch yesterday—his gentle humor, his deep faith, his expressive brown eyes, his to-die-for accent—wouldn't go away.

"Oh, really, Anne!" Jenn slid down from her perch, arms crossed. "When are you going to give up on the idea of love at first si—" She jerked and grabbed for the cell phone hanging from her tiny waistband. "Sorry, gals, it's the restaurant." She whizzed out the door, phone to ear.

"Don't mind her." Meredith stood and stretched. "She and Clay Huntoon broke up."

Anne frowned. "Clay Huntoon? The sports reporter for Channel Six who sings at church occasionally? Did I know she was seeing him?"

Meredith smiled and shook her head. "That's how she met Danny Mendoza—Danny and Clay work together."

"I swear she changes boyfriends like socks." Anne fingered the waxy petal of one of the stargazer lilies. "Do you think maybe that's why she's so keen to find out if I plan to see Danny again? Do you think she might be interested in him?"

"Dunno. Maybe." With a shrug, Meredith crossed to the door. "Hey, have you heard from Major O'Hara the last couple of weeks?"

Anne shook her head. "No, why?"

"He asked about you this afternoon—mentioned we haven't worked any events with you recently, was wondering how you are, and said he'd probably give you a call to see if you have any small events he might pick up freelance."

"Really? Are things so slow there that he has time to cater non-B-G events? I mean, it must really eat into the time he gets to spend with Debbonnaire."

"You really are behind the times, Anne. Major and Deb broke up before Christmas. She wanted him to propose—after dating only two months, if you can believe that." Meredith pressed her lips together. "Well, I'd better get going. I'll tell Major tomorrow you'll be calling." Meredith pulled the door closed behind her. "Good night, Annie."

" 'Night, Mere. No, sweet dreams instead." She grinned when Meredith stuck her tongue out at their long-standing joke.

After putting her kitchen to rights, Anne slid the chain lock into place and put a pot of English toffee–flavored decaf coffee on to brew.

The news that Major O'Hara was once again available hadn't struck her the way it would have a few weeks ago. Twenty years ago, when he'd started working for Aunt Maggie, fifteen-year-old Anne had been sure she was going to marry him one day. Although he seemed to enjoy flirting with her, he never hinted he would consider asking her out. Then she met Cliff Ballantine and allowed her relationship with Major to fall into a comfortable friendship.

She forced Major's dimpled smile to replace George's sharp features and brown eyes in her imagination. If she was going to obsess about someone, better for him to be someone available. She concentrated on Major, trying to remember the last time she'd seen him. Hadn't it been at church a month or so ago?

Had George found a church to attend yet?

"Stop it."

She carried her laptop computer into the bathroom and set it on a low stool. Perching on the side of the tub, she held her hand under the faucet, and when the water reached a comfortable temperature, she measured out two capfuls of the black-tea-and-red-currant bath oil.

Going back into the kitchen, she filled a latte mug with the richly scented coffee, doctored it with a bit of half-and-half and sugar, then went into the living room to grab a DVD. She hadn't indulged in a bath and movie evening in quite a while.

Not even twenty minutes into *My Fair Lady*, Anne stopped it and brought up the computer's media player to listen to music instead. Why did Professor Henry Higgins remind her of George? Was it his influence over Courtney that made her seem older than her nineteen years? Had he seen her as a diamond in the rough and fallen in love with her as he taught her etiquette? Or was he just a wealthy man who wanted a beautiful wife and decided to get one young enough that he could mold her into the kind of woman he wanted her to be?

How had they met? He self-admittedly had never been to Bonneterre before. In fact, aside from the New York area code on the business card he'd given her, she wasn't sure where he lived.

And where had his money come from? Probably some old, aristocratic family in England, with the legacy fortune passed down to and doubled by each successive generation.

Closing her eyes, she sipped her coffee as the strains of Frank Sinatra's "Come Fly with Me" wafted through the steamy room.

She'd opened up with him over lunch yesterday more than with anyone outside of Meredith and Forbes. Not even Jenn knew all of the details of Anne's parents' deaths or of why she had started her own business.

The next song started, and rather than picturing Dean Martin, she could clearly imagine George Laurence serenading her with "Return to Me," her favorite song.

She jumped out of the tub, not caring that she splashed water all over the rugs and tile floor, and turned the music off. Jamming her arms into her bathrobe, she fled to the kitchen, where she grabbed her planner and flipped to the address book.

"Please let him still have this number." She picked up her cell phone and dialed. It rang once. . .twice. . .

"Hello?"

"Hi, Major, it's Anne Hawthorne. . . ."

Soft amber light pooled on the brick walkway from the faux gas lamp outside Anne Hawthorne's office. George stopped. Why had he come down this way? There weren't any restaurants on this side of Town Square.

He had to stop thinking about Anne Hawthorne. He was here to do a job, and once finished, he'd go away. She would stay here with her family and her successful business.

Maybe if he confided in her—no. If he told Anne he wasn't the groom, he would be breaking the contract, and it would put her in an awkward position with her cousin Forbes. Anne would ask questions George couldn't answer, and that would only make matters worse.

After lunch yesterday, though, he was hard pressed to deny the growing attraction he felt for her. He wanted to spend more time with her, wanted to be the one to whom she told all her secrets, in whom she confided her dreams and fears. Asking her to go out socially was out of the question as long as she thought he was the groom. He couldn't do anything to compromise his employment or Anne.

Why was he still here? Nothing he could do or say would justify his lurking outside of Anne's office at nine o'clock in the evening. He crossed Town Square toward the lights and music emanating from the Riverwalk. He fruitlessly wished Anne had still been working so he could have invited her to dinner.

He grimaced. Yes, a romantic dinner with someone he'd spent the last two weeks purposely deceiving. What a brilliant idea.

He chose an open-air café, and the hostess showed him to a small wrought-iron table. He took the chair that faced the river. Although his stomach clenched with hunger, his appetite was gone. Nothing on the menu piqued his interest. He ordered a Caesar salad and let the waitress talk him into trying their peach-flavored iced tea.

What did Anne do outside of her work? His own job was such that he was always on call, necessitating that he drop his own plans whenever his employer wanted something. Anne was self-employed. She could set her own hours. What interests did she pursue? Did she have hobbies?

He'd had a glimpse of that outside life yesterday when she turned on the music in the car. To hear the strains of his favorite singer coming from her stereo. . . He'd never met another woman who enjoyed listening to the classics. Most women thought he was odd for not enjoying the latest noisemakers.

With whom did she spend her free time? Obviously, she had family in town. He shook his head, remembering her cousins. Jennifer Guidry—pretty, young, and flirtatious—had mentioned seeing Anne again on Thursday night. Not for the first time did he wish he had a group of friends or relatives to spend time with. Although he guarded his personal space and private time jealously, he still needed fellowship and companionship.

Lights from the buildings behind him twinkled on the surface of the river. He leaned forward, resting his elbows on the small table.

Are you testing me, God? Is this attraction supposed to be a test of my ability to keep my word to my employer while not lying to Anne? How am I supposed to do both?

He gave the waitress a tight smile as she set the glass of tea down. Absently, he lifted it and took a sip, then groaned. It had taken him years to learn to enjoy cold tea, but he'd forgotten restaurants in the South always overloaded theirs with sugar.

He flagged down another server and requested a glass of water with no ice and a slice of lemon.

He envied Anne. She'd found what she enjoyed doing and had created a flourishing business. He was jealous of Jennifer Guidry's precocious success as a restaurateur. The girl couldn't be thirty years old yet had built a restaurant that seemed to thrive in an out-of-the-way town when the chances for failure in the food-service industry were high.

Both women had found a way to make their dreams come true, while his still remained only a fantasy. Maybe he wasn't praying about it often enough or listening for God's answer hard enough.

"George?"

George started at Forbes's voice. He stood and extended his right hand. "Good evening, Forbes."

The lawyer smiled, his eyes reflecting the glow of the Japanese paper lanterns strung around the café. "I'm glad to see you're getting out and enjoying Bonneterre."

"Yes. The city has many charms." George glanced around at the women gaping or batting their eyelashes at Forbes. "Won't you join me?"

"Ah, I'd love to, but—" Forbes nodded toward a nearby table at which sat a breathtaking redhead. He grinned. "It's a business dinner, but that doesn't keep her from wanting my sole attention."

George smiled. "If you have to do business over dinner, at least the company is pleasant to look at."

"Speaking of dinner company, do you have plans Thursday night?"

"Not particularly. Just work."

"Now, George, you know what they say: All work and no play makes George a dull boy. I know you've got a reputation to protect, so bring Courtney along with you, if you don't think that'll make things too uncomfortable."

"Miss Courtney is in Paris." George's mind raced. Thursday was the night Anne and Jenn were supposed to be having dinner.

"Then you must come. I'll make sure no one asks you any probing questions. You can't just sit around at home by yourself for the next four months."

"Just how many will be at this dinner?"

"Oh, five or six others—Anne, my sisters Jennifer and Meredith, a few other miscellaneous cousins." Forbes squeezed George's shoulder. "Say you'll come. Anne will never forgive me if she finds out you're spending the night by yourself when you could be with us."

"When and where?"

"The Fishin' Shack—it's Jenn's restaurant. Take River Road south out of town and go about twenty minutes to the town of Comeaux—"

George held his hand up with a smile. "I've been there once already, so it should be no trouble to locate again."

"Excellent. We'll see you there around seven Thursday night."

George sank into his chair. He'd get to see Anne in a social setting and meet more of her family. Would she be happy to see him? She seemed to enjoy the time they'd spent together yesterday—

No, he was deluding himself. The attention Anne showed him amounted to nothing more than professional courtesy. She thought he was a client—someone who was getting married—but he was letting it go to his head, thinking that somehow, deep down, she must know he wasn't the groom, imagining she was as attracted to him as he was to her.

The story of his life—he liked a woman he couldn't have because of his social status or job. He had to find some way to cure himself of the attraction and refocus on the job at hand.

Chapter 10

With a wave and return greeting, Anne swept past the hostess and made her way through the crowded restaurant to the large round table in the back. She wasn't the first to arrive, as several cousins sat around talking and laughing over their iced tea and hush puppies.

Meredith scooted out the chair beside her for Anne, who slid into it gratefully. "Working late?"

Anne nodded. "Probably would have worked straight through dinner if Forbes hadn't called me to tell me he was leaving the office later than usual. I didn't tell him I was still at work myself."

"Big wedding this weekend?"

"Yeah, so I'm going to have to eat and run."

"I'm just glad you've been able to make it to as many dinners this summer as you have. When you're not out on dates, that is." Meredith winked.

Anne grabbed a glass and filled it from the pitcher of sweet tea in the middle of the table. Thursday night dinners with the family were easier to work into her schedule than dates with men she didn't know and didn't particularly want to meet. With her family, she could be herself; she could put aside the persona of the outgoing, vivacious professional woman everyone else wanted to see her as. She could let her vulnerabilities show, could let someone else support her for a little while.

"I'm a little surprised Forbes isn't here yet." She looked over her shoulder toward the door. "If he left downtown around the same time I left. . ."

Meredith turned to answer a question from one of their cousins, leaving Anne to her own thoughts. Oh, to meet a man she could feel as comfortable with as she did her family. To be able to talk to him like she had with George here in this very restaurant three days ago.

She wasn't supposed to be thinking about him in that way. He'd already made his choice of partner, and she'd no more try to win him away than she would try to break up a married couple. She had to overcome these feelings. She *had* to.

"Oh, Anne, did you ever talk to Major?" Meredith asked.

"I did. We're having dinner—so I can go over a couple of upcoming events with him to get bids on catering them. That's all." At least, Anne told herself, she didn't have any other motives for getting together with the handsome chef whom longtime Bonneterre residents still remembered as a high school and college football star.

"Hey, y'all."

Forbes's voice startled her. She hated sitting on this side of the table where she had her back to the main part of the restaurant.

"I've brought a guest tonight."

Anne twisted around and nearly fell off the seat. Behind Forbes stood George Laurence, looking handsomer than ever in a cobalt blue button-down and khakis. The shirt hugged his muscular shoulders, and the bright blue hue turned his eyes from cinnamon brown to a deep chocolate.

Anne had to tear her gaze away from George before he caught her staring at him as Forbes introduced him around the table. When Forbes had called her half an hour ago, she'd been begging God to take away the attraction she felt toward her client. God hadn't answered her prayer.

"We're so glad you could join us, George," Meredith said after shaking hands with him. "I believe the seat beside Anne is unclaimed."

No! Anne wanted to yell at her cousin. The last thing she needed was to spend time with George Laurence outside of work.

She was forced to paste on a smile when George looked at her. She couldn't be rude to him. He was her most valuable client, after all. "Yes, please. There's always room for one more."

George sat next to her; Anne's nerves crackled like a live electrical wire. He had some kind of magnetic aura that pulled at her soul, drawing her to him, making her want to know him better. She buried her nose in the menu and tried to calm herself with a few deep breaths.

"Hey, y'all. Sorry I'm late."

The final member of the party, Rafe Guidry, tall and slender with strawberry blond hair like his older sisters, arrived and took the last available seat beside Forbes.

Before Forbes or Anne could make the introduction, Rafe half stood and extended his right hand to George. "Rafael Guidry."

George stood. "George Laurence."

"What kept you?" Jenn leaned over Rafe's shoulder to hand a menu to her younger brother.

"Meeting ran late." Rafe didn't even look at the menu before he handed it to the server while giving his food and beverage order. "Forbes, I now understand why you decided to go to law school instead of taking over the family business."

"Rafe—no business talk at the table, please." Forbes gave him a look only an older brother could get away with, then turned to George. "Our parents are the proprietors of Boudreaux-Guidry Enterprises—the company that owns most of the convention spaces and several hotels and buildings in town. We got our fill of shop-talk around the dinner table when we were kids."

"Which is why Forbes and Jenn got out." Meredith's entry into the conversation surprised Anne, as she usually let Jenn and Forbes overshadow her around nonfamily members.

"But not you." George leaned forward a fraction, though his posture remained perfect.

Anne recognized the same interest in his expression he'd had when their conversation had become personal over lunch the other day. Annoyance filled her for being disappointed her cousin could illicit that reaction from him, too. The man was already engaged to someone else; any interest he'd shown in her had been strictly on a professional level.

Meredith's mouth twisted ruefully. "I decided to major in art history in college. Needless to say, since I didn't want to teach, there really weren't many opportunities out there, so I started working as Anne's assistant at B-G. I took over when she left to start Happy Endings."

George turned to look at Anne. "I'd be interested in hearing, sometime, why you decided to start your own company."

"Anytime." She tried to still the fluttering in her stomach at his intense gaze. At thirty-five, she was far too old to have a schoolgirl crush on a man who was completely unattainable.

"George, do you find Bonneterre to your liking?" Meredith asked.

George answered, and Anne let out a relieved breath. She hated when everyone's attention was on her.

With each word that came from his mouth, Anne's pulse skipped and jumped like a kid on the last day of school. *He's engaged. I'll never work in this town again if word gets out that I've fallen in love with a client. Lord, please help me!*

"All right, George, we're all curious," Rafe interjected, shoveling crawfish cheese dip onto a small plate. "What do you do for a living?"

When George didn't immediately answer, Anne's gaze snapped to him. Why would being asked about his job cause his smile to vanish, his posture to stiffen? She hadn't asked him personal questions because she was afraid that the more she knew about him, the more she'd like him.

He cleared his throat. "I am a household manager and personal assistant."

Anne frowned. Not what she'd expected.

"Okay. . ." Her cousin Jason drawled the word. "What does that mean?"

She was torn between throwing her spoon at her cousin and thanking him for voicing the question in her own mind. She didn't want her family to alienate George and make him decide he didn't want her to plan his wedding, but she really wanted to know everything about him.

"I oversee and attend to all of my employer's personal needs—such as travel plans, social calendar, household organization, setup for entertaining."

"So you're familiar with event planning?" Meredith asked.

He smiled, and his posture eased a bit. "Quite. My employer entertains large numbers of guests at home frequently."

"What a great help for you, Anne." Jenn slipped into her seat as the servers arrived with the entrées. "Who do you work for, George? CEO of a major corporation? An ambassador? A Hollywood megastar? Come on, fess up."

He shook his head, the lines around his eyes tightening. "Part of my job is maintaining discretion."

"I know who it has to be," Rafe said, winking at Anne. "I'll betcha he works for Mel Gibson."

Everyone laughed, and Anne saw George's posture ease again.

"Sean Connery? No? Tom Hanks?" Rafe continued teasing.

Eating gave a much-needed diversion for everyone's attention. Jenn had to excuse herself twice and disappear into the kitchen, and Rafe and Meredith talked shop for a few minutes.

Exhaustion rested heavily on Anne's shoulders. She'd only gotten about four hours of sleep the last three nights. She picked at her crawfish étouffée, eating only the chunks of meat.

"Hey, Annie." Jason speared a shrimp from Jenn's unattended plate. "I talked to Mom on the way over here. She said that she may have to bring the cake for Amanda and David's wedding earlier than planned on Saturday, since she has a birthday cake she has to finish for someone else that afternoon."

"I'll call her first thing in the morning. But it shouldn't be a problem." Anne was keenly aware of George listening to their conversation.

He had a thoughtful expression on his face when she glanced at him. "You have a family member who makes wedding cakes?"

She nodded. "My Aunt Maggie. I would like to set up a time after Courtney gets back in town to do a tasting so y'all can choose the flavor of the cake and the fillings."

"I will check the calendar to arrange a time." He pushed a chunk of salmon toward the edge of his plate and speared a few pieces of romaine and a crouton. "Do you work with your aunt often?"

"I've worked with her since I was nine years old. My first paying job was as her catering assistant." Anne dug the fingernails of her left hand into her palm. Why did she always run on at the mouth whenever he asked her a question?

His smile was inscrutable. "So, in essence, you entered the family business as well."

She blinked a couple of times in surprise and then couldn't stop her smile. "I've never thought about it that way, but I guess you're right."

"But she's bossy, so she wanted to be the one telling everyone else what to do." Jason swiped another shrimp off Jenn's plate. "That's why she started her own business."

"I'm not bossy." Anne laughed as Jason waggled his eyebrows at her. Six years her junior, he'd only been three when she'd come to live with his family after her parents' death. "Okay, maybe I was a little bossy growing up."

Jenn, Meredith, and Rafe scoffed.

Forbes leaned forward to look at her around George. "I hate to be the one to break it to you, my dear, but you do like to be the one in control. . .at least when it comes to your weddings. That's why you work around the clock to make sure everything's up to your exacting standards."

"But that's what makes you so good at what you do." Meredith could always be counted on to defend her.

Anne laughed to keep from groaning. What kind of an impression was George Laurence going to have of her after tonight? Would he still respect her in the morning?

"Anne was featured in one of the bridal magazines a month ago." Jenn jumped into the conversation, slapping Jason's hand away from her plate as she regained her seat. "She's gotten calls from brides all over the country since it came out. Of course, now we can get away with calling her an 'obsessive perfectionist' since it appeared in print from an objective outsider."

"Jenn!" Heat crawled up Anne's cheeks.

"Yes, I saw the article."

George's admission startled Anne.

"That is why Miss Hawthorne was hired to plan this wedding," he continued. "The bride was very impressed by her credentials and the portfolio of photographs from other weddings that were featured."

"So your fiancée decided to get married here just because she read an article about Anne?" Rafe asked.

George shook his head. "No. The bride is originally from Bonneterre and wished to get married in her hometown."

"So that's how you ended up here." Jenn gave George an appraising glance. "You know, George, I'm going to keep bugging you about who you work for until I get it out of you."

The servers returned to the table to remove their dinner plates and offer a dessert menu.

"No dessert for me," Anne said as she handed him her plate, "but I would love a hazelnut cappuccino."

"Brilliant idea." George's voice was soft, as if meant only for himself. "I'll have one of the same, please," he told the waiter.

The talk around the table turned to travel. Anne listened with unbidden fascination to George's descriptions of the distant and exotic places he'd visited. She fought the desire to ask her own questions about his personal life. What had led him into his profession? For whom did he work? Was it someone famous or just wealthy? And how was Courtney—

She gasped, nearly choking on her cappuccino. *His employer!*

Coughing, she grabbed her napkin as Meredith pounded her on the back. "I'm okay—just went down the wrong way," she assured her cousin, her voice raspy. She breathed a little easier when George excused himself from the table.

What he said he did for a living didn't sound like a job that would make him try to shroud his wedding with mystery. What if it was his employer and not himself he was trying to protect? What if he did work for someone famous like Rafe had been teasing about, and that person was embarrassed by George's marrying a girl so much younger?

She needed to go down to the Blanchard Leblanc bookstore, grab as many gossip magazines as she could find, and do some research. If his employer was someone famous, maybe there were pictures of him or her at some event with George hovering in the background—a movie premiere, a black-tie fund-raiser. . . . The coffee scalded her tongue, but she didn't care. Somehow, she had to find out who George Laurence really was.

Yes. Focusing on figuring out who he really was might help her overcome her growing attraction to him.

The house lights lowered. Anne glanced at her watch. How had it gotten to be nine o'clock? She really needed to go back to the office and finish her to-do list for the next two days.

She leaned over to grab her purse from under the table but snapped back upright when the strains of "Volare" started—sung by someone who sounded so close to Dean Martin, chills danced up and down her arms.

She blinked twice just to make sure her eyes weren't playing tricks. Entranced, she couldn't move, couldn't breathe. George Laurence stood on the karaoke stage—now crooning the song's bridge in Italian—sounding just like Dean Martin and giving every indication this was something he not only enjoyed doing, but did often.

Tears burned her eyes. Everything. Every detail about this man fit her long-held mental image of her soul mate. Cliff's weaknesses, the things about him that had driven her crazy, were George's strengths: his ability to socialize with grace, his discretion, his apparent good stewardship of his money. . . . She had a feeling George would never pretend to be in love with a woman just to gain his own end, the way Cliff had used her.

How could God do this to her? Bring the perfect man into her life only to force her to help him marry someone else?

She fled the restaurant. Her car's engine came to life with a roar. But instead of putting it into gear and driving away, she pounded her fists on the steering wheel.

"This is my punishment, isn't it, God?" she cried. "You're punishing me because I've never been able to forgive Cliff Ballantine for what he did to me, aren't You? I don't want to forgive him! He ruined my life. I dropped out of graduate school to work and send him money, and then he dumped me so he could go off and become a famous movie star and I could work myself practically to death to pay off all the debt I went into for him. Why is it fair that You're punishing me by showing me what I can't have, and he's had everything go right for him?"

She slammed the car into gear and screeched the tires pulling out of the parking lot. Taking a deep breath, she tried to calm down. "Lord, I know You have a plan for my life. But if it includes forgiving Cliff Ballantine, I'm not sure I can do it."

Chapter 11

The coffee shop inside the Blanchard Leblanc bookstore was Anne's favorite place to unwind on a Sunday afternoon. She sipped her caramel-hazelnut latte and claimed one of the overstuffed armchairs near the front windows. Heavy rain pelted the glass, drowning out the low buzz of noise from the other customers.

She set the stack of magazines she'd just purchased on the floor and pulled *People* off the top. Most of the publications she'd purchased were running celebrity wedding issues, serving dual purpose as research materials. She retrieved an empty folder and scissors from her attaché to save any interesting articles or photos.

Usually she just flipped through the pages, not paying attention to anything but the wedding articles and pictures. Today she scrutinized every photo, read each caption in hopes of seeing George Laurence's name.

The more she saw, the more thankful she was that she hadn't married someone who was always in the public eye. She'd seen the shows on TV about how photographers stalked celebrities. They never got a moment's peace.

She choked on her latte when she flipped a page and was faced with a double-spread layout of photos of Cliff Ballantine. Pushing aside her distaste for the man, Anne found the long caption at the bottom of the page: *Hollywood is abuzz with rumors that America's most eligible bachelor, and this year's "Sexiest Man Alive," is no longer eligible. According to sources close to the actor, his recent solo appearance at premieres and events may be due to a relationship he's managed to keep out of the tabloids.*

A few months ago, she'd thrown the local newspaper across her office after opening it to see Cliff's face in full color on the front page when he'd come to town for his college fraternity's one hundredth anniversary. Thank God his visit had coincided with her trip to Shreveport as an exhibitor at a bridal show. She didn't know what she would have done or said if she'd run into him while he was in town.

She chewed the inside of her lip as she looked at the photos of Cliff at different red-carpet events in Hollywood and New York. His hair was shorter than he'd worn it ten years ago, his body more sculpted, his wardrobe top-of-the-line. But he was still the same full-of-himself Cliff with the smile that had charmed her out of all good sense. . .and thousands of dollars. To think that she was the one who'd enabled him to become what he was today—but no, she didn't want to go there.

The surprise came from seeing him alone in all the pictures. In the past when the magazines featured him on the cover so that she couldn't avoid seeing him, he had a buxom blond starlet hanging off his arm.

Anne shook her head and turned the page. She was tempted to send a letter to the editor expressing her condolences to the anonymous girlfriend.

Her cell phone began playing the theme song from *The Pink Panther*. She grabbed it out of her briefcase. "Hey, Mere. What's up?"

"Didn't see you at church this morning and you didn't come to family dinner, so I wanted to make sure you're okay," Meredith said.

Anne arched her back to ease her bunched muscles and found a more comfortable position in the cushy chair. "I overslept, so I slipped into the back, and then I had lunch with David and Amanda before they left town."

"Stayed up too late partying last night, huh?" A crackle of static sounded through the phone connection as lightning flashed outside.

"It's not every day one of my friends gets married. Even a wedding planner is allowed to cut loose once in a while." Anne tore out a page that listed restaurants that had catered celebrity events.

Meredith chuckled. "It was a gorgeous wedding. I thought it was so sweet that David got choked up when he was repeating his vows."

"It was the first wedding in a long time where I've shed a few tears. They're so cute together." She pressed the phone to her ear with her shoulder to free her hands and cut out a photo of a gorgeous wedding cake that Aunt Maggie would adore trying to recreate.

"Hey." Jenn's voice replaced Meredith's. "Do you have plans for dinner tonight?"

"I'm not going on another blind date." Anne pulled the magazine closer to try to see someone in the background of a picture.

"What makes you think I'm trying to set you up on a blind date?" A hint of laughter betrayed the falsely innocent tone Jenn tried to adopt.

"Because you asked if I have 'plans for dinner.' That's what you always say when you're trying to set me up. What an awful dress." Anne tore the page out of the magazine for her file of what *not* to do.

"What are you talking about?" Jenn asked.

"Oh, it's a celebrity who got married in a dress that looks like strips of toilet paper strung together with silver shoelaces."

Jenn's laugh mixed with the static crackling through the phone. "Annie, he's a really nice guy. He works in Forbes's law firm."

"No, Jenn. I. . ." Why not? She wanted to get married, didn't she? Then why did the thought of another blind date set off her panic alarm? "This is the busiest time of the year for me. You know that. I don't have time to think about dating right now."

"Okay. You just remember that was your excuse this time. Come fall, you won't be able to use that one."

Anne laughed. "I'll remember. I'll think of a better excuse by then."

"I know you will. We'll catch ya later, gal."

"Bye." She closed the phone and dropped it back into her bag.

Outside, thunder rumbled, vibrating through the building. Anne nestled down into the chair and sipped her latte, amused by the amount of money celebrities were willing to spend on simple items. Dresses that cost more than most normal people's entire weddings. Florists who charged more for one event than most flower shops' annual incomes. Imported crystal and china. Flamboyant gifts for attendants. And all of this for marriages that would last only a few years before they did it all over again with someone else.

Lord, thank You that Cliff broke off our relationship before we actually got married. I don't think I would have survived a divorce. It was a painful reminder that people aren't trustworthy, but I'm glad I learned it sooner rather than later.

"May I join you?"

Startled out of her prayer, she looked up. George Laurence stood in front of her, a shopping bag tucked under one arm, a grande cup in his free hand. His hair was damp, and he wore jeans, a dark T-shirt, and a long-sleeved denim shirt. Water spots on his shirt and pants betrayed his lack of preparation for the unpredictable Louisiana weather. Anne swallowed hard. He was even handsomer dressed down than in his expensive, tailored suits.

Her skin tingled. She should say no. She should remind him that he had a fiancée. She should insist their meetings be chaperoned. "Yes, please do."

"Catching up on some reading?" He nodded toward the stack of magazines beside her chair.

She showed him the wedding-themed front of the one in her hand. "Research."

"Ah. No one gets married like the rich and famous." He settled down onto the adjacent love seat.

"Been to many celebrity weddings, have you?" She had to know who this guy was and for whom he worked. Coming right out and asking wouldn't work.

"I've witnessed several—shall we call them events?—in my time." He grinned, and Anne tried to keep her heart from flipping out of her chest. "Of course," he continued, "the weddings here are much different than those I've seen in England."

"Did you do the same type of work there?" She laid the magazine on her lap and sipped her latte.

He crossed his legs, his left ankle resting on his right knee. "In a way. Working for a member of Parliament is much different than working for someone. . .not in government service."

He didn't work for a politician. She hadn't thought so, but it was nice to know for sure. "Which do you enjoy more?"

His expression turned thoughtful. "It's hard to say. In the years since I've worked at this level, I've enjoyed postings because I liked the person I worked for, or I've enjoyed postings because of where I lived, or I just haven't liked postings at all."

"Postings? Does that mean that you get assignments as to whom you're going to work for?"

"Oh, no." He sipped his coffee and pulled a hardback book from the shopping bag. "I suppose it's just a difference in British and American terminology. A posting is the same as a job, a position."

She grinned. "I'll bet there're a lot of differences in what you're used to in England and how we do things here." To see him like this—relaxed, casual, and chatty—was addictive. She could imagine spending every Sunday afternoon like this with him. *He's engaged to Courtney Landry.*

"Most of the cultural differences are minor. Though the distances one has to travel to do anything—and the lack of public transport in most places—was a rather difficult transition."

Anne slipped off her shoes and pulled her feet up under her. "What would you say is the strangest thing you had to get used to over here?" *Get up. Leave now. He's not available. He's already spoken for.*

"Drive-throughs."

She stared at him a moment. "Drive-throughs? Restaurants? You don't have drive-throughs in England? But haven't all of the American fast-food places opened up over there?"

The lines around his eyes deepened; the corners of his lips pulled up with such warmth Anne nearly started fanning herself. "They have, but you walk in and either dine there or order takeaway. And I'd never heard of such a thing as driving up to a window to collect dry cleaning or even prescriptions."

She laughed, her heart racing. She really needed to get out of here. "Yeah, that's the old, lazy American mentality at work. Drive-through everything, pizza and groceries delivered to your door—and now we don't even have to go out to rent movies. Just get online and click a button and wait for it to come in the mail. Same thing's happening to our language. Laziness has turned to ignorance, and what used to be incorrect is now 'acceptable usage'—" She stopped, embarrassed, at the odd expression on George's face. Why did she become such a geek around him, running on about something that no one she'd ever known—outside of her professors—had ever shown the least interest in?

"Please continue. Your conclusions are fascinating. It sounds as if you've spent a lot of time thinking about this."

Her pulse did the jitterbug. Was he serious? "I used to. My master's thesis was on the impact of the popular culture of the 1970s and '80s on American English."

"You've a master's degree in English?" George set his book aside, shifted to the edge of his seat, and leaned forward, elbows resting on his knees.

She tried to swallow the emotion that threatened to cut off her breath. She'd ventured into treacherous territory; he belonged to someone else. *I have to get out of here. I have to put an end to anything but a professional relationship between us.* "Linguistics—though I was about ten hours from finishing when I had to leave school for financial reasons."

"I'd be interested in reading your thesis sometime. The study of language has always fascinated me." He couldn't be for real. No one—not even a family member—had ever asked to read her work.

The sincerity and warmth in his gaze made Anne want to cry. "I'll see if I can dig it up."

He leaned back again. "I enjoyed dinner with your family Thursday evening."

"I'm sorry they gave you such a hard time with all those questions." Her cheeks burned in memory of some of the things said at dinner a few nights ago.

"Don't fret about it. My brothers would probably be much worse. Do you eat together every week?"

"It's a long-standing tradition. Forbes, Meredith, and I started it a couple of years ago to help support Jenn's restaurant." She remembered Jenn's request. "How many brothers do you have?"

"Two, both younger."

"And do they both still live in England?"

"Henry just moved to Australia. Edward still lives in London. My mum writes occasionally to say they're doing well."

"It must be hard to be so far away from your family." She would never want to live anywhere but within a short drive of her relatives.

He shrugged, and the sadness in his gaze tore at her heart. "I left home at sixteen for a live-in apprenticeship. Henry and I have grown closer since the advent of e-mail, but I don't have much contact with Mum or Edward."

Stop asking him personal questions. "Have you gotten to know Courtney's family?"

He looked away and cleared his throat. "No. Since I moved Courtney out of her mother's house, we've had no contact with her family."

Her heart constricted. "You. . .you're living together?"

"We are living in the same house, yes."

Anguish choked her, and she struggled for breath. She stuffed the magazines into her bag. "You must not have read the entire contract. I'm sorry, but I'll have to resign as your wedding planner. The morals clause states that unless the wedding is to be immediate, I don't plan weddings for couples living together." Standing, she flung the strap of her briefcase over her shoulder.

"Wait—let me explain." He jumped up from the sofa, panic edging his voice.

Grabbing her empty cup from the floor, she stuffed her unused napkins into it, unable to meet his gaze. If she looked at him, the moisture burning her eyes would turn into full-fledged tears.

"I had to get her out of her mother's house. You've met Mrs. Landry, yes?"

Anne nodded.

"Then you understand why I couldn't leave Courtney there. But you must believe me—there is nothing untoward happening. She is staying in a room on the third floor, while my suite is in the basement—right beside the housekeeper's room."

"Right beside. . . ?"

"The housekeeper's room. So you see, even if Courtney weren't currently in Paris, we have a chaperone. There is no need for you to resign. I would—I know Courtney would be most distraught if she discovered my decision to get her away from the negative influence of her mother caused you to break the contract."

He'd thought of everything, hadn't he? Could he be a more perfect gentleman? She swallowed hard. "I see. Well, in that case, I suppose we should set a time to meet this week and finalize the plans for the engagement party, since it's only two weeks away."

Based on several bids still out, she scheduled George for Wednesday afternoon, at which time she planned to have her presentation for the engagement party finalized. She just hoped the plan wasn't too ambitious to pull off in less than fourteen days.

She had to get out of here. "Oh, wow, look at the time." She rummaged for her keys. "I've got to run." Keys found, she extended her right hand. "George, it was good to see you. I'll see you Wednesday. Don't forget you can park in the alley and come in the back door."

His warm, smooth hand wrapped around hers. "I'm glad I ran into you. Cheerio."

Anne tried not to look back as she exited the store but did take a peek over her shoulder as she reached the door. He'd sat down again, his back to her.

She wanted so badly to go back, to sit and talk to him as if they were the only two people in the world. . .like they had for the last hour. *Walk away. Don't give in to temptation. Lord, give me strength.*

She opened the exterior door and got a face full of rain. She'd left her umbrella on the floor beside the armchair. Unable to face him, she ran to her car. She didn't start the engine but leaned forward and rested her dripping head against the steering wheel.

"God, why are You torturing me like this? Please, please take away these feelings I have for him. Why is it that the only men I've ever been attracted to haven't felt the same way for me? Lord, what have I done wrong? I do the best I can—every task You've ever put before me, I've poured myself into one hundred and ten percent. Why are You asking me to plan a wedding for a man I'm falling in love with? What are You trying to teach me?"

A tear burned down her cheek as she visualized George standing under a floral-bedecked arbor, awaiting his bride. . .and it wasn't her.

Forcing himself to stay seated and not run after Anne was the hardest thing George had ever done in his life. He'd nearly blown his cover this afternoon by revealing more of his feelings than he should.

He gave her a few minutes to drive away, shoved the copy of the latest spy thriller from his favorite author back into the bag, and edged around the coffee table. He tripped and looked down to see her red and black University of Louisiana umbrella tangled between his feet.

Grabbing the umbrella, he headed for the exit. He pulled out his phone, scrolled to the entry for Forbes Guidry, and selected his mobile number. Anne's umbrella came in handy as he splashed through the parking lot to the car.

Thunder nearly drowned out Forbes's baritone voice. "George? Is everything all right?"

"I need to speak with you. About Anne."

Leaden silence transmitted through the phone for a moment. "I had a feeling. Come on over to my place, and we can sit down and figure this out."

Since George couldn't stop to write down the directions, Forbes stayed on the phone with him until he pulled into the driveway of the redbrick row house not too far from Town Square.

The front door opened to reveal the man who could be either George's enemy or his ally in sorting out the mess he'd gotten himself into with Anne. He dashed up the front steps, glad to take the thick green towel Forbes held toward him.

Forbes led him down the shiny, dark wood–floored hall into a masculine leather and wood–furnished study. "Make yourself comfortable. I can put on some water for hot tea. Or coffee, if you'd prefer."

"Nothing for me, thanks." George spread the towel over the leather club chair before sitting. He leaned forward, elbows braced on his knees. Now here, he didn't know how to start the conversation.

Forbes sat in a stiff-looking blue Queen Anne wing chair.

Queen Anne. Yes, she had all the makings of royalty.

"I was afraid when I first met you that things between you and Anne might get complicated." Forbes templed his fingers, looking as if this were a casual Sunday call rather than one of the most important meetings of George's life.

"Complicated? Bit of an understatement. I—" He glanced down at his clenched hands. "I cannot continue being dishonest with her. I respect her too much to continue the charade."

"And that's how I know you're perfect for her."

Surprise rushed through George. "Excuse me?"

The younger man nodded. "You'll find that I haven't been completely forthcoming with you, George. You see, I wanted to be able to observe you for a while. I'm very protective of my cousin. She's been through a lot in her life."

George bolted out of the chair and paced the perimeter of the room. "Yes, she's told me some of what she's been through."

"Such as?"

"Her parents' deaths, having to quit graduate school for financial reasons, the decision to start her business. . ." George stopped pacing and braced his hands against the frame of one of the tall windows. "Do you think she'll be affronted when she learns I've been deceiving her?"

"Probably. But she'll get over it quickly. She's not one to hold a grudge. Well, in one case, but otherwise I've never known her to be unforgiving. And I think she has good reason to want to forgive you quickly." Forbes's voice took on an amused tone.

George studied the pattern of the rain washing down the paned glass, his emotions in turmoil. Fear balled in the pit of his stomach. "If I tell her I am not getting married, I'll be in breach of contract."

"I'll handle that part. By this time tomorrow, that part of the contract will be null and void."

"How?"

Forbes held his hands up in front of him. "I've known your employer a very long time. Suffice it to say I do have some measure of influence with him."

A glimmer of hope burned in George's soul. "I'm unsure of how to tell her."

Forbes rose and crossed to join him at the window. "Don't worry. When the time's right, you'll know."

"What if I blow it? What if the time isn't right?"

"Tulips. Purple ones. Lots of them."

Chapter 12

With a couple of hours before the meeting with George Wednesday afternoon, Anne headed upstairs to what used to be bedrooms in her converted Town Square row house. She sang along with Nat King Cole's "Unforgettable" while she rearranged supplies in the larger of the two storage rooms. She loved having music piped through the building over the stereo system her cousin Jason had installed last year. And the five-disc CD changer she'd bought on his recommendation kept her from having to change them but once or twice a day.

The machine cycled to a new track. "I've got you under my skin," she sang along with Frank Sinatra. She stopped singing. The lyrics fit exactly how she felt about George. She clamped her lips shut and refused to let the words affect her. Was she going to have to stop listening to everything because it reminded her of George Laurence?

She kicked off her black pumps and got up on the stepladder to move her Christmas decorations on the top shelf. Last Christmas had been her first in the Town Square Merchant Association, and she had joined with the rest of the members in decorating her storefront in the Victorian Christmas theme. With her love of literature, she'd tried to make hers as Dickensian as possible.

Would George have liked it?

No! She couldn't allow herself to think about him, nor be worried about his likes and dislikes.

Sinatra faded out to be replaced by Dean Martin crooning "I Can't Give You Anything but Love." Anne tossed a wreath onto the top shelf, jumped off the ladder, and ran downstairs. She yanked the CDs out of the changer and replaced them with more innocuous classical music. Hopefully that would help keep her mind from wandering down treacherous paths.

Strains of Mozart, Strauss, Beethoven, Handel, and Chopin filled the office. With renewed determination not to think about George Laurence, she returned to the storage room and tried to lose herself in organizing.

As she cleaned, she mentally laid out the tables at Lafitte's Landing for the Landry-Laurence engagement party. She still couldn't understand why George didn't want her to send out the invitations, but with as much other work as she'd had to do in the past two weeks, his insistence turned out to be a blessing.

The first few notes of "The Blue Danube" came over the speakers. She shook out the eight-yard length of tulle even as her feet started the one-two-three pattern of the waltz. She usually tried to get her clients to incorporate this piece into their reception music. Most under the age of forty didn't.

Letting the music fill her, she twirled around the room, a cloud of yellow fabric billowing about her. If only—

"May I have this dance?"

Anne yelped and spun toward the door. The fabric tangled with her feet and sent her sideways into a tall metal shelving unit. Hand over her pounding heart and cheeks burning, she righted herself and turned to face George Laurence. "I didn't hear you come in."

George stepped forward and took the hazardous material from her, rolled it into a ball, and deposited it on a shelf beside her. Turning, he bowed and extended his right hand. "May I?"

No. She shouldn't. It wasn't appropriate. She placed her hand in his and let him whisk her around boxes and stacks of fabrics and bunches of silk flora.

His cinnamon eyes burned into hers. She wanted to look away, to regain some control over her actions and reactions. She couldn't. The heat of his gaze held a future that would never come true. He belonged to someone else. He spun her as the song swelled to a close, then ended with a dip. As he brought her upright, still tight in his embrace, his breath caressed her cheek.

Fire swept through her. She wanted him to kiss her more than anything she'd ever wanted in her life.

He reached up to brush back a lock of hair that had fallen over her forehead.

As soon as he touched her cheek, she pushed away from him. "I'm sorry." She took several steps back and tried to catch her breath.

He moved toward her, but she held her hands out to stop him.

"George, I can't. . . . I don't think I can continue as your wedding planner."

"That's what I came here to speak to you about." His deep voice was soft, comforting. "You are not *my* wedding planner. I am not getting married."

Lava-hot tears burned the corners of her eyes, and her chest tightened. He wasn't getting married—

Oh no. If he'd broken off his engagement because of her, she'd never be hired to plan another wedding again. She shook her head. "No. Please don't tell me that. I can't—"

"Let me explain."

She shook her head. He wasn't getting married? She didn't want to believe him. The possibility of making more money in four months than she had netted in the last five years vanished. She turned and escaped downstairs to the kitchen. She pressed her back against the cool wall above the air conditioner vent in the floor, her head swimming.

He descended the stairs at a more civilized pace. "Anne?" He reached for her hands. "Anne, we need to talk."

She loved the way he said her name: *Ahhnne*. No. She wasn't supposed to find any pleasure in this situation. She needed to be professional. To express her condolences and cut off all communication with him in the future. But never to talk to or see him again. . . ?

She pulled away. As she yanked, though, he let go and the momentum threw her off balance. She reached for the wall to steady herself.

Lord, what do I say to him? I don't know what to do. Help me, please. She took as deep a breath as her constricted chest would allow and turned to face him.

His eyes were soft, like melted milk chocolate. "Are you all right?"

She nodded but looked away. Why couldn't she resist this attraction?

"Until yesterday, I've been bound by a contract my employer asked me to sign."

My employer. When would he just be forthright and honest with her? She tried to speak, but her voice came out as a squeak. She cleared her throat and tried again. "I'm sorry things didn't work out for you. I'll call all of the vendors we've already signed this afternoon and let them know to cancel the contracts."

He frowned. "No, no. You don't understand. I'm not the groom. I never was. The groom is my employer. He wants to remain anonymous—to keep the wedding plans out of the media. He sent me here as his stand-in—to plan his wedding by proxy."

Stand-in. . . Anne's knees buckled, and the ivy-stenciled walls started to go dark in her peripheral vision. She felt an arm around her waist, and suddenly she was sitting on a hard chair with her head being pushed down.

She waved her arms above her head and knocked his hand away. "I can't breathe." She sat up and wished she had done it slower, pressed her hands against her temples, and closed her eyes.

"Can I get you a glass of water or something?"

She opened her eyes. George knelt in front of her. *George*. She'd wished for this all along. He wasn't getting married. "I think I'm having a nervous breakdown and hallucinating all at the same time."

Chuckling, he reached for her hands, folded them atop each other, then held them between his. "You're not hallucinating. Nervous breakdown, maybe. I didn't mean for it to happen this way, but now you know."

Anne's heart connected with the imploring look in his eyes. "Let me make sure I'm clear on this. Everything we've discussed—the vendors we've booked, food we've tasted, venues we've visited—none of that was for you?"

The skin around his eyes crinkled in the way she loved as his smile grew. "Correct."

Concentration on the subject at hand was hard when he looked at her that way, but she persevered. "The contract *you* signed with me isn't for *you* but for someone else?"

"Yes." He leaned forward.

Anne shifted to her right a bit so her knees didn't impede him from getting closer. "And you couldn't tell me before, but now you can?"

He shrugged. "I should have found a way to tell you from the beginning. But my—"

"I know. Your employer." She tried to ignore the tingles that climbed up her arms from the way he rubbed his thumbs against the backs of her hands. If George was here on behalf of his employer, and George and Forbes had been working on something together—this wasn't just a case of George withholding his identity from her. Both of them had been lying to her for nearly three weeks.

She pulled away from him and crossed the kitchen to lean over the sink, just in case her churning stomach decided to give up its contents.

"Anne?"

"Forbes has known all along, hasn't he?"

"Known? Yes. He is the one who presented me with the contract." George's voice faded out as if he realized he was revealing too much.

She backed away, holding her hands out in front of her, palms out. "I don't believe this." She closed her eyes. "I don't know what to believe anymore."

She should have known better. She'd forgotten the only thing Cliff had ever taught her—never trust anyone.

George moved closer. Anne's Wedgwood blue eyes turned a stormy gray, her cheeks went pale, and she wouldn't make eye contact with him. "Anne, it's not what you're thinking."

"You have no idea what I'm thinking." Anger, quiet but potent, laced her words.

He should have known it wouldn't go well. "I'm sorry. Can we sit down and talk?"

"No. I just need you to leave." Her smooth alto voice was emotionless, flat. She gave him a wide berth and opened the back door.

Fear—deep down and abiding—took root in George. Only once before had he ever fancied himself in love. That had been a mistake. Looking at Anne, he now knew the true nature of love. He couldn't risk losing her.

"Anne—" His cell phone interrupted him with Courtney's ring. He ignored it. He had to talk to Anne. To explain. To apologize. To beg her forgiveness. To have her look at him again with the longing in her eyes even her best expression of professionalism hadn't been able to mask.

"Please leave." Tears escaped onto her porcelain cheeks.

His heart ached. He'd caused this pain. "Anne, I'm so sorry." His voice cracked and he cleared his throat. "Please. I'll do anything to make this up to you."

She wouldn't look at him, just turned her flooded eyes toward the floor.

Rather than stay and cause more damage, he opened the glass storm door and trudged down the steps. The door clicked shut behind him with a crack that ripped through his heart like a bullet.

God, what am I going to do? No immediate answer came.

The carriage house–style lights lining Main Street flickered past as he drove down the wide, tree-canopied boulevard. How happy he could have been here! Even with the nearly unbearable heat and humidity, Bonneterre was the first place in more than twenty years that had truly felt like home.

For the second time in his life, he'd taken someone else's advice on how to tell a woman he had feelings for her. The first time, he'd merely been embarrassed by the outcome. He could only pray this time he hadn't ruined the chance for future happiness for both of them.

He couldn't leave things like this. He grabbed his PDA and scrolled down to Anne's number. He was immediately connected to her voice mail.

"This is Anne Hawthorne. I am sorry I cannot take your call at the moment. Please leave me a message, and I'll get back with you as soon as I can. Thanks!" Her cheerful recorded voice twisted his innards with guilt.

"Anne, George here. Please call me back. I desperately need to speak with you. Words cannot express how terrible I feel about what transpired this afternoon. I know you're angry and have every right to be so. But please, you must let me explain—"

A tone sounded and the connection cut off. He quickly dialed her number again. "Please, Anne, call me. It doesn't matter what time. We need to talk."

Later that evening, although he prepared for bed and turned off the lights, George couldn't sleep. He stared at the small black phone on his nightstand, praying it would ring and he'd hear Anne's voice.

He jumped out of bed and paced, chewing on the tip of his thumb. Why didn't she call? The grandfather clock in the upstairs entry hall chimed twice. They'd parted more than ten hours ago.

The rattle of plastic against wood startled him. His phone vibrated, then started to play "I Can't Give You Anything but Love."

Anne!

He leaped for the phone. "Anne? I'm so glad you called."

"George, it's Forbes." The lawyer's voice was gravelly. "Has Anne contacted you? Do you know where she is?"

George dropped to sit on the edge of the bed. "No, I haven't heard from her. How are you calling me on her phone?"

"I'm at her apartment. Her cell phone was here. She had your number programmed into it. I'm calling everyone on the list. She didn't show up for church tonight, which isn't like her at all."

"She's not home?"

"That's what I just said." Frustration clipped Forbes's words.

"Where might she go? Is there a friend she might stay with? Another of your relatives?" Where was it she'd said she liked to go when things got hectic? "Your grandparents?"

"Meredith has already driven out there. No one's talked to or seen her since this morning. What happened this afternoon?"

George ignored the accusation in Forbes's voice. "I told her the truth—not all of it, just my role. She didn't react well."

"How 'not well' did she react?"

"She asked me to leave, wouldn't look me in the eye, went dead quiet." He rubbed his forehead. That day they'd driven down to Comeaux to view sites, what was it she'd said about getting away from it all?

"That's what I was afraid of."

"Does she have another mobile? One that she uses for personal calls rather than business? Might she have that phone with her?" George stood and resumed pacing.

"I don't think so. At least, none of us has the number if she does." Forbes sighed. "I'm so sorry things turned out like this, George. I guess I didn't realize she'd be so sensitive about it."

"The fault is not yours to bear alone. Is there anything I can do to help in the search?" He stopped and rested his forehead against the armoire.

"Pray."

Chapter 13

George rolled from his stomach to his back, kicked the duvet off, and shifted onto his right side. The glowing hands of the alarm clock stood straight up and down. Six in the morning, and still no word. Where could she be?

"Please, dear Lord, please let her work through this and forgive me."

He sat up. Perhaps that prayer had already been answered. He hadn't prayed for her to be found. Rising, he shrugged into his robe. Pink light edged the blinds. He grabbed his Bible, journal, and phone and went out through the kitchen to the veranda. Sinking into the plush deck lounger, he breathed deeply of the early morning air and soaked in the colors of the sun rising over the duck pond behind the house.

"Heavenly Father, You are all-knowing and all-seeing. I have faith You are protecting Anne. She's a rational woman. If she needs this time to herself, don't let us find her before the right moment. When I do see her again, please give me the appropriate words to say to gain her forgiveness." The stress of the night melted away, and he rested his head against the thick cushions of the chaise.

When he woke, his neck was stiff, and the sun was well risen in the sky. A glance at his watch confirmed he'd been asleep for over an hour.

Comeaux. What was it Anne had said when they were in Comeaux that day? As they'd driven to the restaurant. . .a large Victorian house. . .the Plantation Inn Bed and Breakfast.

"I've stayed here a couple of times, too, when I just needed to get away," she'd said.

He picked up his phone and dialed information. He let the computer automatically connect him with the inn. His heart pounded as the proprietress answered.

"Plantation Inn Bed and Breakfast. How may I help you?"

"Good morning. I'm a friend of Anne Hawthorne's, and I was calling to see if she got checked in all right yesterday." He held his breath, praying he'd guessed right.

"She did. Would you like me to connect you with her room?"

He pounded his fist against his leg as he tried to control his relief. "No, I don't want to wake her if she's still sleeping. Thank you."

"Would you like to leave a message for her?"

"Oh no, that's quite all right. Good day."

"B'bye, now."

He disconnected and rushed inside to dress. It would take him nearly twenty minutes to get out to Comeaux, and by then, Anne should have had sufficient time to get out of bed. He had to talk to her before her family found her and made more of a mess, but he couldn't leave them in suspense. He called Forbes.

"Did you find her?" Forbes answered without preamble.

"I know where she is. I'm on my way to go see her."

"Where? I'll meet you."

"No. I need to see her alone." George grimaced, imagining what Anne's reaction would be at both of them showing up at her secret getaway. "I'll have her call you after we have our chat."

Silence met him from the other end of the connection. George checked the phone just to make sure the call hadn't disconnected.

"Fine." The single word betrayed Forbes's frustration. "I'll talk to you later." The line went dead. George hadn't realized until now just how much Forbes liked to be in control of everything and everyone around him.

He didn't take time to shave but brushed his teeth, then wet his hands and ran his fingers through his hair. It was probably his imagination, but there appeared to be a few new gray hairs mixed in with the brown this morning.

At a quarter of eight, he drove into Comeaux. The inn sat on the corner two blocks north of the Fishin' Shack; he turned onto the side street and into the driveway, pulling up behind Anne's dark green convertible and leaving her no room to pull out.

The aroma of bacon, coffee, and whatever sweets the inn was serving for breakfast made his stomach rumble. Perhaps they could converse over breakfast.

He wasn't sure whether to knock or enter until he saw the Dining Room Open, Please Come In sign. The door swung open into an entryway much like the one at his employer's house. He heard soft voices to his left and closed the door to reveal the dining room. A few tables were filled with patrons who looked like they'd stopped for breakfast before work. Anne wasn't among them.

"Good morning, and welcome to Plantation Inn. Just one for breakfast?" A middle-aged woman wearing a pristine white apron over a flowered dress approached him from the other end of the entry hall. She carried a silver coffeepot.

"I'm looking for Anne Hawthorne."

"Oh, Anne is taking her breakfast on the back porch." She motioned with her nearly gray head over her shoulder toward the french doors at the end of the hall. "Can I bring you anything?"

"A spot of coffee would be lovely, thank you." Walking down the hall at a civilized pace was hard, but he eventually made it to the doors. Taking a deep breath, he swung them open and stepped outside.

Anne drew her gaze away from the blue jays fighting in the birdbath when she heard the doors open. George stepped out onto the porch, and her heart leaped. She shouldn't be happy to see him. Her hand shook a little as she reached for her coffee cup.

Finally, he turned toward her. She fought to keep from smiling back at him. She returned her gaze to the birds in the yard, his presence too unsettling for her peace of mind.

He strolled over to the table. "May I join you?"

"It's a free country." Yeah, that was a mature thing to say.

He walked around the small scrolled-iron table and sat in the only other chair, which happened to be immediately to her left. If she stared straight ahead, he was in her peripheral vision. She wanted to look at him, to memorize the contours of his face, to gaze into his brown eyes. But she was still mad at him.

"Anne, I cannot begin to express to you how utterly sorry I am. I never set out to hurt you—that is the very last thing I would ever want to do."

She closed her eyes and tried to swallow. His voice was so soft, his accent so endearing. She'd picked up the room phone to call him three times during the night to demand an explanation. She'd wanted to hear his story, to understand what had happened. "George, I—" She stopped when his hand covered hers on the table.

"Please, allow me to say this. I came to Bonneterre expecting to meet a middle-aged woman who wouldn't question anything I said to her. Instead, I met you, my beautiful Anne. I wanted to tell you the truth from the beginning, but I was bound by the contract my employer made me sign that I wouldn't reveal to anyone my true role. I was legally bound to pretend to be Courtney's fiancé. They thought it would be easier, thought there'd be fewer questions that way." He paused, and she could feel him searching her face for some reaction.

"Who's 'they'?"

He cleared his throat. "My employer. . .and Forbes."

Her cousin had a lot of explaining to do.

George rushed to continue. "But that was before I'd met you. As I started to get to know you, the deception was already in place. When Forbes realized that I had. . .come to care for you, he interceded on my behalf with my employer and got that clause removed from the terms of my contract. He told me you would understand."

"I'm sorry Forbes misled you. He knows how I feel about people lying to me."

"I'm not here to talk about Forbes." George made lazy circles on the back of her hand with his thumb, sending shivers up her spine. "I'm here to apologize for not telling you the truth from the beginning and to beg your forgiveness, even though I don't deserve it."

Part of her jumped at his words, ready to forgive him and move on to explore what their relationship could be. The other part kept her silent for a long time. Her confidence in him was shattered. She'd always dreamed the man she fell in love with would be as honest with her as she always tried to be with everyone around her. Would George lie to her again if his employer told him to? The whole situation didn't do much for her opinion of his ethics.

The slight whoosh of the doors opening broke the silence. Cheryl appeared with a coffee service tray, which she set on the low side table behind them. "Y'all doing okay?" she asked. "Hon, are you sure I can't bring you anything more than coffee?"

"I'm not certain how long I'll be here," George answered.

Anne finally turned to look at him. She sighed and shook her head. "Cheryl, go ahead and bring him your breakfast special. We're going to be here for a while."

He continued to hold her hand but didn't say anything while they waited for his food. There were so many things she wanted to say to him, so many questions.

After his food arrived, she gave him a few moments' peace to start eating while she pushed the remainder of her omelet around the plate. The birds in the centuries-old oak trees that shaded the large yard provided background music, and a light breeze brought the fragrance of roses and honeysuckle.

When he stopped to spread Cheryl's homemade strawberry jam on his toast, he broke the long silence. "Whatever you're thinking, whatever questions are on your mind, I can handle it."

She rested her fork on the edge of the plate and folded her hands atop the white napkin on her lap. "How am I ever supposed to trust you again?" She'd meant to lead up to that question, not just blurt it out. She didn't take her gaze away from his face, though.

He grimaced, then let out a slight chuckle. "That's my Anne, always straight to the point."

She tried to stop her heart from fluttering at being called "my Anne" but wasn't entirely successful. She was woman enough to admit to herself she was enjoying watching him eat breakfast. He was so fastidious. Not a crumb hit the table as he bit into the toast.

He swallowed and wiped his mouth with the napkin. "The irony of the situation is if I promise I will never lie to you again, you won't know whether or not to trust me. So all I can do is promise to try to earn your trust and regard." He reached for the coffeepot and leaned closer to refill her cup. "Will you allow me to do so?"

He smelled wonderful. And the stubble on his face gave him a rugged look she'd never imagined. What was he wanting her permission for? Oh yes, he wanted to try to regain her trust. "Yes, I'll allow you to do so."

His grin tugged at her heart. "Excellent." He lifted her left hand from her lap. "Now, more to the point, will you forgive me for deceiving you?"

Charm is deceitful. . . . Was he for real, or was he trying to charm himself back into her good graces? But she couldn't call herself a Christian and not forgive someone when asked. "Yes, I forgive you."

He kissed the back of her hand. "Thank you. You have no idea what it means to me."

The silence that fell between them brought a sense of comfort. He returned to his food, and she picked up her coffee, watching him over the cup's rim. "How much of what you told me about yourself is true?"

He frowned and cocked his head to the side as if surprised by her question. "Everything. I've never lied to you about anything—other than who the groom is."

"How did you do it? I mean, didn't it bother you to have to live a lie?"

"Yes. It bothered me very much. There were times I couldn't sleep at night, when I almost called you at 3:00 a.m. to tell you the whole truth."

"I wish you had." She set her cup down and started to relax. He hadn't lied to her about anything else. . .if she could believe his statement. She wanted to. "How did you know where to find me?"

"You told me the day we were out here you occasionally escape to the inn. How is it none of your family know you come here?"

"My family?" Anne frowned. "Why would they need to know?"

Instead of answering, he handed her his phone. "Call Forbes. He was sick with worry looking for you last night."

"He could have called me."

"You left your mobile at home."

She groaned and accepted his, immediately dialing Forbes's number. It didn't ring twice before he picked up.

As soon as he heard her voice, he said, "Anne? Where are you? Do you realize how much you've upset Meredith and Jennifer by disappearing like this?"

"I'm sorry I worried everyone." Her guilt over the concern she'd caused her family was tempered by anger at the way Forbes had handled the entire situation. "After family dinner tonight, you and I are going to have a long talk."

"So you're going to be at dinner tonight?"

"Practice begging my forgiveness between now and then."

Forbes laughed. "Will do, Anne-girl."

When she finished with Forbes, she dialed her own number to check her voice mail. Several from Forbes, which she deleted. Then one from George. She glanced at him as she listened to it. He sounded even more distraught than her cousin had.

She waited until he finished refilling their coffee cups to hand him the phone. "Why were you so frantic to find me?"

He reached up to cup her face. "You were upset, and I didn't know what you were thinking. I couldn't bear to think you might hate me and would never want to see me again."

Emotion gathered in her throat. "I was upset, yes, but not like that."

He glanced at her; then his cinnamon-hued eyes scanned the yard. "Why don't we take a walk?"

She nodded and stood. George assisted with her chair, then offered her his arm. When she slipped her hand into the crook of his elbow, she could feel his tension. "George, there's more to this than your worrying about me being mad at you, isn't there?"

He led her down one of the many gravel paths that led to the gardens hidden beyond the tree line. "It's not important."

"You're going to try to regain my trust by being honest with me, remember?"

He grimaced and patted her hand. "Right." Their shoes crunched on the gravel path, and the daytime symphony of locusts, birds, grasshoppers, and other insects started to warm up as the sun grew hotter. He stopped at a marble bench hidden beneath an enormous oak tree. They sat in silence for a few moments.

George took a deep breath. "This isn't the first time deception has nearly ruined my life. A very long time ago, I fancied myself in love. Felicia was unlike any woman I'd ever met. We were both too young—I nineteen and she seventeen. I'd been forced to leave home three years before, give up my dream of attending university, and start working to support my mother after my father suffered a debilitating stroke. I'll admit I was as attracted to the idea of the daughter of a duke falling in love with me as I was to Felicia herself, but I convinced myself I was in love with her, despite our youth, despite her immaturity."

He picked up a leaf and twirled it between his fingers. "She talked about eloping, running away together, and then surprising her parents. I told her I couldn't bear lying to her parents and insisted on going to them and telling them everything." He let out a rueful laugh. "I know now that she never wanted to marry me. She was just trying to manipulate her parents into sending her to Paris for the summer. The man she really loved—an earl, married with three children nearly her age—summered there and wanted to set her up as his mistress.

"Of course, my employment was terminated immediately, much to Felicia's amusement. Felicia was sent to Paris in the care of the governess who'd introduced her to the earl in the first place." He dropped the leaf on the bench, rose, and paced, hands clasped behind his back.

"What did you do?" Anne retrieved the leaf and pressed it between her hands.

"Rumor spread amongst the aristocracy as to what had happened—all from the point of view that I'd lead dear, innocent Felicia astray—and I couldn't find employment anywhere. I went to work for a British actor. That gave me entrée into other circles and allowed me opportunities for travel and employment I wouldn't have gotten elsewhere."

"Thank you for telling me." She couldn't meet his gaze. Dare she trust him enough to confide her own story of falling for someone who was only using her for his own end?

George knelt in front of her. "I've never told anyone else—aside from my mother and brothers—about it. I'm glad you know."

"I'm sorry I frightened you by disappearing." The thought of opening up old wounds with George when the new ones weren't yet healed kept her from sharing that part of her past with him.

"I trusted God would keep you safe. I prayed He wouldn't let us find you until the time was right." His brown eyes sparkled. "Was the time right?"

She couldn't resist his grin. "Apparently so."

"Speaking of time." He glanced at his watch, then stood and offered his hand. "If we're going to finish planning *my employer's* engagement party, we'd best be going."

"It's a good thing I cleared my calendar for today." She got a schoolgirl thrill when he intertwined his fingers with hers as they walked back up to the inn. Cheryl had cleared the table and left the check anchored under the vase of fresh-cut roses.

George reached for it, but Anne snatched it from him.

"Anne, please, it's the least I can do."

"The least? George, you've already paid enough in worry and stress for this date. It's the least I can do."

He nodded his agreement. As she settled up with Cheryl, his phone started to beep. He winked at her, then stepped out onto the front porch to answer the call. After paying for breakfast and her room, she went upstairs and quickly threw everything into the bag she'd packed in haste last night before her getaway.

When she joined George outside, he was still on the phone, deep frown lines etching his forehead and mouth. "Yes, sir. I understand. Yes, she called me last evening. . . ." His frown dissolved into a smile. "No, I did not plan on calling them. . . . I agree, sir. I will run anything like that past you before any calls are made. . . ." He reached his free hand out toward Anne and she took it. "Yes, I believe I will be able to speak with the wedding planner about it sometime today. Good-bye, sir." He ended the call and clipped the device back to his belt. Over her protest, he took her bag from her. "My employer. Courtney called me last night and asked if we could call to see if Cirque du Soleil would perform at the reception."

Anne laughed. "Really? And was your employer putting the brakes on that?"

"Fortunately, yes." He opened her car door for her. Before she could get in, he leaned close and kissed her cheek. "I'll meet you at your office." His voice was caress-soft.

On the drive back into town, Anne had plenty of time to think about everything George had said. Although she wanted to be upset with him for deceiving her, her relief he wasn't a client and her attraction to him made it easy to rid herself of her anger. And since he'd been burned once in love before also, he'd understand why she would want to take their relationship slowly.

George got ahead of her going through a couple of lights she got stuck at and was sitting on her back steps when she pulled up in the alley behind her office. Her heart fluttered in anticipation of being with him and not having to hide her feelings.

Chapter 14

Forbes skipped out on Thursday night dinner. But by the time she sat down with her family—and George—at Jenn's restaurant, Anne was the happiest she'd been in a very long time. George had agreed they needed to take their relationship one step at a time while he tried to rebuild her trust.

Her other cousins' reactions ranged from bland astonishment to squealing excitement from Jenn and Meredith. And every single one of them insisted George attend Sunday dinner with the whole family.

George twined his fingers with hers as he escorted her from the restaurant. "I think they like me."

The twittery feeling in her stomach intensified. Was it okay to hold hands if they were taking things slowly? "Yeah, I think so, too."

"Which is good, as I plan to be around them for a long time."

A long time. She reminded herself she was thirty-five and not fifteen as her heart jumped up and down like an entire championship-winning Little League team. She barely knew this man, and he didn't have a great track record for honesty.

He opened the door to the convertible Mercedes and offered his hand. She caught the tip of her tongue between her teeth. *God, don't let this be too good to be true!*

Pointing the car back toward Town Square, he reached across for her hand and lifted it to kiss the back. "What time shall I call for you Sunday morning for church?"

Her whole arm tingled. "What? Oh, uh, service starts at eleven, but we'd better leave my place around ten thirty."

"Will you be tied up all day tomorrow and Saturday with your clients?"

"I probably won't get home until well after midnight Saturday."

"You put so much time and energy into your work. Is it that rewarding for you?"

She nodded, stifled a yawn, and leaned back against the leather headrest. "I love my work. I never imagined I'd find planning other people's weddings so fulfilling. It's not a profession I'd ever dreamed of entering—although I did it as a maid of honor in a couple of weddings in college. I always planned to be a college professor."

"Yet you had to drop out of graduate school."

"Not by choice. I—I had to quit school to go to work full-time. Cl—the guy I was dating at the time—had moved elsewhere to pursue his career and borrowed a lot of money from me." She glanced at George, whose sharp profile reflected the lights from the instrument panel in front of him. He'd been honest about his relationship. "He asked me to marry him. Since I figured I could continue graduate school after his career took off, I withdrew from school and went to work full-time for my aunt and uncle at B-G. But even that wasn't enough. I had to give up my apartment and move back home—back with Uncle Errol and Aunt Maggie—just to be able to afford to pay for my car and insurance and the minimum on all the credit cards I'd taken out that year to help support him."

"What happened?" Soft, deep concern resonated in George's voice.

"His career took off, and once the money was flowing in, he didn't need me anymore. I made excuses for his inattention for a long time, but he finally called me two days before the wedding was to take place to call everything off. I haven't heard from him since." She sincerely wished she didn't hear *of* him all the time, too. She was probably the only person in the country who didn't idolize

Cliff Ballantine, mega–movie star, humanitarian, and most eligible bachelor with the charming Southern accent.

"I wish I could say I'm sorry."

She raised her eyebrows. "But you can't?"

"No." He turned and grinned at her. "Because if you'd married him, we never would have met."

Her insides turned to jelly. She hadn't thought of it like that.

In the alley behind her office building, George came around and assisted her out of the car, then turned and opened the door of her car for her. He reached for her hands and once again kissed the backs. "Good night, my Anne."

No good-night kiss? She pushed her disappointment down. *Slow, remember?* "Good night, George."

Sunday, Anne spotted Forbes as soon as service ended and beckoned to him across the crowded sanctuary with her crooked finger. She wasn't going to let him off easy.

He enveloped her in a bear hug when he reached her. "I'm so glad you're okay. Don't ever do that again. Or at least take your phone with you next time."

"While we're on the subject of things never to do again. . ." She cocked her head toward George. "No more surprises, please."

Forbes raised two fingers. "Scout's honor."

She pulled his hand down. "You were never a Scout."

"Same difference." He kissed her forehead. "I'm sorry, Annie. Really, I am."

"Forbes, may I speak with you a moment?" George's voice matched his serious expression.

Her cousin immediately switched from big brother to lawyer mode. "Certainly. Out in the vestibule?" He motioned toward the back doors of the sanctuary.

Anne frowned as they walked away. Something was going on or George would have said whatever he needed to say to Forbes in front of her. Fighting her desire to follow them, she slipped out of the pew to make her way up front where Jenn was holding court, surrounded by several guys from the singles' group.

"Anne, I was so hoping to see you today." A former client stopped her. "I wanted to ask if you would speak at this month's Bonneterre Women in Business luncheon."

"Speak?" Her heart quickened. "About what?"

"About being an entrepreneur. About being a small-business owner in our city. What it took to start your own business. You've been a BWB member for years now. Every month, we get suggestion cards requesting to have you speak."

More than a hundred women attended those lunches. Anne had barely made it through the required public speaking class in a college class of thirty. "Let me get back to you?"

The woman handed her a business card. "Call me at my office anytime this week. I'll need to know by Thursday."

Anne nodded and tucked the card into her planner. She'd almost made it to Jenn when she was stopped again.

"I'm so glad I found you, Miss Anne." A blonde who could grace any fashion runway in New York or Paris gave her a quick hug. "I wanted you to meet my fiancé, Heath."

The young man she shook hands with looked like he'd stepped right off a magazine cover. He was fashionably dressed with boyish, curly golden hair, hazel eyes, and a grin that could melt steel. "It's nice to meet you, Heath. Congratulations. You've found yourself a wonderful bride."

"I know." He put his arm around Elizabeth's miniscule waist and gazed down at his fiancée in a way that twisted Anne's heart with envy. "God has truly blessed me."

Elizabeth's color was high when she pulled her gaze away from Heath. "And thanks to your advice, we're getting married the first weekend in August. Would you have time to work with me? I can't afford much, but I'd really like your help, since it's so soon and you have all the connections."

"Of course." Anne rested her hand on Elizabeth's shoulder. "And don't you worry about the cost. We'll work around what you can afford."

The young woman's eyes filled with quick tears, and she threw her arms around Anne's waist again. "Thank you so much—for everything."

Laughter bubbled up in Anne. "Of course. Call me this week, okay?"

"Okay."

Oh, to be young and in love. Anne shook her head and turned, only to be practically tackled by Jenn. Ending the hug, Jenn slipped her arm around Anne's waist as they strolled toward the exit. "Did I see you and George come in together this morning?"

"Yes. He came and picked me up this morning. We've worked a lot of stuff out this week." But even though he'd promised he wouldn't lie to her again, he was holding something back. He and Forbes had been gone a long time.

"Is that a blush I see?" Jenn teased. "Did you ever find out if he has a younger brother who's as good looking as he is?"

Anne rolled her eyes and shook her head. "Is that all you ever think about?"

"What?"

"Men!"

Jenn laughed. "What else is quite so entertaining?"

Meredith joined them from the direction of the choir room and gave Anne a long, gentle hug. She didn't ask questions like her sister. Emotion lumped in Anne's throat. Meredith's deep understanding of her need for quiet or space was one of the reasons they were so close.

Anne put her arms around her cousins' much smaller waists. "I guess we should head out for Uncle Errol and Aunt Maggie's."

Jenn gave Anne's arm a light pinch. "Is George coming?"

"Yes. Do you think he would dare risk offending any of you?" The rest of the family was going to have a field day with him. If he thought Jenn and Rafe had given him a hard time at dinner Thursday night, once again trying to pry his employer's name from him, he was in for a surprise.

The brass chandeliers overhead went dark, casting the sanctuary into dimness accented by the light flowing through the windows. She'd tried to talk several of her brides into leaving the majority of lights off in this sanctuary to showcase the beautiful stained-glass images of scenes from Jesus' life, but so far, none had. If she got married in this church. . . Anne stopped her fantasy as soon as it started. The faceless groom she'd seen dimly for so many years had been replaced by George Laurence. *Slow, remember.*

"There you girls are." Forbes's voice echoed from the rear of the nearly empty church. "We've been waiting for you out in the foyer."

Her heart skipped a beat at the sight of George, who stood in the doorway with Forbes. She took a deep breath and pushed her emotions back. She couldn't let her feelings get the better of her. When she reached him, his closed expression set her ill at ease.

Her skin tingled when his hand cupped her elbow. Forbes took her other elbow and started to lead her across the vestibule.

She stopped and pulled away from both men. "What have you two been talking about out here?"

"Nothing." Forbes gave her his most charming smile.

Anne wasn't buying it. She turned to George. His mouth was set in a grim line, and he wouldn't meet her gaze. "George? Remember what we talked about Thursday morning? About honesty and trust?"

He closed his eyes and nodded, then turned and rested his hands on her shoulders. "It's just some business I needed to take care of with Forbes for my employer."

"That's all?" She hated to doubt him but couldn't help it.

"That's the truth." His voice, soft, deep, and holding promises she hoped would come true, settled her doubts.

She nodded and took his arm. "All right, then, let's go."

How was he going to tell her the truth? Anne deserved to know what she was in for when the identity of the man she was planning this wedding for broke in the media. On his way to pick her up this morning, his employer had called to warn him that reporters were starting to bug his publicist with questions about the rumor of his engagement. He had returned to New York, leaving Courtney in Paris to eliminate the risk they would be photographed together.

"George?" Anne's mellow voice broke into his worries.

Some of his anxiety ebbed away when he locked gazes with her. He squeezed her hand. He loved that she'd taken it without hesitation as they walked through the very modern part of the church building.

Her fine brows drew together in a frown. "What were you thinking about so intently?"

She didn't like surprises, but he couldn't breach what remained of the confidentiality clause. He needed, however, to be as honest as possible. Forbes, Jennifer, and Meredith had walked faster and disappeared around a corner.

He bit his bottom lip and took a deep breath. "I'm worried that my employer's confidentiality about his relationship with Courtney may have been breached." He paused, and she turned to face him. "If anything happens and I have to suddenly disappear, please don't hold it against me. If anyone connects me with Bonneterre or Courtney Landry, all may be lost."

"I still don't understand the need for such secrecy. What would happen if someone found out why you're here?"

He stepped in front of her to open the door to the parking lot. "If my employer's secret engagement leaks to the press because of me, I would most likely lose my job, which means I would have to return to England."

"Would that be such a bad thing? To go home after so many years?" Anne looked like a movie star when she slipped on a stylish pair of sunglasses and ran her fingers through her hair to push it back from her face. The late June sun and steamy humidity never seemed to affect her.

How long would he have to live here to become acclimated? He probably wouldn't get the chance to find out. "Given the dwindling need for full-time personal assistants with the advent of modern technology, it would be difficult for me to find a position that's the equivalent of what I have now. Aside from that, it's not really the occupation I'd like to keep for the rest of my life."

"Well, just from what I've seen in the short time I've known you, I know you'd do well as an event planner wherever you decide to settle."

"Thank you." *Wherever you decide to settle. . .* Disappointment attacked him through her words. He'd hoped she'd want him to settle here, maybe even go into business with her. They would make a perfect team—her connections and his attention to detail. If he went into business with her, he could get his work visa changed. . . or he could marry her and get a green card. There were much worse fates than being married to a woman he was already attracted to.

They reached the car, and he used the remote to unlock it. He opened the door for her.

She lowered her glasses and winked at him. "Have I warned you about my family? Almost all of the extended family will be at lunch. And they can be somewhat overwhelming."

He winked back. "I have survived a couple of dinners with Jennifer and Rafe."

She laughed. "Oh, they can't hold a candle to the whole family being together."

George followed Anne's directions through town. What had she meant by "overwhelming"? He'd experienced many large dinner parties and gatherings throughout his career—of course as someone who had to service the guests—so he couldn't imagine a meal with her family would be that different.

He was going to meet the rest of her family. He and Forbes

had formed a strong friendship in the short time since they'd met. He also enjoyed the weekly dinners he'd attended with Anne's cousins. Not all of them came every week, but they accepted him and offered him friendship even when he couldn't divulge much personal information to them.

From the examples he'd seen in Anne, Forbes, and the others, her family was the epitome of his image of Southern charm. Anne, never ruffled, always had a smile and encouraging word for everyone she met. Forbes played the dapper gentleman for whom chivalry was a way of life, not an ancient fairy tale. Jennifer, the flirtatious Southern belle. . . He laughed. Henry would love Jennifer. His youngest brother would definitely fall for the beautiful charmer with the strawberry blond hair.

The sunlight barely peeked through the dark green foliage that canopied Oak Alley Drive as they traveled through the garden district toward midtown. She instructed him to turn left on Tezcuco Avenue before reaching the commercial district. Deeper into the heart of the residential area, the smaller houses on Oak Alley gave way to large, immaculate Victorians set far back from the street and surrounded by lush green lawns shaded by oaks, magnolias, and other trees he didn't recognize.

Another left onto Destrehan Boulevard, and the lots grew larger, the landscaping more elaborate. Homes ranged from sprawling Victorians to enormous Greek-revival manses, red brick with fat white columns lining the front.

The first indication that this "family dinner" was beyond what he'd imagined was the number of cars lining the street in front of the multi-gabled, three-story house Anne had him stop in front of.

"This is Aunt Maggie and Uncle Errol's house. They bought this house after I went to college, but it's still home."

He helped her out of the car, and she led him up the driveway toward the sidewalk that snaked across the yard to the wraparound front porch.

Maggie and Errol. He was about to meet the people who'd

stepped in to raise Anne after her parents' deaths. His heart pumped a little faster. He hoped to make a favorable impression on them. If he was going to spend the rest of his life with her—but no, he couldn't indulge in that kind of thinking yet. She needed time to get to know him better, and he had to regain her trust.

His thoughts were interrupted when the front door flew open and an older woman—who bore a remarkable resemblance to Anne—stepped out onto the porch.

"It's about time," the woman called as George and Anne approached the house.

"What are you talking about?" Anne looked at her watch. "It's only twelve forty-five. We never eat dinner before one."

"You're thirty-five years old. It's about time you brought a man home for Sunday dinner!"

Chapter 15

Just when she'd thought her family couldn't possibly embarrass her any further. . .

Anne stepped up onto the porch and bent forward to accept Aunt Maggie's kiss on her cheek. "Good afternoon to you, too, Mags." She turned. "George, this is my aunt, Maggie Babineaux. She's the vendor I suggested to you for the wedding cake."

He nodded, brown eyes twinkling as he took Maggie's hand and lifted it to his lips. "The pleasure is mine, Mrs. Babineaux. I've heard much about you from Anne."

Maggie regarded him with calculation in her gaze. "I wish I could say I've heard more than rumors about you, George Laurence." With a wink at Anne, she took hold of his arm and directed him into the house. "But we'll remedy that today, won't we?"

Anne shrugged and wrinkled her nose in an apologetic grin when George glanced at her over his shoulder. She nearly laughed at the expression of trepidation in his eyes. He'd never experienced anything like a large Cajun family gathered for Sunday dinner. This afternoon would be a trial by fire of his professed feelings for her.

She inhaled deeply as she crossed the threshold into the house. The aroma of roast beef and fresh yeast rolls brought instant images of her childhood to mind. Aunt Maggie and Uncle Errol had bought this house not long after Anne had left for college, but every time she walked in, she was *home*. Her happy memories from childhood started the day she moved in with Maggie, Errol, and their four sons twenty-seven years ago.

The buzz of voices from the back of the house created a tingle of anticipation in Anne. Would George, mostly estranged from his own relatives, understand the importance of family to her? She grinned. Would he survive her family?

George refrained from turning to make sure Anne was still behind him as her aunt led him through the large, well-appointed home. The food smelled wonderful, and even though breakfast had been more than satisfying, his stomach rumbled in response to the tantalizing aromas.

Beside him, Maggie Babineaux kept up a constant chatter about the family, trying to tell him the connections of everyone he'd meet today. She lost him after the name of her oldest son, daughter-in-law, and grandchildren.

The front rooms were formally furnished and appeared rarely used. From what he could see, each room had wood floors covered with expensive, probably antique, Oriental rugs. Anne came from money. He shouldn't be surprised by that, given her education and refinement. He fought disappointment. He'd assumed her background was more like his—enough income in the family to meet their necessities, but not a lot left over for luxuries.

Anne gained his attention with her hand on his arm. "Mamere, I'd like you to meet George Laurence. My grandmother, Lillian Guidry."

He swallowed his surprise as he took the petite, dark-haired woman's hand in his. "It's very nice to meet you, Mrs. Guidry."

"We're pleased you could join us for lunch, Mr. Laurence." She turned to Anne, who leaned over to receive a kiss on each cheek. "You look beautiful, Anne Elaine."

The two women couldn't be more opposite in appearance—Anne, tall, curvaceous, and blond; her grandmother, petite, thin, and brunette. As he watched them converse, he did notice similarities around their eyes and mouths. Each was beautiful in her own way.

"George!" Forbes clasped his shoulder and shook his hand. "Get out of the kitchen before they put you to work."

He looked around for Anne.

"Don't worry, ol' man. She'll join us when the aunts finish questioning her about you, which they can do better if you're not around." Forbes introduced George to his parents, aunts and uncles, siblings, and cousins as they crossed the crowded family room to a sunny, glass-enclosed porch beyond.

Jason, Rafe, Jennifer, and Meredith stood to greet him. George let out a relieved breath when he sank into the thick cushions of an oversized wicker club chair, glad to be around people he knew.

Meredith perched on the ottoman in front of him and leaned forward, her hands clasped in front of her. Genuine concern gleamed in her gaze. "I assume by the fact that you're here that you were able to work things out with Anne?"

He shrugged. "Somewhat. We've agreed to take things slowly and get to know each other better."

The ginger-haired woman nodded slowly. "Good." She stood, then leaned over and pressed her cheek to his. "Because if I ever hear that you've lied to her again, you'll have more than just Anne to answer to." She kissed his cheek, held his gaze for a long moment, then crossed to sit beside Forbes on a leather love seat.

He held his grin in check. The love Anne's family displayed pleased him. Like him, they wanted only the best for her. But he could see why she needed a secret getaway.

"By the way, how did you find Anne the other day?" Forbes loosened his tie and stretched his arm across the back of the sofa behind his sister.

"I simply recalled something she'd told me while we were out visiting sites one afternoon." He returned Forbes's courtroom stare with a challenge of his own. There was a reason her family hadn't known where she was, and it wasn't his right to reveal the location to them.

Before Forbes could interrogate further, two twentysomething women bubbled into the room: a strawberry blonde who turned out to be a younger sister to Forbes, while the other, with brunette hair, belonged to yet another branch of the Guidry family. After being introduced to George, they retreated to a corner to flip through magazines they'd brought and converse in whispers.

After a few minutes, the two young women flittered across the room and dropped something into Forbes's lap. "I knew you weren't telling me the truth the other night," the redhead said.

"Where did you get my high school yearbook?" Forbes reached for the large volume, but the young woman held it out of his grasp.

"From that old trunk of stuff that's still in Mama and Daddy's attic. You told me you didn't know Cliff Ballantine when you were in high school. But how come there's a picture of the two of you together?"

Forbes's expression tightened. "Let it go, Marci. We were on student council together. That doesn't mean we were friends or hung out together."

"But you *knew* him."

George caught sight of Anne from the corner of his eye as a relative waylaid her from entering the sunroom.

Meredith snatched the yearbook from her younger sister. "Marci, please don't bring up his name again."

The uncharacteristic vehemence in Meredith's voice surprised him. What had happened between this family and Cliff Ballantine?

"You know. . ." Marci sighed and stood, hands on hips. "One of these days I'm going to find out what all the secrets in this family are." She put her arm around her young brunette cousin. "We're not children anymore. We deserve to know."

Forbes took the book from Meredith. "When the people in the family who have those secrets feel like telling you, you'll know. Until then, try to keep to your own business. That includes not invading my personal property."

The two young women left in a huff.

Anne stopped them in the doorway. "Marci, Jodi Faye, what's the matter?"

"Ask Forbes." Marci's full lips were set in a pout when she glared over her shoulder at her oldest brother. "He seems to know everything."

Anne's fine brows wrinkled into a frown when she entered the room. "What's going on?"

Forbes held up the school annual and tossed it onto the coffee table in front of him, where it landed with a thud. "They just wanted an ancient history lesson, and I wouldn't give it to them."

Her blue eyes widened at the sight of the book. "Oh." Her shoulders drooped for a moment, then squared; her lips pressed together, then turned up at the corners. "Well, no sense in letting the past spoil the present, right?" Her gaze seemed to search her cousin's for reassurance.

Forbes nodded. "Right. You survived the aunt gauntlet?"

She blushed, and her eyes turned toward George for a brief moment. "Standard questions—who is he, what does he do, when are you going out again. . . . You've been through it before."

"And will probably go through it again. That's why I rescued George and brought him out here, so he didn't have to witness the mayhem."

A ringing echoed through the house, like the triangle and clapper that cooks used as a call to dinner in all the old Western movies. The exterior door flew open and children flooded the sunroom from the backyard.

"Dinnertime." Anne extended her hand to George with a warm smile. "Papere—my grandfather—will say grace, and the children's plates will be served. Once they're all situated in the breakfast room, we'll get our turn."

He rose and placed his hand in hers—even as two children ran between them. They joined the rest of the family, congregated in the great room and kitchen. The feeling of Anne's hand in his offset any feelings of discomfort he had from being surrounded by such a crowd of people. It might take him years, but he could probably learn to love attending Guidry family gatherings.

The dining table's length hindered conversation with anyone other than those immediately surrounding him. With Anne on his left, Forbes on his right, and Meredith, Jason, and Rafe across the table, George found Sunday dinner not much different than the Thursday night suppers he'd attended. And the food. . . He stopped at two servings of roast beef and mashed potatoes with gravy, green beans, corn, and what Anne said were collard greens. He did take a third yeast roll, however, and followed Forbes's example of dipping the bread into the gravy that remained on his plate.

Forbes laughed and took the fork out of George's hand, then put a piece of roll directly between his fingers. "You can't sop like a Southerner if you're using your fork and knife."

George glanced around the table and did see he was the only one not using his hands. "This is called what again?"

On his left, Anne laughed. The sound sent tingles up his spine. "Soppin'. You're soppin' up the gravy with your roll." Her eyes twinkled at him.

"And this is appropriate dinner-table behavior?"

"It is in this family." Across the table, Meredith held up a piece of roll between her fingers. "You might not want to do it at the Ritz in New York, but you'll find pert-near everyone in Bonneterre won't fault you none for soppin' up your vittles."

"I'm flabbergasted as to what you just said, but"—he took the piece of roll and sopped up some of the gravy on his plate—"I'll take your word for it."

When everyone finished eating, the women, including Anne, rose and cleared the plates from the table. When George started to push his chair back and offer to help, Anne stopped him with the gentle pressure of her hand on his shoulder. "It's family tradition," she whispered in his ear. "The women clear the table and bring dessert. The men do the dishes afterward."

As soon as the women were out of the room, Anne's grandfather, Bonaventure Guidry, an imposing, tall man, spread his arms to rest his palms on the corners of the table. "Well now, Mr. Laurence, what are your intentions toward our Anne?"

George sputtered to keep from spitting out the water he'd just sipped. He swallowed and wiped his mouth with the blue fabric napkin. "Sir?" He glanced around the table. Without exception, Anne's male relatives stared at him, awaiting an answer to the preposterous question. "My intentions. . ." He cleared his throat. "My intentions toward Miss Hawthorne are honorable, I assure you, Mr. Guidry."

Beside him, Forbes burst into laughter, and the rest followed suit. "They're just giving you a hard time. Means they like you."

Not sure he understood, George nodded and smiled. He was saved from any further embarrassment by the reappearance of the women. He started to stand, but Forbes stopped him with a hand on his shoulder. "They're going to serve dessert, so you'll just be in the way if you do that."

"I see." He edged his chair closer to the table.

Maggie directed the presentation of the desserts on the sideboard. A white cake with strawberries on top became the centerpiece, surrounded by pies, dishes of petits fours, and other confectionaries.

"Coffee?" Anne leaned over his right shoulder with a carafe and a cup.

"You know me." He winked at her.

She set down the cup and poured. "This is the real thing—genuine Louisiana coffee with chicory. Dark roast." Her voice held a hint of warning.

He sipped the dark, rich, bitter liquid. "My favorite. Although I haven't had it quite this strong anywhere else."

"That's the way Aunt Maggie likes to make it." She squeezed his shoulder and moved on to serve coffee down the table.

Meredith placed a square plate in front of him with a sampling of each of the desserts, arranged on the plate as he would expect to see in a fine restaurant. Maggie did this for a living. Anne had suggested her aunt to make Courtney's wedding cake. If what he'd seen today was what she did for a regular family gathering, he'd love to see what she could do for a reception for seven hundred guests with no holds barred on the price.

He stood and held Anne's chair for her. "Everything looks wonderful. I'm not even certain what all of it is."

Anne picked up her dessert fork and used it as a pointer. "White amaretto cake with strawberries and raspberry filling. Banana pudding. Chocolate petits fours—some have a berry filling, some are vanilla crème, and some are mint—I'm not sure which kind you got. Lemonade icebox pie. We don't usually have this many desserts. Aunt Maggie catered the Junior League tea yesterday afternoon and had all this left over."

"Annie, did Madeline catch you at church this morning?" one of her aunts asked as she leaned between them to refresh their coffee.

"Yes. I figured you were one of the key people who put her up to asking me to speak."

Forbes handed George the cream to give to Anne before she had to ask for it. She answered her relatives' questions about the invitation to speak at the Bonneterre Women in Business luncheon but fidgeted as if uncomfortable with the focus of attention on herself. As soon as the discussion turned to something else, she stopped twisting her napkin in her lap, sipped her coffee, and nibbled at her desserts.

Anne smiled at George when he brought the carafe of coffee over to refill her cup before following the rest of the men into the kitchen to help clean up. As soon as the kitchen door stopped swinging, her aunts and cousins exclaimed over him—his sweetness, good looks, charm, impeccable manners, and especially his British accent.

"Is it serious?" Aunt Maggie's question brought everyone else to attention.

Anne shrugged. "Not really. Less than a week ago, I thought he was marrying someone else."

Meredith leaned forward. "But could it be serious?" Her expression told Anne what answer she wanted to hear.

"I'm really not sure. I haven't even known him for a month. I know y'all want me to find someone and settle down, but give us some time, please." She smiled at the women staring at her to soften her words. "I promise you'll be the first to know if it turns serious."

Each of the younger single women was then given the opportunity to be the center of the aunts' appetite for romance. When the masculine voices and laughter in the kitchen grew louder than the clank of dishes being washed, the women's conference ended. Anne took the opportunity to slip off to the powder room.

On her way back, one of her younger cousins waylaid her at the entrance to the sunroom and pulled her back into the now-empty kitchen.

"What's up, Marci?" Anne reached over and pushed a lock of the twenty-four-year-old's honey-streaked red hair back from her face. She knew the young woman was struggling to get her parents and even Jenn, Mere, and Forbes to recognize her as an adult. But there was a lack of maturity in the way she acted around her family, compounded by the fact that she still hadn't chosen a college major after five years, that kept her a perpetual child in their eyes.

"Annie, you're the only person in the family who'll tell me the truth."

"Of course I will. What do you want to know?"

"Earlier, when I asked about Cliff Ballantine, I know Forbes was lying to me about not knowing him. Did y'all know him in high school?"

Anne's stomach twisted. She didn't want to lie to her cousin, but she also didn't want the story to get beyond the family. She crossed her arms and leaned against the edge of the island. "If I tell you, you have to promise me it goes no further. There's a reason why he's not discussed by anyone, and that's because of me. I've asked everyone in the family to keep my secret, which has become harder as he's gotten more famous." She took a deep breath. "Yes, we knew Cliff in high school. I tutored him in English and helped him write several papers."

"Even though you're two years younger than him?"

Anne harrumphed. "He was only a year ahead of me in school, but I was in advanced placement classes. He wasn't. When he started college, I kept helping him. You have to understand—I was very shy as a child and had very low self-esteem from all the teasing I got because I hit a growth spurt and was nearly six feet tall by the time I was thirteen. I never had a boy show the kind of attention to me that he did just for doing something I was good at. When I got to college, though, I wasn't just helping him with English—it was all his classes: history, anthropology, even his drama classes. When I told him I didn't have time to continue, he really turned on the charm. We started 'dating.' " She made quotation marks in the air with her fingers. "I'll spare you all the gory details. But when Cliff moved out to Hollywood my first year of graduate school, I sent him money every month to help him make ends meet. It got to the point where I was getting every credit card I could and maxing it out with cash advances just to have money to send to him. When the loan company threatened to repossess my car, I told him I couldn't afford to send him any more money. That was when he suggested we get married. I was naive and wanted to be married, especially to someone as handsome and talented as he, so I agreed. I quit grad school and went to work full-time as the event planner for B-G."

"The job Meredith has now?"

"Yes. I started planning my wedding. It was going to be small, just our families. We couldn't afford much, and I didn't want to ask Uncle Errol and Aunt Maggie for money because they'd already helped me out by giving me a loan to pay off all of my past-due bills and letting me move back in so that I could use my rent money to pay them back. Half of each paycheck went to them, half to Cliff in

California. We set a date. I reserved the chapel, the reception hall, worked out the menu with Maggie, and had a gown on layaway at Drace's."

"What happened? I mean, obviously you didn't end up marrying him. . .*did you*?"

Anne had to laugh at Marci's incredulity. "No, I didn't marry him. Two days before the wedding, he called me and told me to cancel everything. He'd gotten a callback on a movie role he'd auditioned for and would have to stay in California another week."

"What a pig."

"Yeah. So I canceled everything and lost most of the money on nonrefundable deposits. For a month, I didn't hear anything from him. The next thing I know, I see a photo of him with some blond bombshell of an actress on the front cover of one of the gossip rags at the grocery store. Time went by, and eventually I gave up hope that I'd ever hear from him and accepted the fact he'd only been dating me to get me to do stuff for him."

The glaze of admiration for the actor in Marci's eyes had been replaced by disillusionment at the revelation of the man's character. "It's no wonder you don't want anyone else in the family to talk about it. Did he ever pay you back all the money?"

Anne shook her head. "Nope. Never saw a penny. I suppose I could have blackmailed him by threatening to run to the media and show them all the canceled checks with his signature on the back, since he takes great pleasure in telling everyone how he struggled to make it on his own in Hollywood until he got his big break. It was a hard lesson to learn."

"What lesson is that?"

"Don't pour all of your emotions and energy into a relationship unless both parties are willing to give one hundred percent to it. Cliff was a taker, and he was willing to take whatever I was stupid enough to offer—my skills and education, my emotions, and my money. I'm just glad he's out of my life."

Chapter 16

"How could you not tell me?" George brushed past the secretary who'd opened Forbes's office door to announce his arrival early Monday morning.

Forbes gave his assistant a curt nod and laid his gold pen atop the paperwork on his desk. "And what is it I'm supposed to have told you?"

Although the woman closed the door behind her, George strained to keep his voice low. "That Anne was engaged to be married to Cliff Ballantine!" He crossed the office and leaned on the desk, his hands on either side of the desk blotter. "Have you lost your senses? How do you think she's going to feel when he arrives in town next week for the engagement party and I turn around and say, 'Surprise, you've been hired to plan your ex-fiancé's wedding'?"

"It wasn't my place to tell you."

"Not your—" Fury clogged George's throat. Was it all just a game to Forbes? He liked Anne's cousin, had thought they were getting on famously and becoming fast friends. But now. . .

"You are the only person in this farce who knows all the players and their roles. How could you let Anne take on this contract?"

The lawyer leaned back in his chair, his fingers steepled and resting on his chin. "Are you more upset because you didn't know or because of how you think this might affect Anne?"

George straightened and dropped his hands to his sides. "Don't play the barrister with me, Forbes." His so-called friend's calm exterior only fed his anger. He wanted to see some kind of emotion, some kind of remorse or embarrassment. He took a calculated risk. "Did it make you feel powerful, knowing that you could manipulate this situation? Or do you hold some kind of shares in Anne's business to make you trick her into taking this wedding on just to increase the return on your investment?"

Forbes exploded out of his chair, and it slammed against the credenza behind him. "There are a lot of things I'll put up with." Menace edged his low voice. He braced his fists against the edge of his desk. "But being insulted isn't one of them. A hundred years ago, we would be headed to a field with dueling pistols about right now."

"And gladly would I have defended Anne's honor and my own." George matched his pose, trying not to let the other man's larger build and height intimidate him. "I've read about the corruption of lawyers in Louisiana, but I never expected to see it in you. To use your own flesh and blood—"

Forbes grabbed the front of George's shirt and nearly dragged him onto the desk. "You have no right to accuse me of wrongdoing. I love Anne, and I would die before I brought her harm or unhappiness."

Some of George's anger dissipated at Forbes's passionate speech. "Then tell me everything. Make me understand. Because from where I stand, you look guilty as sin. And I don't want to be caught in the middle."

Forbes released him, and George stumbled back a step. Balance regained, he smoothed his shirt and tucked it back into his trousers.

Letting out a low growl, Forbes straightened his tie and raked his fingers through his hair. He pulled his chair forward and sank into it with a sigh. "I never meant for you to be caught in the middle, George, and I apologize if you feel that way." He motioned for George to sit. "How did you learn of Anne and Cliff's engagement?"

George perched on the edge of one of the leather armchairs, guilt nibbling away at his anger. "I did not come by the information honestly. I overheard Anne telling the story to your younger sister yesterday, after you'd already left your aunt and uncle's home."

"Then to answer your first question. . ." The lawyer had replaced the outraged man again. "I didn't tell you about Anne and Cliff because it wasn't my secret to share. Just as you swore to Cliff not to reveal his identity to anyone, I swore to Anne I would never tell anyone she had a relationship with him."

"But. . ." Logic and reason failed George. A man had to honor his promises. That still left the second issue. "Why didn't you counsel Cliff against hiring Anne as the wedding planner?"

Sheepishness overcame Forbes's professional demeanor. "Cliff doesn't know Anne is the wedding planner. As you may have experienced, he's leaving the details up to Ms. Landry." He spun his pen on top of the papers that were now strewn across the desktop. "Anne needs to plan this wedding. I think it'll be cathartic for her."

George frowned. "How is planning the wedding for the man who bilked her for thousands of dollars and practically left her standing at the altar going to bring her healing?"

"Two ways. She needs to forgive him; but until she gets closure, until she's able to show him what she's made of herself—and maybe say a few things to him that she's had locked up inside of herself for years—she'll never be able to close that chapter of her life."

Manipulation for Anne's own good. It still didn't sit well with him, but was easier to understand. "And the second way?"

"How much is he going to end up paying her to plan this wedding?"

Understanding rolled in like a London fog. "So she gets closure and revenge all at the same time."

"Oh no, not revenge. . .just what he owes her—with interest." Forbes gave him a conspiratorial wink. "Now was there something else you needed to see me about?"

George left Forbes's office with twenty minutes to get from downtown to Town Square to meet Anne at her office.

Anne had been engaged to his employer. Wanted to marry him. Loved him enough to drop out of graduate school so she could support him. Thought he was *handsome* and *talented.* She would have gone through with it. She would have married Cliff all those years ago if he hadn't gotten his big break and discarded her like a used tissue.

Oh, Anne. . . The disillusionment she must have suffered from being so ill used. No wonder she'd reacted with such vehemence when she discovered his own deception of her. . .on behalf of Cliff Ballantine.

The old adage couldn't be truer than in this situation: *What a tangled web we weave when first we practice to deceive.*

If she'd been so angry at him for simply pretending to be getting married, how angry would she be when she discovered whose wedding she was really planning? And would that anger, justified though it would be, destroy any chance of their relationship growing into something serious?

By the time he reached her office, he dreaded walking in and looking her in the eye. Would she see his misgivings? Would she sense something amiss? He needed to distance himself until the truth came out. If he allowed himself to fall in love with her and then lost her when she found out about Cliff, his heart would never mend. "Above all else, guard your heart, for it is the wellspring of life," King Solomon had written in Proverbs. And Solomon had had his own issues with women, so he knew from whence he wrote.

George parked in the alley behind Anne's office and killed the engine. With trepidation, he mounted the steps to the back door. He crossed the threshold into the kitchen, and cool air washed over him. Making his way from the kitchen through the hall to the front office, he could hear voices. He didn't want to interrupt and stopped out of sight of the doorway.

His skin tingled at the sound of her voice. She would be sitting in the wing chair facing the bow window, her sapphire blue eyes sparkling as she discussed wedding details with her clients.

He leaned against the wall and enjoyed listening to her guide the potential clients through the same questionnaire he'd been given to fill out at Courtney's first appointment. When he heard the telltale jingle of the bell over the front door, he entered the front office.

Anne rose; the intensity of her gaze nearly unraveled him.

"I am so glad I heard you come in." She dropped into the wing-back chair. "I'm not sure I want to sign a contract with the couple who was just here. They can't make a decision to save their lives, and all she did was ask me about Cliff Ballantine. If I didn't know any better, I'd think they were undercover reporters trying to dig up some kind of scandal from his past." She cut her gaze at him. "Of course, if that were the case, why would they come to me?" Her laugh had a nervous quality to it.

What had she said about honesty? If she wanted him to be honest with her, she needed to grant him the same courtesy. He needed to know she was over Cliff, that she'd forgiven him and could move on with a new relationship without the specter of being hurt in the past coming between them in the future.

"What's wrong?" She stood and crossed to stand in front of him, resting her hand on his crossed arms. "I do declaiyah, you look jus' like an ol' thundahcloud."

He loved it when she put on that thick Southern accent. His tension started to melt, and he smiled at her. "Nothing's wrong. It's just been a busy day already."

She gave his arm a gentle squeeze, then went around her desk to retrieve her handbag and keys. "You ready to go to the rental lot and choose decor for the engagement party?"

Cliff's engagement party. The event where Anne would learn the true identity of her client. The thundercloud returned to his heart, but he schooled his expression to mask it. "Certainly. Lead on."

He let her make the decisions on what columns, greenery, linens, tables, and chairs to rent. The only thing he ordered was the gold flatware and table service, per Courtney's request. Anne laughed and chatted with the proprietor, a friend of hers from childhood, as she completed the paperwork and George paid with the expense-account credit card.

Headed back toward her car, Anne's stomach growled. "Where do you want to go for lunch?"

"I. . ." He had to get away. Distance. He needed distance to guard his heart. In one week, she might decide she never wanted to see him again. "I can't. I'm interviewing for several house staff positions this afternoon and need to get back." The interviews didn't start for another three hours but made a convenient excuse.

"Oh. How about brunch on Friday? It's the Fourth of July, and I'm officially taking the day as a holiday. . .except for the wedding I have to set up at noon." She unlocked the car doors with the remote on her key chain. "Then later you can join us for our family Fourth of July celebration."

He slipped into the passenger seat. How could he say no to her when she caressed his face with her azure gaze? "I'll check my schedule and get back with you."

For the next three days, George vacillated between his desire to spend time with Anne and his fear of ending up with a broken heart. The only person he could talk to about it was Henry, and his brother had been no help whatsoever.

"Just tell her the whole tale and have done with it," he'd said. "Honor be hanged."

George couldn't let go that easily. He'd given his word and signed a contract. He couldn't go back on that. But he agonized over the thought of spending time with Anne, because he wanted to lay before her the whole of his situation, especially the part about Cliff, so he could learn her true feelings.

The days dragged. Thursday, as he had every day that week, he went into the study on the main floor to work on the travel arrangements for Cliff and Courtney's party guests. Most had their own personal assistants, but he had a lot of information to convey to get the two hundred guests from all over the world into Bonneterre, Louisiana. He'd started a spreadsheet to track the RSVPs and now used it to enter travel itineraries.

The data swam on the computer screen, and after mangling three entries, he gave up and turned the leather executive chair around to stare out the picture window. The gray clouds and pelting rain matched his mood.

He couldn't do it. He couldn't face her. He picked up the phone and dialed Forbes's private number. The line didn't ring but went straight to voice mail, thank heavens. Forbes would ask too many questions.

"Forbes, George Laurence here. I'm calling to let you know I won't be attending dinner tonight. Something has arisen that I must handle. Please make my apologies to. . .everyone." He ended the call and let the cordless receiver drop into his lap.

The rhythm of the rain lulled him into a semiconscious state. He imagined every possible scenario of how Anne would react. She might be absolutely nonplussed at the revelation. She could be angry enough to break the contract.

"Baby, are you all right?"

George started when he realized Mama Ketty stood over him.

"I'm sorry, but you didn't answer when I knocked on the door." She clucked her tongue. "You're too young to be bearing such a heavy weight. Tell Mama Ketty all about it." She settled into one of the chairs across the desk.

He blinked. She didn't budge. Words tumbled out of his mouth—he couldn't stop them. He told her everything, including his fear that Anne might never want to see him again.

She sat very still when his verbal torrent ceased, her dark face not revealing any hint of her thoughts. She closed her eyes for a moment, and when she opened them, warmth flooded him. Her soft voice drowned out the storm outside. " 'For thus the Lord God, the Holy One of Israel, has said, "In repentance and rest you will be saved, in quietness and trust is your strength." ' I'm thinking Isaiah knew what he was talking about when he wrote that. Until you find peace with God, you ain't gonna have happiness with yourself nor no one else around you." She stood and smoothed her floral dress over her ample figure. "Now come into the kitchen and have some of my snickerdoodles."

Who did she think she was coming in here and telling him—exactly what he needed to hear? The words had been given to her by God, and they convicted him to the core of his soul. He had to heal his own scars before he could give his heart to someone else. He picked up the phone and dialed Anne's cell number. Until he figured his life out, he needed to keep her at arm's length. She didn't answer. He left a message canceling their brunch date tomorrow. He would go to her family's Independence Day celebration in the park. She wouldn't be there until late, and they'd be buffered by the number of people surrounding them.

The aroma of cinnamon and baked goods rolled over him. He inhaled deeply. How had he not noticed before? He rose and followed the amazing smells downstairs.

Mama Ketty bustled about the kitchen. "You just set down at that bar and don't move a twitch. Mama Ketty's gonna put some meat on them bones if it's the last thing I do." She placed a plate of cookies and an enormous glass of milk in front of him. "I know you haven't been eating any of my cooking. How long's it been since you ate proper?"

When was the last time he'd had a decent meal? Sunday afternoon at Anne's aunt and uncle's home. "Awhile."

She clucked at him again. "Uh-huh. I suspected as much. Sit tight, and you'll have a meal that'll stick to your ribs."

Contentment settled into him along with the milk and cinnamon-dusted cookies while he watched her work. "Mama Ketty, do you believe that everything happens for a reason?"

"Baby, I believe that nothing happens without God knowing about it. And when things do happen, if we turn toward Him, He'll make the best of the situation, be it good or bad." She set a plate in front of him. "This here's a good Louisiana-raised, sugar-cured ham steak, fresh corn on the cob, purple-hulled peas from my son's garden, tomatoes from there, too." She turned back to the stove and lifted a small pan. She glopped something akin to porridge onto the plate. "Those are the finest grits in all of Louisiana. They'll stick with you, too. No one leaves Mama Ketty's table hungering after they've had some of my grits."

George had heard of the Southern delicacy but hadn't really thought he'd ever have to eat them. With Mama Ketty's hawklike gaze on him, though, he didn't dare leave a morsel of food on the white ceramic plate.

Seasoned with butter, salt, and pepper, the grits melted in his mouth. She'd salted the tomatoes to bring out their full flavor, and butter dripped down his fingers as he bit into the crisp, sweet corn. The ham steak was among the best meat he'd ever put in his mouth.

She took the plate as soon as he laid down his fork. "Now you get on out of here and let me get back to work." She shoved a small plate of cookies into his hands when he stood. "And take these with you. You children these days, wanting to be skin and bones." She shook her head and mumbled to herself.

He carried the cookies back up to the office to start over on the spreadsheet. His position as head of the household staff had just become an empty title.

Instead of getting straight to work, he opened the Bible program on the computer and searched for the verse Ketty had quoted. Isaiah 30:15. "In repentance and rest you will be saved, in quietness and trust is your strength." He printed the verse, cut it out, and taped it to the bottom of the monitor.

"In quietness and trust is your strength."

"Father, help me to be quiet and trust You for strength. You know I'm going to need it."

Chapter 17

"George is acting weird." Anne tipped her wide-brimmed hat forward to better shield her face from the midmorning sun. She couldn't show up at the church with a sunburned nose.

"Hmm?" Meredith's distracted voice came from behind a biography of Claude Monet.

"I said George is acting weird."

Meredith slipped a bookmark in to keep her place and scooped her strawberry blond hair over her shoulder. "Define *weird*."

"Ever since he came to lunch last Sunday, he's been. . .acting funny—not like himself, like I've said or done something that offended him and he doesn't know how to tell me." Once again, she went over everything that had been said and done at Maggie and Errol's Sunday afternoon, trying to figure out what might have upset him.

"Have you asked him about it?"

"I haven't had a chance. He's been avoiding me all week." Something tickled her ankle, and she jerked her foot out of the inflatable kiddie pool. A leaf from the ancient oak tree overhead careened away on the wake caused by her movement. She put her foot back in the tepid water. As long as it wasn't a bug.

"Maybe he's just been busy with getting ready for his boss coming into town for the engagement party next week." Mere fanned herself with her straw hat. "Jenn better get back soon with that ice.

It's gotta be nearly a hundred degrees out here. But at least it's not raining like last year."

"He didn't come to Thursday dinner last night and canceled brunch with me today."

"Do you think maybe someone said something to him when you weren't around Sunday? Something that scared him off?"

"Are you kidding me? With as much as the whole family wants to see me married?" Anne paused. "Maybe *that's* what frightened him. Maybe they tried to pressure him into making a commitment."

"Or he could've overheard you telling Marci about Cliff, and he's scared he can't compete with a movie star."

"Bite your tongue!" Anne splashed water toward Meredith with her foot. "I can't stand Cliff Ballantine. He's nothing compared to George. He's nowhere near as kind, considerate, funny, caring, compassionate, generous—"

"Okay, okay," Meredith splashed back. "I get the picture. Sheesh. All George needs is a dragon to slay to ensure his sainthood."

Anne smiled, but it faded quickly. "I hate Cliff Ballantine. If it weren't for him, I never would have dropped out of school. I'd be Dr. Anne Hawthorne now, teaching English at some fantastic, quaint little four-year college, redbrick buildings covered with ivy. . . ."

"Yeah. . ." Meredith's voice had the same dreamy quality Anne's had taken on. "Instead, you have your own business, you're a leader in the community, you love what you do." She leaned across the low table between them and poked Anne's arm. " 'God causes everything to work together for the good of those who love Him.' God has blessed you, Annie."

"Did someone send for ice?"

An avalanche cascaded over their shoulders and into the shallow water.

Meredith yelped and yanked her feet out of the pool. Anne laughed and kicked hers to mix the ice in with the warm water.

"That was a twenty-pound bag." Jenn flopped into the third chair, breathless. "And the only one Bordelon's Grocery had left.

I'll take the coolers out to the restaurant and fill them from the ice machine there for tonight." She kicked off her sandals and dunked her feet into the cooling water. "You know, if our landlady would get the real swimming pool fixed, we could be floating around on inflatables instead of sitting around a wader like three rednecks."

"I told you before that there's no way I could get someone out here on the Fourth of July." Anne scooped up a few ice chips and tossed them in Jenn's direction. "Besides, I wouldn't be able to do more than this even if we could use the pool."

"What time do you have to be at the church?" Meredith tested the water with her toes, then slipped her feet in with a sigh.

"I have to be there at noon to get the setup started, then I'll run out to the park to meet the caterer and get them situated. I'll be running back and forth all afternoon." She glanced at her watch. She needed to leave in half an hour. "I'm so glad Jason agreed to help out. He's a natural, but he insists on staying a cop instead of joining me as my assistant."

Meredith laughed. "You know him. He wants to be chief of police someday so that if Forbes ever gets elected mayor, the two of them can work together to make all the changes they think this city needs."

"You have so much work, you need to hire a full-time assistant, not just temporary part-timers." Jenn dug a piece of ice out of her glass of tea and rubbed it across the base of her neck.

Anne sipped her tea and resumed fanning herself with her book. "I've been thinking about that. I've got George's wedding in October—"

"His employer's, you mean." Meredith winked and flashed a grin.

She shrugged. "Same difference. Between now and then, I have a wedding, engagement party, or other event every weekend but two. Then the mayor's wife called me about planning the fall debutante cotillion in September. That's on top of a couple of reelection events for her husband's mayoral campaign and the LouWESA conference

Labor Day week in Baton Rouge."

"Louisa conference?" Jenn asked.

"Louisiana Wedding and Event Specialists Association. That's the week before the cotillion."

"Speaking of debutantes," Jenn said as she crunched ice from her tea, mouth open the way that made Anne's skin crawl. "You'll never guess who I ran into at the grocery store."

Anne didn't bother guessing—Jenn would tell them anyway.

"Patsy Sue Landry." Jenn drawled out the name, imitating the middle-aged Southern belle. "She remembered me from when I used to babysit her younger girls after you started college, Anne. She asked about you."

Anne cringed. She hoped the woman wasn't going to call her again. She didn't know if she could avoid the woman's questions without lying to her about George and the plans for Courtney's wedding.

"She said she's leaving for the Riviera next week and will be gone four or five weeks."

"Thank goodness."

"While we were chatting, I saw on one of the local rags on the magazine stand that Cliff Ballantine might be coming to town next week. Something with his fraternity, they figure."

Anne snorted. "I'll make sure to be on the lookout so I can avoid him, then."

"Don't you think it's time you forgave him?" Meredith's sincerity and concern soothed Anne like a squirt of lemon juice in the eye.

"Look at the time." Anne jumped up from the lounger. "I'm going to be late." She rushed inside and took the stairs to her second-floor apartment two at a time. *Coward.* The passage she'd read from Matthew in her quiet time that morning came back to haunt her. "For if you forgive men for their transgressions, your heavenly Father will also forgive you. But if you do not forgive others, then your Father will not forgive your transgressions."

She had no right to withhold her forgiveness from Cliff for

what he'd done to her. After all, Jesus was willing to give His life to forgive her for all of her sins.

She slammed the apartment door behind her. "Okay, Lord! I forgive him! Does that make You happy?" She felt stupid even as she yelled at the ceiling. Of course her outburst didn't make Him happy. She said the words, but her heart wasn't in it. She just wanted the Holy Spirit to leave her alone with the whole guilt thing.

Halfway through changing clothes, she sank onto the edge of the bed. "Jesus, You're going to have to teach me how to forgive him, then give me the strength to do it. I'm not going to be able to do this on my own."

George's image flashed in her mind. "I can't be with George until I rid myself of Cliff once and for all. I don't know what's going on with him right now, Lord, but give me the strength to resist my attraction to him until I've worked through the Cliff issue and can approach the relationship without baggage."

"Why don't we go back to the church for your car later?" Jason handed Anne her duffel bag. Behind them, the wedding reception limped on, not as much fun for the guests now that the bride and groom had left. "We're already at the park, so we might as well take my Jeep over to the pavilion, have dinner, watch the fireworks, and then get your car on the way home."

Her change of clothes was in her tote bag in the backseat of Jason's vehicle. She glanced at her watch. "You're right. Papere would have fired up the grill about half an hour ago, so the first hamburgers and hot dogs should just now be coming off." She slung the duffel's strap over her shoulder. "Let's go."

On the other side of Schyuler City Park, she dashed into the public restroom, changed, and then tossed everything into the open-top Jeep. Mamere reserved the same pavilion every year for their Independence Day cookout—the one between the playground and the privy, with an unobstructed view of the fireworks.

Her mouth watered at the smoky barbecue aroma that wafted over from Papere's huge charcoal grill. She jogged straight toward the gaggle of children running amok in the grassy field.

"An-Anne! An-Anne!" Seven girls under the age of ten surrounded her.

"We saw the wedding people when we drove into the park." Ten-year-old Jordyn Babineaux hooked her arm through Anne's. Slim with long dark hair, the tween would be unintentionally breaking hearts in a few years. "Was it a beautiful wedding?"

She tweaked the girl's nose. "Of course it was. I planned it, after all."

"An-Anne, when are you gettin' married?" eight-year-old Kaitlyn Guidry asked.

"Probably not for a long time, sweetie." At a tug on her shorts, Anne turned.

Six-year-old Megan's brown eyes beamed up at her. "But Mama said you're gonna marry Mr. George, sooner better than later."

Kaitlyn covered her younger sister's mouth none too gently. "Shush, Megan. You don't know what you're talking about."

Anne's cheeks burned. She knew if the girls' parents had been discussing her at home, the rest of the family was, too.

"Do you like him?" Jordyn ducked her head and kicked at something in the grass.

"Sure I like him. He's a very nice man."

The adolescent heaved a dramatic sigh. "That's not what I mean. Do you like. . .*like* him?"

Good grief! Even the children were getting in on the matchmaking. "I'm not sure, Jordy. I need to get to know him better."

"He's here." Megan tugged on Anne's shorts again. "Over there with the boys, fishin' in the lake."

Anne shielded her eyes against the setting sun. Her heart thumped. George sat on a pier between Cooper, seven; and Christian, four; kicking his feet back and forth in the water. The boys giggled and yelled as the water sprinkled them.

Lord God, I want this man to be the father of my children. She stopped dead in her tracks. Never in her life had she given serious thought to having children of her own. Just the opposite. She'd *never* wanted children of her own.

A bell clanged at the pavilion. With war cries Geronimo would have been proud of, the girls beat a path to go get their supper.

George sprang lightly to his feet and helped the boys gather their fishing poles, shoes, and tackle box. She should turn around now and go into the pavilion. Shoes tucked under his arm, he stopped when they made eye contact.

She smiled and raised her hand in a weak greeting. She couldn't let him see how he affected her. She had to remain distant until she got the rest of her life sorted out.

He smiled and angled over toward her.

What to say to him? Should she tell him about Cliff? What if Meredith was right and he'd be jealous or upset to hear it? He was within a few feet. She had to say something. "There aren't any fish in that pond, y'know."

He shook his head and laughed. "I'd surmised as much. But there's more to fishing than catching fish." He motioned toward the pavilion.

She fell in step with him. "More than catching fish? I thought that was the whole point." What an inane conversation. . .inane but neutral, casual, easy.

"For a professional fisherman, yes, I suppose that would be the general idea. However, for the man of leisure, fishing is an exercise in relaxation, in getting to know oneself and one's companions better."

She laughed, relaxing. "Except for the accent, you sound like one of those fishing show hosts on TV."

"You don't fish?" He clasped his hands behind his back.

He clasped his hands behind his back. Five days ago, he'd taken hold of her hand as they'd walked out of church. Something *had* changed between them. *Focus. Keep things casual.* "I've only been on one fishing trip with my family, and I got yelled at for talking too much when we were sitting there in a boat in the middle of the lake. How can you get to know your companions better if you can't talk?"

He chuckled, a deep, rich sound that tugged at her heart. "Men don't need words to bond."

"Ah, so it's a male-bonding ritual, then." She stopped when they reached the edge of the crowd gathered in the pavilion.

"Precisely." In the waning sunlight, his eyes took on a coppery glow.

Papere called the family to order to say grace, for which she was grateful. Around them, everyone joined hands. George enveloped hers in his. She hadn't noticed Sunday how large and strong his hands were. During the prayer, she stole a glance at him. *Don't you hurt me, George Laurence. If I give you my heart, please be the man who's going to watch over me and protect me from pain. Don't break it the way Cliff did.*

When the prayer ended, Jenn and Mere grabbed her by each arm. "How'd you do it? You said no one could come out today." Jenn waved at someone over Anne's shoulder.

Anne laughed. "I called in a favor."

Meredith pursed her lips. "Let me guess. . .a classmate from high school."

She shook her head. "Nope, college. I didn't tell you earlier because he didn't know for sure if he'd be able to come out today."

" 'Grief, Anne, you know everyone in this city. We should have known you'd know someone who could fix the swimming pool." Jenn kissed her cheek. "Thanks. We enjoyed it this afternoon. It sure was hot outside."

"Tell me about it. I had an outdoor reception to work—" She shoved Jenn when her cousin rolled her eyes. "Quit rubbing it in. I plan to make full use of it tomorrow and Sunday."

When she'd filled her plate, she turned and scanned the long tables under the open shed. George stood and waved her over. She laughed when she got closer. On each side of him were his two fishing buddies. She went around and sat opposite the threesome.

"Mr. George, can you help me with this?" Cooper held up a hamburger hemorrhaging ketchup from all sides.

"Of course." With a plastic knife, he scraped away the excess condiments, then cut the sandwich in four pieces. "Better?"

"Yes, sir!" The boy did his best to shove one of the wedges into his mouth whole.

George turned to his right and did the same for Christian and his hot dog.

"You're going to be a wonderful father someday." She'd said it out loud! She couldn't take it back. She might as well have come out and told him how she felt.

"Thank you, Anne." George's gaze burned into hers.

Embarrassed, she dropped her attention to her plate. So much for being low-key.

The boys vied for his attention, leaving Anne to eat in peace. . . and to fall in love with him a little more with each passing moment. *God, You're supposed to be helping me* resist *him! Not making him more irresistible.*

Peace didn't last long. After less than fifteen minutes, leaving mangled bread and soggy chips behind, Christian and Cooper left the table to expend their now-refueled energy.

"Where's Forbes tonight?" George consolidated the remains onto one plate and stacked them.

"He'll be here shortly. Some kind of emergency conference call came up at work." They were watching. All her relatives. Their gazes bored into her. She glanced around, and no one seemed to be looking in her direction. But she knew what they were thinking and hoping and plotting.

He pushed the plates out of the way and leaned on the table on his crossed arms. "Tell me what to expect tonight."

"Well, about eight thirty, Papere will read the Declaration of Independence. We'll sing 'America, the Beautiful,' 'My Country,

'Tis of Thee,' and the national anthem, and if we've timed it right—which we usually do—the fireworks should start."

"No stage show?" Disappointment furrowed the space between his well-groomed brows.

"Stage show?"

"A concert by the local philharmonic while the fireworks are being shot."

"Oh, they have that up at the amphitheater. But it's always so crowded on that end of the park, so we crank it up on the radio—the public station broadcasts it."

"How big is this park?"

"It's triangular—about two miles long and about a mile wide down here at the base. The north end is only about two hundred yards wide. That's where the stage area is. They shoot off the fireworks from about halfway between." She rested her chin on her hand. "How many Fourth of July celebrations have you been to?"

"I witnessed the Washington, DC, celebration last year because my employer was in town—for work. I've seen it in New York, too."

"Is it strange for you to watch us celebrate our independence from England? After all, what we're celebrating today is basically the declaration of war between our two countries."

The twinkle in his eyes was as addictive as hazelnut crème lattes. "We Brits have taken on a very pragmatic attitude toward the countries that were once a part of the British Empire. As long as no one is currently declaring war on us, we don't mind people celebrating wars that happened centuries ago."

Around them, everyone headed for the field. George took her plate to throw away, and she took his cup to refill with Diet Sprite, no ice. They joined Jenn, Meredith, Jason, and Rafe, who'd overlapped the ends of two quilts on the ground.

Forbes flopped down beside Anne as she got settled. "Miss anything?"

She returned his kiss on the cheek. "Just dinner."

"George came?" he whispered.

Odd question. "Of course. Why wouldn't he?"

"Oh, I thought—never mind." Forbes leaned forward and greeted his sisters by pulling their hair.

After he finished reading the Declaration of Independence, Papere led young and old alike in singing, "America, the Beautiful." Anne added her alto to Forbes's tenor, Jason and Rafe's bass, and Jenn and Mere's soprano. The dumbfounded expression on George's face ended their harmony with laughter.

Forbes held up his hand. "We know, we've heard it all our lives: 'You're just like the Von Trapps from *The Sound of Music*.' "

George recovered himself. "Not exactly what I was thinking, but it did sound nice. Pray, continue."

When they segued into "My Country, 'Tis of Thee," Anne made the mistake of looking at George to see what he thought of the co-opted British national anthem. He leaned over and sang low in her ear, "God save the Queen!"

"You're bad," she whispered.

"I'm bad? Your ancestors stole our song, and I'm bad?" He shifted position, turning his torso toward her, their noses almost touching. A few inches, and they would be kissing. His grin faded. Emotion flooded his gaze. "Anne, there's something—" With a whoosh of breath, his forehead banged hers.

"Ow!" She rubbed her head and leaned away. "Hello, Christian, Cooper."

The two boys hung from George's neck, one in his lap, the other on his back.

The boys' mothers rushed over. "Oh, George, Anne, we're so sorry. Boys, come on with us."

He waved them away. "It's quite all right, Andrea, Keeley. Let them stay. We've been bonding today."

The second time he was with her family, and he'd remembered everyone's name so far. Each moment she was near him, he revealed even more how he fit the image of her perfect mate.

Forgiving ol' what's-his-name didn't seem so hard all of a sudden.

Chapter 18

"It had to be you," Anne sang with the music flooding her office. She smiled, recalling the warmth in George's cinnamon-hazelnut eyes as he'd talked at length with her grandfather Friday evening at the picnic. He'd been such a good sport to put up with the ribbing Papere and the uncles had given him. But he still had to prove himself. She couldn't just fall head over heels for him because he got along with her family.

She wound pink tulle onto a heavy cardboard bolt, pulling the fabric yard by yard out of the white trash bags that nearly filled the floor of her storage room. Her bride Saturday afternoon had taken the wedding from *Steel Magnolias* as her model, with pink bunting draped over anything that would stand still. Anne's own wedding would be much more sophisticated—

Whoa. Thinking in terms like that could only bring disappointment. Sure, she liked George now, and he seemed to like her, but what if the glow wore off? What if she discovered him lying to her about something important again?

The future without George Laurence in it looked dim and dismal. But it was a possible reality she needed to face. At thirty-five, she was too old to indulge in a crush. She couldn't pin her hopes on him. She could, however, have fun exploring the possibility of something permanent.

The room filled with Frank Sinatra's voice crooning "I Get a Kick Out of You." Anne sang along, swirling around in the tulle. She wished more brides would choose standards for their receptions. Easier to dance to, the words and music also spoke to a larger audience than the inane pop music of the moment her clients tended to choose.

George listened to the same kind of music, and oh, how he could croon it! But could he dance—more than just the waltz they'd already shared? If not, they could always take ballroom dancing together. She knew a few—the waltz, the fox-trot, and the cha-cha. She spun around, her feet tangled in the tulle, and she fell, landing on the soft pile of bags of fabric.

The bell on the front door echoed throughout the town house. Oh no, her ten o'clock consultation! She struggled to her feet and managed to reach the door. "I'll be with you in a moment," she called. Her own laughter didn't make extrication from the pink cloud easy. Once out, she had to dive back in to find her left shoe and hair clip. She slipped into the eggplant-colored pump, then crossed to check her reflection in the mirror on the back of the storage room door. She ran her fingers through her hair, tossed the clip on the nearest shelf, opened the door, and rushed down the stairs.

The couple seated on the love seat under the front window stood. He was in his late thirties, slender, just over six feet tall, well dressed, wearing expensive shoes, and would look good in a single- or double-button coat, charcoal or black.

"I'm sorry I kept you waiting." She extended her right hand to the bride first. "I'm Anne Hawthorne."

"Kristin Smith. I'm so glad you were able to fit us into your busy schedule. This is my fiancé, Greg Witt." Kristin looked several years younger than her fiancé. She stood about five and a half feet, with shoulder-length blond hair that would look good in an updo and a crown headpiece, and a pink skin tone that would look best with pure white.

Anne shook hands with the groom, then motioned for them to sit. She grabbed her planner off her desk before taking her place in the armchair across the coffee table from them. The purple tulips were starting to wilt a little. She'd have to call April's Flowers to see if they'd gotten in another shipment.

"Let me start by saying congratulations. I know this is an exciting time for you as you start planning the biggest event of your life. My job as a wedding planner is to take the stress off of you on the administrative end so that you can relax and enjoy your day." As she did with all potential clients, Anne reviewed her business credentials, association memberships, and certifications. Almost every potential client came in with a list of questions from the Internet to ask. Every list started with questions about the planner's professional qualifications. She found most clients relaxed more if she got that information out before they had to ask.

"We saw the article about you in *Southern Bride*. That was one of the reasons I wanted to come to you." Kristin tapped a black Waterford pen against her pink notepad. "How many weddings do you coordinate in an average month?"

"During the summer, I typically handle three to five weddings per month—about one a week. Some of those are just consultations—I help the bride plan ahead of time, and she handles everything the day of the wedding—while with others, I handle everything for the bride, allowing her to sit back and not have to worry about coordinating anything. Of course, during the fall, winter, and early spring, I don't have as many clients. Did you have a wedding date in mind?"

"We're looking at a couple of dates in the fall—October maybe?" The young woman pulled out a well-worn, checkbook-sized calendar.

Anne flipped to October in her planner, nodding. "October's a good month, especially if you're thinking about an outdoor wedding. I have a couple of events already on the books for the first and third weekends but would be able to assist you either as a consultant if you choose one of those weeks or as your on-site planner any other week."

Both bride and groom made notations in their calendars. "Do you have an assistant or someone who can fill in for you if something happens and you're unavailable on our wedding day?" Kristin asked.

"Yes, if something happens and I am unavailable, I will line up a substitute to work with you at a discounted cost, although I have never missed a client's wedding, so that shouldn't be an issue."

Kristin made another note and continued down the list of standard questions, becoming more open and chattier as Anne answered each concern. With the interview list complete, Anne guided the couple into talking about their ideas for what they wanted. She took copious notes, including the fact that neither seemed locked into any firm decisions. That could be good if they would be open to her suggestions. Bad if it meant they were indecisive.

When their half hour was almost up, Anne set her planner on the coffee table. Time to close out the consultation with chatty conversation. "So are both of you from Bonneterre?"

"No."

"Yes."

Anne blinked and glanced from bride to groom.

"What Greg means is that he's not from Bonneterre but I am." Kristin's explanation was rushed, her tone embarrassed. "What about you?"

"Bonneterre born and raised. Where'd you go to high school, Kristin?"

"Governor's Academy." The boarding school that cost more per year than an Ivy League university. "What about you?"

"Acadiana High."

Kristin exchanged a glance with her fiancé. "Really? Were you there when Cliff Ballantine went to school there?"

Of course. Everyone always asked that when they heard what school she'd attended. "He was a year ahead of me. But it's a really big school." Her standard reply.

"I read somewhere that he's getting married here." Kristin gave her a sly grin. "You wouldn't be planning his wedding, would you?"

Anne forced a smile. "I hadn't heard he was getting married."

"I just think it would be awesome to know what his wedding's going to be like. It's going to be the social event of the year, no matter where he gets married. But could you imagine planning his wedding? Whoever that wedding planner is, she's set for life." Kristin tucked her notepad and calendar into her pink gingham purse and stood.

Anne shook hands with the couple and walked them to the door. "Please let me know if you'd like me to write up a contract."

"Oh, we'll be in touch soon."

Anne stood at the front door and watched as the couple crossed the square toward the restaurants on the other side. For a newly engaged couple, they weren't very affectionate with each other. Oh well. Everyone showed their love in different ways. Odd that they didn't even hold hands, though.

Where had they heard that Cliff was getting married—and in Bonneterre of all places? She prayed that wasn't the case, although if it was true, it would have been on the front page of the *Reserve*. Planning his wedding, indeed. Besides the fact that he would never hire her personally, he would never stoop to hiring a local to plan what Kristin had aptly called *the* social event of the year. He probably had some overpriced Beverly Hills event planner on retainer—someone like the character Martin Short played in the remake of *Father of the Bride*: pretentious, foreign, and way overpriced.

The phone rang and interrupted her ponderings.

"Happy Endings, Inc. This is Anne Hawthorne."

"Good morning, Anne." George's silky accent brought her fully to the present.

She sank into her chair and leaned her elbows on the desk. "Good morning, yourself. I guess you got my message?"

"I did. I would love to have dinner with you tonight. Shall I meet you or pick you up at the office?"

Her heart did a happy dance. "Actually, I'm coming to you."

A warm chuckle melted through the phone. "I'd love to cook

for you some night, but with no advance notice and Mama Ketty's not being here. . ."

"The chef will be there at four o'clock to start cooking."

"The chef?"

She laughed. "Major O'Hara, the executive chef for Boudreaux-Guidry. Tonight is the only time he has available to do a tasting menu for the rehearsal dinner. Since you didn't have a chance to taste his food before agreeing to his catering the engagement party, I hope to set your mind at ease tonight."

"Ah. And here I was thinking you were trying to surprise me with a romantic, home-cooked dinner."

Were he standing in front of her, he would wink and give her that enchanting crooked grin of his. She bit her bottom lip and took a calming breath. *Have fun but don't indulge.* "I'll see you at six o'clock."

The caterer arrived at four. After a brief interview, George turned him loose in the kitchen and returned to his quarters. Less than two hours before Anne arrived. Plenty of time to get ready.

He rummaged through shopping bags until he found the table linens. He hadn't expected the enormous discount store to have quality linens, but the ivory fabric with an embossed pinstripe was at least as nice as what he could find at the local department stores. He ironed the creases out of the tablecloth and napkins and carried them into the small room off the kitchen that would serve as the employees' dining and break room, once he hired a full house staff.

Covering the large round table with the cloth, he placed a glass vase of lavender tulips in the center. He'd gone to nearly every florist in town trying to find Anne's favorite flowers, eventually securing the last two dozen at April's Flowers—finalizing the purchase just as someone else called in looking for some.

He opened the french doors onto the promenade that ran the length of the back of the house. The small iron café table with a glass top and two matching chairs, which he'd found at a locally owned hardware store, made for a perfect alfresco dinner for two. He whistled as he arranged the table, finishing with the second vase of tulips and two taper candles.

Distance, remember. Don't let's get in too deep, aye, old boy?

His watch beeped. Five thirty. He'd taken too long with the decorations. He left a book of matches on the table and closed the doors to keep the cool air inside a little longer.

He moved the rest of the spoils of his quick shopping trip into the walk-in closet. He made up the bed with sheets freshly laundered by Mama Ketty, a new duvet, and pillows. In the extra bathroom, he put out the towels Mama Ketty had insisted on laundering before being used. The navy and gold colors were the same he'd used in his quarters in Cliff's two other homes. His brother Henry would laugh and call him set in his ways. He liked to think of himself as consistent.

He showered, then dressed in gray pants, a blue button-down, and a colorful tie. His short hair dried quickly. He leaned close to the bathroom mirror. The dark brown around his temples seemed to sprout new grays every day, and it needed trimming.

He heard a sound and realized it was his phone playing "I Can't Give You Anything but Love." *Anne*. His heart leaped, then stalled. She couldn't be calling to cancel. "George Laurence here."

"Anne Hawthorne here." Her voice sounded amused. "I'm pulling up to the house now, but I thought I should ask—should I come to the front door or. . . ?"

Only someone else who worked in a service industry would even think about that. "Since my employer is not in residence, the front entrance is fine."

"Okay, I'll see you in a sec."

George switched the phone to silent mode, then snapped it into the holster on his belt. He needed to know if Cliff or Courtney called but didn't want dinner disturbed. He straightened his tie, then headed to the front of the house. Through the etched glass in the door, he could see Anne, hand raised to knock. He opened the door and ushered her inside.

Her tremulous smile betrayed a surprising nervousness, given this had been her idea. "This is for you—a kind of housewarming/host gift."

He took the white gift bag from her, surprised by its weight. "Thank you." He kissed her cheek, then turned and made a sweeping gesture with his free hand. "Welcome to my employer's home. Would you care for a tour?"

She smiled. "Maybe the upstairs part. I'm pretty familiar with the ground floor. Aunt Maggie used to cater events for the Thibodeauxes here a few times a year. Once I was old enough, I came out to help with setup, service, and cleanup."

"Ah. That's why you asked about the service entrance."

She stuck her head in to glance around the formal front parlor. "This is the first time I've ever come in through the front door."

He took her by the hand and led her upstairs. "Obviously, it's not fully furnished yet. I expect a shipment later in the week, and once Courtney returns"—he winked at Anne—"she will address decorating the guest bedrooms."

"And the thought of that frightens you?" She glanced in each room as they wandered through both upper levels.

"Not so much as the thought of her mother doing it." He should have known she'd see through him. He opened the door at the top of the service stairs at the back of the house to take her down to the kitchen. "The one time Mrs. Landry came into the house, she suggested a pink faux-fur rug for one of the upstairs rooms."

Her laughter resonated like chimes in the enclosed stairwell. "Hopefully she's not planning to give Courtney the one that's in her own house as a wedding present. Maybe you should find an interior designer to recommend to her."

"I'm meeting with three on Thursday."

The chef turned when they entered the kitchen. "Hey, Anne." He wiped his hands on the red-and-white-striped towel draped over his shoulder and crossed to embrace her.

"Hey, Major. I've been looking forward to this dinner all day."

He cut his gaze toward George. "I'm sure you have."

George wasn't sure how to read the look that passed between Anne and the caterer, who was not wearing a wedding band. George led her out of the kitchen. "How do you know him?"

"Major? He started working for Aunt Maggie when we were in high school."

George smiled and shook his head.

"What's so funny?"

He led her through the dining room and opened the french doors. "I grew up in London. For the last five years, I've shuttled back and forth between Los Angeles and Manhattan. I knew Bonneterre was smaller, but with a quarter of a million population, it's not a village. Yet listening to you, seeing how you cannot go outside of your office without seeing someone you know. . .it's very quaint." He held her chair as she sat.

She looked over her shoulder with a grin. "It used to be a lot more 'quaint' than it is now. The city has nearly doubled in size in the last ten or fifteen years."

He sat as she told him about how Bonneterre had changed over her lifetime. At the first lull in the conversation, he stood. "May I offer you a beverage?"

"Oh, that reminds me, you never opened your gift." She pushed the white bag on the table toward him.

"Quite so." He reached through the tissue paper and wrapped his hand around something rectangular and solid, with a smooth surface. Drawing it out, he grinned when he saw it. "Is this a hint for later?"

"I thought you liked flavored coffee." Her protest was overshadowed by the laughter lacing her voice.

"Yes, but if I guess correctly, hazelnut caramel is your favorite flavor."

She bit her bottom lip, and her smile grew wider. "Busted."

He loved her laugh. "Would you like some now?"

"No, save it for dessert. I could really go for some iced tea."

"The only kind we have is without sweetening."

"That's fine. I can drink it either way." She started to stand.

He stopped her with his hand on her shoulder. "No. You're my guest. Stay there and let me serve you."

Anne's blue eyes sparkled, and she squeezed his hand. "Thank you."

The dinner Major O'Hara put before them was nothing short of perfection, from the spinach salad with muscadine vinaigrette to the medium-rare London broil with Cajun garlic mashed potatoes and sautéed baby asparagus.

"I hope this sets your mind at ease," Anne said after O'Hara cleared their dinner plates. "Major is one of the best chefs I've ever worked with. He's done a ton of catering for me over the years."

George reached across the table and covered Anne's clasped hands. "I'm happy you came."

The candlelight glittered in the sapphire pools of her eyes. "I'm happy you didn't mind the intrusion."

Slow. Take it slow. "Your presence would never be an intrusion." He leaned closer to her.

They both turned at the sound of a cleared throat. "Are you ready for dessert?" O'Hara stood in the doorway, a silver tray balanced on one hand, a coffee service cart beside him.

Anne groaned dramatically. "I don't know how I could eat another bite. What is it?" She leaned back to make room on the table as he stepped forward.

"White chocolate crème brûlée with raspberries." He put the individual dishes in front of them. "The coffee is hazelnut caramel."

George couldn't stop looking at Anne. The chef poured the steaming, fragrant liquid into fine china cups, set the silver coffeepot on the sideboard, and withdrew.

She closed her eyes and sighed as she savored the first bite of the custard dessert. Tonight had been a revelation to George. When she wasn't in business mode—when she was relaxed and not on a time schedule—she truly enjoyed the experience of dining.

"What?" She'd caught him staring.

"I just like watching you." He was going under deep and fast. Was the pleasure of falling in love with her tonight worth the risk of losing her in a few days?

Her cheeks glowed in the candlelight. "Why?"

"Because you're beautiful." He sipped his coffee.

She laughed and shook her head.

"Yes, you are." He set down his cup and reached over to lift her chin, forcing her to look him in the eye. "You *are* beautiful, and I don't know who would have told you otherwise."

She didn't speak for a moment, her gaze never wavering. "It was never in so many words." She put her spoon down. "But the intent was the same."

"Well, I'm here now—and I'm right, so you'd best believe me."

The smile he'd become addicted to returned. He tweaked her chin between his thumb and forefinger, then lifted his dessert spoon.

The symphony of crickets, frogs, and other indigenous fauna filled the silence between them. The sky turned red and purple as the sun set on the other side of the house.

Anne sighed and cradled her coffee cup between her hands.

"What is it?" Although his father would have been appalled, he propped his elbows on the edge of the table and leaned toward her.

She swallowed and blinked a few times. "It's just been a really long time since. . ." Her voice caught and her bottom lip quivered.

"Since?" Now that he had her to himself, he wasn't about to let her clam up.

She shrugged, her gaze fixed on the horizon. "Since I stopped to let myself enjoy a quiet eve—" She flinched and reached for the phone clipped to the waistband of her pants. Her shoulders fell when she looked at the caller ID. "I'm so sorry. It's my client who's getting married next week."

He stood and kissed her on the forehead. "I need to go speak with Mr. O'Hara anyway."

The chef turned as George entered the kitchen. "Is everything all right?"

"Yes. It was a wonderful dinner. My compliments—"

"George, I have to run." Anne breezed into the kitchen. "There's a problem with the wedding dress, and I have to go find out if it's something I can fix or really a problem."

"I'll walk you out." He helped Anne into her suit coat and rested his hand on the small of her back as he escorted her to the front door. "What seems to be amiss?"

"I'm not sure. She was so hysterical she wasn't coherent. So I'm driving out to her house to see what's wrong. Hopefully it'll be an easy fix. If not. . .well, I have a few days to figure out what to do." She stopped at the door and turned toward him. "Thank you for a lovely evening. I'm sorry work interfered."

"Thank you for making it a lovely evening." He brushed back a lock of hair that had escaped to fall across her forehead. How was it possible that no man had claimed this wonderful woman? "I'll ring you tomorrow about the final arrangements for the engagement party." He flinched as the vibrator on his phone startled him. He reached for it as he kissed her on the cheek.

"Good night."

She graced him with another full smile. "Good night."

Cliff's number scrolled across the phone's screen. He waved goodbye to Anne and lifted the phone to his ear. "Yes, Mr. Ballantine?"

"Courtney may have blown our cover. If any reporters show up there in the next few days, you have to let me know immediately. We'll have to change all the plans."

Chapter 19

By Wednesday, George started to relax. No news of the engagement or wedding had appeared in the celebrity press. Cliff had announced he'd be giving a press conference in Bonneterre on Friday, and a private service had been contracted to provide security that night since Cliff didn't want the local police brought in. Courtney would arrive tomorrow, ostensibly to attend a friend's wedding.

"George, dude, what is up with you tonight?" Rafe's voice brought him back to the present—the Fishin' Shack, where Anne's cousins had gathered for dinner a night earlier than usual so both Anne and George could attend this week.

"Sorry. I've lots on my mind tonight. What did I miss?"

"We were wondering where Anne is. We thought she was coming with you."

"She had a last-minute meeting with a client. Something about a dress fitting. She assured me she would arrive by seven." George glanced at his watch. She was nearly twenty minutes late. "Obviously the meeting ran longer than she expected."

The restaurant's back room partially muffled the sound of the large dinner crowd in the main dining room. Jenn fluttered in with a couple of baskets of the fried balls of seasoned cornmeal they called hush puppies. When he'd asked about the name last week, Jenn had spun a tale about Southern soldiers in the American Civil

War feeding bits of fried meal to their dogs to "hush" them from giving their position away to the enemy.

He'd researched it that night on the Internet and hadn't found a more definitive answer—just a few other tall tales. Whatever their origin, he enjoyed Jenn's version of the savory pastry, even though cornmeal didn't rank high on his list of favorite flavors or textures.

"You gonna try something different tonight, sugar?" Jenn asked, resting her hand on his shoulder. "I'm proud that a real Englishman likes my fish 'n' chips so much, but. . ."

He closed the menu and handed it to her. "I'll make you a deal, ducky. Bring me your favorite dish—on or off the menu."

The delighted gleam in Jenn's eyes amused him. "Oh, George, we're going to have so much fun teaching you to suck crawfish heads!" She left the room without taking anyone else's order.

"George, you're going to get a trial by fire tonight of what it means to be in Louisiana." Jason watched Jenn as she flitted from table to table.

"My dear fellow, you forget that I am British. I've eaten haggis in Edinburgh and jellied eels in London. I've also traveled extensively and eaten so-called delicacies ranging from insects to parts of animals that were never meant to be eaten. Crawfish presents no challenge I cannot overcome."

The expression on Jason's face said he believed otherwise, but the young man held his tongue.

"Hey, y'all. Sorry I'm late." Anne slid into the vacant chair beside George before he could stand and offer his assistance. Although smiling, the tight lines around her eyes betrayed her heightened stress level.

"Did everything work out all right?" Forbes, on her other side, put his arm around her.

Anne blew out a long breath and rolled her neck from side to side. "No. I'm taking the bride dress-shopping next week. She decided she didn't want to pay the dress shop to alter her gown and instead asked a coworker to do it. Unfortunately, the coworker didn't measure correctly, and rather than leave extra fabric to make corrections with, she trimmed all of her seams down to less than a quarter of an inch. Now the dress is too tight and too short and can't be let back out. I know. I tried." She rubbed her forehead, then reached into her purse and withdrew a small bottle of aspirin. "George, may I?" She pointed at his water.

He handed his glass to her. "How will she afford to purchase a new dress if she couldn't afford to pay for alterations to the first one?"

Anne swallowed two pills with a big gulp of the water with no ice. "I can't tell you. It'll make Forbes mad."

Why would Forbes care how one of Anne's clients paid for a dress?

"Please tell me you're not letting her take it out of your final fee." Forbes's voice had a growl to it that didn't sit well with George. How Anne conducted her business was just that—her own business. Yet who was he to step between her and her cousin?

"If I don't tell you, will you let the matter drop?" She sounded tired—defeated.

"Anne, the contract you sign with your clients is as much for your protection as it is for theirs. I drew it up specifically to make sure that if something went awry, you would still be paid. The more you do this, the more people are going to hear and take advantage of you."

She rested her fists against the edge of the table. George wished there was some way he could help. Without knowing her any better than he did, he wasn't sure if she would see any action or words on his part as support or as butting in.

"Forbes, I know for you, as a lawyer, this is going to be hard to understand. My client's happiness matters more to me than if I get paid next Saturday or if I get paid in miniscule installments for the next six months. It's not as if I'm hurting for income now like I was a few years ago. This girl is a nursing student who works part-time as a waitress." As she talked, her voice got softer, her words faster. "She's already spent more money on the wedding than I advised because she's trying to make both mothers happy, even though they've refused to pay for anything. What should I tell her, Forbes? What?" She shrugged and held her hands up toward him. "Should I tell her she should just wear her next-best dress? Maybe see if she can borrow a friend's old wedding gown? Tell me. You apparently know better than I do how to run my business."

Stunned silence filled the room. Jason and Rafe stared at Anne, mouths agape. Jenn dabbed at the corners of her eyes with her napkin, moved to emotion either by Anne's story or by the conflict between her cousin and older brother. Meredith glared daggers at Forbes. George suppressed a smile, proud of Anne for taking a stand.

Forbes cleared his throat. "Anne, I apologize. It's not my place to lecture you on how you run your business. I know if you wanted legal advice, you'd come to me. I just don't want to see you lose that business because you let clients overspend their budgets and then not pay you."

"I have never had a client not pay me everything due, including my fee. Sometimes it just takes longer." She rested her hand on her cousin's arm. "How do you think I got as successful as I am? Not because I was a hardnose about people paying me every penny the moment I thought it should be paid. My brides recommend me to their friends because I'm willing to work with them and do what it takes to make their weddings the most joyous events of their lives. I'm so sad for this young woman because the happiness that she should be feeling this week has been overwhelmed by the fact that she made an error in judgment and her dress was ruined. Forbes, what if it were Mere or Jenn or Marci or Tiffani? I can be a blessing to this girl, show her the true generosity of Christ's love, and maintain my integrity and my conscience. We've already worked out a payment plan that she can afford."

Forbes rested his hand on the back of her neck and pulled her close to kiss her temple. "I am so happy you never decided to become a criminal defense lawyer."

Lafitte's Landing echoed with the hushed tones of student workers late Thursday afternoon. Anne dropped her duffel bag on the floor just inside the main ballroom. Her cousins Kevin, Jonathan, and Bryan and several of their friends approached her.

"Thanks for coming, guys. Here's the deal. Within the next couple of hours, I expect several deliveries of large items. I'll need y'all to help unload the trucks and bring everything in. Once it's all here, then we'll worry about where it goes. Any questions?"

"Yeah—what time's dinner?" Bryan elbowed one of his friends and winked.

"Pizza. Six o'clock. On me." Even though she was paying them to be here, college boys couldn't go but an hour or two without eating. Instant gratification to keep them happy until they received their paychecks next week. "Oh, and there's a big ice chest full of sodas in my car if one of you will go out and get that."

Footsteps reverberated from the tiled entry. She tingled from blond hair to pedicured toenails. George strolled in, twirling his key ring around one finger. How could she not have noticed his muscular physique before? His snug, heather gray T-shirt clung to the contours of his shoulders, chest, and upper arms as if he should be on a TV commercial for exercise equipment. His worn-in jeans looked like they'd been tailored to fit. He'd had his hair trimmed since she last saw him, and his milk chocolate eyes sparkled when their gazes met. He had no right to look so utterly sensuous when she was trying to maintain a safe emotional distance.

"Hello! Delivery!"

Anne jerked out of her trance at the shout from the opposite end of the building. She grinned at George. "Looks like you timed your arrival perfectly."

His forced frown couldn't quite draw down the corners of his perfectly shaped lips. "And here I'd hoped I'd missed all the manual labor and would be able to stand back and direct."

"Nope. That's my job." With a sweeping motion of her arm, she invited him to join the boys, who trooped toward the service entrance. "What was it you said earlier this morning on the phone about doing whatever I need you to do?"

"You thought I was serious?" He tucked his hands into his pockets and rocked from heel to toe.

That dangerous grin of his nearly dismantled her resolve. " 'Deadly serious,' if I recall correctly."

His laughter filled the cavernous room. . .and her heart. "You've got me there. I'd best go see where I can lend a hand, then."

To keep from watching him walk across the room, she turned to her bag and withdrew several CDs. She'd gotten keys to everything in the building from Meredith, including the cabinet containing the sound system components. She dropped five discs into the CD changer, switched on the surround sound, and enveloped the hall with the classic tunes and sultry vocals of Dean Martin, Frank Sinatra, Dick Haymes, Bing Crosby, and Nat King Cole.

"Annie, these are so cool." Jonathan and three of his buddies grasped the corners of an enormous board. She'd gone through thousands of stock photos of Mardi Gras to find images that would add ambience. Each had been enlarged, cut into four pieces, and mounted to twelve-feet-wide-by-eight-feet-high boards and would cover the walnut paneling of the room, stacked two high.

"They should be numbered on the back, so put the face against the wall." She directed them toward the far corner as George and the other three boys carried in another.

"What's this music?" one of the boys asked, but a sound pelting from her three cousins stopped him from further comment.

"Guys, I'll tell you what I've told these three." Anne put her arm around the shoulder of the boy who'd asked and drew the others in with her gaze. "If you really want to woo a woman, don't play any of that hip-hop, R&B junk. Show her you have style. That you appreciate the finer things in life—like the classics. This is the most romantic music in the world. And it's a lot easier to dance to."

"Don't laugh," Jonathan chimed in. "It really works. How d'you think I got Kelli to go out with me?"

Anne laughed with them as they trooped out to bring in the next two boards. She pulled out the diagrams she'd composed with the designer, along with her measuring tape.

"Looking for a carpenter?" A woman about ten years Anne's elder entered, juggling two-by-fours more than twice her height.

"Hey, Pamela! The pictures look fantastic." Anne reached for the end of the boards. "I'll help you bring the rest of this in."

"Nah, Trevor came with me to help. You just get to marking where everything goes, and I'll get to work on these brackets."

Following the measurements on the chart, Pamela and her husband installed the mounting boards, which would be removed and the holes filled and stained to match the paneling afterward. They used an impressive arsenal of power tools and laser levels that shot a line all the way down the length of the room. Anne took the thumbnail printout of the pictures around and slapped the corresponding panel numbers up where she wanted them, using the high-tech tools of a Magic Marker and sticky notes.

She hummed along with the music, singing when she didn't have to concentrate so hard.

The rented ironwork arrived as the last of the mural boards were unloaded. "Just stack those up there in front of the stage area. We have to get the pictures up before we can do anything with those."

"I hope you're going to take lots of pictures of this for your Web site, Annie." Bryan kissed her on the cheek. "I can't wait to see what it looks like all put together."

"Don't worry. You'll have plenty of opportunities to see the photos." George cuffed the younger man around the back of the neck and escorted him back out the door.

She frowned, trying to figure out what that comment meant. His employer was supposed to be media shy, given that he'd gone to great lengths to make sure his wedding planner didn't know for whom she was working.

Her timer beeped at a quarter after five as she posted the last two numbers. Time to order pizza. She snagged her planner and phone and perched on top of the ice chest to call her favorite Italian restaurant. No fast-food pizza for this crew, with as hard as they were working.

She stood when George and the boys approached, pointing at the cooler. "What do y'all want on your pizza?" A cacophony of answers showered her and she reduced it down to one word: *everything*.

George fished his wallet out and handed her a credit card. "Expense account."

Excellent. One less thing for her to have to keep track of. "Thanks." With the boys' chatter, Pamela and Trevor's power tools, and the music, which the guys had turned up to hear over the rest, Anne stepped into the office and pulled the door closed behind her. She ordered from Giovanni's all the time, and they always accommodated her, no matter the volume of food she needed.

When she opened the door, all she could hear was music and voices—no power tools. Hopefully Pamela hadn't run into a problem. She hurried down the hall into the ballroom.

The seven college boys swayed back and forth, arms around each other's shoulders, singing "That's Amore" at the top of their lungs, doing their best to drown out Dean Martin. Pamela and Trevor Grant waltzed across the empty parquet floor, sawdust and all.

"See, *that's* what I was talking about." Anne had to raise her voice for the guys to hear her. "That's romantic music." She gasped when George grasped her hand, pulled her out onto the dance floor, and twirled her around.

"Yes, it is." His breath tickled her ear as he drew her close and swung her around the room.

The grace she'd only had a taste of that afternoon when he'd surprised her in the supply room proved to be greater than she'd suspected. Heat burned through her T-shirt at the small of her back where he held her. Muscles rippled under the gray cotton fabric where her hand rested on his shoulder. Her trainers squeaked against the shiny wood floor.

Then he started to sing. No, not sing. Croon. Just like Dean Martin. Her knees wobbled. His gaze captured hers, and the rest of the world disappeared. The song ended, and he twirled her, then pulled her back into his arms and dipped her. Gently, he raised her until their noses almost touched.

His gaze dropped to her lips, and he swallowed hard. "We need to talk." His voice cracked.

"Yes." She allowed him to take her hand and used the silent walk to the office to regain her composure. Once inside the small room, she perched on the edge of the old wooden desk.

He closed the door and leaned against it. "Anne, there's so much I want to say to you, but. . ."

"But you're bound by your word to your employer not to." She smiled. "I know I've put you in a difficult place by demanding that you be completely honest with me. I don't expect you to tell me what you've sworn to keep secret." She dropped her gaze to her clasped hands. "We all have secrets." She had to tell him about Cliff. Before he found out from someone else. "Speaking of secrets, there's something I need to tell you." She glanced at him.

His relaxed posture encouraged her. "Anne, no matter what you tell me, it won't change the way I feel about you."

The way I feel about you. . .and that was? Her heart careened. Not what she was here to discuss with him. *Focus!* "Before we figure out what our relationship is, there's something in my past you should know. I. . ." It was one thing to tell a family member. Quite a different thing to tell the man working his way into her affections. "I've told you I was engaged to be married a little more than ten years ago."

His easy expression didn't change, except for a slight raising of his dark brows. "I never expected you wouldn't have broken relationships in your past."

Oh, it had been broken, all right. "That's not the whole story."

Trepidation coursed through her. "I was engaged to Cliff Ballantine. Back before he was 'Cliff Ballantine.' "

"And?"

"And. . ." She shrugged. "I just thought you should hear it from me before someone else in the family slipped up and let it out."

He nodded, seeming to contemplate her words. "May I ask you a question?"

"Of course."

"Do you still. . .have feelings for him?" He crossed his arms and leaned his head to the left.

"If contempt counts as having feelings for him, then yes. You know what happened—he took advantage of me and then left me in the lurch when he didn't need me anymore." At his silence, she dropped her gaze. Meredith had been right. The truth about her past upset him.

The tips of his athletic shoes appeared beside hers. He cupped her chin and raised her head. "Then he's the biggest fool in the world." He leaned forward and kissed her, his lips warm, soft, and electric.

Tears burned twin trails down her face. She touched his cheek, and he trembled. He raised his head, gave her another quick kiss, then pulled her into his arms. "Oh, I've wanted to do that for so long."

Lightning bolted through her when he kissed the side of her neck. "I've wanted you to do that for a long time." She stepped back. "But George, until I've figured out how to forgive Cliff, I'll never be over him. I've been praying about it, but I just can't seem to get over the anger."

He took a tissue from the box on the desk and dried her face. "Perhaps if you talked to him."

"Ha!" She shook her head. "There's no way I'd ever be able to get in touch with him. He's probably surrounded by people whose only job is to keep commoners like me away from him."

George traced the contours of her face with his fingertips. "You'd be surprised what God can bring about."

"You're such an optimist." She stepped back into his open arms and relaxed into his embrace. "The only way I'd be able to talk to Cliff Ballantine is if he were to walk through those doors."

A sound rumbled in George's chest. "Stranger things have happened."

Chapter 20

Headlights flashed in Anne's rearview mirror. Who in the world would be pulling into her driveway at three o'clock in the morning? She parked and cut off the engine, then reached into the center console for her pepper spray.

The car pulled up beside her, and she released a shaky breath when she recognized Jenn's classic Mustang. Wearily, she climbed out and fumbled with her keys to locate the master for the back door.

"You just getting in?" Jenn called in a hushed voice.

Anne nodded. "And I feel guilty about leaving when I did. There's still so much to finish tomorrow—I mean today."

Jenn skirted her car and put her arm around Anne's waist. "If Fridays weren't one of my busiest nights of the week, I'd offer to help."

"I know. Thanks. How come you're getting in so late?"

"I went out with some of the staff for midnight breakfast after closing. Sort of a celebration. We scored a ninety-eight on our latest health inspection."

"The surprise inspection? Jenn, that's great." Anne looked down to find the right key for the back door.

"So was George there tonight?" In the yellow glow from the porch light, mischief glimmered in Jenn's eyes.

Anne's cheeks burned, and she focused on getting the door unlocked.

"Anne?" Jenn grabbed the keys. "Something happened tonight, didn't it?"

The memory of George's kisses—the one in the office and his good night just a few minutes ago—sent goose bumps racing up and down Anne's body.

"Oh my goodness. He kissed you, didn't he?"

Was she that easy to read? She nodded, unable to speak.

Jenn hopped up and down, her blond-streaked red ponytail bouncing about her shoulders. "I knew it! I knew it! I knew the first time I saw him he was the one for you."

Anne laughed. "Jenn, the first time you saw him, you thought he was a client I was planning a wedding for."

She shook her head. "Nope. Even then. I knew somehow the two of you would end up together. He was too interested in you to be engaged to someone else." She waved her hand to fend off a dive-bombing june bug. "Meredith and I started making plans as soon as she met him."

"Making plans?" With Jenn's attention on avoiding the bug, Anne unlocked the door into the hall that connected all three apartments to the back porch.

"Yeah—for your wedding."

She dropped the heavy key ring on her foot and stifled a yelp. Her *wedding*? She hadn't let her own mind go down that path. She didn't want to be disappointed again when things didn't work out.

"I mean, it's not like we've actually gone out and booked the Vue de Ciel or anything. We just started looking at dresses. . .and flowers. . ."

Crazy. Mad as hatters. Her cousins— "What did you just say?"

"What? That we were looking at dresses and flowers?"

"No, before that."

"The Vue de Ciel? Could you imagine having your reception there? Of course it would have to be at night when all the stars are out." Jenn's tone turned dreamy. "Being on the top floor of the tallest building in downtown; surrounded by glass overlooking the city; the moon and stars glittering like diamonds on velvet. . ."

Anne dropped the keys she'd just retrieved and grabbed her phone, speed-dialing George's number as she raised it to her ear.

Jenn stopped gushing about the location. "Who are you calling at this hour?"

Come on, George, I know you can't be at home in bed yet. As soon as she heard the click of connection, she started talking. "George, I've got it. I know Courtney was disappointed that we can't have the reception at Jardin. But I know where we can do it."

"Slow down. Breathe. What brought on this sudden inspiration?"

She smiled in reaction to the barely suppressed laughter in his voice. "Oh, a conversation I was having with Jenn. Next week we'll go see the Vue de Ciel."

"Is it large enough?"

"A long time ago, I planned a served dinner for nearly a thousand attendees and still had room for a dance floor and bandstand." Fatigue faded as ideas started to take shape. With approximately seven hundred guests, she could have the room set with a mixture of two-, four-, and eight-person tables. The long head table would go on the west side, so they'd have the best view of the city—

"Anne? Are you still there?"

"Sorry. Just formulating some ideas. I need to get it down on paper while I'm thinking about it." She bent down and picked up her keys.

"Are you going to get any sleep tonight?"

"Probably not. I may try to grab a thirty-minute nap tomorrow afternoon when I know everything is going smoothly." Black and white linens with mirrors and candles as centerpieces. Only candlelight—no ambient lighting to distract from the view.

"Do try to get *some* rest, please?"

Well, a bit of electric lighting so it wasn't so dark people would trip and hurt themselves. "I can't make any promises, but I'll try."

"See you at seven for breakfast?"

The enormous cake, fabulously made by Aunt Maggie, would

grace a large table on the south wall. Of course, the photographer would have to figure out how to do the pictures surrounded by so much glass. "Yes, seven at Beignets S'il Vous Plait on Spring Street."

"Good night, then."

"G'night." She flipped the phone closed and started up the stairs.

"Annie? You okay?" Concern laced Jenn's voice.

"Yeah. I've just got to get this all written down before I forget." She turned and kissed her cousin on the cheek. "I probably won't see you until Saturday."

"Bring George by the restaurant Saturday night if he's available. Y'all need to go on a real date and have some alone time."

Somehow, the two of them going to dinner at Jenn's restaurant didn't sound like "alone time" to Anne. "I'll mention it to him and see if he can get away."

"You got in awful late last night."

George gratefully took the blue ceramic mug full of Mama Ketty's chicory coffee and sank onto a stool at the kitchen island. "We had to leave quite a bit undone to get home at that hour." The rich, slightly bitter, extremely hot liquid woke up his mouth. Hopefully the rest of him would follow suit soon. After only three hours of sleep, he felt every one of his forty-one years. . .and then some. He'd gotten soft. Many times in the past few years, he'd had to attend to tasks for Cliff late at night and still be up at six in the morning to keep up with both their schedules. Two months away, and he'd lost the ability to hop out of bed without a minimum of seven hours of sleep when the alarm first sounded. "What time did Mr. Ballantine get in last night?"

" 'Bout an hour before you. He was mightily fearsome when he found out you weren't back yet." Ketty covered her bread dough and set it aside. "Did that young man never learn how to pick up after himself?"

George snorted. He'd picked up Cliff's discarded couture clothing from the bedroom, bathroom, and dressing-room floors this morning. "Apparently not. But it keeps me in cash."

"You gonna clean up after the little miss like that, too, once they're hitched?"

"In the three days she's been back, have you seen her put anything down where it doesn't belong?" His brain started clicking better as the caffeine took effect. "No, Miss Courtney appreciates the fact I have enough to do with looking after Mr. Ballantine. She hardly allows me to do anything for her." *And treats me like I'd always hoped a daughter would. . .* That poor girl. Did she know what she was getting herself into? He had no doubt Cliff was head over heels in love with her. But as soon as Cliff announced their engagement, the media would pursue her as they had Princess Diana. George hoped he'd be able to protect Courtney from the worst of it.

"I s'pose y'all will be getting in late again tonight." Disapproval dripped from Mama Ketty's words.

He caught her about her thick waist as she tried to brush past him. "I'm terribly sorry, lovey. I know you worry."

The muscles in her cheeks twitched as she tried to hold on to her scowl. "Don't go tryin' to butter me up. I told you when you first came here that I work better with a regular schedule. Now you got people coming and going at all hours. . . ." She harrumphed, kissed the top of his head, and continued to the pantry.

"Sorry, what people coming and going?" He checked his watch. Six thirty. He needed to leave in a few minutes to meet Anne for breakfast—and coffee. He swirled the bit of black liquid still remaining in his cup and chuckled. He needed a cup of coffee to wake up enough to go to a coffee shop for breakfast. He really was getting old.

"Them movers that came yesterday after you left."

Frowning, he followed her into the storage room. Fresh spices and dried herbs mingled with the odor of the onions and garlic cloves in the wire basket suspended by a long chain from the high ceiling. "What movers?"

Mama Ketty balanced near the top of the stepladder. She glanced over her shoulder and handed him a large sack of cornmeal. "They came to the service entrance and knocked. Said they had furniture for the upstairs that they was to deliver to Mr. George Laurence. I figured since you and Mr. B. weren't here it was okay, so I let them in. I had Miss Courtney's dinner just coming out of the oven, and I came back to the kitchen. But when I checked on them half an hour later, they weren't moving any furniture, and one of them was coming out of the office. Said he was leaving you a note that they had the wrong furniture and had to go back to the store."

"Oh, love a duck!" The pantry door slammed against the wall in response to George's hasty retreat. Had they been reporters? Had they found anything? He hadn't thought it would be necessary to lock the office when he was out of the house. He kept the file cabinets locked unless he needed something out of them.

The dark wood door swung open at his touch. Nothing appeared to be out of place.

The computer. He dropped the bag of cornmeal and turned the machine on. It didn't require a password to get into the main operating system. Most of his files were encrypted, but what if they'd copied them and had a computer elsewhere that could get into them?

"What's wrong?" Ketty wheezed, out of breath from running after him. "Did I do something I oughtn't have?"

He stared at the blue WELCOME screen. How difficult would it be for them to figure out his password for the confidential files was anne0608? The "anne" part they might figure out if the perpetrators knew Anne was planning the wedding. What they didn't know was that he'd first met her on June 8.

The image of the Big Ben clock tower with a purple evening sky behind it replaced the start-up screen. A yellow bubble popped up in the right corner. YOU HAVE FILES WAITING TO BE WRITTEN TO THE CD. TO SEE THE FILES NOW, CLICK THIS BALLOON. His heart sank when the window opened and he saw the list. Five files. The RSVPs and travel arrangements for the engagement party. The guests for the wedding ceremony. The invite list for the reception. And the detailed questionnaire he'd filled out for Anne.

He hoped the thieves had been thwarted by the unreliable CD burner. But half the time when he used it, that message popped up even after the files had been successfully copied to a disc. He closed his eyes and rubbed them with the heels of his hands, hard enough to see stars.

The dulcet chime of his Westminster clock marked forty-five minutes past the hour. Mama Ketty's warm hand rested on his shoulder, and she leaned over him to look at the screen. "What's all that?"

He let out a defeated breath. "Confidential documents about the wedding. Those blokes weren't movers."

"Oh, honey, I'm so sorry. I knew I should've called you when they showed up. But they knew your name. . . ." She squeezed his shoulder. "Do you s'pose they're reporters?"

Nodding, he shut down the computer. "I'm certain of it." He patted her hand. "Our saving grace is that Mr. Ballantine will make the announcement just a few hours from now. If they can get through my password and figure out what the files mean, we can only hope they try to keep the information for themselves. After the press conference this afternoon, everything will be public knowledge, and they'll lose their exclusive story. Just pray they can't break those passwords."

Anne checked her watch again and flipped open her phone. She didn't even have to look at the keypad as she punched in the code to speed-dial George. He was always on time. She hoped he hadn't overslept. Too much still needed to be accomplished before the florist arrived at noon.

After one ring, he answered. "Good morning. Sorry I'm running behind schedule a bit."

"I was starting to worry about you. What's your ETA?"

"I'm turning onto Spring Street as we speak. As soon as I overtake this lorry that's pootling down the lane, I should be within sight of the coffee shop."

She laughed. "*Pootling*? That's a new one on me." She craned her neck to see down the road. "Ah, there you are. See you in a bit."

"Toodle-oo."

Taking a deep breath to calm her racing pulse, Anne tucked the phone in her pocket. Would he regret his actions last night? They'd spent so much time trying to avoid the attraction between them, she didn't know how easy showing affection for each other would come for either of them. Yet as she watched him unfold his lanky frame from the low-hung convertible, she wished he'd stop *pootling* and get over here and take her in his arms and—

She tried to control the size of her smile as he approached.

He clasped her hands and gave her a quick kiss on each cheek. "Good morning."

Disappointment surged, but she tamped it down. Standing on the front porch of one of the most popular coffee shops in midtown probably wasn't the best place for the kiss she'd hoped for. "Good morning. You look tired."

"And you, m'lady, look fresh as if you'd just returned from a long holiday." He tweaked her chin, then motioned her toward the door. "Shall we? I don't know about you, but I could use a lot more coffee this morning."

"More? As in, you've already had some?" Anne reached for the door handle, but George was faster. She loved being treated like a fine lady. . .especially by him. Her male cousins were all gentlemen, but sometimes they forgot to open doors or allow her to enter ahead of them. George never forgot. More often than not, he asked her to wait for him to perform his chivalrous duty.

He gave her half a grin. "I had to or I was afraid I might fall asleep driving here."

"Good morning, Anne!"

She turned and greeted the three young women behind the counter, introducing George. While he read the menu board, one of the girls handed Anne her usual.

"That looks good." George leaned over and took a whiff of the enormous muffin.

"This is a tall caramel vanilla latte with a splash of hazelnut and a glorious morning muffin, still warm from the oven." Her stomach growled at the aroma of the dark bran pastry filled with raisins, grated carrots, walnuts, and dates, not to mention the cinnamon, nutmeg, brown sugar, and honey. She took a sip of her coffee and closed her eyes as she imagined the tingle of the caffeine rushing to every nerve in her body. She'd have to have at least one more of these before she'd have enough energy to get anything accomplished this morning.

The three baristas gave Anne a pitying look when George ordered a "large coffee, black." She rather liked the fact he was a no-frills kind of guy. Forbes had probably given closing arguments in court that were shorter than the description of the specialty espresso he drank.

Melted cheddar cheese oozed from George's croissant, and the salty fragrance of the ham made Anne wish she'd ordered that instead. Oh well. Maybe next time. She found an unoccupied table on the back deck that overlooked Schuyler Park and pulled out her list. Halfway through, though, George's attention seemed to be elsewhere.

She set the notepad down on the table and pinched off a chunk of her muffin. "What's going on, George?" She popped the bite in her mouth and savored the chewy sweetness.

The faraway glaze slowly left his eyes. "I'm sorry, what were you saying?"

"Just trying to find out why you haven't heard a word I've said since we sat down." She really didn't have time for him to be unfocused today.

He sipped his coffee and dabbed the corners of his mouth with the white paper napkin. "I do apologize. Pray, continue."

She shook her head. Keeping secrets again? Or just fatigue? Maybe she was overreacting, but she couldn't take that chance. Disheartened, she took a swig of her latte to try to wash down the lump in her throat. She didn't know him well enough to discern if his blue funk was because of her or something else he didn't want her to know about. Truth be told, she hardly knew anything personal about him. She wanted to remedy that, but when he wouldn't open up to her. . .

Exhaustion pushed her emotions to their limit, and she blinked back sudden tears. She'd gone and done exactly what she'd feared—given in to her feelings and made herself vulnerable to him. Just like before, she'd end up with a broken heart after he'd gotten everything from her that he wanted. Just what did he want from her?

She jolted when his fingers touched hers. She pulled her hand away and rested it in her lap, focusing on the now unappetizing lump of muffin on her plate.

"Anne? Anne, I'm sorry. I don't mean to shut you out." He let out a deep breath. "I discovered this morning that some confidential documents may have been stolen from my computer. Documents containing information about the wedding."

Her gaze snapped to his. "Someone hacked into your computer at home?"

"Not exactly. Someone got into my office and may have copied the files onto a CD. I don't think they can do anything with them. But. . ."

She no longer felt sorry for herself, but for him. "Oh. George. What happens if they figure it out? Will you lose your job?"

He shrugged. "There's nothing for it now. We can just pray. . . ."

"Yes." She nodded and reached across to take his hand. "Let's pray. That's why everything feels so overwhelming to me. I didn't start my day in the presence of God." She closed her eyes and bowed over the small round table. George lowered his head, his forehead nearly touching hers. She took a deep breath and cleared her thoughts. "Most merciful and gracious Father, only through the grace of the blood of

Your Son, Jesus Christ, can we come before Your throne. Humbly we give You thanks for Your goodness and mercy, for the blessing of life, and most especially for Your grace and love. Please give us strength today to do what needs to be done, to put aside fatigue and concerns, to make this the best event for the client. Help George to set aside his worries over the crime committed against him. We ask that You keep the thieves from ruining his employer's special day and endangering George's employment. Help me to be a conduit of Your Spirit of love and hospitality with everyone who crosses my path today. Amen."

George squeezed her hand. "Almighty God, I come before You with a humble heart this morning. Grant that I may be able to put aside all anxiety to be prepared to be of service to You and to Anne today. Help us to trust Your guidance and not be carried away by our own plans or preoccupations. Drive away wrong desires, incline our hearts to keep Your law, and guide our feet in the way of peace; that, having done Your will with cheerfulness throughout the day, when the night comes, we may rejoice and give You all the glory. Amen."

Chapter 21

"Have you seen George?" Anne looped a gold-beaded garland around her neck and picked up a string of white twinkle-lights.

"Not recently." Her cousin Bryan came down a few rungs and reached for the end of the light cord. He scrambled back up the ladder to complete the faux starry sky. "You might try in the office. Last time I saw him, he was griping about not being able to get a good signal on his cell phone. He might've gone in there to use the landline."

What could possibly be so important as to take him away from the work he'd promised to help with? "How long ago?"

"Probably more than an hour ago."

"Thanks." She crossed the ballroom to deliver the strand of beads to the student workers decorating the parade float. Continuing through the heavy pine door, she tried to get hold of her anger. How could he disappear on her like this? She'd hoped to turn things over to him for half an hour so she could sit down and regroup—and maybe close her eyes for a few minutes. She was getting too old to keep these kinds of hours. With her business's financial future secure, she needed an assistant—or a partner.

The office door stood open. No George. Frustrated, she dropped into the tall executive chair behind the desk, picked up the phone, and dialed his number.

He answered on the third ring. "George Laurence here."

"Where are you?" She grimaced at the accusation that managed to slip into her voice despite her best efforts to affect a light tone.

"I am in the hot sun at the top of a very tall ladder trying to hang purple, gold, and green garlands while talking on the phone without plunging to an early and grizzly demise."

Embarrassed relief washed through her. "Oh. I thought. . ."

"Anne." His deep voice caressed her jumbled emotions. "I promised I would be here for you. Unlike. . .other people, I always hold true to my word."

Her throat tightened. His ability to understand what she was thinking continued to amaze—and comfort—her. "I'm sorry I doubted you."

"No apology necessary. Why don't you close the office door and rest for a few minutes? I'll fetch you should any problems arise."

The idea of being "fetched" by him like a stick by a golden retriever brought her to irrepressible laughter. She couldn't explain her mirth to him at his inquiry. She repeated his "Ta-ta for now" and hung up.

Indecision hit her when she crossed to the door. Three o'clock, and so much left to do. Could she afford to disappear for fifteen minutes? Or, being honest with herself, could she depend on George? Happy Endings, Inc., and her reputation as an event planner represented what she valued most in life, outside of her family.

She closed the door. If the relationship between them stood any chance of developing into. . .something, she must learn to trust him. Besides, what could happen in the few minutes she needed to get her second—or was she already on her third—wind?

At five o'clock, George found Major O'Hara and asked him to bring all of the workers together in the break room behind the kitchen. Cliff's press conference would begin in half an hour, and George wanted the staff to be made aware of the ground rules for tonight's event.

He found one of Anne's cousins in the crowd of student workers. "Have you seen Anne recently?"

Jonathan shook his head. "Not for a couple of hours. I thought maybe she'd gone to run some errands."

"Thanks." George asked O'Hara to keep everyone together until he returned. He jogged across the ballroom-turned-French Quarter and down the hall to the administrative office. He turned the knob softly and swung the door open.

Anne never stirred. Even when she was sound asleep, stress drew her forehead into worry lines. He eased the door closed and released the handle centimeter by centimeter until it latched. He wanted to reveal the guest of honor's identity to her in private anyway. Best let her get all the rest she could. She'd need it. As soon as he finished with the staff, he'd come back and tell her.

The buzz of voices in the break room stilled when George entered. "I know many of you have been curious as to whom this event is for. That's why I wanted to call you together. Our guest of honor this evening is Mr. Cliff Ballantine."

Astonishment swept through the room, and the initial gasp turned to excited whispering, especially among the females. He held his hands up to regain their attention. "Obviously I don't have to explain who he is. There are, however, some ground rules everyone must agree to before his arrival. If you cannot agree, or if you break any of these rules, you will be asked to leave."

He pulled a manila folder from his bag. "First, Mr. Ballantine will not be signing any autographs tonight. Please do not approach him with any such request. He has been kind enough to supply autographed photos for each of you instead." He passed the stack of black-and-white head shots to the young woman at his right. "Second, you may not, under any circumstances, call anyone to let them know he will be here tonight. You are more than welcome to talk about it after the event to whomever you please." He reached for a cardboard box on top of a stack of chairs. "Please deposit your cell phones in this box. They will be locked in the office until the end of the event."

Excited twittering turned to groans. George gave them his sternest look. "If you cannot abide by these rules. . ." The thud of phones dropping into the box drowned out the complaints. "Third, there will be many other people here tonight whom you may be tempted to ask for autographs. Don't. After the event is over, if they offer to sign something for you, that is permissible. But don't solicit them. Finally, for those of you who will be greeting guests at the door, if they do not have an invitation, please call me over the radio before allowing them admittance."

A hand shot up at the back of the room.

"Yes?"

"Even if it's someone we recognize, we're not to let them in?"

He didn't want any of the guests offended, but he didn't want any paparazzi or reporters gaining entrance, either. Most of the guests would understand. "Please call me no matter what." He pulled another stack of papers out of his bag, split it in half, and started them around the room. "This is a release stating that you have heard and understood the guidelines I've just enumerated for you. Please sign it and return it to Mr. O'Hara or me, and then you can go back to your duties."

They were signing the releases when Anne's cousin Jonathan burst through the doors. "George, I think you should come outside."

He left Major to gather the paperwork and ran across the building. His phone beeped and he pulled it out to answer the call from Cliff's publicist.

"We were on our way to the hotel in downtown, and Mr. Ballantine decided he wanted to have the press conference at Lafitte's Landing instead." Tracie's voice betrayed her state of near-panic. "You'll need to figure out a podium and some sound quickly." A black stretch limousine, followed by innumerable vehicles, wound its way up the long drive toward Lafitte's Landing.

"Oh, my sainted aunt!" He spun and ran back inside. "Keep Mr. Ballantine in the car until we get everything set up," he called into the phone, then disconnected and clipped it back in place.

One of the staff directed George to a storage room where he found a large lectern and portable sound system. As the boys who'd worked with the equipment before rushed to get everything plugged in, George arranged the stanchions and black velvet rope, originally set out to line the red carpet leading to the entrance, as a barrier to keep the reporters and cameras out of Mr. Ballantine's face. Like locusts, they swarmed toward the building, but the college students did an admirable job of keeping them behind the barricade.

After a thumbs-up from Jonathan, George descended the porch steps and crossed to the limousine. Blinding flashes combined with yelling reporters competed for Cliff's attention as George opened the door and the movie star stepped out.

What was he wearing? Blue jeans and a University of Louisiana baseball jersey? George shook his head. If he hadn't been here all day. . . But he'd promised Anne.

Anne! She still didn't know. He whirled to return to the building and find her before she woke up and walked out into the middle of her worst nightmare.

Cliff grabbed George's shoulder to stop him. "Tracie, call the hotel and have them send over any other reporters still waiting for me there. Laurence, show me what's been done inside."

No, no, no! He had to get to Anne. He had to tell her himself. *Please, dear Lord, let her sleep through this. Let her stay in the office until I can get to her*. "Yes, Mr. Ballantine."

The diminutive, dark-haired publicist stepped up to the lectern to announce that Mr. Ballantine would give his statement in approximately fifteen minutes.

As soon as his eyes adjusted to the dim interior, George's gaze scoured the room for the statuesque blonde he'd come to love in the last month. He sighed when he couldn't spot her.

Like a politician, Cliff greeted the college students still working on the decorations, table settings, and final preparations. George kept his eyes trained on the door at the back of the room. When Tracie gave him the word, he'd get Cliff back out front and go tell

Anne. He couldn't let her hear this from someone else.

Standing in the middle of the ballroom, Cliff turned in a full circle, nodding his head. "Looks great, Laurie. Good job."

"I can take no credit, sir. Your wedding planner, An—"

"Why aren't any of them asking for my autograph?" A fierce frown marred Cliff's world-famous face.

Oh no! A worker, with the box holding everyone's cell phones under her arm, went through the door at the back of the room. George moved to stop her, but Cliff grabbed his shoulder again. *God, please don't let Anne wake up!* "Everyone working here tonight signed a release that they wouldn't. We gave them signed head shots a few minutes ago."

The frown melted into relief. "Oh. Good. I thought I was losing my touch for a minute there." He inhaled deeply. "Take me to the kitchen. I want to sample what we're eating tonight."

Yes. The kitchen. Anne probably wouldn't go in there.

The frenetic preparations in the kitchen came to a dead stop when Cliff entered. Major O'Hara commanded them all back to work and came toward him, his face a study in granite.

"As I live and breathe, Major O'Hara." Cliff extended his hand jovially.

The caterer's smile seemed forced. "Cliff Ballantine. It's been a long time. Welcome."

"So what's on the menu?" Cliff seemed not to notice the frosty reception.

George followed them as Major allowed Cliff a taste of each of the dishes. He knew why Anne and her family would give Cliff a frigid greeting. What had happened with Major O'Hara?

Tracie beeped through on his phone while Cliff taste-tested the jambalaya. George stepped to the double doors and peered out into the ballroom. No sign of Anne. "Tracie, please tell me everyone is here and we can get started."

"Yes. The natives are getting restless. They're ready for the human sacrifice."

"I'll have him out there in a moment." He had to wait for Cliff to finish slurping down a glass of iced tea. Through the doors and fifty feet across the ballroom, and Tracie would take over. He pushed the swinging door open, and it bumped someone on the other side.

"I beg your pardon—" Not now! Not when he was so close to success.

"It's okay. Oh, hi, George." The beautiful, trusting smile that crossed Anne's face broke his heart.

"Thanks, guys, everything looks great!" Cliff called over the din of kitchen equipment.

George's shoulders dropped. "Anne, I was going to tell you—"

"No!" She shook her head and backed away from him. "No." The dead calm of her voice worried him more than the shock on her face.

"Laurence, why—" Cliff stopped beside him and muttered a surprised expletive under his breath. "Annie Hawthorne. I never thought I'd see you again."

George clenched his hands into fists and bit the insides of his cheeks. "Mr. Ballantine, may I introduce your wedding planner?"

"Wedding planner?" Cliff looked from George to Anne. "You're kidding, right?"

Anne's face had gone pale, her posture so stiff George worried she might faint. His phone beeped again. "Sir, the press conference."

"Right. Anne—we'll talk later." Cliff brushed past her on his way out of the kitchen. She jerked away from him and exited into the ballroom.

When George came out of the kitchen, Anne stood with her back to him. "Anne. Anne, I wanted to tell you privately, but then he came here instead of going to the hotel, and. . ." He shook his head. "And things spiraled out of my control." He touched her arm.

She whirled to face him. "Cliff Ballantine? You work for *Cliff Ballantine*?" Her gaze shot electric blue anger at him. "Did you have a good laugh last night? I poured my heart out to you. I told you how much he'd hurt me. And you stood there and said nothing. Nothing!

If you really cared about me, you would have told me. Right then. *Stranger things have happened*? That's all you could say?"

Although she never raised her voice, he felt as though she'd yelled at him. He looked around the room. A few students working nearby quickly turned their attention back to their tasks. He clasped her elbow. "Let's go to the office—"

She yanked out of his grasp. "Afraid I'll embarrass you with my outburst?" She took a deep breath, and before he could blink, her expression changed from fury to calm professionalism. "If you'll excuse me, I have a job to do." She stalked away.

Oh, Anne, Anne! I'm so terribly sorry. He turned to exit the building. Now the truth had been revealed, Anne wouldn't want him here. His responsibility lay solely with Cliff and Courtney. . . and in figuring out how to convince Anne to forgive him. Perhaps after she got over the initial shock, she'd be more open to listening to his explanation.

A red haze surrounded Anne. Cliff Ballantine. She'd been planning Cliff Ballantine's wedding. To see him standing there behind George. . . Tears burned her eyes. How could he do this to her?

He? Whom was she most angry with? George? Cliff? God? She hated to admit it, but of the three, Cliff's surprised expression at seeing her acquitted him of any guilt. He hadn't known about her any more than she'd known about him.

"Keep the walkways clear of streamers and confetti. We don't want anyone slipping and hurting themselves." The college students jumped to do her bidding.

George. She'd trusted him to be honest with her. She'd told him—

"Make sure to tape the plugs connecting those light strings so they don't come undone. Also, tape the extension cord down along the floorboard so no one trips on it. If y'all are finished with that, you need to go change into your uniforms."

God, how could You do this to me?

In response, her own voice echoed through her memory. *The only way I'd be able to talk to Cliff Ballantine is if he were to walk through those doors.* She hated it when God took her at her word.

Several students stood in the front hall, gawking through the windows on each side of the front doors. "If y'all don't have anything else to do, you need to go change clothes and get your stations ready."

They scattered, and Anne took their position at the window.

Had Cliff always been so broad through the shoulders? Between them stood George, hands clasped behind his back. Compared to his employer, he looked half his real size.

He glanced over his shoulder, and their gazes met. He turned and slipped inside. "Anne."

She stepped back, shaking her head. She opened her mouth but had no words. Pressing her lips together, she closed her eyes and turned away.

He moved closer. "Anne, I wanted to tell you last night, but I couldn't. I truly was going to tell you this afternoon, but he changed his plans at the last minute and came here instead of going to the hotel to give his press conference. He showed up just as I was coming to tell you."

The din outside rose in volume as reporters started shouting questions over each other. Anne stopped but kept her back turned to him. "I don't want to talk about this right now. I just want to get through tonight with as little drama as possible." She walked away, praying he wouldn't follow. The sound of the heavy front door closing gave her some relief.

She crossed the French Quarter at Mardi Gras–themed ballroom into the kitchen. Major O'Hara looked up from where he was supervising one of his cooks. She jerked her head toward the staff break room. He nodded and joined her a few moments later, closing the door on the noise and confusion of the final preparations.

"Did you know?" Major asked. He perched on the edge of a

stack of four dining room chairs. Ten years ago, Major had agreed to cater Anne and Cliff's reception for a miniscule amount of money.

She released the large clip at the back of her head and ran her fingers through her hair. "No. I can't believe George didn't tell me."

"Does he know you have a history with Cliff?"

"Not until I told him everything last night." She sank onto an ancient sofa and then decided she'd have been more comfortable on the floor.

"And he didn't tell you then?" Major crossed his arms, a familiar storminess coming into his expression. She'd forgotten what a short fuse he had when he thought someone he cared for had been wronged.

"He—" What was it she'd said to George last night just before telling him about Cliff? *I don't expect you to tell me what you've sworn to keep secret.* She leaned her head back and stared at the water-stained tile above her. "He promised Cliff he wouldn't tell anyone."

"Then why did he pull everyone together and tell all of us right before Cliff got here?"

Anger surged anew. Why indeed. "You're right. He could have told me last night. It's not like I'm going to go out and blab to some supermarket tabloid reporter. He should have shown me more respect than that. 'Stranger things have happened,' my foot! If he has so little respect for me, after tonight is over, he can just plan the rest of the wedding by himself."

Chapter 22

She would put all the Hollywood royalty present tonight to shame.

George ran his finger under his collar, suddenly unable to breathe. Dressed in a modest floor-length, black column dress, Anne glided around the perimeter of the room, double-checking the readiness of each station and each server. If her idea had been to blend into the background, she'd failed miserably. He turned at a tug on his sleeve.

"George, how do I look?"

Courtney Landry stood before him, no longer a cherubic nineteen-year-old, but a grown woman dressed in a clinging, plunging silk gown the same electric blue as Anne's eyes. He wanted to drape his tuxedo coat about her bare shoulders and hold it closed just below her chin. He cleared his throat and reached for her hand. "Like a princess." He brushed a kiss on her knuckles.

She blushed and touched the chestnut curls piled up on top of her head. "He's introducing me to all his friends tonight. What if I trip? Or drop food down my dress?"

"Now, Miss Courtney, I know you paid more attention than that during our etiquette lessons. Chin up, shoulders square, make direct eye contact." She followed his commands like a well-trained soldier. "And remember, tonight is about *you*. Not Cliff, nor anyone else in the room. Now. . ." He tucked her hand under his arm. "It's time for you to greet your guests."

Cliff stopped pacing when George arrived in the foyer with Courtney. "It's about time. Laurence, check my tie. I think it's crooked."

George squeezed Courtney's hand once more and stepped forward to pretend to adjust the perfectly straight knot of white silk at Cliff's throat. In his ear, a short burst of static came over the radio, followed by, "Mr. Laurence, a limo's coming!"

He touched the button on the side of the pack clipped to his belt. "I'll be right along." Returning his attention to Cliff, he brushed invisible lint from the lapel of the black Valentino. "If you're ready, sir?"

Cliff waved him away. "Yeah. Enough. Go. Don't keep people waiting."

"Wait!" Anne's voice stopped George cold. She ran into the foyer and skidded to a stop, breathless. "You forgot your jewelry, Miss Courtney." Anne's maternal smile as she clasped the diamond-and sapphire-encrusted choker around the girl's throat curled George's toes. Yes, she would be a wonderful mother to their children.

She left without even a glance in George's direction.

"Laurence. I believe it's time to let the guests in." Cliff motioned toward the front doors.

"Yes, Mr. Ballantine." George stepped out onto the front porch, rolling his shoulders to release some of the tension.

Over the next two hours, he stood vigil on the porch, keeping the photographers beyond the ropes, welcoming guests, overseeing the valets, and, in general, trying to keep the chaos to a minimum. Every so often, Anne's voice came over the radio in response to one worker or another's panic. The calm reassurance in her tone acted as a soothing balm for everyone. Just the awareness that she had everything under control made the evening successful.

The radio crackled as she came over the connection. "George, I need your assistance. Please come to the administrative office." Something had to be terribly wrong for Anne to call him away from his post. But her voice betrayed nothing.

"I'll be right there." He motioned to Jonathan to take over supervision. Inside, around a hundred guests milled about, exclaiming over the decor and devouring the Cajun food. He looked around to check on Courtney. His heart thudded when he didn't see her, and he quickened his pace.

He pushed open the ajar office door. Courtney sat in one of the guest chairs, Anne kneeling on the floor in front of her. When the young woman saw him, she burst into tears, pulled away from Anne, and flung herself at him. He caught her in an embrace and looked over the top of her head at Anne. She shook her head as she stood.

"They hate me," Courtney wailed against his black waistcoat.

He patted her back, trying to soothe her. "No one could possibly hate you. What happened?" He directed the question at Anne.

"Apparently she overheard some not-so-kind remarks about herself in the restroom."

"They called me a gold-digging, trailer-park redneck." Courtney pulled away enough to look in his eyes. "I did everything just like you taught me."

"I'm certain you did." He disentangled himself and sat her in the chair again. He knelt on the tile floor in front of her while Anne perched on the edge of the other chair. "Courtney, I wish there were some way I could protect you from people saying terrible things about you. But this is the life you've chosen by agreeing to marry Cliff. You must become inured to being insulted for no reason."

Courtney's fine brows pinched together in confusion. He looked to Anne for assistance.

Her lips twitched, and she wouldn't meet his gaze. "What George means is that you have to get used to people insulting you. You're going to be in the public eye, and you're the envy of every woman in this country." What had it cost for her to say that? "Hell hath no fury like a scorned—or jealous—woman. I'm certain you remember what it was like when you were in high school. Everyone hated the girl who dated the most popular guy, and said horrible things about her behind her back, and made up stuff to make her look bad."

Courtney ducked her head and blushed. "Yeah. I remember. I was like that. I guess it's payback time now, huh?"

Anne patted her hand. "Whenever you hear or read bad things about yourself, just remember the people who love you and think you're one of the most wonderful people in the world—like us."

Courtney looked from Anne to George, moisture still glittering in her brown eyes. "Really?"

With a tissue, Anne dried the young woman's tears. "Really." She handed her a makeup compact. "Now. Powder your nose and go show those jealous biddies what you're made of."

Courtney giggled and did as instructed, then swept out of the office with her chin up, shoulders straight.

George tried to get Anne to meet his gaze. "You're very good at what you do, Miss Hawthorne."

"Thank you for your assistance. I don't know if I could have handled her on my own." She turned her back on him, reaching for the doorknob.

Disappointment filled him. He'd hoped when she called him in here that she might have gotten over her anger and decided to forgive him. "You would have managed one way or another."

Anne surveyed the crowd milling in the ballroom, exclaiming over the genuine Mardi Gras parade float, admiring the life-size murals of the historic buildings lining the French Quarter, and devouring Major's excellent Cajun food nearly to the exclusion of the caviar and other delicacies she'd worked so hard to get brought in from the New York and Los Angeles restaurants. Of course, the list had been Cliff's idea. No way would Courtney have ever come up with that.

George came out of the kitchen, and her heart thumped even as she narrowed her eyes. How could she feel so torn about him? Part of her was ready to forgive him, while the other part never wanted to talk to him again.

Halfway to the front door, a vaguely familiar young woman grabbed George's arm.

"George, you have to introduce me to the event planner!" The girl's voice carried over the din of guests and the zydeco band playing their hearts out on the other side of the room.

His tight smile and the slight bow he made gave a good indication the girl wasn't an acquaintance of his. He led the girl to Anne. "Miss Alicia Humphrey, I'm pleased to present Miss Anne Hawthorne, who is solely responsible for planning this gala."

Embarrassment crept up to burn her cheeks. "I wouldn't say *solely* responsible." She smiled and finally recognized the young actress. "It's very nice to meet you, Miss Humphrey."

The girl, who couldn't be any older than Courtney, took Anne's proffered hand in both of hers. "I want to hire you to plan my wedding. Court's been telling me all about what you're doing for her, and I just have to have you do mine. I'm getting married at Christmas at home in Baton Rouge. With me living in Malibu, I can't do it myself."

Anne's heart raced. Another celebrity wedding meant another influx of income. She really would have to take on a partner. George bowed and excused himself.

George. She didn't know another person who possessed more experience in planning high-profile social events. He wanted to stay in America but disliked his current employment. Would he consider. . . ? More to the point, would she consider taking him on as a partner? Could she trust him?

"Miss Hawthorne?"

"I'm terribly sorry—my mind wandered there for a moment." She smiled at her newest potential client. "Tell me about what you want for your wedding."

Twenty minutes later, Alicia Humphrey floated away on her director-fiancé's arm, Anne's card in her hand. Although Anne didn't usually make house calls, nor appointments to meet with clients on Saturdays, she'd be visiting Miss Humphrey at her hotel at eleven tomorrow morning.

Throughout the evening, she made a point of speaking with the local VIPs in attendance, including the mayor and the state senator from their district, just so they might keep her in mind should they need any event-planning services.

As the locals began to leave, more of the Hollywood crowd trickled in. She walked past the food tables, pleased to see all the dishes were as full as if the party had just started. As usual, she'd been impressed by Major O'Hara's staff. All evening, she'd switched over to the frequency channel they'd chosen and listened to the constant chatter between the kitchen and the table staff. He'd also taken charge of the student employees working as servers and made them part of his battle-ready army.

At midnight, as the crowd waned, she signaled Major to pare down the savory foods and put out more sweets and coffees.

She stifled a yawn. Speaking of coffee. . . Slipping into the kitchen, she smiled at the sous-chef, then stopped at each of the four commercial coffeemakers and inhaled the fragrance of each.

There, the one that was still brewing. Cinnamon hazelnut. Had to be. Like a pro, she slipped the carafe out and slid a cup under the basket, not letting a drop of the precious liquid go to waste. She turned with her stolen treasure to find Major standing behind her, hands clasped behind his back like a drill sergeant.

"Hi."

"Anne Hawthorne, you know no one is allowed in my kitchen except my staff."

She held the mug toward him. "You don't happen to have any cream on hand, do you?"

He tried to stare her down, but she knew him too well. His frown broke, and he pulled a carton of half-and-half from behind his back. He even poured it and produced a spoon and crystal bowl of sugar. "I'd started to wonder how long it would be before you had to have a caffeine fix. You know I only make that sissy-flavored coffee because of you. Why a Louisiana gal like you can't be happy with good ol' chicory."

She leaned against the counter beside him. "Thanks, Major. I love you, too." She sipped her treat while he reviewed his evening. Around them, his staff cleaned up their work areas and packed away equipment, leftover food, and unused ingredients.

"I can return a lot of the unused items."

"No." Anne downed the last of her coffee and poured another cup, letting Major doctor it for her again. "Donate it to University Chapel's food closet. Put the cost for all of it on the invoice. He can afford it."

"He? You mean Cliff?" Major spat the name out.

Anne leaned into his side. "I know why I'm angry at him. Can I assume your bad feelings are on my behalf?"

"He stole my girlfriend." He put his arm around her shoulders.

"I was never your girlfriend."

"I wanted you to be."

"You never asked."

"I didn't think your aunt and uncle would approve."

"Aunt Maggie loved you like a son—still does, even though you're her competition now instead of her favorite employee."

"Am I going to have to hate this George character now, too?"

Anne leaned her head to the side to gaze at her friend. "What are you talking about?"

"I've watched him all night. He's in love with you, y'know."

She frowned at him. "Weren't you the one who sat there in the break room just a couple of hours ago, egging me on in being angry at him?"

Major quirked the left side of his mouth. "Yeah. But I've had more time to think about it. He was looking for you for a while before he gathered the staff together. I think he was planning to tell you privately."

Guilt started to replace the righteous indignation she'd used as a shield between herself and George all night.

"You don't know how hard this is for me to say, but you need to forgive him."

Tingles started at her toes and shot all the way to her scalp. "I know."

He crooked his elbow around her neck and pulled her close to kiss her temple. "See if you can convince this George fella to stay around. He sorta grows on a body."

She patted his arm where it rested across her throat. "Oh, I'll see what I can do."

At 2:00 a.m., Cliff and Courtney's limousine drove away from Lafitte's, taking the last of the paparazzi with them. George pulled the radio earpiece off and let out a big sigh. "Wonderful job tonight, gentlemen. Let's go find Anne and see if we can call it a night."

"Amen to that," Jonathan agreed. "Fourteen hours is *way* too long to work in one spell."

George shook his head as the man twenty years his junior trudged into the building. Oh, to have to work only fourteen hours at a spell. Several of the service staff passed them, dressed in their shorts, T-shirts, and thong sandals. The boys ahead of him picked up the pace, ready to be released to go home.

Anne sat at one of the tables near the kitchen signing time cards. Major O'Hara straddled a chair behind her, his denim chef's tunic unbuttoned to reveal the UL–BONNETERRE T-shirt beneath, massaging her shoulders.

George tried not to be jealous, recalling they were old friends, and continued around to the coffee service cart beyond them.

"Plain coffee is brown; flavored is white," Major said, leaning his head back to tell him.

George lifted the brown carafe.

"Man after my own heart." The caterer raised his Styrofoam cup in salute.

George returned the gesture and sank into the chair on Anne's other side. She wrote the time and signed each card as fast as she could, trying to get the kids out as soon as possible. How many of them would leave here and go out now? He'd heard his valet-parking boys discuss some kind of big event going on tonight down on Fraternity Row. Knowing college kids, it would still be going on at this hour, if the police hadn't been called in yet.

Anne's makeup couldn't hide the dark circles beneath her eyes. Limp tendrils of her hair had come out of the french twist at the back of her head, and she tapped the fingernails of her left hand on the table as she worked. She wouldn't leave until everything was finished and the place locked down for the night.

"Are some of the staff staying to help clean up?" Major asked, looking around at the mess.

"We have a cleanup crew coming in tomorrow," George answered. "Meredith is supervising that so Anne doesn't have to come back up here."

She glanced up at him in surprise. "What? When was that decided?"

"Meredith and I discussed it last week. She said if they run into any problems, she'll call you. She talked to Pamela and Trevor yesterday and arranged for them to come remove the murals. You've already scheduled the rental company to come pick up what belongs to them, and I supplied Meredith with my copy of the list so she knows what to set aside. The rest belongs here, and it's her staff who will be working, so she didn't feel your presence would be necessary. I wholeheartedly concur."

Rather than argue, she surprised him with a smile—the first she'd given him since she'd walked into the kitchen and seen Cliff. "Thanks. I really wasn't looking forward to spending another full day up here."

Major rose and returned the coffee service to the kitchen. He returned a few minutes later, a large bag hanging from his shoulder. He leaned over and kissed Anne's cheek. "Great party, Annie."

"Wouldn't have been without you. Fax over that final invoice as soon as you have it, and George will write you a check." She patted the caterer's hand. "Won't you?"

George nodded. "Just ring me up when you have the total, and I can drop it off."

"I'll call, then. Probably Monday morning after I have a chance to do a complete inventory and go over my staff's time cards. Mere and I have that banquet tomorrow night, so it's unlikely to be any earlier."

"Monday's fine." Anne signed the last time card with a flourish and sent the student away. "I'll be talking to Mere next week about a couple of other projects we'll need you for."

"I look forward to hearing about them." Major's gaze shifted to George for a brief moment, then back to Anne. "And remember what I said."

Anne's cheeks reddened. "I will. Now get out of here so I can, too."

"Okay. Kitchen's locked down tight; lights are off. G'night, you two." Major beat a path out the front door.

Anne stood and stretched, then bent over to pick up her shoes from under the table. "George, I. . .I'd like to talk to you if you have a minute."

For her, he had hours, days, weeks, years. He followed her back to the office, where she shoved the shoes into her bag and pulled out her trainers. He grinned as she put the white athletic shoes on with the black evening gown.

When she finished tying the laces, she didn't stand but leaned back in the chair, her hands folded at her waist. "I wanted to apologize to you."

He raised his brows and leaned against the edge of the desk.

"I've treated you unfairly tonight. I was angry with you because you didn't tell me about Cliff. But I can't hold that against you, for the very reason you didn't tell me in the first place."

"I'm not sure I follow."

She rubbed her temples. "I'm not making any sense, am I? Too long without sleep. I guess what I'm trying to say is, will you forgive me for being mad at you for being an honorable man and keeping your word?"

Grinning, he knelt in front of her, took her hands in his, and kissed her palms. "Gladly and wholeheartedly."

Leaning forward, she wrapped her arms around his neck. "I'm sorry for being so hard-hearted. It was just. . .seeing Cliff like that with no forewarning. . . I guess I really have a lot to work on when it comes to forgiving him, because that isn't going to come easily. I know that now."

He held her for a few moments until his knees started to ache on the tile floor. He kissed the side of her neck, rose, and stretched as stress rolled off his shoulders.

She slouched back in the chair. "There's something else I want to ask you."

He perched on the edge of the desk facing her, curiosity aroused. "All right."

She bit the right corner of her bottom lip as she searched his face, then sat up straight, her knuckles turning white as she gripped her hands together. "I know we've only known each other for a little over a month. And during that time, we've had our share of misunderstandings and communication issues."

Her skill with euphemistic understatements would put a parliamentarian to shame. He nodded, encouraging her to continue.

"I feel like we have a lot in common, and we obviously work well together." She smiled nervously. "What I want to ask is: How about making this permanent?"

He nearly fell off the desk. Permanent? Had Anne Hawthorne just proposed marriage to him?

She rushed to continue. "As I said, I know it hasn't been that long. And I know you'll need time to think about making a major step like this."

Every fiber of his being cried out, *Yes! Yes, I'll marry you*. The miniscule part of his brain that clung to reason still controlled his tongue. “I'm flattered. But, Anne, have you thought this through? Are you sure this is what you truly want, and not just a reaction to seeing Cliff tonight?”

She frowned. “Cliff? What does he have to do with my asking you to be my business partner?”

Business partner? He chuckled and shook his head. Yet another example of their typical misunderstandings and communication issues. “Nothing, I suppose.”

“I mean, you may not make as much in a year working with me if we're splitting the profits equally, but the cost of living here is a lot lower.”

And he'd get to see her every day. He tapped his thumb against his lips a moment. If he were going to stay here, he wanted the whole package—and he meant to have it before Courtney's wedding. But given her nervousness at asking him to go into business together, convincing her to marry him would be a considerable undertaking. “Draw up a business plan, and I'll take a look at it. I'll have to look into the legality of changing jobs with my current work visa.” Of course, being married to an American citizen, he wouldn't have to worry about work visas ever again. Not that where they would live mattered. He'd be happy living in a thatch-roofed hut in the bitter cold of Scotland, as long as he had Anne at his side.

Chapter 23

Anne tried to ignore the pounding by pulling a spare pillow over her head. There. The noise stopped.

Something heavy hit her bed. She shrieked and bolted upright, nearly colliding with Jenn, who bounced up and down on her knees.

"When were you going to tell us?"

Anne glanced at the alarm clock. Not even eight o'clock. Less than four hours of sleep—again. Never before had she thought ill of a relative. But right now she hated the two auburn-tressed sisters staring at her like baby chicks waiting to devour a worm. She fell back against her pillow with a groan. "Go away! Let me get some sleep."

"I told you we should have left her alone," Meredith scolded her younger sister. "Come on, let's go."

"No. I want to hear it from her. Is it true?" Jenn crawled over and straddled Anne.

"Is what true?" She could very easily toss the skinny-minnie off the bed, maybe even out the window.

"You're planning Cliff Ballantine's wedding."

She could have gone all day without being reminded of that. "Go away." She pushed Jenn away, rolled onto her side, and covered her head with the pillow again.

"You're on the front page of the newspaper, Annie." Meredith's soft voice filtered through the thick down covering Anne's ears. "You looked really nice last night."

She bolted upright again, this time bumping Jenn's nose with her forehead. She snatched the paper from Meredith. Below a giant color photo of Courtney and Cliff on the front porch of Lafitte's Landing was a smaller image of herself. When. . . ? Oh, she'd gone out to give Jonathan batteries for his radio pack.

"I'm surprised your phone isn't ringing off the hook." Jenn rubbed her nose.

"I turned the ringer off when I got home last night. I thought that would thwart anyone who might try to disturb me before I had a decent amount of sleep. I guess I'll have to start using the door chain."

"She would have just stood there pounding on the door until you opened it." Meredith came around and sat on the edge of the bed. "Did you know?" She pointed at Cliff's picture.

Anne shook her head. "No. George was under strict orders to keep his employer's identity secret. No one knew until just before the press conference."

"Hello?" Forbes's voice rang through the apartment.

"In here," Jenn yelled.

"What is it with you people and Saturday mornings?" Anne flipped the folded paper over to look at the top of the page again. BALLANTINE TO MARRY LOCAL GIRL, the headline proclaimed. Poor Courtney. She tossed the paper aside as Forbes entered her bedroom.

"Aren't you going to read the articles?" Jenn caught the section before it slid off the far side of the bed.

"I was there. I planned it. I think I know what happened." She propped a couple of pillows against her headboard and scooted up to sit against them. She reached for the tall paper cup of coffee Forbes held in his hand and took a big gulp before handing it back to him. "Ugh. Gross. Skim milk and artificial sweetener. I always forget."

"Everything okay?"

Why did he look so nervous? "Mostly." She cocked her head to one side. "Did you know anything about this? No, wait." She held up her free hand. "I don't want to know. Anything you say will probably just make me mad, and then we'll sit here all morning analyzing why I'm mad and I'll never get any more sleep. So now that everyone is reassured that I'm okay, can you please leave so I can go back to sleep?"

His relief palpable, Forbes leaned over and kissed her forehead. "Yes. Yes, we can do that."

Meredith patted Anne's knee through the quilt. "Yeah. Sorry we woke you up like that."

"Jennifer, let's go." Forbes stood at the end of the bed like a nightclub bouncer.

"But—"

"No buts. Now." He snapped his fingers and pointed at the door. He waited until his younger sister huffed out of the room, then turned back to Anne. "Rest up. If what they wrote in the paper is true, you're not going to be getting a lot of rest anytime soon."

As he walked out the door, Anne rearranged her pillows and curled into her favorite position. She yawned and closed her eyes. Ah, sleep.

If what they wrote in the paper is true. . . Forbes's words bounced through her mind. What had they written about her in the paper? The feature they'd done on her after the article in *Southern Bride* had been extremely complimentary and had driven most of this summer's business. But with whom had the reporter spoken last night?

Her head throbbed. She wouldn't worry about that now. She needed sleep. Sleep. She tapped her fingers on the mattress. Sleep. Yes, that's what she needed.

One professional photographer had been allowed in last night. George said Cliff's publicist, that very nice young woman named Tracie, would choose certain photos from inside the party to be released to the major entertainment magazines. Anne hoped she wasn't in any of them. She hated what the camera did to her already large frame.

Stop thinking about it. Sleep!

How many messages would she have on her voice mail at work? After the *Southern Bride* article, she'd changed her home number and kept it unlisted. But not only was her cell phone number on her business cards; she'd bought a display ad in the Yellow Pages this year. She was the only one out of the five planners listed in the category who'd done so. She was also the only one to ever be featured in a regional magazine. Or to have her own office in Town Square, just a few doors down from the store that did the most bridal clothing business in town. How much was this kind of national exposure going to grow her clientele?

She tossed onto her other side. She already had the answer to that in her appointment with Alicia Humphrey in a few hours. The girl was by no means a major star like Cliff, but her fiancé's latest film had won several awards at this year's independent film festivals. Buzz had already started about the possibility of an Academy Award nomination for best director. At least, that's what she'd heard most often last night.

What if Alicia wanted Anne to come out to California to meet with her? She rolled onto her back and stared at her high, white-plaster ceiling. No. Not even for a client could she board a plane. In this day and age, technology should allow her to do whatever necessary from here. Baton Rouge was only a two-hour drive, so that was no problem. But she had to make Alicia understand that Anne Hawthorne would *not* be flying anywhere.

All possibility of falling asleep again gone, Anne pushed up into a sitting posture and reached for the newspaper. The article contained mostly fluff. A truncated guest list. The reporter should have stayed later, as the most interesting names weren't on it. A reference to the Mardi Gras–themed decor with Pamela Grant and the Delacroix Gardens Nursery & Florist both mentioned. Excellent, free publicity for her vendors. When she found her name, she took a deep breath before continuing on.

> *The event was planned and executed by Bonneterre's own Anne Hawthorne, an event planner whose business, Happy Endings, Inc., is well known throughout Louisiana and the Southeast. Hawthorne has planned many high-profile events, such as the mayor's inaugural ball, the annual Bonneterre Debutante Cotillion, and the society wedding of Senator Hawk Kyler's daughter Aiyana Kyler-Warner.*
>
> *"I totally relied on Miss Anne for everything," bride-to-be Landry said. "She talked to me about what I wanted and then did everything just like I imagined. No, even better than I imagined."*
>
> *Hawthorne, a Bonneterre native, first appeared in the pages of the* Reserve *twenty-eight years ago as one of five survivors of a commuter plane crash that took the lives of twelve others, including her parents, world-famous photographers Albert Hawthorne and Lilly Guidry-Hawthorne.*
>
> *According to sources, Hawthorne and Ballantine knew each other as students at Acadiana High School and UL–Bonneterre. Neither Hawthorne nor Ballantine could be reached for comment.*

"Nor am I likely to comment." She tossed the paper aside. At least they hadn't written anything negative about the event or her company. She climbed out of bed and winced as her sore feet hit the hardwood. She hadn't even worn heels last night, and her feet still ached.

Thank goodness she'd set the coffeepot up without changing the timer before climbing into bed in the wee hours. She poured a cup of the chocolate-caramel-pecan-flavored brew, stirred in half-and-half and sugar, and padded across to her giant chair-and-a-half. Cradling the blue ceramic mug in her left hand, she grabbed the

TV remote and clicked the TV on. The screen came to life showing CNN Headline News.

". . .confirmed all the rumors when he announced yesterday he is getting married." The picture cut away from the cutesy reporter to footage of Cliff's press conference. She smiled to see George in his butler-esque stance behind him. If George agreed to go into business with her, he'd never have to debase himself the way she'd seen him do with Cliff several times yesterday.

She clicked up one channel. MSNBC. Same story, same footage. Click. Fox News. Different news story—but then the scroll at the bottom of the screen ran the announcement. Click. Regular CNN. A repeat of *Larry King Live* from earlier in the week—with the announcement of Cliff's engagement in the scroll at the bottom. Click. E! Entertainment Television. The *True Hollywood Story* of Cliff Ballantine. Couldn't be all that "true" since they'd never interviewed her or Aunt Maggie, his employer for four years. Click. The Style Network. The fashion critique of a movie premiere event last night—and chatter between the hosts about the engagement announcement "a few minutes ago." Click. Bravo Network. A repeat of *Inside the Actor's Studio* featuring Cliff.

Okay, maybe she needed to go to a different set of channels. She punched in the number for TBS. They usually ran romantic comedies on Saturday mornings. Commercials. She sipped her coffee. Hopefully something that would put her to sleep. The movie came back on. She squinted to read the caption in the lower right corner. "You're watching *Mountebank*."

She nearly threw the remote at the TV. Cliff's first movie. The one that had made him a star and her a nobody. She jumped out of the chair, crossed to the armoire-style entertainment center, and grabbed the blue box of the extended edition of *Return of the King*. Nothing like the Battle of Pelennor Fields and the destruction of the ring to get her mind off things—

"Anne, it's you!"

She glanced down at the TV. Cliff's face, ten years younger, filled the large screen. She recognized that expression. She'd seen it when he suggested they get married.

"Anne, you're the one I love. You're the one I want to marry—"

She turned the DVD player on, mercifully sending the TV to a blue screen while she inserted the first disc.

No wonder he'd gotten that part. He already had the fake emotions—and the lines he had to say—down pat from practicing on her. She slouched down in the deep cushions of the big chair.

What would his marriage to an overweight, provincial, hometown girl have done for his career ten years ago? He'd spent the past decade creating the image of a happy-go-lucky bachelor, only too happy to have a different starlet on his arm at every red-carpet event he attended. Women turned out in droves to see his action-adventure movies on opening night. Would he have become such a phenomenon with Amazon Anne on his arm at every event?

No. She sighed. Not only would she have hampered his rise to megastardom, she would have hated all the attention; and being honest with herself, the stress of living in the public eye would have driven a wedge between them. She was woman enough to admit they would have been divorced within a few years.

He had an ulterior motive for dating her all those years. Could he be marrying Courtney now to improve his image? He'd gotten lots of press about being a playboy, gracing the cover of several magazines as the Bachelor of the Year multiple years running. Which was fine as long as he made action films. According to several conversations she'd overheard last night, Cliff wanted to be "considered for dramatic roles." He'd never get those roles and garner an Academy Award nomination as long as he lived a life worthy of the cover of the *Enquirer*. And he'd wanted to win that particular award ever since she'd known him. He'd even practiced his acceptance speeches on her. "I'd like to thank the Academy, the wonderful casting agent who had the foresight to choose me for this role, the fabulous screenwriters who wrote this role with me as their model, the director who took my advice on every scene. . . ." She'd laughed then, not truly understanding the size of his ego.

Did Courtney really comprehend what she was getting herself into? Could the poor girl ever hope to compete with Cliff's first love—himself?

The struggle between good and evil on her TV screen no longer interested her, and she turned it off. She needed to have a heart-to-heart with Courtney Landry before things went any further. If the girl got in over her head and ended up brokenhearted when Anne could have done something to head it off. . .

She went into the kitchen and grabbed her cell phone from her purse. She scrolled down to Courtney's name and hit the button to dial.

No answer. Her voice sounded so young in her voice-mail greeting. "Hello, Courtney, it's Anne Hawthorne. I hope you enjoyed yourself last night. You looked beautiful, and everyone in America loves you already. I know—I saw it on all the news channels this morning. Listen, I wanted to schedule a time for the two of us to go to lunch this week. We've never really had a chance to sit down, just the two of us, and chat. We've got some big events coming up that I'd like to get your ideas for. So just give me a call." She left her cell, home, and office numbers and hung up.

Out of curiosity, she called into her voice mail at work.

"Ms. Hawthorne, hi, my name is Alaine Delacroix—you've worked with my family at Delacroix Rentals and Delacroix Nursery many times. I'm the social scene reporter with Channel Six—" Anne skipped forward and listened to the first few seconds of twenty-three more messages—all from reporters wanting exclusives about the wedding. She deleted them with no remorse.

She needed to go to her office and get her planning calendar. She hadn't picked it up yesterday morning as she didn't need it for the engagement party. But for her meeting with Alicia in an hour, she'd need it. So much for a leisurely shower.

She hopped in and out, put a little bit of makeup on so she didn't look like death warmed over, and drove to the office with the convertible top down so her naturally straight hair would be dry enough to pull into a clip at the back of her head.

She deactivated the alarm at the keypad just inside the back door. She didn't bother turning the lights on and passed through the dark hall into the front office, lightened enough to see from the bright sunshine outside. Shadows passed in front of the windows. *Lots of people out shopping today.*

She grabbed the leather planner and glanced out onto the sidewalk. Several people stood outside her storefront. People with huge cameras strung around their necks. Good thing they didn't have the back entrance covered.

She slipped out the back door and speed-dialed George as she drove down the alley.

"Good morning, Anne." His voice had an early morning, gravelly quality that sent shivers down her spine.

"You sound like you just woke up."

"Not exactly. I have to keep regular hours when I'm with Mr. Ballantine. Early morning is the only time I get to myself to read the Bible and spend time in prayer." He yawned and begged her pardon. "Did you get plenty of rest this morning?"

"Not exactly. Jenn, Meredith, and Forbes practically beat down my door at seven forty-five, wanting to make sure I was all right, waving the newspaper under my nose. I couldn't go back to sleep after that."

"You need to get away somewhere they can't find you."

"No kidding. Hey, speaking of not being found—I had to run up to the office to grab something for a meeting, and there were photographers hanging out on my front porch."

"At home?"

"No, at the office. They didn't see me. I went in and out the back. But I think you and I need to sit down with Tracie and come up with a game plan for how I'm supposed to handle the phone calls and paparazzi on my front stoop."

"Yes, we do. They'll lose interest as soon as Cliff leaves for New

York Tuesday. Or if not lose interest, all you'll have to deal with is the phone calls, as the photographers will follow him."

"Pictures of me aren't worth much, I gather."

"Not without either Cliff or Courtney with you. But that's good, yes?"

"Definitely." She turned into the hotel parking lot. "I'm at my appointment, so I'd better go."

"You're working?"

"Remember Alicia Humphrey? She wanted to sit down before she leaves for California this afternoon."

"Oh. Good for you. I'll talk to you later."

He sounded less than enthusiastic, but she didn't have time to ask why.

Toodles? You, too? No, I love you. . . .

She went with "Toodles" as if she were an old school friend. Oh well. She'd known going in that she needed to take this slowly. And, although empirically she'd thought forgiving Cliff would come easily, seeing him last night sent her back to square one without passing Go or collecting two hundred dollars.

An hour later, she dialed George as the elevator doors shut.

"How'd your meeting go?" he asked by way of greeting.

"Why didn't you forewarn me?"

"Didn't want you to think I'm a spoilsport."

"Her third engagement in less than two months? Is she trying to beat out Elizabeth Taylor for a most-broken-relationships award?"

George chuckled. "You never know. He could be 'the one.' You know how it is with those Hollywood types. So quick to move on to greener pastures. . ."

"Is that going to happen to Courtney? Is she 'the one' for Cliff, or is she just 'the one for now'?" She climbed into the car and started for home.

"Do you mean, is he using her to gain something? I'm not certain. If he were just looking for a token wife to, say, give him a more serious image, there are a lot of other women out there he could have chosen. He's opened himself up for some fierce criticism from the public by announcing he's engaged to a woman half his age." He sighed. "You know better than I how people marry for many reasons other than love. I do believe he cares for her. I know she cares for him."

"Will caring be enough, though?"

"Let me pose this: What's more important in a marriage? Being madly in love or having a strong friendship based on mutual respect and admiration?"

Anne had the funny feeling he wasn't talking about Courtney and Cliff anymore. "I'm not married. I can't answer that."

"Oh, you know the answer. You surprise me, Anne. I thought after so many years of working with couples—especially with as much counsel as you provide them—you'd have lost some of your ideals of romanticism."

Her heart thudded in her chest. What did he mean? Could he just be playing devil's advocate, as he did so often? "I think the best marriages are built on love that grows out of that strong friendship and mutual attraction." She'd seen the failure of too many couples' marriages because they'd fallen madly in love but never taken the time to get to really know one another. "But I want to be madly in love with the man I respect and admire when I get married."

His pause grew so long she checked to make sure she hadn't lost the connection.

"Well, how does a romantic dinner at a restaurant overlooking the lake sound as a start?"

Chapter 24

Anne watched Meredith over the rim of her iced-tea glass as she took a sip. She'd just finished spewing all the shock, anger, hurt, confusion, excitement, and flutterings of the past forty-eight hours. Fortunately, the second-story veranda at the Plantation House restaurant was empty except for the two of them. The sound of the river below and the light breeze rustling the ancient oak trees worked in tandem with Meredith's calm presence to soothe Anne's spirit.

"It sounds like George really is in love with you." Meredith pushed a chunk of tomato to the edge of her salad. "I know he would have told you about Cliff if he could have. I admire him for being a man of his word."

Warmth wrapped around Anne. "I do, too. And there's one other thing. That's one of the reasons why I wanted to have lunch with you before I see him again tonight." She put her glass down. "I've asked George to become my business partner. Now, I know I've always told you that I want you to be my partner—"

Meredith held up her free hand, a smile playing about her lips. "And there was always something in my heart that kept me from saying yes. It's not that I don't trust your ability as a businesswoman. And we've always enjoyed working together. But every time I would get to the point of agreeing, something held me back. Don't you see, Annie? God knew I wasn't the right partner for you."

"I hadn't looked at it that way." She smiled, skin tingling. "It's always so much easier for us to see how God works in others' lives than it is in our own, isn't it?"

Meredith grinned. "You know the family is expecting him to come to lunch tomorrow, right?"

"I'll have to find out his schedule now that his employer"—Anne cleared her throat and winked—"is in town. Who knows what all Cliff will have him doing."

"Speaking of, are you going to try to talk to Cliff about—well, about what happened between the two of you?"

The euphoria from thinking about George vanished. "I know I need to, but every time I think about it, I start feeling sick to my stomach. I don't want to dredge up the past if it's going to make him resent me and possibly fire me as the wedding planner. I can't do that to Courtney."

"Do you think he's told Courtney about y'all's relationship? I mean, really, she was only eight or nine years old when that happened, so it's not like she's a contemporary who would know that the two of you even dated."

"And now that the media knows about their engagement, they're bound to start digging into Cliff's history for dirt about past relationships. All it takes is one or two people outside of our family to mention we dated, and the reporters will be beating down my door wanting all the details. Can't you just see the headlines?" Anne held her hands up as if framing the words on a marquee. " 'Movie star Cliff Ballantine hires ex-fiancée to plan his wedding.' Wouldn't that make great publicity?"

"You can't worry about what some reporters might or might not do. You just have to make sure that your life is straightened out. If you don't talk with him, if you don't forgive him, how will you ever be happy moving forward in a relationship with George? That bitterness you hold inside of you toward Cliff will always be there, keeping you from fully giving your heart to George. Cliff will own you more fully than he did when you went into debt to support him back then."

"I know. I've gone through all of the arguments in my head. I know I have to talk to him."

"Knowing in your head isn't enough." Meredith set down her fork and reached across the table to grasp Anne's hand. "You have to know it in your heart, too. You have to ask God to break through those walls you've built up—whether from the teasing you got in school about being an orphan or losing your parents or finding out Cliff never really wanted to marry you. God can heal your hurts, but He can only do so if you choose to trust Him and forgive."

Tears burned the rims of Anne's eyes. No sermon could have come to a more laser-honed point. All her life, Anne had allowed every hurtful thing that happened to pile up like so much garbage in her soul. Then whenever someone came along and tried to get through to her vulnerabilities, she assumed she would be hurt again and turned away, isolating herself and blaming those who'd hurt her in the past.

"I'm not sure how to start," she whispered.

"You just did." Meredith squeezed her hand. "If you really want my opinion, I think that before you talk to Cliff, you should start with forgiving your parents."

"My parents?" Anne shook her head. "What do they have to do with George and me?"

"Everything if you're going to have a healthy relationship with him. Annie, every time we're with any of our relatives who have kids, I can see the hurt in your eyes. You think you hide it, but I know you better than most."

Not wanting to have an emotional breakdown in the middle of a restaurant, Anne gathered her wits—and defenses—took a deep breath, and dabbed the corners of her eyes with her napkin. "How did you get so smart?"

"Well, I do have a master's degree in art history, even though I don't use it most of the time. That's almost as good as a professional therapist, right?" Meredith grinned and took out some cash and laid it on top of the tray with the check. "I know this is a lot to handle over lunch on a sunny Saturday afternoon. And I didn't mean to push you so hard. But I also don't want to see you lose the best thing that could ever happen to you. So please, if you need help with any of this, come talk to me. You know I'm at your disposal twenty-four-seven."

"I know. Thanks." Anne put her money down, too. She hugged Meredith and kept her arm around her cousin as they left the restaurant.

Half an hour later, alone in her apartment, Anne pulled several storage boxes out of the large hall closet until she found the particular one she sought. Stacking the rest neatly in place, she heaved the large plastic bin into the living room, set it in front of the ottoman, and sat with it between her feet.

She stared at the blue plastic. Could she do this? She hadn't looked in this box since she'd given up hope on Cliff. Steeling herself—and rising to pull a box of tissues closer—she popped the clasps and laid the lid aside.

Like wild creatures released from captivity, memories ravished her as she recognized the items at the top of the container. The notebook she'd put together for the very first wedding she'd ever completely planned—her own. Inside the plastic front cover, a photo of her with Cliff—she smiling and looking like nothing would ever go wrong, and he practicing the smile that would grace the front of every entertainment magazine and supermarket tabloid for the next ten years.

Today wasn't the day to deal with that particular part of her past. She put it aside, along with the album of photos of the two of them during their nearly six-year relationship—well, more pictures of him in his various stage roles through those years than actual shots of them together. The one in the front of the notebook was one of the few when he wasn't hamming it up.

Next, she pulled out the scrapbook Meredith had created for her college graduation. Nostalgia and regret mingled as she set it down on the floor. The high school graduation scrapbook went on top of that.

Now she was getting down to it. She pulled out a red photo album with a brass spiral spine and gingerly lifted the cover. In her bad teenaged penmanship on the title page she read, *Trip to Baton Rouge and State Capitol Building. Anne Elaine Hawthorne, Freshman Civics Class, Acadiana High School.* One of the better memories from her earlier years. She closed it and added it to the stack beside her right foot.

Three more albums joined it until she finally got to what she was looking for. The padded cover had a faux wood-grain finish with a large script *H* engraved in a metal plate shaped like a shield in the middle. Her skin tingled when she opened it to see her mother's handwriting on the first page. *Hawthorne Family Photos. Copyright Lilly Guidry-Hawthorne and Albert Michael Hawthorne. Amateur photos by Anne Elaine Hawthorne.*

Her mother had written the beginning date—Anne's fifth birthday. Anne had written the ending date—the one-year anniversary of the plane crash four years later. Her throat tightened. She hadn't looked at these pictures since then, as her grandmother had become visibly upset every time she caught Anne looking at photographs of her parents the year she'd lived with them. And she hadn't wanted Aunt Maggie and Uncle Errol to think her ungrateful by making herself sad looking at them.

Like an old-fashioned television warming up, Anne's memory slowly faded in as she flipped through the album. She remembered her mother and father with cameras in front of their faces most of the time. Not little ones, but big black monstrous ones that made the most wonderful whirring and clicking noises. Her gaze rested on a photo of her father teaching her all the different parts of the camera. She couldn't have been more than six years old but knew all of the terminology—from f-stop to parallax to field flattener. Her first few attempts at taking pictures with the cameras she could barely lift followed on the next few pages. She'd helped her mother develop them in the converted-garage darkroom. For her birthday that year, she'd received her mother's first camera—a 1958 Kodak Signet 35mm—and twenty rolls of film. Her grandmother had taken a picture of her with her parents at the New Orleans airport before they left for some exotic locale like Bora-Bora, Nepal, or Taureg. Their parting instructions were to use all twenty rolls of film in the four months they'd be gone.

Apparently she hadn't had a precocious talent at it, as the scene when they sat down to critique her work popped into her mind with picture-perfect clarity. Only ten photos—out of the hundreds she'd helped her mom develop—made it into the album. After that session, seeing the disappointment in her mother's beautiful face and her father's bright blue eyes, Anne had carried the camera with her everywhere—until her first grade teacher confiscated it because she wasn't doing her schoolwork. When her grandmother gave it back to her after a week without it, Anne spent all of her free hours trying to practice what they'd taught her about focus, light saturation, contrast, and composition so that when they came back from taking photos sure to win them more national and international recognition, they wouldn't be disappointed again.

Examples of her "much better" work followed—a close-up shot of ladybugs on a leaf. The branch of an old oak tree dipping down into the creek behind Mamere and Papere's farmhouse. Uncle Lawson teaching Forbes to play chess. A wide shot of the entire family—except Lilly and Albert—eating Sunday dinner.

She flipped the next page and something slipped out. She caught it before it hit the floor, and her heart lurched. She unfolded the newsprint. There, on the front page, above the fold. A photo of the skeleton framework of the "tallest building ever to be built in Bonneterre" with which she'd won the newspaper's amateur photography contest. She had to admit, the composition was pretty spectacular, taken from the roof of a nearby office building. *Maybe now my parents will see that they can stay in Bonneterre to take pictures and still have them printed,* she had thought when she had found out about winning the contest.

The adult Anne snorted. At thirty-five, she knew why her parents had to leave to do their work. The child within her still wanted to know why they loved doing it more than being with their daughter.

Of course, they'd been thrilled. Had bought her a new camera. Had taken her out to dinner to celebrate.

Then the Smithsonian called. They wanted to display her parents' photography in a special exhibit in the months leading up to the announcements of the Pulitzer prize, which everyone in the country was sure her parents would win for their photo essay on a flood that ravaged a previously unknown village in the Appalachians. They wanted Lilly and Albert to be there for the opening.

Anne begged to go with them, now that she was an award-winning photographer herself. They laughed at her earnestness, but she got through to them because after a couple of days, they agreed she could go. They'd take a week and make it a family vacation. So many things for Anne to practice her photography skills on in Washington, DC.

Never having left Bonneterre before, Anne had been excited but tried to imitate her parents, to whom the trip was nothing out of the ordinary. She kissed Mamere and Papere good-bye at the gate at the Bonneterre airport—then just a small regional outfit—and followed her parents outside and up the steps into the small plane, lugging her heavy camera bag. The commuter jet had two seats on one side of the aisle and one on the other. She sat beside her daddy, in the window seat, the thrill of finally getting to go with her parents ready to boil over.

Her stomach lurched as she remembered the sensation of the plane picking up speed down the runway. She swallowed hard and closed her eyes. She was holding Daddy's hand, looking out the window at the buildings and trees whipping by. The front of the plane lifted up.

She swallowed again, cold sweat breaking out on her face.

Farther and farther back in her seat the g-force had pressed her as the plane lifted off the tarmac. Daddy pointed out the steeple of Bonneterre Chapel and the tree-shaded campus of the university. There was Town Square and the river.

The plane gave a sudden loud *pop* and jerked drunkenly to the right. Other passengers gasped. Daddy's hand on hers tightened. What was happening? She looked up at Daddy, who wasn't smiling anymore as he looked across the narrow aisle at Mama. The plane jerked again, and Anne could smell smoke. Something was on fire! A woman behind them started praying, calling Jesus' name over and over.

The memories came back so real, so clear; tears streamed down Anne's face, and she wrapped her arms around her churning stomach.

With a sickening screech, flames had erupted outside her mother's window as the engine exploded. Anne remembered screaming. With gathering speed the small plane hurtled toward the woods. Daddy wrapped his arms around her, tucking her head into his chest, whispering, "It's going to be fine, sugarplum. It's going to be okay."

Smoke filled the cabin; flames backlit her mom. *Mama, get away from the fire—you'll get hurt! Mama!*

Anne leapt off the ottoman and dashed to the bathroom just in time as her stomach emptied all its contents. She collapsed on the cool white tile, sobbing, trembling, her heart racing.

She'd woken up in the hospital three days later. Lilly had died instantly. Albert lingered a few hours—his chest impaled with a twisted piece of metal, the same piece of burning metal that seared a scar along the left side of Anne's neck. He'd protected her as best he could during the impact of the crash, shielding her from burning debris, but her injuries had still been extensive: her left foot and ankle crushed by her heavy camera bag, second- and third-degree burns where his hands and arms couldn't cover her, the gash along her neck into the shoulder muscle.

Her father had only been thirty-four years old, her mother

thirty-two. Still so much life ahead of them.

Why, God? She pulled herself off the floor and proceeded to brush her teeth. *Why did Lilly and Albert have to die? Why did I have to be deprived of my parents growing up? You could have saved them, but You didn't. I don't understand.*

She took some Pepto-Bismol to try to calm her stomach.

God was no more to blame than her parents for their death. Yes, He could have worked a miracle and stopped them from dying. But He hadn't. Accidents happened. She wasn't the first child to have lost her parents, and she wouldn't be the last. But she could take comfort in the knowledge that they'd believed in Him, had accepted that their salvation was only to be found in the blood of Jesus. They had been with Him from the very moment their lives here ended.

Leaving Anne to have to go on without them. To have the stigma of being the girl who had to depend on the charity of relatives for a place to live. The girl who was teased when changing clothes for gym class in the locker room because of all the burn scars on her back. No boy would ever want to be with a *monster* like her.

That legacy followed her through junior high into high school, combined with the fact that she had a burning need to please every adult she came into contact with, including all of her teachers. What other students saw as Anne trying to ingratiate herself by volunteering to help or getting the best grades had been no more than her need for approval by anyone in a pseudo-parental role—at least, that's what a friend had written in a psych paper about her in college. The teasing had followed her, too. Especially being nearly six feet tall at thirteen with no athletic ability whatsoever.

She returned to the living room and started replacing items in the box. The trip to Baton Rouge in ninth grade had been great because only the kids with the top grades—other nerds, geeks, and social outcasts like herself—had gone. No one had teased her about her height, her grades, her lack of "real" parents.

She cracked open her high school scrapbook. A photo of her

with her "older brothers" and Forbes slipped out. Maggie and Errol's three older sons, Whit, Andre, and David, along with Forbes had done their best to protect Anne from the worst of the teasing. But they'd had their own lives and couldn't be around all the time.

Tucking the photo back into the book, she continued flipping through. She stopped in the pages representing her junior year. A piece of paper with purple ditto-machine ink glared back at her:

Acadiana High School
Nominees for Junior Prom Court

As a joke, someone had nominated her for prom court. She'd tried to make light of it, not to take it seriously. That was hard when Aunt Maggie heard, though. Since Maggie had no daughter of her own, she and Anne had a strong relationship. But Aunt Maggie couldn't understand why Anne wasn't excited about being nominated, until Anne finally confessed that she didn't have a date for the dance and knew no one would ask her to go.

Maggie had suggested Anne ask one of her cousins to go as her date. It was the only major argument she and Aunt Maggie ever got into. Anne won but felt terrible for disappointing her mother's sister, who'd been so kind as to take her into her home to live.

Once the flyers had been passed out among the junior class, the teasing intensified and started getting nasty when the chess team, chemistry club, and honor society started campaigning for her.

She could remember that worst day like yesterday. Three of the cheerleaders had cornered her outside the gym on her way out of PE—one of them was her cousin David's girlfriend. They threatened her with all sorts of retribution stolen straight from the Molly Ringwald movies they'd seen too many times. She was doing her best to get away when a masculine voice rang across the hall.

"Leave her alone!"

The three cheerleaders had squeaked and spun around.

Cliff Ballantine—tall, slender, and well liked, with dark hair and brooding good looks—stood over the three twits like an avenging angel. She'd only seen him in the school plays or across the room at assemblies. The cheerleaders scurried away, and Cliff had escorted her to her next class.

Anne didn't go to junior prom by her own choice. By the end of the school year, Cliff was working for Aunt Maggie part-time, and Anne was helping him with his English homework so he could graduate.

Maggie had taken every opportunity that summer to have the two of them work together. Although with every appearance of being outgoing and happy-go-lucky, Cliff let only a few people, including Anne, see his vulnerable, somewhat introverted side. She was the only girl at school who knew he lived with his mom in a trailer park on the edge of town instead of at his deceased grandparents' address that he used to be in the Acadiana High district—the school with the best drama program in town. He was the only person outside the family she ever told all of the details of the plane crash to. She also recognized that he used his good looks and charm to get people to do what he wanted. She'd confronted him about it the year before he graduated from college, but he just laughed, patted her cheek, and asked her if she could go to the library and find him some books for a sociology research paper he had to write.

She put the scrapbooks, the wedding plan book, and everything else back into the box and snapped the lid on.

If Cliff hadn't really wanted to marry her, why had he asked in the first place? They'd never really been "boyfriend and girlfriend"—he'd gone on dates with other girls in college. But when he moved away to California, he'd seemed to cling to her like a lifeline—and, of course, a constant source of money when he quit whatever part-time job he was willing to take on.

Ask him.

She lugged the box back to the closet and returned to the bathroom to start getting ready for her date. She stared at herself in the mirror as a slow smile spread across her face. After all these years, she'd finally figured out how to talk to Cliff. She'd make an appointment with his personal assistant, George.

Her cell phone buzzed and started playing "That's Amore."

"Hello, George."

He didn't respond immediately, and her smile faltered.

"Anne, I—we—something has come up."

She trudged into the living room and sank into her big chair. "That's okay if you have to cancel tonight."

"Oh no, it's not about tonight—well, it is, but it isn't—" He let out a frustrated breath into the phone. "I'm making a muck of this. Here's the issue. Mr. Ballantine just received word from his agent that he's gotten a call for Mr. Ballantine to star in what's sure to be one of the biggest movies he's ever done. Mr. Ballantine doesn't want to turn it down."

Anne frowned. "Okay."

"The movie starts filming in September in New Zealand for ten weeks."

"Ten—oh. So they want to postpone the wedding?" A tingle started at the base of her skull. Postponing the wedding would mean George would be around that much longer.

"Well, no. They'd like to move the wedding up to the last weekend in August."

Anne's fantasy of George being around for an additional two or three months crashed into a heap of anxiety. "Last weekend in August? With everything we have left to do? Are they still determined to have it the same size?"

"Yes. Everything still the same, just moved up almost two months. Anne, I know this is an imposition on you. But Mr. Ballantine has instructed me to spare no expense in making it happen. Do you—do you think it can be done?"

Her stomach started churning again. Six weeks to do what was going to be difficult in four months. "Of course. But I think instead of going out for dinner tonight, we should have something delivered to my office and work on a new timeline."

The relief in his sigh was palpable through the phone. "I'll meet you at your office at six. I lo. . . I'll pick up dinner. What do you fancy?"

Anne left the choice of meal up to him—she wouldn't be able to eat anything anyway—and bade him farewell for the time being.

So much for a leisurely, romantic dinner.

Chapter 25

The weeks between the engagement party and Courtney's wedding sped by, even though Anne did everything to utilize every minute of every day. After a quick trip to New York to get Cliff settled into his Manhattan condo, George returned to Bonneterre to assist her with anything she needed.

He helped her avoid the media—including Kristin and Greg, the couple who'd pretended to be potential clients to try to pump her for information on the wedding. The looks on their faces when George had walked into the office and recognized them brought a smile to her face every time she thought about it.

She admired and respected him. . .and she was falling madly in love with him. She couldn't start her day until she'd talked to him on the phone, and she couldn't sleep at night until they'd prayed together to close out the day. At least once a week, they went out on what she called "real" dates—just the two of them with none of her family present—where they didn't discuss anything remotely related to their jobs.

He enjoyed spending a lot of time with her family, which was understandable, given his estrangement from his own relatives. She could be happy for him that as adults, he and his youngest brother had reconnected with each other and were now friends, even though Henry lived in Australia. George's pride in his brother's success as a barrister specializing in entertainment industry law shone through whenever he spoke Henry's name. She imagined Henry to be a lot like Forbes, explaining the close friendship between George and her cousin.

As the wedding drew closer, Anne saw more of George but spent less time connecting with him. She was past the point of no return in the relationship, yet had no confirmation George felt the same.

The memory of their conversation about whether a marriage based on friendship could survive continued to haunt her, especially given the fact George didn't exhibit any more romantic interest than he had in the beginning—saying good-bye with a kiss on the cheek, taking her hand only when assisting her in or out of the car or when they prayed over their meals.

Between the doubts over their relationship and the details of the impending wedding, Anne barely slept the week before the event. She needed every minute of each day to make sure everything was ready, every contingency plan in place, every reservation confirmed.

In the early hours of Friday morning, she tossed and turned, going over the schedule for that night's rehearsal and dinner. She'd only seen Cliff a few times since the engagement party. If she was going to resolve her past, she had to do it this weekend. She had to talk to him. No longer did she seethe with anger whenever she saw him. From the way he treated Courtney, she could tell he genuinely loved the girl. But he still had a lot of explaining to do.

Thunder shook the house, and she groaned. She couldn't understand why anyone in Louisiana would want an outdoor wedding. One of two things inevitably happened: unbearable heat or torrential rain. Or both. The weather guy on Channel Six said the rain would move through today and the weekend would be clear. She hoped for once he knew what he was talking about.

She crawled out of bed and stumbled down the hall to her home office. She jiggled the mouse, and the computer screen came alive, showing the rain contingency she'd been working on before trying to go to bed at midnight.

Why couldn't George just come out and say it? *I love you.* Did he? Maybe it was a British thing, this reluctance to be demonstrative or say the words aloud. A cultural difference. Given his loveless childhood, he might even be afraid of saying it. Yes. That was most likely the case. He loved her but was afraid to say so for fear of. . . what? Losing her?

She grimaced in wry understanding. He had as many issues with cultivating a relationship as she did. She just needed to give him time. If he could get his visa status worked out and join her as a partner, they'd have all the time they needed.

She saved the document, shut down the computer, and returned to bed, lulled to sleep by the rhythm of the rain against her bedroom windows.

George rolled out of bed before the alarm sounded. He took his Bible and prayer journal out onto the back porch, along with a large mug of Mama Ketty's strong coffee, and tried to still his thoughts long enough to concentrate on God's Word.

"I know the plans that I have for you," God had said through the prophet Jeremiah. "Plans for welfare and not for calamity to give you a future and a hope."

He clasped his hands, elbows on the edge of the iron scroll table, and leaned his forehead against his thumbs. "O God, the King Eternal. I haven't always tried to follow Your plan for my life. But now I ask You to bless my steps as I walk in what I believe is Your plan in asking Anne to marry me. I love her more dearly than I ever knew possible, and she is my hope for the future. I know it was Your divine plan that brought us together. Thank You for blessing me with her. Please prepare her heart to receive my proposal. . .and to understand the haste with which I will ask her to wed with me so we do not have to part.

"As we go into the whirlwind this weekend, I ask You to strengthen Anne and give her the courage and grace she needs to speak with Cliff and finally, once and for all, forgive him. I pray You'll bless Courtney and Cliff in their new life together. Amen."

He leaned back in the chair and sipped his coffee and watched as the rain fell in sheets across the lush green yard. Even if it stopped in an hour or two, would the ground still be soggy Saturday? It wouldn't do to have the guests' chairs sinking into the newly leveled and sodded yard.

"George, what are we going to do?"

He stood at the sound of Courtney's voice. "Don't fret. It's not supposed to last the day."

In loose-fitting, blue-plaid seersucker pants and a misshapen white T-shirt with no makeup and her dark hair pulled into a ponytail atop her head, Courtney looked more like a thirteen-year-old desperately in need of loving parents than a young woman about to get married in a public spectacle. She sat in the other chair, pulled her knees up, and wrapped her arms around them.

"What are you doing downstairs? I thought we discussed how the ground floor is for employees. It's not appropriate for you to be down here. Mama Ketty or I will bring your breakfast to you upstairs—on the balcony, if you wish."

"It's boring upstairs. George, before I moved here, I was living in a sorority house just off the UCLA campus with two other girls in the same room, and nearly one hundred others in the house. I'm not used to being alone so much." She rested her chin on her knees. "I wish Cliff hadn't gone off to New York right after the party. Or at least that he'd been able to come back for longer than two days at a time. It's so hard to be separated from the one you love."

He tried not to laugh at the philosophical tone of her voice as he regained his seat. "Yes. It's hard."

She leaned her head to the side to look at him. "But you don't have that problem, do you?" She grinned. "You and Miss Anne are hardly ever apart."

His face burned and he scowled, staring out at the rain.

Courtney laughed, leaned over, and wrapped her arms around his, resting her head on his shoulder. "I'm happy for you. I'm just sad, because I have a feeling it means you won't be working for Cliff much longer, which means I won't get to see you anymore, except when we come home for visits."

He rested his right hand atop hers. "Yes. We'll always be here for you, whenever you need to get away from the chaos of life under the examining glass."

"Mama's coming back from the Riviera today. I don't think she's going to be happy with the wedding."

He squeezed her hands and reached for his coffee. "It's not her wedding, so what does it signify?"

"I don't want her making a scene. Miss Anne has worked so hard on everything, and I don't want Mama to say something to offend her."

"I believe Anne has a clear understanding of mothers of the bride. Perhaps, though, your mother's jet lag will keep her from raising too much of a stir."

"George, I can't find—" Mama Ketty stopped and propped her fists on her ample hips. "Young'un, you're supposed to be upstairs for your breakfast, not down here mingling with the hired staff."

Courtney didn't budge from her clinging position. "Oh, Mama Ketty, you and George aren't just hired staff. You're *family*."

Mama Ketty clucked and went back inside, shaking her head.

Contentment nearly burst his heart. Only one person missing and his family would be complete. Soon, though. . . He kissed the top of Courtney's head. "I don't know about you, young miss, but I for one am famished."

Instead of letting go, Courtney hugged his arm tighter. "George. Do you think. . . I mean, would it be inappropriate. . . ?"

He rested his cheek against her hair. "Spit it out, lass."

"Do you think it would be okay for you to walk me down the aisle? Do you think people would think it's weird?"

He swallowed hard. Walk her down the aisle? Take on the duty of the father of the bride? He cleared his throat. "It's your wedding. You can do whatever you wish, weird or not."

"Then I want you to walk me down the aisle. I want you to give me away like my daddy would have if he was still alive. Do you think Anne will think it's okay?"

He squeezed her hands. "We'll talk to her this morning." Despite his best efforts, his voice came out gruff with barely suppressed emotion.

"She's more like the mother of the bride than Mama. I wish. . ." She heaved a sigh. "I wish I didn't have to invite Mama, that I could have just you and Miss Anne there with me. And then when y'all get married, I'll be like your adopted daughter."

"*When* we get married?" He chuckled. "You're assuming quite a lot."

"Oh, y'all will get married. And soon, too, I figure. You may think I'm oblivbious to what goes on around me, but I know you picked up the engagement ring when we went to get my jewelry last week. So when are you going to propose?"

He didn't have to hide his smile at her *oblivious* mispronunciation. "Saturday night, after the wedding."

"At the reception?"

"Most likely. Probably after you've made your exit. She won't be able to slow down a moment before then."

"But I want to see her after you give her the ring."

"All right. I'll find a time to propose that's convenient for you." He kissed the top of her head again. "Come on. Let's go eat before Mama Ketty comes after us again."

Humidity rose in nearly visible waves from the wet ground as the sun started its western descent. Anne slogged barefoot through the soggy yard toward George, holding the end of a measuring tape in one hand, cradling a clipboard in the other.

"There's nothing for it. We're just going to have to figure out some way to make the ground hard by Saturday."

George laughed and wrapped his arms around her waist from

behind. "*There's nothing for it?* Where do you pick up such idiosyncratic phrases?"

"Some strange English guy I know. He says weird things like that all the time."

He squeezed her tight a moment longer, then released her. "Has Courtney talked to you?"

"About what?"

"About me."

Anne's right eyebrow shot up. "About you?"

"Yes. She's gotten it in her mind that she wants me to walk her down the aisle." He took Anne's hand, tucked it under his elbow, and began to practice by walking her back toward the house. She released the end of the tape measure, and it snaked back toward her cousin Jonathan.

"Oh, that's so sweet. I don't have a problem with it if that's what she wants. But what will Cliff think?"

"That's the crux of the matter. I don't think he would appreciate his hired man escorting his bride down the aisle." He smiled in remembrance of Courtney's outburst of emotion this morning. "Even if the bride considers me to be part of her family."

"I guess the question then becomes, whose wishes are more important to us at this point in time? Cliff is footing the bill for this shindig but has taken no interest in the proceedings."

"I'm all in favor of giving Courtney whatever she wants."

She squeezed his arm. "I know you are. And she deserves to have someone in her life who feels that way about her."

"And she does—two of us." He sighed. "Mrs. Landry returned from France a few hours ago. Courtney's afraid she'll make a scene tonight."

"I'll do whatever I can to rein that woman in. I managed to keep her down to a dull roar at Courtney's sisters' weddings. I'll try to find some trivial—but time-consuming—task for her so she feels like she's being helpful but is out of the way. She's really not going to like the idea of you giving her daughter away. She didn't even like it when one of Courtney's sisters asked their brother to be her escort."

"Courtney has a brother?"

"He hasn't had any contact with the family since that fiasco, about three years ago. Courtney was fifteen, so she should remember it pretty clearly."

"I'll talk to her again and make sure it's what she really wants to do."

"I've always thought that if anyone in that family were ever going to stand up to that woman, it would be Courtney. She has an inner strength that most of her sisters could never hope to possess. They all let Mrs. Landry run roughshod over them. I tried to manage her, but they gave in to her demands so easily, I ended up planning the weddings to her liking rather than the brides'."

They ascended the steps to the porch behind the service entrance. Above, Anne's staff hung pink floral swags from the upper balconies that wrapped around the house. They'd be doing it all again on Saturday with fresh garlands of white flowers. Nothing but the best for their girl. Maybe in another twenty or so years, she and George would get to do this for their own child.

He stopped and pulled Anne into his arms and kissed the side of her neck.

Her hands rested on his shoulders, one hand toying with the hair at the back of his neck, a bemused expression in her eyes. "What was that for?"

He winked and took her by the hand to lead her into the house. "Just because."

At six, Cliff's limousine arrived from the airport. George instructed the butler's assistant to meet the car at the service entrance and carry the luggage up back stairs. He'd had difficulty training the Americans on the staff the proprieties that the British butler he'd hired took as a matter of course, but his efforts were proving rewarding. In the last few days with the full staff on the job every morning by seven o'clock, the house ran with English precision. Even Mama Ketty had been impressed.

Electronic planner in hand, George met Cliff in the front foyer. "Good evening, sir. Welcome home. How was your trip?"

"Long and tiresome." Cliff started up the stairs. "Have someone bring me a Mountain Dew and a fried bologna sandwich."

George nodded at the butler, who left his post at the door to relay the message to Mama Ketty. "Would you like to go over your schedule?"

His employer stopped in the middle of the wide staircase. "Yeah. I guess we have to. Come on up."

At George's request, the valet he'd hired for Cliff for the weekend had laid out several outfits across the bed. The young man followed the assistant butler into the bedroom-sized dressing closet and proceeded to unpack for their employer. George nodded his dismissal at the assistant butler and took out his stylus.

The schedule Anne had e-mailed him for the evening made up the majority of today's agenda. George read through the line items as Cliff went about the suite from bathroom to closet.

"What am I wearing tonight?" Cliff interrupted.

"Your valet has laid out some clothing here on the bed, sir." George returned to reading the agenda.

Cliff exited the closet and examined the outfits. He pointed at one and motioned for the valet to assist him in changing.

"If that's all, sir, I would like to check on Miss Courtney."

Cliff dismissed him with a wave of his hand. "Yeah. Go. Hey, boy—what's your name?"

George left him to get acquainted with his valet and went down the long hall to the bedroom suite on the opposite end. The door stood open. Courtney sat on the window seat reading, Anne in a cushioned armchair with her back to the door.

Courtney looked up and held one finger to her lips, then pointed at Anne. He walked around until he faced the chair, and smiled.

"She came in to go over the schedule with me," Courtney

whispered, "and the next thing I know, she's asleep. I don't think she's been sleeping well at night, worrying about my wedding. It was too much for her to take on by herself. She really needs an assistant."

"Yes, she does." George sank onto the window seat.

"Did I hear Cliff come in?" Courtney tried to sound disinterested, but the hurt still came through her small voice.

"He's changing." After four weeks apart, the least he could have done was greet his fiancée upon arrival. "I'm certain he'll be along directly."

"Then you probably ought to wake up Anne so he doesn't see her right off. I know he's not happy I hired her." She reached over and patted his arm. "Don't look so uncomfortable, George. Anne told me everything after the engagement party. She even offered to resign and help me find another planner. But I wouldn't let her."

He crossed to Anne and gently shook her shoulder.

Her eyes popped open. "George?"

"You have a wedding rehearsal to oversee, madam. I suggest you quit dillydallying and get to it." He kissed the tip of her nose and offered his hand.

"How long. . . ?" She looked at Courtney, her cheeks bright red.

"Just a few minutes. I didn't wake you because I knew you needed the rest."

"I'm so sorry. I'm so unprofessional." She gathered up her planner and paperwork from the small coffee table.

"No, just overworked." Courtney came over and hugged Anne. "Just in case I don't get a chance to say it again this weekend, thank you for everything. You've made every dream come true."

He heard a door down the hall and held his hand out toward Anne. "We should go."

She nodded, kissed Courtney's forehead, and followed him out of the room. Cliff's new valet caught up with them at the door to the service stairs.

"He sent me away when his food arrived. Should I just wait

outside the door? He's not changed clothes yet."

"Yes. Wait outside the door. Did you finish unpacking the suitcases?"

The young man nodded. "Most of it needed to go to the laundry, he said. So I put it in the orange bags like you showed me. In England, are there really people who do this for a living? Like, all the time for one person?"

"Yes. That was one of my first positions as an adult." He squeezed the college student's shoulder. "But not a career path I'd recommend for most."

"Thanks."

George followed Anne down the two flights of dark, narrow stairs to the kitchen. The serenity above the stairs belied the pandemonium below. He and Anne had to give way on the landing between the main floor and the lower level to several young women running up with table linens and silverware. In the kitchen, Major O'Hara commanded his staff like a general while Mama Ketty directed the young men loading the china into the dumbwaiter.

They got separated by different people needing their help. He winked at Anne as she went outside to approve the setup at the gazebo.

After a few minutes, he disengaged himself from Mama Ketty's string of complaints about the hired-on linens and went to see if he could help Anne with anything in the last few moments before the bridal party started to arrive.

At the gazebo, her young cousins Jonathan and Bryan checked the sound system. George stood at the rear of the area staked off for guest seating and gave them a thumbs-up on the volume before approaching.

"Where's Anne?"

Her cousins exchanged a look. "He came and got her. Mr. Ballantine, I mean," Jonathan said. "Said he needed to talk to her."

George's heart jumped into his throat. *Lord, let her say what needs to be said. Let her forgive him, but don't let him hurt her.*

Chapter 26

When Cliff's hand closed around her elbow, Anne's skin burned as surely as it had from the debris from the plane crash. He led her back into the house and to the office on the main floor where she and George had spent many happy hours working side by side on the wedding. She stopped behind a tall wing chair; Cliff crossed to look out one of the two tall windows.

"Do you remember the time I invited you to go on that weekend ski trip with a bunch of my friends from the fraternity?" Cliff asked, his back to her.

She smiled in spite of her anxiety over this tête-à-tête. "I said I couldn't go because it involved flying."

"I thought it was just an excuse to get out of spending time with my frat brothers. I knew you didn't like them much. I knew you didn't like the person I became when I was around them." He turned to face her, arms crossed. "Did I ever tell you how horrible that weekend was?"

She shook her head. "Aside from breaking your arm? I had a feeling other stuff happened from the fact that you didn't really talk about it after you got back."

"All they did was drink and try to get the girls who did go into bed with them. And a lot of the girls gave in. I was so glad you weren't there to witness it all. I knew you'd be disappointed."

Anne moved around to sit in the chair. This was going to take awhile. "You really worried about that?"

Nodding, he clasped his hands behind his back and ambled around the room, pausing to look at objects on shelves, books, the large painting hanging behind the desk.

"Cliff, I—" Now alone with him, Anne didn't know how to start. "I'm happy for you and Courtney."

He turned to face her, surprise in his expression. "When I found out Courtney had hired you, I wondered if God was punishing me for what I did so many years ago."

Laughter bubbled up in Anne's throat. "When I found out it was your wedding, I wondered nearly the same thing."

He crossed the room and sat in the adjacent chair. "Anne, you have to understand. You were one of the few true friends I ever had. I never felt as close to anyone as I did to you. You understood me. You knew what it was like to feel alone in a room full of people. You didn't have any expectations of me." He hung his head. "And I took advantage of that friendship. I let you give and give and give—your time, your money, your friendship—without giving you anything in return. I wouldn't have made it out of school if it hadn't been for you. I wouldn't have gotten where I am today if it hadn't been for you."

Anne studied her recently manicured nails, the remaining bitterness and accusations she'd harbored for the past decade replacing her amusement of moments before.

"I wanted to marry you, Anne. Really, I did. I wanted us to get married just like you'd planned and then bring you out to California to be with me. God knows I needed you those first few years after—" He jumped up and started pacing again.

"Then why?" She gripped her hands to keep them from shaking.

He tossed his hands in the air. "It sounds so stupid now, really. When I signed the contract to make *Mountebank*, the studio hired a publicist for me. They wanted to make me into a star. When I told them I was supposed to be getting married, they went ballistic. Told me it would have to be postponed. Made me call you to tell you that. I didn't want to disappoint you, Anne. And I never wanted to hurt you."

Tears burned her eyes. It hadn't been his idea to call off the wedding.

He spun and came to kneel in front of her. "They wouldn't let me call, but I could at least have the studio secretary mail letters for me."

Anne shook her head. "I never got any letters. I thought once you got your big break, you had everything you wanted and didn't need me anymore."

"I needed you, Anne." He clasped her hands in his. "I needed you more than anything. I was miserable making that movie—especially since my character fell in love with a character named Anne. I poured my heart into those scenes, the dialogue between us, because I hoped if you ever saw it, you'd know I was talking to you."

She stared at the ceiling, blinking to keep the tears from spilling out.

"When I never heard back from you, I got mad because I thought you didn't want to talk to me because I'd postponed the wedding. I hadn't wanted to think you were that shallow, but then when I got your letter. . ." Cliff shrugged his broad shoulders.

Her gaze snapped back to his. "*My* letter? Cliff, I never sent you a letter. I thought you never wanted to hear from me again."

A frown furrowed the area between his well-groomed brows. He let go of her hands and reached into his jeans pocket. "This letter."

She took the yellowed piece of paper from him. The folds were fragile, the edges darkened from years of handling. In old dot-matrix print was a brief note with what looked like her signature under it. It was dated nearly six months after he called off the wedding:

Dear Cliff,

Congratulations on your new career as an actor. I wish you all the best as you follow your dream. I don't want to hold you back, and I feel that if we marry, that's what I'll be doing.

Please know that I will always support you from afar. Please do not try to contact me again. This is for the best.

Anne

"I didn't write this, Cliff. That's not my signature. It's a good forgery, but it's not mine." She handed the page back to him.

He folded it and put it in his pocket. "I always suspected. It didn't sound like you. You'd only typed one letter to me before that—you'd handwritten the rest of them. But I just wasn't sure."

"Why didn't you call? Or come see me whenever you came back to town?"

He stood and ran his fingers through his stylishly tousled hair. "I was going to. The first time I came back after the movie came out, I went by Aunt Maggie's house, but they didn't live there anymore. The people who did live there didn't know where y'all had moved to. I finally tracked down Forbes's phone number. I went to his office to meet with him. He told me how hurt you'd been, how you'd dropped out of graduate school just to be able to send me money."

Forbes. Anger started to rise. How dare he try to manipulate her life!

"Before you get mad at Forbes, let me explain what I told him. I told him that I wanted to see you, to apologize. He asked me if I still intended to marry you. I had to be honest with him, Annie. I'd just started dating someone else. I thought I was falling in love with her. He thought it best that we didn't see each other again. You had been my best friend. But—" He pressed his lips together as if unwilling to continue.

"But you were never really in love with me." Anne pressed her hands together and rested her forefingers against her lips.

"He thought it would hurt you more to see me on those terms than to never see me again. I'm so sorry."

Closing her eyes, she sat in silence for a long time, trying to remember when she'd stopped loving him. She'd loved the idea of being married to a handsome, talented, interesting man—the only one who'd ever shown any interest in her. But in all honesty, he hadn't broken her heart. He'd broken her trust—an emotion stronger than love.

"I forgive you, Cliff." The words, softly spoken, came from a place in her heart she hadn't felt in a very long time. "I was angry at you for so many years—especially while I was still trying to pay off all that debt, knowing how rich you were getting."

"Wait a minute! I asked my manager to have a check cut for you—I had kept a running tally of everything I owed you. The least I could do was pay you back with interest."

Anne shook her head. "Didn't get the letters, didn't get the check, either. I hope whoever that manager was doesn't work for you anymore."

Cliff started to puff up the way she remembered when he was angry. She bit her bottom lip as a smile threatened. Nice to know some things didn't change.

She stood and rested her hand on his arm. "Never mind about that. God knew what He wanted from both of our lives and that we were better off not together. And now look." She waved her hand toward the window overlooking the lawn where members of the wedding party were starting to congregate. "You do get to pay me back—with interest. You know, I never would have gotten into this business if it hadn't been for you borrowing that money and my dropping out of graduate school. Thank you."

He opened his mouth, but no words came out.

She laughed—a feeling of freedom overwhelming her. "Come on. Let's go practice getting you married."

"How did it go?" George asked when she joined him in the kitchen moments later.

She smiled and slipped her arms around his waist. "Better than I expected. I'll tell you about it later. Right now, I need to get to work."

He kissed her cheek. "Righto." He released her and pressed the button on the battery pack clipped to his belt. "Places, everyone."

Anne took the headset he offered and got wired up to be able to direct the proceedings.

Courtney's ten bridesmaids kept her busy for nearly half an hour, trying to get them in some semblance of order, while George tried to do the same with the groomsmen down at the gazebo. Once aligned, Anne clicked her headset microphone on. "George Laurence, I need to see you, please."

He appeared at her side a few seconds later. "Yes, ma'am?"

She nodded at Courtney, standing at the back of the long line of giggling girls on the back veranda. "You have a duty to perform, sir."

If Cliff was surprised to see George escorting Courtney down the aisle, he didn't let on. George returned to stand beside Anne, his hands clasped behind his back, very much the same as the position he'd maintained during Cliff's press conference. The man certainly didn't believe in public displays of affection. She wouldn't have minded if he'd put his arm around her or taken her hand. But, she sighed, they were working, and how professional would that look?

Before the rehearsal ended, George vanished to oversee the setup for dinner up on the wide front porch. Anne wrapped up a few minutes later and sent everyone in that direction.

She was stopped from following them by a bone-jarring hug from Courtney. "Thank you for everything, Miss Anne. I know this is going to be the most beautiful wedding ever, and it's all because of you."

Cliff grinned at Anne over his fiancée's head.

She smiled back at him. "It'll be the most beautiful wedding, Courtney, because you're going to be the most beautiful bride ever."

Courtney stepped back to be engulfed by Cliff's huge arm. "I hope you have lots of business cards with you tonight, Anne. Lots of the girls were asking me about you."

Anne shooed them toward the house. She set the crew George had hired to breaking down everything and followed them.

Throughout the evening, she tried to find a few minutes alone with George but couldn't seem to find him when he wasn't surrounded by people or on his way to run an errand for Cliff. She was a bit disconcerted by his inattention but reminded herself he had a job in addition to helping her, and if she knew Cliff, he kept George running at all times.

But tomorrow night. . . She sighed. Tomorrow night, it would all be over. Cliff and Courtney would be gone on their honeymoon. And she and George. . .

She couldn't wait to see what happened then.

Chapter 27

Anne watched from a distance as Cliff and Courtney fed each other a piece of the enormous cake Aunt Maggie had labored over for weeks. Cliff had insisted on being at Vue de Ciel when the cake was scheduled to be delivered just so he could see Aunt Maggie. Anne shook her head. She never thought she'd see the day when she'd be happy to witness Cliff Ballantine getting married.

Where was George? She'd only had glimpses of him throughout the evening, and he'd slipped away while Anne arranged the cake-cutting. A casual perusal of the warehouse-sized Vue de Ciel ballroom didn't reveal him.

She'd hoped they'd find a few minutes alone tonight. They needed to discuss the partnership. She wanted a yes or no answer out of him before the end of the night. Every time she'd broached the topic in the last few weeks, he'd come out with one excuse or another about his work visa. She was beginning to feel like he'd decided against it but just couldn't bring himself to tell her.

Something about the distance that still remained between them kept her from fully trusting him, held her back, made her want to retreat behind her old emotional walls and protect herself. Even talking at length with Meredith about her parents' death and the expectation she carried with her since then—that everyone who professed to love her would eventually leave or disappoint her—hadn't helped her put her fear aside.

Working her way around the perimeter of the room, she spoke to guests as she was spoken to, nodding at the service staff who caught her gaze.

As she neared the corridor that led to the kitchen, Major intercepted her.

"We're running low on caviar," he divulged in a hushed whisper. "Only half of what we ordered came in, and there is no more to be had in town anywhere—I know because I've called every grocer in a hundred-mile radius."

Anne looked over her shoulder at Cliff and Courtney. Neither of them liked caviar. They'd only put it on the menu because it was expensive and would impress people. "Don't worry about it. If it's gone, it's gone." She looked down the hall toward the kitchen.

"What are you looking for?" Major looked over his shoulder in the same direction.

"You haven't seen George in the last few minutes, have you?"

A smile spread across her friend's face. "I think I saw him headed out onto the observation deck a few minutes ago." He caught her arm as she turned to go. "Am I going to have to compete with your aunt for the privilege of catering your reception?"

Anne forced a smile. With the way things stood between them now, would there ever be a Hawthorne-Laurence wedding? "I think I can probably put both you and Aunt Maggie to work." She spun around with a wave and headed for the opposite side of the top floor of Boudreaux Tower. Although the room, with its glass walls and roof, gave a spectacular view of downtown Bonneterre, the observation deck allowed visitors to experience the view unobstructed.

George Laurence wouldn't leave tonight without discussing their future partnership—whether business or personal.

"I've got to wait until the time's right. If I do this wrong, she's likely to bolt." George paced the width of the deck overlooking the twinkling lights of the sleeping city. While he stood at the top of the tallest building in Bonneterre, Louisiana, in the middle of the night, his brother Henry sat in evening rush hour traffic in Sydney, Australia.

"Look, mate. You've been in love with this woman since the first time you clapped eyes on her. You've spoken of little else since you met her." Henry paused to yell a few colorful phrases at another driver. He had adapted to his new environs quickly.

"It took me awhile, but I know Anne is the woman God created especially for me." George sighed and leaned against the waist-high safety wall. "But if I resign my post, I'll have to return to England for six months and apply for a new visa—I'll lose my years of residency toward becoming a citizen."

"So what's to keep you from just courting her until she's ready to marry you?" Henry asked.

"Because in two weeks when Mr. and Mrs. Ballantine return from their honeymoon, I'll be going to New Zealand with him for nearly three months. After that, it's off to who knows where. I'm afraid she'll give up on me. I can't lose her."

"Listen, Brother, I'm almost to the harbor bridge, and traffic is bad so I need to go. There is one idea that I don't know if you've thought of. You could always marry an American and stay in the country that way. You already have the ring for your Miss Hawthorne, do you not?"

George reached up and felt the slight bulge in the inside pocket of his tuxedo jacket. "I do."

"Well. . . ?" Henry prompted.

"What you're saying is that I should propose to Anne tonight and convince her to marry me in two weeks so that I can stay in the country?" He had a feeling Anne would say yes to his proposal, but would she want to get married that quickly?

"I don't think you'd have to get married in two weeks. I think if you got engaged and could prove it to the immigration services office, they would probably give you an extension until you do get married. That way, you can resign your post and stay there with her. At the worst, you'd have to go back to England for a few weeks until you're issued a temporary green card."

"Marriage to Anne would be the perfect solution." George paced as he ruminated on the idea. "She'll have the business partner she longs for, and I'll get to stay in the country."

"Oh, and spending the rest of your life with the woman you're madly in love with doesn't factor into the equation?"

"Well, there's that as well." Anxiety tingled through him. Would she say yes? He took a few moments after the phone call to compose himself, then returned to the ballroom in search of Anne. He had to propose before Courtney left, or the girl would never forgive him.

He didn't immediately spot Anne in the room, no surprise among seven hundred guests. He stopped a few servers, who said they'd seen her come through recently but weren't sure in which direction she'd gone.

Courtney gazed adoringly into Cliff's eyes as they glided about the dance floor. The one area where she'd disagreed with Anne had been music. Anne just couldn't convince her to have a swing band instead of one that would cover the current hit songs. When he and Anne married, he'd suggest "That's Amore" or perhaps a more traditional "Someone to Watch over Me" as their first dance. He slipped into the crowd to avoid Cliff's seeing him.

Anne didn't seem to be anywhere in the ballroom, so he went down the hall to the massive kitchen.

Major O'Hara greeted him with a wink and a smile. "Anne was just in here looking for you. I sent her out toward the observation deck a few minutes ago."

"Cheers!" George spun and headed back in the direction he'd come. She'd probably gone out the door on this side of the building. He slipped through the door and looked for the woman who stood head and shoulders above the rest. . .almost literally. He'd never imagined falling in love with a woman who, when she wore heels, stood the same height as he. Just one of her many beauties.

Finally, he found her on the observation terrace in the far corner near the emergency exit. Perfect. Hidden from the view of those inside, and far from the best views of downtown.

"Anne?"

She didn't turn.

He stopped beside her, his shoulder touching hers. "I hoped I would find you out here."

Strange distance filled her gaze when she finally looked at him. She must be exhausted. She hadn't been sleeping at all.

"I know you'll be glad when this is all over."

She shook her head. "You have no idea."

He leaned against the safety wall, facing her. "You need a long holiday."

"I can't. I have a business to run and lots of events already booked."

She wasn't making this easy. *Just do it. She's tired.* "Anne, I know we haven't been acquainted long. But I've always believed in quality over quantity. I also remember our conversation about marriage and how we both believe that it should be based on mutual respect and admiration."

Tears filled her eyes.

He smiled and reached for the ring box. Clasping her hand, he dropped to one knee with a flourish, holding the ring box toward her. "Anne Hawthorne, will you marry this man who not only admires and respects you but is madly in love with you?"

The darkness made her expression hard to read. She pulled her hand away and took the ring box. She studied the jewel for a moment, then closed the box and handed it back to him. "No."

He rose. "No?"

She gestured for him to take the box. When he didn't reach for it, she grabbed his hand and pressed it into his palm. "No."

He blocked her retreat, heated embarrassment replacing his earlier thrill. "May I have the honor of an explanation?"

She crossed her arms. Tears glittered in twin trails down her cheeks. "I was a fool to believe. . .to believe you would ever be honest with me."

"To what are you referring, madam? Please make sense!" What had changed from their stolen kiss after the wedding ceremony to now?

She pointed to the ring box. "Proposing as if you meant it. Saying you're madly in love with me to manipulate me into marrying you."

Cold anger flooded him. "Manipulate. . . ? Anne, when have I ever tried to manipulate you? I've done everything I can to prove my love to you."

She swiped at the moisture on her face. "I have to be the biggest idiot in the world. At least Cliff's actions I can blame on immaturity and bad counsel. But you? All this time you talked about honesty, about how important it is to found a relationship on trust. And all along, you were just reeling me in like the catch of the day."

"I have no idea to what you are referring." Instinctively, he handed Anne his handkerchief.

She pushed it away. "No? Let me refresh your memory. You propose, and we both get what we want: I get a business partner, and you get to stay in the country."

His heart sank. His phone call with Henry. She'd only heard one side. But she should have trusted him rather than jumping to erroneous conclusions. "Anne, you didn't hear the whole conversation."

"No. But I heard enough. This is why you've been avoiding answering me about the partnership—why you've kept me at arm's length." Her voice caught, and her face contorted as she tried to control her emotions. She shoved past him but stopped after a few feet. "I thought you really loved me. I guess you're as good of an actor as your employer. I would have been better off if you had stayed the groom!" She composed herself as she turned to reenter the ballroom.

He should go after her. Explain. Make her understand.

But how could she accuse him of trying to manipulate her? He genuinely loved her. He would never intentionally hurt her.

She was too angry right now to listen to reason. . .and he was too hurt and angry to try to reason with her. He just needed to give her a couple of days to cool off.

Monday morning, George stopped in front of Anne's office, surprised to see the Closed sign hanging in the window. Finally, she'd decided to take a day off.

He dialed her cell phone number as he walked back toward his car. No answer. Her cheerful answering machine greeting brought him the first smile in days. "Hello, Anne. I know you may still be angry, but I would like a chance to explain. Remember what you said about misunderstandings and communication issues. That's all this is. Please call me so we can talk. I love you."

When he hadn't heard from her—or anyone else in her family—by Thursday, he decided to take matters under his own control again. Forbes's secretary ushered him into the large office.

The dark look on the lawyer's face told George everything he needed to know. "She told you her side of the story?"

"Her side? She told me what happened, yes. And to think I trusted you not to hurt her."

"It's all a horrible misunderstanding." George paced the width of the room. "She overheard a conversation I had with my brother. He and I were joking around. I would never consider marrying Anne for a business partnership or a green card."

Forbes nodded, his blue-gray eyes piercing. "Really?"

"Really!" He threw his hands up. "What do I have to do to convince you people?"

"Go home." The words were growled more than said.

"I beg your pardon?"

"You want to prove to Anne you don't want to marry her just for a green card? Go back to England. Prove you love her and not just the idea of staying in the States."

He sank into a chair and dropped his head into his hands. "Go home? I don't have a home to go to." If Henry's apartment hadn't sublet yet. . .

Forbes was right. He had to regroup, show Anne it was her, not this place, not her business, that he loved. "All right. I'll go back to England."

Forbes's expression neutralized. "I'll help you take care of things on this end—liquidating your assets, transferring accounts."

"Thanks." George stood and offered his hand. "Thanks for everything. Tell Anne. . ."

Forbes nodded. "I'll tell her."

On his way out, his phone beeped. "George Laurence here."

"Hi, George," Courtney's voice chimed through the line.

"Hello, Miss—Mrs. Ballantine. How may I be of assistance?"

"George, Cliff is going to have to cut his trip short. They need him on the movie set earlier than they thought. He wants you to meet me in Paris this weekend. *We're going to buy a villa!*"

He needed something to pay the bills while he tried to convince Anne. While this wouldn't be as grand a gesture as resigning and returning to England to live in squalor while waiting, it would serve his purpose.

"Very good, ma'am. I'll make flight arrangements this afternoon."

Chapter 28

The light clink of silver against china and the din of hushed voices reminded George of his very first meeting with Forbes. As a farewell, his friend had suggested dinner at Palermo's, bringing everything full circle.

"I've closed up the house. Mama Ketty will check in every few weeks." Emotion threatened to close George's throat.

"I'll take care of adjusting her contract. When does your flight leave?"

"Sunday afternoon at three, with layovers in Memphis and Atlanta." He pulled a copy of the itinerary out of his attaché. "Here's the schedule. I've given Henry your number in the event of an emergency."

Forbes gave the schedule only a cursory glance before folding it and sticking it in his suit-coat pocket. "Six months is a long time. When I said to take time to prove your love for her, I didn't mean *that* long."

"I know. But maybe the distance will be good for us." He grinned wryly. "And I do have all that vacation time I never take. I can be back in a trice if she decides she's ready."

Forbes chuckled. "She'll miss you, George. She probably does already."

"I hope so." He handed his friend an envelope. "Can you give her this for me? I had to at least try to explain before I left."

"She'll come around. We'll make sure of it."

"You're not going to interfere, are you?"

"*Interfere* is such a negative word, my friend. Think of it as encouraging her to reconsider her hasty and emotionally motivated actions."

Somehow, that didn't make George feel better. "Thanks."

"No problem. You realize I'm just doing this because Meredith and Jennifer have already planned your wedding, and I hate to disappoint my sisters, right?"

"Right. Tell them thanks for me."

"Will do."

For the first time in his life, George didn't want to leave a place. He had friends—no, family—who loved him. He'd made a life here in a few short months. He'd started to dream of building his future here. His happiness resided in Bonneterre, Louisiana. . . because Anne would never get on an airplane to go anywhere else. "Tell Maggie and Errol. . ." He shrugged, unable to continue. They'd welcomed him into their home and treated him like a son.

"I will."

When they parted, George barely managed to hold his emotions in check. Forbes dropped him off at the hotel where he'd stay until he took the shuttle to the airport in two days. As soon as he entered the room, he hit his knees, begging God to change her mind.

"Miss Anne, are you okay?" The bride turned, her wedding gown swishing with the hidden whisper of the multiple petticoats holding out the bell skirt.

Anne dabbed the corners of her eyes with a tissue. "I'm okay. You look so beautiful."

The young woman rested her hand on Anne's shoulder. "Thank you for everything. I know it has to be hard with your breakup and all. . . ." She bit her bottom lip.

Anne swallowed back new tears. "You're welcome, honey. Now

there's a wonderful young man waiting in that sanctuary for you. Let's get you married."

As she had every night for the past week, Anne cried herself to sleep Saturday night. Sunday, she woke up with a migraine, gave in to her self-pity, and stayed in bed. Why had she been so stupid and let George walk away? She hadn't heard the entire conversation. What if he had just been joking around with his brother? After all, George's dry sense of humor was one of the things she loved most about him. The least she could have done was let him explain.

Her anger that night had quickly melted into embarrassment, embarrassment into shame that kept her hiding out, avoiding everyone, including Forbes, Meredith, and Jenn. Tomorrow she'd work up the courage to call George to beg his forgiveness. But she needed one more day to prepare herself.

Shortly after noon, a familiar pounding started on her door.

"Go away!"

The unmistakable rasp of a key in the dead bolt followed. "Annie?"

She pulled her pillow over her head. The bed bounced and gave beside her. "Go away," she moaned.

"No. Enough of this already." Meredith pulled the pillow off her head. "We're tired of you moping around just because you're stupid enough to let the best thing that ever happened to you walk out the door."

Jenn pulled down the covers. "You're going to get up, get dressed, and go with us down to Riverwalk for an ice cream cone."

"I know I was stupid." Anne pushed their hands away. "He deserves better than me. He deserves someone who'll trust him."

Jenn grabbed one arm, Meredith the other.

"Anne." Meredith's tone stilled her. "George Laurence loves you. We saw it the first time we met him. You love him, too. But you've treated him unfairly, and you should be begging his forgiveness."

Anne closed her eyes and pressed her lips together. She knew they were right—she had no one to blame but herself if George didn't forgive her, if he didn't want to marry her now.

Regret tightened her throat. Married to George. It was all she'd dreamed of the last two months. Marrying George, working with him, restoring this house together. . .

Elizabeth d'Arcement's wedding yesterday hadn't given her the same sense of completeness she'd felt at every other wedding. A part of herself had been missing. George.

"Anne, this is ridiculous." Forbes's deep voice sounded from the doorway. "You've been avoiding me for a week, but time has run out."

Jenn and Meredith retreated, and Forbes came around to take Meredith's place on the side of the bed.

"When I agreed with Cliff that George should stand in for him, that George should keep his own identity secret, I did it never having met George before, not knowing that he's the man God created specifically for you, Annie." Forbes took hold of Anne's hand. "Once I realized that you and George had feelings for each other, the scheme was already in motion. George and I did the best we could under the circumstances. I can understand why you might still be mad at me, but if you don't stop wallowing in self-pity, you are going to lose George. And if that happens, I'm not sure I want to be around you—because you'll be miserable for the rest of your life."

Anne couldn't look at him. To her surprise, rather than try to convince her she needed to go to George on bended knee and beg forgiveness, Forbes pressed a cream envelope into her hand, kissed her forehead, and departed, taking his sisters with him.

Anne nearly wept when she saw her name in George's compact script on the envelope. Oh, she missed him. The feel of his arms around her when she was tired, his reassuring talks, the strength of his hand around hers. . .

Why, God? Why does this keep happening to me?

"I know the plans that I have for you," declares the Lord, "plans for welfare and not for calamity to give you a future and a hope."

"I love him. But I'm afraid of being hurt again."

"For God has not given us a spirit of fearfulness, but of power and love and discipline."

"Fill me with that power and love and discipline," she cried out to God. "Show me how to love and be loved without fear."

She opened the letter:

My dearest Anne,

I do not know how to begin to apologize to you for any hurt I've brought you. You are the most wonderful blessing God has ever brought into my life. I was an idiot to joke with Henry about my feelings for you. You are so deep in my heart that when you're not near I feel like I can't breathe properly.

I leave Sunday for France. Forbes has information on how to contact me. As soon as I arrive, I will contact him. . .and write you.

I love you so much, I ache when we're apart. Somehow, I will manage to survive the coming separation with only the hope you will be waiting for me when I return.

Please forgive me for hurting you.

I love you, and I miss you already.

With all my heart,
George

Sunday. Today. He was leaving today. She could still stop him. He couldn't go. She loved him. She had to tell him. She wanted to marry him and spend the rest of her life with him.

Forbes. He knew where George was going. Why had she avoided Forbes all week? If she hadn't given in to embarrassment and shame, she and George could already be back together.

Jumping out of bed, she grabbed the first pair of jeans and T-shirt she could find and combed her hair back into a ponytail as she stepped into an old pair of canvas sneakers.

She ran upstairs and pounded on Jenn's door. No answer. Down two flights and pounded on Meredith's door. Same result.

She ran back to her apartment and grabbed her purse, keys, and phone, dialing Forbes's number as she flew down the stairs.

"Anne?"

"Where is he?"

"Who?"

"What do you mean *who*? George! Where is he? He said you know where he's going. I have to find him. I have to tell him not to go."

She skidded to a stop on the back porch.

Forbes climbed out of his black Jaguar and snapped his phone closed.

She jumped down the steps and grabbed his arms. "Where is he?"

Jenn stuck her head out the back window. "He's at the airport, Anne."

Forbes shook his head. "His flight for Memphis left fifteen minutes ago."

"You have his itinerary?" She snatched the page out of his hand before he had it fully out of his pocket. She looked at her watch. "His flight to Atlanta leaves in three hours. Memphis is a six-hour drive."

Forbes grabbed her arms. "Anne, there is a way."

Looking into his steel blue eyes, she saw the answer and started shaking her head. "I can't."

"How much do you love him?" His gaze bored into hers.

Her heart raced; her stomach churned. With fear's cold fingers choking her, she nodded. "I have to go."

"I'll call Rafe. He can have the jet ready by the time we get you there."

"Is that what you're going to wear?" Meredith slid out through the front passenger window and sat on the frame like the car was the General Lee from *The Dukes of Hazzard*.

"I—no—I don't know."

Forbes squeezed her arms and gently pushed her toward the porch steps. "I'll call Rafe while you put on a clean shirt and real shoes."

In less than five minutes, Anne was ready to face a fear even bigger than falling in love.

The last remaining Guidry company jet gleamed in the sun like a sparkling coffin. She was going to plummet to her death. She touched the scar on the side of her neck, the reminder of the last time she'd been on a plane.

George. She had to get to George. If he left, she might never see him again. Swallowing hard, she put her foot on the first step. Then the second. Too soon, she was hunched over, walking into the living room–like seating area.

Forbes sat on the sofa beside her and tightened her seat belt. "Do you want me to come with you?"

She shook her head. "Just tell Rafe to get this flying death trap off the ground before I change my mind."

He kissed her forehead, said a prayer for her safety, and departed.

Rafe came back and prayed with her, too, then returned to the cockpit.

She didn't stop sobbing until the plane had been in the air nearly twenty minutes. With all the window blinds closed, she could pretend she was riding in the back of the RV Errol and Maggie had rented that time they took a family trip out to the Grand Canyon. She'd just started to relax when Rafe's voice came over the intercom to say they were about to land in Memphis.

She pulled her makeup compact out of her purse. There was nothing for it. Her eyes were red and puffy, her nose, too.

Throughout the landing, she gripped the edge of the seat and prayed that if God wanted her to come home, He'd let her die upon impact. Then the wheels touched the tarmac, and the small jet coasted into the private plane section of the Memphis airport.

She nearly cried again when she saw the length of the line at the ticket counter. She kept checking her watch. Thirty minutes. Twenty. Fifteen.

Finally, with ten minutes to spare, she got to the front of the line. "I need you to page a passenger who's on this flight." She handed the woman George's itinerary.

The woman looked down at her computer screen and handed the paper back to Anne. "I'm sorry, ma'am, that flight has already boarded and pushed away from the gate. There's no way to page him."

No. So close. She'd survived the flight here. She couldn't lose him now.

"What's thc next available flight to Atlanta?" Rafe asked, grasping Anne by the arm when she wavered, nausea nearly overwhelming her at the thought of boarding another plane.

"We have one that leaves in about thirty minutes. But it'll take that long to get through security, and if you have any luggage—"

"No luggage." He slapped his corporate credit card down on the counter. "Get her on that flight. First class."

Boarding pass in hand, Anne ran behind Rafe through the airport to the security gate. Only a few people milled about in front of her.

"Take your shoes off and put them in the bucket. Put everything in the bucket—cell phone, too."

She did as told, numb with fear. This time, the fear wasn't of flying. She was afraid she'd lost her only chance at happiness. If she couldn't find him in the Atlanta airport. . .

On the other side of the security gate, she waved at Rafe, slipped her shoes back on, then jogged down the corridor to the appropriate gate. At the desk, the airline employee told her to go ahead and board, as she was one of the last to arrive. She handed the boarding pass to the ticket taker and walked down the long, hollow-sounding hallway. She paused at the gaping door at the end, looking like a mouth ready to devour her, like the great fish in the book of Jonah.

She sank into the plush seat and secured her seat belt.

God, please let me find him. I have to ask him to forgive me, to come home with me.

What was taking so long for the plane to take off?

They shut the door, and the plane rolled away from the building. Then they sat.

Panic rose in her throat with each minute that passed. He had a two-hour layover in Atlanta. But she was already an hour behind him. And she'd heard the Atlanta airport was huge.

Twenty minutes later, the captain came over the intercom, apologized for the delay, and told his staff to prepare for takeoff.

Please let him still be there. Please let me find him.

An hour and ten minutes later, she rushed up the Jetway into the bustling metropolis known as an airport. She stopped at the check-in desk and thrust George's itinerary at the airline worker.

"Can you tell me where this flight takes off from?"

"That's an international flight." The woman clicked a couple of color-coded keys at her computer. "That flight leaves from E-11."

"Where am I now?"

"A-20. If you're trying to catch that flight, you'll never make it. Shows here they're already boarding."

"Can I have a passenger from that flight paged to come back here?"

"We can try. But if he's already boarded, they're not going to let him off the plane, or he can't get back on."

"Okay. Page him, please."

The woman dialed the other gate to have George paged. Anne paced. Other people came to the gate to check in for a flight to Nashville.

Where was he? Which direction would he be coming from?

Ten minutes passed. Twenty. Thirty. Past time for his flight to leave. She returned to the counter. "Did they page him?"

"That flight's already left, ma'am. The gate agent said no one got off the plane."

Anne fought tears. He hadn't gotten off the plane. "Okay. Thanks. How can I purchase a ticket to go home?"

After going through an embarrassing search as she came back through security, Anne found her departure gate and sat facing the windows, watching the planes come and go. He hadn't gotten off the plane.

Music wafted from a nearby karaoke bar. She grinned ruefully. Dean Martin. Her favorite.

Wait a minute! The man singing "Return to Me" sounded just like Dean—

She shot out of her seat and whirled, looking for the source of the music. An Asian man stood at the microphone crooning the sad ballad.

She felt someone stop behind her. Warm breath tickled her ear as someone whispered the heart-touching lyrics of the song, entreating the man's beloved to return, to forgive, to say she belongs to him. . . .

Closing her eyes, she turned, not wanting to see if it wasn't really him.

Warm, strong fingers cupped her chin. She opened her eyes, and tears escaped down her cheeks. George's warm chocolate gaze melted her lingering fear.

"I'm sorry," he whispered. "You can't know how sorry."

She touched his face, just to make sure he really stood there in front of her. Real tears dampened his real face. A sob caught in her throat as he pulled her into his arms. "They said you didn't get off the plane."

"What?"

"When I had them page you earlier. They said no one got off the plane. I thought you were on your way to Paris because you didn't want to see me."

His chuckle vibrated in his chest. "Did you ask them to see if

I checked in for that flight?"

"No." She gulped for air. "How did you find me, then?"

"I got here and realized I couldn't leave. I went downstairs and bought the first available ticket back to Bonneterre—this flight." He held her at arm's length. "How did you get here?"

"Rafe took me to Memphis on the company plane. I hoped to catch you there, but your flight had already left."

"You got on a Learjet and a commercial airliner just to come after me?" Emotion thickened his voice.

She nodded, drinking in the sight of him. She never wanted to be away from him ever again, ever, ever.

"You got on a *plane*—no, on *two* planes to come after me?"

Laughter bubbled up through her tears. "Yeah. Two planes." She held up two fingers.

He kissed her, his tenderness fulfilling her every dream. "Two planes."

"I had to see you." She touched his hair. He was grayer now than he'd been when she first met him. "I have a question I wanted to ask you."

He smiled and pulled her out of the path of onlookers. She hadn't meant to make a spectacle. She took his proffered handkerchief and dried her tears.

"What question did you want to ask me?"

My, my, but he was smug. "Well, I feel like we have a lot in common, and we obviously work well together." She grinned. "What I wanted to ask is: Would you consider joining me as an equal partner in Happy Endings, Inc.?"

Smugness deflated into speechless disappointment.

Oh, she couldn't resist. "I know you'll have to figure things out legally with your work visa and all."

He cleared his throat. "I—well, that is to say. . . "

She pressed one finger to his lips. "Of course, I've decided I cannot take on any business partner but my husband. So if you still want to work with me, I guess you'll just have to marry me."

He laughed and pulled her close, caressing the back of her head. "I think that's the best business proposition I've ever heard."

The touch of his lips on hers sent blue sparks through her body. "I love you," she whispered. "Always, always, always."

He traced the curve of her jaw with his forefinger, kissed the bridge of her nose, and tucked her back into his arms. "Now that's what I call a happy ending."

Discussion Questions

1. Anne Hawthorne is a single woman who helps other people get married. Have you ever been in a situation where you've had to do something for or give something to someone else that you really want for yourself but can't have? Read Philippians 4:11–12 and Hebrews 13:5–6 and discuss what it means to "be content with what you have."

2. When we first meet George Laurence, he is signing an agreement to pretend to be something he is not—to be dishonest with others around him. Have you ever been asked to be dishonest by your employer or someone in a position of authority over you? How did you handle the situation? How do you think George should have handled it? What could he have learned from the story of Jacob and Esau before getting himself into this situation (Genesis 27:1–42)?

3. Many of the Psalms mention fear and how God is greater than our fears, and in 1 John 4:18, we read that there is no fear in love. But some people, like Anne, live with fears and phobias that can be debilitating. Discuss how the idea that there is no fear in love helped Anne face her fear of flying and how love can help us face fears in our own lives.

4. What does it mean to hold a grudge? How did the grudge that Anne held against her ex-fiancé affect her life? Have you ever held a grudge against someone? Who did it hurt more—you or the person you held it against? How does Matthew 6:15 apply to holding grudges?

5. Anne's cousin Forbes Guidry decided to keep information from Anne that affected Anne's and George's lives in this story. Have you ever been tempted to try to keep information from

loved ones because you think it might hurt them? Have you ever had someone do that to you? How did you feel when you discovered the truth?

6. Mama Ketty quotes Isaiah 30:5: "For thus the Lord God, the Holy One of Israel, has said, 'In repentance and rest you shall be saved, in quietness and trust is your strength'" (NASB). She then tells George, "Until you find peace with God, you ain't gonna have happiness with yourself nor no one else around you." Do you agree with Mama Ketty? What does the verse mean when it says, "in repentance and rest you shall be saved"?

7. In Chapter 19, when Anne and Forbes argue about Anne letting a client take money for a new wedding dress out of Anne's fee, Anne tells Forbes that by doing this, she has shown the client Christ's love. What do you think Anne meant by this? Has anyone ever done something like that for you?

8. Even though his contract specified complete confidentiality, should George have found a way to tell Anne about Cliff Ballantine before Cliff showed up at the site of the engagement party? Was Anne justified in being angry with George over keeping Cliff's identity secret?

9. In Chapter 24, Meredith tells Anne that before Anne can move forward in her relationship with George—in order to have a happy life together—Anne needs to forgive her parents and God. Why did Anne need to forgive her parents? Why was she still carrying anger at God for their deaths? Have you ever been angry at someone for dying? Have you ever been angry at God for taking a loved one from you?

10. When Anne overhears George's phone conversation at the reception, she jumps to the conclusion that he has once again been dishonest with her—just like she thought her ex-fiancé had been. What would have been a better way to handle the situation? Have you ever assumed someone was untrustworthy based on your past experiences then found out later they deserved your trust all along? Have you ever made a decision based on a misunderstanding and come to regret it later? What did you learn from those situations?

Menu for Romance

Dedication:

To the real-life Corie, Lori, and Pam—wonderful sisters-of-the-heart who're always there for me.

Acknowledgments:

This book wouldn't be here if it weren't for my brilliant agent, Chip MacGregor, and my incomparable editor, Rebecca Germany. My sincerest thanks to both of you for believing in me. Most sincere thanks go to my copyeditor, Becky Fish. Thanks for everything you do! As always, my deepest gratitude goes to my family who are my biggest supporters and greatest fans. And greatest of all, praises to God for granting me the desire of my heart: the opportunity to stay home and write.

CHAPTER 1

"Happy New Year!"

Her thirty-fourth New Year and still no kiss at the stroke of midnight. . .or any other day or time. Meredith Guidry stood in the doorway leading into Vue de Ciel—the cavernous, sky-view event venue at the top of the tallest building in downtown Bonneterre, Louisiana—and swallowed back her longing as she watched hundreds of couples kiss.

A short burst of static over the earpiece startled her out of her regrets.

"Mere, we're going to set up the coffee stations and dessert tables." The executive chef's rich, mellow voice filled her ear.

She clicked the button on the side of the wireless headset. "Thanks, Major." Turning her gaze back to the main room, she tapped the button again. "Let's slowly start bringing the houselights back up. I want us at full illumination around twelve thirty." She strolled into the ballroom, the floor now covered with shiny metallic confetti, the hundreds of guests milling about wishing each other a happy New Year. Out on the dance floor, a large group of men stood swaying, arms about shoulders, singing "Auld Lang Syne" at the top of their lungs, accompanied by the jazz band.

"Let's make sure tables are bussed." Pressing her finger to the earpiece to speak over the network made her feel like those secret service agents in the movies who were always talking into their shirt cuffs. "I'm seeing several tables with empty plates and glasses."

She kept to the perimeter of the room, doing her best to blend in with the starlit sky beyond the glass walls, barely repressing the feeling of being the loner, the schoolgirl no one else paid any attention to... the woman no man ever gave a second glance.

"You look like a kid staring through a candy store window, wishing you could go inside."

Meredith's heart thumped at the sudden voice behind her. She turned. Major O'Hara grinned his lopsided grin, his chef's coat nearly fluorescent with its pristine whiteness.

"How're you holding up?" He squeezed her shoulder in a brotherly way, his indigo eyes gentle.

She sighed. "You know me—I operate on pure adrenaline at these things no matter how little sleep I've gotten the night before. So long as I stay busy and don't slow down, the fatigue can't catch up with me."

"And stopping to grab a bite to eat would have meant slowing down?"

"Yep."

Coldness embraced her shoulder when Major lifted his hand away. "I set aside a few take-home boxes for you—and Anne. I told her I'd be sure to save a little of everything."

Anne. Meredith's cousin and best friend. Her inspiration and mentor. Owner of a stellarly successful wedding- and event-planning business, Happy Endings, Inc. And friends with Major O'Hara on a level Meredith could never attain.

"If you see George, tell him I've been experimenting with that plum pudding recipe he gave me. I'll need his expert opinion before I can officially add it to my repertoire."

"I'll tell him—but you see him more often than I do."

"Yeah, I guess so. I'm glad we convinced Anne to fall in love with him. Finally, having another man's opinion when we're all working an event together." He winked.

Meredith quickly turned her eyes toward the milling crowd so he wouldn't see how he affected her. It would only embarrass him—and mortify her.

He tweaked her chin. "Come on. Back to work for the bosses."

Over the next hour, Meredith poured herself into her work to try to keep exhaustion at bay. The last few guests meandered out just after one thirty. Meredith turned on all of the lights, their glare on the glass walls and ceiling nearly blinding her. She tasked her staff to stack chairs, pull linen from tables, and clear the room.

She directed the sorting of the rented decorations and materials into different dump sites around the room. Early Tuesday morning she would meet all of the vendors here to have their stuff carted away so the building maintenance staff could get in for a final cleaning before resetting the room for lunch service.

"Miss Guidry, are these your shoes?" Halfway across the room, one of the black-and-white-clad workers held aloft a pair of strappy, spike-heeled sandals. Meredith's medium-height, pointy-toed brown pumps rubbed her feet in a couple of places after six hours—but nothing like the pain those sandals would have caused.

"Lost and found," she called over the music throbbing through the room's built-in PA system. Not what she would choose to listen to, but it kept the staff—mostly college students—happy and working at a brisk clip. That made three pairs and two stray shoes, five purses, sixteen cellular phones, and one very gaudy ruby ring—and those were only the items Meredith had seen herself. Her assistant would be fielding phone calls for days.

Vacuum cleaners roared to life—a wonderful sound, as it meant they were getting close to quitting time. A couple of guys loaded the last of the large round tables onto a cart and wheeled it down the hall to the freight elevator, followed by several more pushing tall stacks of dark blue upholstered chairs on hand trucks.

Vue de Ciel expanded in all directions around her. She hugged her arms around her middle. She'd survived another New Year's

Eve Masked Ball—and the eight hundred guests seemed to have enjoyed themselves immensely. Hopefully her parents would deem it a success.

The soprano of flatware, alto of china, tenor of voices, and bass rumble of the dish sterilizers created a jubilant symphony that thrilled Major O'Hara's heart.

Simply from the questions the food-and-wine columnist from the *Reserve* had asked, the review in the morning newspaper wouldn't be good. It would be glowing.

"Chef, stations are clean, ready for inspection." Steven LeBlanc, sous chef, wiped his hands on the towel draped over his shoulder. Though Steven's white Nichols State University T-shirt was sweat-soaked—much like Major's own University of Louisiana–Bonneterre tribute—the kid's blond hair still stood stiff and tall in mini spikes all over his head.

Major hadn't yet been able to find anything that would keep his own hair from going curly and flopping down onto his forehead in the heat and humidity of a working kitchen. Yet asking Steven for hair-styling tips—Major grunted. He'd rather slice his hand open and stick it in a vat of lemon juice.

He followed Steven through the kitchen, inspecting each surface and utensil, releasing some of the staff to clock out, pointing out spots missed to others.

"Civilian in the kitchen," rang out from one of the line cooks.

Meredith, stately and graceful, light hair set off to perfection by her brown velvet dress—like strawberries served with chocolate ganache—swept into the kitchen, drawing the attention of every man present. If she knew she had that effect on his crew, she would laugh her head off and call them all nuts.

"I'm ready to release my staff, unless you need any help in here." Meredith came over and leaned against the stainless-steel counter beside him. She even smelled vaguely of strawberries and chocolate—

or maybe that was just his imagination.

He cleared his throat. "I think we've got it covered."

"Dish-washing station cleared, Chef!"

"See?" He grinned at her.

She graced him with a full smile then covered her mouth as a yawn overwhelmed her. "I'll let my guys go, then." She pressed her hands to the base of her neck and rolled her head side to side. "I've got to run down to my office to get my stuff."

"Why don't I meet you at your office, since I have to come downstairs anyway?"

"Don't be ridiculous. I'll be fine—"

"Mere. Stop. I will come to your office to walk you to your car. You're lucky I'm not insisting on driving you home myself."

Her nutmeg eyes flickered as if she were about to argue; then her smile returned. "Thank you, Major. I'd appreciate that."

Good girl. "That wasn't too hard, was it?" He limited himself to once again laying his hand on her shoulder instead of pulling her into a hug. "Go on. I'll make sure all the rest get clocked out and then shut everything down for the night."

Meredith nodded and departed. Major rounded up the last few stragglers and watched them run their cards through the computerized time clock. Returning their "Happy New Year" wishes, he ducked into his office at the rear of the kitchen, grabbed his dry-cleaning bag along with his duffel, turned off his computer and light, and locked the door.

The brass nameplate winked in the bright kitchen light. Major O'Hara, Executive Chef. He grimaced. What pride he'd taken eight years ago when Mr. Guidry had offered him the position—saving Major years of working his way up the chain of command in restaurants.

He heaved the two bags over his shoulder. Meredith's parents had been better to him than he deserved, had given him the flexibility in his schedule to take care of family matters no other employer would have given. They had also given him their blessing—their encouragement—to strike out on his own, to open the restaurant he'd dreamed of since working for Meredith's aunt in her catering company throughout high school and college. The restaurant he'd already have if it weren't for his mother.

Major shut down the houselights, guilt nipping at his heels. Ma couldn't help the way she was. The mirrored elevator doors whispered shut, and he turned to stare out the glass wall overlooking downtown Bonneterre from twenty-three floors above.

His descent slowed then stopped. The doors slid open with a chime announcing his arrival on the fifth floor. Before he could turn completely around, Meredith stepped into the elevator.

"How long were you standing in the hall waiting for one of these doors to open?"

Meredith busied herself with pushing the button for the basement parking garage. "Not long."

"*Not long*," he imitated the super-high pitch of her voice. "You've never been a good liar, Mere."

"Fine." She blew a loose wisp of hair out of her eyes. "I was out there a couple of minutes. I didn't want you to have to wait for me. Happy?"

"Not in the least. But I appreciate your honesty." Due to the tenseness around her mouth, he changed the subject. "Your mom invited me to drop by their New Year's open house. You going?"

Meredith shook her head. "No." The simple answer held a magnitude of surprise.

"She said she had something she wanted to talk to me about."

The porcelain skin between Meredith's brows pinched. "Hmm. No—I don't usually go over for the open house, just for our family dinner later. Instead, I'm fixing to go home, sleep for a few hours, and then head over to the new house. I'm planning to get the paint stripped from all the woodwork in the living room and dining room tomorrow."

"In one day?" Major grunted. Meredith's *new* house was anything but: a one-hundred-year-old craftsman bungalow everyone had tried to talk her out of buying. "Wouldn't you rather relax on your holiday?"

"But working on the house is relaxing to me. Plus, it gives me a good excuse to go off by myself all day and be assured no one's going to disturb me."

The elevator doors opened to the dim, chilly underground parking garage. Major took hold of Meredith's arm and stopped her from exiting first. He stepped out, looked around, saw nothing out of the ordinary, then turned and nodded to her. "Looks safe."

"Of course it's safe. You lived in New York too long." She walked out past him.

"Meredith, Bonneterre isn't the little town we grew up in anymore. Even before Hurricane Katrina, it was booming." He stopped her again, planted his hands on her shoulders, and turned her to face him. "Please don't ever take your safety for granted. Not even here in the garage with security guards on duty. If anything happened to you. . ."

Meredith blushed bright red and dropped her gaze.

"Look, I don't mean to alarm you. But in this day and age, anything could happen." He kept hold of her a moment longer, then let go and readjusted the straps of the bags on his shoulder.

Meredith released a shaky breath. "So, what are you going to do on your day off?"

"Watch football." He winked at her over his shoulder as he approached her Volvo SUV. The tinted windows blocked him from seeing inside. Perhaps he had lived in New York too long. But Bonneterre had changed even in the eight years he'd been back. Crime rates had risen along with the population. And he would have done this for any other lady of his acquaintance, wouldn't he?

He heard the lock click and opened the driver's-side door for her—taking a quick peek inside just to make sure that the boogey man wasn't hiding in the backseat.

"Oh, honestly!" Meredith playfully pushed him out of the way and, shaking her head, opened the back door and heaved her large, overstuffed briefcase onto the seat.

Major moved out of the way for her to get in. "Drive safely, okay?"

"I always do."

"Call me when you get home. Nuh-uh. No arguments. If you don't want to call, just text message me—all right?—once you're in your apartment with the door locked."

"Hey, who died and made you my keeper?" Meredith laughed.

He didn't let his serious expression crack. "Just call me safety obsessed."

"Okay, Major Safety Obsessed." She leaned into his one-armed hug then settled into the driver's seat. "Thank you for your concern. I will text you as soon as I arrive safely home, am safely in my house, with my door safely locked."

He closed the car door and waved before walking over to Kirby, his beaten-up old Jeep, a few spaces down. As he figured, Meredith waited to back out until he was in with the engine started. He followed her out of downtown and waved again as they parted ways on North Street.

A few fireworks flickered in the distance against the low-hanging clouds. He turned the radio on and tuned it to the southern gospel station. Always keyed-up after events, he sang the high-tenor part along with the Imperials. Though it had taken him a while to build the upper range of his voice—having always sung baritone and bass before—when he, George Laurence, Forbes Guidry, and Clay Huntoon started their own quartet, Major had been the only one who could even begin to reach some of the high notes. Sometimes it was still a strain, but he practiced by singing along with the radio as loudly as he could to keep his voice conditioned.

When he pulled into the condo complex parking lot, his cell phone chimed the new text message alert. He shook his head. Of course she texted instead of calling. He pulled the phone out of the holster clipped to his belt and flipped it open to read the message:

> *Safely home. : -)*
> *happy new year*
> *Mere*

While Kirby's engine choked itself off, Major typed out a return message:

Home too
Sweet dreams
MO'H

The phone flashed a confirmation that the message was sent, and he holstered it. Grabbing his black duffel from the back, he left the orange dry-cleaning bag to drop off at the cleaners Tuesday.

To blow off some steam and try to relax enough to fall asleep, he turned on the computer and played a few rounds of Spider Solitaire. About an hour later, his whole body aching, eyes watering from yawning every other minute, he grabbed a shower before turning in. At thirty-eight years old, he shouldn't feel this out of shape—of course, if he still made time to go to the gym every day and didn't enjoy eating his own cooking as much as he did, he probably wouldn't be this out of shape. He weighed as much now as he had playing middle linebacker in college—except twenty years ago, it had all been muscle.

But who trusted a skinny chef anyway?

Thunder grumbled, and rain pattered against the window. Major kicked at the comforter that had become entangled in his legs during the night and rolled over to check the time.

Eight thirty. What a perfect day to don ratty old sweats, sit in the recliner watching football on the plasma TV, and eat junk food.

If he had a plasma TV. Or any junk food in the condo.

Alas, though, he'd promised Mrs. Guidry he would drop by. Best check the schedule of games, see which he cared least about, and make the visit then. He pulled on the ratty old sweats and an equally ratty ULB T-shirt, though. As he passed down the short hallway, he tapped the temperature control on the thermostat up a couple of degrees to knock a little of the chill out of the air.

His stomach growled in concert with the thunder outside. The tile in the kitchen sent shockwaves of cold up his legs. Shifting from foot to foot, he yanked open the dryer door, dug through the clothes in it, and found two somewhat matching socks. Sometimes having the laundry hookups here did come in handy, even though they took up more than a third of the space in the small galley kitchen.

The fridge beckoned. Not much there—maybe he should hit the grocery store on the way back from the Guidrys' open house.

Half an hour later, with the Rose Bowl Parade providing ambiance, he sank into his recliner and dug into an andouille, shrimp, potato, mushroom, red pepper, onion, jack cheese, and bacon omelet spread with Creole mustard on top.

Maybe he should consider making a New Year's resolution to cut back on calories this year. What was missing? Oh yeah, the grits. He'd left the bowl sitting by the stove.

Halfway to the kitchen to retrieve the rest of his breakfast, the phone rang. He unplugged it from the charger as he passed by.

"Hello?"

"Mr. O'Hara, this is Nick Sevellier at Beausoleil Pointe Center."

Major stopped. So did his heart.

"I'm sorry to bother you on a holiday, sir, but your mother has had an episode. She's asking for you."

Chapter 2

Meredith poured herself another mug of coffee. The machine might have cost only twenty dollars, but it sure did keep the liquid hot. Careful not to jiggle the tray table when she replaced the carafe, she blew through the steam rising from the cup and turned to survey her house.

She thrilled at the thought: *her* house. She owned it. She'd dreamed of owning a craftsman bungalow ever since she could remember. Now that Anne and George were getting married, they wanted to convert the three-story Victorian from apartments—where Meredith, Anne, and Meredith's sister Jenn lived—back to a single-family home. Ready to get out of such close proximity to anyone—even family—Meredith decided to buy a house. She hadn't been looking a week when she found this one.

From the outside, she'd been afraid she wouldn't be able to afford it—the previous owner had restored the exterior and landscaped the front yard to complement it. Inside was a totally different story.

Meredith sipped her coffee and leaned against the door frame between the dining room and kitchen. Pipes stuck out of the wall where the sink should have been. A few remnants of cabinets hung from the walls, and the plywood subfloor moaned and bowed whenever she walked across it.

Her parents had tried to talk her out of it. The previous owner had gone into foreclosure trying to restore the house for resale. But Meredith didn't mind the gutted kitchen, nor the bare bulbs swinging from wires in every room. She'd be able to fix up the inside exactly how she wanted.

But not if she just stood around looking at it.

Jazz music echoed through the house from the radio. The two large space heaters worked overtime to chase away the damp chill of New Year's Day. Meredith slipped on her safety goggles and mask, opened the can of paint stripper, and started on the built-in bookcase in the living room. Between the music and the vision of what the house would eventually look like, she lost herself in the project.

She'd just started the fourth shelf when her phone's earpiece beeped. She grabbed it from the mantel and stuck it in her ear. "Hello?"

"Hey, it's Anne." Her cousin yawned. "Sorry. What time did you get in last night? I never even heard you drive up."

"After two o'clock."

"And you're already out and about?"

"You know how it is when days off are few and far between."

"Ah. You're at the new house."

"Right you are, my dear."

Anne yawned again. "It's not even nine yet. Did you sleep at all?"

"A few hours." Meredith continued stripping the absolutely gross, moss-colored paint from the original, hand-detailed woodwork beneath.

"It can't be healthy for you to get only five or six hours of sleep a night."

Meredith let out a derisive snort. "And I'm hearing this from the woman who doesn't sleep at all during wedding season?"

The thunder outside nearly drowned out Anne's chuckle. "Point taken. Anyway, that's not why I called. I'm looking at the Style section of the newspaper. Looks like you really outdid yourself last night."

Tingles of trepidation and pride danced up and down Meredith's skin. "The article is good?"

"Article? Try the whole section! Looks like the writers had the time of their lives. All of the quotes from guests are glowing. And the food reviewer couldn't find enough adjectives to describe Major's food."

"Good. Mom and Dad will be happy." Meredith released her breath and rolled her head to try to ease the tension in her neck.

"Of course they will. Their oldest daughter is the best event planner in town."

"Second best."

"Oh no," Anne disagreed. "I left Boudreaux-Guidry because all those huge events daunted me. I'd never have been able to pull off a party like that."

"Oh, spare me. You did last summer—or have you already forgotten the wedding and reception you put together for the most popular movie star in the country?"

"But you and Major really helped me out with that. Take the compliment, Meredith. I wouldn't say it if I didn't mean it."

Why did Anne's praise make Meredith feel like a complete fraud? "Well, thanks, I guess."

"You're welcome. I'll leave the paper on your kitchen table before I go."

"Wedding today?" Meredith started on the fifth shelf.

"Yeah. And I'd better get a move on."

"Okay—oh, Major sent some leftovers home for you and George. They're in my fridge. I wrote your name on them so they wouldn't get mixed in with all the other boxes I have in there."

"I'll get them. Thanks. And thank Major for me, too."

Meredith put the earpiece back on the mantel. She tried not to imagine what Anne would think of the interior of the fridge. Hardly a day passed when Meredith didn't bring home at least one Styrofoam box filled with a more-than-ample serving of the lunch entrée from Vue de Ceil.

She knelt to work on the cabinets below the open shelves. Until now she hadn't thought about missing her afternoon visit from Major. He'd started bringing her a box of lunch-service leftovers every day about a year ago—after she accidentally confessed to almost always eating out because she hated to cook. Every day around three o'clock, her pulse quickened, and she had to stop herself from rushing to the restroom to reapply her lipstick, fix her hair, and make sure she looked her best for him.

Heart racing as it did whenever she expected his appearance, she sank back onto her heels. She had to get over this. Eight years was way too long to carry a torch for someone who'd shown no indication he had any interest in her other than friendship.

Her earpiece beeped again. She took a deep breath to try to settle her emotions then stood to retrieve the phone. "Hello?"

"Hey, it's me." Her older brother's voice filled her ear.

"Hey, Forbes."

"I didn't wake you, did I?"

"Nope—I've been at the new house for a while. You and the boys having fun at the lake?" Her brothers always spent New Year's Eve at their family's lake house on Larto Lake.

"Yep, though it's been really wet and cold. But the fish are biting, which makes it all worthwhile. We'll be headed back to town around noon, and then we'll go over to watch football with Dad."

Watching football with her father and four brothers was something that Meredith usually dropped everything to do. "Aw, that sounds like fun."

"But not as fun as whatever construction project you're doing today?" The tone of amusement in Forbes's voice came across as almost patronizing. Along with their parents, Forbes had been very vocal in his disapproval of Meredith's purchase of the house.

"Exactly. I'll miss y'all, but this is where I want to be." *So please don't make a fuss and try to convince me to come over.*

"Okay. Well, if you decide to knock off early, there might be an inch of sofa for you."

"I'll keep that in mind."

"You are planning on coming over for family dinner tonight, right?" Forbes asked.

"Of course. Why?"

"I just wanted to make sure. Um. . .there might be a non–family member there tonight as well."

"Is Marci's boyfriend coming?"

Her brother paused a little longer than necessary.

"Oh, Forbes!" She groaned. "Please tell me he isn't going to propose to her in front of the whole family."

"He'll be okay."

"It's not *him* I'm worried about. Marci came to me a couple of weeks ago, worried about whether or not he's the right one for her. If he does this in front of all of us, she's going to feel obligated to say yes, just so she doesn't disappoint us or hurt him."

"You're not giving her enough credit, Mere. Or him. I've talked to Shaun at length. He really does love Marci and will provide her with a good life."

"You've talked. . . Did you talk him into doing it this way?"

"No." A little sharpness crept into Forbes's voice. "Look. I realize you still haven't forgiven me for what you think was my interference with Anne and George's relationship—"

"Forbes, you told George to lie to her—not once, but twice. She was so angry with him she almost let him walk away forever."

"Whatever happened last summer is between them and me." Forbes's voice strained with forced softness. "Besides, I don't really think you're upset with me."

Meredith's annoyance started turning to anger. "Are you a psychologist now? Is that something they taught you in law school?"

"Whoa there, girl! I'm not trying to psychoanalyze you. I just wonder if the idea of a sister who's ten years younger than you getting married first is the main issue."

"You don't seem to have a problem with it. She's only twenty-four!" Meredith slammed the scraper on the floor and paced the living room. "She isn't finished with her bachelor's degree yet. How can she be thinking about getting married when she can't even commit to a major?"

"Uh-huh."

Frustration, disappointed hopes, self-recrimination for her still-single status wrapped around her chest in tight bands, cutting off her air. Her head spun for a moment. She hadn't wanted to admit it, but she could no longer deny the fact that there was something wrong with her. Why else would she still be single at thirty-four?

She took a deep breath and tried to gather up the shattered pieces of her emotions, then let out a bitter laugh. "I guess I should thank you for the forewarning. Now I won't have a meltdown like this tonight."

"You're welcome." Forbes spoke with a gentle laugh.

"I'll get home in time to make sure Jenn is ready to go at six."

"Great. I'm going to let you go then."

"I'm sorry I yelled at you."

"I'm sorry I deliberately provoked you."

In spite of the remaining tightness in her chest, Meredith smiled. "Yeah, well, I guess I can forgive you. I love you."

"I love you, too, Sis."

When the call ended, she tossed the earpiece back onto the mantel, wishing she hadn't answered—but also grateful she knew what was coming. She grabbed her coat and trudged out to the back porch, where she sank onto the wet top step, the rain having momentarily paused. The old cypress boards sagged, just like her spirits.

"Lord, what's wrong with me?" She glared up at the dark clouds. "Why is it that a twenty-four-year-old without a clue can find a man who'll love her, and I haven't been able to get a guy to take me out on a date even once in my life? Why is it that the two men I've fallen in love with haven't even noticed?"

Wrapping her arms around her legs, she rested her forehead on her knees. "It's not fair. I've been asking You ever since I turned fifteen for a boyfriend—for a husband ever since I turned twenty. What have I done so wrong that You've kept that from me?"

A large raindrop plastered hair to the top of her head. The cold water running down her neck made her feel even worse, adding insult to injury. She scooted back up the porch to lean against the house wall and pulled her coat closer. Driving rain sliced the air, eliminating her view of the tree-lined fence at the back of her half-acre lot. The squeaky moan of the floorboards did nothing to help her mood—one more thing that needed to be fixed.

She was just like this house. The part the world saw was complete, pulled together, polished; but inside, everything was a mess. The difference was that she could fix the house.

Lightning streaked, followed by booming thunder, the sky nearly black, water forming in vast pools in low-lying places in the yard. The porch boards moaned—no, that wasn't possible. She wasn't moving. Something else was making the noise.

The pounding rain nearly deafened her. She leaned over and pressed her ear to the crack between two floorboards.

Was that something whimpering? She crawled to the edge of the porch and leaned over, her head and shoulders instantly soaked. The trellis that enclosed the area under the porch broke away easily.

With one hand trying to keep her hair out of her eyes, the other sinking into the mud to keep her balance, Meredith hung half off the porch, trying to see under it.

No good—too dark.

She pushed herself up, and not caring about the rivulets of water—and mud—she tracked in, she ran into the dining room. From the bottom drawer of her tool chest, she grabbed the giant flashlight.

Back outside, she once again leaned over the edge of the decking. She flicked on the high-powered beam and swept it slowly from one side to the other—

There. Light reflected in two small eyes. Too big to be a rat, not close enough together to be a possum—or were they? No, the rounded shape of the shivering body was wrong.

Though the edge of the porch dug into her diaphragm, Meredith whistled. "Come 'ere," she called in a high-pitched voice.

The shape moved—Meredith nearly lost her balance in surprise.

"Come on. That's it. I'm not going to hurt you." She ignored the water running up her face, filling her nose, and stinging her eyes but kept offering encouragement until she could finally see the puppy clearly.

A few long moments brought it close enough for her to make a grab for it—Meredith landed shoulders-first flat out on her back in the grass, face fully exposed to the drowning rain. And now she had a cold nose whuffling in her ear.

She grabbed the squatter, mud squishing between her fingers. Numb, soaked, and trembling, she struggled to her feet, puppy clenched firmly before her, and went inside.

"Look at the pair of us! Good thing we've got hot water, huh?" The heavy pup nearly wagged itself out of her grip. In the utility room, she set him down in the deep sink and hosed him off with the sprayer—revealing what looked like a puppy that was mostly black Lab, though his gangly legs, large muzzle, and huge feet indicated he had some other, bigger breed in his blood, too.

The caked mud and dirt gone, fur soaked down smooth, she could see the poor little guy's ribs and hip bones. "I'll bet you're hungry."

The tail thumped against the side of the sink. Meredith grabbed a towel off the stack of old ones she kept there for emergencies and did her best to wrap up the little bundle of energy. She carried him into the living room, dragged a drop cloth over in front of the space heater with her foot, and sat down to towel-dry the dog.

The towel proved too tempting, and the puppy grabbed a corner and started to play tug-of-war with her. After unsuccessfully trying to get him to behave, she finally gave in and just played with him.

Once they'd both stopped shivering, Meredith walked over to the small, dormitory-style fridge in the dining room. She crouched in front of it and, keeping the puppy at bay, pulled out the half loaf of bread. "I don't know if you'd be able to eat roast beef." She pushed the Vue de Ceil box back into the fridge, took out a slice of bread, and put the rest of it away.

After nearly snapping her fingers off the first couple of tries, she finally convinced him to take the bits of bread politely from her fingers. She held him over the utility sink to let him lap water from the faucet, then put him down.

She followed him around as he explored all the rooms in the house. After about twenty minutes, he curled up on the drop cloth in front of the space heater, heaved a huge yawn, and fell asleep.

Meredith shook her head and glanced at the ceiling. "If this is Your idea of a joke, God, I'm not laughing. I asked for a husband, not a dog."

Chapter 3

"I want grandchildren, Major."

Major tucked the blanket around his mother's legs in the recliner. Her private room in the assisted-living facility was as homey as they could make it. "Ma, let's just concentrate on getting you better."

"I am better. My boy's here." She reached over and patted his cheek with her smooth, dry fingers. Though not quite sixty, his mother's hard life showed in her sunken, dark-circled eyes and white hair.

He sank into the chair he'd pulled over beside her recliner. "You're sure there was no episode?"

"That little boy just panicked. He's an intern. He doesn't know anything."

"He said you were pacing the hall and yelling and wouldn't stop when the nurse asked you to return to your room." Major leaned forward, elbows propped on his knees.

"I was bored."

"You were bored."

"It's boring here, if you haven't noticed, son. Everyone who lives here is crazy—there's no one to carry on a conversation with."

No, no, no. She couldn't want to move again. Beausoleil Pointe Center was the only assisted-living center for the psychologically challenged in this part of the state—over the last eight years, she'd lived in every other inpatient facility in the parish that would take psychiatric patients; she'd either demanded to be taken home, or Major had been told by the staff he had to remove her. If it happened again, he'd be forced to look at properties in Shreveport or Baton Rouge, both about two hours away. Which would mean moving. Leaving behind his friends, his job. And his dreams of possibly opening his restaurant this year—or ever—would vanish.

He clenched his fists and pressed them against the tops of his legs. "I thought you liked it here. Every time I come, you're always in the lounge playing Rook or gossiping with the other ladies. Aren't they your friends?"

"Yeah—the crazy ones." She smiled, her blue eyes twinkling. "Crazy—I guess that's me, too, or I wouldn't be here, would I?"

Major shook his head and swallowed hard. "You're not crazy. You're schizophrenic. It's nothing to be ashamed of. You've always done the best you could for me." The words oozed with thick bitterness in his mouth. He hated feeling this way, hated resenting the fact that her illness kept him from pursuing his goals, from making his dreams reality.

"Sometimes I think I am crazy. Sometimes when the meds wear off and the hallucinations creep in. . ." She took hold of his hand. "Maybe I didn't. . .take my pills last night like I should have."

Truth. Finally. "Maybe?"

"I wanted to watch Dick Clark on TV. The meds make me sleepy—they want us all doped up and asleep by eight o'clock. But it was New Year's Eve. I always watch Dick Clark on New Year's Eve. Although some young kid was on with him, and I didn't like him at all. Looked like he was up to something. I think he's trying to take that show away from Mr. Clark."

"Well, Dick Clark is getting awfully old now. He needs help with that show. What did you do with the meds, Ma?"

"But I've *always* watched Dick Clark on New Year's Eve—since Guy Lombardo went off. Talk about a great musician. That Guy

Lombardo was something. Good-lookin', too, before he got so old. Why don't you like Guy Lombardo, Major?"

"I like Guy Lombardo just fine, but he died when I was just a kid. Ma, what did you do with your pills last night?"

"I think Dick Clark may have died a few years ago and was reanimated by scientists in some kind of experiment."

"Ma—what?" Major rubbed his palms up and down his face.

"Well, you know they do it for commercials all the time—Fred Astaire and Frank Sinatra. Natalie Cole did a duet with her reanimated father. And they brought back the popcorn guy, too—that Knickerbocker guy."

"Redenbacher. And they're not reanimated. They just use old footage of them and splice it into the new stuff—Mother, quit trying to throw me off the subject." He paused for a moment to try to take the anger out of his voice. "What did you do with your meds last night?"

"I wanted to watch Dick Clark."

"Yes. I got that part." Inside, Major shouted with frustration.

She held her left hand out in front of her, forefinger and thumb pinched together. "Plop." She opened her fingers. "Dropped them in the commode and flushed them away. Let the fishes go to sleep early on New Year's Eve."

He dropped his head into one hand and rubbed his eyes with the other so hard he saw white dots.

"But then when the nurse came to check on me later and saw I wasn't asleep, she told me that I had to turn the TV off. Well, no one tells me to turn off Guy—Dick—whoever it was. But I wasn't watching that anymore because there was a John Wayne movie on another channel, and I really wanted to watch that. They don't understand about John Wayne here. Can you make sure they understand about John Wayne?"

He raised his head to look at her again. If it had been John Wayne they'd tried to take her away from, her reaction was starting to make more sense. "I'll make sure they understand. What did you do then?"

The papery skin between her barely there eyebrows furrowed. "I went out into the hall to find her supervisor, but then that little boy came and tried to tell me I was disturbing all the other patients. I told him they were all so doped up that none of them would hear me."

"What little boy?"

"That Nick kid. He says he's a doctor, but he can't be old enough to shave yet. Not like my Major." She patted the top of his head.

"Ma, you can't do this anymore. If you don't take your meds on your own, you know what's going to happen, don't you?"

Her thin lips twisted into a grimace. "They'll start observing me while I take them. Danny, I don't want them to do that."

His stomach lurched. She hadn't called him Danny in years. Not since just before the first time she set fire to their apartment when he was in high school.

"Why aren't you home watching football? Isn't that what you usually do on New Year's?"

"Yeah, Ma. I'm here because they called me to say you had an episode, remember?" He rubbed his forehead, a headache coming on like an iron rod being shoved through his temples.

"Well I didn't. And I'm not going to. I took my meds like a good girl this morning. So, get. I know you worked hard all weekend. And I've got a date in a little while, anyway."

Major snapped his head up. "A *date*?"

She grinned. "Gotcha. The girls and I are going down to the kitchen to watch that new young cook fix our dinner—he's almost as cute as you, hon. He told us he might let us help."

"No handling anything hot."

"I'm not a child, Major Daniel Xavier Kirby O'Hara."

Major allowed himself a measure of relief. She hadn't been able to remember his full name in a while—at least not with all the names in order—so she must be doing okay. "No, but the last time you were in a kitchen and paying more attention to the cute cook. . ."

"You drove me to distraction with everything you were telling me to do. I forgot the burner was turned on. But it's healed okay." She held her left hand out, palm up.

He took hold of her fingertips and pulled her hand forward to kiss the burn scar. "Try not to forget this time, please? I don't want to have to leave my football game in the middle to rush back out here because you've set your hair on fire, okay?"

She leaned forward and gripped his cheeks between her thumb and forefinger, pushing his lips into a pucker. "Don't give me ideas. Now, get out of here." She kissed him. "Go live your life."

"Do you want me to put a movie on for you before I go?" he asked through her pinch.

She released his face. "Yeah. *Flying Leathernecks*—no, *Fort Apache*—no, wait. . .*North to Alaska*."

He knelt by the small TV stand, hand hovering over the DVDs. "Are you sure? *North to Alaska*?"

"Yes, definitely. *North to Alaska*. That's what was on last night that they wouldn't let me watch."

He put the disc in, stood, and headed for the door. She was better at handling the remotes than he was. "I'll see you Wednesday night."

"Are you ever going to find a girlfriend and bring her out here to meet me? I want grandchildren."

Major leaned his head back and started to smack the door frame, then stopped himself and slowly lowered his palm to press against it. "We're not having this discussion again today."

His stomach roiled. He couldn't tell his mother he was in love with someone, because he couldn't bring himself to tell the object of his affection about his mother and her condition. That was a burden no one would choose to bear and something he wouldn't wish on his worst enemy.

"You're thirty-eight, son. It's time for you to find a girl and marry her. But bring her here before you propose. I want to tell you if I like her or not."

Weary to his soul, Major leaned his forehead against the back of his hand. "Yes, Ma."

The intro music for the movie started playing. "You're still here," she singsonged.

He straightened. "I'm going. I love you."

"I know. Me, too."

He closed the door of his mother's room and made his way down the wood-floored hall to the nurse's station that looked more like a concierge desk at a five-star hotel in Manhattan. "I need to speak with. . ." He pulled the crumpled envelope out of his pocket and smoothed it. "I need to see Nick Sevellier."

"Yes, Mr. O'Hara. I'll page him."

Major crossed to the common room, where he had a clear line of sight to the desk, and sank onto one of the plush sofas. He slouched down, leaned his head back against the cushion, and covered his eyes with his right hand. This was definitely not how he'd expected to spend the morning.

"Mr. O'Hara?"

He uncovered his eyes and stood. Ma had been right—the young man in front of him couldn't be old enough to be responsible for patient care, could he? Aside from the fact the kid wasn't even as tall as Meredith—and she must be about five-seven—the wire-rim glasses he wore did nothing to add maturity to his baby face.

"Yes. I'm Major O'Hara."

"Sorry—Major, sir."

Major eased his stance. "No, it's not a title. It's just my first name."

"Oh." The kid set his miniature laptop computer on the coffee table and seemed to relax a little. "I'm Nick Sevellier. Let's sit."

Major resumed his place on the couch but leaned forward, elbows on knees again, hands clasped.

"You've seen your mother?"

"Yeah, I've been with her for about an hour. She told me she didn't take her meds last night. No insult meant, but how long have you been working here?"

Sevellier's mouth twisted into a wry smile. "Everyone asks that. I know I look like Doogie Howser, but I really am old enough to be almost finished with my med school internship. I've been here since August. I was assigned to your mother's case a few weeks ago when the other intern rotated out."

"And what have you observed?"

"That she seems to be handling the medications and managing her condition quite well. That's probably why I panicked last night. I was so sure that no one could go as long as her charts indicated without having an episode." Sevellier picked up the laptop, slid a stylus out of the side of it, and began tapping things on the screen. "How did she appear to you this morning?"

"A bit disoriented—some of her thought processes were disjointed. But nothing I haven't witnessed before."

Sevellier typed something into the computer. "You're her only family?"

Major nodded. "She was a single mom—a great one."

"How old was she when she first started exhibiting symptoms?"

"I was just a kid—so she was in her late twenties or early thirties."

"And she was in and out of the hospital?"

"Not in the beginning." Major reclined against the back of the sofa. If Doogie wanted to know the whole history, they might be here awhile. "She had her first real psychotic break when I was in high school. She was committed to Central State Hospital over in Pineville. Since then, she's been in and out of residential programs, until eight years ago when she finally agreed she needed to move to an assisted-living facility."

The kid doctor didn't look up from the notes he was making. "What precipitated that decision?"

Major crossed his arms. "She set fire to her condo, and several other residents of the complex were injured. It wasn't the first fire she'd set."

"She was living alone?"

Here it came. The accusation. How could he have left her alone to fend for herself when he knew how bad off she was? "I was working in New York at the time. She'd been taking her meds and going to therapy regularly. But I moved back immediately afterward. I tried taking care of her myself for several months, but it didn't work."

Sevellier nodded as if gaining new understanding. "I see. She's come a long way since then."

"There is something you should know—and it's supposed to be in her charts. She is sort of obsessed with John Wayne movies. That was why she had. . .why she was such a problem last night. It wasn't just that she hadn't taken her meds; it was because she was watching a John Wayne movie. She doesn't like to be interrupted when she's watching one of those."

"I see." Sevellier typed some more. "But if she'd taken her meds, it wouldn't have been a problem?"

Major bit the inside of his cheek. These guys never really understood her. "Probably not, because she would have been asleep before the movie came on. But I'm telling you, she's watching one right now. If you want to see how she reacts to having her John Wayne time interrupted, be my guest."

"I. . .uh. . .I don't think we need to upset her again. I've noted it on her chart." He stood and extended his right hand. "It was nice to meet you, Mr. O'Hara."

Major rose and shook the kid's hand. "You, too. Please don't hesitate to call me if anything like this happens again."

"Will do." Sevellier moved away then turned back. "Oh, I hear congratulations are in order."

Major frowned. "For what?"

"You mother has been telling everyone for weeks that her son is getting married."

Ma! "She's mistaken—she just wishes I would get married and is trying to force me into it."

"Oh." Doogie Howser blushed. "Sorry."

"No problem."

Major shrugged into his coat and exited the center into the frigid, pouring rain. He pulled the collar up around his ears and ran toward Kirby. His cell phone vibrated against his waist, and as soon as he climbed into the vehicle, he unholstered the phone and flipped it open. "Hello?"

"Hey, Major. It's Forbes."

His best friend's voice came as a welcomed relief. "Hey. What's up?"

"Wondered if you might have time to get together one day this week."

His mind still occupied with his mother and her issues, Major couldn't think clearly. "I think I should be able to get free one day, now that Steven's handling lunch service. But I'll have to check my calendar once I get back to the office tomorrow to let you know for sure."

"Okay. Good. I've been reviewing the paperwork you gave me on your restaurant idea, and I wanted to talk to you about it."

No more bad news. Not today. Major slumped forward until his forehead pressed against the top of the steering wheel. "My restaurant proposal?"

"Yeah. I don't really want to get into it over the phone. Let's just try to get together as soon as possible next week."

"Sure. I'll shoot you an e-mail tomorrow to let you know when."

"You all right?"

"Just exhausted. You know, the event last night. . ." He wasn't really lying to his friend—just not divulging the truth.

"Why don't you come over and watch football with us this afternoon—Dad and the boys and me—over at Mom and Dad's house?"

"Thanks for the invite, but. . .I'll be at the open house for a few minutes; then I'm going to head home for some peace and quiet."

"I gotcha. I'll talk to you later."

After they disconnected, Major tossed the phone into the passenger seat. "Lord, why did I get out of the bed today?"

Chapter 4

"You'd better not mess up my car, buddy-boy."

The puppy thumped its tail a couple of times against the floor then put its head back on its paws. The veterinarian at the quick clinic had said the little guy would be out of it from some of the shots.

Meredith pulled her jacket over her almost-dry hair and dashed across the small lot to the store's front door.

"We close for lunch in thirty—oh, hey, Glamour Girl." The proprietor rounded the sales counter and shook Meredith's hand. "To what do we owe the honor of your visit today?"

One of the things she loved about Robichaud's Hardware was the fact that no one cared if she arrived in paint-splattered clothes, wearing no makeup, and looking no better than that puppy had when she'd pulled him out from under the porch.

"Since you're having your big New Year's Day sale, I figured I'd come in and clean you out of the rest of that paint stripper. And I need some wood epoxy, as well. Same aisle?"

"You know where stuff is in here better than I do, gal." He handed her a shopping basket. "If you think of anything else you need, or if I don't have exactly what you're looking for back there, give me a holler."

"Thanks, Rob. Will do." Meredith dropped her wallet and keys into the basket and headed for the painting supplies section in the back of the store. Her work boots thudded slightly on the wide-plank pine floor.

She breathed deeply and let it out as a sigh. The smell of wood and metal and turpentine and hard work welcomed and embraced her. She was certain she could get what she needed at the warehouse-like home improvement center a few miles closer to the house, but she preferred the sounds, scents, and service she experienced here.

She grabbed the last two one-gallon cans of the gel-style solvent she liked best for removing old paint and moved down the aisle to the display of all the caulks, glues, and epoxies. The few products that she needed to look at were, naturally, on the bottom shelf. She set the heavy basket on the floor and crouched down to read the labels.

In the stillness, the front-door bell chimed faintly, followed by Rob's echoing voice calling out that the store would be closing for lunch in twenty minutes. Meredith turned her attention back to the product labels, not wanting to leave her leather seats at the mercy of the puppy any longer than necessary.

The light above her dimmed. She glanced up—and nearly lost her balance.

"Do you need help finding something, miss?" The man who asked towered over her.

She jumped to her feet, balancing the can, bottle, and tube of epoxy in her hands. "No, thank you. I'm just reading to try to see which one I want to buy." The can shifted and her fingers spasmed and cramped trying to keep hold of it—to no avail.

Before it could fall, the giant with curly dark hair caught it. "Whoops. Don't want that falling and popping open. We might be stuck here forever." He had a jaw like a sledge hammer and a grin like a teen idol.

She shook her head. So he was good-looking—so what? "Thanks."

"You're buying wood epoxy?" His gray eyes twinkled.

"Yes." She shifted the tube and bottle into her left hand and reached for the can.

He didn't immediately let go, a crease forming between his thick brows. "Are you sure this is what you're looking for?"

Annoyance prickled up Meredith's spine. "Unless you know of something else I can use to fill in years' worth of wear and tear in my woodwork."

"If it's molding or baseboards, you'd be better off just replacing the piece of trim completely."

She pulled a little harder and finally succeeded in getting him to let go of the can. "If they weren't period and prohibitively expensive to replace, I might consider it. But I can't replace all of the moldings, baseboards, and cabinets in a craftsman house."

His brows elevated in tandem with his low whistle. "A craftsman—not the cedar-sided one over on Destrehan Place?"

She stepped back, hugging the epoxies to her. "Yes."

"Whaddya know? A buddy of mine owned it—bought it to flip right before the market crashed. I helped him as much as I could with the exterior. We'd just started on the interior when he ran out of money."

"As in, y'all ripped the kitchen out completely without any means of putting another one in?" The corners of Meredith's mouth twitched.

The six-and-a-half-foot-tall giant rubbed his hand over his short curls. "Yeah," he drawled. "I told him not to do that until he knew for sure he could get another line of credit. You—" He regarded her curiously. "You aren't actually living in that house with no kitchen, are you?"

Meredith smiled at him for the first time since the conversation began. "No. I'm not currently living in the house. But at the rate I'm making progress, it's not going to be in much better shape when I do need to move in a few months from now."

"Lease on your current place ending?" He motioned for the bottle and tube she held, took them at her nod, and set them back on the shelf.

"Sort of." More like Anne and George would be returning from their honeymoon to England and wanting to get started on restoring the Victorian.

"So are you thinking about hiring a contractor?" He rested his elbow against the second shelf as if settling in for a long chat.

Who was this guy? "Yeah, I'm thinking about it. Why—do you know one?"

His full lips split into a smile, revealing too-white-to-be-natural teeth. He reached into the pocket of his denim shirt and produced a business card.

Meredith read it—then did a double take.

"What's wrong?"

"Nothing. I just didn't read your card right the first time." She looked up at him. At his quizzical look, she decided to confess. "I've just never actually met anyone named Ward before."

"I know—it's odd, isn't it? But Edward's a family name, and my parents didn't want me being 'Eddie the fourth.' I've never seen it anywhere else as a first name."

"You've never heard of Ward Bond?" She slipped the card into her pocket.

Ward Breaux shook his head. "No. Who's he?"

Meredith's jaw unhinged momentarily. "*The Searchers*? *Rio Bravo*? *The Quiet Man*?" At the title of each film, the contractor shook his head. "Surely, you've at least seen *Fort Apache*?"

"Um. . .if those are westerns, I can guarantee you I've never seen them."

"They're not just westerns, they're John Wayne classics—Ward Bond costarred in all of those and a bunch more with John Wayne."

"Well, there you go." Ward winked at her. "I've never seen a John Wayne movie."

"Never? Oh, you don't know what you're missing. *Fort Apache* and *She Wore a Yellow Ribbon* are my two favorite movies."

Ward's eyes crinkled a bit at the corners when he smiled. "Then I guess I'll have to watch them sometime if they're your favorites."

Movement behind him caught Meredith's attention, and she bent to grab her basket. "Sorry, Rob. I'm ready—" She glanced askance at Ward and held up the can in her hand. "At least, I think I am."

"That's the putty I always use." Ward turned toward Rob. "I'll be done by the time you finish ringing up Miss. . . ?" He swung his head around, brows raised.

Her skin tingled at the way his dark lashes perfectly framed his gray eyes. "Meredith Guidry."

"Miss Guidry."

Meredith tried her best not to look back as she followed Rob to the sales counter. She nearly bounced on each step, buoyed by high spirits. Never before had a man flirted with her like that.

After handing her check card to Rob, she pulled a business card out of her wallet. She stared at it a moment. Meredith E. Guidry, Executive Director, Events & Facilities Management. Her title always made her feel pretentious, though she supposed it did reflect her real job better than "the event planner," which is what most people called her. She signed her receipt and willed Rob to move slower in bagging her purchases.

Her heart jangled like a cartoon telephone when footsteps approached from behind. She drew in a calming breath. Strange. In the eight years since she'd first met Major, she'd never experienced this level of attraction toward anyone else. Maybe she was finally getting over him.

She handed Ward her business card while Rob scanned Ward's three cans of primer.

"Impressive." Ward's flirtatious gaze made her almost want to forgive him for having been so condescending to her a few minutes ago. "Never would have expected someone as young as you to be such a bigwig with a company as huge as B-G Enterprises. You must be good at what you do."

Rob's chuckle brought flames of embarrassment to Meredith's cheeks. All of a sudden, all she could think of was her grubby appearance. Who was she kidding, thinking that a man like Ward Breaux was flirting with her?

"E-mail or call me, and we can set up a time for you to come by the house to look it over and then review my plans so that you can start putting together a bid." She grabbed her bags off the counter. "Thanks, Rob. Happy New Year."

She didn't usually take the coward's way out, but she pretended not to hear Ward calling for her to *wait up* and ran through the rain to her SUV.

The puppy awoke with a yip when the can of epoxy fell off the seat and bumped him.

"Oh, goodness—I'm so sorry." She leaned over the console and rubbed his head before returning the can to its bag and putting the supplies on the floor behind her seat. One glance at the rearview mirror showed Ward exiting the store. Stomach churning, Meredith started the engine and pulled out of the parking lot.

"Stupid, stupid, stupid. How could I be so dense as to think he was flirting with me for any reason other than wanting my business?"

The rain slapped the windshield all the way back to the house, doing nothing to improve her mood. She sat for a moment after parking under the protection of the carport.

He probably hadn't seen her as anything more than a potential client. How many people had she sucked up to in the past, believing they could potentially become clients? But she couldn't deny that while the delusion lasted, she had felt the stirrings of attraction toward him.

Maybe, just maybe, she was finally recovering from her eight-year affliction—the affliction that went by the name Major O'Hara.

Cars—mostly expensive, foreign models—lined the street of the upscale subdivision. Major parked a few houses down from the Guidrys', pulled his coat collar up, and ran through the rain to the cover of their wide, wraparound porch.

He reached the front steps at the same time as a pair of other guests—familiar looking and smart enough to be carrying a huge black and red umbrella. One of Major's part-time staff opened the door and grinned at him, dressed in the standard black pants and white tuxedo shirt all servers at B-G events wore.

Major stepped aside for the woman to enter first. As she passed, the small dog draped across her arm snapped and growled at him. Behind her, folding the umbrella, the man rolled his eyes and sighed—and Major finally recognized him. Gus McCord, Bonneterre's new mayor. Major hadn't realized how short the man was. He always looked much taller on TV.

When the mayor drew even with Major, he extended his right hand. "Sorry about the dog. She can't go anywhere without that thing. You look familiar, but I can't place you."

"Major O'Hara, sir." Major returned the politician's firm, brief grip.

The quick processing of Major's name registered in Mayor McCord's brown eyes. "You played football with my son at ULB."

Major reined in his surprise. "Yes, sir. He was a couple years ahead of me."

"And now you're the most popular chef in Beausoleil Parish—if not all of Louisiana." Mr. McCord handed his dripping umbrella to the doorman.

Maybe Major shouldn't have voted for the other guy last fall. "Mr. and Mrs. Guidry would be pleased to hear you say so."

"I'll be sure to tell them, then." Mr. McCord motioned Major to enter ahead of him.

Major stopped just inside the door, awestruck. He didn't know much about architecture, but this house reminded him of the big plantation houses down on the river he'd seen on school fieldtrips. The dark-wood-floored entryway echoed with a hum of voices coming from all around. To his left, the walnut and green library featured a large, round table laden with a display of fruit, guests hovering around it like hummingbirds in a flower garden.

For a moment, professional jealousy reared up in his chest. Why hadn't they asked him to cater? Then, before the envy could take full root, he spotted Maggie Babineaux, Mairee Guidry's sister—the caterer who'd taught Major more about food service than they'd ever imagined teaching in culinary school. She waved at him but didn't break away from her conversation. He waved in return.

To his right, circulating around the twenty-person dining table piled high with exquisite displays of pastries, he recognized a few people—the mayor's wife and her little dog, the state senator for Beausoleil Parish, the pastor of Bonneterre Chapel. . .who motioned Major into the room.

"We've missed you the last couple of Sundays." Pastor Kinnard shifted his plate and extended his right hand.

Major smiled and shook hands with him. "I've missed everyone, too, but I was filling in for the chaplain out at. . .one of the nursing homes."

Reverend Kinnard nodded. "When are you boys going to sing for us again?"

Major shrugged. "Everything's been so crazy with the holidays and then with the Christmas musical before that—we haven't practiced in months."

"Three weeks enough notice?"

To pull together four professional workaholics to learn the intricate harmonies of a southern gospel song and have it memorized? "Shouldn't be a problem—oh, but I think Forbes said something about going to a conference in Baton Rouge in a couple of weeks, so let me check with him—and George and Clay—and I'll try to let you know by Wednesday."

"Sounds good—ah, Mairee, no doubt you're here for our chef extraordinaire."

Average height, like Meredith, with dark auburn hair, Mairee Guidry entered the dining room with a majestic air. "I hate to steal him away, Frank, but I do have some business to discuss with everyone's favorite chef." She hooked her arm through Major's and, though ever polite, steered him through the crowd without interruption.

She led him up the back staircase from the kitchen. "I know you probably want to get home and relax on your day off." She pushed open a set of double doors at the end of the hall. "So I'll keep this as short as possible."

The study was at least the size of Major's living room and

bedroom combined. Mairee led him to a raised area in a bay window and motioned for him to take one of the wing chairs while she enthroned herself in the other.

"How's your mother?" she asked, settling back as if ready for a long chat.

"She's fine. I just came from seeing her, actually."

Mairee's eyes flickered to the door. "Oh, good, Lawson—there you are."

Discomfort settled in Major's gut. What in the world would they want to talk to him about that they couldn't do at the office? He blanched. *Please, Lord, don't let anyone have come down with food poisoning last night!* But Mairee had told him early yesterday evening she wanted him to come by today.

He stood and offered the chair to Lawson, but Meredith's father waved him off and pulled one of the ottomans beside Mairee's chair.

Mairee folded her hands in her lap. "I know you've got to be wondering why we asked you to meet with us today, outside of business hours."

Major nodded and swallowed, trying to ease the dryness in his throat.

"We wanted to discuss your future with Boudreaux-Guidry Enterprises. Your annual appraisal is coming up in a couple of weeks, and Lawson and I wanted to take some time to talk to you about your goals and plans for the future."

Rubbing his tongue hard against the backs of his teeth, Major nodded again, flickering a glance at Lawson then back at Mairee. Meredith looked more like her father than her mother.

"You told us a long time ago that one of your dreams is to open a restaurant here in Bonneterre." Mairee uncrossed and recrossed her ankles, leaning forward slightly. "We have recently purchased a bundle of properties in the Warehouse District—all of which has been rezoned to commercial and retail space. You may or may not have heard that we have just contracted with another company to develop the area into a village square–style shopping area—boutiques, specialty stores, high fashion, and the like."

The knot in Major's stomach stopped twisting.

Lawson took over. "One of the properties in the parcel was a cafeteria. It's a separate building with a large industrial kitchen. While it would need a complete overhaul, we believe you're up to the task."

His heart tripped and fell into his feet, then leaped back up into his throat. "Me? You want me to overhaul the cafeteria?"

Lawson chuckled. "No. Not a cafeteria. A restaurant. *Your* restaurant. Well, technically, we would own most it—but with an investment, you'll be a co-owner in addition to being executive chef. And over time, we expect you to buy us out of it—even if it's just 10 or 20 percent at a time—until it truly is your restaurant."

Investment. He prayed he had enough money saved. So long as nothing happened with Ma anytime soon, he could be on the road toward becoming the restaurateur he had always dreamed of being.

Mairee laid her hand on her husband's arm. "We don't need to get into all of the business details right now—Forbes will take care of that. What we do want is for you to take some time to think about this. You'd still be working for us—drawing a salary—and we would need you to continue to oversee the event catering division. I know that will put quite a strain on your time, but no one ever said opening a restaurant would be easy."

"No, ma'am, no one ever did." Major's heart pounded so hard, he could feel it in the tip of his nose.

Lawson stood and stepped over to the large writing desk nearby, returning with a thick manila folder. "Forbes is handling all of the legalities—the restaurant will be incorporated separately from B-G Enterprises. I believe he's already called you to set up an appointment."

Rising from the chair, Major took the folder with trembling hands. "Yes, sir."

"We don't expect you to make this decision quickly or without a lot of thought," Mairee said. "In fact, if you said yes today, I would withdraw the offer because you hadn't thought through all of the pros and cons. We do ask for an answer by Easter, though. Groundbreaking is scheduled for the first week of May."

Lawson extended his right hand to Major. "We want you to know that if you feel this isn't the right time for you to take on something like this, we'll still consider ourselves fortunate to have the best chef in the Gulf South working for us at B-G."

Hand so numb he barely felt the pressure from Lawson's, Major thanked his employers.

"Will you stay a little while?" Mairee asked, standing. "Several people hoped to see you to compliment you on last night's food." She raised her brows.

Networking—one of the most important skills he'd learned about the food service industry. Personal relationships with the right people could ensure a restaurant's success. "Of course I'll stay awhile."

Mairee beamed. "Come along, then. I believe I saw Kitty McCord looking at you with adoring eyes just before we came up."

He followed his employers downstairs. No sooner had he cleared the bottom step than a woman dressed in pink tweed took hold of his arm.

"Major O'Hara, isn't it?"

"Yes, Mrs. McCord." Major eyed her little dog speculatively, but for the moment it appeared calm.

"Just call me Kitty. I'm sorry I didn't recognize you when we came in. When Gus told me who you were, I just had to find you to tell you how fabulous the food was last night—though really I should be reprimanding you, making me have to start the New Year off with a resolution to lose the ten pounds I know I put on with all of your wonderful dishes."

"Thank you."

"Now, come with me. There are a few people I want to introduce you to."

Feeling very much like the dog clasped in her other arm, Major allowed himself to be led around the Guidrys' home and introduced like a prized pet to Mrs. McCord's friends.

"Were you responsible for last night?" the state senator's wife asked. "That was one of the most wonderful galas I've ever attended—and we've been to ever so many in Baton Rouge and New Orleans."

"I wish I could claim full responsibility, ma'am, but that praise rightfully goes to Meredith Guidry, the executive director of events. She planned and organized everything." He wished Meredith were here, listening to the accolades. She tended to be too hard on herself, taking a few minor complaints to heart and not enjoying the copious amounts of praise for her events.

"Yes. . .Meredith. Bless her heart. I met with her the other day to start planning Easter in the Park. I never would have guessed she'd be capable of pulling off an event like last night, though. She must rely greatly on you." Mrs. McCord's simpering voice and flirtatious expression were repeated by the retinue of ladies circled around him.

Major stiffened, and the tiny hairs at the back of his neck prickled. "Actually, Mrs. McCord, the truth of the matter is that we all rely on Meredith more than we should. She's such an organizational genius that all I have to do is show up and follow her plan to make everything go smoothly."

"Hmm." Kitty McCord's smile tightened. Before she could say more, a commotion caught her attention. "Oh, here's someone you *must* meet."

Major turned to look the same direction and quickly closed his eyes against a blinding beam of light. He blinked a couple of times and finally was able to open them enough to see the source—a large TV camera.

The mayor's wife held her hands out toward an exotic young woman with dark hair and features. "Alaine Delacroix, what a surprise to see you here." The two women exchanged a kiss on the cheek.

"Mrs. McCord, how lovely to see you. Might I impose on you for an interview?"

"Naturally, you know how much I love talking to you." Mrs. McCord clamped her hand around the reporter's elbow. "But first, there's someone I want to introduce to you."

Major's skin tingled as the two women drew closer, even with as much as he tried to quell the purely epicurean reaction to the younger one. What man wouldn't react to such a beautiful creature?

"Alaine, this is Major O'Hara. He's the chef responsible for the New Year's Eve Ball."

The young woman shook hands with him. "Alaine Delacroix, Channel Six News. I would love to get an interview with you, Mr. O'Hara. Would you have time this afternoon?"

Held enthralled by Alaine Delacroix's chocolate eyes, Major swallowed a couple of times. "I. . .yes, I'm. . .I have time."

Alaine's full lips split into a smile revealing perfect, dazzlingly white teeth.

"Did I hear someone say something about Major being interviewed for Alaine's show?" Mairee Guidry joined the cluster of women. She gave Major a significant look. "What a wonderful opportunity."

Major wiped his clammy palms on his khakis, unsure of how he'd gotten himself into this situation. Yes, being featured on a news show would be great publicity for B-G Enterprises—and potentially for the restaurant—but that kind of publicity would only lead to people asking questions, finding out about his background. . .about his mother.

He cleared the rising apprehension from his throat. "Yes, it would be a wonderful opportunity." Collecting himself, he gave a slight bow. "Ladies, it was a delight to meet you. Ms. Delacroix, I just recalled a previous engagement, so I won't be able to do that interview right now—" Catching sight of Mairee's raised eyebrow, he fished into his back pocket, slid a business card out of his wallet, and handed it to the reporter. "But do call me sometime, and we'll reschedule."

Alaine's fingers brushed his as she took the card, sending quivers of sensation up his arm. "I will call you tomorrow morning, Major O'Hara."

Major excused himself, retrieved his coat from the kid at the door, and barely waited for the door to close behind him before he took off toward Kirby at a full-out run. The cold rain in his face helped calm him, and by the time he reached the Jeep, his thoughts had stopped swirling. He hadn't had a reaction like that to a woman's mere presence in. . .ever. Now that he was away from her, shame over his reaction seeped through him. He'd foresworn dating, realizing that he'd never be able to saddle a woman he loved with his life—between the hours he worked and never knowing when the day might come that his mother would have a complete psychotic break.

Meredith's image slipped into his mind. Of any woman he knew, she was the only one who would understand his life, the only one who gave him a sense of fulfillment, of companionship. She wouldn't care about his hours—she worked longer than he did and spent the rest of her time refurbishing that house—but still, the specter of her reaction when she found out about Ma turned his stomach.

Kirby's engine roared to life. No. He couldn't do that to Meredith. She deserved better, better than the pittance of a life he could offer her. Major would have to settle for finding fulfillment in work—in opening a restaurant.

Chapter 5

After a day of falling in the mud, scraping paint, and hauling in a twenty-pound bag of puppy food, Meredith stood in the shower for several minutes, letting the hot, pulsating water work on her sore muscles. On the other side of the shower curtain, snuffling sounds and nails clicking on tile kept her well aware of the fur ball's movements around the small bathroom.

"I still can't believe I let myself think that guy was interested in me."

The puppy barked in response to her voice. Meredith smiled and worked honeysuckle-scented shampoo into her hair. "Maybe it is a good thing I found you, if you're going to talk back to me. Now people won't think I'm quite as crazy when I talk to myself out loud. I just don't know if I'm ready for a dog."

Meredith nearly tripped over the puppy when she got out of the shower. She pushed him back with her foot to keep his claws from her bare legs. His wagging tail caused his whole body to wriggle. How could she give up such unadulterated, uninhibited love? "Okay. I'll put signs up, and if no one has contacted me in a week or so, I'll take them down and you can stay with me."

She took extra time styling her shoulder-length hair and applying makeup. Even though she would only be with her parents and siblings, if she showed up the way she preferred—jeans, sweatshirt, and well-worn work boots—Mom wouldn't speak to her all night. But Meredith would definitely hear about it in undertones and insinuations all day tomorrow.

Her sisters could wear designer jeans and nice tops. But none of them worked for Mom and Dad. Meredith bypassed the closet full of denim and comfortable clothes and went instead to the closet holding her more expensive, work-appropriate attire.

After twenty minutes, she sank onto the side of the bed amid a pile of tops and pants. She hated feeling like she had to be "on" all the time around her family. But it kept at bay the whispers and hints that her choice in casual clothes might have something to do with why she was still single.

"What will I be most comfortable in?" she asked the clothes now strewn across her bed.

She chose her utilitarian black slacks—the size twelves that were somewhat loose in the waist—and a light turquoise cashmere twinset with a little beading around the neck. She stepped into her favorite loafer-style black pumps and turned to admire the look in the antique cheval mirror. Knowing Mom, she'd be dressed similarly.

"No, no, no!" She pushed the puppy away with one foot as he pounced on the hem of her pant leg. "If you're going to stay with me, you're going to have to learn better manners than that!"

Unabashed, he sat and hunched over to scratch at his new collar.

"Get used to it, bubba. Come on. We'd better take you out before it's time to go."

Pleased with his performance outside, she took him back into the bathroom, where she picked up the rug and draped it over the shower curtain rod. In its place, she put down a triple layer of newspaper and an old towel for him to sleep on.

As soon as she closed the door, he cried and whined his displeasure. She ignored him.

With the lint roller in hand and balancing on one foot so she could get the dog hair off the hem of her pant leg, she buzzed the intercom to Jenn's apartment.

"What?" Her sister's voice crackled through the speaker.

"You about ready to go?"

"It's only—crimenetly. I didn't realize it was already six. I'll be down in five minutes."

"Jenn. You know how I hate—"

"Being late. I know. But everyone will blame me, not you."

Eight minutes later, Jenn clattered downstairs and entered without knocking. "Wow, Mere, you're awfully dressed up." Jenn, of course, looked fabulously stylish in her dark indigo jeans with penny loafers and a bright green turtleneck sweater.

Meredith quirked the corner of her mouth in a grimace. "You know how it is with Mom."

"Yeah, I know. She gives you a hard time. But that's only when you show up in the rattiest stuff you own—" Jenn cocked her head. "What in the— Is that a *dog* I hear?"

"A puppy. Come on—I'll tell you about him in the car."

"I want to see him." Jenn barreled through the apartment and opened the bathroom door before Meredith could stop her.

"He's so *cute!*" Jenn's voice reached the extreme high pitch usually brought on by a baby sighting. She crouched and scooped up the puppy. "Let's take him over to Mama and Daddy's."

"No. Jenn, look—you already have fur all over your sweater. Can you imagine how Mom would react if he had an accident in the house?"

Jenn's expression shouted incredulity. She stood and tucked the squirming pup under her arm. "Mom loves dogs. She's the one who kept Daddy from getting rid of Jax, even after Jax completely lost control of his bladder. He's coming." Jenn marched past. "Why you've gotten it in your head that they're going to disapprove of everything you do or say. . ."

Because I'm the only sap who went into the family business. Well, that wasn't true. Rafe had worked for their parents for a couple of years, flying one of the corporate jets. But he didn't have to work with them day in and day out—and he'd left the company late last year to work for a charter airline.

The only reason Meredith had seven siblings was because her parents thought that all of them would run B-G so they could retire early. With a master's degree in art history, Meredith hadn't really had any job options other than going to work as an assistant event planner ten years ago.

Sometimes she wished she'd been brave enough to pursue her dream of working in home design, but as that had not been deemed a viable job choice by her parents—

"Hey! We going or what?" Jenn stepped back into the apartment.

"Coming." Meredith grabbed her keys and wallet off the table and followed her sister outside.

"Can we take your car?" Jenn asked, walking around to the passenger side of the SUV. "The 'Stang's top is still leaking."

Meredith rounded the tail end of Jenn's classic Mustang, already expecting to be the one driving. She climbed into the Volvo and started the engine.

"So, how'd you end up with this little guy?" Jen nuzzled the puppy, who joyously licked her chin.

Meredith buckled her seat belt and pulled out of the driveway, relating what had happened. By the time she parked under one of the centuries-old oak trees in front of their parents' house, she'd gotten to the part about taking the pup to the quick clinic at the pet store.

"Yeah? Well I think I'd be kinda wiggly, too, if someone was trying to stick a thermometer there." Jenn cooed gibberish at the dog and climbed out of the vehicle, tucking the puppy under her raincoat for the dash to the front porch.

Sighing, Meredith popped open her umbrella and followed her sister up the sidewalk.

With the exception of all the furniture still being shoved up against the walls in the front rooms, little evidence remained of the hundreds of people who'd likely crowded the house for most of the day.

The front door opened behind her, and she turned. Forbes closed his umbrella and stowed it in the rack beside the door. She waited for him; he hooked his arm around her neck and kissed her temple.

"Did you have a good day?" He eased the headlock and settled his arm across her shoulders as they strolled down the hall.

"Yep—well, for the most part. My stupid brother provoked me into an argument this morning."

He squeezed his arm tightly around her neck again. "I apologized."

She nudged his side with her knuckles; he released her and danced away, squirming. "I know. And you were right—it was better for me to find out ahead of time instead of being blindsided by it. Did you forewarn Jenn, too?"

"Uh. . .no. You know she can't keep a secret to save her life."

Meredith wrinkled her nose. "She might not take it as well as I did."

"I know. But we'll cross that bridge—"

"There you two are." Mom greeted them as soon as Meredith and Forbes entered the kitchen. She looked Meredith over from head to toe. "Do you have a date after this or something?"

Meredith glanced at Forbes, in his form-fitting black turtleneck and jeans, then back at their mother—also in jeans. She plastered on a smile. "Oh, I thought I'd try to make everyone else feel completely *under*dressed for a change." Would she ever be able to do *anything* right when it came to her parents?

"Well, come on and get some food."

As in years past, almost every inch of counter space in the generously sized kitchen was covered with trays and pans of food. Growing up, Meredith and her siblings had always looked forward to dinner on New Year's Day because they got to eat the leftovers from the open house—including as much dessert as they wanted.

Family members milled about, filling plates, while some had already migrated into the great room beyond the kitchen's breakfast bar.

Rafe vacated the rocking chair and offered it to Meredith. "Don't want you getting your fancy duds messed up." Though his voice lilted with teasing humor, his eyes held sympathy and understanding.

"Thanks."

At her youngest sisters' high-pitched voices, she looked across the room and saw them feeding bits of Aunt Maggie's gourmet food to the puppy. Her brothers were more interested in the football game on the flat-panel TV mounted above the crackling fireplace—even Forbes seemed to be getting involved in the game between two teams from faraway colleges no one in this family had ever cared about before.

Finally, at eight o'clock, Meredith's father turned off the TV. "Well, here we are, at the start of another year. This time we have a new face with us." He motioned toward Marci's boyfriend with an outstretched hand. "Welcome, Shaun. I'm not sure if Marci explained exactly what it is that we do here on New Year's."

"Yes, sir, sort of like what most families do at Thanksgiving."

"Right—except we're giving our goal for the upcoming year and what we intend to do to reach it. Last year I believe Forbes went first?" Lawson shot a raised-brow glance at his oldest son.

"Yes, sir."

"Then it's youngest to oldest this year. Tiffani, take it away."

As her youngest sister started talking about her upcoming semester at college and grades and school projects, Meredith mentally rehearsed her goal: finishing renovations on the house and getting moved and settled in. No, it wasn't creative or soul-searching, but really, what else did she have in her life?

An image of Major flickered in her mind's eye. She wished she had Major in her life—more than as just an infatuation that wouldn't go away. She forced her mind to replace his image with one of Ward Breaux. Had he been flirting with her before he knew she might need a contractor? Sure, he'd been a little condescending, but he'd seen her as a woman, not as "just one of the guys" as most of the other men she'd ever known did.

Jonathan and Kevin gave their goals—both also talking mostly about college. When Marci's turn came, Meredith set her own relationship musings aside and paid attention. Marci launched into her goal—changing her major to nursing and, in another two years, finally finishing school.

"That's an admirable goal, Marci. You know we'll support you no matter what career path you choose." Dad's eyes twinkled, and the corners of his mouth twitched. Like Jenn, he was horrible at keeping secrets. "Shaun, would you like to participate?"

Though almost thirty years old, Shaun squirmed like a schoolboy in the principal's office. "I'm really happy to have been included in your family's tradition." His gaze darted around the room, but he didn't make eye contact with anyone. Seated on the floor in front of her, he turned to face Marci and raised up onto one knee. "Marci, we've been together for four years now. I can't imagine spending my life without you by my side. Will you marry me?"

Marci shrieked a yes. Meredith swallowed and blinked hard.

Jenn fled the room.

Meredith groaned. Not good. Fortunately, Marci and Shaun were too preoccupied with each other to notice Jenn's reaction. Meredith dabbed the corners of her eyes with a napkin and stood, waving her mother back down. "Let me."

She passed through the kitchen and down the main hallway, calling her sister's name. She followed the sound of sobbing to the powder room under the elaborate staircase. She knocked softly. "Jenn?"

"Go away."

"Jennifer." Meredith tapped on the door again.

"Go away! I don't want to talk about it, okay?"

"Do you want me to go get your stuff and tell the family you're sick and we're going home?"

A long pause. "No."

"Then talk to me. You can't stay in there all night."

The doorknob rattled and clicked; Jenn didn't come out, though. Meredith pulled the door open. "May I come in?"

Jenn perched on the closed commode, elbows on knees, weeping into a wad of toilet paper.

Meredith closed the door behind her and leaned against the edge of the pedestal sink.

"It's not fair," Jenn wailed.

"What? That Marci's engaged? Or that she's twenty-four and engaged?"

Jenn moaned into her fistful of tissue.

"Look, I understand—"

"How could you possibly understand what I'm feeling?"

Meredith rocked back, the words hitting her like a sucker punch to the gut. "Wait just a minute. You haven't forgotten that I'm almost three years older than you, have you? And that I'm having to figure out how to accept the fact that my sister who is *ten* years younger than me just got engaged?"

"But you've never been in love—you've never even dated! How could you understand what this means to me? I've been trying for half my life to find what Marci found with her first boyfriend."

Meredith separated the hurt and anger Jenn's words caused from the need to counsel her sister through this emotional crisis. She'd deal with her own emotions later. "Just because I've never dated doesn't mean I've never been in love."

Once again the specter of Major flickered in Meredith's mind, but she shoved the thought aside. "When I was in college, I fell in love with someone who didn't return my feelings, and I had to stand by and watch him marry a girl who was supposed to be a friend of mine: my roommate, who knew I was in love with him. So how do you think it makes me feel to know my younger sister has found something I'm still searching for? Something I've been searching for longer than you? How do you think I feel every time a handsome, interesting man asks you for a date? Or when Rafe doesn't come to Thursday night dinner because he's on a date? Or being maid of honor for Anne?"

Jenn sniffed, but her sobs subsided.

"We can't begrudge Marci the fact that she found the love of her life at a young age. We both know all she's ever wanted out of life is to be a wife and mother—yes, I know you want that, too. But you and I both had aspirations for our education and for careers. Look at how successful you've been with the restaurant. Do you think you could have done that with a husband and babies to take care of?"

"But I've been praying so hard for God to send me my husband. What's wrong with me?"

Meredith moved to kneel in front of her sister—after shifting the rug closer with her foot—and rubbed Jenn's upper arms. "Remember that just because it seems like God isn't giving us the main desire of our hearts doesn't mean He's not working in other areas of our lives—blessing us in ways we can't see because we're focusing so hard on the one thing we want but don't have."

"How can you be so calm about this?" Jenn grabbed a fresh wad of toilet paper and patted her face dry.

"Because I've had all day to think about it."

"Forbes?"

"Forbes."

Jenn rolled her eyes. "I swear he knows everything everyone in this family is going to do three days before we know we're going to do it."

The continued celebration of Marci's engagement created enough chaos that only their parents, Forbes, and Rafe looked at Meredith and Jenn in concern when they returned.

Though she smiled and laughed, Jenn remained subdued for the rest of the evening, cuddling the puppy on her lap. As they walked out, Forbes wrapped his arm around Jenn's shoulders and leaned his head close to hers. Rafe came up beside Meredith and encircled her waist in a quick half hug and walked with her toward the front door.

"Crazy, huh?"

"What do you mean?" Meredith tilted her head to study her younger brother's profile. Though he would turn twenty-nine in a few weeks, she could still trace elements of the pudgy-faced, red-haired little boy.

"I mean that Marci is the first one of us to get married. I always figured it would be Jenn."

Rafe's words pressed salt into the gaping emotional wound Jenn's had ripped open. "Gee, thanks."

"Oh, come on, you know what I mean—Jenn had her first serious boyfriend when she was barely fifteen."

"The first one Mom and Dad knew about, you mean."

"Yeah." Rafe opened the door.

Meredith shivered in the cold, damp air and buttoned her jacket.

"She's taking this kinda hard, isn't she?" He nodded toward Jenn and Forbes, standing next to Meredith's SUV. Jenn hugged the puppy to her, like a shipwreck survivor hanging onto a buoy.

"She'll get over it—as soon as she finds a new boyfriend. And that won't take long." But Meredith wasn't certain about herself. She'd known a day would come when her younger siblings started getting married, but she hadn't expected to still be single when it happened.

"So long as she doesn't make any rash decisions, like eloping with the next guy who asks her out."

Meredith laughed and dug her keys out of her purse. She used the key fob remote to unlock her car. "You know Forbes would never let any of us make a rash decision about anything."

"He's so. . .I don't know, anal retentive or obsessive-compulsive or something. He needs serious psychological profiling."

"I think all they'd be able to tell us is that he's a massive control freak."

"Y'all talking about me?" Forbes turned to face them while opening the car door for Jenn. "Because there's only one control freak allowed in this family." He waggled his eyebrows.

"Rafe, are you in town Thursday?" Jenn settled the puppy on the floor while she fastened her seat belt.

"I think I get in late in the afternoon, so I should be there for dinner." He blew her a kiss then hugged Meredith.

"Fly carefully."

"I always do." Rafe clasped hands with Forbes then trotted off to his classic red Corvette in the driveway.

Forbes closed Jenn's door then walked around the SUV to stand with Meredith. "What're you thinking about?"

She couldn't bring herself to admit to her emotional turmoil over tonight's events, not even to Forbes. "Just stuff."

"Marci-related stuff?"

"Yeah—sort of." She leaned against the door—then regretted it when the beaded raindrops soaked through her jacket.

"You want to share?"

Tell Major's best friend in the world that she'd had a crush on Major for eight years? "I don't think so."

He reached over and squeezed her shoulder. "I think it would be good for you—you know how you get when you keep things bottled up too long."

"I'll take it out on the house." She sighed. "Are you coming to dinner Thursday night?"

"Of course. I have to be there to orchestrate my siblings' and cousins' lives, control freak that I am." He opened her door and waited until she was in with her seat belt fastened before closing her door, then waved as she drove away.

Jenn stayed quiet on the fifteen-minute drive home, staring out the window and slowly stroking the sleeping puppy in her lap. Approaching the large Victorian—one of the largest on the block of turn-of-the-twentieth-century houses in Bonneterre's garden district—Meredith could see lights on in the second-floor windows. Once in the driveway, she recognized the dark Buick parked behind Anne's convertible.

George was over—probably for dinner and a movie. . .with a little work mixed in, now that he was officially Anne's business partner as well as her fiancé.

Melancholy caught in Meredith's throat. She was tired of praying the same prayer Jenn had lamented earlier: *When, oh Lord, will it be* my *turn?* At least Jenn dated—a lot. Meredith didn't even have that opportunity. Even if she weren't in love with Major, she never seemed to meet eligible men anymore. None of the single guys at church had ever shown the least interest in her; they'd always vied for Jenn's attention. Meredith had even tried the online dating thing. But whenever she started getting close with someone, a feeling of dread—of wrongness—overwhelmed her, and she withdrew.

"Can I keep the puppy with me tonight?" Jenn asked as she trudged across the back deck.

"Sure. You'll need to let him run around the yard before you take him inside, though, since he hasn't been out for a while."

"I know how to take care of a puppy."

Meredith forgave her sister's snappish tone and bade Jenn good night. Meredith didn't bother turning on the lights but felt her way through the dark apartment to her bedroom. She changed into her favorite pajamas—an old Bonneterre High School T-shirt and stretchy cotton-knit shorts—and climbed into bed.

The tears she'd been fighting all evening welled up and overflowed onto her pillow. She couldn't deny it anymore—Major would never return her feelings. She had to move on, find someone new.

Meredith turned on her back and stared at the shadowy ceiling. Though she'd told her family her goals about the house, a new, more important goal begged to be made, to be spoken aloud.

"Lord, my real New Year's resolution is that I won't still be single by this time next year."

Chapter 6

Great spread this morning, Major. I meant to tell you earlier."

Major accepted Lawson Guidry's proffered hand, his stomach twisting. "Thank you, sir." He hadn't slept much this week, visions of and plans for the restaurant running constantly through his mind. This morning he'd given up on sleep around three o'clock and been at work at four, half an hour early, to prepare breakfast for Mr. Guidry's weekly prayer breakfast.

"What brings you down here at this time of the afternoon?" the older man asked.

Major looked beyond Mr. Guidry toward the offices at the end of the hallway. "I came down to bring Meredith's takeaway box for her dinner, but she's not in her office. I need to talk to her." At her father's raised-brow look, Major quickly added, "About my part of the financial report on the New Year's event." Which was sort of true, though what he needed to ask her about could be done over the phone.

Maybe he read too much into Mr. Guidry's expression, but he was pretty sure Meredith's dad didn't believe him. "She had to go out to meet clients at Lafitte's Landing—probably won't be back for a while."

"Oh. Okay. I'll catch her later, then."

"Don't you have an interview scheduled for this afternoon anyway?"

Major checked his watch. "Yes, sir. I guess I'd better get back up to the kitchen, since that's where I told them to meet me."

"You'll have to let us know how it goes." Lawson raised his hand palm forward, his own unique good-bye wave. "I'd wish you luck, but you don't need it."

"Thank you, sir." Major nodded his farewell, then booked it back to the elevator and returned to the twenty-third floor.

Several kitchen and service staff stood facing him when the doors opened.

"Bye, Chef."

"Have a great afternoon, Mr. O'Hara."

"See ya tomorrow, Chef."

He tossed a good-bye over his shoulder as he exchanged places with them, then headed across the expanse of Vue de Ceil to the kitchen on the opposite side. Vacuums' whines filled the cavernous space, run by two of the waiters, both of whom had changed from their black pants and white button-downs into droopy jeans and sweatshirts.

In the kitchen, only Steven and the sauté chef and two dishwashers remained. Steven and his second-in-command hovered over the whiteboard, which they'd taken down and laid on the long prep table in the middle of the room, discussing tomorrow's lunch menu and assigning components to the various staff who would be here.

Major stepped into his office and closed the door. He opened the wardrobe behind his desk, planning to wear his white chef's jacket for the interview—but it wasn't there. He smacked his forehead. He'd dropped it off at the dry cleaner Tuesday and had meant to pick it up after the prayer breakfast this morning.

He swapped his navy polo for the burgundy tunic and watched himself in the mirror on the back of the armoire's door as he buttoned the double-breasted placket. Hmm. Must have shrunk when he had it cleaned. At least, he didn't remember the buttons around his gut pulling like that last time he'd worn it.

He sat down at the desk to write a note reminding himself to go to the cleaners tomorrow. The computer dinged, indicating a new e-mail received. Meredith usually checked her e-mail regularly when offsite, so maybe she'd finally decided to respond to him.

But the message was from Anne Hawthorne to set up a time to discuss the menu for her rehearsal dinner and wedding reception. He flagged it for follow-up later, then scanned the rest of the unread messages in his inbox. None from Guidry, Meredith.

If he didn't know better, he'd think she was avoiding him.

The five-minute warning of the time scheduled for the interview popped up on the screen. He quickly straightened up his desk, though that consisted of making sure the stapler and tape dispenser were at a perfect right-angle to the desk blotter and that the blotter lay exactly one inch—as measured by the tip of his thumb—from the edge of the desk.

Back out in the kitchen, the dish sanitizers had stopped rumbling, and a solitary Steven was hanging the whiteboard back on the wall.

"Everyone else gone?" Major paused to glance over tomorrow's menu.

"Yes, Chef. I'm about to call it a day, too, unless you need me for something." He glanced pointedly at Major's attire.

Have Steven hanging around for the interview? "No. It's already after four o'clock. Go on home."

"Thanks. I'll see you tomorrow." Steven slung his denim chef's jacket over his shoulder, tucked his knife case under his arm, and swaggered from the kitchen.

Major gave him half a minute's head start then stepped out into the warehouse-sized, sky-view room. Just as one set of elevator doors closed behind Steven, another set opened.

Though he thought he'd prepared for it, the sight of Alaine Delacroix once again disarmed him. No woman had the right to be so distractingly beautiful. She held the door while the burly guy with her muscled out a large duffel bag and a couple of equipment cases.

Major jogged over. "Can I help with any of that?"

The guy looked up at him, apparently offended. "Naw, man. I

can get it."

"Chef O'Hara, it's good to see you again." Alaine extended her hand.

Heat rushed into Major's face when he took her hand in his enormous paw and tried not to hurt her. "Ms. Delacroix. Welcome to Vue de Ceil." He swept his arm toward the room.

Alaine strolled past him. "It looks so different. I've only been here at night—and with five or six hundred other people, like at New Year's."

More like eight or nine hundred, but who was counting? He followed her. Alaine Delacroix was the kind of woman who could be admired from afar but not someone Major had any interest in getting to know better on a personal level.

Not like Meredith. He didn't have to worry about hurting Meredith on the rare occasion that called for him taking her hand in his—which he wished happened more often. He also didn't feel like a prepubescent boy at his first school dance around Meredith the way he did right now. And to put final nails in the coffin in which he would bury his reaction to Alaine, he decided he much preferred strawberry blonds with nutmeg-colored eyes to brunettes with eyes so dark he couldn't distinguish the pupil from the iris.

". . .your office?" Alaine stopped in the middle of the room and turned to face him, those dark brown eyes gazing at him askance.

What about his office? Oh, the interview. "Right through here."

He led her down the service corridor and pushed open the ENTER ONLY door into the kitchen, motioning for her to pass through ahead of him—and for the overloaded cameraman to do the same.

"Wow. I've seen some professional kitchens on TV before, but this one takes the cake." Alaine ran her hand along the stainless-steel countertops. "Nelson, we'll want to get some footage of this kitchen. In fact—" She whirled around to look at both men. "I know we discussed filming the cooking segments in the executive kitchen downstairs, but I wonder now if maybe we should do it up here."

Nelson thunked the equipment cases down on the floor and

crossed his arms. "I'd have to see the other space to find out which one'll be easier to light."

Alaine returned to her perusal of the kitchen. "Mrs. Guidry said they'll help us out with getting some new lights installed if our portables won't be sufficient."

Major felt as if he'd walked into the middle of a movie. "Cooking segments? I wasn't supposed to have prepared a cooking exhibition for today, was I?"

"No, no. Your weekly guest spot for my show."

"Oh." Now he really needed to talk to Meredith. It wasn't like her not to tell him when she made decisions that impacted his work. And even if the decision had come from farther up the food chain, the least Meredith could have done was to give him a heads-up. She was his *boss* after all.

"After we finish the interview, can you show us the other kitchen?"

"Sure." That would give him a good excuse to see if Meredith was back yet and talk to her. He had to talk through this restaurant thing with someone. He couldn't talk to Forbes—Forbes was representing his parents in the business deal. Meredith was the only other person he trusted.

Then why can't I bring myself to tell her about Ma?

He pushed the wayward thoughts aside and led Alaine and Nelson into his office. He'd think about his relationship issues with Meredith later. Much, much later.

"Hey, kiddo. Good meeting this afternoon?"

Meredith looked up from her computer at her dad's voice. "Yeah. I think we've got that wedding reception in the bag."

"How much are they wanting to spend?"

"At least six figures."

"That's my girl."

Yep. That's when her parents were proud of her: whenever she brought more money into the company coffers. "It's not signed yet."

"I'll put the pressure on the father of the bride—I'm playing golf with him Saturday morning. You hooked the fish; I'll just reel it in." He leaned his shoulder against the doorjamb. "Major was down here a little while ago looking for you. Said he needed to talk to you."

Meredith's insides cringed, but she kept her expression neutral. "Yeah, I've got a couple of e-mails from him that I haven't gotten around to yet—it's been such a busy week."

"Well, before you talk to him, there's something you should know." Her father rubbed the back of his neck. "Your mother and I offered to become investors in a restaurant with Major. He'd still work for you as the head of the catering division while the restaurant is in the start-up phase. But as soon as it opens, he'd be running the restaurant full-time."

Meredith took several deep breaths to try to settle her churning stomach. Major was going to leave B-G? She wouldn't get to see him every day. She might not see him ever again.

But you're supposed to be getting over him, remember? Maybe this is God's way of helping with that goal.

She cleared her throat. "I see. I guess I'll have to ask him to help me find a replacement executive chef."

"He hasn't accepted the offer yet, and we're not pushing him to make the decision quickly. Let him get through the Hearts to HEARTS banquet."

"Sounds reasonable." Meredith dug her thumbnail into the opposite palm. "Anything else?"

"He said he needed to talk to you about the financial report for New Year's Eve, too." Dad gave her his stop-sign farewell wave. "See you tomorrow. Don't work too late."

"'Night, Daddy." As soon as he disappeared, she rubbed her forehead. Her head—and heart—split in two: one part of her wanting to be happy that both she and Major would have a chance to move on, move forward; the other part mourning the loss of what she'd always wished would happen.

Major's Jeep—that old green thing he called Kirby—had still

been in the garage when she'd driven in a few minutes ago. Steeling herself to see him for the first time since making her New Year's resolution, she left the B-G corporate offices and got onto the elevator before second thoughts hit.

The orange, red, purple, and navy of sunset gave Vue de Ceil the aura of a cathedral. She paused for a moment just to appreciate the view.

Is this a sign, Lord? A sign that I'm doing the right thing by letting go of my childish crush on him? Of course it was. As was the fact that he would leave B-G to start a restaurant, and she'd rarely—if ever—see him again.

She entered the kitchen through the EXIT ONLY door, since it was closest—and then stopped. Voices came from Major's office. His, followed by—a woman's. Meredith took a step back, bumped the door, and covered her mouth with her hand. He was up here alone with a woman?

He said something; then both he and the unknown female laughed. The refrigerators and other equipment in the kitchen made too much noise for Meredith to clearly make out the words, and through the cracked-open door, she could see only the corner of the wardrobe that stood behind his desk.

Though she gulped, her lungs wouldn't fill with air. What more sign did she need to prove Major did *not* return her feelings and that it was time for her to move on?

Dazedly, she backed out through the door and somehow ended up at the elevators. When she'd voiced her resolution, it hadn't seemed like it would be hard—at least not *this* hard. But as her mother would say, *a goal that's easily attained doesn't bring the satisfaction that comes through sacrifice, hard work, and sometimes even tears.*

She held her breath to keep the tears at bay, staring out over the darkening city as the glass elevator descended. She refused to go through the pain she'd experienced in college. At least she was fairly certain that Major wasn't about to marry one of her closest friends as Brent had.

Back in her office, she sat down to work on her report—after all, the more she could get done now, the less she'd have to take home over the weekend. But the tinkling laughter of the mystery woman continued ringing in Meredith's head.

Who was she? What was it about this other woman that caught Major's attention—what quality Meredith didn't have?

Okay, stop. She had to concentrate on the report. See, this was why it was good she didn't have a relationship with someone she worked with. If she got this distracted by his having a conversation with another woman, what would she be like if Major actually returned her feelings—if they were dating?

Her head started throbbing, so she turned to grab a soda out of the mini-fridge. She'd just laid her hand on the neck of the last bottle when the Styrofoam carryout box caught her eye. Major's bold scrawl across the top of it sent chill bumps down the back of her neck:

Meredith—sorry I keep missing you. Hope you enjoy. I think this is one of your favorite meals.

M O'H

A raft of tears flooded her eyes, but she blinked hard to make them go away. She jumped when her cell phone buzzed against her waist and began trilling her general ringtone. An unfamiliar number scrolled across the screen.

With a deep breath, followed by clearing her throat, she clicked the appropriate button and pressed the device to her ear. "This is Meredith Guidry."

"Well, hello there, Meredith Guidry," came a deep voice. "This is Ward Breaux. You didn't answer the e-mail I sent earlier in the week, so I figured I'd give you a call."

Yeah, she'd been meaning to get around to reading that e-mail. "Hey, Ward. I guess you want to talk about my house, huh?"

"That wasn't my primary reason for calling, no." The humor that filled his voice conjured an image of him towering over her, giving her that grin and looking at her with flirtatious eyes. "I was hoping I could take you out for dinner tonight."

"Tonight?" Thursday. Dinner with the other unmarried adult cousins and siblings. "I can't tonight. I already have plans."

"Tomorrow then."

She pulled the phone away, stared at it in astonishment, and put it back to her ear. "Hold on. Let me check my calendar." She already knew what it would show her. No event tomorrow night that she needed to be at—the event planners were doing that—which meant that her Friday night might include going upstairs to watch a movie with Anne and George if they weren't going out.

"Am I freaking you out by moving too fast?" Ward's voice tingled on her skin like ice chips followed by a warm shower.

"No—not at all." She was freaked out by someone she'd only met four days ago calling her and asking her out for a date, since it had never happened to her. She tried to swallow the knot of nerves blocking her air passage. "It looks like I'm free tomorrow night."

"Great. Why don't I pick you up at your office—say around five thirty? Or is that too late for a Friday evening?"

Meredith pulled a pen from under the untidy stack of papers beside the computer and started drawing question marks on the back of a legal pad. "Sure. Five thirty. Here. Sounds fine."

"I hope you like jazz music. I know the greatest little club down on the river. I thought maybe we could get dinner in downtown and then drive over to Town Square, stroll along the Riverwalk, and then sit and have coffee and listen to some jazz."

The word *JAZZ* appeared in big, bold letters under her pen. "I love jazz. And if you're talking about the Savoy, I've been wanting to go there since they opened."

"Excellent. I'll see you at five thirty tomorrow evening, then. I can't wait."

"Me, too." She repeated his "Bye-bye now" farewell and hung up. She tapped the phone to her chin and glanced around the office, looking for some confirmation of what had just occurred.

Aside from the fact that for the last three months she'd been trying to think of some way to invite Major to go to the Savoy with her, she was excited about tomorrow night. The idea of going out with someone she didn't know the first thing about—well, she knew he was a contractor, so didn't know the second thing about—frightened her a little. But not as much as the blind dates Jenn wanted to set her up on.

Besides, if she was going to end her single status by this time next year, how else did she expect that to happen?

She leaned back in her chair and stared up at the ceiling. "Lord, please let him be a nice, normal, Christian guy—with no weird fetishes or obsessions. And if You could keep him from getting distracted by an attractive woman while we're on our date, I would so appreciate it."

Chapter 7

Major filled the thermal carafe with chicory-flavored dark roast, covered the platter holding warm croissants, strawberries and raspberries, bacon, shelled hard-boiled eggs, and a large ramekin of honey butter—everything he'd watched Meredith pile onto her plate the last time he'd seen her at one of her father's prayer breakfasts—and added them to the rolling service cart. Preparing a meal for someone he was mad at always helped him overcome the feelings and approach the situation in a positive frame of mind.

The silverware rattled against the porcelain plates when the cart's wheels bumped over the threshold of the freight elevator. He checked his watch again: 7:53. As long as she hadn't decided to come in early this morning, he should be able to get everything set up on the small conference table in her office before she arrived.

With a grinding squeal and an unnerving bounce, the elevator stopped on the fifth floor. He swiped his security card on the reader beside the door directly across the hall. Dark quiet enveloped the smaller-scale kitchen—the place Alaine Delacroix decided would be *just perfect* for the cooking segments on her midday news show. The segments Meredith had never told him about.

He rubbed his tongue against the backs of his teeth. Maybe Meredith had a good reason for why she'd failed to tell him she'd volunteered him to do a weekly cooking demonstration in addition to his regular job. His *full-time* job at which he worked nearly fifty hours a week—even longer when gearing up for big events, like the upcoming Hearts to HEARTS banquet.

The soft wheels of the cart whispered across the wood floor in the executive dining room and hallway. Meredith's office door stood open, and the lights were still off. Good. She wasn't here yet.

He glanced around as he raised the dimmer switch to bring the lights up. The dark wood along the curved juncture of wall and ceiling, copper ceiling tiles, cream walls, and dark-wood floors made the room look like a Boston cream pie. His stomach rumbled. But the rest of the office—he cringed. Unkempt stacks of paperwork sat on her desk. She'd obviously done some work at the small round table, too, because the vase of bright pink flowers sat near the far edge, as if shoved aside.

Three minutes until eight o'clock. He moved the vase to the center of the table then set out the plates, napkins, silverware, and cups and saucers. He measured distances between utensils and china using his fingers—the way Maggie Babineaux had taught him—then stepped back to make sure everything looked uniform and symmetrical.

"What's this?"

His stomach jumped at Meredith's voice. He stepped aside so she had an unhindered view of the tablescape. "Breakfast."

The shoulder strap of her overloaded briefcase fell from her shoulder into the crook of her elbow. She jolted to the side from the shift in weight, then hugged her arms around an opaque garment bag. "Breakfast?"

"Yes. You know, the meal that one usually eats first thing in the morning. Which for you typically consists of a child's-size box of Cheerios, dry, and possibly a tub of applesauce, if you get around to eating it, with several cups of coffee, I believe."

"What—do you have a nanny cam in here somewhere to keep up with my eating habits?" She smiled, but wariness still filled her eyes. She hung the garment bag on the coat hook on the back of the door then went around her desk, divested herself of her briefcase and purse, and turned on her computer.

"No, we've just had enough early morning meetings for me to observe the fact that you take a very haphazard approach to breakfast." He clasped his hands behind his back to try to stop the itching sensation in his fingers from wanting to go to her desk and straighten up all of the paper stacks, line up the several sticky notes on the edge of her computer monitor, and close the partially opened file drawer in the credenza behind her desk. The office hadn't looked this disheveled when he dropped off her dinner box yesterday afternoon.

"Do we—are we supposed to be meeting this morning?" She grabbed her thick leather planner out of her briefcase and flipped it open on top of the papers strewn over her desk blotter.

"No, but I saw on the computer that you don't have any meetings this morning—at least Outlook showed your time as free—and I hoped to be able to get half an hour with you."

Being in the same room with Meredith made yesterday's frustration with her evaporate. The dark gray suit she wore highlighted her figure to perfection—making him wonder what was in the hanging bag on the back of the door.

"Are you working an event tonight?"

"Tonight? No. Pam and Lori are overseeing a couple of functions—I thought they'd worked out the catering with your staff." Concern troubled her usually calm, golden brown eyes.

"Yes, I have staff assigned to both events. I just saw you'd brought extra clothes and wondered. . ." His thought drifted off when Meredith turned deep red.

"Oh, that." Her voice squeaked. "I have plans after work and didn't want to spend the evening in a suit."

Major stopped rubbing his tongue against his teeth and caught the inside of his cheek between them instead. Plans? A *date*? With whom?

"So what did you want to meet with me about?" She carried a legal pad and pen over to the conference table.

"Meet? Right. Why don't you get started serving your plate." He picked up the carafe and poured coffee for both of them.

"This looks wonderful, Major. Thanks for thinking of it." She sat down and draped the cloth napkin over her lap.

He cut open a croissant, slathered it with honey butter, arranged a layer of raspberries on one half, then replaced the top.

"A raspberry sandwich?" Meredith grinned at him as she layered her bread with bacon and the egg she'd just sliced. "Not a bad idea."

Of course she had a date tonight. Any man would have to be an idiot to pass up the chance to date Meredith Guidry. *Call me an idiot, then.* "Something I picked up from my roommate during culinary school."

"How's the week been? Sorry I've been missing you, but clearing everything up after the New Year's gala and trying to get things going for the H to H banquet have kept me running." Meredith took a big bite out of her bacon and egg sandwich.

Major hid his amusement. One thing he'd always appreciated about Meredith was the gusto with which she ate—no pretense, no falsely dainty bites, just a sheer enjoyment of the food in front of her. He washed down his raspberry croissant with a slug of coffee then gave her a recap of everything the catering division had done that week.

Meredith refilled both coffee cups. The recap of the catering division's week turned into a discussion of the New Year's Eve gala and what they could improve upon next year.

But I might not be here next year.

The last bite of his sandwich stuck in his throat. That was something he hadn't taken into consideration about the restaurant deal: not working with Meredith day in and day out. But *not* seeing her every day might help him stick to his resolve of never dragging her into the uncertainty of his life, the fear that at any time a call would come that his mother'd had a psychotic break and would have to be removed from the assisted-living facility and find a new place.

"So are you going to tell me what you wanted to meet with me about?" Meredith rested her elbows on the edge of the table and cradled her coffee cup in both hands.

He pushed his plate back, grateful for the derailment of his train of thought. "I guess you know that I had an interview with Alaine Delacroix from Channel Six yesterday."

"Alaine Delacroix? The girl who does that talk show at noon? Interviewed you?" Meredith's brows flattened into a frown.

Major didn't know what to make of her response. "Yeah. Apparently she's going to be doing a story on the Hearts banquet and wanted to interview me about that, and the New Year's gala. And she also wanted to talk to me about the cooking segment."

"The cooking segment?" Meredith almost dropped her coffee and set it down quickly. "What cooking segment?"

He rubbed his forehead. Obviously she was as much in the dark as he'd been. "You didn't know that I'm apparently supposed to be doing a weekly cooking demonstration for Alaine Delacroix's show?"

She shook her head. "This is the first I've heard about it."

"Oh." His heart twisted at the pained expression that filled Meredith's eyes—and the knowledge that he'd probably just put her in a very awkward position. "I thought maybe, since the catering division falls under your department. . ." Shame sloshed around in his gut at the memory of the accusatory anger he'd held toward her since yesterday.

"Catering does, yes. But you know that my parents sometimes like to make decisions without department directors' input." Meredith didn't pull her gaze away from her clasped hands.

He opened his mouth then clamped it shut. Asking Meredith if she really thought her parents did that with any of their other executive directors probably wasn't the best direction to take the conversation. He wanted to apologize, to take back the knowledge he'd just thrust upon Meredith that her parents didn't respect her authority and position. But once the soup was spilled, there was no getting it back into the pot.

"I'll talk to my mom and pass along whatever details she can give me." Meredith's soft voice and the weariness in her eyes when she finally looked up tugged at Major's heart. He wanted to reach over and hug her, wanted to express the sentiments he'd kept bottled up for years, wanted to make her a permanent fixture in his life.

But she deserved better. She deserved more than what he could offer her. She deserved a man who could devote his whole attention to her, who hadn't been a coward and hidden his schizophrenic mother from her.

"Is there something else on your mind?" Meredith asked.

He frowned and stared into the little bit of coffee remaining in his cup. "I had a meeting with your parents Monday. They want me to consider investing in a restaurant with them."

With what looked like a conscious effort, the remnants of her earlier frown disappeared. "Dad told me yesterday. It's a great opportunity for you. When would it happen?"

"I'm not sure. Forbes and I are supposed to be setting up a meeting to discuss the details." Major checked the carafe to see how much coffee remained before offering it to Meredith, but she waved him off.

"I knew this would happen eventually. You're too good to be kept from the general public by catering B-G events for the rest of your life."

"Thanks."

"It kills me to say this, but you have to do it. You've been wanting to open a restaurant for so long."

Major leaned back and hooked his arm around the top of the vacant chair beside him, all the fear and doubt that had kept him awake at night returning. "Meredith, you're one of the closest friends I have. I can't tell your parents or Forbes this, but I don't know what to do. I'm afraid."

An odd expression crossed her face before sympathy replaced it. "Afraid of what?"

"Failure. Of disappointing your parents. Of disappointing all those VIPs I met at your folks' house Monday."

The corner of her mouth quirked up. "And you've never worried about that here? I'm jealous."

Through the jocularity of her tone, her words hit home. "I guess. . .I guess because here I've always been working on someone else's orders—working someone else's plan—I've never had the sense of being completely responsible for the success or failure of an event. Not the way I would be as the person in charge of everything at a restaurant."

Meredith didn't say anything for a long moment. "This is probably going to sound like a patronizing question, but have you prayed about it?"

"Nonstop since I left their house."

"What is God telling you to do?"

"I'm not sure. A verse keeps running through my head, but I'm not sure how to interpret it."

"What verse?" She stood and crossed to her desk and sat at the computer.

" 'For to everyone who has, more shall be given, and he will have an abundance; but from the one who does not have, even what he does have shall be taken away.' I think it's in Matthew somewhere." He moved around and leaned against the edge of the desk where he could see her screen. He recognized the Web site she accessed—he used it all the time when it was his turn to lead Bible study, or when he filled in for the chaplain out at Beausoleil Pointe Center.

"Matthew 25:29, to be exact. It's in the parable of the talents—where the master gave each of three slaves some money. . . ."

"Two went out and doubled what they received; the third hoarded his and did nothing useful with it." Major dragged his fingers through his hair. "So is God telling me that if I don't take this opportunity, I'm acting like that third slave who risked nothing?"

Meredith turned to face him. "In my experience, faith is a lot like the money Jesus was talking about. Unless you use it—unless you invest it in some worthy endeavor—it will never grow. It'll never do you any good." She looked back at the screen. "Did you read this verse—15?"

" 'To one he gave five talents, to another, two, and to another, one, each according to his own ability. . . .'"

"'According to his own ability.'" Meredith repeated. "Do you think maybe *that's* what God is trying to tell you? He is rewarding your ability and wants you to go out and invest that reward?"

He squeezed her shoulders. "Thanks." His phone beeped, and he angled it from his belt to see the screen. "That's Steven wondering where I am."

"Reports by noon?"

"I'll send everything to your assistant." He loaded up the remnants of their breakfast onto the cart and departed—but turned to take one last look over his shoulder from the door.

Meredith sat at her desk, face buried in her hands.

His insides twisted around all that food he'd just eaten, hating himself for having caused pain to the woman he desired to please above all else.

Meredith pounded the backspace key on the computer's keyboard. She'd made the same spelling mistake five times while typing the memo that would go to her parents along with the spreadsheet her assistant was even now finalizing. Her brain buzzed with everything Major had told her this morning, and her emotions swung from despair at the thought of Major leaving B-G to start a restaurant to frustration and anger that her parents—Mom, most likely—had once again made a major decision that would impact one of the divisions in Meredith's department without alerting Meredith first.

She had no delusions that her parents would seek her advice or input on something like asking Major to appear on TV weekly, adding to his already overloaded schedule. But they could have at least informed her of their decision ahead of time so she didn't come across looking like such a complete imbecile in front of Major.

"Oh, for mercy's sake!" She smacked the edge of her keyboard with the heels of her hands when she misspelled the seafood vendor's name a sixth time.

"Everything okay, Meredith?" Corie, her administrative assistant, hesitated in the doorway, a thick folder in her hands.

"Just frustrated with myself." Meredith turned away from the computer and reached for the bottle of soda that usually sat next to her phone—but she hadn't replenished her stock yesterday. "What's up?"

Corie crossed the office and extended the folder. "I finished the spreadsheet and e-mailed it to you. Here's all the receipts and invoices."

"Does that include everything from catering?" Meredith took the file and set it on her desk without looking at it. Though just seven months out of college, Corie was the most efficient and organized assistant Meredith had ever had.

"Yes. Major got everything to me this morning."

"And the payroll report?"

"Included."

"Really? I was expecting to have to get on the phone with HR this afternoon and pull rank to get the information from them before deadline." Finally, something was going right today.

Corie filled her in on everything she'd done to get the report finished before the end of the day so Meredith could take it home to work on over the weekend.

"Good job. I owe you lunch big-time." Meredith glanced at the clock. "It's four o'clock. All I have left is to finish the memo, so if you don't have anything else you need to do today, why don't you go ahead and knock off early."

"Thanks, boss!" Corie bounced out of the office.

Once more, Meredith reached for the soda bottle, only to find empty air. "Good grief." She dug into her purse and pulled out a handful of coins.

"Did I miss something?" Corie asked when Meredith came out of the office.

"Nope. I just need a Coke."

"I can go get it for you." The assistant put her tote down on her desk.

"That's sweet. But you go on home. I'm perfectly capable of going down to the shop and getting a drink." No way was Meredith going to become one of those spoiled executives whose assistant did nothing but get her coffee, pick up her dry cleaning, and answer her phone—like her mother's executive assistant.

"I'll walk down with you."

On the five-flight trek down the stairs, at Meredith's inquiry, Corie talked about her plans for the weekend, which included a trip to Baton Rouge for a concert of some band Meredith had never heard of. Once they reached the first floor, Meredith bade the girl farewell and crossed the large, atrium-style lobby to the coffee shop–newsstand–convenience store.

"Afternoon, Miss Guidry."

She greeted the cashier and made a beeline for the refrigerated cases at the back of the small shop. She vacillated between ginger ale and root beer and finally chose Cherry Coke instead, figuring the caffeine would help with the dull headache she'd been trying to ignore all day. Plus, she wasn't sure how late she'd be out tonight, so the boost might be helpful.

She paid and headed back toward the bank of elevators—but was diverted when she saw one of her building maintenance managers and a couple of his guys at the security desk. When she joined them, the manager explained that several complaints had been made about trip-and-fall accidents on the twelfth floor near where new tenants were remodeling their office space.

Meredith tucked the information away to ask about in the facilities staff meeting on Monday if the manager forgot to mention it.

Back in her office, fortified with caffeine and sugar, Meredith returned to the report, recapping everything that happened from planning through execution of the New Year's Eve gala. Finally, at a quarter of five, she e-mailed the memo and spreadsheet to herself at home, then stuffed the folder of receipts and invoices into her bag.

She switched over to her e-mail program. . .and groaned. More than a hundred unread e-mails just since lunchtime. She scanned the subject lines. Nothing vitally important that couldn't wait until Monday. She shut down the computer and reached for the phone.

As she took a long swig of soda while listening to her twelve new voicemail messages, her eye caught on the garment bag hanging from the coat hook on the back of the door. Her stomach gave a little flip. In half an hour, Ward Breaux would arrive to take her on a date. A *date*.

She wrote down the messages on the page for Monday in her planner. Finished with those, she scanned the sticky notes scattered around her desk and stuck to the sides of her computer monitor. Half of them referenced completed projects, so she threw them away. The rest she stuck to the appropriate pages in her planner to deal with next week.

The phone rang, and she picked it up without looking at the caller ID window. "Events and Facilities Management. This is Meredith Guidry."

"Well, hello there, Meredith Guidry." Ward Breaux's voice sent goosebumps racing down Meredith's arms. "I just wanted to give you a heads-up that I left my job site earlier than I thought, so I'm probably going to be there about ten or fifteen minutes early. I hope that doesn't mess up your schedule."

She glanced at her watch. "No, I was just wrapping things up, as a matter of fact."

"Great. I'll see you in a few minutes then."

As soon as she hung up, Meredith jumped up from her desk and closed her door so she could change clothes. The dress was something Anne had talked her into buying a couple of years ago, and it had hung in Meredith's closet ever since. The chocolate brown matte-silk sheath topped with a three-quarter sleeve bolero had a very 1940s vibe to it, which was the only reason she'd been cajoled into buying it. Her round-toed brown pumps had a similar retro feel to them. She hoped she didn't look like she was wearing a costume.

Hanging the gray tweed suit in the garment bag, Meredith slipped into the marble and cherry powder room that connected her office with her mother's. She added a little makeup—but didn't go for the full war paint that she wore for formal events—and let her hair down from the clip she'd pulled it back with at the height of her frustration this afternoon.

The intercom on her phone buzzed. She jogged over to grab the receiver.

"Miss Guidry, there's a Ward Breaux here to see you."

"Yes, thank you. I'll be out in a moment."

Heart trying to make a jailbreak through her rib cage, she grabbed the small purse she'd tucked into her larger bag that morning, draped her burgundy wool car coat over her arm, and left the security of her office.

Most of the lights were out except for in the main hallway and the reception area, which the girls were getting ready to close down. Standing with his hands clasped behind his back, engrossed in the images of all the Boudreaux-Guidry properties mounted on the wall, was Ward Breaux. His charcoal overcoat made him look even larger than she remembered, and instead of the jeans and boots she'd seen him in before, dark pants and shiny black shoes showed beneath the hem of the coat.

She stopped, stomach knotted, and nearly turned tail and ran back to her office. No. She could do this. She *needed* to do this.

"Ward." Could she have sounded more breathless? She moved forward and extended her right hand. "It's good to see you again."

"Meredith." His grin was somewhat lopsided. She hadn't noticed that before. His large hand wrapped around hers, not in a businesslike handshake, but as if he were going to raise it to kiss the back of it. "When I met you, I thought you were beautiful. But I was wrong. You're gorgeous."

Her toes curled in their cramped confines. Heat prickled her face, knowing the two receptionists were gawking at them. "Thanks."

"Ready to go?" He turned and swept his arm toward the main doors.

"Yes." She allowed him to take her coat and assist her into it, and her breathing hitched when he settled his hand in the middle of her back to walk her to the door. Deep smile lines appeared in his cheeks when she looked up at him.

The front door swung open before they got to it. Meredith stopped, mortified.

Of anyone who could possibly walk through those doors at five twenty on a Friday evening, why, oh why, did it have to be Major O'Hara?

Chapter 8

Major stopped and did a double take of the couple standing in front of him. Some guy had his arm around Meredith—who looked absolutely stunning. Something hot and sticky and. . .and. . .green oozed through every piece of Major's being.

She had the decency to blush almost as dark red as her coat. "Major? Did you need something?"

The temptation to hide the Styrofoam box behind his back and make up some other excuse for his presence made his hand start to shake. How could he have forgotten she'd mentioned she had plans tonight?

"I—one of the sauté chefs didn't show up, so we got into the weeds this afternoon, and I forgot. . ." He held up the box. "I forgot to bring you a dinner box."

"Oh." An expression that looked quite close to pity flickered across Meredith's face. She glanced at her companion then back at Major. "It'll keep till Monday, won't it?"

He was the biggest idiot in the world. "Yeah. . .yes, it should. I'll put it in the fridge in the executive kitchen just to make sure it stays cold enough."

"Thanks. I have so many meetings on Monday, it'll be nice to know I don't have to worry about scrounging up lunch." She twisted the shoulder strap of her briefcase with her left hand.

When Meredith again glanced at the man beside her, Major turned his attention in that direction as well. Because he was six foot one, not many men made Major feel short—but this guy did. He towered over Meredith, even in her high heels, by almost a foot.

"I'm sorry. I should have introduced you. Major, this is Ward Breaux. Ward—Major O'Hara, B-G's executive chef."

The curly-haired giant didn't even have the decency to take his left arm from around Meredith when he shook Major's hand.

"So, how do you two know each other?" Major cringed, but the words were out of his mouth before he could stop them.

"I had the very good fortune of running into Meredith at the hardware store on New Year's Day. I knew it must be fate—how often does a guy run into a gorgeous lady like this buying wood epoxy on a holiday?" Breaux smiled down at Meredith with a proprietary gleam in his dark eyes.

Molten heat roiled in Major's stomach. "Really?"

Meredith cleared her throat. "Ward is a contractor. He's going to give me a bid for finishing the work on my house."

"Oh." That didn't explain why Meredith was wearing a silk dress and looking like a movie star.

"Yes—but I do have to admit, I'm much more interested in the *owner* of the house right now." The interloper glanced at his watch—and returned his arm around Meredith's waist. "If we're going to make our six o'clock reservations, we should go."

"I'll put this away for you." Major wanted to draw her into his arms and show his previous claim but settled for giving her the warmest smile he could muster. "I'll see you Monday."

"Bye."

He turned when he reached the executive dining room, hoping to see Meredith watching him with longing in her gaze. But she and Breaux were already disappearing through the frosted-glass doors.

"Stupid, stupid, stupid, stupid," he mumbled, making his way through the dining room by the dim light from the cityscape beyond the windows. In the kitchen, he felt his way along in the dark until he found the handle on the door of the reach-in refrigerator.

The reception lobby was dark when he came out, and he had to unlock the doors to exit. He fished his keys out of his pocket and locked up before heading toward the elevators. They took too long, so he opted for the stairs instead.

He should have been happy for Meredith finding time to date, having a social life, allowing room for romance in her busy schedule. But seeing her with another man only made Major want to make her part of his life all the more.

Who was he kidding? He'd seen the amount of work she was taking home with her to do this weekend. If he had the added pressure of getting a restaurant started, not only would his social life become nearly nonexistent, but what little personal time he might have would need to be spent with Ma. He had to let go of Meredith.

Knowing his brain wasn't going to easily let go of the image of Meredith with the Jolly Green Giant, he pointed Kirby toward Beausoleil Pointe Center.

The receptionists greeted him by name at the front desk, and many of the residents did the same as he made his way to Ma's apartment. When she didn't answer the door, he walked down the hall to the common room.

"Major, what are you doing here?" Ma looked up from her hand of cards when he approached her table.

"I came to see you."

"Today isn't your regular day to come. I'm busy. You'll have to come back another day."

After all these years, his mother telling him to go away shouldn't have stung like it did. But after being rejected by Meredith a little while ago, albeit in a roundabout fashion, it hurt that the person he was giving Meredith up for didn't want to see him either.

"Fine. You know how to reach me if you change your mind."

He trudged back out to the Jeep and squealed the tires a bit pulling out of the parking lot. If he were already running a restaurant, he'd be there on a Friday night and not worrying about how the two women in his life didn't want him. He also wouldn't have to face the fact that he'd done such a good job of keeping everyone out of his personal affairs that he found himself in this situation.

Would it really be so terrible if Meredith knew about Ma?

Major's mind went back to the last time his mother had a real, full-blown schizophrenic episode. He shuddered. Yes, it really would be so terrible if Meredith had to witness that. Just like the few other women he'd dated, if she found out, she would look at him in disgust, wondering when that was going to happen to him—and then hightail it out of there. And he wouldn't blame her. There were times he wished he could do the same.

He stopped at the international market on the way home and picked up a bunch of random, interesting ingredients. Back at the condo, he put *The Fighting Seabees* DVD on and started cooking—thinking about and planning for what he might put on the menu of his restaurant.

The opportunity offered by the Guidrys looked more and more like the only future Major had.

"You've hardly touched your *cordero*."

Meredith cut another small piece of the braised lamb. Cooked with honey, garlic, and onions, and topped with crumbled Cabrales cheese, the strong flavors burst in her mouth. But nerves kept her from enjoying it as she should.

She set her fork and knife on the edge of the plate and raised her napkin to wipe her mouth. "I think I ate too much of the tapas. Of course, they gave me enough of this"—she indicated the large lamb chop atop a mound of garlic mashed potatoes—"to feed three people." And plenty to take a sample to Major, who always liked trying new dishes.

Her chest once again felt like it would cave in at the memory of the look on Major's face when he'd seen her with Ward. Had she imagined the flicker of jealousy in his eyes?

Ward waved the server over and asked for a takeaway box. "And two flans for dessert with *café con leche*." He gave Meredith a slow smile.

She couldn't help but smile back at him, though his high-handed manner was starting to grate on her nerves a bit. Just because they were in a Spanish restaurant and he spoke the language didn't mean she couldn't order for herself.

Nevertheless, it was kind of charming and old-fashioned in its way. And if she were out with Major, she'd allow him to order for her. But of course, she had good reason to trust Major implicitly when it came to food.

"You were telling me about your college major," Ward reminded her.

"Art history. I specialized in the arts and crafts movement."

"Thus your love of the craftsman style of architecture?"

"Yes. I've wanted a craftsman bungalow since I was a little girl." She grinned. "And now I have one."

"One that isn't livable." His dark brows arched over gray eyes twinkling with amusement.

His flirtatiousness had made her uncomfortable at the beginning of the meal, but now she rather enjoyed the focused attention. "But you're going to help me remedy that, aren't you?"

"I'll do my best."

"I do have one request—I'd like to ask Major O'Hara to help with the kitchen design. He worked with the architects who designed the kitchens at B-G—the large one for Vue de Ceil and the smaller executive kitchen—and I've seen some of his ideas for his dream home kitchen that I hope to incorporate in my house." Of course, when she'd originally come up with this idea, it had been with the thought in mind that the kitchen might one day be his, if he ever woke up and realized she was in love with him.

No. She couldn't allow herself to think like that anymore. He'd had eight years. She couldn't waste any more time on him.

"That's an excellent idea. When we get to that point, I'll be happy to work with him." Ward looked down at his buzzing phone.

Meredith grimaced but quickly schooled her expression. While Ward hadn't actually answered his cell phone during dinner, several times he'd looked down when it vibrated to see who was calling him. She'd have to check with Anne and Jenn, but she was under the impression that proper etiquette was to turn one's cell phone off when out on a date. That's why hers was currently just a deadweight in the bottom of her purse.

He glanced across at her. Some of what she was thinking must have shown in her expression.

"Sorry. I'll turn this off. I'm such a phone addict, it's hard for me to ignore it." He looked up and leaned back when the server brought their desserts.

The baked custard with the burnt-sugar syrup was almost as good as Anne's favorite dessert—crème brûlée—but not quite as good as cheesecake. She savored each bite slowly.

"If you majored in art history, how did you end up becoming a big-time corporate executive? I mean, I know it's your parents' company and all, but it seems like you'd have gone into some kind of design work, or maybe become curator at an art gallery."

"I thought about that—actually, I minored in interior design as an undergrad." She put her spoon down after about half of the rich dessert. "When I finished my master's degree, I was ready to get out of Mom and Dad's house, to live on my own. But the part-time job I had at the city art museum wasn't enough to pay rent and utilities and buy groceries."

She tried not to stare at the way Ward's long, tapered fingers curled around his spoon. She could get used to eating out with him.

Clearing her throat, she continued. "At that time, my cousin Anne was the event planner for B-G—and the company was much smaller then with just a couple of event venues. But they'd just acquired Lafitte's Landing, which almost doubled the amount of work Anne had to do, so she needed an assistant. And I needed a full-time job."

"And your cousin. . .she doesn't work there anymore?"

"She started her own wedding- and event-planning business almost six years ago. As the only person left in the department, I was promoted."

"Now you're an executive director." He spooned up the last bit of syrup on his plate. "And from your title, it sounds like you do a whole lot more than planning events."

"Yeah." Meredith let out a sardonic chuckle. "I do a lot of paperwork."

"That's not what I meant, and you know it."

"It's my job. I do what's required of me." *And I try to live with the fact that my parents have no respect for my title or authority.*

"So the reason you bought a house that's gutted inside is because you wanted to get back to your first love—designing?"

She shrugged. "I guess that had something to do with it. I love renovation projects. I've done most of the interior renovations in the triplex."

"Triplex?"

"Where I live. About a year ago, Anne bought the old Victorian where we live—it's split into three apartments. She and my sister Jenn and I have lived in those apartments for five or six years." She sipped the café con leche—rich, bitter coffee tempered by scalded milk.

"You live with your cousin and your sister; you work for your parents. Do you ever get away from your family?"

"Get away from them?" She thought about the glorious hours she'd spent at her house Monday, relieved that after Anne's and Forbes's phone calls, everyone had left her alone. "Not very often. But I have a large family—immediate and extended—and we're all very close to each other."

"I'll bet I could beat you on family size. I'm one of six." Ward pushed his dessert plate aside and lifted the delicate china cup. It could have looked awkward in his large, calloused fingers, but he moved with grace, making it look as if he was accustomed to such finery.

"I have four brothers and three sisters." She pursed her lips together, daring him to challenge her, ready to pull out a family photo to prove it.

"You've got me there. Do they all live in town?"

"Every single one."

"Let me guess. You're the oldest?"

"Second. I have one older brother."

"And does he work for your parents' company as well?"

"No. He's a lawyer."

"A respectable choice if he wasn't going to go into the family business." He swirled the liquid in his cup. "You said your sister lives with you. I guess she's next oldest to you?"

"We don't actually live *together*—we do have separate apartments." Which was a good thing, given Jenn's penchant for not picking up after herself.

"Let me guess—doctor?"

Meredith laughed at the image of Jenn dealing with sick people. "Restaurateur. She owns The Fishin' Shack down in Comeaux."

"I've heard about that place. You'll have to take me there sometime."

Ward continued questioning her about her family until he'd heard what each of her brothers and sisters did, about Marci's engagement, and what Meredith knew of the plans for Anne's wedding.

When the bill arrived, Meredith reached for her purse.

"What are you doing?" Ward asked, his thick, dark brows drawn together.

"I. . .I guess I'm just used to going out with friends and having to pay my own way."

"If you haven't already figured it out, Meredith, I'm sort of an old-fashioned guy. Which means that when I ask a lady out on a date, I pick up the tab." He slipped a platinum card into the bill folder and laid it on the edge of the table.

A few minutes later, Ward helped her back into her coat and escorted her from the restaurant, carrying her takeaway box for her.

On the drive to Town Square, Meredith turned the tables on him and questioned him about his siblings, learning that two of his brothers worked in the construction business with him—one as a painting contractor, one as an electrician.

The Savoy was pretty crowded when they got there. She followed Ward through the forest of bodies, glad for his large size, as people tended to get out of his way. He left her at the table to go get beverages.

Meredith shrugged out of her coat and draped it across the back of her chair, glad to have a moment to reflect and regroup.

She liked Ward, was enjoying the evening with him. But being completely honest with herself, the chemistry just wasn't there. His lopsided grin didn't make her heart zing the way the faintest hint of a dimple in Major's cheek could.

Maybe it was just a matter of time. She'd known Major a lot longer. Maybe Ward just needed to grow on her.

She frowned at a sudden thought. She'd known Major for almost a decade, Ward for less than a week. Yet she already knew more about Ward's family than she knew about Major's. The only thing she knew for sure about Major was that he'd been raised by a single mother. She assumed he was an only child, since he never mentioned brothers or sisters. But he never really mentioned his mother, either, so she couldn't be sure. She knew his mom was still living—she'd overheard Forbes asking Major about his mother awhile back.

Maybe they'd had a falling-out. Maybe he didn't really see or talk to her anymore. Her heart ached for him and made her want to include him in her family all the more.

"Here you go. One Sprite with a twist of orange." Ward set her glass down on the table. "You looked so serious just a second ago. Everything okay?"

"Thanks. Yes, everything's fine. Just thinking about. . .a friend who isn't as fortunate as we are to have big, close-knit families." She took a large gulp of the soda, enjoying the tangy taste and the slight burn of the fizz going down her throat.

"There is a downside to families like ours." Ward twisted the cap off his bottle of sparkling water.

"What's that?"

"They're always in our business. You know, I didn't tell my brothers why I needed to leave the job site early this afternoon. I knew if I told them I was going on a date with a girl I picked up at the hardware store, there wouldn't have been an end to the grief they would have given me."

Meredith laughed. "I know exactly what you mean. I had dinner with some of my siblings and cousins last night, and there was no way I was going to tell them about tonight. Especially my older brother."

"Protective?"

"Yes—and somewhat high-handed. If he can't control something, he doesn't like it one bit."

Ward grinned, showing his perfect, ultrawhite teeth. "I think that's an affliction all oldest brothers have. I'm that way with my siblings—especially my sisters."

"It's one thing to be protective, but Forbes is actually a genuine control freak. I could tell you stories about him that would make you reconsider classing yourself in the same category with him as an oldest brother." Guilt over bad-mouthing her brother rushed in. "Now, don't get me wrong; I love my brother dearly—"

Ward leaned forward and caressed her cheek, stopping her excuse—and all coherent thought. "I understand."

Meredith sat frozen, mesmerized by the warmth in Ward's eyes. What was it about chemistry she'd been thinking a few minutes ago?

"Well, well, well. What's this?"

The all-too-familiar voice drew her out of her entrancement. She looked over Ward's shoulder and cringed to see Forbes, one hand on his hip, an inquisitive light in his eyes.

Ward turned to look.

No way to get out of the situation now. "Ward Breaux, this is my older brother, Forbes Guidry."

Ward stood and shook Forbes's hand enthusiastically. "We've just been talking about our families. It's wonderful to meet you. Won't you join us?"

Meredith's stomach felt as if it was about to reject that huge, expensive dinner she'd just eaten.

"Thank you, but no. I'm entertaining clients tonight. I just thought I'd come over and say hello."

"Hello, Forbes," Meredith said. "Good-bye."

He had the audacity to wink at her.

Chapter 9

"Can I catch a ride with you to church this morning?" Jennifer helped herself to a large mug of coffee.

"Hey—I haven't had any of that yet!" Meredith reached for the cup, but her sister twirled to keep it out of her reach. Typical.

"You can make more."

"I don't know how you're going to survive when we don't live in the same house." Meredith tightened the belt of her robe and crossed her arms.

Holding the cup to her lips, Jenn blew across the surface of the steaming liquid, sending a few drops of it over the opposite side. "I'll have you know I signed a lease on a house—not an apartment mind you—a house less than half a block from the restaurant."

Meredith stopped halfway through grabbing a napkin from the holder on the table and sank into the nearest chair. "You're moving to Comeaux?"

Jenn shrugged and slurped the coffee. "Why not? I'm at the restaurant eighty or so hours a week. It's wasteful for me to be driving the twenty or thirty miles back to an apartment in Bonneterre when I can walk to work. And the rent's a lot cheaper down there, too."

For all that Meredith had enjoyed teasing her sister over the past few months about how lost Jenn would be without being able to raid Meredith's or Anne's kitchens or catch a ride somewhere with one of them, she hadn't really thought through how *she* would feel without her sister so close by. They'd shared a room until Meredith was eighteen and moved into the dorms at college.

She swallowed hard against the emotion swelling in her throat. "When are you going to move?"

"The house won't be ready until March first. But I'm going to rent a storage unit down there and go ahead and start packing up books and stuff that I'm not using right now. That way I don't have quite as much to do when the time comes. What about you? Are you really going to hire someone to finish that house of yours?"

Meredith shook off the melancholy and crossed the small kitchen to the coffeepot. She poured what was left into her mug then started another half pot brewing. She added flavored, powdered creamer to her cup and stared into it as she stirred and the liquid turned a kind of grayish brown. She smirked, remembering the last time Major had seen her use powdered creamer in her coffee. He'd looked like he was about to be sick or cry—or both.

"Mere?"

"Who—oh, yeah, I've found a contractor."

Ward Breaux's darkly handsome features replaced Major's in her mind's eye. She'd had a surprisingly good time Friday night, and he'd been everything she'd always imagined a romantic date would be. As they said good-bye at her SUV in the parking garage, her heart had raced—with nervous energy only, she was certain—when for a moment she thought he was going to try to kiss her.

She touched the back of her right hand where his lips had landed instead.

"Are you even awake this morning?"

An oven mitt smacked the back of Meredith's head and knocked loose the towel wrapped around her wet hair. "Cut it out, will ya? I just have a lot on my mind." She turned and leaned her hip against the cabinet.

"So can I?" Jenn stood with her hand on the knob of the door out to the common stairwell.

"Can you what?"

Her younger sister heaved a dramatic sigh. "Look, I'm sorry I took your coffee—obviously you need it more than I do this morning. Can I get a *ride* with you to *church*?"

"Yeah. Of course. But if you're not down here ready to walk out the door at nine o'clock, I'm leaving without you."

"You say that every time, and you never do," Jenn called over her shoulder, leaving Meredith's door standing open.

"And every time, we walk in late wherever we're going." Meredith closed the door and sent up a quick prayer that Jenn would be better about closing doors—and locking them—when she lived by herself. Sometimes Meredith was amazed that Jennifer was thirty-two and owned a successful business instead of still seventeen and playing her way through high school.

She poured a full, fresh cup of coffee and carried it with her—but stopped in the middle of the living room. Jenn hadn't said anything to indicate she'd heard about Meredith's date Friday. More than twenty-four hours was usually ample time for everyone in the family to find out what one of their siblings had been up to.

Maybe, for once in his life, Forbes had decided to allow Meredith to have some semblance of a private life. He'd left the Savoy much earlier than Meredith and Ward had, and surprisingly, her brother hadn't called or e-mailed about it yesterday.

Worries about what Forbes might say to the rest of the family plagued her as she finished getting ready for church. Finally, dressed in a tailored suede jacket over a brown tweed skirt, she retrieved her Bible from the nightstand and took it and the pumps she'd worn Friday night into the kitchen.

A bowl of cereal and another cup of coffee later, she sat at the kitchen table, staring at the clock on the back of the stove as the minutes ticked away. At 8:55 she returned to the bathroom to brush her teeth and put lipstick on. At nine o'clock on the nose, she stepped into her shoes, grabbed her Bible and purse, and walked out to the SUV.

It only took ten minutes to get to church, and Sunday school never started at nine fifteen like it was supposed to. But she was tired of Jenn's taking advantage of her. Just like everyone else did.

At five minutes after nine when Jenn still hadn't appeared, Meredith started the engine. Movement caught her eye, and she waved at George, who pulled his car up behind Anne's on the parking apron. Anne appeared almost immediately, and they were off.

She shifted into reverse, feeling guilty that she was about to leave her sister behind. But Jenn had her own car; and since it wasn't raining, the fact that the ragtop leaked shouldn't be an issue.

Besides, what message was she sending Jenn if she didn't follow through on her threat? Jenn treated Meredith just like their parents did. They made decisions and just expected Meredith to go gladly along with them.

She backed out and drove away.

No more. She liked making people happy, but she wasn't going to let anyone walk all over her any longer. Not Mom and Dad. Not Jennifer. And not Major O'Hara.

Jenn didn't show up for Sunday school but caught Meredith in the vestibule outside the sanctuary before worship service.

"I can't believe you left without me."

Meredith raised her brows. "I warned you I would."

"But you didn't mean it. I was counting on you to call me, or else I wouldn't have gone back to bed."

"I guess you have less than two months to acclimate yourself to getting up and out the door on Sundays. Don't forget, it's going to take you half an hour to get here after you move."

Jenn rolled her eyes and flounced away like a petulant teen.

Forbes intercepted Jenn and gave her one of his headlock hugs, greeting her with a, "Hey, kiddo."

Jenn launched into blaming Meredith for making her late, and it looked like Forbes would take Jenn's side—as usual.

Meredith shook her head and moved into the sanctuary to the opposite side from where she usually sat with her brother and sister in the midst of the singles group. Until now, she hadn't realized how juvenile Forbes's standard greeting for his sisters appeared.

A rustling beside Meredith caught her attention. Anne, followed by George, sidled in and sat beside her.

"Everything okay?" Anne didn't hug her, headlock her, kiss her, or touch her in any way.

Meredith appreciated it. "Just needed a break from the sibs."

Across the large sanctuary, Meredith's brothers and sisters gathered with the rest of the single adults and college students. Though some of the other people did hug each other in greeting, they were quick, almost perfunctory gestures.

"Anne, is my family abnormally touchy-feely?"

"What?"

"Do you think that my brothers and sisters are too physically affectionate?"

"You make it sound like something bad."

Meredith combed her teeth over her bottom lip but stopped when she tasted lipstick. "That's not what I mean."

Anne cast a sidelong glance at George—her fiancé sat a modest few inches away from her, and though his arm rested along the back of the pew behind Anne, it wasn't as if he really had his arm *around* her.

"Yeah," Anne drawled the syllable out. "You and the rest of your siblings tend to be a little more touchy-feely than what makes some people comfortable. But y'all practically lived on top of each other most of your lives. It was bound to make you extremely close and comfortable with your lack of personal space, or it could have made you hate each other and never want to be near each other once you grew up and left the house."

"I think it's why they have no respect for me," Meredith murmured.

"What do you mean? Of course they respect you."

Meredith gave her cousin her most exasperated look. "No, they don't. Everyone takes advantage of me. And it's because of what you said: no boundaries." She had to raise her voice slightly as the organist began playing the prelude. "How can my parents take me seriously as an executive in the company when Rafe comes in and tackles me on the sofa in front of them? Or Jenn makes me her alarm clock and chauffeur?"

The organ's bellowing almost drowned out the end of Meredith's question. She leaned closer to her cousin. "None of them treat you that way. And when you were in charge, Mom and Dad would never have made decisions affecting our department without discussing it with you first."

Anne reached over and laid her hands atop Meredith's balled fists. "I'm sorry you feel that way. Why don't we plan dinner early this week, and we can talk about it and figure out what you can do."

Anne's calm acceptance of what Meredith said reassured her, and Meredith stood to sing the first hymn with a lighter heart.

When the service ended, Meredith lagged behind the rest of her relatives, debating whether or not to skip the weekly gathering of the full extended family. But making the decision to stand up to her parents and siblings and then hiding from them seemed counterintuitive.

Aunt Maggie and Uncle Errol's house rang with voices when Meredith entered. All of the single and young adult cousins would be out in the sunroom. Meredith detoured into the kitchen where her grandmother, aunts, Anne, and a few older cousins and cousins' wives put final preparations on dinner. If any of them were surprised by Meredith's offer to help, they didn't let on.

Once seated at the enormous table, which fit everyone over college age, Meredith glanced around at her immediate family members with new eyes. Sunday dinner with the entire Guidry clan was a given—just like going to church or going to school when they were growing up. There were a few times Meredith had wished it otherwise: most especially her first few years out of college and in the singles group at church, when every week she turned down the invites to go out to lunch with them. Eventually, the invitations stopped.

She couldn't remember the last time she'd participated in a social activity that didn't consist of mainly her relatives. Ward's question Friday rang in her head. *Do you ever get away from your family?*

"Hey, earth to Meredith."

She snapped out of her thoughts when Marci poked her shoulder. The men had already cleared the table and disappeared into the kitchen to wash the dishes.

"It's your turn." Marci pushed her auburn hair back with her left hand, her engagement ring catching the light.

"My—oh. I had a rather uneventful week after the New Year's Eve gala was over. Lots of paperwork to do. Nothing exciting."

"Yeah, except leaving people stranded when they're counting on you for a ride." Jenn could pout with the best—worst?—of them.

Meredith tried to laugh it off. "Don't be so melodramatic. You have a car; you weren't stranded."

"The roof leaks—I told you."

"It isn't raining—" Frustration bubbled up in Meredith's chest, but she did her best to squelch it. Arguing with her sister over something so stupid wouldn't help gain her family's respect.

She turned to face her grandmother again. "Anyway, nothing too exciting." Should she tell them about Ward?

Marci's glittering diamond hinted that Meredith would come across as desperately trying to one-up her younger sister if she blurted out, "I went on my first real date ever."

Meredith refolded her napkin and set it on the table. "A friend and I went to the Savoy Friday night."

"The new jazz club?" Across the table, Anne leaned forward, blue eyes dancing. "George and I have been talking about going. How was it?"

Perfect, until Forbes showed up. "Great. Their house band could give anyone in New Orleans a run for their money. I'd never heard of the headline act, but they were great, too."

"Next time you go, let me know—George and I might tag along with you."

A double date? Meredith considered the possibility but dismissed it pretty quickly. Until she knew Ward better—and her tummy tingled at the idea—it might be nice to keep at least that small part of her life private. Because once everyone found out about him, they would bombard her with questions and would want her to bring him to Thursday night supper or Sunday dinner so they all could meet him.

Before she could think of an excuse to leave the table, the male members of the family returned, signaling it was time to head home. She'd just started to push her chair back and disappear in the general melee, but the chair bumped into something and wouldn't budge.

Hands clamped onto her shoulders in a squeeze. She hunched her shoulders and pulled away, slipping sideways from the chair to stand up.

A confused frown formed an upside-down Y between Forbes's eyebrows. "What's with you today?"

"I don't know what you're talking about." Meredith skirted around her brother and tried to escape. She made it to the quiet of the front foyer before Forbes caught up with her.

"Meredith, stop."

"Please don't tell me what to do." She hooked her arm through her purse straps and dug out her keys.

"I'm not trying to order you around. I just want to find out why you're mad at the world today."

She sighed. No one in the family—least of all control-freak Forbes—would easily understand her sudden need for privacy. "Just because I don't feel like being touched doesn't mean I'm angry. I simply need my personal space."

Forbes folded his arms. "Personal space I can understand. But running off this morning after you told Jenn she could ride to church with you?"

"Forbes, she's thirty-two years old! She's not a teenager anymore. And she needs to start taking responsibility for her own life and for getting herself the places she needs to go."

"This doesn't sound like you, Mere."

"Well, it is me. Or at least the me I am when I'm not trying to be the person everyone else thinks I *should* be."

One of Forbes's brows arched up. "No one has ever asked you to be something you're not."

Meredith matched his crossed-arm stance. "Really? Then why is Mom still mad that I bought a house that needed to be renovated—and that I chose to do it myself?" Moisture burned her eyes, but she blinked it away. "No one in this family really knows me, knows who I am—except Anne—and I'm tired of having to hide behind this veneer of the perfect daughter, the one who never stands up for herself, the one who always defers to someone else's decision or opinion." She caught her breath before she hyperventilated. "I'm tired of constantly trying to please everyone else. And I know that sounds selfish, and maybe I am. But that's what's 'up' with me today."

Sadness filled her brother's blue-gray eyes. "I wish you'd said something before you got to the point where this has hurt you so much." He reached for her, but Meredith stepped back.

The hurt expression that replaced the sadness nearly made Meredith feel guilty. "I'm sorry, but I need space. I need time—time away from being with the family every waking minute—to figure out who I really am, to figure out what it is I truly want out of life."

Forbes looked as if he wanted to argue, but he restrained himself at great effort. "I understand. And I'll try to cover for you with the family while you sort things through. But I hope you know that I'm here for you—for the *real* you—no matter what. You can tell me anything."

"Thanks." She smiled, keeping her lips pressed tightly together to keep the bottom one from quivering. Not wanting to leave things between them quite so tense, she cast around for something to lighten the mood.

Of course.

"Oh, and I'd like to also thank you for not saying anything to the family about Friday night. I already know that rumors are going to get around at the office—since he picked me up there and several people saw him." Including Major, which still wrenched Meredith's heart. "But I'd rather not have the family know just yet that I went out on a date."

Forbes tried his best to look offended. "I? You think that I would immediately run off and tell everyone that I caught you out on a date with someone we've never met before?" Humor danced around his mouth. "I'll make you a deal. You tell me all about him, and I'll keep it to myself until you're ready for the family to know."

She sighed and shook her head. Change wasn't going to come easily. She just hoped she was up for the challenge.

Chapter 10

"Please tell me my face isn't really that puffy."

"No, Chef."

"Of course not, Chef."

Somehow, Major didn't believe Steven and Jana's denials. There, for all of Bonneterre to see, his pudgy face filled the TV screen. Sure, the antique-reproduction wardrobe behind him looked good. The bright lights hadn't washed him out as much in the burgundy coat as it would have if he'd worn the white one, but he couldn't deny that he looked like a chipmunk on an acorn binge.

"I don't think I can watch the rest of this. Y'all can stay and watch the whole thing, but don't forget, we have lunch service going on right now."

Eyes glued to the TV, his sous chef and head server waved him out of his own office.

"You can handle it, boss." Steven moved from the edge of the desk into Major's chair without even looking at him.

Indeed, the kitchen and waitstaff had Monday lunch service well under control. Major headed out into the main room and walked from table to table, chatting with regulars and introducing himself to those he'd never met before. News about this year-old project seemed to be spreading around downtown, and people working in nearby buildings had started coming to Vue de Ceil for weekday lunches, since they would probably never get another chance to see the famed event venue. After all, this was where local-boy-turned-movie-star Cliff Ballantine had held his wedding reception last year.

Not only was Major happy his idea had proved a good one, making him look even better to the Guidrys, but he was happy that it had allowed people like Steven and Jana—who'd been his most loyal part-timers—to work for him full-time instead of just when he needed them for events. And the Guidrys had been happy to put Vue de Ceil to use five days a week, instead of having it sitting empty for weeks and even months at a time.

If only he could have this kind of success in the restaurant's first year. His stomach twisted. That had been a line of questioning he hadn't expected from Alaine Delacroix last week. Obviously, Mrs. Guidry had filled the reporter in on every aspect of it except one: that Major hadn't officially accepted the offer yet.

A flicker of light to his left caught his attention. One set of the reflective elevator doors slid open to reveal Anne Hawthorne, along with several other people—including Meredith. Major tugged the hem of his coat to straighten it and resisted the urge to run his fingers through his hair.

In a bright blue sweater, Meredith reminded him of a soothing waterfall. He tried to smile at her when she looked over at him; she smiled back but glanced away again quickly. Avoiding her at church yesterday had been easy, since he always went to the early service and a late Sunday school class; and looking at her now, he couldn't help but see her standing next to that guy Friday night, dressed to the nines and looking too beautiful for words.

He met them at the perimeter of the room.

"As you can see," Meredith told the potential clients, "Vue de Ceil definitely has enough capacity to host your event, with room to seat everyone at four- and eight-person tables, if that's what you want." She barely spared Major a glance, as if embarrassed to meet his eye again.

Anne stepped forward. "This is Major O'Hara, executive chef for all events held at Boudreaux-Guidry properties." Anne introduced her clients—a bride who appeared to be hardly out of high school, along with her parents, future mother-in-law, and a couple of grandmothers.

"Oh yes! I was at the New Year's ball just a few days ago," the future mother-in-law gushed. "What a wonderful spread of food. If that's the quality we can look forward to, I definitely recommend this place."

"Thank you, ma'am." Why wouldn't Meredith look at him? "It's my goal to try to serve the best food possible at every event—to make it delicious and memorable."

"That's just what we want," said the mother of the bride. She turned to Anne. "When do you think we can get this booked and set up the menu?"

Anne raised her eyebrows in question to Meredith.

"We can go back down to my office now and look at dates for your event. Once we have that scheduled, Chef O'Hara will develop several sample menus for you to choose from. After that, we'll set up a tasting."

This seemed to please everyone, and Meredith herded them back to the elevator.

"Are we still on for two o'clock tomorrow afternoon?" Anne asked, slowly bringing up the rear of the group.

"Yeah." Major frowned. Something was definitely wrong with Meredith. Was she afraid he was going to ask her about her date Friday? "I'll bring the cost analyses for the menus we talked about."

Anne nodded. "All right. I'll see you then." She glanced over her shoulder at Meredith, who was engrossed in listening to something one of the grandmothers said. "Yes, we have a lot to talk about." The elevator whisked her away before Major could ask her to clarify that last statement.

Shaking his head, he went back to the kitchen. Steven and Jana came out of his office laughing, though their amusement died as soon as they saw him.

"Great interview, Chef." Steven smirked.

Jana elbowed Steven hard enough to send him off balance. "It was a good interview. But why didn't you tell us you're starting a restaurant?"

Major groaned. So much for asking Alaine not to include that part in what she aired. "It's not a done deal. I'm still thinking about it."

"What's to think about?" Jana's eyes widened. "Chef, it's a great opportunity. You'd be wonderful at running a restaurant. And there are a lot of folks here who'd love to work in a restaurant owned by you."

Major studied Steven's face. Was his second in command thinking about the day when he'd be running this kitchen? A chill ran down Major's spine at the thought. Though Steven was a good chef, his people-management skills left a lot to be desired.

He looked back at Jana. In a restaurant environment, she could make three or four times as much money as she did working this lunch service every day. Everyone in the industry knew that people didn't spend as much or tip as well at lunch as they did for supper—even when ordering off the same menu. Yes, he would definitely take Jana with him.

"As I said, nothing has been decided yet. Believe me, when the decision is made, y'all will be amongst the first to know." He stepped aside. "Now, please get back to work so I don't have to fire you for slacking off."

Sitting at his desk, Major stared at the blank TV screen, wondering if he really wanted to watch the recording of the program when he got home tonight. Just what had he gotten himself into, agreeing to appear on television? Not just the interview, but every week. Would the potential for publicity really be worth the public humiliation?

"Hey. I'm not late am I?"

Meredith jumped at Major's voice, her pen striking a blue mark across the page before her. "N–no. I'm just making a list of everything we need to get done today."

A soft smile hinted at his dimples; Meredith ignored her squirmy stomach—just as she tried to ignore the fact that the dark green shirt he wore made his eyes a vivid violet-blue.

"So, what's on the agenda?"

What? Oh, right. Meeting. "Hearts to HEARTS: menu and final food budget, staffing requirements, space planning. . ." She let her voice drift when her mother appeared in the doorway.

"Oh good, Major, you're here already. Would you both step into my office?"

"Of course." Meredith glanced at Major, who looked as if he shared her confusion. She took her pen and legal pad with her. At the threshold to her mother's elaborate office, Meredith hesitated, and Major bumped into her.

One of the most beautiful women she'd ever seen sat in front of her mother's desk. Black hair lay tumbled in voluptuous curls around the woman's shoulders—the kind of curls Meredith had prayed for every time she'd subjected her own poor fine, limp hair to perms back in her teens.

Pushing envy aside, she slapped a smile on, armed herself with professional confidence, and strode into the office. The woman stood and extended her right hand.

"Alaine Delacroix," Mom said, beginning the introduction, "this is Meredith Guidry, our executive director of events and facilities."

"It's very nice to meet you." The name clicked in Meredith's memory. "Alaine Delacroix—from Channel Six?"

Perfect, full lips parted to reveal dazzling white teeth. "Yes. It's nice to meet you, too. I've heard so many wonderful things about you—about how you're practically a miracle worker when it comes to planning these social events everyone wants to attend."

Dreaded heat tingled in Meredith's cheeks. She hated that compliments still made her blush at her age.

Alaine looked over Meredith's shoulder, and her nearly black eyes sparkled like diamond-studded onyx. "Hello, Chef."

Meredith's heart crashed into an iceberg and succumbed to hypothermia. Stepping aside, she avoided looking at Major, not wanting to see the drool hanging from his mouth at the reporter's overly warm greeting. She followed her mother to the table and sat.

Ever the gentleman, Major waited to sit until all three ladies had taken their places.

"Alaine is here"—Mom looked from Major to Meredith—"because she has come up with an idea that I'm really excited about. Alaine, why don't you explain it?"

"I'd be happy to, Mrs. Guidry."

"Oh, please, it's Mairee."

Alaine's smile beamed at Mom. Meredith thought she might be ill. She could handle when her mom turned on the fake charm for gold key clients. But she wasn't sure she could stomach these two women fawning over each other.

"The idea actually came to me because of meeting you, Chef O'Hara." The dark eyes twinkled at Major again. "I thought it would be a good idea to create a news special on all of the planning that goes into the Hearts to HEARTS banquet. Kind of like the shows they do on the food channel—but not just about the food. About everything that goes into the event."

"That's where you come in, Meredith." Mom leaned forward, more excited than she'd been when Meredith landed the contract for Senator Kyler's inauguration ball. "Alaine is going to set up a time to talk to you so you can explain everything you've already done. And she's brought her cameraman with her today so that they can observe your planning meeting."

Meredith balled her hands together in her lap and tried to maintain a neutral expression. "I'll do whatever I can to help." A reporter following her around, scrutinizing every decision she made? Great. Just great.

"Now, Major, the other part involves you," Mom continued. "Alaine is to be given access to the kitchen during the week before the event so she can get footage of y'all making everything, so you'll need to let her know that schedule. Oh, and you two still need to work out the schedule for the weekly cooking segment on her program."

Meredith swallowed hard, gritting her teeth against the desire to ask why she'd ever been made an executive director if Mom and Dad were going to continue making these kinds of decisions without consulting her. Meredith was beginning to believe Anne hadn't been completely honest about why she'd decided to leave B-G and start her own business.

"Major, if you can come back when you and Meredith finish your meeting, we'll discuss the details." Mom placed her palms flat on the tabletop and stood. "I know you have a lot of work to do, so I'll let you get to it. Alaine, Major, if you'll go ahead, I need a few words with Meredith."

Partially out of her chair, Meredith sank back into it, pulse thudding. Had she not done a good enough job hiding her reactions to her mother's pronouncements?

Mom made sure the door closed firmly behind Alaine and Major before rejoining Meredith at the table. "I have a couple of questions now that I've had time to dig into your report." She flipped open her thick planner.

Meredith cringed. If Mom took the time to write everything down, this would be no quick chat.

"First, you sort of glazed over this in our meeting earlier, but the final financial report. . . I noticed the expenditure was nearly twenty percent below last year's. What happened?"

Any other employer would have been praising Meredith for saving the company money, not questioning her as if she'd done something wrong. "I spent a lot more time this year negotiating rates and working out trade agreements."

"No cutting corners anywhere? Nothing that takes advantage of anyone?"

Disbelief and shock pulled at Meredith's bottom jaw, and she stared at her mother. "I would never compromise my integrity—nor B-G's—like that."

"Calm down. I'm not saying you did. I was just confused by how the final number could have been that much lower." Mom looked back down at her list, asked about some of the complaints detailed in the report: valet parking attendants too slow; tables bussed too fast; band too loud; lights too dim—"Pretty much the same complaints as at every event, so just keep working on that."

Same complaints. . .probably by the same people. Meredith scrawled something illegible on her notepad as if taking it seriously.

Mom studied her notes for a moment then closed the planner. "It's come to my attention that you've been keeping something from me."

Ward. Of course. The receptionists had no doubt blabbed about his coming here to pick her up. She hated the idea that her personal life was fodder for watercooler gossip around the office. But she also knew her mother's way of getting information out of people. "What are you talking about?"

"Jenn told me you've hired a contractor for your house."

Defensive words gathered in a ball in the back of Meredith's throat. "What? Oh, yeah—well, I haven't officially hired him. I ran into him at the hardware store last Monday and asked for a bid."

"I can't tell you what a relief that is to me." Mom smiled—the first real smile she'd shown since Meredith entered the room. "I probably haven't told you, but the only reason I counseled you against buying that house is because I thought you would be stubborn and insist on doing everything yourself. I can't wait to see it when it's finished."

Relief tripped up Meredith's thoughts. "Thanks, Mom."

"You're welcome. Now, best not keep Alaine and Major waiting any longer."

"Right." Meredith took her notepad and returned to her own office, smiling. But her good mood vanished as soon as she walked in. Alaine sat in Meredith's regular place at the table, having what looked like an intimate conversation with Major.

"How's that? Can you see both of our faces?" Alaine asked.

The guy behind the camera gave a thumbs-up, and Alaine stood.

"Oh, Meredith, I didn't hear you come in. We're ready to get started whenever you are." Alaine waved Meredith toward the table. Toward *Meredith's* table in *Meredith's* office.

Meredith turned around, pretending to look for something on her desk. She closed her eyes and drew a deep breath, reaching as far down inside as she could to draw upon whatever confidence she could find in this situation. She couldn't let this woman's beauty and command of the situation rob her of what little professionalism she had left. She caught sight of the tube of her favorite tinted lip balm next to her phone and quickly swiped a little on.

"We're mostly here to get footage of you two working together. That will become part of a montage with a voice-over, most likely. Meredith, if you don't mind, after you're finished, I'd love to do an on-camera interview with you to get caught up on everything you've already done."

"I don't mind." Good. Her voice hadn't sounded as if she'd been inhaling helium. She took her seat and avoided making eye contact with Major. She couldn't let him see how much this was getting to her.

"Remember, just pretend like we're not even here."

"Right." Meredith scooted her stack of files closer. "Okay. Menu and final food budget. . ."

Even though Major seemed to have no problem ignoring Alaine and the camera and the big, fuzzy microphone catching every word they uttered, Meredith had never been so uncomfortably aware of her body in her life: her hands, her legs—should she cross them or just her ankles?—her facial expressions, her posture.

"Next week, the board and Mrs. Warner are coming in for the tasting so we can finalize the menu." Great. Now she was saying things Major already knew because she was thinking about that microphone hovering below the edge of the table. "What have you decided to make?"

Major pulled out a stapled-together packet and handed it to her. "Everything we discussed, and I added a few things at your suggestion."

Beyond the camera, Alaine Delacroix scribbled something on her steno pad.

"Uh, okay. Great." Meredith hadn't been this nervous since the oral presentation of her master's thesis. Major handed her another piece of paper. She read, scrawled in his bold handwriting, *Hang in there, you're doing fine.*

Some of the anxiety ebbed away. She looked up in time to see a bead of sweat trace its way down his hairline and along his jaw then disappear under his shirt collar. The confirmation that Major wasn't as cool and collected as he appeared filled Meredith with the first traces of genuine confidence. She delved into his tasting menu, and soon she had almost forgotten anyone but she and Major were in the room.

When they turned to determining how many staff Major would need—kitchen porters, servers, cleanup crew—Meredith went to the small fridge built into the wall unit behind her desk and retrieved four bottles of water. Without interrupting Major's monologue of calculations, she gave Alaine and the cameraman two of the bottles and the third to Major.

"Thanks." He opened it and took a long swallow. "So that's two servers per table of ten, one per eight-top, and one per two four-tops."

"And we need to get them all to bring in their black pants a couple of days ahead of time to make sure none of them are stained or faded and that we don't end up with anyone in chinos again." The cold water soothed the dryness of nerves and extensive talking in Meredith's throat.

"Agreed." He made a note in his binder. "And as soon as Jana gets the schedule confirmed, I'll have her get the sizes to Corie so we can make sure we get the shirts ordered early this time."

"Don't fancy a drive to Baton Rouge to pick them up the morning of the event?" Meredith teased. The sound of a pencil scribbling madly etched through her jollity.

"Not particularly, no." Major winked at her then returned to talking through the number of employees he'd need on the schedule.

At three thirty, the facilities supervisor for Vue de Ceil came in with a copy of the floor plan so they could work out the arrangement of the room—tables, dance floor, and stage.

"Oh! Do you mind if we reset the camera so we can get more of an overhead of y'all working on that?" Alaine piped up for the first time since the meeting started.

Meredith glanced at Major and Orly. Both men shrugged. She nodded at the reporter then returned her attention to the large sheet of paper covering her table. "I don't want it set up just like we did at New Year's. Too many of the same guests are expected, and I want it to look distinctly different."

Orly slid another roll of paper out of the plastic tube he'd brought with him and spread it out on top of the blank one. The heavily notated and revised plan from New Year's. Meredith stood and leaned over the table, resting her right knee on the seat of her chair.

Almost as if someone covered her back with a blanket, she felt Alaine's presence behind her, trying to get a look at the plan. But the reporter didn't interfere, didn't come in closer, didn't say anything. Grudgingly, Meredith admired her restraint.

After quite a bit of discussion, the location of the dance floor was set. Major and Orly started sketching in tables, determining the proper distribution of sizes and the spacing so the servers could easily move around them.

The room went suddenly dim. Meredith, Major, and Orly all stood and turned to see the cameraman taking his equipment apart.

Alaine had the good grace to look apologetic. "I'm sorry. It's four thirty, so he has to get back to the studio."

Meredith checked her watch. "I hadn't realized it was so late. I guess we'll just have to set up another time for that interview?"

"Yes. I'll call you in the morning to schedule it." Alaine helped wrap up cords and pack everything into large canvas bags.

"I can have my assistant call one of the building maintenance staff to help you carry all of that out." Meredith took a few steps toward the door to the outer office.

"Oh no, it's not necessary." The cameraman waved her off. "I've got it."

He did indeed manage to heave everything but one small bag up onto his large shoulders and carry it from the office.

"Do you mind if I come back up and continue taking notes?" Alaine asked. "After I help him take this to his car?"

"That will be fine." Meredith returned to the schematic and pretended to be oblivious to the fact that Major and Orly both watched Alaine leave the room. "Okay, let's see if we can at least get the preliminary layout finished by five o'clock."

When she returned, Alaine stood beside the fourth chair at the table, notepad in hand, making occasional notations while Major and Orly drew in tables, then erased them, then drew them in somewhere else. If Meredith moved just a foot to her right, she might be able to see what Alaine was writing.

"Miss Guidry?" Corie appeared at the main door to the office. "Do you need anything before I go?"

Meredith almost laughed at her assistant's formality. "No, Corie. Thanks. Have a good evening."

"You, too." The young woman grinned and closed the door behind her.

At five fifteen, Orly finally rolled the schematics and stuffed them in the tube. "That's a good start, I b'lieve."

"I think so. Putting the bandstand in front of the east windows will give us a lot more room, even though it means losing the view from that side." Meredith pressed her hands to the small of her back and stretched away the stiffness from two hours' leaning over the table.

"Guests are always happier when there's more room between the tables." Major stacked his papers and files. "And the servers are as well."

"We'll get together again next week to finalize the plan after the board's tasting. I'll e-mail you both to set up a time."

Orly raised the plastic tube in salute. "See y'all later."

"How do you spell his name?" Alaine asked.

"It's actually Orlando Broussard. But he goes by Orly—O-r-l-y." Meredith dropped her stack of work on her desk with a thud.

"Thanks. I really appreciate you letting me do this, Meredith.

This is going to be a great way to publicize the Hearts to HEARTS charity and hopefully raise a lot more money for the hospital."

"I'll do whatever I can to help." Meredith smiled, though dreading the added stress having a reporter and cameraman around all the time would create.

"Mere, I'll bring your take-out box back by on my way out if you're going to be here for a little while." Major hovered near the door.

"Yeah. I have some projects I need to write up for my staff, so I'll be here another half hour or so." She extended her right hand to Alaine. "It was very nice to meet you, and I look forward to working with you."

"Same here. I appreciate everything. Really." That high-wattage smile returned. It seemed much warmer than it had in Mom's office.

Alaine turned to leave. "And Chef, I'm looking forward to seeing a lot more of you soon."

"Why don't you come up to my office, and we can look at my schedule." Major motioned Alaine out the door ahead of him.

Her charitable feelings toward Alaine Delacroix vanished, crushed under a block of ice. Meredith had been right. Major would never feel *that way* about her. Ward seemed to like her, though she couldn't quite figure out why. But how long would that last before he met an Alaine of his own?

Chapter 11

I'm happy you had time in your schedule to meet with me today." Alaine Delacroix finished fiddling with her camera and settled into the guest chair facing Meredith's desk.

"I'm pleased to be able to accommodate you." Meredith clasped her hands atop her desk blotter and tried to force her shoulders to loosen up.

"Chef O'Hara had so many wonderful things to say about you when I interviewed him last week—I couldn't wait to come talk to the miracle worker myself."

"I'm sure he was exaggerating." Meredith didn't know why she always felt the need to deflect compliments rather than just say thank you and move on. "So I take it the interview with him went well?"

"Yes—I aired a twenty-minute segment on today's show as a promo for his cooking segment starting in a couple of weeks. And it made a nice follow-up to the part of the interview I aired on the New Year's Eve Masquerade Ball."

In spite of herself, Meredith returned Alaine's perfect smile. She seemed pretty genuine. Maybe Meredith was overreacting to the reporter's presence and Major's reaction to her. Of course, that shouldn't matter anyway, since she was supposed to be getting over Major.

"Okay—ready?"

"As I'll ever be." Meredith rearranged her hands on her blotter.

"Should I look at you or the camera?"

The cycloptic lens stared at her over Alaine's shoulder. "Let's just have a conversation, you and I. Don't think of this as an interview, just think of me as. . .as a potential client who's curious about the event you're working on right now."

Laughter released some of Meredith's nervousness. "I think I can do that."

"Great. Let's start with the history of the Hearts to HEARTS banquet. How did Boudreaux-Guidry Enterprises get involved with a charity to raise money for the cardiac care unit at University Hospital?"

"About five years ago, my father, Lawson Guidry, suffered a heart attack. He was taken first to Bonneterre General, where his condition was misdiagnosed as severe angina, and he was sent home."

Meredith picked up a pen and was about to start twirling it between her fingers until the little red light on the camera caught her attention. She put the pen back down. "Later that night, he passed out during dinner. This time, he was taken to University Hospital and immediately admitted to the cardiac care unit. Dr. Warner personally treated him and attended the surgeon during Dad's bypass surgery. After that, the Warners became like part of our family.

"When Dr. Warner passed away a year later, my parents wanted to do something to honor him and decided the best way was to help raise money for his research foundation, HEARTS."

"Is that an acronym?"

"It is: Heart-disease Education, Awareness, Research, Treatment, and Survival." She grinned, pleased with herself for being able to say the whole thing without having to stop to remember what any of the elements were.

Alaine segued into questions about the actual nuts and bolts of planning the events. Meredith was only too happy to talk about what went into organizing an event like this, being sure to give her event planners and Corie plenty of credit for all of the work they did to help her.

After an hour, Alaine changed her line of questioning. "Tell me a little about yourself, Meredith. How long have you been in this job?"

"I've been the executive director of events and facilities for about six years. Before that, I was an event planner under Anne Hawthorne when she was head of the department."

"Anne Hawthorne—the wedding planner?" Alaine clicked her tongue. "If only I'd known you last year, I might have gotten that interview with her I kept trying for." She laughed. "So Anne Hawthorne worked here before she started Happy Endings, Inc. How long did you work for Anne?"

"About four years. I started working here as soon as I finished grad school."

"Let me guess—MBA?" Alaine grinned.

Meredith shook her head, laughing. "No. Not even close. Art history. My dad wanted me to follow in his footsteps and get my degrees in business, but I chose to go the fine arts route instead."

Alaine's dark eyes glowed from deep within. "I can't believe it! I started out as an art history major—then I took a journalism class for a liberal arts requirement, and I was hooked. But whenever I got a chance, I took art classes to fulfill elective hours."

"What movement did you want to study?" Meredith leaned forward on her elbows, thrilled at the rare opportunity to talk to someone who knew something about art.

"Impressionists. I have Monet and Renoir and Pissaro lithographs all over my townhouse—and a few framed postcards I got at the Louvre several years ago."

"Oh," Meredith half sighed, half groaned. "I've always wanted to go to Europe and tour all the great art museums."

"Have you at least been to the Metropolitan Museum of Art in New York?" Alaine seemed to forget the camera and her notepad, leaning toward Meredith in her interest.

"No. Closest I've been is the National Gallery of Art and the Hirshhorn in Washington, D.C. I've also been to the Art Institute of Chicago."

"What's your movement?"

"Art deco. Everything about the era—the art, the jewelry, the architecture. That's why I jumped at the opportunity to buy a craftsman bungalow a few months ago—even though it did need a complete overhaul inside."

"Really? I'd love to buy an old place and fix it up." Alaine laughed and rolled her eyes. "Well, have my brother fix it up."

"Your brother?"

"Tony. He's a contractor."

A tingle of interest tickled the back of Meredith's neck. Even though she was pretty sure Ward would give her a reasonable offer, having another bid on the work might be good. "A contractor? Here in Bonneterre?"

"Yeah. He actually has his degree in architecture. But he decided he liked getting his hands dirty instead of sitting in an office drawing every day, so he became a contractor instead." Alaine jerked her head then jumped up to turn the camera off. "Sorry. I'll erase all of that personal stuff."

"Not a problem." Meredith stood and walked around to perch on the front edge of her desk while Alaine broke down the camera equipment. "What kind of construction work does your brother do?"

"Home remodeling. Hey, you know what?" Alaine stopped half-way through wrapping up the power cord. "You and Tony would have a lot in common. Would it be weird if. . . ?"

"I'd love to meet him."

"That's great." Alaine gave a little hop of excitement. "I don't usually go around trying to set up the people I'm interviewing with one of my brothers, but I know the two of you would really hit it off."

Meredith's stomach dropped into her left knee. A setup?

"I could give him your phone number or e-mail address and have him get in touch with you." Alaine crouched down to pack everything away in a black canvas bag. "If I can get another one of your business cards, I'll tell him to e-mail you." She caught the tip of her tongue between her teeth when she looked up and wrinkled her nose in a big grin at Meredith.

"I. . .uh. . ." How did she expect to end her years of singleness if she passed up opportunities for dates, or get her house finished if she worried that every contractor might ask her out? She swallowed hard and handed Alaine another business card. "Okay."

Meredith walked Alaine out to the main entrance and shook her hand in farewell. Back in the solitude of her office, Meredith allowed the stunned disbelief to swallow her. Had she really agreed to let Alaine Delacroix set her up with her brother?

"Do that later. The movie's starting."

"I'll be there in a second Ma. I can see the TV from here, y'know." Major continued dusting the top of the mirror over his mother's dresser in her studio apartment. A large archway separated the bedroom from what she called the "front parlor"—a sitting area that held her recliner, a loveseat, and a small entertainment center. While Beausoleil Pointe Center sent someone in to clean the bathroom every day and to vacuum once a week, the responsibility of caring for and cleaning any personal furniture items lay solely with the resident. And his mother had never dusted a piece of furniture in her life that Major could remember.

"You just did that last time you were here. It can't be that bad."

"Actually, Ma, I've been here twice since last time I did this. It'll just take a minute." He spritzed window cleaner on the mirror and polished it until all the streaks disappeared. "I take it you haven't changed your bed since last time I dusted either."

Beverly O'Hara waved her hand dismissively. "I don't remember."

Major pulled down the comforter. Yep. Still the same pink-and-yellow-striped sheets he'd put on there two weeks ago. In less than thirty seconds, he had the bed stripped, the linens bundled up and set by the door to take home and run through the laundry—since he was pretty sure that after almost two years here, his mother still didn't know where the laundry room was.

The opening score of *Flying Leathernecks* filled the room. Major hummed along with the melody.

"You're missing it, son!" His mother's voice gained a shrill edge.

"I'm right here. The opening credits are still running, aren't they?" He pulled a clean set of sheets off the top shelf of the closet.

"But this is the one."

"The one what?"

"For heaven sake. If I can remember, you should be able to. The one I named you for."

Major tossed the folded sheets onto the bed and went into the sitting room where he leaned over the back of his mother's chair and pressed his cheek to hers. "Oh, you mean this is the one in which the Duke plays Major Daniel Xavier Kirby, United States Marine Corps."

She pressed her cold hand to his other cheek. He whispered the first few lines of the voice-over introduction in her ear then kissed the top of her head. "Let me finish making the bed. Then I'll put on some coffee, make popcorn, and watch the John Wayne War Movie Marathon with you." He refrained from pointing out that she had the DVDs of all of the films that were going to be shown.

"You'll stay for the whole marathon?"

"I'll stay as long as I can." He returned to the other part of the room and made up the bed with the precision corners his roommate in New York during culinary school—a former army drill sergeant—had taught him.

As promised, before he settled into the cushy loveseat, he'd fixed decaffeinated coffee and microwave popcorn. And Ma was already asleep in her chair. Their typical Sunday afternoon.

"You've got enough troubles of your own for one man." John Wayne said on the TV screen. *"Stop trying to pack everybody else's around."*

Major had been able to quote nearly every line of this movie since he was a little kid. But that particular line had never hit home with him as it did today. Ever since he'd seen Meredith's date a week ago, he'd given himself indigestion ruminating over whether or not he should tell her about Ma and see if there was any chance to work things out.

The idea of telling Meredith both relieved and frightened him. He couldn't imagine anyone else he'd be more content to spend the rest of his life with. Yet would she understand? Would she be able to accept Ma's condition as a very intrusive and volatile part of their relationship?

Ma snuffled a little in her sleep.

No. He couldn't do this to Meredith. While he'd love to truly become a member of the Guidry family—instead of just an accepted outsider—he couldn't reciprocate and bring Meredith into his family. Guilt gnawed at his stomach, souring the coffee he'd just downed.

"I've got enough troubles of my own."

Meredith, while not a high-maintenance girl like some he'd dated, worked in a high-stress job with long and unusual hours. If a restaurant were to become a success, it would have to be Major's life for the next few years.

Resentment vied with the guilt in curdling the contents of his stomach. He had to make a choice: spend what little free time he would have developing a relationship with Meredith, or spend it with his mother.

"Lord, I don't know how I got myself into this mess. All this time, Ma's been telling me she wants me to meet someone and get married. If only I'd listened to her before now. I've known Meredith for eight years."

The reality of his words sank in. He'd known Meredith for eight years. In the beginning, she'd been like a younger sister. When he'd first started working at B-G, he'd toyed with the idea of finally allowing himself to do something about the crush he'd had on Anne in high school and college. But she'd just gone through the breakup of her first engagement, so he offered a brotherly shoulder for support. It had been only natural that he would treat Meredith the same way when she took over Anne's job—and took the job beyond anything Anne had ever done.

In every respect, she was the ideal companion for someone in the restaurant industry. She understood the late nights, the long hours—because she had the same demands in her own job. She was wonderful with clients. And though he always made sure his numbers were exact and balanced before he turned reports in, he depended on her for many of the business aspects of the catering division.

"She'd never leave an executive director position and come to work at a restaurant. That would be ridiculous."

The movie ended, *The Fighting Seabees* started, and his mother napped on. Major rubbed his eyes hard enough to see stars. Truth be told, if he were going into business with Meredith as his sole partner, he would have signed the papers the day the offer had been made. He'd watched her become MacGyver and fix a broken table with rubber bands, paper clips, and chewing gum; solve any audio-visual problem their equipment could throw at them; make fifty tablecloths work in a room with a hundred tables; and never let on to the client or the rest of the staff that there'd been a problem to begin with.

"She's perfect for me." When he realized he'd spoken aloud, he glanced at Ma, but she hadn't budged. He'd become too accustomed to talking to himself from living alone for so long.

He collected the popcorn bowls and coffee mugs and took them to the kitchenette—one counter along the far wall of the sitting room—to wash. He wished he could find a way to let Meredith know he cared for her, that he'd like nothing better than to be with her forever, but that right now he couldn't.

"Why can't I just bring myself to be honest with her?" He looked over his shoulder to make sure neither the sound of the water nor his voice had awakened his mother. He was starting to get a little concerned—she wasn't usually a deep sleeper like this.

Because if Meredith got wind of the truth—the truth that Major had been concealing his mother and her condition from everyone in his life ever since he returned to Bonneterre eight years ago—she'd never want to talk to him again. And who'd blame her? He deserved to be censured for the shame and resentment he'd allowed to fester in his heart. How would Meredith ever be able to trust him fully?

His watch beeped. Football playoff game started in forty-five minutes. He tidied up the rest of the small apartment. His gut wrenched with what he was about to do. Because his mother had been asleep so long, and because a different movie had come on, he could take his leave without having to make up an excuse—she wouldn't know how long he'd been here.

He almost made up his mind to stay, to salve his conscience. But he had laundry to do tonight, and he had to be at work at five tomorrow morning to cook breakfast for a meeting for some company or another located in Boudreaux Tower.

Promising himself he'd make it up to Ma another Sunday, he leaned over her chair and shook her shoulder.

Her eyes popped open immediately. "You leaving?"

"Yeah. I've got a bunch of stuff I need to do at home tonight, and then it's an early day tomorrow." He kissed her forehead. "You be good, and when they come in here and tell you to turn off John Wayne, don't make a fuss, okay? You have all these movies on DVD and can watch them anytime."

"I know. I promise, I'll be a good little crazy person."

"I'm counting on you. I don't want to get a call in the middle of the night saying you've whacked out on them again. Even if it is fun to scare 'that Nick kid.'"

She laughed, a rusty, rattling sound he didn't hear often enough. "Okay. I tell you what. I'll turn it off at the end of this movie. And I won't raise a fuss."

"Thank you. Love you."

"I know."

He kissed her forehead again. "Good night."

Ma patted the top of his head. "G'night, yourself."

Major's smile faded as soon as he turned his back. How could he just walk out on his mother like this?

"Oh, son?"

He turned around, the fake smile straining every muscle in his face. "Yes, Ma?"

"So who's this Meredith you've been muttering about, and when do I get to meet her?"

Chapter 12

"Is she in?" Major paused at Corie's desk Thursday afternoon and nodded toward Meredith's partially closed door.

"Her client meeting ran late, so she isn't back yet. You can go in and put that in the fridge if you want."

"Thanks." Major carried the takeaway box into the office. She'd obviously straightened up yesterday for her meeting with Mrs. Warner after the tasting—making the room feel oddly devoid of any indication it belonged to Meredith. . .with the exception of the soft jazz music permeating the space. The ornate decor bespoke Mairee's taste, not Meredith's.

He stowed the Styrofoam box in the mini-fridge hidden in the credenza, then sat at her desk to leave a note. He went through four green sticky notes before he finally had something he didn't feel embarrassed for her to read:

Mere—

Sorry I missed you. Dinner is in your fridge. Enjoy.

M.

Looking around the office once more, he tried to imagine what it would look like if Meredith had been responsible for decorating it. When arranging events—from the table layout to centerpieces to color schemes—her design skills never failed to impress him. He was curious to see her house once she finished; it was bound to practically ooze with her personality.

He shook himself out of his reverie. If he was going to make it to Forbes's office on time, he needed to get out of here. He waved at Meredith's assistant on the way past.

When he got to the end of the hall, he paused. Leaning casually on the high counter of the reception desk stood Ward Breaux.

The receptionist hung up her phone. "I'm sorry. Apparently Miss Guidry is out of the office right now. Did you have an appointment?"

"Not today, no. I was in the building for another meeting and thought I'd stop by."

"Is there any message—?"

The front door swung open, and Meredith breezed in, drawing everyone's attention. She stopped when she spotted the dark-haired man. "Ward. What are you doing here?"

Molten heat roiled in Major's stomach at the way the contractor's face lit up when he looked at Meredith. Major forced the jealousy aside.

The giant enveloped Meredith's right hand in both of his. He gave the same song and dance about being in the building for another meeting, which Meredith bought hook, line, and sinker.

The flush that bloomed in her cheeks filled Major with dread. She glanced away and looked right at Major. He tried to smile at her, unsure if he succeeded by the slight crease that formed between her brows. She pulled her hand free and motioned Major over.

"Major, you remember Ward Breaux."

Major grudgingly shook hands with the guy.

"The chef, right?" Breaux asked. "Good to see you again."

"Same here."

Meredith glanced at the contractor. "I wasn't really expecting to see you again before tomorrow night."

Tomorrow. . .*night*? Jealousy returned full force. Meredith's going out with this guy once was one thing. But was she seriously considering dating him? A guy who'd picked her up at the hardware store?

"I thought maybe, if you have time this evening, you might let me follow you over to your house so that I can get a better idea of what you're wanting to do with it." Ward grinned at Meredith as if Major weren't standing right there. "And then maybe we could bump up our date to tonight."

"I. . .uh. . ." Meredith, looking more embarrassed than ever, cut her gaze toward Major—then turned and really looked at him. "Major, I thought you were meeting with Forbes this afternoon to talk about. . .that business thing."

The duty of keeping his appointment warred with the desire to stay right here and demand to know what Ward Breaux's intentions toward Meredith were. Duty won. "I put your dinner in the fridge in your office." He gave her shoulder a squeeze on the way past. "I'll see you tomorrow."

"Bye."

Major paused at the front doors, tempted to turn around and look, but a quick glance at his watch spurred him into motion. Wouldn't look good to show up late to the business meeting that could be the first step toward deciding his future. He took the stairs down to the parking garage instead of waiting for the elevator.

He slammed Kirby's door a little harder than he meant to. Okay, he really couldn't walk into the meeting with Forbes to go over all of the legalities of the restaurant deal still upset about Meredith's choice to have a life.

Easing the Jeep out into traffic, Major tried to switch his mind into gear for the upcoming meeting—but the blush on Meredith's cheeks when receiving the compliment from Ward proved too distracting.

Ever since the first time he'd seen Meredith getting ready to go out with Breaux, Meredith had hardly spoken to him about anything other than work stuff.

What kind of name was *Ward* anyway? The only real-life Ward he'd ever heard of was Ward Bond, a character actor who'd been in several of John Wayne's movies.

He slammed on the brakes to keep from running a red light that sneaked up on him. He couldn't compete with someone like Ward Breaux, with his perfect teeth, professional athlete's physique, and a business of his very own. Unlike Ward, Major had always been too cowardly to step out and start a business.

No, not cowardly, just afraid of what might happen to his mother if he gambled everything and lost. Every week he watched a television program in which a celebrity chef went around to failing restaurants and tried to get them back on their feet. No one would come in and do that for Major. He'd always known that if it came to sink or swim, with the added weight of responsibility for his mother, he'd sink. Straight to the bottom.

He pulled into the parking lot of the three-story, red-brick building just as his radio clock flickered over to four o'clock. He grabbed his paperwork, and entered the office of Folse, Landreneau, Maier & Guidry, Attorneys at Law.

Feeling extremely underdressed in his khakis and a denim shirt with the B-G Enterprises logo, Major followed a dark-suited assistant up to the second floor. Everyone they passed wore expensive suits and shoes that looked like they'd just come out of the box, unlike Major's scuffed Top-Siders.

"Mr. O'Hara to see Mr. Guidry," the receptionist told the secretary seated at the desk outside of Forbes's office.

The secretary stood. "Of course. Mr. Guidry is expecting you, Mr. O'Hara."

Major cringed at their formality. It was one thing for his staff to call him Chef—it had become more like a nickname. He was so glad he didn't work at a place where everyone had to go by "Mr." or "Ms."

Forbes stood when Major entered the richly appointed office.

"Come in, Major. Samantha, please hold calls," Forbes said by way of greeting as he shook Major's hand.

"Yes, Mr. Guidry."

"Have a seat, Major." Forbes motioned to a small table on the other side of the large room. Even though he'd been friends with Forbes Guidry since junior high school, Major found himself intimidated by his friend in this setting. He pulled out one of the heavy wooden chairs and sank into it.

Forbes carried a stack of folders over and set them down before sitting. "Now that you've had a couple of weeks to think about my parents' proposal, I'd be interested in knowing your thoughts."

Major quickly recapped the conversation he'd had with Meredith two weeks ago. "I've been spending a lot of time in prayer. And I believe the Lord is telling me this is an opportunity I can't pass up—if all the financial stuff works out."

"I told Mom and Dad that would probably be a concern, since they want you to start off as an investing partner and not just an employee. I believe we've come up with a plan that will work for all parties involved."

From the stack in front of him, Forbes pulled a legal-sized folder with what looked like at least fifty pieces of paper in it. Major swallowed hard. He'd done well in his business law classes in college and culinary school, but that had been so many years ago. This was the part of starting a restaurant that turned him into a blithering idiot.

"According to the start-up plan you gave me to help you with a few months ago"—Forbes pulled it out of the folder—"you proposed to start a restaurant based on an initial investment of $150,000 cash and $600,000 in venture capital. I've presented this to my parents, and they like this plan."

Major's skin tingled, anticipation rising.

"That will make you a 20 percent co-owner in the restaurant. I believe they discussed with you that you will continue to have responsibilities in the catering division of B-G while the restaurant is in start-up phase?"

Major nodded. "Yes, and that I would continue to draw a salary—for a while, at least. I wasn't too sure on that part."

Forbes's gray-blue eyes dropped back to the paperwork in front of him. When he found the document he sought, he passed it across the table to Major. "Here is the five-year buyout plan." He grinned. "This was my idea, actually. It's the plan I came up with for Jenn's restaurant. She was able to buy me out after three years instead of five."

Oh, that Major would be able to do the same. His eyes darted across the numbers and words on the page in front of him, unable to focus on anything.

"Once the restaurant begins to turn a profit—which we know may take at least two years—you will have the opportunity to buy out the 80 percent of the business owned by my parents." Once Forbes started explaining all of the line-items in the spreadsheet, Major could see how it worked—that as he bought the Guidrys out of their investment in the restaurant, his share of the restaurant's proceeds would increase.

The best part was that, even though he'd be taking everything out of savings and cashing out a few investments to buy into this deal, he wouldn't be losing the security of a steady salary in the beginning. He would still be able to pay for his mother's residence at Beausoleil Pointe Center in addition to his own expenses. Of course, he'd be working eighteen to twenty hours a day to get everything done, so he'd never *see* his mother, but in the end, it would all be worthwhile, wouldn't it?

He forced himself to focus while Forbes detailed the rest of the legal and financial arrangements. Mairee and Lawson wanted the restaurant to be Major's—he would be in charge of the menu, the decor, everything. They trusted him to make it a success.

They *trusted* him. They were taking a pretty big risk on him. He would do his best to deserve it and live up to their expectations.

"I know I've hit you with a lot of stuff." Forbes handed the thickest folder to Major. "Take everything home with you, and spend some time reading through everything. Whenever you see something you have questions about, just holler, and I'll explain it to you. I believe my parents told you they don't expect an answer before Easter, right?"

"Right." Which was a good thing. It would take him longer than the eight weeks between now and then to read through everything.

"Let's plan to get together again in a couple of weeks. We can go back through everything, go over any questions that come up, and you can pull together your financial paperwork and the other business applications that are detailed in there." Forbes pointed at the folder.

"Okay."

"Look, Major. We've been friends for a long time. I wouldn't be sitting here talking to you about this if I didn't think it's a solid plan that will be extremely profitable for you in the long run. I also know that you have some concerns about your mom and her health, but I think it's time that you start looking toward your future, start chasing your dream."

Major fanned the edge of the paperwork in the folder with his thumb. The man sitting across the corner of the table from him was his best friend in the world. And even he didn't know the whole truth about Ma—if he did, he'd probably counsel his parents to run, not walk, away from this deal.

He flattened his hands atop the folder. "I'll read through all of this and get back to you."

"That's all we're asking." Forbes stood and returned to his desk, motioning Major to follow.

The chair across from Forbes's desk was much more comfortable than the one at the table. "I appreciate everything you've done."

"It's my pleasure." Forbes loosened his tie and leaned back in his leather executive's chair. "I know that right now, there's no way you'd be able to afford my retainer. Technically, I only represent my parents in this venture. But I want to let you know that if you need anything—*anything*—I'm here for you, pro bono."

"I don't want you having to do that for me. Maybe we can work out some kind of trade agreement—I mean, you've got to have some events for the office, right? Stuff you bring in food for? Special client dinners at restaurants?"

"Yeah—sure, of course. And that'll benefit you, too, because it'll get the restaurant's name out to everyone here."

An unreasonable surge of envy filled Major. How could it be that he and Forbes were the same age—had graduated from high school together twenty years ago—yet here Major was barely starting on his career journey and Forbes was a partner in the largest law firm in town with his own office and his own secretary?

"You're a brave man, Major."

Major blinked a few times, startled. "What do you mean?"

"I mean—to take a step like this. To risk it all on what you've always wanted to do. Not a lot of people would be willing to do this at our age. It's almost like you're getting to start over."

"Start *over*?" He had never thought of it that way. "Up until now, I've always felt like I was waiting to begin my life. Like everything I was doing was just waiting—building up to this."

"You may feel that way, but that's not how it looks on paper. If you were unproven, unknown, do you think my parents would have given you this opportunity? You're a name, brother, a commodity in this town. Sure, part of that comes from your working at B-G for years, but everyone in the business community knows that Mom and Dad don't suffer fools—if you lasted that long with them, you've got what it takes. Plus, just about every one of them has been to one event or another that you've catered."

Forbes's words took a few moments to filter through Major's brain. "Benefits of a city that still has a small-town mentality?"

Forbes laughed. "Something like that. Hey, speaking of small-town mentality, what are you doing for supper?"

"Figured I'd just throw something together at home."

"Not tonight. You ever been to my sister Jenn's restaurant down in Comeaux?"

"The Fishin' Shack? A couple of times. I don't make it down to Comeaux very often."

Forbes removed his tie and reached in his top desk drawer, withdrawing keys and his PDA. "Come on, then. I'm meeting some of my siblings and cousins for our standing Thursday night dinner."

"Okay. . .sure, I'd love to. How about I follow you down there?" Major had heard about this Thursday night family dinner tradition through Anne a few years ago. She'd invited him many times in the beginning, but back then he'd spent almost every evening with his mother. Eventually, the invitations stopped coming; then his mother insisted she didn't want to see him every day.

And if he went, he'd be able to find out if Meredith had foregone bumping up her date with Ward Breaux in favor of her family without having to try to find some way to wheedle it out of her subtly tomorrow.

Chapter 13

"You did all this work yourself?"

Meredith leaned against the pillar in the opening between the living room and front foyer while Ward inspected the refinishing she'd done on the built-in cabinets flanking the fireplace.

"I did." She held her breath and followed him around the room with her gaze, praying he wouldn't find fault with any of her work.

He turned and gave her a winsome smile. "Ever considered quitting your job and becoming a subcontractor?"

Only in her dreams. "You can see how much needs to be done if the house is going to be ready for me to move in three months from now."

The toe of his shoe scraped along the row of carpet tacks still stuck in the hardwood near the wall. "For one person, yes, it would be impossible." He continued around the room until he leaned his shoulder against the pillar opposite her. "I'd be very interested in submitting a bid to complete your remodel."

Meredith's face grew hot under Ward's intense gaze. "What will you need me to do so that you can do that?"

"I need to come by some time with my apprentice so we can measure all the rooms and so you can tell me exactly what you want done."

"I'll have to check my schedule at work. With the Valentine's banquet coming up so soon, I'm not sure what my days are going to look like."

His lopsided grin was rather disarming. "That's fine. It means I don't have to make up an excuse to call you tomorrow."

Oh, she shouldn't have skipped lunch today. Her empty stomach knotted and twisted with the rush of pleased embarrassment that blasted through her. Never before had a good-looking, eligible man flirted with her like this.

"I'm sorry. I didn't mean to embarrass you, Meredith. But I just can't seem to help myself whenever I'm around you."

The chirping of his phone saved her from having to think of a response.

He cringed when he looked at the device. "Ooh, I really need to take this. Forgive me?"

"Sure. No problem." She escaped the living room and headed upstairs to make sure the almost constant rain since Christmas hadn't generated any problems.

A few minutes later, footsteps announced Ward's presence on the stairs.

"Meredith?"

"In the guest bathroom." She balanced herself on the edge of the claw-foot tub and ran her hand along the top edge of the wall and around the window casing to check for dampness.

"What are you—"

Her left foot slipped off the narrow edge of the tub. She pitched backward—straight into Ward. He swung her up easily into his muscular arms. Mortification burned every inch of her skin.

"Yes, now I see why you shouldn't be trying to do this renovation all by yourself. What in the world were you trying to do, besides break your neck?"

"There was some damage to the roof in the last big storm. It's been patched, and I was just checking to make sure the patch is holding."

"Well, if you approach everything that way, it's a wonder you haven't broken something—like your neck."

"Speaking of, could you put me down?"

He took a few steps away from the tub and gently set her on the floor, not removing his hands from her waist until she assured him she had gained her balance. He moved around her, bent over, and leaned his weight on the edge of the tub, which promptly began to tip toward him.

"Yeah, that's what I thought: so old the bolts securing it to the floor are either missing or rusted through." He rotated around to face her, returning to his full height. With crossed arms and a frown crinkling his forehead, he could have passed for an avenging angel. "One thing I want you to promise me, whether I get the contract or not."

The back of her neck began to ache from looking up at him in such close quarters. "What's that?"

"You'll follow some basic work site safety guidelines—and you'll make everyone who sets foot on the property do the same. I'd hate for you to get sued because a worker breaks something when he falls off the edge of the tub that isn't secured.

Impressed by his concern not just for her safety, but for anyone else's, she nodded. "I will. And I don't usually do that. It was just expedient tonight."

He grimaced. "And that's how most on-the-job injuries occur. You don't want to start your life in a new home with a huge claim on your insurance, do you?"

Laughter bubbled up and escaped.

"Meredith, I'm serious."

She patted his folded arms. "I know. And I do take safety seriously. I was laughing because you reminded me of my older brother and our mom just then. That's the same lecture either of them would have given me in the same circumstance. When all else fails, appeal to the financial aspect of the situation."

His expression eased, his dark eyes no longer stern, but amused once again. "They sound like very smart people."

"Come on, let me show you the rest of the upstairs."

"Hey, Major!"

At Forbes's younger brother's greeting, the handful of people sitting at the ten-top table turned and greeted Major with the same warmth. Why did he always assume they would see him as an interloper—as an intruder? They'd never treated him with anything but affection and friendship. Most of those present were too young to remember the couple of years that Major worked for Aunt Maggie two decades ago, yet they still acted as if he were a member of the extended family.

"Oh, mercy!" Jennifer Guidry came out of the kitchen. "Now I'm going to feel self-conscious. Forbes, did you have to bring a professional chef to my restaurant?" She winked at him. "Hey, Major."

"Hi, yourself." He looked around with interest at the interior design. "I don't know what you're worried about. I think everything is fantastic. The pirogue is new since the last time I was here." He pointed at the flat-bottomed, pointy-ended boat suspended upside down from the beamed ceiling overhead.

"One of my suppliers down in Jeanerette thought I needed that for some authenticity. So he built it and put it up there a couple of months ago."

Major watched Jenn as she talked with a couple of her siblings or cousins—he could never keep all the relations straight in this clan. He hadn't seen her in at least a year. He used to think that she and Meredith were nearly identical—in fact, when he'd first met them as teenagers, he'd thought they were twins. But Jenn had cool, blue-gray eyes like Forbes's, not wide, nutmeg brown eyes that glowed with an emberlike intensity. Jenn's hair was a little redder, too. She flitted from person to person like a hummingbird. Meredith would have just found a place to sit and observe those around her.

"Chef, we need you in the kitchen."

Major turned along with Jenn—and shook his head at the gut reaction.

"I'll be right back," Jenn called over her shoulder as she followed her employee around the fishing tackle–decorated wall that buffered the dining room from the kitchen. The snap and bustle of working in a restaurant—he missed it.

Sitting beside Forbes, Major found he had a good view of the front door across the large room, because he saw Anne as soon as she entered.

She paused in her confident stride toward the table when she noticed Major. "What—my invitations weren't good enough for you? You had to wait until Forbes invited you to come to family dinner?"

Major stood and greeted her with a handshake. "He's a lawyer—trying to argue with him would just be a losing battle." He held the chair to his right for her.

She glanced around, a frown forming between her brows. "Where's Meredith?"

Finally, someone had voiced the question that had been bouncing around in Major's brain for the last fifteen minutes.

"She's going to try to come later," Forbes said. "She called as I was driving down here to say that something came up, and she made other plans for dinner."

Major's guts melted into a disappointed puddle.

"What do you mean, 'other plans for dinner'?" Anne asked.

Major assisted Anne with the chair and waited to hear how Forbes would answer her question. Jenn returned with a couple of baskets of hush puppies and took the seat on the other side of Anne.

Forbes refilled his glass from the pitcher of tea on the table. "I don't know. I guess something came up at work." He glanced askance at Major.

Major lowered himself into his chair and shrugged. It would serve her right if he told her somewhat meddlesome kin that she wasn't working but was on a date. . .but that would be petty. "I don't know. It could be any of a million things that sidetracked her."

"Well, hopefully she'll be able to get here soon." Anne glanced at the printed list of the day's specials then placed her order. "It would be a shame for her to miss such a historical event as Major O'Hara attending a Guidry family function after so many years."

And to think, if he'd been paying attention and hadn't been so wrapped up in his own little life, he might have recognized his feelings for Meredith soon enough to have actually become part of the Guidry family.

He hardly knew what he was ordering when the waiter came around to him. He could almost hear a game show announcer in his head: *All of this could have been yours, but the price wasn't right.*

As dinner progressed, Major was slowly able to set his thoughts aside, though the self-recrimination remained. But no one could be around this crew for very long and spend any time inside his own skull. Conversations flew fast and furious around the large, round table, ranging from the bizarre case police officer Jason had just worked to the latest plans for Anne's wedding.

On that point, Major could contribute to the discussion, teasing Anne about the lack of extravagance in her menu choices.

"That's our Annie—always suggesting all the frills and frou-frou for everyone else, but never indulging in them for herself." Jenn rolled her eyes.

"I blame it on George—since he's not here to defend himself." Anne's blue eyes twinkled.

"Oh, please." Jenn stood and went to the wait station to refill their pitcher of iced tea. "George would let you do anything you want."

"Well, as brother of the bride, I have to say that I'm glad it's not one of those really over-the-top kind of weddings," Jason Babineaux said.

"Yeah?" Forbes challenged him. "All you have to do is usher. You don't have to stand in front of the hordes of gawkers who are going to be sitting there just waiting for someone to flub up."

"You could always be removed from the list of attendants, Forbes, if the idea bothers you so much." Anne's eyebrows arched up, her expression stern, though she couldn't wipe the smile from her eyes.

"And leave George with only his brother up there with him for moral support? I couldn't do that to the poor sap. Someone's got to commiserate with him on his life as he knows it being over."

Anne turned to Major. "I'm so happy that you could finally come and witness for yourself just how much everyone in this family loves each other." She winked.

Melancholy wrapped around Major's chest. Did the people sitting at this table have any idea just how blessed they were to be part of a family at all? To have what Major had dreamed of his whole life, had imagined when he was a kid?

After everyone had overindulged in Jenn's peach cobbler, people exchanged places at the table as if at a signal. It happened before Major realized it, and suddenly, he found himself not between Anne and Forbes, but next to their young cousin Jodi.

"I'm so glad I was able to get over here to you. I've been hoping to see you again for a while now." Jodi flipped her long, brown hair over her shoulder and gazed at him with wide, dark eyes.

Major straightened and cleared his throat, uncomfortable with what felt like flirtatiousness in the young woman's demeanor. He was certain he was just flattering himself by thinking she was actually interested in him. But when she leaned closer and rested her hand on his arm, a sense of foreboding stole through him.

"What can I do for you, Jodi?"

"Oh, I don't want you to do anything *for* me." She batted long lashes. "It's what I think we can do together."

Meredith leaned against the side of the SUV, her neck starting to ache slightly from looking up at Ward. The in-and-out flow of people from the gourmet deli marked the passing of time as they stood chatting. And while she enjoyed his company and getting to know him better, she couldn't help but think about the fact that, right now, her siblings and cousins were all down at Jenn's restaurant.

When she'd agreed to grab a quick sandwich with Ward, she'd

been proud of herself for the ease with which she'd called Forbes to tell him she wouldn't be there for dinner. But over the past hour, the idea that they were all down there having fun without her kept intruding on her thoughts.

Ward reached out and took her hand. She pressed against the back door of her SUV. He was quite handsome; she couldn't deny it. But the thought that she'd rather be here with Major kept her from enjoying the moment.

"Ward, I hope it won't offend you that I'm going to have at least one other contractor bid the house."

The corners of his eyes crinkled. "I'd think you a fool if you didn't." He rubbed the palm of her hand with his thumb. "But I hope that even if you don't accept my bid, you'll still go out with me."

Come on, heart, flutter! "Of course."

"Good." He looked down when his phone buzzed. "That's my cue to say good night and let you get back to your previous plans." He leaned over and kissed her cheek. "G'night, Meredith."

She blinked twice, stunned that the kiss had been so quick—and so chaste. "Good night, Ward."

He held her door and shut it once she was in with her seat belt fastened. She waited until he'd started the engine of his massive, four-door pickup before pulling out of the lot and heading toward Comeaux.

Though she hated doing it while driving, she pulled out her phone and speed-dialed Anne's cell phone number.

"Hey, Mere." Loud music nearly drowned out Anne's greeting.

"Y'all going to be there awhile longer?"

"Oh, yeah. Karaoke just started, in case you can't tell. Jason just did 'Mack the Knife,' and Forbes and Major are about to get up there and sing 'My Favorite Things.'"

"What—from *The Sound of Music*?" Meredith cautiously but quickly overtook someone piddling around in the left lane. Major was there? And she'd missed it?

"Yeah. Are you on your way? If so, I'll tell Jenn to have them bumped down the list. They've already done a couple—and believe me, you don't want to miss this. They're in rare form tonight."

For the remainder of the twenty-minute drive, Meredith fought the urge to speed. Major was at family dinner, and she'd missed it. How had he—

His meeting with Forbes to go over the details of Mom and Dad's offer on the restaurant. Of course. She'd promised to pray for him before and during the meeting and had completely forgotten.

The gravel crunched and popped under her tires when she pulled in to the overflow lot adjacent to Jenn's restaurant. Yes, indeed, there was Major's green Jeep.

She jogged a few steps then forced herself to slow down. She had no reason to think he'd come because he expected her to be here—only to hope it.

Music spilled out when she pulled open the front door. Though not dark, the houselights had been dimmed to direct attention to the brightly lit stage.

The hostess greeted her by name, as did several servers. Meredith's heart thumped in time with the upbeat country song someone was singing. She skirted the perimeter of the main dining room toward the separated party room at the back.

She strained to see who all was there. Her heart flip-flopped when she saw Major—then almost stopped completely when she saw him with her younger cousin Jodi. Her *much* younger cousin Jodi.

Meredith stopped and watched as Jodi wrote something down on a drink napkin, folded it, and tucked it into Major's shirt pocket.

More clearly than she could see anyone at that table, Meredith could see the choice now standing before her. She could let this bother her, or she could remember that she'd just been taken to dinner—a second time—by a handsome stranger.

She slapped a smile on and approached the table.

"Hey! You're here." Anne pulled out the chair beside her.

Fortunately, everyone else was involved in poring over the lists of available karaoke tracks and barely spared her a glance, much less forced her into hugs and kisses.

Anne leaned close. “So what happened tonight?”

“Oh, it’s—” On Anne’s other side, Meredith saw Forbes turn his head their direction as if expecting to hear the explanation for her lateness as well. “It’s nothing. I’ll tell you about it later.”

“Hey, Mere, what’s this I hear about some guy coming to pick you up at the office a couple of weeks ago?” Rafe called across the table.

So much for her personal life staying private. She tried to laugh it off. “Who told you that?”

“Tonya. She said he was very good-looking and that you were very dressed up.”

She’d forgotten Rafe occasionally dated one of the front-desk receptionists. Around the table, everyone focused on Meredith. Except Major, who gazed at Rafe through narrowed eyes.

“Yes. I had a date the other night. What’s the big deal?”

Anne squeezed her wrist. “What’s the big deal? You had a date, and you didn’t even tell me?”

Though feeling bad for not telling Anne immediately, Meredith started getting angry. “It’s not announced around the table every time Jenn goes out on a date—or Rafe or Jodi.” She flickered her gaze at Major and hoped that pairing would never come to pass. “So why is it worthy of the family grapevine when I have a date?”

“Duh—because you *don’t* date. What—did you decide to give up *not* dating as your New Year’s resolution?” Rafe teased.

She couldn’t look at Major now; in fact, she wasn’t sure she’d ever be able to face him again.

“That’s enough,” Forbes admonished their younger brother. “Meredith deserves to have a personal life that she can keep private if she wants to.”

“Aww, come on, Forbes. She hasn’t had a date in ten years and—”

Meredith jumped to her feet and grabbed her purse. “I knew this was a mistake,” she muttered. “Good night. See y’all later.” She almost ran from the restaurant, molten-hot embarrassment propelling her steps.

Halfway across the small, main parking lot, she dug in her purse for the car keys—and promptly dropped them on the pavement.

"Meredith, wait." Major's voice echoed over the dull sound of the music inside the restaurant.

Her eyes tingled and burned, and she had to blink quickly to eliminate the gathering moisture. She picked up the keys and stood—but couldn't face him.

Chapter 14

Major hesitated when Meredith wouldn't turn around to face him after picking up her keys. He could understand why she might not want to talk to a family member right now, but what had *he* done?

He approached with caution. "Meredith, is everything okay?"

The smile she wore when he got around to where he could see her face was the same one she wore when dealing with difficult clients. "Everything is fine, thank you. I just—it's just been a really long day, and I have a puppy that's been cooped up in my apartment since I ran home to let him out at lunchtime. He's probably destroyed my bathroom, so I really need to get home." She shivered and rubbed her arms.

Without thinking, he shrugged out of his leather jacket and wrapped it around her shoulders.

"Thanks." She clutched the front closed.

He cleared his throat. "May I walk you to your car?"

She shrugged. "Sure."

They walked in silence all the way to her Volvo. After she unlocked it, he opened the front door and looked in to make sure no one waited within to accost her—drawing a real smile from Meredith.

He'd missed seeing that smile from her. "When did things get weird between us?"

The streetlamp illuminated the surprise in her eyes at his question.

"I'm not. . .I don't. . ." She swallowed hard and licked her lips.

Major's breath caught in his throat. Those perfectly shaped lips.

"Major—I don't know how to say this without coming across sounding stupid and juvenile and potentially making things even more awkward between us." She wrapped his jacket tighter.

He leaned his shoulder against the back window and tried to draw his gaze away from her lips to her eyes. "You know you can say anything to me."

She laughed—but it turned into a groan; her brows puckered, and she shook her head. "I don't think I can. It'll just make things worse between us."

He leaned closer but clasped his hands behind his back to keep from taking her in his arms and declaring his undying love to her. "Whatever it is, I think I'm man enough to handle it."

Tears welled in Meredith's nutmeg eyes, and her breathing increased. "I can't." She swallowed a couple more times, and an odd expression overtook her face. "I didn't realize you knew my cousin Jodi so well."

The sudden change in subject threw him. "What?"

"You. . .and Jodi. I saw you together when I walked in." She reached into the pocket of his shirt. "I saw her give you this."

She pulled out the napkin Jodi had stuffed in there a few minutes ago. He laughed and enclosed Meredith's fisted hand with both of his. "Your cousin told me she'd heard about the restaurant on Alaine's program. She offered to come up with a marketing plan and some materials for me—as part of her portfolio or internship or something for grad school—if the time comes. She doesn't have any business cards, so she wrote her number down for me. I'm supposed to call her when I know what my schedule's going to be like the next couple of weeks."

"Marketing plan?" Meredith's cheeks darkened. "I thought—I mean I didn't think—"

Hope kindled in Major's chest. "You thought Jodi was flirting with me and that I was lapping up the attention of a girl about fifteen years younger than me?"

She nodded, her throat working hard as she swallowed, face as red as a five-hundred-degree oven.

He tried to contain his smile. "So, you were jealous?"

"I—no—I was surprised—"

"You were surprised that someone like Jodi would show interest in me? Or that I would show interest in any woman?" *Other than you.* He wanted her to admit it, to say aloud that she loved him. Of course, he would never be able to act on it, but he really wanted to hear the words.

"It's not quite like that—"

He used the leverage he had by his grasp on her hand and pulled her closer. "Then what is it like?"

Her eyes widened—but not with fear. He leaned his head closer to her, heart thundering.

"Hey, is everything o—" Anne skidded to a stop as she came around the back end of the Volvo. "Oh, dear." She shielded her eyes as if to keep from seeing anything else. "I'm so sorry. I'll just leave now."

"No, it's all right." The breathy huskiness in Meredith's usually smooth voice stirred the smoldering embers in the pit of Major's stomach. She pulled her hand, and he released it, though he didn't want to. "I really need to be getting home anyway."

Major gulped a couple of deep lungfuls of the chilly air to settle his nerves and slow his still-racing heart. Had he really almost just kissed Meredith Guidry?

Meredith was certain she was about to have a heart attack. Unless she was seriously deceiving herself, Major O'Hara had been about to kiss her before Anne interrupted them.

"Oh—okay, well, good night." Anne gave an apologetic grimace and backed away to her own car a few spaces away.

Sweat beaded on Major's upper lip, and he rubbed his forehead with the heel of his hand. "Meredith, I have to tell you something."

The hyperventilating feeling returned to her chest. Would he now declare his feelings for her? Put her out of years of agony? "Yes?"

"I need you to know how I feel about you. . . ." He wiped his hand down his face. "About you and Ward Breaux. I'm—I'm really. . .happy that you've managed to find time to have a life outside of work. You deserve to have some fun and joy in your life, and I hope that you find it."

Nooooo! Emptiness swallowed up all the warm, pleasant feelings she'd had this evening. He wasn't supposed to be happy for her. He was supposed to be jealous, insanely jealous, over the fact she'd gone out on a couple of dates with someone else.

"Thanks, Major. That means. . .a lot to me." She slipped his jacket off her shoulders and handed it back to him—but she'd started shivering before the cold air hit her. "I guess I'll see you at the office tomorrow."

"Ten thirty, right?"

"Ten thirty?"

"The meeting to finalize the Hearts to HEARTS menu?"

"Right. Ten thirty."

"I'll bring coffee and snacks. I'm sure we'll need them." His grin didn't quite deepen his dimples the way it usually did.

"See you then." She climbed into the car, ready for this night to be over. She returned his wave and pulled out of the parking lot.

Meredith was about to give in to the tears that wanted desperately to be released, but her phone rang. She fumbled in her purse for the hands-free earpiece, hooked it over her right ear, and answered.

"Meredith? Antoine Delacroix. I hope it isn't too late."

"No." She grabbed a tissue and dabbed away the moisture from her eyes and nose. "Thank you for calling."

"Of course. My sister has told me some stuff about you. But I have to admit, it confused me. I couldn't tell if she was trying to set us up on a date or if you have a job you want me to bid."

Was Alaine Delacroix the reason Major was happy Meredith had started seeing someone else? "I have a house I'm remodeling, but I've about reached the limit of what I can do on my own—and time is a factor as well."

"Oh. If that's the case, the sooner I come by to evaluate the property, the better, huh?"

"Yes. But I don't have my calendar with me. Can I call you back tomorrow morning once I have it in front of me?"

"I don't really do mornings, so why don't I give you a holler some time tomorrow afternoon?"

A contractor who didn't "do" mornings? "Okay. I'll talk to you tomorrow. Bye."

"Later, dude."

Meredith disconnected with a derisive huff and took the earpiece off. Had he really just called her *dude*? Even the college students they hired to work large events were trained better in customer service than that.

At home she heard the puppy's howls as soon as she opened the back door into her kitchen. She stepped out into the rear hall again at the sound of footsteps on the wooden stairs.

"I was just coming to see what the noise was." Anne hesitated on the bottom step.

"Just the puppy. I'm sure there's a mess to clean up, but come in if you want to." Meredith had no doubt that Anne's visit had nothing to do with the racket the puppy continued to make.

Meredith changed clothes first before daring to open the bathroom door. But surprisingly, the puppy had managed to keep his mess to the newspaper. She still fought retching at the smell as she wadded it up, and she carried it at arm's length out to the large trash bin outside, the puppy doing his best to trip her up.

Anne followed them out, and Meredith joined her on the deck.

"Are you going to keep him?"

Meredith smiled over the dog's antics. "I'd like to. It would be nice to have a dog for some nominal protection once I'm living alone. I just don't have time for him right now."

"What about Jenn? I know she'd love to take him."

"And how does she have more time than I do? She's at the restaurant six days a week. Besides, she double-checked, and the lease she signed doesn't allow pets other than cats, birds, or fish."

"Too bad. He's so cute."

"Yep. But he needs a family with kids who'll play with him every day. I might get a cat, just for the companionship. They sleep twenty hours a day, so it wouldn't care that I'm hardly ever home." She crouched down as the puppy came up the steps, and scooped him into her arms. He lavished her chin, jaw, and neck with kisses.

"I know it's getting late, but I hoped you might want to talk." Anne held open the door.

Wariness settled over Meredith. She trusted Anne implicitly, but how much should she tell her cousin about Major?

"Come in. I'll put some coffee on." Meredith deposited the puppy on the floor, washed her hands, and put on a pot of decaf dark roast. They talked about Anne's wedding plans while the coffee brewed and Meredith fed the dog.

Finally, both cradling Meredith's favorite large green mugs in their hands, they settled in the living room.

"So tell me what's going on."

"It was nothing. We were just talking."

Anne frowned then seemed to understand. "No, we'll get to that in a minute. I mean what's this about your going out on a date for the first time in ten years and not telling me?"

"I'm sorry I didn't talk to you. There's been so much going on in my life the last week, I kind of lost track of what day it is." *And I wanted to have something completely of my own for just once in my life.*

"You know I want all the details: who is he, where'd you meet him? Is he the 'friend' you went to the Savoy with Friday night?"

Meredith told Anne everything. She even pulled up Ward's company Web site to show Anne his picture. Anne seemed duly impressed, but grew silent when they returned to the living room from the second bedroom/office.

"What about Major?" Anne asked.

"What about him?" Meredith picked at a loose thread in the arm of her sofa.

"You've been in love with Major for a very long time."

Meredith got up and went back into the office for a pair of scissors to take care of that pesky thread.

"I didn't really allow myself to recognize it until last year when we were all working on Cliff's wedding reception. I guess being in love myself made me finally recognize it in you."

Meredith really didn't want to delve into the whys and wherefores of her feelings for Major, but if anyone could understand falling in love with someone who didn't return the feelings, it would be Anne. At least, Meredith hadn't been in Anne's position—having to cancel a wedding two days before it took place because the groom chose his career over her. But look how that had turned out for Anne in the long run.

"Yes." Meredith's voice came out wispy. She took a swig of coffee to try to clear away the nervous dryness. "Yes, I have been in love with him for a long time. At least, I thought I was."

"Is that what I interrupted tonight?"

Meredith shook her head. "No. I almost made the mistake of telling him but chickened out at the last minute. Which was a good thing, because he told me that he's happy that I've started to have a personal life, that I've met someone."

"Hmm." Anne's mouth twisted to the side. "Looked to me like he was about to kiss you when I walked up. Do you think maybe he was just trying to hide his own feelings for you because you have started seeing someone else? That maybe he's realized he could possibly lose you to someone else?"

"I doubt it. We've known each other for eight years. If he were interested in me, he'd have told me long before now." Meredith stopped toying with the scissors and put them on the coffee table.

"Mere, I've known him a lot longer than you, and one thing I do know about Major is that he has a really hard time opening up and letting people in. There are things I still don't know about his family and his upbringing."

Meredith's interest piqued. "What do you know?"

"Just that he was raised by a single mom, but that on a couple of occasions he was in a foster home. I think the only reason he told me that much is because he knew I'd lost my parents and had been raised by a foster family—even if they are blood relatives. I don't even know if his mom is still alive."

"She is. I heard Forbes ask about her several months ago." Mentally, she made a note to ask her brother about Major's family.

"So can you see why he might not feel like he can express his feelings to you? He got comfortable with the way things were—he knew you'd always be there, that because you gave your full attention to the job, it was like you were giving your full attention to him."

"I think you're reading too much into it." Meredith put her head down on the arm of the sofa. "As far as I'm concerned, Major and I are friends and work colleagues and nothing more. I made a New Year's resolution to get over this crush on him and move on."

Anne sat in thoughtful silence for a moment. "If you think that's the best course of action, I'll support you wholeheartedly."

Meredith pushed herself upright again. "Anne, I'm thirty-four years old—I'll be thirty-five in four months. I want to get married. I'm tired of being alone. I'm afraid that if I don't do something now, I'm going to be alone for the rest of my life."

Anne smiled. "I know exactly how you feel. Of course, I was pushing thirty-six by the time I met George."

"And you had already started trying to meet someone—you were letting Jenn and Forbes set you up on blind dates and introduce you to people."

"Is that what you want—do you want them to start setting you up? Because I'm sure they'd be only too happy." Anne's expression of apprehension was so comical, Meredith had to laugh.

"I don't know about the blind date thing. Especially when it comes to who Jenn might pick out for me. And Forbes is the *last* person I want involved in my dating life." Meredith gave Anne a pointed look.

"I'm right there with you on that one." Anne picked up her mug, looked into it, and set it down again. "I'll keep on the lookout for you. Oh, George's brother, Henry, will be coming to town in a few weeks for a short visit—to get fitted for his tux and meet the family—and it's usually customary for the maid of honor and best man to spend some time getting to know each other. Plus, when we go out while he's here, it'll be nice to have a foursome so Henry doesn't feel like a third wheel."

"As long as it's not the week of the HEARTS banquet, I'll be more than happy to accommodate you."

"No—not that week. I have a huge wedding Valentine's Day. I think it's the week after that." Anne stood and stretched, then carried her coffee cup into the kitchen.

Meredith followed her. "When does George get back from Paris?"

"Not soon enough. He flies into New Orleans next Wednesday, and I'm driving down to meet him—I have a couple of vendors down there I'd like to talk to face-to-face for this Valentine's wedding. We'll spend a few hours down there and then drive back—should be back in time for church that evening."

"That'll make for a long day for you."

"I know, but it'll be worth it once George is with me."

A pang of envy ripped through Meredith's soul at the contentment in her cousin's voice. Yes, coming clean with Anne had been the right thing to do—because now she had the person who specialized in Happy Endings on her side.

Chapter 15

"Come on, push it. Push it. Push it!"

The only thing Major wanted to push was the stupid trainer out the nearest window. With each impact of his foot on the treadmill, sharp pains shot up through his calves, quads, and hamstrings; and his lungs felt like he was trying to breathe through soggy bread.

When had he gotten this out of shape?

Unfortunately, the personal trainer assigned to take him around and put him through his paces on his first visit to the gym had recognized his name as a former football player at ULB. Though how this whippersnapper could remember someone who played almost twenty years ago was a miracle.

The only thing that kept him from hitting the emergency stop button was the memory of how puffy his face had looked on TV. Sure, no one should trust a skinny chef—but who wanted to look at a pudgy one week in and week out?

He ran as hard as he could to keep from being flung backward off the machine while Mr. Universe called encouragement at him. Finally, the kid reached over and knocked the speed down to three and a half miles per hour.

"Walk it off. Walk it off." He made a notation on the clipboard he carried. "Yeah, I think you can start with running fifteen minutes at. . .seven miles per hour, then walk half an hour at three and a half. Gradually, you'll work it up so that you're running the entire forty-five minutes."

Major followed him over to the weight machines and spent the next forty-five minutes pretending that he already had more muscle than flab, and planning to decrease the amount of weight on each one next time he came in. If he survived tonight.

After the last apparatus, Major was ready to dissolve into a puddle of melted lard on the floor. Sheer strength of will was the only thing that kept him upright when the trainer smacked his shoulder.

"Good workout, man. Come in four or five times a week and do that, and you'll be back in your playing condition in no time. See ya later!" The trainer jogged away.

Major grabbed the top of the bicep curl machine as the floor wavered beneath him. Sweat dribbled down his spine. . .and his face and his chest and his arms. Why should sweating in the gym feel entirely different from sweating in the heat and humidity of a busy kitchen?

And why had this stupid gym put the locker rooms on the second floor? He stared up the long flight of stairs, trying to talk his legs into carrying him up them.

"Hey—Major O'Hara, right?"

He turned at the man's voice—and groaned inwardly when he recognized Ward Breaux. He knew he should have come in the morning instead of waiting until after work. He wiped his hand on his towel and shook the man's proffered hand. "Yeah, good to see you."

"Didn't know you worked out here."

"Just joined today."

"What'd you think?" Ward started up the stairs two at a time.

Pride—that ghastly beast—refused to allow him to let Breaux leave him behind. Clenching his teeth against the pain, Major ran up the steps to keep up with the contractor. "To be perfectly honest, it kicked my butt. It's been since college that I've made an effort to exercise regularly."

"Yeah? What did you do back then?"

"Played football."

"Really? Me, too. Where'd you play?" Ward nodded at several beautiful young women who smiled and eyed him hungrily when they passed them on the stairs.

None of them noticed Major. "Here, at ULB. Where'd you play?"

"Miami. I guess in your line of work, it's hard to find time to stay fit."

If Major could move his arms, he'd deck the guy. He didn't need someone else to point out to him how out of shape he was. His legs were already screaming that they'd be sore for days to come. "It is. But I figured if I'm about to be on TV every week, I'd better shape up."

"You're going to be on TV?"

Finally, something he had that Breaux didn't. "I'm going to be doing a weekly cooking segment on Alaine Delacroix's show."

Ward's dark brows shot up. He opened the locker room door. "That hot chick who does the midday show on Channel Six?"

"Yeah." Major wasn't sure if he liked the fact that someone who was seeing Meredith had just called another woman a "hot chick."

The contractor let out a low whistle. "No wonder you're here. If I were still unattached and about to be spending that much time with Alaine Delacroix, I'd want to get in shape, too."

If I were still unattached. A little piece of Major's heart died. Things between Meredith and this guy must be more serious than Major originally thought if Breaux considered himself attached to her. Major didn't see any reason to correct Ward's notion that he would be spending time with Alaine, when it had been made pretty clear that it was only the production and camera people he'd see each week on Tuesdays when they came to film.

"Oh, by the way, Meredith told me she'd like to bring you in on planning the kitchen design in her new house. I'd like to pick your brain on that so I can include your ideas in my bid."

Lovely. Just what Major wanted to do. Spend more time with the guy who was stealing Meredith away from him. "Sure. Anytime."

"Great. I'll get your number from Meredith when I see her later. Well, I'll catch you another time." Breaux flung his towel over his shoulder and went around to a different part of the locker room.

Major stuffed everything into his duffel and headed for home before he had to speak to Ward again. The cold air outside turned his sweat to clamminess, and since Kirby's ragtop was more like a colander than a roof, he was shivering by the time he got home a few miles away.

He stood in the shower for a long time, letting the hot water work on his sore muscles and trying to clear his head. But he had to face the truth. He'd lied to Meredith last night. He *wasn't* happy about Meredith and Ward Breaux. He was especially not happy that he'd had the perfect opportunity yesterday to tell her the truth—about Ma, about his feelings—but like a coward, at Anne's untimely interruption, he'd allowed all of his doubts and insecurities to come flooding back.

He couldn't blame Ward Breaux for wanting to have a serious relationship with Meredith. And when he compared himself to the tall, fitness-club-commercial-perfect contractor, he couldn't blame Meredith for choosing Ward over him.

After the shower, he took a couple of aspirin to hopefully head off some of the soreness he was sure would come, pulled on a clean pair of sweats and long-sleeved T-shirt, and went into the kitchen to fix supper. He opened the fridge and bent down to make sure he didn't miss seeing anything in there.

Another Friday night, and here he was at home, alone. Alone, while Meredith was probably at this very instant getting ready for another date with Ward Breaux.

He should win her back.

The thought jerked him upright, and he cracked his head on the bottom of the freezer door. Win her back? He'd never had her to begin with. Had he?

He pulled stuff out of the fridge without really paying attention. The only thing that had kept him from asking her out all these years was fear—fear that once she found out about Ma, she wouldn't want anything to do with him. Once burned. . .

But Meredith wasn't anything like the other women he'd dated in the distant past. He should give her a chance, tell her the truth, see how she reacted.

He remembered the way the women in the stairwell had looked at Ward. Tossing a package of lemon fish onto the cabinet, he let the fridge door swing shut with a condiment-rattling slam. He couldn't compete with that. He'd only look more like a fool if he tried.

But Major had known Meredith a long time; Ward, only a few weeks. Surely Major could call upon his greater knowledge of Meredith's likes and dislikes to draw her attention back to him.

He loped into the living room and sank—painfully—into the desk chair. The notebook in which he'd been writing his sample menus was on top. He flipped to a clean page and started writing a new menu—a menu of ideas for romancing Meredith away from Ward Breaux.

"I ran into your friend, the cook, at the gym this evening." Ward Breaux held open the door of Palermo's Italian Grill and ushered Meredith in before him.

She tried to think which of the cooks he might have met who would have claimed to be anything but an employee of hers. "Which one?"

"Major O'Hara."

"Oh, he's a chef, not a cook."

Ward chuckled. "Isn't that the same thing?"

"No. The title 'chef' is usually reserved for someone who's been to culinary school."

"And that's a big deal?"

"It would be like me calling someone a contractor who doesn't have a license."

"Yeah—I guess it is a big deal when you put it that way. Anyway,

I saw *Chef* O'Hara at the gym tonight. Told him that you wanted him to be involved in the kitchen design, so I'm going to set up a time to get together with him to get his ideas."

The idea of Ward sitting down one-on-one with Major scared her for some reason. "Let me know when so that I can give you my input as well."

Ward launched into his ideas for the kitchen design. Meredith only half listened as they followed the hostess through the large restaurant to a table near the rear windows overlooking the University Lakes. As usual when in public, the other half of her attention was focused on looking around to see if she knew anyone in the room. It wouldn't do to walk past a former client without at least a greeting—that was one of the first things she'd ever learned from Anne.

Meredith opened the large, leather-like menu and started perusing the many selections. She'd eaten here only a couple of times since they'd open a year ago, and then with the family, so they had ordered the family-sized dishes and shared.

The waitress came to the table, introduced herself, and asked if they wanted drinks and an appetizer.

"Go ahead and bring us a basket of fried mushrooms and two iced teas."

"Actually, make mine Sprite with a twist of orange, please," Meredith hastily corrected, miffed Ward had assumed what she would want.

As soon as the waitress departed, Ward covered her hand with his. "Sorry, I should have asked instead of guessing."

"That's okay. I do usually drink iced tea, but sometimes I get in the mood for something else."

They discussed the menu items, and Meredith wasn't any more ready to order when the waitress came back with their drinks than before.

"Do you need more time, Mere?" Ward looked at her with those heavenly eyes.

She wished her heart would pitter-patter or skip a beat or

something. "Go ahead and order, and I'll make a decision by the time you're finished."

After the waitress finished flirting with Ward with her eyes, Meredith ordered crawfish and shrimp alfredo and gave the waitress her menu along with a warning glance. The girl had the good grace to look apologetic.

Though the tight waistband of Meredith's skirt warned her she shouldn't indulge in the fried mushrooms, once she tasted one with the sweet horseradish dipping sauce, she couldn't help but eat a few of them. She didn't want to go back to the much larger size she'd gotten to in college—turning to food after Brent announced his engagement to her roommate—but she wasn't so concerned about her weight that she wouldn't allow herself to indulge in treats every so often.

As they ate dinner, Ward told stories about his siblings, and Meredith shared a few about hers.

"Do you ever get to a point where, while you still love them, you're just good and sick of your relatives?" Ward asked.

"Yeah, that's what I've been going through for the last two weeks, as a matter of fact."

"Really? What happened?"

"You." Meredith grinned at him.

"Me? Was it because we ran into your brother?"

"Sort of, but it was what you said on our first date—asking me if I ever got away from them. And I realized, I never do. That project house has become something of a refuge for me, and I didn't even realize it until you put it into words. The whole reason I've been so gung ho about doing the renovations myself is because that was the only place I could think of where I could get away from all of them."

"Good for you."

"Yeah, it was amazing—I realized I had no private life with my family, and that I needed to take a stand. I decided not to tell them about you." Meredith kept her face straight—because Ward's was so expressive when she teased him.

"You don't want them to know about me?"

"That's right. Unfortunately, one of my younger brothers occasionally goes out with one of the receptionists at the office, and she told him about you coming to pick me up last week; so he asked me about it in front of a bunch of siblings and cousins last night." And Major. She still cringed at that. But everything had seemed pretty normal during their meeting this morning.

"And what did you tell them?" Ward swirled his tea in his glass. The sugar sludge in the bottom barely budged. She still couldn't decide if it was endearing or just gross that he added sugar to already sweetened tea.

"I didn't have to say anything. Forbes—the brother you met—came to my defense. Of course, that was only after I blasted him Sunday afternoon for prying." And then she'd run out like a child. But he didn't need to know that part.

"Can I interest you two in dessert? Tiramisu or apple crostata or amaretto cheesecake?"

Meredith's mouth watered at the mention of cheesecake, her favorite dessert.

"What do you want, Mere?"

"We have a chocolate Gianduia cake that's to die for."

"I'm not real big on chocolate." It shouldn't be that hard of a decision. "I think I'm going to have to pass. My rule is usually that I can have either appetizers or a dessert, but not both. And since I'm taking half my meal home with me. . ."

"What about this?" Ward reached across the table and took her hand. "Why don't you order whatever you want, and I'll split it with you?"

How could such a completely generous and caring man engender absolutely no emotional response from her other than gratitude and a general liking? "Okay. Do you have a cheesecake that doesn't have almonds or amaretto? I'm allergic."

"We have a mascarpone cheesecake, but it has walnuts in the crust."

"Walnuts are fine. Let's go with that."

"I'll be right back with it."

Meredith liked the warmth of Ward's hand around hers—and the idea that anyone in the restaurant looking at them would think they were really a couple. . .that she really had feelings for this handsome man, that someone had chosen her.

"You slipped away from me there for a minute." Ward's thumb circled her palm. "Where were you just now?"

"My mind wandered."

He grinned. "Fine, keep your secrets."

"I have to start somewhere. I need the practice." The feel of his thumb rubbing her palm nearly sent her into a trance. She squeezed his hand to get him to stop.

"Do you already have plans for Valentine's Day?"

"I do. I'm working that night. It's one of our biggest events of the year—a charity banquet and auction to benefit the cardiac care unit at University Hospital."

"Let me see if I've got this straight. You work New Year's Eve. You work Valentine's Day. Let me guess. . .you work the Fourth of July?"

"Not usually. But you did skip Easter."

"Easter?"

"Yes. The multichurch sunrise service followed by the Easter egg hunt in Schuyler Park."

"I thought the mayor's wife did that. That's what they always say on the news."

"I know. The mayor's wife is responsible for leading the events and awarding the prizes. So it's a marquee event for her—show her involvement in the community."

"But you plan and organize all of it?"

She shrugged and nodded. "It's my job. I don't need any special recognition for it."

"Uh, yeah, you do. With all of these events falling within a couple of months, I'm surprised you have time to go out to dinner. Glad, but surprised."

"I have a good team of planners and assistants who work with me. I learned early on in this business to identify people's strengths and delegate responsibility to them." Just as Anne had done with her. She'd zeroed in on Meredith's need to please the people she was working with and put Meredith in charge of working with customers. Learning how to stand her ground with vendors had been a hard-won battle.

"I can tell you don't take enough credit for the amount of work you do and that your coworkers probably take you for granted."

He saw things so clearly—things that until she'd met him, her eyes had been closed to. "Maybe."

"Have you ever considered leaving and doing something totally different?"

Only every time she worked a major event. "Occasionally."

"Like becoming an interior designer—maybe one who works hand in hand with a particular contractor?"

"Why, Ward Breaux—are you offering me a job?" She laughed, but it faded quickly when his expression remained serious.

"I haven't seen your design aesthetic, but I can imagine it's got to be impeccable, just from what I know about you and the work you've done on your house."

The waitress chose that moment to return with the dessert. "Here you go. Enjoy."

Meredith hardly tasted the first bite, still stunned by Ward's offer. Leave B-G and go to work with him? Do the kind of work she'd gone to school for?

"Of course, I know you wouldn't make nearly what you make as an executive director with a huge corporation. But there's something to be said for job satisfaction."

She couldn't let him believe she didn't like her job. "I do have satisfaction in my work." She thought about the happy faces of the people at the New Year's Gala. "I make people happy by giving them the best event possible."

"But is that what you really want to do for the rest of your life? If you say yes, I promise I'll never mention designing again. But if you can't say yes, I want you to think about what I said."

She opened her mouth to answer in the affirmative, but something stopped her tongue from forming the word.

Ward nodded. "I won't pressure you, but I just want you to think about it, 'kay?"

"I don't think I'll have any trouble doing that."

Chapter 16

"So, you know what I'm thinking? Concrete floors."

Meredith prepared to laugh, then realized that Antoine Delacroix looked like he really meant what he said. "Concrete floors?"

"Yeah. We rip out all this old wood—it just makes everything dark and closed in—and do painted concrete floors."

The months of lovingly restoring the crown molding, the door and window facings, the built-ins made Meredith's fingers tingle with indignation. "Rip out the wood?"

"Yeah. And I'm thinking a totally modern kitchen—colored, laminated, stainless steel and glass, very streamlined."

Mouth agape, she could only stare as Alaine's brother—her much *younger* brother—wandered from the dining room into the barren kitchen. When he'd shown up—almost an hour late—she'd been surprised that someone as young as he appeared to be was already a licensed contractor. And when he'd handed over his credentials, the recent date on the license had confirmed her suspicions.

"Maybe I didn't explain properly over the phone." Meredith followed him into the kitchen. "I want this house *restored* not *remodeled*."

"Same diff." Antoine waved his hand over his shoulder and continued on into the utility room. "Hey, that den is on the other side of this wall isn't it?" He knocked on the back wall. "We could knock this wall out and put in a kickin' wet bar."

This walk-through couldn't end soon enough. What had Alaine been thinking? If she'd meant to set Meredith up with Antoine romantically, she'd overlooked the fact that Meredith was a good ten to twelve years older than this kid. If she thought Meredith would like Antoine's aesthetic, she'd been sorely mistaken.

She leaned heavily against the back door. "You know, Antoine, what I'm really looking for is someone who can come in and restore the house and keep the historical integrity while bringing the utilities and features, like kitchen and bathrooms, up to date."

The wall-knocking stopped, and he stuck his head out of the utility room. "Really? Most folks I talk to want everything modern these days."

"Well, call me old-fashioned, but I bought a craftsman-style house because I love the craftsman style."

"Dude. You should have told me. I really don't do old stuff."

"I guess there's no reason for me to waste more of your time, then, Antoine. I'll walk you out." Meredith waved him toward the front of the house.

"Yep. You're probably right." He preceded her to the front door. "But you really should think about that wet bar idea. It would be sweet."

"I wouldn't have any use for a wet bar." Besides, Ward had suggested taking away half of the space. And Ward knew an architect who could draw up plans before the end of the week so that he could get started soon and have it finished before Anne and George returned from England at the end of March.

Antoine grabbed the front door's handle but turned before opening it. "So, wanna go out sometime?"

Meredith cleared her throat to mask a chuckle. "While I'm flattered by the offer, I. . ." Was she really going to turn down an offer for a date? Yes. Yes she was. "I'm seeing someone."

"Cool."

She should be indignant at the relief that showed in his dark eyes, but she couldn't quite conjure it. "Bye."

"Later, dude." He loped down the porch steps and sidewalk to his monster-sized luxury SUV, which dug trenches in the driveway and sprayed gravel everywhere when he gunned the engine backing out.

High-pitched yapping from behind the house caught her attention. She hurried through and out onto the back porch. The fuzzball stood with his forepaws on the trunk of one of the massive oaks, barking his head off at a tabby cat.

Meredith put her fingers to the corners of her mouth and whistled. The puppy—who really needed a name if she was going to keep him any longer—whipped around. Overjoyed to see her, he broke out into his lumbering puppy run, tripping over his too-big feet a couple of times before he reached her.

She brushed off a few dead leaves and scooped him up, holding him low enough that his tongue couldn't reach her face. So he concentrated his kisses on her hands instead.

"Come on, li'l booger. Let's drop you off at home so I can get back to work."

Since the afternoon had turned out somewhat pleasant, Meredith decided she could take the risk of leaving the puppy outside in the small fenced area beyond the swimming pool Anne figured had been set up as a dog run by previous residents.

She put him in it then ran inside to get the kennel she'd borrowed from her parents, the bottom padded with the old towels he'd been sleeping on, along with his water dish.

Anne's cell phone went straight to voicemail—must be with a client—so Meredith left her cousin a message to check on the dog if she wasn't home when Anne got there. She pulled out of the driveway headed north, toward downtown.

Corie was just clearing her desk when Meredith hurried in.

"Hey. Everyone's been looking for you." Corie handed her several sticky notes with messages.

Meredith flipped through them quickly. "I already talked to most of them on the way back here. I'll call this one back tomorrow." She wadded the unnecessary messages and handed them to Corie to throw away. "Any deliveries come while I was out?"

Corie shook her head. "I called them several times. They said the linens were on the truck to be delivered today." The assistant put her satchel down in her chair. "Need me to stay and help out with anything so you're not here all night?"

"No. I've got that meeting in"—Meredith glanced at her watch—"two hours. And then I'm out of here."

"Want me to go pick up something for you to eat?"

"Won't be necessary."

Meredith whirled around at Major's voice. He carried a tray with several dome-covered dishes, a pitcher of tea, and a glass full of ice.

Warm gooiness—like a chocolate chip cookie straight from the oven—stuck to Meredith's insides. "Is that for me?"

"Who else?" He nodded toward her door. "Unless you don't want it."

"Don't be ridiculous." Meredith stepped out of his way and motioned him into her office.

"I remembered you said you had a late meeting tonight, and I figured you might appreciate not having to reheat cold leftovers." Major slid the tray onto her table and began putting out a place-setting, complete with cloth napkin and placemat.

"I guess you're taken care of, then." Corie joined Meredith in the doorway. "Here's all the stuff you'll need for the meeting."

"Thanks." She took the stack of folders. "Have a good night."

Corie's gaze cut toward Major; then she grinned at Meredith. "You, too."

Instead of correcting her assistant's erroneous conclusion, Meredith bade her farewell and carried the thick stack of folders to the table.

"You look like you've gotten some sun." Meredith's voice just over his shoulder startled Major, making him clank the plate cover against the ceramic.

Embarrassment kept him from looking up at her; instead, he concentrated on setting the dishes out just so. "Yeah. Alaine suggested I go to a tanning salon and get a little more color so they don't have to use so much makeup on me tomorrow."

"Oh." Meredith picked up one of the folders she'd just put down. "So, that starts tomorrow, huh?"

"Mmm." Major was so not ready to get in front of the camera again. How had he ever agreed to do this? Oh, yeah, that's right. He hadn't. He'd been *told* he'd agreed to do this.

"Do you know what you're going to cook yet?" Meredith perched on the edge of a chair across the table.

"Alaine suggested starting off with a kitchen basics lesson—talking about different techniques, different utensils that most people will be using at home." He swallowed hard. "We're going to be doing it at my condo."

Meredith's head rocked back slightly, and her eyebrows shot up. "Really?"

"Something about not wanting to intimidate the viewers by showing me only in a professional kitchen." Of course, once they saw his kitchen at home, they'd kick him off as a fraud. No professional chef had anything at home as laughable as what he had. "Then it'll mostly be based on viewers' suggestions and questions as to what I cook each week."

"Sounds like a good idea." Meredith fingered the edge of the folder her arm rested atop. "How is this going to affect your work schedule? I heard the filming is pretty much going to eat up your whole day on Tuesdays."

Major added a last-minute garnish of chopped chives and parsley to the blue cheese mashed potatoes and pulled out the chair for Meredith. Really looking at her for the first time since their meeting last Friday morning, he was surprised by how exhausted she looked.

"Can you stay a few minutes?" she asked before sitting.

"Sure." He sank into the chair she'd just vacated. "I'm not sure yet how this thing is going to impact the work flow. Steven has been pretty much running lunch service upstairs for the past five months, so he's ready to step up as *chef de cuisine* and handle everything. I'm just a little concerned that we only have three and a half weeks until the banquet. Normally, tomorrow would have been my day to start calling vendors and placing orders. I did some of that today, but Monday's a really bad day for getting in touch with anyone in the food industry."

Meredith finished off her Caesar salad quickly and started on the blackened lemon fish with the citrus beurre blanc. At the first bite, she closed her eyes and sighed.

Major relaxed. It had been a favorite of his to prepare in culinary school, but he hadn't made it in years, before Friday night. It was definitely going on the short list for the restaurant menu.

"Is that something Steven can help out with?"

"With vendors for the banquet? I'd rather have him concentrating on lunch service. I'm going to have him do the final inventory and budget this week, as well as have him start ordering for next week. I'm going to work closely with him on it, but it's something he should pick up pretty easily. He's a quick learner."

"He's got a good mentor." Meredith gave him a soft smile.

His insides turned into goo. "Thanks."

"Hey, when are you guys going to sing at church again?" Meredith moved her cleared dinner plate aside and pulled the dish of sliced baked apples forward.

"Forbes said something Thursday night about a few new pieces he'd found for us. It's just a matter of us all having time in our schedule to get together and practice. With Clay working most nights, George off gallivanting all over the world, and Forbes and me working long hours, we hardly cross paths anymore."

"That's too bad. Everyone loves to hear y'all sing. It's the only time we ever get to see Forbes doing something that seems completely out of character for him."

Major laughed. "Yeah, he doesn't seem the southern gospel type. Of course, he's the main reason we dress in suits rather than just making sure we're wearing similar color shirts up there."

Meredith lapsed into silence for a moment, stirring the baked apples around in their sauce. "Major, I don't mean to pry into your personal life, so tell me if I'm overstepping bounds here, but I've always been curious about your family."

Frozen iron settled in Major's gut. "Curious about what?"

"Well, you never talk about them. You know so much about mine—have practically been part of our family for a really long time."

His forearms started twitching from how tightly he gripped his fists. "I don't talk about my family because there really isn't much to say." He should tell her. He would tell her.

Meredith looked over at him, head cocked, a half smile playing about those very inviting lips.

No, he couldn't tell her. He didn't want that open, carefree gaze to be tainted with suspicion, wondering when he was going to go off his rocker, too. "I'm an only child who was raised by a single mom."

"And your mom is. . . ?" She pressed her lips together.

As tempting as it was to let her think his mother had passed away, he couldn't lie to her. "Still living."

"Does she still live in Bonneterre?"

"No." Because technically, Beausoleil Pointe Center was outside the city limits.

"That's too bad. So you probably don't get to see her very often." She looked genuinely sad for him.

Guilt pounded in his head and chest. Why couldn't he just bring himself to tell her the truth? "I see her as often as I can." Like every Wednesday evening and Sunday afternoon.

"Well, if she ever comes in town, let me know. I'd love to meet her and tell her how much I. . .appreciate her son."

Wouldn't Ma love that? Someone to rave about him to. "I'll keep that in mind." He refilled her tea glass. "Want me to leave the pitcher? Jeff and Sandra can pick it up when they come down with the snacks for the meeting."

Meredith's eyes lit up. "Is Sandra making cookies?"

Major stood and started collecting the dinner dishes. "Yes—that's why I only brought you baked apples for dessert." He winked at her.

"You know me too well, Major O'Hara."

But not as well as he'd like—oh, there was no use in entertaining those kinds of thoughts anymore. He'd created the recipe for their relationship; now he had to live with the product.

Meredith rose and stretched, her back audibly popping a couple of times. "Guess I'd better get back to it." She leaned across the table and dragged the pile of folders toward her.

"You'll be careful leaving tonight?" He made sure his expression was as stern as he could make it.

"In addition to my facilities maintenance managers, I'll have all of my security supervisors here. Do you think any of them would let me walk to my car alone?" She laughed. "I'll be okay, you old worrywart."

"If I didn't worry about you—" An all too familiar ring interrupted his retort. His heart sank as the ringtone he'd chosen for Beausoleil Pointe Center's main switchboard trilled into the silent office.

Giving Meredith a tight farewell smile, he hefted the service tray up on one shoulder, grabbed the phone with his free hand, and backed out of her office.

"This is Major O'Hara."

"Danny, it's Ma."

Major hurried down the hall to the executive dining room and through to the kitchen. "Ma, what's wrong?" He slid the tray onto the island and went back to stop the swinging door's flapping.

"Does anything have to be wrong for a mother to call her son?"

"No, but you don't usually call me unless something's happened. So what's wrong?"

"Well, you see, Joan and I were going into the dining room for supper—but they call it dinner around here, and I don't know why. You need to tell them that dinner is lunch and dinner at nighttime is supper."

"Ma, focus. What happened?" Major snapped the lights on,

tucked the phone between shoulder and ear, and set to hand-washing the dishes.

"We'd just gotten our trays, but Gene—he's the one with the daughter I was telling you about, the one that just got married." She paused, obviously expecting a response.

"Yes, Gene with the daughter who just got married."

"Right. Anyway, Gene was behind someone else who stopped right in front of him, and Gene ran into her and both of them spilled their iced tea, see?"

"No, Ma. I don't really see yet. Keep going."

"So, Joan and I were talking and we weren't paying much attention to Gene. You know, all he ever talks about is his daughter who just got married. It's like he's rubbing it in that his kid is married and mine isn't. I want grandchildren, Major."

He needed to bang his head against something hard. "What happened, Ma?"

"I fell."

His hands stilled—but his heart pounded faster. "Fell? Are you hurt?"

"No. But they're trying to make me go to bed. I don't want to go to bed, Danny. Tell them I don't have to go to bed."

Head throbbing, he set the clean dishes on the drain board and found a clean towel to dry his hands on. "Put the doctor on."

"There's no doctor, just that little boy who keeps saying he is one. But I don't think he's old enough. You need to come out here and tell them I don't want to go to bed."

"Give the phone to him, please."

"You're coming, right?"

"Yes, Ma, I'll come. Now give the phone to. . .the little boy."

A bit of fumbling on the line ended with, "This is Nick Sevellier."

"Dr. Sevellier, how bad is she?"

"She's a little banged up and hit her head pretty hard when she fell. But it's not a concussion, so we see no reason to have her taken to the emergency room."

Major'd taken his share of spills, working in kitchens since he was fifteen, and he knew just how dangerous even falling on a wood floor like those at BPC could be. "Was she knocked out?"

"Not at all. But she's developing a pretty good knot on the back of her head."

"And your medical opinion is bed rest?" The kid called himself a doctor, but Major didn't know this kid's credentials.

"My previous rotation was in the emergency room, Mr. O'Hara. I had to deal with a lot of head traumas there. I'm more worried about how sore she's likely to be tomorrow. She wrenched her back a little bit, so I'd like her to lie down and let the nurses give her an ice and heat treatment."

"Okay. Thanks. Put her back on the phone." Major sighed.

"Did you tell him I'm not going to bed?"

"Ma, let them take care of you. I'll be there in a few minutes."

By the time he convinced her, he was back in his office gathering his coat and duffel. "Ma, I've got to go," he said quietly, to avoid Jeff or Sandra hearing him out in the kitchen. "Hang up the phone and let the nurses take you back to your room. I'll be there in about twenty minutes."

"I don't like you very much right now." The line clicked and went dead.

"I love you, too, Ma." Major threw the phone into his bag and turned off the office light.

"Everything okay, boss?" Sandra asked. The cookies she'd just taken from the oven filled the large space with a heavenly aroma.

"Yeah, just fine." He slung his bag over his shoulder. "Jeff, there are some dishes on the drain board down in the executive kitchen. Will you bring those up and run them through the sterilizer with everything else before you leave tonight?"

"Can do, Chef." Jeff didn't look up from the cheese straws he was piping onto a large baking sheet with a pastry bag.

"Meredith is in her office if you need anything."

"Yes, Chef," both cooks responded.

Once in the elevator, Major leaned heavily against the wall, rubbing his forehead. Though he hated keeping secrets from Meredith, tonight's episode with Ma reminded him of why he needed to keep her as far away from Meredith as he could, lest she ruin Meredith's life, too.

Chapter 17

Major rubbed his dry, burning eyes and looked around the condo one more time, just to make sure he hadn't missed anything. Which he knew he hadn't, since he'd been up at 4:00 a.m. to clean an already spotless apartment.

Maybe he should vacuum one more time.

No. He'd vacuumed twice already. He stepped into the kitchen and caught sight of the clock on the back of the stove. They would be here in less than fifteen minutes, and he wasn't even dressed.

The producer from Alaine's show who'd called yesterday had suggested Major not wear his chef's jacket for the segments. He slid the closet door open and shuffled through his button-down shirts. Solid blue in a variety of shades; blue with stripes and patterns; white with blue stripes of various widths. . .didn't he have anything other than blue? Yes—gray. The producer had wanted him somewhat casual—"weekend wear," she'd called it. Well, he didn't really think that sweats and a ULB T-shirt were appropriate. Instead, he donned a plain white T-shirt, khakis, and a blue-gray waffle-weave pullover that allowed a bit of the white undershirt to show at the neck.

With just a few minutes remaining, he ducked into the bathroom to brush his teeth, again. He should have gotten his hair cut before today. It was going to be flopping down onto his forehead all day.

After cleaning the sink and counter with a disinfecting wipe, he straightened the hand towels one more time.

He jumped at the rifle-shot sound of the knock on the front door. When he opened it, a plain woman of indeterminate age wearing a Channel Six–logoed Windbreaker stood on the other side.

She extended her right hand. "Major O'Hara? I'm Pricilla Wilson. We spoke on the phone yesterday."

"Yes. Please come in." He stepped out of the doorway into the space between his living room and dining area.

The cameraman who'd come with Alaine to the tasting last week entered behind her, pushing a cart piled with equipment cases.

"Can I help with anything?"

The cameraman grunted, which Major took as a no, and Major pointed him toward the kitchen.

"While he sets up the lights and cameras, let's sit and discuss the plan for today." Pricilla pulled out one of the chairs and sat at the table, scattering a stack of papers all over it in a matter of seconds. "We've got a lot of stuff to film and not a lot of time to do it."

Eight hours sounded like quite a lot of time to Major.

"The girl doing your hair and makeup will be here in about forty-five minutes—"

"Hey, Priss"—the camera guy came around the corner—"you'd better come look."

Major followed them but stood in the hallway outside the kitchen, since three people wouldn't fit.

Pricilla hit a couple of keys on her phone and pressed it to her ear. "Hey, it's me. We've got no joy here."

Mortification rang in Major's ears and burned every surface of his body.

"Kitchen's way too small for the equipment we need for filming." Pricilla came out of the kitchen to pace the length of the living room. "Of course not. We expected a chef would have at least a decent home kitchen. . . . You want what?"

She brushed past Major again and pulled the phone away from

her ear. "Nelson, pack it all up. We're going." Back to the person on the other end of the phone, she said, "Yeah. We'll see you in about twenty minutes."

Major followed her back to the dining table, where she scraped up all her papers—and the placemat.

He reached over and rescued the mat. "What's going on?"

She stuffed the papers into her bag. "We can't shoot here. Your kitchen's too small. So we're taking all this elsewhere."

"Where?"

"Alaine's place."

Major stopped cold. "Where?"

"Alaine Delacroix's place. She thinks her kitchen will work better, so bring what you might need that she may not have, and let's get going. We're on a tight schedule today." Pricilla turned her back on him and made another phone call.

Major had to wait until Nelson got all of his equipment cases out of the kitchen before he could go in. He looked around for what to take with him and grabbed his knife case right away. No chef ever went anywhere without his knives. But what about everything else? Food processor, blender, steamer, butane warmers. . .

The whole point of what they were doing today was to familiarize people with stuff they already had in their home kitchens. What better way to do that than in the kitchen of someone who didn't have professional-quality products? He tucked his knife case into his duffel bag and joined the production assistant and cameraman at the door.

"I'll follow you over there." He locked the door behind them and trailed them out to the parking lot where, this time, Nelson accepted his help in loading all of the equipment back into their van.

The van headed toward Old Towne and into an older part of the townhouse development where Forbes lived. Major had looked at a couple of units here when he'd moved back to town, but even though he'd much preferred the kitchens, the price on his condo had been more palatable.

He parked one space away from the van to give them room for taking equipment out, just as a small, sporty Mazda with dark windows pulled into the driveway at the townhouse across the roadway.

Alaine sprang out of the little black car—but if Major hadn't known she was meeting them here, he might not have recognized her. Dressed in jeans and a black sweater, she wore her hair pulled up at the back of her head haphazardly as if done on the fly, and she didn't have any makeup on, making her look pale and wan.

"I had a great idea on the way over here." Alaine jogged across the street to help with equipment. "Hey, Major."

"Hi, Alaine."

"What's this idea?" Pricilla asked.

"Were you working at the Food Network when Gordon Elliott did that show where he went around and dropped in on people and made a meal from whatever they had in their kitchens?"

"That was before my time, but I watched it pretty regularly." Pricilla heaved a large case onto the cart. "You want him to do something like that?"

Major loved being talked about as if he weren't standing right there with them.

"Similar idea. What if he were to fix a meal just from whatever I have on hand in my kitchen? He could explain what he's doing but also go ahead and give recipes and tips and a cooking demonstration along the way." Alaine finally turned to acknowledge his presence. "What do you think?"

Considering he hadn't wanted to do this in the first place? "Sounds like it would be better than me trying to demonstrate how different things work or explain what they're used for."

"Try to use as much of the stuff that I have in my kitchen as you can—there are a bunch of things in there that I don't even know what they are. My mom gives me stuff for my kitchen every year on my birthday and at Christmas. I guess she hopes I'll eventually stop hating to cook and start using all of it." She wrinkled her nose like

Samantha on *Bewitched* when she grinned.

He couldn't help but laugh. Why did everyone he know hate to cook? "I'll see what I can do. But if you don't like cooking, am I going to have any ingredients to work with?"

"I went to the grocery store last night. I always have the greatest intentions, but I never follow through. Fortunately, Mama likes my kitchen better than her own, so she usually comes over one night during the week and cooks up a bunch of meals for me."

Oh, to have a mother who could do stuff like that without burning down the building. "Great. Let's go see what you have, and I'll come up with a menu."

He followed Alaine through the one-car garage—which was empty, so it looked as if she actually used it for her car—up several steps, and into a utility room/pantry. He stopped and looked at the dry goods on the shelves. Flour, sugar, baking powder and soda, spices, dried herbs, canned vegetables and fruits, and cereal—lots of cereal.

Alaine's cheeks were red when he finished his perusal. "I'm a big cereal-for-supper girl. And breakfast."

Meredith had been that way, too, until he'd stepped in and started making sure she had decent meals to take home with her every day. "Show me to your kitchen."

Jealousy struck instantly when he stepped out of the utility room and into the main part of the house. Though not huge, the fact that the kitchen was completely open to the living and dining rooms made it feel huge. And she had upgraded stainless appliances, including a gas stove built into the eat-at island that divided the kitchen from the rest of the space.

"So, Chef, tell me what you think." Pride laced Alaine's voice.

"It's great. I didn't know any of these units had kitchens like this. The ones I looked at were much smaller and more closed off—they just had pass-through windows."

"The people who owned this before me completely renovated it based on something they saw on TV. The colors were hideous—tomato red walls and a green tile backsplash so it looked like Christmas all the time—but that was a pretty easy fix. And I got the place for a song—I mean, most buyers can't stand the fact that the front overlooks a bunch of old, dilapidated warehouses across the highway."

"But you don't care about the view?"

Alaine turned slowly around, her arms extended. "When I could have this?"

"I see your point."

She looked at her watch and sighed. "While I'd love to stay and watch you work, I've got to get back to the station and finish writing some stories for today's show. Have fun, and leave me some leftovers." She winked and lcft.

Pricilla and Nelson brought in the equipment and went to work setting it all up while Major explored Alaine's kitchen. At first, he felt odd going through all the drawers and cabinets, until he started seeing the quality of her cookware and small appliances. Not quite professional quality, but definitely top of the line.

Once familiar with where everything was, he pulled his spiral notebook out of his duffel and went to the fridge. Inventorying its contents, he started writing down ideas for dishes that were moderately simple and quick, that pretty much anyone could cook if given the right instruction. The freezer offered up even more ideas, especially once he saw the lamb shoulder steaks and artichoke hearts. He took them out, filled half the sink with cold water, and put the plastic-bagged meat in it to start thawing.

The makeup gal, Charla, arrived and had Major sit on one of the stools from the island, which had been moved into the middle of the living room. She tucked paper towels around his collar and went to work. Pricilla took the opportunity to wire him up with a lapel microphone—which she had to run up under his shirt from the battery pack clipped to the back of his belt. As he could throughout the process, he wrote recipe ideas, trying to figure out exactly how to explain the processes and eliminating several ideas as too complicated to explain.

"Have you ever thought about getting your teeth whitened?" Charla asked.

"No. Can't say as I have." What—were his teeth *that* bad?

"Hmm." Charla shrugged and made a face as if to say, *Your funeral.*

Great, one more thing to be self-conscious about. Pudgy face, check. Bad hair, check. Hideously discolored teeth, check. He'd hit the trifecta.

He held his breath to keep from sneezing when Charla dusted powder over his whole face. "Now, whatever you do, don't touch your face. Don't scratch your nose or rub your eyes."

Immediately, his entire face started itching. "I'll do my best. What about sweating?"

"This makeup can withstand a lot of moisture, but try not to sweat too much. If you feel like you're going to need it, turn the thermostat down or open some windows to cool off." She closed up her makeup kit—which looked like a fishing tackle box—and shrugged into a coat with a huge furry collar. "I'll be in and out all day for touch-ups."

"Thanks."

"Keep those paper towels in your collar except when you're filming. I guess they didn't tell you not to wear white up on your neck."

"No. Sorry."

"That's okay. Just try to keep your head up at all times so your makeup doesn't rub onto the white shirt."

Great. Now everyone involved in this project was frustrated with him. "Will do."

"Chef, we're ready to get some test shots of you," Pricilla called.

They'd set the tripod camera up across the island from the cooktop, and Nelson had another one on his shoulder.

"Here's the deal." Pricilla pulled one of the stools over beside the tripod and set her clipboard down on the seat. "This is the camera you're going to talk into, and I'm going to be running it. Nelson is going to be getting shots from more of an over-your-shoulder perspective. We may have to run through some of the steps a couple of times so that he can get close-ups of what you're doing."

"Did I hear Alaine say you used to work at the Food Network?"

"I did two internships there as an undergrad and as a graduate student and then worked there a couple of years after college." Pricilla smiled for the first time this morning. "Having a cooking segment on Alaine's show was my suggestion."

Now he knew whom to blame for this entire fiasco. He went around to the stove. Pricilla adjusted the fixed camera's angle. "Move around as if you're cooking—go to the sink and the fridge, move to the side of the stove where you'll chop vegetables. . . ."

Major moved around the kitchen as directed, doing his best not to be freaked out that a big guy with a large camera on his shoulder was following his every move. The lights they'd put up in every corner of the triangular kitchen were really heating up the place, and he hadn't even turned on the stove or oven yet.

"You good, Nelson?" Pricilla asked.

"Yep."

"Let's go through your menu, Chef, and figure out the best order for doing this. We want it to be real time as much as possible—meaning that if someone was really making this for a meal, they'd have to be working on multiple projects all at once. We aren't just going to do a dish at a time."

Forty-five minutes later, he pulled the paper towels out of his collar and began explaining to the camera how to thaw frozen meat safely.

"Let me stop you for a second, Chef." Pricilla came out from behind her camera.

His heart pounded, and he really needed a bottle of water from the case he'd seen in the pantry. "What's wrong?"

"First, you need to remember to breathe. You're talking way too fast."

"Right. Breathe. What else?" He took a couple of gulps of air to prove he could do what she said.

"Don't say *all right* at the beginning of each sentence and end each sentence with *okay*, okay?" She nodded her head.

"Right. No *all rights* or *okays*."

"Ready to go again?"

He gave her a thumbs-up. "Ready." He launched into his explanation of defrosting meat again, trying to slow down the words tumbling out of his mouth and stumbling each time he was about to say the no-no words.

"Let me stop you again, Chef." Pricilla sounded a little more frustrated this time. Major knew just how she felt.

"Still too fast?"

"A little bit. But the problem is that you don't sound like you're talking to a person. You sound like you're talking to a camera. Forget that it's a piece of equipment. Pretend that there's someone you know really well, who doesn't know how to cook, sitting right here across from you. Talk to that *person*. In your head, carry on a conversation with them. Imagine their reactions to what you're saying. Can you do that?"

"Imagine a person, right." A person. A person who didn't know how to cook. Slowly, a grin split his lips. Meredith. Of course. The one person he'd love to spend time with in the kitchen more than anyone else. Imagine Meredith sitting here, taking cooking lessons from him. Imagine this was his kitchen and Meredith was here with him, lending her moral support and gazing on him affectionately with those wonderfully expressive brown eyes.

"Let's try it again." Pricilla made another notation on her clipboard and moved back behind the camera.

For the next six hours, Major talked to Meredith—through the camera—and created dishes he knew she would be able to recreate if she put her mind to it. Finally, at four o'clock after Nelson got close-up shots of the plated dishes, Pricilla called it a wrap.

Having cleaned as he went—as he'd been taught to do by Aunt Maggie—Major didn't have much cleanup to finish, so he immediately set to it, eager to run up to the office to find out how everything had gone today.

"Now, when you come in Thursday to do the voice-over—"

He whipped around at Pricilla's words. "What? Where am I supposed to go Thursday?"

"Didn't I tell you we'd need you to come in and do some voice-overs for where we've edited the segment down?" The corner of her mouth pulled down in a sheepish expression.

"No. I wasn't told I'd have to do more than just filming on Tuesdays. How much time do you think it'll take?" He couldn't afford any more time away from work. And if he started the restaurant, he'd need every hour he could get.

"An hour, maybe ninety minutes. You'll get to watch the edited segment through and write out what to say to bridge where we've condensed. Remember, this is fitting into a fifteen-minute segment. It's just too bad that everyone at the studio won't get a chance to taste it, because just what you fixed us for lunch was fabulous."

"Thanks." Yeah, having to cater lunch for all of Alaine's co-workers would be the cherry on top of this hot-stress sundae. He rummaged around in her cabinets for storage containers. He separated all the food out into single serving sizes and labeled everything with the masking tape and marker he found in one of the drawers. Too bad he hadn't thought to bring a disposable takeaway box so that he'd have something to take back to Meredith.

He hummed as he worked, enjoying the sense of accomplishment that washing the last few dishes gave him. By the time Alaine's kitchen was as spotless as it had been when he'd walked in, Pricilla and Nelson had finished loading their equipment in the van.

Pricilla came back in and closed the garage door then ushered Major out the front, locking the door behind them. She gave Major a funny look as they walked down the steps.

"What?"

"You're going to want to wash that makeup off as soon as you get home. Most people complain that their faces break out pretty bad if they wear it for more than a couple of hours."

His face suddenly started itching again. "Thanks. I'll do that." He had to go right past his complex on his way to the office, so he might as well stop and do it there.

"See you Thursday," Pricilla called, swinging up into the passenger seat of the van.

He waved and climbed into Kirby. As he drove home, he reviewed the day. Thank goodness Pricilla had the idea to tell him to imagine talking to someone. He'd be forever indebted to Meredith for helping him make it through his first day of filming. Maybe one day he'd really have the chance to spend that much time with her one-on-one.

He just hoped it wasn't so she could cook for Ward Breaux or any other man.

Chapter 18

As the weeks dwindled down to days and then hours before the Hearts to HEARTS banquet, Meredith began to realize just how hard her New Year's resolution was going to be to fulfill. Though she had been asked out twice since Antoine's invitation, and had even gone out with one of the guys, she just couldn't seem to find anyone she wanted to spend a whole evening with, let alone the rest of her life. And while she enjoyed Ward's company, she couldn't force herself to fall in love with him.

She stared out over the city from the glass-front elevator. Truth of the matter was, no matter how hard she tried to get over Major, each man she met seemed to reinforce just how deep her feelings for him ran.

Fat lotta good being in love with him would do for her, though. That he was falling for Alaine Delacroix couldn't be any more apparent—from the tanning to the teeth whitening to going to the gym and losing weight, he seemed to be doing everything he could to make himself fit the image of a man someone like Alaine would deign to be seen with.

Shame tingled on her skin. Alaine had never been anything but friendly with Meredith, and she couldn't allow her own jealousy to shine an unflattering and untrue light on the reporter.

The elevator doors slid open on the twenty-third floor. Speaking of Alaine. . .

The facilities staff swarmed the enormous floor space of Vue de Ceil, with a cameraman and his spotter hustling around in the chaos getting shots of the setup. Meredith jinked and dodged through the mayhem to get to the service corridor on the other side. She wished she could stop and enjoy the way the red and orange sunset made the banquet facility glow, but she did at least spare it a moment's glance, hoping tomorrow's sunset would be just as spectacular.

The pandemonium in the kitchen wasn't at quite the fevered pitch of the banquet hall, though the presence of another cameraman and spotter, along with Alaine and her producer, did make it feel much more crowded than usual.

"Hey, Meredith." Alaine waved in greeting.

Meredith slipped through the busy cooks and porters to join her. "How long have y'all been here?"

"Since nine this morning. Well, not me, because I had to do my show. But Pricilla and Nelson were here at nine to start filming prep. I brought everyone else with me after the show wrapped. Good thing this was Major's regular day for filming and that the banquet is our feature for his segment this week."

Meredith moved out of the way as a prep cook came out of the walk-in refrigerator behind them with a crate of pears. "My mother said something to me about Major and me meeting you at the studio Friday?"

"Yes—didn't my intern call you?" Alaine shook her head, her plump curls bouncing around her shoulders. "I'll have to have a word with him. You and Major are my featured guests on the show Friday."

"On the show—*on* the *show*?" Meredith's legs wanted to give out on her.

"Yes. It's going to be clips of the event—and all of the stuff we've filmed up until now—interspersed with live chat with the two of you about it. Don't worry; you'll be fine. You did great in our interview."

"Yeah, well, that was just the two of us in my office. I'm sure you've got a bunch of people in the studio watching when you do your show." She stuffed her hands into her pants pockets to keep from wiping the sweat on the ivory fabric.

Alaine patted her shoulder. "It'll be okay; I promise." She glanced over at the prep cook who was in the process of peeling and coring the pears. "What are those for?"

"Poached pears with ginger crumble. One of the three dessert choices the diners were given." She was particularly glad Mrs. Warner and the board had stayed away from the two desserts containing tropical fruit. Though she trusted Major's staff to be cautious about cross-contamination of foods such as raw meats, most prep cooks didn't worry about cleaning and sanitizing a work surface between cutting up different types of fruit. And if someone who'd been working on the tropical fruit touched something else that then touched something Meredith might eat that night. . .

She shuddered. The memory of the last time she'd eaten something that had been cut on the same surface as kiwi wasn't pleasant. Her throat had been sore from the breathing tube for nearly a week afterward. But at least it'd kept her from suffocating when the swelling from the allergic reaction nearly closed her windpipe.

"How did that whole thing work? I know you and Mrs. Warner narrowed down the choices from what was presented to the board a few weeks ago." Alaine pulled her pen from behind her ear, ready to write on the steno pad in her left hand.

"Once we narrowed that down, I had menus made up giving each banquet attendee a choice of starter salad, protein—from red meat, poultry, seafood, or vegetarian—and dessert. The menus will be at each place, and the wait staff will take the guests' orders as they serve beverages." Meredith glanced around for Major but didn't see him. She didn't really need to talk to him, but coming up to ask Alaine about Friday had been all the excuse she'd needed for an opportunity to bump into Major.

"But all of the meals are served at the same time?" Alaine scribbled on her notepad.

“Yes. Dinner service is at seven o’clock sharp.”

“How do you know how many of each dish to prepare?”

“Based on the percentages of how many chose similar dishes last year,” Major said, and Meredith turned, heart thrumming. “Hey, there.”

“Hi.” She wanted to think that the warmth of his smile, the soft expression in his eyes were for her—but who was she kidding? No man in his right mind would look at her like that when she was standing next to someone like Alaine. Just as she’d only seen that kind of expression in men’s faces whenever she was with Jenn.

“What brings you up to the kitchen? Everything okay?” Though he looked at Meredith, his attention was most definitely divided between her and what was going on in his domain.

“I needed to ask Alaine a question about Friday.”

“Yeah.” He crossed his arms as his gaze wandered over his staff. “That sort of took me by surprise, too. But it’ll be easier to do it together.”

“Chef!”

“Gotta go.” He squeezed Meredith’s shoulder and disappeared into the intricate ballet dance of a frenzied kitchen.

“I guess I’d better head back downstairs and get back to work myself.” Meredith sighed.

“What are you working on today?” Alaine looked as if she wanted to follow Meredith back to her office, which was the last thing she needed.

“All of the last-minute details—confirming all vendors and deliveries for items not arriving until late tonight or tomorrow, coordinating with all departments involved to make sure the work is getting done”—her cell phone started ringing— “and fielding lots of phone calls.”

Alaine grimaced. “I won’t keep you, then. See you around.”

“See you.” Meredith answered the phone as soon as she stepped out into the nominally quieter hallway. “This is Meredith.”

“Mere, it’s Corie. You’d better get down here. I’ve got the florist on the phone—he says it’s urgent.”

“I’ll be there in a minute.” Instead of risking the stop-and-go pace of the main elevators, Meredith opted for the freight elevator across from her, which let her off just across the hall from the executive kitchen on the fifth floor. She swiped her security card and dashed through the dim kitchen and dining room to her office.

"Which line?" Three of them flashed, signaling they were on hold.

"Two."

Meredith took a deep breath. "This is Meredith Guidry."

What had sounded like an emergency turned out only to be a glitch with the schedule for delivery of the centerpieces. She dealt with it and moved on to the uniform supplier on line one and the symphony director on line three, who wanted to inform her she was getting four violins and two violas instead of three and three as originally planned.

In a brief respite between phone calls, Meredith finally took the aspirin she'd been thinking about taking for her headache all afternoon.

Corie knocked on her open door and stepped inside the office. "I just got off the phone with Giovanni's. The pizza is on its way."

"Great. Thanks for handling that." Meredith picked up the phone and dialed the extension for the Vue de Ceil kitchen.

"Catering division, Steven LeBlanc speaking."

"Steven, it's Meredith. Is Major easily accessible?"

"Sure. Hold on just a second." The freight-train sound of the busy kitchen was replaced by soft classical music for a moment until Major picked up.

"Hey, Mere. What's up?"

"The pizza's on the way here. How do you want to handle sending folks down to eat?"

"Let's send the facilities staff down first. It'll be easier for them just to stop what they're doing and take a dinner break. Once they're fed, I'll have my crew come down as they get to stopping points. I'll send a couple of porters down with the ice chests of sodas, but other than that, the executive dining room should be set up for buffet service."

"Mind if I keep your porters and have them help sort pizzas and get everything organized?"

"I figured you would. They'll be down in a minute."

Meredith rubbed the back of her neck. "Remind me why we decided against canceling lunch service today?"

"We?" He chuckled. "I thought that command came down from on high."

"Hmm. Yeah, I guess you're right."

"See you in a bit."

"Bye." Her hand lingered on the receiver for a few seconds after she hung up. How would she do this without him? She almost snorted at the irony. Maybe if he did decide to start the restaurant, she should take Ward up on his offer to work as his interior designer so she didn't have to find out how horrible this kind of event would be without Major at her right hand.

She leaned back in her chair and let her eyes wander over the features of her office—wrecked though it was currently. Seeing Corie, Pam, and Lori bustling around in the outer office warmed the cockles of her heart. And though right now it seemed crazy, she was actually excited about the banquet tomorrow night. She couldn't wait to see the looks on the board members' faces when they walked in and saw how the thousands of candles sparkled off the glass walls and ceiling.

She thought about Easter in the Park and the library fund-raiser in May. She couldn't think of anyone her parents might hire to replace her who would put heart and soul into those events the way she would. She pressed her thumbs and forefingers to the corners of her eyes.

Truth of the matter was—she liked her job. Despite the fact her parents had little respect for her position, doing her job gave her pleasure. And even with as much as she enjoyed working on her house for the past couple of months, she knew she wouldn't get as much pleasure from remodeling and redecorating houses as she got from planning events. God had given her the heart, mind, and soul to be doing exactly what she was doing.

And there was always the slight possibility that Major might not take her parents' offer.

Around seven o'clock, Major went to each station in the kitchen and told his people to go down to eat as soon as they got to a point where they could stop.

Steven returned from his quick dinner break, allowing Major the opportunity to go grab a bite. Out in the main room, the facilities staff were just getting back to work, and Alaine stood over to one side, talking to her people as they packed up equipment.

He detoured over to them. "Calling it a night?"

"They are. I'm going to stick around awhile longer if that's okay with you." Alaine pulled her hair back into a ponytail.

"That's fine. Why don't y'all come down and grab some pizza before you go." He nodded toward the freight elevator. "This one takes us practically right to where the food is set up."

Only one of the camera assistants didn't want to stay. Major led the rest of them down to the fifth floor. Most of his kitchen staff sat around the carved mahogany tables in the executive dining room—a place none of them had probably ever dreamed of eating a meal, even though the pizza was served on paper plates.

The two event planners, Pam and Lori, along with Meredith's assistant, sat with pastry chefs Sandra and Jeff, having what looked like a very entertaining discussion. Major glanced around the room again. He hadn't been mistaken—no Meredith.

Corie got up and came over to him. "She's still in her office. Maybe you might have better luck convincing her to take a break and come get something to eat."

"I'll give it a shot." He went across the hall to Meredith's office. Her door was half shut. He knocked lightly and pushed it open.

Meredith and Mairee looked up from the large piece of paper they were leaning over, spread on Meredith's table.

"Everything okay?" Meredith asked, her eyes begging him to

say yes.

"I was just getting ready to ask you the same question." He nodded toward the table-layout schematic.

Meredith rubbed the back of her neck. "Just a few last-minute RSVP changes, so we're having to rearrange some of the seating assignments."

"Additions?" He joined them at the table.

"Yes." Meredith pointed to an eight-top table she'd penciled in. "But it works here. Remember how you and Orly kept saying that side of the room looked unbalanced? Well, now it's balanced."

He nodded. "I reviewed the original with Jana this afternoon for server assignments, so I'll be sure to inform her of the change tomorrow before the staff arrive so she can adjust coverage if she needs to."

"Well, I'm going to leave this in your more-than-capable hands." Mairee put her hand to the small of Meredith's back. "Meredith and Major, you've done a wonderful job on the preparation, and I know tomorrow night is going to be spectacular." With a smile trailing behind her, she turned toward her own office, her gait a bit stiff.

Meredith left the floor plan on the table and went around to collapse in her desk chair.

Major followed and grabbed her hands. "Nope, come on. You need something to eat."

"I'm too exhausted to eat." She resisted his gentle tugging for a few seconds, then, with a sigh, got back out of her chair. "All right. I'm coming."

It was all Major could do to let go of her once she was back on her feet. Her hands fit perfectly in his, felt just right clasped there. He tried not to think about Ward Breaux, with his big catcher's mitts, holding Meredith's hands.

Corie passed them on their way into the dining room, and she grinned at him. "See, I told you that you would have better luck convincing her."

Meredith didn't seem to hear—or care about—what her

assistant said. "Corie, do you mind staying until I get back? I'd hate to think what would happen if someone else calls and I'm not there to answer it."

"I already told you I can stay as late as you need me."

The fatigue in Meredith's face vanished when she smiled. "Thanks. You're sweet as a Georgia peach."

"And twice as sassy." Corie cocked an eyebrow and laughed.

Meredith went over to talk to Pam and Lori, so Major fixed plates and grabbed sodas for both of them. He chose a table a little bit away from where the few remaining kitchen staff sat, wanting to give Meredith a few minutes' peace before she dived back into work.

On her way to join him, she made a full tour of the room, speaking to everyone, including Alaine and her camera crew. Compared to Alaine, on whom the toll of the long day was evident, Meredith looked as if she were just starting her day—shoulder-length hair perfectly in place, cream-colored pantsuit not in the least rumpled or wrinkled, skin as luminous as ever. Alaine, on the other hand, with her hair pulled back in a limp ponytail, looked like she'd been through the wringer. She'd slung her suit coat across the back of her chair, kicked her shoes off under the table, and rolled her shirtsleeves up. But it was in her face, in the dark circles beneath her eyes and the slight downward turn of her mouth, that her fatigue showed the most.

His chest tightened with pride in Meredith and how she thrived in a whirlwind like tonight. Finally, she joined him. He asked a blessing, and they launched into eating.

After her third slice of pizza, Meredith leaned back, popped open a second can of Diet Coke, and took a long swig of the soda. "Ah. I needed that. Thanks for making me come eat."

Major weighed the pleasure of a fourth slice against the pain of the extra running he'd have to do on the treadmill later on. The pizza won. "Want some more?"

"Some apple dessert pizza would be great." She handed him her plate.

After getting her dessert and his fourth slice, he turned to see

Alaine had joined Meredith at the table. He grimaced. He'd hoped to have Meredith to himself for at least a few more minutes before he had to get back up to the kitchen.

"Major, I've been wondering something," Alaine said before he could regain his seat.

"What's that?" He handed Meredith a fork to go along with her dessert.

"I was a little surprised to see that you actually wear your chef's jacket to cook in. I always thought those were just for show—you know, something you put on before you come out of the kitchen to take a bow. Hardly any of the chefs on TV wear one."

Every muscle in his body cringed. He hated it when people compared what he did to what the celebrity chefs did on TV. Wait a minute—*he* was now one of those TV chefs. Oh, the irony. "The jacket is actually a very practical piece of the kitchen uniform in addition to looking good. It's double-breasted to protect from burns, but also, if something gets spilled, it can be rebuttoned with the other side out to hide the stain." He went on for another minute or two on the design and proper usage of the chef's jacket.

"So, would it be better if we had you wear one in your segment?" Alaine propped her elbow on the table and rested her cheek against her fist.

"Probably not. Since I'm supposed to be preparing what people can do in their home kitchens, it would probably look pretentious if I started wearing it after I've already been on the show for two weeks without it." He ate a few bites of the pizza before he realized he wasn't hungry anymore.

"Yeah, that probably wouldn't go over very well." Alaine raised her hand to cover her yawn. "Sorry, I've been up since five this morning."

Major caught Meredith's eye—they'd walked in together from the parking garage at a quarter of six this morning. The corner of Meredith's lips quirked up, but she turned her attention to her apple pizza.

"I've been meaning to tell you, though, that the feedback we've been getting from viewers has been overwhelmingly positive. You're a big hit with my viewers, Chef O'Hara." A little bit of the glimmer returned to Alaine's dark eyes.

"That's good to know. I'd hate to think I was tanking and taking your show down with me." Actually, he'd tried not to think of it, because he knew finding out wouldn't be good for maintaining a healthy level of ego.

"The feedback we get most often, from our female viewers of course, is that they feel like you're talking straight to them. Some of them were afraid that you might do stuff that was way over their heads or too fancy or that you would use terminology or techniques they didn't understand. But they say they feel like you're just a friend who's come into their kitchens to give them a one-on-one cooking lesson." Alaine stifled another yawn. "Which is exactly what we were hoping for."

This time, Major didn't risk looking at Meredith. If only Alaine knew to whom he was really talking when he explained what he was doing. If only Meredith knew that he sometimes imagined she was there with him, sharing and participating in his favorite thing to do.

Lord, I love Meredith. I want to marry her. Please, show me what to do.

Chapter 19

When the first guests arrived at six thirty, Meredith breathed a relieved sigh, thankful they'd never know how frantic Vue de Ceil had been mere moments ago. But now, all of the tables were set, candles lit, place cards where they were supposed to be. In their white tuxedo shirts, black bow ties, and black pants, several servers waited with her near the elevator foyer to show guests to their seats.

"Good evening, Mr. and Mrs. d'Arcement. Good to see you again. You are at table twenty-three. Jeremy will take you. I hope you have a wonderful evening." Meredith glanced down at her list to double-check that the d'Arcements were indeed at table twenty-three. She had to keep reminding herself there had been too many last-minute changes to rely totally on her visual memory of the seating chart.

After more than half of the three hundred expected guests had arrived, one of the newer workers looked at Meredith in awe. "Wow. You know everybody. You haven't once had to ask anyone's name."

"I've been doing this a very long time, and most of the people who are coming tonight have come to this event every year since we started. A lot of them come to most of the events we do." She looked over as two of the elevators opened at the same time. Her parents and several other couples came toward them.

Meredith greeted everyone by name and handily sent them with servers to their tables. She stepped away from the service staff to speak with her parents, while still keeping an ear out for the chime that indicated an arriving elevator.

"How's it looking?" her father asked, craning his neck to glance around the venue.

"We'll have a few latecomers as usual, but it looks like the majority have chosen to show up on time this year. It really helped to put on all of the mailers they received that dinner would be served *at* seven o'clock." Her gaze caught on the black-clad cameraman and his spotter in the corner near the orchestra. She was glad she'd won the battle, insisting on one stationary camera out of the main line of sight of the guests rather than the two or three cameramen wandering around in the room Alaine had wanted, their bright lights interfering with the mood set by the thousands of candles now reflecting off the walls and ceiling.

Mom, instead of looking around the room, scrutinized Meredith. "You look gorgeous tonight, Mere. Is that new?"

Meredith looked down at the wine-colored gown. "I picked it up at a consignment store down in Baton Rouge last time I was there."

"The color's perfect on you. I know you get tired of hearing this, but I do so prefer to see you dressed up than in those torn-up, paint-splattered clothes you like to wear on the weekends." Mom reached out as if to touch Meredith's cheek but lowered her hand again. "Forbes told us that you were feeling like we don't respect you or your position in the company."

Meredith closed her eyes and rasped her breath in the back of her throat. "He shouldn't have said anything. It wasn't his place."

"No. It was yours. Why didn't you ever say anything?" Instead of looking affronted, sadness filled her mother's expression.

"I guess because I thought that you'd eventually realize you were riding roughshod over me. I thought if I put up with it long enough, you'd see that you treat me differently than any of the other executive directors." Meredith wished she hadn't taken her jacket off. Chill bumps danced up and down her arms.

"You're right." Dad rested his hand on her shoulder. "We have been taking advantage of the fact that you're our daughter. And we promise that's going to stop."

"But you have to make us a promise in return." Mom smiled. "You have to promise that you'll come to us and talk about these things before they make you so mad that you take it out on other members of the family. Okay?"

Leave it to Forbes and Jenn to make it all about them. "Okay."

The elevator chimed, saving her from more awkward parental attention. They moved on to take their seats, and Meredith returned to her post.

The room buzzed with voices, the twelve-piece orchestra barely discernible above the din. Meredith couldn't wipe the smile from her face. Though the lead-up to tonight had been anything but easy, seeing their guests—dressed in their glittering best—talking and laughing and enjoying themselves was one of the moments she lived for.

A Bible verse strayed through her thoughts: *"Give her the product of her hands, and let her works praise her in the gates."*

She hoped her parents meant what they said about showing her more respect from now on, but if not, she would learn how to be content with knowing that by creating a good "product" through hard work and dedication, God would reward her with fulfillment and the pleasure she could take in the praise of her guests' enjoyment.

A burst of static startled her. "It's five till seven." Major's voice came over her earpiece. "Jana, please send the rest of the service staff into the kitchen."

Meredith pressed the talk button on her module. "I'll let my father know to get things rolling."

He must have checked his watch, because before she could leave her post, Dad glanced over at her with raised brows. She nodded, and he stepped up onto the stage. To the side of the platform, the sound tech gave him a thumbs-up.

"Good evening, friends." Dad's voice boomed over the crowd, which immediately quieted. "Happy Valentine's Day and welcome to the Eleventh Annual Hearts to HEARTS Banquet and Charity Auction to raise funds for the Warner Cardiac Unit at University Hospital. I hope you came prepared to enjoy a wonderful dinner. . .and to spend lots of money at the auction. I've been told that we have some fabulous items that you're all going to want to bid on. Now join with me in asking the Lord's blessing on the meal."

While her father prayed, Meredith moved around the perimeter of the room to the opening of the service hall leading to the kitchen. As soon as he said, "Amen," she motioned the servers to disperse throughout the dining hall, not envying them the trays they carried, piled with covered dishes. She would never have survived in that job.

Major brought up the rear of the line of servers and joined her. "Sounds like everything's going well."

"It is now. I wasn't so sure there about forty-five minutes ago. But once Manny figured out that the elevator system hadn't been reset since the fire alarm went off this afternoon, things have been flowing just fine."

"Yeah, getting this many guests up twenty-three flights without elevators wouldn't have been pretty." Major's phone rang—she'd heard that ringtone once before, and that time Major had paled and left her office immediately. Now he grimaced. "If you'll excuse me." He disappeared down the hall and into the kitchen.

She sighed. By now she should be accustomed to his shutting her out of anything remotely personal, no matter how much she really wanted to get to know what was going on in his life outside of this place.

Major shut his office door before answering the phone. "Major O'Hara, here."

"Where are you?" His mother's voice was shrill and sharp.

"I told you five times today already that I have to work tonight,

Ma." His jaw ached from grinding his teeth a little harder every time she'd called tonight.

"But it's Wednesday night. You always come on Wednesday night."

"I know, but as I already explained, I have to work tonight. I'll be out there tomorrow night. It's just one day, Ma." *Lord, please help her understand so that I can get through this evening without any more interruptions.* "Isn't this the night that the chef teaches cooking lessons? Don't you usually do that before I come?"

"I don't want to do that. I want to see you."

"Then why don't you put on a John Wayne movie. What about *Without Reservations* or *The Quiet Man*?"

"I don't want to watch John Wayne. I want you to come like you're supposed to."

Frustration throbbed behind his eyes. "I can't come, Ma. I have to get off the phone now. I have to work tonight. But I will see you tomorrow, okay? So don't call again tonight unless it's an emergency."

The line clicked and went dead. He closed the cell phone and pressed his forehead and nose against his desktop. "God, I don't know how much more of this I can deal with."

But he didn't have time to wallow in his problem. He dropped the cell phone in his pants pocket and returned to the kitchen, allowing the controlled chaos to calm his frazzled nerves.

Plating the main course and sides continued apace. He stepped in and assisted where necessary when garnishes didn't suit his taste or when a plate was unnecessarily messy. But he had a good team of well-trained and -educated chefs and cooks, so not much coaching was required.

Fifteen minutes after service began, servers returned with trays stacked with mostly empty salad plates. As soon as the servers divested themselves of the empties, they reviewed the lists of requested meals for their assigned tables and worked with the kitchen staff to get the appropriate dishes. Thankfully, Meredith had managed to convince Mrs. Warner that everyone should have the same side dishes—

roasted baby veggies and garden risotto—instead of giving guests a choice there, too.

More than half of the mains had gone out when Major's phone started ringing again. He almost ignored it. But knowing his mother, she'd just keep calling until he answered. He couldn't step away from the kitchen right now, though.

"Major O'Hara." He inspected the dishes on a tray and nodded his approval.

"Mr. O'Hara, this is Gideon Thibodeaux, facility director of Beausoleil Pointe Center. I'm calling regarding your mother."

A wave of nausea struck so forcefully, Major wavered. "What's she done now?"

"She had an accident and started a little fire in the kitchen."

Horrible memories and visions from his childhood assailed him. "Was anyone else hurt?"

"No one but her. She has at least second- and possibly third-degree burns on both arms. We've called for an ambulance to take her to the emergency room. I suggest you meet her there instead of trying to come all the way out here."

Major pressed his thumb and fingers to the outside corners of his eyes. "I'll be there as soon as I can." He closed the phone and released a heated, angry breath.

"Boss, is everything okay?" Steven approached with trepidation in his steps.

"I've had a. . .situation come up. I have to go to the emergency room. I need you to take over and make sure that desserts get served right at eight o'clock. Jana knows, but because of the schedule with the auction, it can't be any later than eight, even if some of the guests aren't finished with mains yet. Okay?"

"Yes, Chef." But Steven's brow remained furrowed.

Major didn't have time to stay and try to alleviate his sous chef's concerns. He grabbed his keys from his office and dashed out of the kitchen, hitting the call button for the freight elevator.

No, he couldn't leave without telling Meredith. But what would he tell her? He tapped the talk button on the earpiece he'd forgotten to take off. "Meredith, I need to see you in the service corridor, please."

"I'll be there in a second."

Many seconds later—but not long enough—the perfect vision that was Meredith materialized in the hallway, worry written all over her face. "What's up?"

"I. . .I have to leave. I have to go to the hospital."

Her eyes widened, and shock replaced the worry. She reached over and touched his arm. "Are you okay? Do you need someone to drive you?"

"No. It's not—" He swallowed convulsively and pulled away from her, though it was one of the most difficult things he'd ever done in his life. "I have to go. Steven knows what needs to be done. I'll try to make it back here if I can." The freight elevator arrived. "I'm sorry."

The last glimpse he got of Meredith before the doors closed was of a woman who was both upset and confused by his actions.

He braced his forearms against the elevator wall and rested his head against his fists. "God, why does my mother have to ruin *everything*? She's done it all my life, and she's doing it again."

The fire had been no accident. It was her way of punishing him. She'd always been fascinated by flames but had started setting fires just for the joy of it when he was in junior high. Whenever he did something she didn't like or forced her to take her meds, she started fires. He'd tried to make it hard on her—getting rid of all matches and lighters. But she always got more.

He'd been pulled out of class when he was fifteen, a sophomore in high school, after she'd set a fire that quickly got out of control, destroyed their apartment, and damaged several adjoining units. Fortunately, no one had been hurt—that time. The state had committed her for thirty days, and Major had been sent to live with a foster family. A foster family who owned a restaurant. He continued to work for them even after he went back to live with his mom.

The fire she'd set eight years ago that led to his returning from

New York had severely injured several other residents of the apartment complex.

Maybe it was time to discuss with her doctor a change in her medication levels, especially since it seemed as if her episodes were becoming more frequent. Either that, or it was time to look into having her committed to a full-time nursing facility.

He stopped halfway across the garage to Kirby. If he had her committed, it would mean he'd finally given up on her. And even with as much anger as he had toward her at this very moment, he wasn't sure he was ready to do that.

But he sure wasn't going to be able to forgive her anytime soon.

The tires squealed when he pulled out of the garage. He turned off the southern gospel music he'd been listening to on his way to work. But not before it reminded him what he'd been thinking—dreaming—about on the drive: the restaurant.

His head spun. At a restaurant, he'd never be able to walk away from a dinner service the way he'd just walked away from the banquet. And if his mother did this based on his missing one night's visit with her, what would she do when he wouldn't have time for weeks or months at a stretch to go out to visit her?

He shook with impotent rage. He'd already given up everything for her—his childhood, New York. . .and Meredith. And would Ma ever appreciate it? No. Of course not. He refused to give up his dream of opening a restaurant.

He trudged into the emergency room lobby and went straight to the information desk.

The woman in khakis and a pink sweater looked up over the rim of bejeweled reading glasses. "How can I help you, Mr. O'Hara?"

He frowned at her use of his name. She smiled and pointed at his left shoulder; he looked down and read his name, upside-down, on his coat.

"My mother, Beverly O'Hara, was being brought here by ambulance from Beausoleil Pointe Center." He unbuttoned the jacket.

"Let me call back to the nurses' station and see if she's ready for visitors. In the meantime, you can have a seat there." She pointed behind him.

"Yeah, I know the drill. Thanks." He slumped into one of the stiff upholstered chairs, his back to the few other people in the waiting room.

A few minutes later, the admissions nurse called him over to her window to answer the standard payment and insurance questions.

He turned at the sound of rubber soles squeaking on the tile floor. A vaguely familiar young man ran to the information desk. "I need to see Beverly O'Hara."

"Are you a relative?"

"No—I'm from the center. I was there—it's my fault she got hurt, you see, and I need to make sure she's going to be okay."

Major turned to the admissions nurse. "Do you need anything else from me?"

"No, sir, I think I've got everything."

"Thanks." He went back over to the information desk. "Excuse me. You said you're from the Pointe?"

The younger man turned. "I'm Patrick. . . ." His eyes flickered down to Major's coat. "Oh, Mr.—I mean, Chef O'Hara. I am so sorry about what happened to your mother. It was all my fault. I only turned my back for a second. . . ."

Major led him over to a semisecluded area of the waiting room and forced him to sit with a hand on his shoulder. "Start from the beginning and tell me what happened."

"She came in late, after the cooking class had started. She comes every week and has always done very well—owing to you, I'm sure."

"Go on." Major crossed his arms, displeased with the kid's attempt at flattery.

"Well, I asked her if she would remove a pot from the stove. I warned her it would be hot and to use a towel wrapped around the handle to move it. But I forgot to tell her to turn the burner off first. She must have dragged the tail of the towel in the flame. That's all I can figure."

"But how did it burn both of her arms?"

"Oh, that wasn't what burned her. She jumped back and the pasta water splashed all over her."

"I see." Major rubbed his eyes. Guilty sympathy chiseled away his anger. Burns from liquid could be almost as bad as from oil or open flame. He should know—he'd suffered his share of them.

"O'Hara family?"

He looked over at the nurse standing in the door that led back to the ER.

"May I come with you?" Patrick stood with him. "I want to apologize to her."

"Sure." A short corridor connected the lobby to the actual emergency room facility. As soon as they passed through the door on the other end, he could hear his mother's shrill cries.

All anger toward her forgotten, Major sped up and bypassed the nurse the last few yards to the room where he could hear her.

"Ma?" He pushed the privacy curtain aside. Two orderlies were trying to hold her shoulders down on the bed, while a nurse held a syringe, trying to give her a shot in her upper arm.

"Major, make them stop!" For someone so frail looking, she sure was strong. His throat tightened. No matter what she'd done, she was his mother. For that reason alone, she deserved his respect and love.

He stepped over and pulled the orderly closest to him away, then looked at the one on the other side and nodded. "I'm here, now, Ma."

Huge crystalline tears coursed down her cheeks. "It hurts."

"I know it does. But they're trying to make it better. Let the nurse give you a shot, and it won't hurt as much anymore." He looked around and found a box of tissues on the counter beside the small sink. He grabbed several and dried his mother's face, which was turned away from the nurse with the needle.

"What is that?" He nodded toward the syringe.

"Demerol—a pain killer."

A man in a suit entered the room. "It's all right, Mr. O'Hara. I've already briefed them on your mother's condition and the medications she's on." He nodded at the nurse, who couldn't mask the fear in her eyes when she approached and gave the shot.

Major continued wiping at his mother's tears. "And you are?" He glanced over his shoulder at the man.

"I'm Gideon Thibodeaux."

"I don't know him, Danny." Ma's blue eyes opened and showed that the pain medication was already taking effect.

Major had never met BPC's new director. "He's the manager at the Pointe, Ma."

"Patrick, may I speak with you outside?" Mr. Thibodeaux's grave expression told Major that Patrick might no longer be employed by the center in a few minutes.

"Can I. . . ?" Patrick looked at Major, then at Ma.

"Yeah." Major stepped back and let the kid have his place beside Ma.

"Ms. O'Hara, it's me, Patrick. I'm so sorry about what happened. I hope you're better soon."

Ma's glazed eyes tried to fix on the young man. "I had fun. But you need to go back and make sure the macaroni and cheese isn't burning. I won't eat it if it's burned on the bottom."

Patrick relaxed a bit. "I'll do that. But you don't worry about that. You just worry about healing, okay?"

" 'Kay." She closed her eyes. "Major Kirby, don't leave me."

"I'm staying right here." He pulled over a stool. "I'll never leave you, Ma." Even though it would mean sacrificing everything he wanted in life. He would do his duty.

Chapter 20

"You'll come tomorrow?"

Major pulled the covers up under his mother's arms. "I'll come tomorrow." He set two pillows beside her. "You can put your hands down now."

Gingerly, Ma settled her arms down on top of the pillows. "What if my shoulders get cold?"

He went to the closet and pulled a small lap blanket down from the shelf. He unfolded it and tucked it in around her shoulders. "There. All snug?"

She wiggled farther down into the nest created by the pillows and covers. "All snug." Each time she blinked, it took a little longer for her eyes to open. The emergency room doctor had said she would probably sleep through the night and most of the day tomorrow. And Mr. Thibodeaux had arranged for around-the-clock nursing attention for the next week or so until the bandages came off.

"A nurse is going to be coming in every so often to check on you during the night." He held up a little speaker. "And they're going to be monitoring you, so if you wake up and you're in pain or you need to go to the bathroom, just say something and they'll come help you."

" 'Kay." Her eyes drifted closed.

He leaned over the bed, careful not to bump her arm, and kissed her forehead. "Good night, Ma. I love you. I'll see you tomorrow."

"Me, too."

He stopped and talked to the floor nurse on the way out to make sure they called him in case anything happened. Then with heavy steps, he walked out into the chill night air to his Jeep. He glanced at the clock on the radio as he pulled out of the parking lot. Three o'clock in the morning. In two hours, he needed to be at work to prepare food for Mr. Guidry's Thursday morning prayer breakfast. So that everyone could sleep in and recover from their late night working the banquet before they had to report to prepare for lunch service, he hadn't scheduled a subordinate to assist.

At home he collapsed on the bed without even bothering to undress—but did make sure the alarm clock feature on his phone was set for four thirty. He'd barely closed his eyes when the alarm sounded, it seemed.

More tired than he'd ever been in his life, he dragged himself to the shower and managed, somehow, to get ready for a full day of work and then a full evening out at the Pointe with Ma.

As executive chef and co-owner of a restaurant, he could expect to put in these kinds of hours on a regular basis in the beginning.

He stuffed anything he might possibly need into his black duffel and walked out the front door, then went right back inside for his knife case—remembering after five minutes of wandering all over the condo looking for it that he'd left it at work last night.

At five o'clock in the morning, Bonneterre still slept. Only a hint of pink tinged the sky on the other side of the river. He had to sit through red lights at a couple of vacant intersections and fight falling asleep before they changed to green.

The parking garage security attendant greeted him with a wave and a stifled yawn. Major had to swipe his card twice—the second time making sure the magnetic tape was actually facing the right direction.

His shoes seemed to be made out of concrete. Every step sapped him of a little more of his precious energy reserve. Finally, he made it to his office. Someone—probably Steven—had thoughtfully cleaned and repacked his knives and put the soft-sided case on his desk. He steeled himself against the temptation of collapsing into his chair and closing his eyes for a few minutes, pulled his burgundy jacket out of the armoire, and went down to the executive kitchen to get to work.

By the time Mr. Guidry's breakfast meeting broke up, Major had come to a decision. He gave Lawson a few minutes to get back to his office before following him. He knocked on the open office door.

Lawson looked up from his computer and pulled his glasses off. "Come in, come in."

"Do you have a few minutes, sir?"

"Of course. Have a seat."

"Thank you." Major forced his body to fold itself down onto one of the leather chairs facing Lawson's massive desk.

"Meredith said you had an emergency last night and had to go to the emergency room. I hope you're all right."

"Yes, sir. It wasn't me. It was my mother. Which is why I wanted to talk to you." The nausea that had started with the doctor's call last night returned full force. Good thing he hadn't eaten in more than twelve hours.

"If you're worried that there will be any negative repercussions from us because you left to take care of your ailing mother, don't."

Major wanted to get up to pace but wrapped his hands around the wooden arms of the chair instead. "That wasn't really what I'm here about. But it does bear on what I need to tell you."

Lawson leaned back in his chair and tapped his glasses against his chin. "Am I correct in assuming this is about the restaurant deal, then?"

"Yes, sir." Major swallowed twice, trying to eliminate the bitter acidity in the back of his throat. "After a lot of thought and prayer, I am going to have to say no. I know y'all proposed the partnership based on the plan I gave Forbes to look at for me. And I really appreciate the belief you and Mrs. Guidry showed in me by coming up with the proposal—you have no idea how much I appreciate it. But the truth of the matter is that I can't commit the kind of time that opening a restaurant requires—my mother needs me too much. These last two accidents with her have also shown me that I can't take everything that I have and invest it in a business that might not turn a profit for eighteen months or longer. I need the safety net just in case something else happens."

The words had spilled out in a monotone, his eyes glued to the front edge of Mr. Guidry's desk. But now he dared to look up at his would-be benefactor.

Lawson's expression hadn't changed—still slightly smiling and warm. "I am sorry you feel that way, son. But I understand your desire to want to be sure you can take care of your mother. I was afraid it might come to that. I don't suppose the fact that groundbreaking has been delayed six months would change your decision?"

Six months? Major went over all the numbers and scenarios in his head. The pit of his stomach gnarled. "No, sir. Six months probably won't make a significant difference in the amount of time I will need to spend with my mother, nor in my financial situation." The words *I'm sorry* tripped to the end of his tongue, but a recurring line from *She Wore a Yellow Ribbon*, the John Wayne movie he'd watched with Ma on Sunday, zipped through his mind: *"Never apologize. . . . It's a sign of weakness."*

"It's disappointing. We want to see you chasing your dream of owning a restaurant. But if anyone understands family obligations, we do." Lawson stood and extended his right hand. "We'll look for another opportunity with you in the future."

Major sprang to his feet and shook Meredith's father's hand. "Thank you for the offer, sir. And you can trust that I'll be working extra hard to get to a place where I can do something like this."

"And we'll do whatever we can to help."

Over lunch Thursday, Meredith filled Anne in on the details of everything that happened at the banquet the night before. Their check arrived right as Meredith got to the part about Major.

Anne's pen stopped halfway through her signature on her receipt. "What happened? Was he okay?"

Meredith slipped her signed receipt into the black folder and tried to remember if the pen was hers or the restaurant's. "I think so. Apparently, he fixed breakfast for Daddy's prayer group this morning."

"Who told you that? You haven't been calling in and checking on work on your day off, have you?" Anne took her sunglasses out of her purse and slipped them over the top of her head.

Meredith tried to look innocent, then grinned as she slid out of the booth seat. "Okay, just the one time. Corie told me she saw Major go in to Dad's office after the prayer group broke up."

"What do you think that was about?"

Meredith shrugged and followed her cousin out of the restaurant. "I don't know, and I'm tired of speculating. If Major wanted me to know what's going on in his life, he'd tell me. Since he hasn't, I have to operate under the assumption that he's perfectly happy with our relationship just the way it is. I can't live my life hung up on every little thing he does."

"That's probably wise." A mischievous grin appeared on Anne's face. "So whom are you going to ask as your date to the wedding?"

"I'm in the wedding. I don't need a date. Forbes'll be my date." Meredith feigned interest in the display of handmade soaps in the store window they were passing.

"Forbes has already asked someone."

She stopped. "Really? He's asked someone to be his date to your wedding?"

"That's what he told me yesterday. But he wouldn't tell me who she is."

"Wow. Forbes is actually bringing a date to a family function."

"Speaking of, I think you should ask this Ward fella." Anne hooked her arm through Meredith's and got her moving again.

"Ask Ward?"

"Yeah—you are still seeing him, aren't you?"

"Not in the last couple of weeks—I've been too busy." And even though he'd called and asked her out a few times, she'd told him she was too busy simply because it was easier than admitting to herself that, while she really liked him as a person and enjoyed spending time with him, she had no romantic feelings toward him whatsoever.

Anne let go of Meredith's arm to unlock the front door of her office, located in one of the converted Victorian row houses lining Town Square. "Well, Jenn already has dibs on Henry, so it's looking like Ward's your only option."

"All right, I'll ask him." It took a moment for Meredith's eyes to adjust to the dim interior of the office from the bright sunlight outside. When she could finally see clearly, she saw Anne looking at her expectantly from behind her desk. "What?"

"You have a phone, don't you? If not, you can use mine." She pushed her desk phone closer to Meredith.

"You want me to call him right now?"

"Yes, now. Because if I leave it up to you, you won't call."

How well Anne knew her. Reluctantly, Meredith pulled out her phone. "What should I say?"

"Oh, for mercy's sake. You've known the guy for almost two months now. You'll think of something."

Meredith quick-dialed Ward's cell number, praying he wouldn't answ—

"Hey, pretty girl."

Instead of warmth or tingles, all Meredith felt was embarrassed. "Hey, yourself."

"What's up? Calling to check progress on your house? Right now, we're on schedule to be finished about a week early."

"That's good to know, but it isn't why I'm calling."

Across the desk from her, Anne's expression of encouragement was anything but helpful. Meredith averted her gaze.

"So to what do I owe the honor of a phone call from Meredith

Guidry?" The laughter in his voice conjured a vivid image of Ward's handsome good looks in Meredith's mind.

"I. . ." She forced herself to breathe. She'd never asked a guy out before. "My cousin Anne is getting married a week from Saturday."

"I know. You're the maid of honor."

The fact that he was humoring her made what she needed to do a little easier. "Right. But I was wondering. . .thinking maybe you might like to come as my 'and guest.'"

Anne sighed loudly; Meredith gave her a dirty look.

"I'd love to be your 'and guest' at your cousin's wedding. It's in the evening, right?"

"The ceremony starts at five o'clock."

"Good. I can still go to the hospital, then."

Taken aback, Meredith glanced at Anne. "The hospital?"

"Didn't I tell you? I volunteer in the pediatric cancer unit on Saturday mornings."

Could this guy be any more perfect? He was going to make someone a great husband someday. "No, you never told me. What led you to do that?"

"I've been doing it since I was fifteen and my youngest brother was diagnosed with leukemia." Someone yelled his name in the background. "I'll have to call you back, Mere."

"Okay. I'll talk to you later. Bye." She closed the phone and dropped it in her purse.

"The hospital?"

Meredith told her.

"He sounds like a keeper." Even though Anne leaned over to pull out the binder of her wedding plans from under the desk, it wasn't quick enough to keep Meredith from seeing her amused smile.

"For someone else, maybe."

Anne snapped upright. "What?"

"I just don't feel that way about him."

"Not everyone falls in love right away. Sometimes it needs a chance to grow. I've planned plenty of weddings for people who were friends for years before they fell in love with each other."

Friends for eight years before falling in love? Meredith shook her head. "I'm giving it a chance—it's not like I have a lot of other options at this point in time."

"You know I've been praying for you about this, right?" Leaving the binder on her desk, Anne came around to sit in the chair beside Meredith.

Emotion lumped up in Meredith's throat, forcing her to nod as her only reply.

"Have you been praying about it?"

She nodded again.

"More than just, 'Please, God, send me a husband'?" Anne's blue eyes twinkled.

Meredith laughed. "Sometimes. But most of the time it's, 'Please, God, let me get over Major so I can fall in love with someone else.'"

"Oh, I can so relate." Anne sighed. "Before I found out George wasn't the one marrying Courtney Landry, that was my almost hourly mantra—'Lord, please don't let me be falling in love with a client.'"

"But he turned out not to be the one getting married, and he fell in love with you."

"Right. But what I'm saying is that God did answer my prayer—granted in a rather roundabout fashion, but He answered. You have to trust that God will answer your prayer. . .just maybe not in the way you expect or on your timeline."

Meredith groaned and slumped down in the chair to rest her head against the top of it. "Maybe I should pray instead that He'll take away my desire to get married. Then it won't matter if the man I'm in love with doesn't return my feelings."

"Maybe you should pray for the patience to hold on until Major realizes what he's missing." Anne stood and picked up the binder.

"Right. And let God make me wait another eight years? I know what His sense of humor is like. No way I'm praying that!" She let Anne pull her out of the chair and followed her cousin to the small table in the bay window overlooking Town Square in the front of the building.

"Then I guess you'll just have to muddle through."

"Thanks. You're tons of help." Meredith stuck her tongue out at the woman who'd been her best friend since before she could remember.

"Well, you could always just talk to him."

"Who?"

"Major—I thought that's who we were talking about."

"Talk to him?"

"About how you feel."

"No way. Call me old-fashioned, but I firmly believe that a man should make the first move." Meredith pulled her own folder of information for Anne's wedding out of her bag. "Can we focus on you now, instead of me? You are getting married in a week, you know."

"Nine days."

"Right. Nine days. And there's still lots to do, so let's get to it." Meredith pulled out her to-do list and started reviewing everything they'd accomplished since their last war-room briefing.

But she couldn't put Anne's words out of her head. Talk to Major about her feelings? What if he once and for all told her he could never feel that way toward her?

No, she'd rather live with the pain of unrequited—but hopeful—love than to know for sure that she would never have a chance at love with Major O'Hara.

Chapter 21

"Forbes, I saved you a seat." Meredith waved at her big brother, who'd just entered The Fishin' Shack.

"Thanks, Sis." Forbes looked somewhat frazzled, which served as partial explanation as to why he was so late for the Thursday night cousins dinner. He walked around and greeted everyone at the table before taking the chair between Meredith and George.

"Tough day?" Meredith moved her purse from the table to the floor.

"Somewhat. But I'm no longer at work, so I refuse to think about it further. How was your day off? Did you and Anne get everything done you wanted to do today?" Forbes poured himself a glass of iced tea and doctored it with three packs of sweetener.

"There are still a few loose strings, but Anne will have everything tuned up and ready to go by the time we get to church for the rehearsal Friday evening."

"I'm sure she will. I just hope we can all live up to her exacting expectations."

"Hey—I heard that!" Anne leaned around behind George and poked Forbes's shoulder.

"What? Anne's here?" Forbes winked at their cousin.

Once the subject of the wedding had been brought up, it consumed quite a bit of attention around the table. Certain that no one was paying any attention to her or Forbes, Meredith leaned closer to him.

"What do you know about Major's family?" she asked softly.

"Excuse me?" Forbes looked startled.

Maybe she should have figured out a better way to broach the subject, but she wasn't sure how much time she would have before they were drawn back into the general conversation. "Major's family. What do you know about them?"

"He was raised by a single mom."

"I know that. But do you know anything more specific? I mean, you two are pretty close friends." She twisted her napkin in her lap.

The little upside-down Y formed between Forbes's brows. "I think that's something you should ask Major."

She sighed in frustration. "I have asked him, and he won't tell me much more than what you just did."

"Then I can't believe you're going around behind his back asking me to divulge whatever he may have told me in confidence. Really, Mere, I thought you had higher principles than that." Though his words came across as angry, all she could see in his eyes was discomfort.

"I'm just worried about him. He had to leave the banquet early last night—some kind of an emergency. I wanted to make sure everything's okay, and if not, to see if there's anything I can do to help."

With meticulous movements, Forbes unfolded his napkin and draped it across his lap. "As I said, it's something you'll have to ask him." He turned his attention to the wedding talk, effectively cutting off any further questions from Meredith by the angle of his body.

Eventually, the discussion of Anne's wedding waned. Across the table, Rafe said, "Hey, Mere, how's the work on your house going?"

"Great. I talked to my contractor this afternoon, and he said it's looking like they might be done early."

Rafe's left brow shot upward. "Your *contractor*? Would that be the *contractor* you've been dating?"

"I'm not dating him." Her pulse quickened—she hated being the source of her siblings' amusement. "We're just friends."

"Really? What would you call it when you go out to romantic restaurants for meals alone with him?" Jenn joined in on the teasing.

"I've only been out with him a couple of times. We're still just getting to know each other." Meredith glanced at Anne for help, but her cousin was listening to something George was whispering in her ear.

Rafe laughed. "You met him on New Year's Day, right? Jenn would be practically engaged if she'd met someone six or seven weeks ago who'd asked her out."

"Take it back!" Jenn laughed and punched their younger brother in the arm.

Meredith laughed, too, glad not to be the sole recipient of the ribbing.

"Hey, did y'all know Meredith's going to be on TV tomorrow?" Jenn turned a saucy smile toward Meredith.

So much for not being the sole focus of her teasing-prone family.

The next morning, Meredith's desk was piled with messages and paperwork, as it was every time she took a day off—only today it was compounded by the fact they'd had a massive, midweek event.

"Corie?"

Her assistant appeared in the door, still in her jacket with her backpack hanging from one shoulder. "Yes?"

"What time do I have to be at the TV studio?"

"Let me check the e-mail." She disappeared for a couple of minutes then reappeared sans coat and bag. "It says you should plan to arrive no later than ten o'clock."

Meredith glanced at the clock in the lower right corner of her computer monitor. Seven forty-five. "Can you give me a heads-up at nine thirty if it looks like I'm not paying attention to the clock?"

"Will do. Want to go over the stuff from yesterday so we can get started on reports?"

Not really. "Sure. But give me a minute to get some coffee."

"I'll come with." Corie grabbed her big, hand-painted ceramic mug from her desk and walked with Meredith to the executive kitchen. "How was your day off?"

"Fun. Anne and I got a lot of last-minute stuff done for the wedding." She told her assistant some of the details of what they'd accomplished.

Her mother's executive assistant greeted them in the dining room, coming from the kitchen with three mugs of coffee. Meredith waited until the kitchen door closed behind them then turned and grinned at Corie.

"I guess I'm not letting you live up to your title of executive assistant."

"You know I really wouldn't mind getting your coffee for you."

"Not to demean the other executive assistants, but you're more valuable to me than just someone to fetch and carry at my whims." Meredith pulled out the coffee carafe and poured Corie's coffee first. "In case I haven't said it recently, you're a vital part of this team; and at your annual appraisal in April, we're going to be discussing moving you into a junior event planner position."

Corie's brown eyes lit up.

"Now, I can't promise that will happen. You of all people know what the approval process is like around here. But I think I can make a pretty convincing case on your behalf."

They doctored their coffee with flavored creamers and sweeteners and returned to Meredith's office. Over their morning caffeine fix, Corie reviewed the messages she'd taken on Thursday, as well as everything she'd handled on her own.

Once Meredith was up to date on everything that happened in her absence, Corie went back to her desk with the folder of receipts and invoices Meredith had worked on organizing last night after she got home from dinner. She e-mailed the rough spreadsheet to Corie, who would work some kind of magic on it to generate all kinds of comparisons and charts and departmental breakdowns of how much money Meredith had spent on behalf of B-G on the banquet. Thank goodness someone from the HEARTS Foundation board handled everything connected with the money from the auction. One less thing for Meredith to have to deal with on the back side of the event.

She spent the morning returning phone calls from yesterday—as well as answering those coming in—and was about to go get a second cup of coffee when Major knocked on the open office door.

The sight of him was enough to make her bite the inside of her cheek to keep from telling him how much she wished he wouldn't keep her at arm's length, that he would let her into his life, even just a little bit.

"You ready to go?" He wore his burgundy jacket—the one that made his eyes look almost purple.

She glanced at her watch. "Oh, mercy. I didn't realize it was nine thirty already." She jumped up from her desk then leaned back down to get her purse out of the bottom drawer. She stood slowly. "Are we going together?"

"I figured we could—save gas, you know."

"Oh. I just didn't know if you had to be there longer or something." She shrugged into her suit coat and grabbed her planner from her briefcase—the planner where she had all of the notes she'd written down, things Alaine had asked her to think about so she'd know what to say about the event when Alaine asked her questions live on air. "I'll drive."

He grinned at her. "Don't feel like arriving windblown?"

She returned the smile. "Not particularly."

"Did you have a good day off yesterday?" Major asked as she pulled out of the parking garage.

As she had with everyone else, she talked about what she'd done yesterday. But that filled only enough time to get them halfway to the studio.

Now or never. "Major, I wanted to ask you about Wednesday night—about why you left. Is everything okay?" She glanced at him from the corner of her eye.

He'd gone all stiff. "Everything's fine. I just—something came up that I had to go handle."

"At the emergency room?"

"It was. . ." He swallowed hard. "It was my mom. She got hurt, and I had to meet her at the emergency room."

Finally—something about his mother. "Is she okay?"

"She will be. She burned herself—cooking, actually. Splashed scalding hot water on her arms." Tension pulled in tight lines around his mouth.

"I thought you said she didn't live here—but you met her at the emergency room?"

"She doesn't live in town, but the hospital here is closest. Careful—don't want to miss our turn."

His discomfort with the subject couldn't be any plainer. And though it hurt Meredith that he didn't trust her enough to tell her the truth about his mother—whatever that might be—she was determined to figure out a way to convince him to confide in her. Because she was starting to feel like this secret was the only thing standing between her and a happily-ever-after ending with Major.

Major hoped his tension from the time they got out of the SUV at the TV studio until the cameras turned off would appear to Meredith as nothing more than nerves over being on the live broadcast. But her fishing expedition in the car, trying to find out what had happened with Ma, had sent him into a state of near panic, afraid he might have to lie to her or tell her the truth, both of which would ruin everything.

On the way back to the office from the studio, he talked about the great job Alaine's team had done at putting together the documentary-style footage on all of the preparation leading up to the banquet as well as the event itself. And he'd been right—doing the live broadcast had been much easier to bear with Meredith sitting beside him.

He kept up a steady stream of inane chatter until they got on the elevator to go back to their offices.

"Can you have your reports to me by the end of the day?" Meredith's voice sounded tired.

"To you or to Corie?"

"To me. I've got to take everything home with me to work on this weekend."

"You work too hard." His arms itched to hug her, so instead, he took a step back and leaned against the bumper rail at the back of the elevator car.

"I know, but it's part and parcel of the job of being the executive director of a department. I knew that when I accepted the position."

He wanted to say more, but her cell phone rang. The tension drained from her face when she put the thing to her ear. "Hey, Ward."

He hated the softness, the warmth in her tone.

"Tonight? Well, I have a lot of work to do. . . . Sure, I could do something quick." Meredith waved her farewell when the elevator doors opened at the fifth floor.

Major crossed his arms and stared out the window on the rest of the ride up to the top floor. He deserved every bit of the awful, gut-wrenching pain now ripping apart his insides at the idea of Meredith falling in love with and possibly marrying someone else. He deserved it because he'd brought it upon himself by pushing her away.

The kitchen crew was just finishing lunch service cleanup. He wished them all a happy weekend then cloistered himself in his office for the remainder of the afternoon. Just before five o'clock, he e-mailed his reports to Meredith, then gathered up all of his receipts and invoices in a folder.

Down in the corporate offices, the interior door that connected Corie's office to Meredith's was partially closed.

Corie looked up from her computer when he walked in. "She's on the phone."

Meredith's laugh floated out through the narrow opening.

"I brought these for her. She said she wanted to take this stuff home to work on over the weekend." He handed Corie the folder and tried to smile.

"I'll make sure she gets it."

"Thanks." He couldn't torture himself by standing here listening to the happy tone of her voice any longer. "Have a great weekend."

"You, too."

When he got to the parking garage, he realized he'd forgotten to bring jeans to change into. Oh well. The guys would just have to put up with him in his black-and-white checked pants and the limp New York City T-shirt he'd been wearing under his jacket all day. He pointed Kirby toward church and tried to keep his mind from returning to the ride with Meredith to the TV studio. The look on her face when he wouldn't tell her why he'd had to disappear from the party last night. . .

A light drizzle started as Major pulled into the parking lot. He grabbed his folder of music and jogged in through the side door by the church offices.

George sat at the piano practicing the new piece they'd chosen to sing Sunday. He stopped, stood, and extended his hand. "Hullo."

"Hey. I figured I'd be the last one here."

"No. Forbes and Clay both called to say they're running late."

"Oh. Okay. That's good, actually. I could use a few minutes' downtime before we start singing." Major tossed his folder into a chair and collapsed onto the floor, stretching out flat on his back.

"Nice pants," George chuckled.

"Yeah, they're all the rage in New York," Major shot back. He did some of the stretches he'd learned in physical therapy after tearing his trapezius, ending his college football career. They almost always worked to ease the deep muscle spasms between his shoulder blades he'd been plagued with since then. Recently, though, nothing seemed to work. Every time he saw Meredith and the insane urge struck to tell her everything—about Ma, about his jealousy over Ward Breaux—he would clamp his mouth shut, his shoulders would tense, and the sharp pain would worsen.

He sat up and eyed George, who'd gone back to playing.

George must have sensed the scrutiny, because he looked up, and the music stopped. "What?"

Major hooked his arms around his bent knees. "I need to ask you something really personal. And if you don't want to answer, I'll understand."

"Go on." George turned to straddle the piano bench and leaned over to brace his elbows on his knees.

"When you met Anne and you couldn't tell her the truth about who you were and whose wedding she was really planning, how did you handle it? How did you keep from just blurting out the whole truth?"

George registered no expression of surprise or offense—or any reaction at all—over the question. The man should be a professional poker player.

"I wanted to every day." George rubbed his chin. "Many times I came close to slipping up and saying things that would have shattered my cover story. It was a wrench, I'll tell you, especially once I started falling in love with her."

Major could completely understand that. "But how did you make yourself keep the secret?"

"Because I was foolish enough to believe that the contract I signed was more important. But when I finally realized that it was not only wrong but would hurt Anne more the longer I waited to tell her, I gained permission to at least tell her I wasn't the groom, just his stand-in."

Major rocked back and forth. "So you wish you'd told her everything from the very beginning?"

"Of course." George eyed Major speculatively. "Is there someone you're keeping a secret from that's vital to your relationship?"

Vital to their relationship? "No—yes. I guess so. It's something about me—about my. . .family that very few people in the world know. And I've kept it that way to protect myself from undue scrutiny and judgment."

"But it's something that will affect the person you want to have a relationship with?" Deep lines formed in George's forehead when he raised his brows like that.

"Yeah—it could. It probably will." Major collapsed down onto his back again, covering his eyes with his left arm.

"You must tell her, then. Even if you are not dating currently, putting off the telling of your secret will only serve to make it worse when the truth becomes known later."

The choir room door swung open, and Forbes entered looking like Cary Grant or Gregory Peck in his dark gray, tailored suit and overcoat.

"Still waiting on Clay?" Forbes shook hands with George.

"I imagine he'll be along shortly." George turned back square to the keyboard and began playing again.

"In that case, Major, can I have a word with you? Privately." Forbes motioned to the door leading into the men's robe room.

Major nodded and followed, hoping this conversation wasn't about what he was afraid it would be about. He leaned against the metal storage cabinet in the small room.

Forbes stood in the middle of the room and turned to face him, unbuttoning his suit coat. "I know you don't want to hear this, but you have to tell Meredith about your mom."

Yep. That was what he'd hoped this conversation *wouldn't* be about. "What makes you say that?"

"She asked me about your family last night. She was very concerned about something that happened Wednesday night—you had to leave the banquet?"

"Ma spilled hot water during a cooking lesson and burned her arms. I had to meet her at the emergency room." Major crossed his arms then uncrossed them—he couldn't protect himself from Forbes's penetrating gaze no matter where his arms were.

"Look, I went along with you when you decided not to tell anyone but my parents about your mother's medical condition, but aside from the fact that Meredith is your boss, she's a person who cares a lot about you—I have a feeling more than either of us wants to admit—and you're only hurting her by not telling her the truth."

Major ran his tongue along the backs of his teeth. Twice within five minutes. It couldn't have been any clearer if God had taken a cast-iron skillet and smashed him over the head with it. "I promise, I will tell her the truth." As soon as the right moment presented itself.

Chapter 22

Meredith, you're going to wrinkle your gown if you keep holding it up like that."

At Anne's soft words, Meredith released her death grip on the layers of purple chiffon and satin. "Isn't the bride supposed to be the nervous wreck and the maid of honor the one reassuring her?"

Anne paused in her circuit around the room, ensuring each person knew what to do as soon as they left the bridal room.

Melancholic joy filled Meredith's throat until she thought it might burst. She was overjoyed for her cousin yet at the same time felt as if she were losing her.

"Don't start," Anne warned, her smile wavering. "You know if you lose it, I will, too."

"I know—" Meredith's phone chimed and saved her from dissolving into the unwanted tears. She dug her purse out of her satchel and read the new text message. She deleted it, tossed the phone back in her bag, and turned to Anne. "Ward's here. Do you mind. . . ?"

"We have a few minutes. Go on."

Meredith avoided grabbing the front of her dress to lift the skirt. She didn't need to for walking. She was just used to long skirts that were straighter than this A-line, flared thing. She was also used to being much more covered up on top. Though the straight-cut bodice provided modesty, the spaghetti-straps left her shoulders feeling very bare.

She nodded and smiled in greeting at the guests milling in the vestibule.

Ward's dark, curly head towered above everyone else. Her pulse gave a halfhearted flutter at the sight of him. Dressed in the tailored charcoal suit he'd worn on their first date, he drew the admiring attention of every female near him.

Why, then, couldn't Meredith muster even an ounce of attraction for him? She'd hoped that by bringing him as her date to such a romantic affair as a wedding she might be able to jump-start an interest in him as something more than just a friend.

"Meredith Guidry." Her name came out as almost a low growl when Ward finally noticed her. "You look gorgeous. I'm afraid I'll break you if I hug you."

She rested her hand on his chest as he squeezed her bare shoulders and kissed her cheek. "Thanks. You clean up pretty well yourself."

"When you told me this was going to be a big wedding, I had no idea you meant everyone who's anyone in Bonneterre would be here. I think I saw the mayor arriving as I pulled in the parking lot."

"Anne's worked with him on several events." As had Meredith. "That's why the reception is invitation only—and even still, we expect almost three hundred guests there." She turned and glanced into the sanctuary. The room that seated more than one thousand looked like it was getting pretty full.

"I should probably go in and find a seat, huh?" Ward came up behind her and rested his hands on her waist.

By turning around to face him again, she dislodged his hands, uncomfortable with such a possessive touch from someone she wasn't sure she liked *that way*. "Yeah, I'd better get back to Anne."

Ward gave her a cocky grin. "At least I know I'll be able to find you easily in all this crowd. You're the prettiest girl here."

She tried so hard to get her heart to flutter or her stomach to flip-flop at his flirting, but. . .nothing. "Aww, just what every maid of honor needs to hear." She patted his arm. "Now, go. I've already been gone too long, I'm sure." She grabbed her skirt and hurried back to the bridal suite.

Anne directed Meredith to join the rest of the women for photos, discussing them with the photographer as if she were the wedding planner, not the bride. Everyone laughed when the photographer had to remind Anne that she needed to be in the picture.

After a few posed shots as well as several candid shots of them all laughing again, Anne sent Mamere and Aunt Maggie out to be seated.

Meredith shifted her weight from foot to foot as Anne calmly made one final check to ensure everything was ready. Certainly with just Meredith and Jenn as attendants, she didn't have much to organize. But an aura of peace surrounded her, no doubt from her years of experience planning other people's weddings. Meredith hoped if she ever got married, she could be so annoyingly serene.

A knock on the door jarred all three of them. Uncle Errol stuck his head in. "You girls ready?"

Meredith's throat tried to swell closed again. Anne retrieved her bouquet and a large silver picture frame. Meredith took a few deep breaths and followed Jenn down the hall and back into the lobbylike foyer behind the sanctuary. Jason was just taking Aunt Maggie, the foster mother of the bride, down the aisle.

One tear escaped and trailed down Meredith's cheek when Anne handed the framed photo of her parents to Whitt, her oldest foster brother, to carry down the aisle and place on the pew beside Aunt Maggie.

Jason and Whitt came back to man the doors. Anne motioned a red-eyed, sniffling Jenn to go down the aisle.

Meredith turned to Anne. "I'm so happy for you that I think my heart might explode."

Anne blinked rapidly a few times, and her lips quivered. "Please don't do that—it'll make such a mess." They both laughed. "And thank you. But you need to go, now. And don't walk as slowly as you did last night, please."

"All right, all right. Good grief, I'm going." Meredith winked at her cousin, grateful that Anne had lightened the mood.

Though more than a thousand people crowded the sanctuary, Meredith had never felt more alone, walking down that aisle. At the other end stood George; his brother, Henry; and Forbes. But though Forbes nodded at her, they weren't waiting for her. They were waiting for Anne.

Then she saw him. As soon as she got to the front and turned to face the crowd, his face was the only one she could clearly see. In the back row, on an outside aisle, Major O'Hara smiled and gave her a quick thumbs-up.

Meredith couldn't help grinning like a fool—but fortunately, the doors at the back opened, the organ fanfare at the beginning of the march Anne had chosen started, and the congregation stood to watch Anne Hawthorne come down the aisle on her uncle's arm.

The wedding planner's wedding.

Across from Meredith, George Laurence's brown eyes stayed glued to his bride, his sharp but handsome profile reflecting the joy on Anne's face.

The happiness Meredith had been afraid would burst her heart did—and flooded her entire being with joy that made her want to sit down and weep. Her gaze broke away from Anne and George, now separated only by Uncle Errol, as the pastor began the ceremony in prayer.

Before she closed her eyes and bowed her head, Meredith stole one more glance at Major and witnessed him sneaking out the side door. No doubt to go back over to Lafitte's Landing to finish everything for the reception.

Meredith joined everyone else in a prayer posture. *Father God, I hate to sound selfish on Anne's day, but You know how much I want to get married. Please change my heart toward Major so I can fall in love with Ward—or anyone who'll love me back.*

Major sneaked one last glance through the small, cross-shaped window in the door at the back of the sanctuary. Meredith stood in profile to him, looking at her cousin with such emotion, Major wanted to charge up there and beg Pastor Kinnard to make it a double wedding.

But Major hadn't missed the sight of Ward Breaux greeting Meredith in this very foyer before the ceremony. Major had had his doubts about how serious Meredith was getting with the contractor, but wasn't inviting someone to a wedding a sure sign that things were going beyond the "seeing each other" stage? He backed away from the door, needing to get to Lafitte's Landing to finish setup—and needing to get away from Meredith.

He shrugged out of his suit coat and removed his tie and tossed them in the passenger seat. He grabbed his phone and quick-dialed Steven.

"Anything I need to pick up on my way back?" he asked his second-in-command.

"No, Chef. But you are on your way back?" Steven's harried tone set off warning bells for Major.

"Yeah. I'm headed that way now."

Ten minutes later, he pulled into the narrow service lot behind Lafitte's. Once inside, he changed into his utilitarian work smock. He'd put his presentation jacket on after the cooking was finished and when he would step out of the kitchen to watch his friend and colleague cut her wedding cake—which his staff had picked up from Aunt Maggie's house that morning along with the chocolate groom's cake frosted and decorated to resemble George's omnipresent PDA.

"Why hasn't plating started yet?" Major called over the din of work in the large kitchen. He walked over to Steven, the only one from whom he expected an answer.

"The trays all had to be rewashed, Chef. They're drying them now."

Major glanced at his watch, then looked around, knowing he'd drawn everyone's attention upon his entrance. "The wedding ceremony will end in less than ten minutes, which means we can expect guests to start arriving in about twenty to thirty. I want cold hors d'oeuvres and canapés on the buffet tables in no more than fifteen minutes; passed hot hors d'oeuvres ready for the servers in twenty."

"Yes, Chef," his staff called.

"This is Anne Hawthorne's wedding reception, folks. I know most of you weren't working here when she was the event planner for B-G, but you do know how much business she brings the company—and that she's Mr. and Mrs. Guidry's niece. So let's make this perfect beyond her expectations."

"Yes, Chef!"

He slipped into the staff break room off the kitchen and changed shirts, then plugged in the earpiece that connected him with everything happening outside the kitchen.

"Lori, this is Major. I'm back. How's everything front-side?"

"Fine. Two of my staff showed up late, so we got off to a later start than I wanted, but everything's fine now."

"Good. First guests should be here in about fifteen. Did you and Jana brief the servers?"

"We did. No one is to approach Mr. Ballantine any differently than any other guest—no asking for autographs and stuff like that."

"Okay, thanks." He released the TALK button and returned to the kitchen.

Could it really have been nine months since Major had prepared the food for mega-movie star—and Anne's one-time fiancé—Cliff Ballantine's engagement party in this very kitchen? Ironic that Anne would have chosen to have her wedding reception in the place where she learned George had been keeping Cliff's identity secret from her for weeks.

"Chef, taste," called one of the cooks. He crossed to the station and tasted the cheese grits.

"Needs more pepper." Major tossed his spoon into the sink and went to the meat station. "How's the prime rib coming?"

"It'll be perfect just in time to set up the carving posts."

Major ran down the list at each station, pleased that everything had been timed just right.

"Chef," came Lori's voice through the earpiece, "guests are arriving."

He pressed the Talk button. "Thanks." He clanged a ladle against an empty metal bowl. "Cold trays out now. Hot trays in five." He spoke into the earpiece again. "Jana, send in the servers, please."

Meredith managed to make it through the ceremony with only a couple of tears escaping—sighing over George's British accent as he recited his vows, giggling with Jenn when the kiss lasted a little too long.

"Ladies and gentlemen, please join me in congratulating Mr. and Mrs. George Laurence." The pastor's voice was nearly drowned out by the applause from the wedding guests.

Meredith handed Anne's bouquet back to her, leaned over to adjust Anne's train, then took Henry Laurence's arm to be escorted to the vestibule behind Anne and George. She hugged her cousin and new cousin-in-law as soon as they reached the foyer. Inside the auditorium, the pastor invited everyone to stay while photos were being taken.

Meredith groaned.

"I know—you hate the idea of people watching you while we're taking pictures," Anne said. "But it was either that or a receiving line, since most of these people aren't invited to the reception."

"I guess feeling like a monkey in the zoo is a little better than standing there for two hours—and then still having to get my picture taken." She followed Anne down the side hall to reenter the sanctuary near the front.

For all that everyone had been invited to stay, not many did. Meredith smiled at Ward as warmly as she could when he joined them at the front, while Anne and the photographer discussed the best way to get the shots Anne wanted.

"You looked stunning up there—like a princess." Ward pulled Meredith into a hug.

She sighed, disappointed that Major had never hugged her like this. "Thanks."

When she stepped back from his embrace, she caught a glimpse of her sister hovering nearby. Meredith looked around for Henry Laurence—ah, he and George were deep in a private discussion.

"Ward, I don't believe you've met my sister yet." She introduced Jenn. Was it her imagination or did his gaze linger, his handshake last just a little longer than necessary when he greeted Jenn? Well, even if it had, it wouldn't matter. Jenn had had eyes for no one but Henry from the moment George's youngest brother set foot off the plane.

With Anne's guidance, the photos were finished in short order.

Meredith, Jenn, Forbes, and Henry climbed into the first of the two limousines waiting outside the church. Forbes and Henry sat toward the middle of the stretch vehicle, while Meredith and Jenn—not wanting to trip on and possibly damage their skirts—sat in the back.

"You never told me Ward is so good-looking," Jenn whispered, stealing a glance at Henry to ensure he and Forbes were still in deep discussion about the differences between practicing law in the States and in Australia.

"Didn't I?" Meredith closed her eyes against the inevitable. She'd seen the glaze overtake Ward's eyes when she introduced him to Jenn.

"And if you two aren't dating, as you keep protesting, remind me why you asked him to be your date for the wedding."

"Anne told me I should. And yes, we were sort of dating."

"Meredith! You denied it all this time? After all this time you finally get a boyfriend, and you pretend like it's nothing—what do you mean you *were* dating?"

"I mean I'm going to tell him that I don't think things are going to work out between us."

"Are you crazy?" Jenn smiled at Forbes and Henry when they

looked over at her shouted question. She leaned closer and lowered her voice. "Are you crazy? He's gorgeous."

Would it do any good to try to explain? "Yes, he is very handsome. And he's a wonderfully charming guy. But after seeing him for almost two months, I don't feel anything for him but friendship."

"Try."

Meredith groaned in frustration. "I *have* tried. I've prayed, begging God to let me stop being in love with—" She clapped both hands over her mouth.

Jenn's eyes grew huge. "In love with who? Meredith Emmanuelle Guidry, you have to tell me. I'm your sister. I tell you everything."

Whether I want you to or not. She might as well go ahead and spill the whole can of worms now that it was open. Jenn would never leave her alone otherwise.

"Major."

Jenn stared at her for a few seconds. "Major. . .O'Hara?" she whispered, shock obvious.

"Yes, Major O'Hara. Who works for me—well, for Mom and Dad, but he reports to me."

"Major O'Hara?" Jenn looked as if she was going to laugh, but Meredith quelled her with a withering glance.

"You have to promise you won't say anything to anyone, Jenn."

"But if you're in love with Major, why are you dating Ward Breaux?"

"Because I made a promise to myself that this year I'm going to finally get over this thing I have for Major and not spend next New Year's alone."

"What do you mean 'finally'? How long have you harbored feelings for him?"

"Jenn—"

"No. I want the truth."

"Oh, all right." Meredith huffed, but a sense of release seeped in around her frustration with her sister. It actually felt good to finally tell someone other than Anne. "Eight years."

Jenn's mouth dropped open. "Eight *years*?"

"Yes. Ever since he started working at B-G."

"So if you're not interested in Ward Breaux, can I. . . ?" Jenn tipped her head to one side and waggled her eyebrows.

Meredith snorted. "What about Henry?"

Jenn looked over at George's handsome younger brother. "He's a lot of fun for right now, but he will be returning to Australia day after tomorrow. Ward lives right here in Bonneterre."

While Meredith wished she could be jealous over the idea of Ward turning his very romantic attention onto her sister, the thought brought profound relief—especially since she'd always hoped her sister would find a man as wonderful as Ward.

"Yes, by all means, go for it. . .him."

The limo rolled to a stop in front of Lafitte's Landing. Meredith scrambled out as soon as the door opened, allowing one of the boys taking invitations at the entrance to assist her out of the car.

"Wow, Miss Meredith, you look great."

"Thanks, Jeremy."

Lori met them inside the front door.

"Anne and George's limo pulled up just behind ours," Meredith told her. "Let the kitchen know and go give the DJ the heads-up—" She stopped with an apologetic smile. "Sorry. Old habits."

The veteran event planner shrugged her shoulders. "I was getting ready to defer to you, so I guess we're both operating on old habits." She stepped away from them to do just what Meredith had instructed and rejoined them as Anne and George came in. "Everyone is ready. Bridal party, if you'll come with me."

Meredith reminded Jennifer with one look that as maid of honor it was she, not Jenn, who should be escorted in by Henry Laurence.

It was going to be a long night.

Chapter 23

"Ladies and gentlemen, please join me in welcoming Mr. and Mrs. George Laurence."

Meredith applauded with the other three hundred people in the room, emotion once again trying to get the better of her at the sight of how happy Anne was.

"Miss Meredith?"

She turned. One of their longtime servers stood behind her, a tray of champagne flutes filled with Major's secret recipe fruit tea. Meredith gratefully took a glass.

Henry looked at the beverage contemplatively. "Unlike my brother, I've yet to grow accustomed to the idea of cold, sweetened tea."

"Ah, yes, then you'll want. . ." Meredith touched his arm for balance as she raised up on tiptoe to look around for a server with a different option. She caught the eye of one and motioned him over.

"What's this?" Henry took a glass of the clear, fizzy liquid.

"Sparkling water. George's choice."

"Excellent."

Jenn joined them and slipped her arm through Henry's. "I can't believe you left me at the mercy of Great-Aunt Edith, Mere. You know how much she likes to harp on me because I'm not married yet." Jenn batted her lashes at Henry.

"Why do you think I escaped?" Meredith winked at her sister. On more than one occasion, Edith had offered to set Meredith up with some "fine young man" she knew. She considered that a moment. Edith herself had married quite well—Great-Uncle Rodney had been handsome and wealthy.

If things got dire, maybe she'd take Edith up on her offer. She laughed to herself.

"Here you are." Ward encircled Meredith's waist with one arm and kissed her temple.

Meredith introduced him to Henry and then to Forbes, again, who materialized out of the crowd of people trying to greet Anne and George. "But Forbes, where's your date?"

His eyes scanned the crowd, but his face looked a bit redder than normal. "She. . .she had something come up at the last minute and couldn't come."

"Something?" Jenn cocked her head and gave him a speculative stare.

"She got engaged last night."

Meredith and Jenn both groaned.

"Not another one who agreed to go out with you just to make her longtime boyfriend jealous?" If Meredith could ever figure this dating thing out, she'd have to teach Forbes how to do it, too.

"Yeah, something like that." He shook himself slightly, as if trying to dislodge his embarrassment. "Hey, what are we supposed to be doing right now?"

"This is technically what's considered to be the cocktail hour. At seven, the DJ will announce dinner; once everyone's seated, Reverend Kinnard will say the blessing before food service begins. At seven forty-five, the toasts begin—Henry, then me, then Uncle Errol and Aunt Maggie."

Meredith visualized the list in her head. "At eight o'clock is the first dance—Anne and George. Then Anne will dance with Uncle Errol, and George will dance with Aunt Maggie since his mom couldn't be here, and the attendants will join on that one—me with Henry, Jenn with Forbes. Then the floor's open to everyone for dancing."

Around her, Jenn, Forbes, Henry, and Ward all looked at her in astonishment.

"What?"

"Pray, continue," Henry said. "I had no idea all of this would be happening."

Heat rushed into her face at her ability to be a dork no matter what circumstance she was in. "Well, at nine o'clock, they'll cut the cake. Dancing will resume. And at nine thirty, Jenn, Aunt Maggie, and I will go with Anne to help her change out of her dress into her going-away outfit, and at ten o'clock, they'll leave. Forbes, you'll need to make sure we get out of here with George's tux so we can take it with Anne's dress to the dry cleaner on Monday."

"I'll be sure to do that." Forbes nodded.

"Meredith Guidry, there you are!"

She turned at the somewhat shrill female voice. "Hello, Mrs. McCord." She let the mayor's wife take her hands and kiss her cheek—well, kiss the air with her cheek pressed to Meredith's.

"I tried to find you after the banquet to tell you that it was absolutely the most wonderful event I've ever attended. You outdid yourself, young lady."

"Thank you very much, Mrs. McCord."

"And you looked positively darling on TV afterward. You're so photogenic. And that Major O'Hara—if he isn't just the yummiest thing I've ever laid eyes on. How long have the two of you been together?"

"We've worked together for a little over eight years now."

The mayor's wife simpered. "No, dear, I mean how long have you been dating?"

Meredith was acutely aware of Ward standing right beside her. "I'm not dating Major. We're colleagues, nothing more."

"Well, then you must be blind to the way that boy looks at you—as if you hung the moon and stars. I'm sure everyone watching that program thought the same thing I did, that your wedding would be the next one we'd see announced in the paper."

"Mrs. McCord, may I introduce you to my date, Ward Breaux?" Meredith moved a little sideways to pull Ward into the conversation.

"Oh—my." The older woman looked like she might attempt a swoon after taking her time to drag her gaze up Ward's striking figure to his handsome face.

"Ward, this is Mrs. McCord, first lady of Bonneterre."

He shook the woman's hand and answered her questions about his family and what he did for a living. As it turned out, Mrs. McCord and Ward's mother had been in the same sorority together in college.

Mrs. McCord turned to Meredith. "That means your mother would know Ward's mother as well, Meredith, as Mairee and I pledged Tri-Delt together our freshman year. If I recall, Ward, your mother was two years ahead of us."

"Really?" Meredith exchanged a raised-brow look with Ward. "I'll have to ask her later if she remembers Ward's mom."

"You do that." Mrs. McCord waved at someone beyond Meredith. "I've got to run—oh, but I will be calling you Monday to set up a time to come in and talk about Easter in the Park. It's time we get *in the hunt* on that." Her laughter trailed behind her after she walked away.

"Was that supposed to be funny?" Jenn asked when Meredith and Ward turned to rejoin the group.

"Hunt—the Easter egg hunt. Get it?"

"Oh. Ha-ha." Jenn smirked. "So, Ward, Meredith hasn't told us much about you." Even hanging on to Henry's arm, Jenn seemed to have no shame in flirting with someone else.

Ward talked a little about his family and his business. Meredith allowed her gaze to wander around the room, catching details that most attendees at this soiree would never notice—Lori talking to the DJ, the number of black-and-white-clad servers walking around with the trays of hot hors d'oeuvres, the little knot of servers gathered at the mouth of the hall leading to the kitchen.

Without really thinking about what she was doing, Meredith excused herself and crossed the room to the service hallway. By the time she got over there, the servers had dispersed. But now that she was this close to the kitchen, she might as well stick her head in and see how everything was going.

She'd barely pushed the door open when the nearest person yelled, "Civilian in the kitchen."

Though on a smaller scale, the frenetic pace of the kitchen was very much like what it had been on Valentine's Day.

"May I help—oh, it's you." Major wiped his hands on a towel and draped it over his shoulder. "You look beautiful, Meredith."

She was pretty sure even her shoulders were blushing. "Thanks. How's everything going in here?"

"Is it my imagination, or are you supposed to be *not* working tonight?" The dimple appeared in his left cheek, though he tried to keep his expression stern.

"I just. . ." She shrugged. "Busted."

"Since you are a *guest* and not part of the staff tonight, I have to order you out of the kitchen." He pressed his fingertips to his earpiece. "Especially since I just got the five-minute warning until salad service. So," he reached behind her and pushed the door open, "please vacate the service area of the premises."

She caught the tip of her tongue between her teeth—he was so close to her. All she had to do was raise up on her toes and she'd be within a millimeter of kissing him.

She took a deep breath and swallowed hard. "Yes, Chef." Her voice squeaked, and she turned and fled the kitchen.

She was halfway through her Chateaubriand before her heart returned to a normal rate and she stopped imagining what would have happened if she hadn't backed away and practically run from the kitchen. Major would have been mortified if she'd kissed him in front of his staff, and possibly offended.

Mrs. McCord's words had wrecked Meredith's ability to ignore her romantic thoughts about Major. And even if Major did feel something for her, she couldn't do anything until she had a conversation with Ward to tell him the truth about her feelings toward him.

"And now, the bride and groom will share their first dance."

George led Anne out to the open space in the middle of the room to the guests' soft applause. Out of the three songs Anne had narrowed the choices to, "True Love" had been Meredith's favorite. And she was really glad that Anne had been able to find the recording of Bing Crosby and Grace Kelly singing it, because it was a little slower, more romantic, than the Dean Martin version Anne had played for her a few weeks ago.

As soon as that song ended, the DJ invited Errol, Maggie, and the attendants to join Anne and George on the dance floor. When the first notes of "That's Amore" started playing, Meredith giggled, nerves pressing at her throat. Even though Anne had taught her several different steps, Meredith was by no means comfortable with the task of dancing, especially since Henry was so graceful it made her feel like an elephant trying to balance on a tightrope.

Thankfully, it was a short song. Meredith was just about to escape when Ward stopped her.

"May I?" He extended his hand.

She shook her head. "I'm not really a dancer."

"You looked wonderful out there." He took her hand and led her back onto the dance floor. "If you're truly awful, we'll stop, I promise."

Not only was Ward good, but he also softly sang along with "It Had to Be You" as he whisked Meredith around the floor. But two dances were enough for Meredith. She went and sat down with Forbes while Ward partnered up with Jenn.

"Do you think Jenn's seriously interested in Henry, or is it just because he's new and different?" Forbes asked.

"New and different. She's got her eye on Ward now, too." And from the way Ward was looking at Jenn while they slow-danced to a song Meredith had never heard before, he might not mind spending some time with Jenn.

"You don't think she'd try to steal him away from you?" Forbes leaned forward, concern evident in his slate blue eyes.

"It won't be stealing." She leaned across the table to retrieve her glass of tea.

"I see." Forbes resumed his more relaxed posture. "You've already told Jenn that?"

"Yeah. But I need to tell Ward."

"Best do it now." Forbes nodded at the two of them coming toward the table together.

She'd hoped to put it off as long as possible, but she could see the struggle in Ward's eyes when he sat down beside her.

Forbes sighed and stood. "Come on, Jenn. Dance with your decrepit old brother."

Ward reached over and took Meredith's hand. "You don't look like you're enjoying yourself."

"Ward. . .there's something I need to tell you."

"Sounds serious." He rubbed his thumb against the palm of her hand.

"It is." She pulled her hand out of his and rested it on her lap. "It's something I should have told you awhile back, but I've been putting it off, hoping things would change."

He leaned forward and braced his hands on his knees. "Hoping *things* would change—as in the way you feel about me?"

"Yeah." She drew the word out. "I have had so much fun going out with you, and I have never felt more cherished and admired than I have since I met you."

"But you aren't falling in love with me." Kindness permeated his voice and soft smile. "Would it surprise you to learn that I'm not in love with you either?"

Breathing came a little easier. "A little. Why keep asking me out if. . .?"

"Because I *wanted* to fall in love with you. On paper, Meredith Guidry is the perfect woman for me."

"But I'm not the same person in real life that I am on paper?"

"No, that's not what I mean. I mean that every quality that I've ever dreamed of finding in a woman, I found in you."

"But the spark isn't there." She began to relax, understanding that he really did feel the same way she did.

"Exactly."

"I was seeing definite sparks between you and Jenn." She grinned at his surprise. "Henry leaves day after tomorrow, and while she's having fun flirting with him, when I told her I was going to break up with you, she wanted to know if that meant you were fair game. So I'm giving you the same blessing I gave her: go for it."

And he did. As soon as Jenn came off the dance floor with Forbes, Ward took her right back out and relinquished her to Henry only twice.

"I'm proud of you, Mere."

"Hmm?" Meredith hadn't caught all of what Forbes said. She was too caught up in watching Major make his way around the room. It must be almost time for the cake cutting, since he'd said he was going to make an appearance for that.

A sudden welling of emotion took Meredith by surprise. She'd wished, wanted, hoped, desired, prayed for so long that what Mrs. McCord had said would come true—that she would marry Major O'Hara. The desire to melt into a heap of tears, in private, drew her to her feet, but before she could disappear and give into the temptation, Anne waved her over to the table where the enormous cake Aunt Maggie had created stood.

As soon as Anne and George had finished feeding cake to each other and the servers had taken over cutting the masterpiece into pieces for the guests, Meredith slipped out the front door and followed the wraparound porch to the place overlooking the lake that lay between Lafitte's and the university campus.

She immediately wished she'd stopped to get her wrap as the cool, damp air prickled her arms and cheeks. But she didn't feel like going back inside to get it. She'd come out here to feel miserable, and being cold only added to her self-pity.

Leaning against one of the pillars, she wrapped her arms around her middle and gave into the tears that had been building for weeks, months, years. Tonight she'd lost Anne and Ward. Though Anne would never cease being her cousin and friend, their relationship would never be the same again—she'd seen the hints of that over the past six months since Anne and George met. And even though she hadn't been in love with Ward, at least she'd had the appearance and comfort of having a boyfriend for a couple of months.

"Lord, what's wrong with me? Why doesn't anyone want me? Are You trying to show me that I'm going to be alone for the rest of my life?"

She wasn't really sure she expected an answer. For years, she'd been praying the same prayer in different ways, but basically asking for one thing: a husband. Someone, as the song said, to watch over her. The one person who would not only flatter her vanity and make her feel cherished, the way Ward had, but who stirred the very embers of her soul, the way Major did.

But maybe Anne had been right. Maybe she should be praying for something other than for Major to come to his senses. She closed her eyes. "Lord, I've been begging for You to make Major return my feelings for a long time now. And I've never once prayed to ask You to show me Your will in my relationship with him—or any relationships. Father, please help me to be content with where I am and what I have in my life, and to be looking for the ways in which I can make myself a better person and serve You better."

The muscles in her shoulders cramped with the cold, and she shivered violently. But she couldn't go back inside. Not yet. Not until she got all the tears out of her system. She hoped God would start giving her that contentment soon, because right now, all she had was a great big, empty, gaping hole of loneliness.

"You know, you really shouldn't be out here without a coat."

Warmth enveloped Meredith's shoulders—and the scent that was unmistakably Major's. She snuggled into his leather jacket even as she tried to wipe away any evidence she'd been crying.

"How'd you know where to find me?" Hoping her supposedly waterproof eye makeup hadn't run, she turned, her heart wrenching at the familiar and beloved sight of him in his pristine white chef's jacket.

He reached over and pulled the collar of the jacket closed under her chin. "I always try to make sure I know where you are."

The gruffness in his voice nearly keeled her over. "Oh."

"Meredith, I—" He swallowed a couple of times. "I'm sorry Ward Breaux hurt you the way he did tonight. I couldn't believe it when I saw him blatantly and openly flirting with Jenn right in front of you."

A sob-laugh burst from Meredith's throat. "He didn't hurt me. I told him tonight that I don't have any feelings for him—not romantically anyway—and I gave him and Jenn both my blessing."

"Your blessing?" Major moved closer, clasping her shoulders, his eyes midnight blue in the faint moonlight. "You're saying you're not in love with Ward Breaux?"

"Yes, I'm—"

Major's lips pressed to hers in a kiss that buckled Meredith's knees. She kissed him back with all the intensity eight years of hoping for this moment had built inside of her.

When the kiss finally ended, Major pulled her into his arms and pressed his cheek to her hair. "I love you, Meredith. I have for a very long time."

She laughed. God hadn't taken very long in answering her prayer for contentment.

Chapter 24

"I still can't believe you laughed at me when I told you I love you."

"You're so cute when you're disgruntled."

Major couldn't help smiling back at Meredith. When he'd seen Ward Breaux dancing with Jenn last night, he'd been ready to call the guy out—forget the fact that Breaux had the advantage of at least four inches and a couple tons more muscle. And at that moment, Major knew he couldn't live one more day without letting Meredith know he loved her.

"Are you sure that coming to Sunday dinner with my entire extended family isn't going to be awkward for you? No one knows about us."

"Um, I think they can see us sitting here together." Major looked around the sanctuary and back at Meredith. He wanted to go with her, to have her show her family that they were together, that they loved each other. And as long as this family meal didn't last three or four hours, he would be able to get out to BPC before Ma started wondering where he was—though she had been a lot better since the trip to the emergency room a week and a half ago.

Meredith half turned on the pew to face him. "Major, you know how I feel about you."

He grinned. "Yeah. You've been in love with me since we first started working together." He'd been both surprised and humbled when she'd told him that last night.

"Right. But even though we've worked together for a long time and I love you for who you are as a person, before we can move forward with our relationship, there's something you're going to have to do for me."

The organ music started, and around them, everyone rose to sing the call to worship.

Heart throbbing with guilt, knowing what she was about to ask him, Major stood and opened the hymnal. He leaned over and whispered, "We have plenty of time to talk about our relationship. Let's just take things slowly."

He did have a lot he needed to tell her. She didn't even know yet that he'd turned down her parents' offer to open the restaurant. And then there was Ma. He prayed for wisdom.

It shouldn't have surprised him that Meredith had a special journal in which she took notes on the sermon. The few times he'd attended the late service when the quartet sang, he hadn't taken the time to notice how studiously she paid attention and wrote down ideas sparked by Reverend Kinnard's sermon.

He also found it interesting that Meredith had chosen to sit across the sanctuary from where most of her family were. But as soon as the service ended, Forbes appeared—almost as if magically and instantaneously transported across the large room.

"You don't usually come to this service." Forbes extended his hand to Major, speculation practically dripping from his gaze.

"It was a late night last night." Major glanced at Meredith.

"Forbes, I've invited Major to come to Sunday dinner today."

His friend's speculation disappeared into a knowing smile. "I see. I thought last night things might be moving in that direction."

Meredith leaned left to look around her brother. "Why don't we go on and head over to Maggie and Errol's?" She looked up at Major, a slight nervousness in her smile.

He looked beyond Forbes, too. Jenn, Rafe, and a few others of

Meredith's siblings and cousins were heading in their direction.

Forbes glanced over his shoulder. "You'll have to deal with them one way or another."

"I'd rather deal with them in a less public setting, thanks very much." She shooed Major out of the pew, and he obediently led the way.

"Do you want to ride over with me?" Meredith slid her sunglasses on when they reached the brightness outside.

"I think I'm closer to home at Maggie and Errol's than from here, so why don't I just follow you over there." Guilt nibbled at his conscience like ravenous piranhas.

"Oh, okay. But I thought maybe we could drive out to my house afterward so you can see the progress Ward has made on the kitchen, since you did help him design it."

And when he'd talked on the phone with Ward about the things he would want to see in a home kitchen, Major had experienced jealousy unlike anything he'd ever want to go through again. Not just for the fact he was talking to the man he thought Meredith was falling for, but because he couldn't foresee ever being able to afford a kitchen like that for himself. But now. . .

The drive to Maggie and Errol's sprawling mini-mansion didn't take long, and he and Meredith were among the first to arrive.

"Do my eyes deceive me, or is that Major O'Hara?" Maggie Babineaux stopped stirring the contents of a pot on the stove and came across the ginormous kitchen to hug him. He could understand Maggie's having a kitchen like this—after all, she'd been a caterer and cake decorator for years—but he still didn't quite understand why Meredith, who didn't cook at all, wanted a gourmet-quality kitchen.

"It's good to see you, Maggie."

"I'm glad one of our girls finally wised up and brought you around." Maggie winked at him. "The first time I met you, I knew you were destined to become part of this family."

He endured the ebullient greetings from the rest of Meredith's aunts—and the more reserved welcome from her grandmother. The only outward sign of surprise Mairee gave when she entered a few minutes later was the slight lifting of one eyebrow.

While he'd had an intellectual understanding of just how large Meredith's extended family was, to experience it in reality soon became almost overwhelming. The table in the cavernous dining room seated all the adults, while teens sat at the long central island in the kitchen, and children, at tables set up on the sunporch.

"Anne called before their flight left Atlanta," Maggie announced after Meredith's grandfather asked the blessing and food began making the rounds of the table.

"Did she sound like she was coping okay?" Meredith passed him the bowl of mashed potatoes.

"She admitted she had gotten sick to her stomach before they boarded the plane here, but since the flight to Atlanta was smooth, she's feeling okay about the flight to New York. Still, I could tell she's worrying about the flight to London."

"It's a miracle she's flying at all." Rafe shook his head. "If it hadn't been for George, she might never have had the motivation to get on a plane again."

"Well, she asked everyone to pray that she doesn't have a panic attack along the way, because she doesn't want to ruin this trip for George."

Though the food was what most French-trained chefs would consider "rustic," Major loved every morsel that passed his lips, from the fall-apart-tender roast beef with rich gravy, to the corn pudding, to the mustard greens that had been cooked with a ham hock. Every family should have a meal like this once a week.

After dinner was finished, the women cleared the dishes and returned from the kitchen with thick slices of cake garnished with fresh berries, which they served to everyone at the table. Meredith set Major's in front of him, and he immediately recognized the cake.

"There was this much wedding cake left over? I'm surprised there was any."

"Aunt Maggie made an extra tier that she ended up not using. So now we get to have it for dessert." Meredith scraped a thick swirl of frosting off her piece with her fork and ate it, closing her eyes with a sigh.

Major wasn't a big fan of cake, but Maggie's creations were in a class by themselves. He enjoyed every bite but wished he could take a piece to his mother, who loved cake and never got a chance to eat any but the dry, grocery store cakes that they occasionally served at BPC for someone's birthday.

As soon as the last crumb was eaten, the last dollop of frosting scraped off the plates, the men all stood and collected the dishes. Forbes indicated with a nod of his head over his shoulder for Major to join them. He took his and Meredith's plates and followed Forbes into the kitchen.

Led by Errol, the men scraped and rinsed all of the dinner dishes and put them into the three dishwashers hidden behind panels that matched the cabinet doors.

"Major, how long have you known our Meredith?" her grandfather asked as he scraped the few spoonfuls of mashed potatoes from the serving dish into a plastic container.

"Eight years, sir."

"And it's taken that long for her to invite you to Sunday dinner?" The old gentleman's brown eyes twinkled—just like Meredith's did when she teased him.

"I'm a slow learner."

The head of the Guidry clan threw his head back and laughed. The self-deprecating humor seemed to be all the men in Meredith's family needed to accept him as one of their own, as no one else questioned his presence and what it meant.

But as soon as the dishwashers hummed and swished in the background, Major approached Lawson Guidry. "May I have a word with you, sir?"

"I hoped you might want to." Lawson cuffed his shoulder and led him to a study beyond the kitchen. He closed the door then motioned for Major to take one of the wingback chairs that flanked the fireplace.

Major had occasionally imagined the day when he would sit down with the father of the woman he loved and confess his feelings and ask for the father's blessing. Now that it was here, he wasn't exactly sure where to start.

"Mairee and I cannot thank you enough for the exemplary job you and your staff did at Anne's reception last night. I know Anne appreciated every effort you made on her behalf."

"Thank you, sir. It was my pleasure to give her the best of everything." He wiped his hands on the knees of his slacks. "Mr. Guidry, I'm in love with your daughter."

"Which one? I have four." The corner of his mouth twitched.

Major stopped fidgeting, Lawson's humor breaking the tension in the room. "You mean, I can have my pick?"

Lawson finally gave in and smiled. "I've been aware that Meredith has carried a torch for you for a while now. We were quite surprised when we learned she had started seeing someone else. And when you told me two weeks ago that you couldn't take the restaurant deal due to your need to tend to your mother, I almost wanted to tell you then that Meredith would be the perfect helpmate."

Major swallowed hard. "I haven't told her about my mother just yet."

The humor seeped out of Lawson's face. "Why not?"

Because I'm chicken. "The right opportunity hasn't presented itself yet. But I will tell her, soon."

"See that you do. Honesty is of the utmost importance in any relationship."

"I will."

"Good. Now, if that's all." Lawson rose.

Major stood as well.

Meredith's father extended his right hand. "Welcome to the Guidry family, Major."

His stomach flip-flopped. "Thank you, sir." Following Lawson out of the study, Major looked at his watch. One thirty. Not too bad. As long as he made it out to BPC by three o'clock, Ma should be okay.

When he walked into the dining room with Forbes, Rafe, Kevin, and Jonathan, Meredith's face was beet red. The intrusion of men into the room broke up the hen party, and couples started discussing getting their kids home for naps or homework.

Meredith jumped up from her seat. "Major, are you ready to go see the house?"

"Sure, if you are." He had the distinct impression that her aunts, cousins, and sisters had been giving her a hard time about him, thus her eagerness to escape.

"Let's go, then." She bade a hasty and general farewell to her relatives and practically dragged him from the house, muttering. He caught random words, such as "meddling" and "privacy," which confirmed his suspicions.

She didn't slow down until they arrived at her SUV. "Are you following again or riding?"

"I might as well just follow you over there." Because he could go straight out to BPC instead of taking the time to come all the way back over here.

Meredith's house sat deep within the Plantation Grove area of town, where the lots were enormous and the houses no newer than seventy or eighty years old.

From the street, the craftsman bungalow was half hidden by the two huge oak trees in the front yard. Azalea bushes, which were starting to show hints that they'd be blooming soon, lined the base of the porch on either side of the wide steps. From the outside, the house appeared in perfect condition—until the driveway took him around to the back. A large Dumpster blocked access to the carport and detached garage, and construction detritus littered the side yard.

Meredith climbed out of her SUV and held her arms open wide. "Welcome to my house, such as it is."

"It's great." He pocketed his keys and met her at the gate to the backyard. A high-pitched bark seemed to be coming from nearby. "Is there a dog here?"

"I dropped my puppy off over here this morning before church, since I knew I'd be coming by this afternoon to check on the progress." A much larger puppy than Major had pictured trundled over. Meredith bent down to scoop it up—then apparently changed her mind. "Your feet are muddy."

Major crouched down beside her, drawing the little guy's attention—and muddy paw prints on his pant leg. He scratched behind the floppy ears, then on the tubby tummy when the pup rolled onto his back. "What's his name?"

"I haven't named him yet."

"How long have you had him?"

"Since January first. I found him under the back porch."

"You've had him almost two months and you haven't named him?"

Meredith stood and started for the raised deck. "I don't really have the time to commit to a puppy—housebreaking, obedience training, and paying attention to him in general."

Major rocked back onto his heels. If she didn't think she would have time for a puppy, how could she have time to deal with his mother if he needed her to? But a puppy and a person were different, and her priorities would probably change in that case. "If you were going to keep him, what would you name him?" He joined her on the porch.

"Duke." She had to jiggle the key in the knob to get it to unlatch. She swung the door open and closed a couple of times. "Good. They rehung this door so it doesn't scrape the floor anymore."

"Duke—any special significance?" He followed her into the house.

"It was John Wayne's nickname." She flipped a couple of switches, and light flooded the room they were in—the kitchen.

But for the moment, Major had no attention for anything other than what she'd just said. "John Wayne?"

"I know. I'm a weirdo for liking John Wayne movies. But he's my favorite, and I refuse to apologize for it." She faced him, arms crossed as if daring him to contradict or tease her.

"Have I ever told you my full name?" He bit the sides of his tongue to keep from smiling.

She frowned, appearing uncertain as to the seemingly random change of subject. "No."

"Major Daniel Xavier Kirby O'Hara."

She repeated the name slowly. And a second time. Then understanding flickered in her nutmeg eyes. "Major Dan Kirby. . .the character Duke played in *Flying Leathernecks*?"

"None other. I like John Wayne movies, too. But I am partial to the war movies."

She braced her hands on the edge of her kitchen island. "I knew there was something I liked about you. But I have to disagree—I like his westerns best."

How could he ever have doubted that God meant for the two of them to be together? Once he could drag his gaze away from her, he finally took in the sight that surrounded him, and it quickened his heart. The cherry cabinets had been stained to exactly match the original woodwork of the window casings and crown molding. The grayish green granite countertops needed a good cleaning but looked exactly how he'd imagined. All the room lacked were the appliances—the six-burner, commercial-grade stove with double oven; the stainless-steel refrigerator and dishwasher; and the hood with the warming shelf built in.

Oh, yes, he could create the perfect romantic meals for the two of them in this kitchen. As a matter of fact, that would be a great way to celebrate the completion of this room, as well as a perfect time for him to tell Meredith all about Ma.

It would mean talking to Ward Breaux to find out when construction would be finished—and he wondered if Alaine's crew would mind shooting a segment here, since she said she'd like to get him in some home kitchens every so often.

Meredith toured him through the rest of the house, but Major's mind was occupied with creating the perfect romantic menu—one that would hopefully make up for the fact he'd been keeping a pretty big secret from her.

"Oh, for heaven's sake." Meredith's words drew him out of his thoughts. "See, this is why I don't want to deal with owning a dog. I hate cleaning up messes."

Duke had indeed messed on the protective paper covering the kitchen floor.

"I'll take care of that if you want to put him outside." Major tore the paper in a large square around the little pile, pulled the corners up, and carried it out to the Dumpster in the driveway.

Meredith's attitude about the responsibility of having a puppy niggled him. If she felt so strongly about something as simple as dog poo, how was she ever going to be able to cope with Ma?

Chapter 25

"She said it would be seven o'clock before she'd be able to get here." Ward leaned against the edge of the island.

Major finished emptying the grocery bags. "That's perfect. She doesn't suspect anything even with me here filming today?"

"Just that there's something wrong with the house." Ward crossed his arms and glared at Nelson. The unflappable cameraman continued placing lights around the freshly painted, stained, and polished kitchen.

Pricilla came in with more equipment cases. "I can see why you wanted to film here, Major. Sorry we had to put it off a day."

He introduced her to Ward. "He's the man responsible for all this." Major turned, his hands held out in front of him. "In fact, one of the caveats Meredith gave for allowing us to film here today was to make sure that Ward gets recognition for creating this kitchen. So I'd like to open with a little bit of me talking to him."

"Whoa—you never said anything about me being on camera."

"Think of the free publicity," Major said in a low voice.

Pricilla shrugged. "No problem. The rest of your script is staying the same though, right?"

If one could call the rough outline of what he was going to say a script. "Yes. Want to go over your notes on it?"

He spent the next fifteen minutes going over the plan for the day's filming while Charla did his makeup and Nelson tested the lighting. Once they finished those tasks, Major rehearsed the blocking of his movements around the unfamiliar space, using Nelson's guidance to choose where to place the pans, dishes, utensils, and small appliances he'd brought from home and the executive kitchen.

Major spent the first few minutes of filming talking to Ward about the features of Meredith's kitchen and things homeowners could do to increase the efficiency of their cooking and food-prep spaces. When they finished, Major shook hands with his former rival and invited him to stay and watch, but Ward excused himself, promising to return later.

Nelson did some close-ups of different areas of the kitchen while Major set out his mise en place, carefully arranging all of the utensils, dishes, and food items he would need in the order he would use them.

"Ready?" Pricilla asked from behind the stationary camera diagonally across the island from him. This would be a little harder than usual, since the stove was over to his right instead of behind him, as in the executive kitchen—or in the island, as at Alaine's place. But it would work.

"Ready."

Pricilla gave the take number then pointed at Major to start.

"I'm Chef Major O'Hara, executive chef for Boudreaux-Guidry Enterprises' catering division. Today we're going to be making braised beef short ribs; cheesy potato casserole; sautéed broccoli rabe with lemon and garlic; and for dessert, an easy, rich, flourless chocolate cake."

He got started cooking. Every time he looked into the camera lens, he got a little tickle in his stomach, imagining Meredith on the other side instead of Pricilla. In just a few hours, Meredith would be here, eating the food he was cooking.

At three o'clock, Major designed the presentation plate for Nelson to shoot.

"You were really on a roll today." Pricilla started wrapping up cords.

"It seems to be getting easier every week."

"Let the homeowner know that we're grateful for the chance to film here—and that I'm jealous over this house."

"I'll be sure to tell her." He pitched in and helped break down the equipment and load it in the van. Even though he could use some of what he cooked for the segment, he had quite a bit of work to do before he could run out to see Ma and still get back in time to surprise Meredith.

He grabbed his phone and called Ma's direct line.

"Yes?"

"It's me, Ma."

"Why are you calling? You're coming tonight, aren't you?" A tinge of panic laced his mother's voice.

"I'm coming early for my visit tonight. I should be there around five o'clock." That should give him enough time to do a quick clean of her room and let her tell him everything that had happened to her since Sunday.

"Oh. Okay. But you'll have to leave by six, because that's when we have dinner."

He'd have plenty of time to get back here and sauté a fresh batch of the broccoli rabe, put last minute touches on everything else, and change clothes before Meredith arrived. "I'll see you in a little while, Ma. And I'll be sure to leave by six."

" 'Kay. Bye." She hung up.

He dialed Ward's number.

"Is the coast clear?" Ward said by way of greeting.

"Yeah. Did you get the table and chairs?"

"I did. I'm headed that way with them now."

"Thanks. See you in a few, then." He closed the phone and turned his attention to the romantic dinner for Meredith. He marveled at the irony that in the short span of two weeks, Ward Breaux had gone from enemy to Major's greatest ally.

Twenty minutes later, he slid the pan of hash-brown casserole back into the smaller warming oven to reheat. Tires crunched on the gravel drive. After a moment's panic that Meredith had come early, Major went out to help Ward carry in the table Major had found at a secondhand furniture shop. If she protested his buying it for her, he'd insist it was a housewarming gift, especially since he'd overheard her telling Corie how much she wanted to find a drop-leaf table to put on the newly screened-in back porch.

Major pulled out the tablecloth, candles, and flowers he'd brought. Ward returned with the two chairs.

"You're sure you don't mind staying while I run a last-minute errand?" Major placed the matchbook on the table so he could light the candles as soon as Meredith drove up.

"So long as I don't have to do anything with the food." Ward glanced nervously over his shoulder at the kitchen.

"Nope. Everything's either warming or chilling or braising, so it's good to go until I get back to finish it off. I should only be gone about an hour. Hopefully, she won't come early."

The morning's slight drizzle had turned into a steady rain. He hoped it wouldn't cause any problems. The last thing he needed was to get stuck in a traffic jam trying to get back before Meredith arrived.

Meredith groaned when the radio DJ announced that traffic in midtown was still in a snarl because of a major accident at University Avenue and Spring Street—the most direct route to get to the house from the office. She picked up her phone and quick-dialed Ward's number.

"Hey, pretty girl."

She laughed at his continued use of the endearment. "Hey, yourself. I'm calling to let you know that it looks like it may be seven fifteen or later before I can get there. Traffic through town is bad, so I'm going to have to go around the long way."

"Not a problem. Drive carefully."

"I will. See you in a bit." She ended the call and set the phone in the closest cup holder. She made a U-turn to head north instead of south out of downtown.

But even the winding country roads that led to the back entrance to Plantation Grove were packed with cars barely crawling along. She breathed a huge sigh of relief when she turned into the subdivision and traffic instantly thinned out.

Tension ebbed from her shoulders at the warm, beckoning light shining through the front windows of her house. Almost thirty minutes late, she hoped whatever it was that Ward needed to show her wouldn't take very long.

Pulling her jacket over her head, she dashed up the sidewalk to the front porch. The beveled glass in the top of the door glittered and sent glittering rainbows across the porch and floor when it swung open.

The heavenly aroma of food greeted her. She drew in a deep breath and sighed—then laughed. Best not get used to the smell of food cooking in this house. At least, not in the near future. But maybe someday. . .

She nipped that thought in the bud. Until Major told her everything about himself—about his family—she'd promised herself she wouldn't let their relationship progress past its current stage.

He was supposed to have finished filming several hours ago—so why did it smell like the food was cooking now?

She followed the scent toward the back of the house—and stopped just inside the dining room door. A table with flowers and unlit candles as a centerpiece, formally set for a meal, sat in the middle of the large room. Her heart jumped. Could this be for her? Or something left over from the TV segment?

A noise in the kitchen motivated her to move. "Hello?"

Ward appeared in the doorway to the kitchen.

Her heart dropped. Had he changed his mind? Was this an attempt to win her back?

"Hi, Meredith."

"What. . .what is all this?" She stopped at the table and gripped the spindle back of a chair.

"Uh. . .well, you know that Major was over here today, shooting his TV show. You see, it's like this: He wanted to surprise you with a romantic dinner, so he asked me to call you to come over tonight."

"Oh." Drat the way her voice went all high and squeaky when she was excited. "Is he in the kitchen?" She started around the table.

"No-o-o." Ward's forehead became a washboard of frown lines. "Truth is, I don't know where he is. The only reason I'm here is because he had to run an errand. He said he'd be back around six, but I haven't heard from him since he left."

Meredith looked at her watch. "It's almost a quarter of eight." She reached for her phone but then remembered it was still in the cup holder in her car.

Ward extended his phone. "Here."

She dialed Major's cell phone number from memory. It rang four times; then his voicemail picked up. She dialed it again. It rang twice, then—

A woman's voice answered. "Hello? Who is this, please?"

Meredith's heart pounded. "Meredith Guidry. I'm looking for Major O'Hara. Have I dialed the wrong number?"

"No, ma'am. Are you a relative of Mr. O'Hara's?"

Her knees buckled. Ward grabbed her shoulders to keep her from falling and pulled out the closest chair for her to sit. "I'm. . ." What was she to him? "I'm his. . .his boss."

"Oh. I'm Alison Rihsab, a nurse in the emergency room at University Hospital. We couldn't find any emergency contact information on Mr. O'Hara."

Meredith's head spun, and she doubled over to keep from passing out. "Emergency room? What happened?"

"He was in a car accident."

"How bad is it?"

"I'm sorry, I can't give that information over the phone. Do you have any contact information for an emergency contact for him?"

"I'm his emergency contact, and I'll be there as soon as I can get there." She ended the call and tried to jump up from the chair, but

Ward wouldn't let her.

"Slow down. Tell me what happened."

She repeated what the nurse had told her. "So I have to go. I don't think he has anyone else to be with him."

"Fine. But you're not driving in this condition unless you want to end up in the hospital bed right next to him." He held out his hand. "Give me your keys. You're parked behind me, so it'll be faster to take your truck than mine."

She dropped her keys into his large palm.

"Now, you just sit here and take some deep breaths while I do something about that food."

Meredith's head started spinning again, so she leaned over, arms wrapped around her stomach. "Oh, Lord, let him be okay. Let him be okay. I can't lose him now." She repeated the words like a mantra until she started feeling calmer.

After a lot of clanking and clattering, Ward reappeared. "Come on. Let's go."

"I think I'm okay to drive."

"Are you sure?"

"I'll probably be out there most of the night—you know how slow things move in the ER. I don't want you tied up out there with me when you don't have to be."

"Do you want me to follow you out there, just to make sure you get there okay?"

She reached over and squeezed his hand. "Thanks for the offer, but really, I promise I'll drive carefully."

He handed the keys back to her. "You call me when you get there and find out what happened, okay? No matter how late it is."

"I will."

"And be sure to let me know if there's anything I can do." He walked her to the front door.

"Just pray."

"I already am."

Meredith ran to her SUV and was about to punch the accelerator to get to the hospital as fast as she could—then remembered where she was going and why. No point in getting into an accident herself by speeding on the wet roads. With both hands in a death grip around the steering wheel, she headed for the sprawling medical park that surrounded the largest hospital in town.

She prayed the entire way, never getting beyond *Please let him be okay*.

Trying to figure out where to park to get to the emergency room frustrated her almost to the point of tears. She eventually found the designated lot and pulled into a space, not caring that her right wheels were over the line.

Her heels tapped on the tile floor in a quick staccato as she half walked, half jogged to the information desk.

"May I help you?" the woman behind the glass asked.

"Yes. I'm here for Major O'Hara. He was in a car accident. I talked to a nurse—" Oh, what had her name been? "Amanda or Abigail or. . .Alison! I talked to Nurse Alison, who answered his phone when I called it."

"And your name is?"

"Meredith Guidry."

"Please have a seat, Ms. Guidry."

"But—"

The woman slid the glass closed.

Defeated by worry, Meredith perched on the edge of the nearest chair and dug in her purse for a piece of gum or candy or something. She found a peppermint that had been in there forever and put it in her mouth, tapping her back teeth on its hard surface.

The sitcom on the TV hanging off the wall twenty feet away ended, and another show started. Meredith couldn't sit still any longer. So she paced.

Surely after so many years and so much time wasted, God wouldn't take Major away from her like this.

Chapter 26

Major tried to concentrate on what was going on around him, but the shot they'd given him in the ambulance made his stomach woozy and his head feel like it was stuffed with cabbage. He couldn't move. They had him strapped to a board.

But he needed to get to Ma. She would be frantic when he didn't show up at the time he said he would. She'd have an episode—and she'd caused so much trouble recently that it might be the last straw. He didn't want to have to find another place for her to live.

"I need my phone." He watched as they put another shot of something into his IV.

"Mr. O'Hara, we need to get X-rays of your neck and spine. If those come out okay, we'll unstrap you from the board. Is there someone we can call for you?"

"My mother—she's at Beausoleil Pointe Center. She's expecting me. But if I don't come—I think I'm going to throw up."

The medical staff scrambled to turn him onto his side and stuck a plastic tray under the side of his face. After a few long seconds, the wave of nausea abated.

"I'm okay now." But he wasn't really. His vision started going dark around the edges. Maybe if he just closed his eyes for a minute, everything would be okay when he opened them again.

Painful pressure on his chest woke him.

"Mr. O'Hara, don't go to sleep on us now."

"Won't." But the drifting feeling tempted him, because to follow it meant he didn't have to experience the reality of the severe pain in his left leg or the sharp stabbing in his left side every time he breathed.

"Mr. O'Hara, there's a Meredith Guidry here to see you."

"Meredith? Where?"

"Is it okay if she comes back? She said she's your emergency contact."

"Yes." He closed his eyes. He answered yes or no to the nurses' questions about his medical history. They finally removed the neck brace and back board.

"Major?"

He opened his eyes to the most beautiful sight he'd ever beheld. "Meredith. I love you. Will you marry me?"

Tears dripped from her eyes. "I think that's something we should probably talk about sometime when you aren't doped up on morphine."

"Okay. I need to get out of here. I've got to go—get to Ma." Strong hands pressed his shoulders back against the bed.

"You just need to stay here and let them fix you up." Meredith's fingers grazed his forehead, pushing his hair back.

"We need to take him up to get an MRI on his leg before surgery." A nurse appeared beside Meredith with a plastic bag. "These are his personal effects—his clothes, shoes, wallet, phone... everything he had on him."

"Surgery?"

"For the compound fracture in his leg. I'll take you upstairs to the waiting room near where they'll be doing the procedure."

"Thank you."

Major heard a familiar sounding tune. Ma's song. It was his phone. Ma was calling. But the sound grew fainter, and the ceiling tiles whizzing by overhead were making him sick to his stomach again.

Meredith wiped the moisture from her face and followed Alison to a different set of elevators than the ones they'd taken Major away in.

"The pain killers they gave him were making him say things that he probably didn't mean," Alison said.

"You mean when he asked me to marry him?"

The nurse nodded.

"I told you I'm his boss, but we're also sort of dating."

"Oh, so he might have meant it, then." The elevator doors opened, and Alison motioned Meredith to follow her.

Major's phone started to ring again with that peculiar ringtone she'd noticed on other occasions.

"Whoever that is has called a couple of times already. Once we talked to you as his emergency contact, we didn't want to answer it."

Before Meredith could dig the phone out of the bottom of the big plastic bag, it stopped. "Well, if they call back, I'll answer it, just in case it's something important."

They stopped at the nurses' station for the surgical unit, and Meredith gave them her name and cell phone number.

"You realize he's going to be in pre-op and surgery for a few hours, right?" the nurse asked when Meredith told her she planned on staying around.

"Someone needs to be here for him, and as far as I know, I'm the only someone he's got." Pressure built in her throat. Even though she'd seen him with her own eyes and Alison had assured her he'd be okay, fear laid claim to her soul. Something could still go wrong.

"All right. But it'll be a long evening. If you'd like, the cafeteria is down on the second floor. They serve dinner until nine o'clock, and the coffee shop is open all night."

The heavy plastic bag started digging into Meredith's fingers. "I think I'll go put his stuff in my car—oh, I'm parked in the ER visitor lot. Should I move it to another parking area?"

"Your car should be fine where it is." Alison touched Meredith's arm. "I'll be praying for your. . .friend."

"Thank you." Meredith briefly pressed her hand on top of Alison's.

"I'll take you back down to the ER—that'll be the easiest way to get to your car."

Meredith did her best to pay attention to their route so she could find her way back through the labyrinthine building when she came back. Alison showed her where to go from the emergency room lobby to get back upstairs. Meredith thanked her again then stepped out into the chill March air.

Only when Major's phone started ringing again did Meredith remember to dig it out of the bottom of the bag.

BPC flashed on the screen. It took her a couple of tries to find the correct button to answer. "Hello?"

A slight rustling came over the line then a click and dead air.

"Hmm." Meredith looked at the screen again. CALL ENDED. Well, that was odd.

She'd just gotten onto the elevator when the phone rang again. "Hello? This is Meredith Guidry answering for Major O'Hara."

A slight pause. Then, "Major—I need to talk to him." The voice was low and hoarse enough that Meredith couldn't tell if it was male or female.

"He can't come to the phone right now."

"I need to talk to him." Urgency made the voice sound female.

"I understand, but he's. . .he's been in a car accident, and the doctors are looking at him right now. Is this—are you his mother?"

Dead air was the only response she received. She looked at the screen, but the call timer kept ticking the seconds away. They hadn't been disconnected.

"Hello?"

Nothing.

She kept the phone to her ear and made her way down a myriad of corridors until she found the correct surgical waiting room.

"Hello? Are you still there?"

Silence came back to her.

After another few minutes, she tried again, but to no avail. She disconnected and stared at the screen a moment. What did *BPC* mean? She scrolled through his contacts to find it. Taking a deep breath, not knowing who would answer, she hit SEND.

The line rang twice, then a click. "Hello. You have reached the main switchboard at Beausoleil Pointe Center. Our hours of operation are 7:00 a.m. to 6:00 p.m. If you know your party's extension, please dial it at any time. If this is an emergency, press 6 to page the on-call physician."

Meredith hung up. On-call physician? What was this place?

She went back into his contacts list and scrolled down to the *Ms*. She got a slight smile seeing her name with all of her contact phone numbers listed, but kept scrolling. No *Mom* or *Mother* listed. Closing the phone, she sighed. She'd just have to wait for the woman to call back.

She flipped through a couple of old magazines, called her parents, tried to watch the news program on the overhead TV, called Forbes, paced, sat, called Ward, paced some more, and prayed—prayed hard. The more time dragged on, the more frustrated and worried she became.

"Ms. Guidry?"

She practically ran to the nurses' station. "Yes?"

A male nurse dressed in green scrubs leaned against the counter. "Mr. O'Hara is in the pre-op area. The doctor said you can go back and see him for a minute if you'd like."

"Definitely."

He spotted the cell phone in her hand. "You'll have to turn that off. You can't use it back there anyway."

"Okay." She pressed and held the END button, hoping it worked just like hers. Blessedly, it did, and she dropped it into her jacket pocket. Flipping her phone open, she did the same to it.

Major was the only patient in the pre-op area. Her breath caught. The entire left side of his face looked bruised, with tiny cuts across his forehead, cheek, and jaw. His broken leg, the sight of which had nearly made her ill downstairs, was covered with a sheet.

The anesthesiologist who hovered near the head of the bed introduced himself. "I thought I'd wait until you had a chance to talk to him before I gave him the sedative."

"I appreciate it." She approached the other side of the gurney. "Major?"

His eyelids raised to half-mast to reveal glazed eyes. He blinked a couple of times, and his gaze became a little clearer. "Meredith." He reached toward her.

She grabbed his hand with both of hers. "It'll be okay."

"Will you pray for me?"

"Of course. I have been praying for you." She lifted his hand and pressed it to her cheek.

"I mean right now."

"Miss, I really need to administer this." The anesthesiologist raised a hypodermic needle.

"Major, I'll pray for you while the doctor gives you the sedative." She looked up at the anesthesiologist. At his nod, she leaned closer to Major, keeping one hand wrapped around his and resting the other on top of his head.

"Lord God, I bow before You right now so thankful that You chose to spare Major's life. Father, I pray for the doctors and nurses who will be performing the surgery. Steady their hands, give them strength and wisdom and clarity of mind. And I pray especially for Major, someone I know is precious in Your sight. Watch over him and protect him while he's in surgery, and then we ask for a quick recovery afterward. Amen."

"Amen," the nurse who'd brought her in repeated.

Major grunted, and his head lolled to the side.

The anesthesiologist removed the needle from the port on Major's IV. "It works pretty quickly."

"It's time, Ms. Guidry. We have to take him to surgery now."

She nodded, fighting more tears. Placing her hands on Major's cheeks, she turned his head until he looked at her. "I love you, Major O'Hara, and I'm not giving you up without a fight."

"Love you." Slurred though his words were, they still sounded sweet to Meredith.

She followed them out into the hall, but they went the opposite direction from the door that would lead her back to the waiting area. After standing in the middle of the corridor for a few long moments after they disappeared, Meredith returned to what she was quickly coming to think of as *her* chair.

But she couldn't just sit here all night. Maybe she should go down and get something to eat. The memory of the heavenly aroma of the meal Major had cooked for her in her new house brought the tightness back to her throat, but she ignored it. There would be other romantic dinners in that house.

She let the nurse know where she was going—just in case—and took the elevators down three floors. She took a few wrong turns but eventually found the large cafeteria.

The puppy!

Someone needed to go over to her apartment and let him out—and probably hose down the bathroom. She pulled out her phone—and remembered that she hadn't turned either hers or Major's back on, which she quickly rectified.

She started to call Forbes, but her dear older brother didn't really do well with pets and their messes. She called Rafe instead, but he'd just flown back in and would be at the airport filling out paperwork for a while. So she called her brother Kevin, who was only too glad to help her out.

No sooner did she hang up with him than Major's phone started ringing again. At last, she might finally get to the bottom of the mystery calls.

"Hello?"

"This is Gideon Thibodeaux from Beausoleil Pointe Center. With whom am I speaking?"

Hearing a strong male voice when she'd expected the weak one of the previous call, took her by surprise. "Meredith Guidry."

"Ms. Guidry, I am trying to get in touch with Major O'Hara."

She stepped out of the traffic pattern, though there were few enough people trying to get to the buffet of food. "Mr. Thibodeaux, Major has been in a car accident. He just went into surgery. Is there something I can do?"

"Are you a relative?"

"No. I don't think he has any relatives. Except his mother."

"It's his mother I'm calling about."

Meredith staggered into the closest chair. "His mother?"

"She's having an episode. We don't want to sedate her, but the other residents are starting to get agitated. We need someone to come out and try to calm her down so that we don't have to take extreme measures."

Mouth completely dry, Meredith worked her tongue back and forth to try to form words. "An episode?"

"Yes. We are an assisted-living facility for the psychologically challenged, not a psychiatric hospital. If no one can come and manage her, get her to calm down, we may have to call the state mental hospital and get them to come take her."

Meredith shivered. Was this the kind of call Major had gotten the night of the banquet? No wonder he'd dropped everything.

"I'll come. But I need directions how to get there." Digging a pen out of her purse, she grabbed a napkin from the dispenser on the table and wrote down what the director told her.

She dashed back upstairs to leave word at the nurses' station that she would be leaving the hospital for a while, then out to her car.

The facility lay outside the city on the north side of town. In daylight, it must be lovely. But at night in the rain, the winding drive from the main road kept Meredith's foot hovering over the brake pedal so she didn't accidentally miss a sharp curve and drive off the road.

Finally, the lane widened into an almost empty parking lot, with the hulking, shadowy mass of a large building beyond. Leaving everything but her own cell phone in the car, she ran in through the rain. Mr. Thibodeaux had said to head up to the second floor and follow the main corridor.

She jogged up the stairs and hurried down the wide central hall, the sounds of a major commotion spurring her on. The hall ended at a large room furnished with many cushy-looking sofas and chairs, game tables, and a couple of entertainment centers with big TVs. But rather than enjoying all that, about a dozen people stood in a semi-circle while a woman with thin white hair paced, yelling and crying.

Meredith watched, dumbfounded. The woman screamed if anyone got within five feet of her. She banged her fists against her temples, muttering to herself, shouting occasional random words.

Could this be Major's mother?

"Are you Ms. Guidry?" A tall, middle-aged man in a suit approached Meredith.

"I am. Is that. . .is that Mrs. O'Hara?"

"Gideon Thibodeaux. Do you see why we needed you to come?"

She nodded then shook her head. "I don't know what I'm going to be able to do to help if no one else can get close to her."

"You have to try. It's not good for her to be in a state like this."

"Do you know what triggered it?" Focusing on Mrs. O'Hara, Meredith wracked her brain to come up with something, anything, she could do to help Major's mother.

"She was upset that her son hadn't shown up to see her when he said he'd be here at a certain time. Then she started acting like this. I can only assume the hospital found her phone number in Mr. O'Hara's personal effects and called her and revealed he'd been injured."

Stomach sinking, Meredith looked at Mr. Thibodeaux again. "Actually, I think that's my fault, then. She called Major's cell phone, and I answered and told her."

"Don't blame yourself. Positive energy is what's needed."

"What should I do?"

"Try talking to her. Sometimes, as with babies, a soothing, steady stream of words can lull them into a calmer state of mind."

Right. Just like that. "What should I talk about?"

"See if you can recognize anything she's saying. Get her to focus on one thing and talk to her about it—ask her questions, tell a story together, whatever it takes."

Hands and heart trembling, Meredith took a deep breath. She'd created this mess; she had to fix it. "I'll do what I can."

Chapter 27

Meredith made her way through the people standing around Major's mother until she stood in the neutral zone between them. With a closer view of the woman, Meredith revised her idea of how old she was—her white hair and the gauntness of her face had aged her prematurely. She might be younger than Meredith's own mother.

"Mrs. O'Hara?"

Major's mom didn't stop pacing or muttering.

"Mrs. O'Hara, I'm Meredith. I'm a friend of Major's."

Mrs. O'Hara raised her voice, and Meredith caught the words, "Asked her why. . ." before the muttering became incoherent again.

"Who did you ask, Mrs. O'Hara?"

"Custer is dead."

Meredith shook her head, not sure if she'd heard the woman correctly. "Custer—General Custer? Yes, he's been dead a long time."

"Two hundred twelve officers of men. . ."

"Mrs. O'Hara, I don't understand what you mean. Are you talking about Custer's last stand at Little Big Horn?" Meredith took a cautious step forward.

"No—don't come closer. Where's Major? I want my son! I'll leave here and go find him myself." As suddenly as she started screaming, she stopped and returned to muttering. " 'Ten thousand Indians under

Sitting Bull and Crazy Horse. . .uniting in a common war against the United States Cavalry.' No one understands. No one knows. Where's my son?"

Meredith moved closer. "Wait—Mrs. O'Hara, what were you saying about Sitting Bull and Crazy Horse? I've heard that before." She stilled when Mrs. O'Hara turned and looked directly at her.

" 'The Sioux and Cheyenne are on the warpath.' "

"I'm going to call the state mental hospital." Meredith hadn't noticed the director coming up behind her. "She's making no sense at all."

"No!" Mrs. O'Hara's arm whipped out, and her bony fingers wrapped around Meredith's wrist. "Don't let them take me away. They can't take me away from Danny. They took him away from me before and put me in the loony bin, and they can't do that to me again. Where's my son? Take me to my son."

Before Meredith could respond, Mrs. O'Hara collapsed on the floor and began wailing, yelling Major's name over and over.

Meredith turned to Mr. Thibodeaux. "Don't call yet. I think I know what she was talking about." She knelt on the floor by the rocking, keening woman. "Mrs. O'Hara, were you quoting lines from *She Wore a Yellow Ribbon*?"

" 'Round her neck she wore a yellow ribbon. . . .' " Mrs. O'Hara sang.

Tears of relief sprang to Meredith eyes. She gingerly rested her hands on the distraught woman's shoulders and sang the next line of the song.

" 'When I asked her why. . .when I asked her. . .' " Mrs. O'Hara looked up at Meredith through the fingers she held over her face.

Meredith continued singing. When she got to the chorus, Mrs. O'Hara repeated "cavalry" along with her each time she sang it. Meredith moved from kneeling to sit beside Major's mother and put her arm around the woman's shoulders.

After what must have been at least ten minutes of singing the movie's short theme song over and over and over, Meredith felt Mrs.

O'Hara's taught muscles suddenly relax. She leaned into Meredith's side.

Without the ranting and screaming to entertain them, most of the people who'd been standing around this whole time dispersed.

" 'M tired. Want to go back to my room now."

Meredith helped her to her feet. "I'll go with you to your room."

Major's mother looked at Meredith as if she hadn't seen her before. "Mary Kate?"

"No. I'm Meredith."

"Meredith—Mary Kate." She grasped Meredith's arm. "Come back to my apartment, Mary Kate."

Meredith corrected her twice more but then gave up and answered to Mary Kate, letting Mrs. O'Hara lead her down a couple of halls until they stopped at room number 267.

Mrs. O'Hara pointed to the number. "Twenty-six seven. John Wayne was born on May 26, 1907."

"Was he?" Meredith figured the easiest thing to do right now was just humor her until she was certain the woman would stay calm.

"Such a sad day when he died. Danny was just a little boy."

"Danny? Is that Major's brother?" Perhaps pumping Mrs. O'Hara for information on Major's family wasn't the most honorable thing to do, but she never could get it out of him.

"No. Danny is Major. Major Daniel Kirby Xavier. . .Major Xavier Kirby. . ." Mrs. O'Hara frowned and looked like she was building up again.

"Major Daniel Xavier Kirby O'Hara."

"You know Danny?"

Meredith's forearms were going to be bruised where Mrs. O'Hara kept grabbing her. "I work with Major. I've known him a long time."

"Come on, Mary Kate, I want to show you my apartment." Mrs. O'Hara shoved the door open.

As soon as Meredith entered the room, she finally understood where the seemingly random references to John Wayne stemmed from. Framed movie posters lined the walls of the small studio apartment—*Stagecoach* and *Fort Apache* and *Sands of Iwo Jima* and *Flying Leathernecks*.

But Mrs. O'Hara crossed into the bedroom and pointed to one hanging over her vanity table.

"Mary Kate." She pointed at the poster.

"Of course." Meredith took in the illustrated image of John Wayne with Maureen O'Hara in his arms. "*The Quiet Man*. Maureen O'Hara played Mary Kate Danaher."

"You look like her." She grabbed Meredith's sore arm again and took her around to look at each of the posters.

Finally, Major's mother collapsed into the plush recliner in the small sitting area, which included a TV, DVD player, and a rack full of what looked like just about every movie John Wayne had ever been in.

"Take me to see Danny."

The sadness in his mother's voice broke Meredith's heart. "I'll have to ask Mr. Thibodeaux if I can take you. But Major's going to need to sleep for a long time after he comes out of surgery."

"I want to see him." Large tears dripped from Mrs. O'Hara's faded blue eyes.

"I understand. Let me go ask." She glanced around the apartment. Would Mrs. O'Hara stay here quietly if Meredith left to track down the director? "Do you want me to put a movie on for you?"

Mrs. O'Hara nodded.

"How about *She Wore a Yellow Ribbon*?" Meredith reached for the case.

"No. *Donovan's Reef*."

"Good choice." Hopefully the comedy would get her into a better frame of mind. Meredith put the disc in, and by the time she turned around, Mrs. O'Hara had a remote control in each hand. "You got this?"

"Yes."

"I'll be back in a few minutes, okay?"

" 'Kay."

"You'll be here waiting for me when I come back?"

"Go."

Startled, Meredith did as bade and left the apartment. She didn't have far to look for the facility's director. He came down the hall toward her.

"Sorry I abandoned you. I had to make sure everyone else was okay." He rubbed his left temple. "You did a great job with her. I can't believe you recognized that she was quoting lines from a movie. I've never even heard of that film."

"It's one of John Wayne's westerns—and one of my favorite movies." Meredith turned to walk back to Mrs. O'Hara's apartment with him. "She asked me to take her over to the hospital to see her son."

He shook his head. "After that episode, it'll be better if she stays here. One of our psychiatrists is on the way here. He'll give her something to help her sleep through the night so she doesn't relapse."

Meredith cringed. "I thought you said you didn't want to give her something to knock her out."

"That would have been different. We would have been giving her a powerful antipsychotic drug. Instead, it'll be a mild sleeping pill along with her other medications. It'll keep her from suffering adverse affects from the episode." He knocked then opened Mrs. O'Hara's door. "Hi, Beverly. May I come in?"

"Where's Mary Kate?" Beverly O'Hara asked without turning away from John Wayne on the small TV screen.

Meredith resigned herself to answering to the character's name. "I'm here, too."

"Okay, you can come in then."

She followed the doctor in and sat on the edge of the loveseat.

"Beverly, I don't think it's a good idea for you to go to the hospital to see your son. You wore yourself out tonight. And he's going to need his rest, too. So it'll probably be better for you to stay here and for your son to come see you when he gets out of the hospital."

Beverly looked at Meredith, worry crinkling the papery skin of her forehead and around her eyes.

"Mrs. O'Hara, I think it's a good idea. I promise I will bring

Major out here to see you as soon as he's released. But just so you know, that may be a couple of days."

Major's mother chewed her thin lips. "But what if I need him before that?"

"How about this?" The director spoke before Meredith could respond. "I'll ask Ms. Guidry to leave her phone number for you—but only if you promise that you won't call her unless it's an emergency. Can you promise to do that, Beverly?"

Her gaze flickered back to the TV—and after a little while, it seemed as if she'd forgotten anyone else was in the room. Meredith looked askance at the director, who shrugged.

"I agree. I'll only call if it's an emergency." Beverly reached into the end table beside her chair and pulled out a marker and a pad of sticky notes. "Major uses these to write down things I need to remember."

Meredith wrote her cell phone number in large, clear numerals and handed the pad back to Beverly. "Mrs. O'Hara, I will call you with an update on Major in the morning."

"Promise?"

"I promise."

All three turned at a knock on the door. A nurse came in with a young man in a white doctor's coat.

"Hi, Mrs. O'Hara. I came to talk to you about what happened earlier." The kid-doctor offered Meredith a nod and smile of acknowledgment before scooting past her to sit on the loveseat.

Meredith stood. "Maybe I should go—"

Whip fast, Beverly grabbed Meredith's arm again.

"Why don't you stay," Dr. Sevellier said.

Meredith extracted her arm then held Beverly's hand loosely in hers and sat down.

For the next half hour, the young psychiatrist managed to impress Meredith with the way he drew information out of Major's mother until the woman was speaking coherently. Finally, Dr. Sevellier stood, had a whispered conversation with the nurse, and moved beside the recliner.

Meredith released Beverly's hand and scooted back in her seat to allow him room.

"The nurse is going to bring your meds. And I'm having her add a sleeping pill so you can get some rest and recover from your ordeal." Dr. Sevellier patted Beverly's shoulder and moved toward the door.

Beverly reached for Meredith's hand again. "They're going to put me to sleep. Don't let them put me to sleep. I want to watch the movie. Don't let them take me away from the movie."

Meredith moved back up to the edge of the sofa so her shoulder wasn't in danger of being pulled out of its socket. "Mrs. O'Hara, would it help if I stay until you fall asleep? We can keep the movie on so you can see it from the bed."

Beverly agreed and took all the pills the nurse brought. The director, doctor, and nurse left. Meredith helped Beverly change into her nightgown and took over the task of brushing the baby-fine white hair when Beverly complained that her arms were too heavy to continue.

"Will you sing it for me?" Beverly stretched out and pulled the covers up to her chin.

"Sing what?"

The older lady yawned. "Yellow ribbon song." Her eyelids drooped.

By the time Meredith made it all the way through the tune, Beverly O'Hara was sound asleep. As quietly as she could, Meredith turned off the lamp on the bedside table and straightened up the room, putting Beverly's clothes into the hamper, wiping the water and dripped toothpaste off the sink in the small bathroom, and turning off the TV and video player, returning the DVD to its case and the case to its original spot on the shelf.

"Cavalry. . ."

Meredith jumped at Beverly's muzzy singsong voice. But Beverly didn't move and didn't say anything else. Meredith released her held breath and let herself out of the apartment, releasing the doorknob a smidgen at a time until the latch softly clicked into place.

The director met her in the lobby and got her contact information, then walked her to the front doors.

"Thank you for coming tonight, Ms. Guidry. I'm certain Beverly and her son appreciate it, as well."

"I'm glad I could help." Meredith shook hands with him then headed out to her car. She sat for a moment, fingers steepled over her nose and mouth. *Lord, what did I just step into the middle of?* And why had Major never told her about his mother? He had a lot of explaining to do.

Awareness dawned at about the same speed it took a watched pot to boil. Major became vaguely aware of odd little sounds that he'd never heard in his condo before. A rhythmic beep. A plastic rustle and slight whoosh of air every time he moved. Though there were times when he woke up sore the morning after a hard workout, breathing had never hurt as much as it did this morning. The back of his right hand was killing him, too.

He opened his eyes, and in the dimness, his surroundings took a minute to resolve. He wasn't at home. He was in a hospital room. And then he remembered—

The car in front of him had slammed on its brakes for no apparent reason. He'd lost control of the Jeep on the wet pavement. Kirby had rolled over a few times. After that, he only remembered bits and snatches. The emergency room. Being told he needed surgery on his leg. And Meredith. . .

The beeping sound increased. When she'd appeared at his side in the emergency room, all he could think of was wanting to make sure she never left him again. He'd said. . .he'd said. . .

His face burned. Though he did want to propose to Meredith *eventually*, hopefully she understood that he'd been under the influence of heavy-duty painkillers.

An insistent buzzing sound caught his ear, followed by rustling from the dark corner of the room.

"Hello?" A whispered voice. "No, Beverly, he's still sleeping.

I promise, I'll call you as soon as he wakes up so you can talk to him. . . . Okay. Bye."

Nausea churned Major's empty stomach. "Meredith?"

"You're awake?" Her figure materialized out of the darkness and came over to the bed.

"Was that—were you just talking to my mother?"

A neutral expression masked her face. "I was. I had to go out to Beausoleil Pointe Center last night because she had an episode when you didn't show up to see her."

He groaned.

"Why didn't you ever tell me about her?"

"How am I supposed to explain her? 'Oh, by the way, I have a crazy mother'?" Anger came to his defense against the tears forming in Meredith's eyes. "I learned a long time ago that if I didn't want people wondering when I was going to lose my mind, I couldn't tell them about Ma."

Meredith was silent for a while. "I'm trying to see this from your point of view, but I can only come up with two explanations of why you basically lied to me about your mother—either you don't trust me, or you're ashamed of her."

He was ashamed all right—of himself. "Mere, you don't understand. . . ."

"Then help me to understand. I've known you, worked beside you, for eight years. *Eight years*. And unless I'm remembering incorrectly, a couple of weeks ago, you told me you love me. Yet the next day, when I tried to ask you about your family again, you shut me down, putting me off once again. Were you ever going to tell me?"

He sighed. This was exactly why he hadn't told her. "Last night, over dinner. I was going to tell you then."

"If you didn't chicken out first."

Her words cut like his sharpest knife. She knew him too well. But he'd been right about her, as well. "All I can say is, I'm sorry. This is exactly why I've been trying to keep away from you, to stop myself from falling in love with you. Because I knew once you found out about her, you wouldn't want to have anything to do with either of us. I mean, you're the one who told me you didn't want to take the time to deal with training a puppy. How would you possibly want to take the time to deal with my schizophrenic mother?"

Meredith stood silent for a long time. The only indication she hadn't turned to a statue was her deep, ragged breathing.

He fought the guilt that tried to drown him over the words that had just come out of his mouth. He'd only lashed out at her because he was angry with himself. But he was doing this for her protection. In the long run, she'd thank him for saving her from his fate.

"I'm sorry you feel that way. I think your mother is a lovely woman who has done the best she can do while fighting a terrible affliction, and she's someone I would be proud to know better." Meredith took a few more gulping breaths.

He couldn't look at her anymore, couldn't bear to see the hurt in her eyes—those beautiful eyes he loved so much. *Never apologize. . . . It's a sign of weakness.* And he had to be strong if he was going to let her walk away.

She cleared her throat, but her voice remained heavy with emotion when she spoke again. "I'll let Mom and Dad know it'll be awhile before you're able to return to work. When you are ready, let me know, and we'll discuss your duties and what you can and can't do until you're on your feet again."

Turning her back on him, she returned to the chair in the corner of the room to gather up her things. "Forbes is planning to come out after work tonight. You should arrange with him about getting a ride home when you're released." She flipped the strap of her briefcase over her shoulder and came back to his bedside.

The words of apology, of begging her forgiveness, of pleading with her to stay, nearly tore his throat asunder. He clenched his teeth together to keep from speaking. He had to let her walk away.

She held his phone out toward him. "Call your mother. She's worried about you."

Chapter 28

Meredith fought fatigue the remainder of the day—and angry tears every time someone stopped by her office to find out how Major was doing. Her only saving grace was the amount of work she needed to do to make sure Easter in the Park and the Easter brunch at Lafitte's Landing went off without a hitch on Sunday.

Around three o'clock, she was startled out of a stupor by a knock. Steven LeBlanc stood in the doorway, a Styrofoam box in his hands.

He cleared his throat. "When I talked to Chef earlier about what I'll need to do for Sunday, he told me I should bring you a boxed lunch this afternoon."

The lump of emotion that she'd fought all day tightened into a fist in her throat. "Thanks." She met him halfway across the office to take the box then waved him toward one of the guest chairs facing her desk. She put the box in the small fridge in her credenza and tried to compose herself before she turned back around.

Taking a deep breath, she clasped her hands on top of the pile of paperwork on her desktop and smiled at Major's second in command. "Where are we since we talked this morning?"

"Jana was able to get all the servers she'll need for the number of RSVPs we have. I got with Orly and arranged for the steam tables to be taken over to Lafitte's. I double-checked with all the food vendors to make sure we're still on track for everything to be delivered tomorrow—to Lafitte's. And the pastry chefs guaranteed me that they have everything they'll need to make the doughnuts and stuff for the event in the park."

"I've also talked with Orly," Meredith noted, "and he's arranged for drivers to transport the food out to the park early Sunday morning. Are there some kitchen porters on the schedule to help with loading and unloading and setup once it all gets there?"

"Yes."

"Thanks for stepping up and handling everything, Steven. I guess it's good practice for when Major leaves to start his restaurant, huh?" Meredith shivered. She might be mad at him right now, but that didn't keep her from wanting to continue working with him.

"But he's not—" Steven shook his head. "He told me he'd turned down your parents' offer to start a restaurant."

Did she need more proof of Major's distrust of her? "Oh. That's interesting." Her phone rang. "I guess that's all. I'll call you if I have any other questions."

She waited to pick up the phone until Steven left. "Facilities and Events. This is Meredith."

"Hey, Mere. It's me."

"Hey, Jenn. What's up?"

"I just heard about Major's accident. Is he okay?"

Meredith ground the heel of her hand into her forehead, trying to will away the dull, throbbing headache. "He had to have surgery on a compound fracture in his left leg last night, and he has a couple of cracked ribs and some bumps and bruises."

"Whoa. Sounds rough. He's still in the hospital?"

"Until tomorrow or Saturday. I'm not sure which."

"I guess you'll be spending your evening out there tonight instead of coming for family dinner?"

She hadn't thought about today's being Thursday. "Actually, I've got a ton of work to do for this weekend, and then I'm going home to crash. I didn't really get any sleep last night."

"Let me know what day Major is released, and I'll send some meals over for him."

"Forbes is going to take care of getting him home from the hospital."

Jenn didn't say anything for a long time. "What's going on?"

"It's—it's private. I can't talk about it." But she needed to talk to someone. Why did Anne have to be gone for ten more days?

"Look, I know I'm just your younger sister, and that you've always chosen to confide in Anne about these things; but I *am* your sister, and I am a grown-up who can keep things confidential."

Before she could think twice, Meredith blurted out everything that had happened yesterday—from the dinner-that-wasn't, to meeting Major's mother, to Major's reaction this morning when he learned she'd discovered his secret.

"I had no idea." Jenn whistled. "It's pretty rotten that he didn't tell you a long time ago."

"It's not rotten. He was just protecting himself, I'm sure." With several hours' distance from their encounter, Meredith's anger began to abate.

"There's protecting yourself, and then there's flat-out lying."

Jenn's vehement defense of her brought Meredith's first real smile of the day. "You know, I've replayed every conversation I've tried to have with him about his family, and he's never actually lied to me. He's always just hedged, changed the subject, or told me part of the truth."

"You're going to stick up for him?"

The image of Major lying there in the hospital bed, bruised, scratched, and utterly distraught brought Meredith around full circle. "I love him, Jenn. Yeah, I'm upset that he didn't trust me enough to tell me the whole truth, but it's something we can work through."

"I still think he's a jerk for not telling you."

"Let me ask you this: Do you tell the guys you date everything about our family when you start dating them?" Meredith picked up a pen and started doodling in the margin of her notepad.

"Are you kidding me? If I told guys I'm one of eight kids, they'd immediately think that all I want is to marry them as fast as I can and start popping out babies." She paused. "Oh. I see what you mean."

"Major said he learned a long time ago not to tell people about his mother, or they thought he might have problems, too. I imagine that some of the people that happened with were women he dated. I've heard that some forms of mental illness are genetic."

"Yeah, that's what I've heard, too. Hold on." A rustling sound followed by tapping came through Jenn's end of the line. "What did you say his mom has? Paranoia?"

"Schizophrenia."

"Hold on." More clicks. "How do you spell that?"

Meredith spelled it for her.

"Okay, this Web site—which shows that it was written by a panel of psychiatrists—says that there's only a 10 percent chance that a child can inherit schizophrenia from a parent with the disease. . . condition." Jenn paused for a long time.

The lull gave Meredith time to think—and to listen to her heart. Her shoulder muscles began to relax; her head stopped throbbing.

"It says here that if someone has schizophrenia, they start having problems by their teens or early twenties. So Major's, like, *way* past the age for you to be worried about him having it."

Meredith laughed. "That was never really a concern for me."

"Just the lying part."

"Right—even though he didn't lie to me." She tapped her pen against her chin. "The truth of the matter is that I love him. I've loved him for a very long time. I'm not going to let something as simple as the fact his mother is. . .a little different from ours, scare me off."

Major looked up from the old copy of *Gourmet* magazine one of the nurses had scrounged up for him. "Hey, Forbes."

Dressed in his expensive suit, Forbes looked every inch the lawyer. "How're you feeling?"

"Better now that most of the anesthesia has worn off."

Forbes shrugged out of his coat and started loosening his tie. "Pain?"

"Some. Actually, my ribs hurt worse than my leg right now. But they tell me that won't last long." Using his arms for leverage, Major pushed himself into a more upright position—and grunted at the pain that wrapped around his chest.

"Have they told you yet when they're going to release you?"

"Tomorrow morning, if all goes well."

Forbes pulled one of the visitor's chairs closer to the bed. "You're going to come stay with me until you're up and about."

"No, I can't—"

"How long have we been friends?" Forbes removed his cufflinks and rolled his sleeves up to mid-forearm.

"Since high school." Major narrowed his eyes, pretty sure he knew where this was going.

"More than twenty years. And in all that time have you ever known me to back down or not do something I say I'm going to do?"

"No. But in all that time have you ever known me to rely on anyone but myself?"

"No, but I've always thought you should every once in a while." Forbes waved his hand dismissively. "Besides, the doctors have already told you that you shouldn't be home alone until you can get along on crutches by yourself, haven't they?"

"Let me guess—you talked to the doctor before you came in here."

"Fraternity brother."

Major rolled his eyes. "Fine. I'll come stay. But you can't make me like it."

Forbes's booming laugh filled the room. "I won't try to make you. Did you ever get in touch with your health insurance company this afternoon?"

Major told him everything he'd managed to do since their earlier phone conversation. "What I want to know is how am I supposed to get the ambulance, emergency room visit, and surgery preapproved? I mean, come on!"

Brows raised, Forbes leaned forward. "Are they refusing coverage?"

"No, I just had to go over the head of the gal who answered the phone and talk to someone who wasn't just reading off a script."

"If you have any more trouble with them, just tell them your lawyer will be calling." He relaxed again.

"I will. Now, I'm tired of wallowing in my own issues. Tell me about an interesting case you're working on or something. I've spent too much time in my own head today."

Forbes obliged. Major zoned out a bit, listening to the ramifications of some statute or other that was keeping Mairee and Lawson from moving forward with getting the area around the old warehouse district declared eminent domain, or something to that effect.

"Your dad told me that the groundbreaking had been pushed back six months. Is that why?" Major readjusted his pillow.

"Yes. Apparently some of the property owners out there are putting up a fight."

"I thought you didn't represent your parents—that everything for B-G was handled by one of the senior partners."

"I don't. But I keep up with everything that's going on—because my folks expect me to know about it. Speaking of, Dad told me you turned down the restaurant deal."

Major told him about his mother's accident the night of the Hearts to HEARTS banquet. "It made me realize that as long as my mother's around, I'll never be free to do something like that."

Forbes crossed his arms, his expression hardening. "Did you ever tell Meredith about your mother?"

And here they were—on the very subject Major had hoped wouldn't come up tonight. But if he was going to be staying with Meredith's brother, he'd have to tell him sooner or later. "I was going to tell her last night. I cooked dinner for her at her house but was running out to the Pointe to see Ma when I got in the accident. Apparently Ma had an episode when I didn't show up. Meredith answered my phone and went out to try to get Ma to calm down."

"I see." Forbes's jaw worked back and forth. "I would imagine she was pretty upset finding out that way."

"I wouldn't be surprised if she doesn't want anything to do with me again."

A flicker of anger twitched Forbes's expression. "Once again, you're underestimating my sister."

"You didn't see how mad she was."

"I don't have to. I know her. . .better than you do."

Anger—at himself, at Meredith, at Forbes, at Ma—boiled in Major's chest. "Look, I appreciate your concern for Meredith. I really do. But this isn't any of your business. It's between me and Meredith and no one else."

"If you had a sister, you'd understand why I can't let this go, why it is my responsibility to make sure she isn't hurt."

"Like it was your responsibility to get George Laurence to lie to Anne for weeks about his real identity?" Sure, it was a low blow, but Major wasn't going to be the only one in this room being accused of not treating someone fairly.

"You don't know anything about what happened. Besides, that's a totally different situation." Forbes raked his fingers through his hair. "I think the real issue here isn't Meredith. It's you."

"What's that supposed to mean?"

"I mean you're a coward." Forbes stood, posture stiff.

Major tried to push himself into a straighter position and ignored the sharp pain in his side. "I beg your pardon?"

"You never told Meredith about your mother because you're a coward—you were afraid that if you told her, she might not love you anymore just because of your mother's condition."

No words came to mind with which Major could defend himself.

"I've known you, watched you, listened to you talk about your mother for more than half our lives. The truth is that you're ashamed of her. You didn't keep her a secret from everyone—especially Meredith—because you were protecting her from them. You kept her a secret because you're embarrassed by her condition, mortified that someone might think that you're the same way she is."

Guilt pelted Major like hot grease splattering from a fryer.

"If that's the way you truly feel, you are not the kind of man I want my sister spending the rest of her life with." Forbes gathered his coat and tie and started toward the door.

Through the overwhelming pressure in his chest, Major caught his breath. "Wait."

Forbes stopped, arms crossed. "Well?"

"You—you're right. I am embarrassed by my mother. I always have been. But you don't understand what it was like growing up with a mom who might throw a tantrum in the middle of Sears with everyone watching. You don't know what it's like to be called out of Algebra class and told that your mother set fire to your apartment and she's being taken to the state mental hospital and you're being put into foster care. You don't know what it's been like to have every woman you've ever dated break up with you as soon as they find out about your mom because they're too scared to listen to the facts and find out that I'm *not* going to be like her."

Forbes came back around the bed and sat down.

"You don't know what it's like to give up everything—football, New York, the restaurant, Meredith—because she's had another breakdown, set another fire, had another episode. I've had to live with that my whole life, have had to deal with it with no help from anyone else for thirty-eight years. And I'm tired of it."

As quickly as his anger had flared, it waned. "But mostly, I'm ashamed of myself."

"Why?"

"Because ever since I moved back here from New York, every time something happens with her, it makes me wish she weren't around." His voice cracked, and he tried to clear the pressure out of his throat. "Can you imagine that? My mother, who raised me by herself, who loves me, who did the best she could. And I wish she didn't exist, because I feel like she's ruining my life."

"How do you think your life would be better if she didn't exist?"

Major closed his eyes and leaned his head back. "I don't know. . . . Maybe I'd still be in New York, executive chef in a high-end restaurant in Manhattan."

"Why did you go to New York in the first place?"

He looked at his friend, wondering if he'd really forgotten. "For culinary school."

Forbes stood up again and began pacing the length of the bed. "What made you decide to go to culinary school?"

"I'd been working in food service since I was fifteen." He now knew what a witness on the stand felt like under Forbes's cross-examination.

"You were fifteen?" Forbes paused and raised his brows.

"Yes—you know this already."

"What happened when you were fifteen that led you to taking a job in a kitchen?" The attorney resumed pacing.

"I—" Major clamped his mouth shut.

Forbes stopped and turned to look at him again, his gaze piercing.

Frustration pushed out a big sigh. "The foster family I was placed with when Ma was put into the state institution owned a restaurant, and everyone in the family pitched in."

"But when you went back to living with your mom, you kept working at the restaurant?"

"I needed some kind of stability. Some assurance I could take care of myself." He was starting to see the point of Forbes's probing. He never would have thought of working in a restaurant if he hadn't lived with that foster family for a month. He wouldn't have fallen in love with the industry, wouldn't have gone to work for Maggie Babineaux in her catering business.

"So you admit that it is because of your mother that you entered the food service industry."

"Yes. I'll admit that."

Switching out of lawyer mode, Forbes flopped back into the chair. "And you got to go to college, where you played football until you injured your back, if I recall, not because of your mother."

Okay, yes, he'd used his mother as an excuse as to why he'd had to give up playing. "Yes. I got to do that."

"And you lived in New York for how long?"

"Two years in Hyde Park for culinary school and six years in Manhattan."

"How often did you come back to visit during those eight years?"

Major swallowed hard. "A couple of times—but I was working in restaurants, trying to build my credentials."

"And your mother was doing what during that time?"

This exercise in chastisement was starting to chafe. "Living here alone, doing her best to take care of herself so I could go off and do what I wanted to do."

"How were things going for you in New York?" Forbes looked smugly superior.

"Are you going to make me say it?"

"Yes."

"Fine. I was struggling to make ends meet, living in a rundown apartment with three other guys, working at least two jobs, and making myself sick because I never slept."

"And since you've been back here?"

Major wanted to punch his friend in the face but couldn't reach that far. "I was hired by your parents to be the executive chef and manager of the catering division of Boudreaux-Guidry Enterprises." He crossed his arms—then wished he hadn't when he elbowed his own cracked ribs. "I see what you're getting at. If it hadn't been for my mother, I wouldn't be where I am today."

"Then don't you think it's time you do what the Bible says?"

Wracking his brain, Major couldn't easily come up with whatever Forbes was referencing. "Ask her forgiveness?"

"That's part of it. I'm talking about honoring your mother."

Major nodded. "Tomorrow when we get out of here, I want you to take me to BPC. I've got a lot of years of dishonoring her to make up for."

Chapter 29

"You sure you got it?"

Major glared at his friend but quickly returned his focus to keeping his balance on his right foot while turning to lower himself into the wheelchair.

The wheelchair was bad enough, but not being able to maneuver himself around in it because of his stupid cracked ribs made his embarrassment complete.

Forbes closed the door of the sleek black Jaguar, then pushed Major across the parking lot and in through the sliding glass doors of Beausoleil Pointe Center. Major directed him to the elevators then through the halls to his mother's apartment. Forbes reached to knock on the door, but Major caught his wrist.

"I can knock for myself, thank you very much."

"No need to get tetchy."

"No need to laugh at me." The good mood Major had woken up with at the thought of being released from the hospital hadn't lasted long when he realized how much he *wasn't* going to be able to do for himself for quite some time to come.

"So are you going to knock?" Amusement laced Forbes's voice.

Major glared at him then leaned forward to knock, ignoring the shooting pain the movement caused in his chest and leg.

A few seconds later, the door flew open. "Danny!" Ma put her hands on his cheeks and pulled his head forward to kiss the top of it, bumping his heavily splinted and bandaged leg in the process.

He drew his breath in through clenched teeth. "Careful, Ma."

"We've been waiting for you." She squeezed out the door around him and pushed Forbes away. She grunted with the effort of getting the chair started on the carpet, but once rolling, she had an easier time.

"We?"

"The girls and me. We're having lunch on the terrace. Everyone's been talking about you, and no one wanted to start without you." She stopped at the door to the back stairwell. "Oh. Guess we can't go down that way."

Forbes coughed.

Major glanced over his shoulder, trying to put as much warning in his expression as he could.

"Well, it looks like you're in very capable hands. So, I'll just wait for you to call me when you're ready for me to come back and pick you up, shall I?" Forbes twirled his keys on his index finger.

"Yeah, yeah. *Ooph*, easy there, Ma." Major pressed his hand to his ribs, which had just hit the side of the chair when his mother jerked it around with strength he didn't know she possessed. He glared at Forbes as Ma pushed the wheelchair past him. "I'll call you when I'm ready to go."

Whistling, Forbes waved. "Bye, Mrs. O'Hara. It was good to see you again."

"Uh-huh." Ma didn't turn, just kept pushing Major toward the elevators. The top of Forbes's head hadn't disappeared down the main front staircase before she said, "I don't like him, Danny."

"Forbes? He's my best friend, Ma."

"He's too. . .pretty. He's like Gregory Peck in *Roman Holiday*. You look at him, and you know he's up to no good."

Major laughed. "He's one of the best guys I know. I trust him with my life." Even though he hadn't always trusted him with the whole truth of everything going on in his life.

"Well, don't trust him to throw him."

Now Major was the one who coughed to cover a laugh.

Ma whacked him between the shoulders. "You're not coming down with something are you? You can't be here if you're sick."

"Ow. I'm not sick, Ma."

"You know that most people come out of the hospital sicker than they were when they went in? I saw a program about that on TV. How people pick up all kinds of germs in the hospital when they're suspectable."

"Susceptible."

"You could have picked up meningitis or strep or herpes and not even know it until you keel over and die." She shoved the wheelchair out of the elevator and through the main receiving room.

"Thanks for those cheerful thoughts, Ma." He held his hands out to try to keep his leg from bumping chairs, plants, tables, the corner of the wall as they entered the back hallway. . . . The pain in his ribs to wheel himself around might be worth saving himself the stress of his mother's driving skills.

One of the staffers met them at the door to the flagstone terrace. "You should have called one of us, Mrs. O'Hara. You shouldn't be pushing this by yourself." The young woman took over and pushed Major behind his mother toward one of the farthest-away tables.

He loved being referred to as *this*, as if he were nothing more than a roasted turkey or sack of flour.

Ma's card-playing friends all came over to examine the cuts and bruises on Major's face, to poke at the ACE bandages covering the lower portion of his left leg, and to beg him to lift his T-shirt to show them the wrapping around his chest. Okay. Being called *this* wasn't so bad, comparatively.

The chicken salad on croissants, fruit, and potato salad were a bit cliché for a springtime alfresco meal; but after the bland food at the hospital for the past two days, nothing had tasted better to him in a long time.

After everyone finished eating and dispersed to different activities,

Ma pushed him over to a separate, somewhat secluded area of the patio, partially shaded by a pergola and magnolia trees at three corners. With a fireplace and the privacy the surrounding raised planters gave it from the terrace, he could almost pretend they were at a park instead of an assisted-living facility for the psychologically challenged.

Ma sat at one of the two small tables and fanned herself with a lace hankie. He flashed back to his childhood. For as long as he could remember, she'd always carried a handkerchief instead of disposable tissues. It was more ladylike to use a hankie than a piece of flimsy paper, she'd explained to him when he'd asked about it at age eleven.

"How did you do it all those years?" He manipulated the wheels of the chair until he faced her squarely.

"Do what, Danny?"

"Raise me. Put up with me. Support us. Hold yourself together until I was old enough to take care of both of us." Emotion shredded his voice into hoarse shards.

She shrugged. "I just had to. You were a little boy." She patted her forehead with her fingertips. "I had to think about things because you couldn't do it and because I knew they'd take you away from me. That was the worst time, when they took you away from me." Her eyes filled with tears. "I didn't mean to set the fire, Danny. I didn't mean to."

He stroked her arm until she started to calm down. "I know you didn't. You couldn't help it. Flame has always fascinated you. Like a moth." He grinned. "You can't stay away from it."

"But I was supposed to because you could be hurt in a fire, and I don't want to hurt you."

"Of course not. You've always protected me, Ma. And I've never told you how much that means to me. How much I love you for that."

"Fssh." She waved her hand. "You tell me you love me all the time."

"I may say the words, but I don't always show it. I'm sorry I left you on your own when I went to New York, that I didn't make more of an effort to get back down here and see you."

She pushed wisps of white hair back from her cheek. "You were doing important work. That's what I told all my friends at my jobs I had while you were gone. You were in New York becoming a famous chef. They were all jealous of me because my son was a famous chef in Manhattan and none of their children ever did anything important like that."

"I wasn't famous, Ma. I worked long hours in menial positions so that I could try to get better hours in less menial positions."

Her eyes clearer than he'd seen them in a long time, she patted his hand where it still rested on her arm. "I didn't want you to have to come back here. I wanted you to get out of this town, out of this state. I wanted you to have a better life than what you could have here. I wanted you to go away so you didn't have to watch me become this crazy old lady who drools and doesn't know what she's saying half the time."

He swallowed hard. "You don't drool."

"That's how little you know." She smiled vaguely.

They sat like that for a while, touching but not speaking, the warm spring breeze bringing the scents of early blooming flowers. Major used the time to compose his emotions. If there was one thing that sent his mother over the edge faster than anything, it was to see him in anything but a completely cool and collected state.

"This is a romantic spot, don't you think?" Ma asked.

"It is."

"You should bring her here sometime."

"Who?"

"Mary Kate."

He frowned, digging deep into the recesses of his mind for anyone by that name. "Ma, I don't know anyone called Mary Kate."

"Mary Kate—you know her. Mary Kate." She frowned, her confusion and consternation clear. "Mary Kate—*The Quiet Man*, like the poster."

He shook his head. She must have decided that if he wasn't going to bring a real woman here, she'd set him up with someone from one of the Duke's movies. "I don't think that's possible, Ma."

She shrugged. "She'd come if you asked her."

"I don't think I can ask her."

She patted his hand. "Never mind. I'll ask her."

". . .which leads me to my final point."

Meredith took Pastor Kinnard's words as her cue and slipped out of the back row of folding chairs. The Easter Sunday worship service had gone off without a hitch—she again sent up a prayer of thanks that the forecast rain never materialized. Now for the hard part of her day.

She checked in with Pam to make sure the senior event planner had everything under control to start the Easter egg–related activities immediately after the worship service ended. Mrs. McCord hadn't been too happy when she'd learned Meredith would have to be gone for the beginning of the event, but had changed her tune when Meredith told her of Major's accident and her need to be at Lafitte's to make sure that Easter brunch ran smoothly.

Meredith drove as fast as she dared over to the property just off the college campus but slowed when she reached the drive up to Lafitte's Landing. The azalea bushes lining the road exploded with color—mostly deep fuchsia, but some white and some pale pink—which made springtime in Louisiana her favorite season of all. Though when the crepe myrtle trees that shared the sides of the road with the azaleas were in bloom in the late summer and early fall, they were pretty spectacular, too.

Under the tachometer, the SUV's clock showed 10:30 a.m. when Meredith pulled into a space in the shade of one of the heavy-limbed oak trees surrounding the parking lot. Half an hour until they would begin seating guests. Hopefully by eleven thirty, she'd be able to leave and go back to the park to check on activities there. With Major unable to work and Lori on vacation for the holiday weekend, Meredith's supervisory responsibilities had increased tenfold, but she thrived on it. She just needed to keep telling herself that.

The porters and facilities staff greeted her when she walked into the cool interior of the converted and expanded antebellum mansion.

"Everything looks wonderful, y'all. Keep up the good work," she called, crossing the ballroom to the kitchen in the back.

As she'd hoped, she was greeted by a dull roar of activity in the large room.

"Civilian in the kitchen." The line cook greeted her even as he announced her presence.

"Oh, good. You're here." For the first time since he'd worked for B-G, Steven's appearance betrayed his stress—his cheeks red, his jacket damp with sweat, his usually spiked hair limp and lifeless.

"What's wrong?" Meredith dropped her keys and phone into her suit coat pocket, then stripped the jacket off and stepped into the staff room to lay it over the back of a chair.

"Nothing's wrong. I just wanted to go over everything with you to make sure it meets with your approval." He brushed past her into the room to where several large sheets of paper were spread out on a battered table. "Here's my diagram of where I want to put everything on the steam tables and buffet tables."

Meredith ducked her head down to look at the sketches to hide her amusement from the overeager young chef. And just so she didn't appear to be humoring him, she asked him questions about his decision to place the trays of sausage patties and bacon before the eggs, and if he had made labels for the two different types of quiche listed.

"I asked someone to do that. I'll check to make sure it got done."

"Great. Everything looks fine to me. You've done a good job taking over and making sure this stayed organized and on schedule. I'll be writing an official commendation for your personnel file."

He grinned at her. "Thanks!" He swept up his diagrams and swaggered out of the room.

Though still sticky and hot from the early spring heat wave outside, Meredith put her jacket back on before guests began arriving. Even though the sleeveless sheath dress looked fine, there was something about bare arms that didn't feel professional to her.

By eleven thirty, everyone who'd RSVP'd and prepaid for the first seating had arrived, been greeted, and were now happily filling their plates at the tables lining the long back wall of the ballroom. Jana handled checking names off the reservations list while Meredith assumed the role of hostess, greeting guests before passing them off to a server to be shown to their tables.

Jana confirmed every name checked off.

Meredith came out of her jacket again. "Let Steven known that I've gone back over to the park and that I'll be back before the one o'clock seating begins. But y'all can call me if you need me before then."

By the time Meredith got back out to the park, Pam had already handled getting the hamburger and hotdog grilling under way, and more than half the crowd looked as if they were almost finished eating.

"Cooking's going a little slower than we expected," Pam said, breathless after scurrying over to greet Meredith as soon as she got out of her car. "But everyone seems to be understanding about it, so long as we keep the activities for the kids going."

Meredith couldn't find anything to do at the park but walk around and talk to VIPs, former clients, and family friends she'd known her whole life. Before she left, she reviewed everything about cleanup with Pam who, as Meredith had with Steven earlier, humored her.

"Enjoy your day off tomorrow," Meredith told Pam and waved at the rest of the staff on her way to the car.

Back at Lafitte's, she went through almost the same routine as before, but this time powwowing with Jana and Steven to see how first service had gone and agreeing to their suggestions for how to make second service run more smoothly.

By two o'clock, tired of making small talk and shaking hands, Meredith leaned against the edge of the old table in the staff room, enjoying a piece of spinach-artichoke quiche, not having eaten anything else all day but a bowl of cereal at four this morning.

"You look like you could use a nap." Steven slung a towel over his shoulder and stopped about five feet from her, hands clasped behind his back.

"I could. And that is exactly what I'm about to go do." Though most of the staff had been off Friday or would be off tomorrow to make up for having to work this weekend, as the boss, Meredith didn't have any such luxury. And with the mayor's dinner to honor the top students from all the high schools coming up in a few weeks, as well as the Spring Debutante Cotillion the first weekend in May, followed by the library fund-raiser and three of the high schools' proms at B-G properties after that, she'd be lucky to get a Saturday off to move before the summer wedding and event season hit full force. Of course, once Mom and Dad approved the new third event planner position and she officially promoted Corie, she might be able to get a little more time for things like Saturdays off and naps on Sunday afternoons.

"I think Jana and I can wrap things up if you'd like to go ahead and get out of here." His eager blue eyes begged her to say yes.

"Since we don't have anything scheduled here before week after next, it's okay if not everything gets done this afternoon. We can always send facilities guys over to finish—put tables and chairs up or bring the steam tables back to downtown—sometime this week when we're not having to pay them double time for working on a holiday."

"We'll take care of it." He reached for her empty plate and coffee mug.

"Call me if—"

"We know. Call you if we need anything." He swept his arm toward the door. "If you please."

"You've been hanging around your boss too much." But she obliged and departed.

No more than five minutes after she drove away, her phone's hands-free earpiece beeped. With a sigh, she pressed the button on the side. "This is Meredith."

“Mary Kate,” came Beverly O’Hara’s singsong voice.

“Hi, Beverly.” She had to laugh. Major’s mom had taken to calling her at the oddest times the past few days—usually when Meredith was at her most stressed and needed a reminder that her life wasn’t nearly as hard as it seemed at the moment. “What’s going on?”

“Can you come today?”

“You want me to come out and visit you today?” She pulled to a stop at a red light. Forbes had told her earlier that Major had spent most of the day yesterday at the center with his mother, and that he’d been pretty drained when Forbes picked him up last night. He must have told Beverly he didn’t plan to come today, and she was bored.

“Yes. For tea. Iced tea. Not hot tea. I don’t like hot tea. Do you know I burned my mouth on hot tea at a restaurant once? Major would never have served it that hot, because he knows that I don’t like hot things.”

Meredith stifled her laughter. Bless Beverly for keeping her entertained this stressful weekend. She wanted to go home and nap, but she wanted to get to know Major’s mom better, too. Still, a shower and a change of clothes were a necessity. “It will probably be around four o’clock before I could get there. Is that okay?”

“Four—today, right?”

“Four today—about two hours from now.”

“ ’Kay. See you at four.”

Chapter 30

Meredith opened her eyes and glanced at the clock—blinked away the bleariness and glanced again.

"Oh, mercy!" She scrambled up from her prone position on the sofa and darted to her bedroom. She'd only meant to close her eyes for a few minutes after her quick shower; she'd never meant to sleep for almost an hour and a half. Now she had less than ten minutes before she was supposed to be at Beausoleil Pointe Center for tea—iced tea—with Beverly.

At her closet, she let her hand rest wistfully for a moment on the stack of folded, soft, much-worn T-shirts—the ones that had been neglected for far too long in recent months. But this wasn't a time to dress down. Beverly deserved more respect than that. Meredith exchanged her comfy robe for her best pair of trouser jeans, a sleeveless wine-colored shell, and a three-quarter sleeve, lightweight brown cardigan.

Lastly, she stepped into brown ballet flats before making a mad dash for the car. "Lord, please don't let her have an episode because I'm fifteen or twenty minutes late."

At 4:05, by the clock in the dashboard, her cell phone rang.

"Hello, Beverly. I am on my way out to see you right now."

"You're still coming?"

Meredith wasn't familiar enough with Beverly yet to know if her tone carried panic or excitement. "I'll be there in about ten minutes."

" 'Kay." The click and silence that followed were apparently the hallmark ending of a phone conversation with Beverly O'Hara.

When she arrived at the center, she had to park at the back end of the parking lot. No doubt most of the residents received regular visits from their families on Sundays. Would she ever become part of Beverly's family?

She shook off the thought. Plenty of time to deal with Major later.

Cool air whooshed out the sliding front doors. Meredith started the stairs two at a time but slowed her pace halfway up when she got winded. She really needed to start exercising again.

She took two wrong turns but eventually found Beverly's room. She knocked. And waited. Odd. She knocked again. No answer.

Returning to the lobby, she approached what looked like a concierge station. The young lady behind the high counter—whose name tag included the initials R.N. after her name—smiled up at her. "May I help you?"

"I'm here to see Beverly O'Hara, but she's not answering her door."

"Is she expecting you?"

Meredith nodded. "I just talked to her on the phone about ten minutes ago."

"You're looking for Beverly?" Another nurse approached the desk.

"Yes. I'm supposed to be having tea with her." Saying it renewed Meredith's amusement at how Beverly had described it.

"I think I saw her go out onto the back terrace. If you go down those stairs there"—she pointed to a door with an illuminated Exit sign over it—"you'll come out right by the back doors."

"Thanks." Meredith entered the stairwell and stopped just beyond the door at the bottom to get her bearings. She was in a hallway that looked very much like the one above, except to her right was a large glass door leading onto a patio.

Two women who looked about Beverly's age stood just inside the door. Meredith smiled at them, and they giggled, putting their heads together and whispering as she passed.

Outside, she slid her sunglasses down from the top of her head and looked around. The large flagstone paved area looked like an outdoor café, and most of the tables were filled with residents and their family members—most still dressed in their Easter Sunday finery.

But she didn't see Beverly anywhere. She was just about to head inside when she heard someone calling, "Excuse me, excuse me, are you Mary Kate?"

"I'm—yes, I'm Mary Kate." At least she hoped in this instance she was.

The elderly lady grinned, showing dentures that looked too big for her mouth. "Come this way. Beverly is waiting for you."

"Oh." Meredith released a relieved breath. "Good."

The woman took Meredith's hand and practically dragged her through the maze of tables and down a little path leading away from the main patio. Behind a large magnolia tree, they came upon a second patio—much smaller, covered with a wood pergola. It had only two tables, at one of which sat Beverly. . .and Major.

Meredith's heart pounded. She hadn't seen or spoken with him since Thursday, that awful morning. She sent up one last prayer that he hadn't really meant most of the hurtful things he'd said to her.

Beverly looked up, and a smile transformed her face from gaunt to angelic. "Mary Kate."

Major whipped his head around. Had Ma truly lost it this time?

But instead of the fictitious Mary Kate Danaher from *The Quiet Man*, Meredith Guidry stood framed by the entrance to the gazebo, looking once again like an exquisite dish of chocolate and strawberries with the way her brown sweater brought out the red tones in her hair. He wished he could stand up, go to her, pull her into his arms, and beg her forgiveness for the way he'd spoken to her the other morning. But he couldn't.

As she came around to greet his mother, Meredith touched his shoulder. Fleeting and light, the contact told him enough. She'd already forgiven him. But he still needed to say the words to her.

"I was just telling Danny yesterday how romantic I thought this place was. He was too scared to ask you to come, so I called you myself."

Heat tweaked Major's cheeks.

"I'm glad you did call, Beverly."

His mother grabbed Meredith's forearm and practically forced her into the chair next to him. "You two wait right there." She skipped away with her friend.

Major stared after her.

"What's wrong?"

"I haven't heard her giggle like that in. . .ever." He summoned his courage to face Meredith again. "Since she met you, she's been happier than I've seen her in more years than I care to remember."

"I think she's a wonderful person."

"She is a wonderful person. And I'm. . ." He swallowed back years of following John Wayne's character's advice. "I'm sorry I never told you about her."

"You were trying to protect her."

"No. I was trying to protect me. I was embarrassed by her, ashamed to admit I have a mother with schizophrenia, scared to see how people reacted to that knowledge."

"You *were* embarrassed?" Hope shone in Meredith's brown eyes.

"Was. Past tense." Rustling noises and women's whispers and giggles caught his ear. "There's just one more thing I need to do to make it right."

Ma and her friend returned carrying plates, with two other women behind them holding glasses of iced tea.

"A romantic spot calls for a romantic meal." Ma's forehead creased. "I had to make due with what I had in my apartment."

The plates went down in front of Major and Meredith. Tuna on wheat with a side of Cheetos and a Twinkie for dessert. He had to clear his throat a couple of times before he trusted himself to speak without bursting out laughing.

"Thanks, Ma. This is wonderful."

"You two lovebirds enjoy this." Ma started to leave with her friends, but Major caught her by the hand before she disappeared.

"Wait. I have something I need to say to you, something Meredith needs to hear me say."

"But this is your romantic dinner, and I'm not supposed to be here."

"It'll just take a minute, Ma. Sit down, please." He waited until she pulled over a chair from the other table and sat beside him.

"Ma, yesterday we talked about how much I love you and how sorry I am that I didn't come home more from New York, remember."

"Of course I remember. I'm not an idiot."

No way was she going to get a rise out of him today. "Well, there's more that I need to say. And that's to ask your forgiveness, Ma. You see, all my life I've been embarrassed to tell anyone about you, to let them know what a wonderful mother I have."

"Danny, I'd be embarrassed by me, too." Ma stroked the side of his face with her dry, papery fingertips.

"You have nothing to be embarrassed about. You are my mother, the only one I have. You've done the best you can to give me a wonderful life—which, I've recently been reminded in a very painful way, is precious to me." He pressed his hand to his cracked ribs. "I don't want to think about how bleak and empty my life would be without you in it. So will you forgive me for being an ungrateful son?"

Ma wrapped her arms around his neck and kissed his cheek. "You are my son, and I'll take you any way I can get you. But before I forgive you, there's something you have to do for me."

"Name it."

"Marry Mary Kate."

Molten lava melted his insides. The volcanic heat flared into his face, but he took a deep breath, disentangled himself from Ma's hug, and managed to turn his wheelchair so that he was parallel with Meredith's chair, facing her.

"I had the perfect romantic menu planned and wanted to do this at a time when I could do it right and get down on one knee." He took both of Meredith's hands in his. "I haven't even gotten you a ring yet."

Moisture filled Meredith's eyes, and her breath seemed shallow. But her smile was all the encouragement he needed.

"Meredith will you—"

"Can't find it. Can't find it. Can't find it." Beverly stood up, her hands flapping around her as if she were beating off bees. "Can't find it."

Major cringed but reminded himself that his mother couldn't help the way she was.

Ma took off toward the building. With a sigh, Major looked at Meredith. "It's always something."

"Should we follow her?" Meredith's fine brows knit together.

"Yes. Do you mind?"

Her frown disappeared into a radiant smile. "Of course not." She pushed him back into the building and all the way to his mother's apartment.

But he didn't see her when they entered. "Ma?"

"Where is it? Can't find it." Around the side of the bed, Ma hunkered down on hands and knees, digging for something under the bed. "Ah." She came back up with a shoe box, removed the lid, and dumped the contents in the middle of the bed.

Fascinated, Major wheeled himself closer.

Ma rummaged through thimbles, paper clips, clothing tags, pennies, and other trinkets—and Major understood. This was her collection. The little things she picked up here and there that, somehow in her mind, connected her to memories and coherency.

Finally, she picked up an item, blew on it, wiped it on her shirttail, and handed it to Major. He looked down at the object in his hand. Love unlike anything he'd felt for her before overwhelmed him.

"Thanks, Ma." He turned the wheelchair around to face

Meredith. "As I was saying. Will you—"

"Not here! You have to do it over the romantic dinner on the patio."

Meredith laughed and wiped her damp cheeks with the back of her hand.

"I guess we need to go back outside then," Major said.

Once back out on the secluded patio, Beverly instructed Meredith to resume her seat and pushed Major's chair so he was just where she thought he'd been before.

"Can I ask now, Ma?" He glanced over his shoulder at her.

"What are you waiting for?" She waved her hand then went to hide behind the pillar at the entrance.

"As I was saying before, I had this romantic dinner all planned out. . . ."

Meredith squeezed his hand. "You should have known me long enough by now to know that I'm not one for fancy dinners or gourmet food. Tuna and Cheetos is a romantic enough menu for me."

"Why have I wasted so much time?"

"Because you're crazy!" Ma called.

He and Meredith laughed. "I guess I'd better get on with this before she comes over here and does it for me." Taking her left hand, he slipped the object Ma had given him, his grandmother's engagement ring, onto her finger. "Meredith Guidry, will you marry me?"

She never broke eye contact with him. "On one condition."

His heart stopped. "What's that?"

"You'll go back to my father and tell him you've changed your mind about the restaurant deal."

"How did you—?"

She pressed her free hand to his lips. "That doesn't matter. What matters is that I'm pretty sure your mother is the reason you turned him down. And if I agree to marry you, she's going to be my mother, too, which means I can share in the responsibility of taking care of her while you work at the restaurant."

"But what about your job and your hours?"

"I'm promoting Corie into a new planner position to take some of the pressure off me so that maybe I can go back to just a fifty- or sixty-hour work week." She grinned. "So will you?"

He would never deserve her. "Will you agree to keep the puppy and name him Duke?"

"You'll help out with training?"

"Naturally."

"Then, yes, I'll keep the puppy."

"Good. Now, you haven't answered my other question. Will you marry me?"

"Yes, she will." Beverly's whisper carried to them.

Meredith laughed then leaned forward and kissed him. "Yes, Chef. I'll marry you."

Discussion Questions

1. Even though Meredith loves her family and is close with them, she began to see things about them that she wishes were different. Do you think she chose the right way to go about trying to make changes in her relationship with her family?

2. We've all had a family member who's embarrassed us in one way or another. But is there someone you love dearly of whom you're ashamed, like Major with his mother? Someone you don't want your friends or coworkers to meet? What is at the root of that shame? How does that affect your relationship with that loved one?

3. Part of Meredith and Major's problem in this story is that they don't do a good job of communicating with each other. What is at the root of the problem for each of them that keeps them from being open and honest with each other?

4. Meredith's house is representative of both Meredith's and Major's lives—put together on the outside but needing extensive work done inside. How did each go about doing those emotional and spiritual renovations? Are you putting on a good face for the world and ignoring the mess inside?

5. After his mother's burn accident, Major tells Mr. Guidry he's not going to take their offer to start a restaurant. Have you ever had to give up your dream to care for a loved one? How did that affect your life? What did it do to your relationship with that person? Did you ever get to pursue that dream?

6. Even though Meredith felt that she wasn't given the respect that her position warranted at work, she didn't feel like she could talk to her parents about it. She thought that they would eventually come to respect her hard work. When her brother intervenes on her behalf, her parents acknowledge the situation. Do you need to have a similar conversation with your boss? Or are you more like Meredith's parents, overlooking and taking for granted your employees? Do you tell your children they are appreciated and increase their responsibilities when they prove themselves trustworthy?

7. Major thinks about the quote from the John Wayne movie, "Never apologize, it's a sign of weakness." What do you think of that sentiment? Is apologizing or admitting you're wrong a sign of weakness?

8. Do you assume that people are going to think worse of you if they find out some secret about your past or your family? What happens when you make that assumption?

9. Meredith spent many years praying for God to give her "the desire of her heart"—to have Major fall in love with her. Why do you think it took her changing her prayer to a request for contentment for God to give her the desire of her heart?

10. When Major is in the hospital, Forbes confronts him about telling Meredith the truth about his mother. Forbes tells Major he needs to do what the Bible commands and honor his mother. What does "Honor thy father and mother" mean to you? How do we honor our parents?

A Case for Love

Dedication:

For Ruth Anderson, because she "gets" me.

Acknowledgments:

Great thanks to Meryll Rose and the *Talk of the Town* team at Nashville's News Channel 5 (WTVF) for letting me shadow you for a day. Thanks for giving Alaine her voice. Also, much gratitude to Cara Putman for answering a few legal questions for me.

Chapter 1

"You did what?"

Forbes Guidry sank into the tall-backed leather chair, extremities numb, and stared at the couple sitting across the desk from him. As a partner in the largest law firm in Bonneterre, Louisiana, he'd heard a lot of shocking things over the fourteen years he'd been practicing. But nothing had hit him quite like this.

"We eloped." His sister held up her left hand where a diamond wedding band had been added below the antique engagement ring she'd sported for the past three months. "I know you were looking forward to being Major's best man, which is why we're telling you before breaking it to the rest of the family."

He hardly spared a glance at his best friend—now his brother-in-law—before pinning his gaze on his sister. "Meredith, this is a joke, right? What about the meeting Monday with Anne—the plans we discussed?" Sure, Meredith had been a little too quiet during that meeting, had voiced concerns about how big the wedding seemed to be growing, but she'd been coming off working a huge event that weekend and had been tired. . .hadn't she?

"Things were getting out of hand—had already gone too far."

"Stop." Forbes fought the urge to press his hands over his ears. "Way too much information."

Major chuckled; Meredith frowned at both of them. "Oh, for mercy's sake. I'm talking about the wedding plans. Neither of us wanted a big wedding, but every time we met with Anne—or you, or anyone in the family—it grew exponentially. Especially once Mom and Dad stuck their oars in and started making lists of all of their business acquaintances that needed to be invited."

Forbes stared at his sister, dumbfounded. He prided himself on knowing exactly what each member of his family was thinking before they ever thought it. How had this blindsided him so completely?

He finally turned his attention on Major. "When you came in Tuesday to talk about the restaurant, did you already have this planned?"

"No. Not planned. We'd discussed it, but it wasn't until that night when we made the decision." Major had the good grace to look abashed.

And you didn't call me? Forbes reined in the childish words with a tight fist of control. He faced his sister again. "When and where did you get married?"

"Yesterday, when Mom and Dad met us at Beausoleil Pointe Center for lunch with Major's mom. We'd asked the chaplain to perform the ceremony, and we got married in the pavilion where Major proposed to me."

Forbes turned away from the dewy-eyed look Meredith gave her new husband, feeling ill. That would explain why Meredith hadn't shown up for dinner with the siblings and cousins last night. He'd just assumed she was working overtime preparing for an event this weekend.

When the silence stretched, Forbes looked at them again.

Meredith's eyes narrowed speculatively at Forbes. "Major, would you mind if I had a private word with my brother?"

"Sure. No problem." Major stood, smoothing the front of his chinos. "I–I'll wait for you out in the car."

"Thanks." Meredith never pulled her gaze away from Forbes—giving him the look that had always been able to make him squirm.

Forbes watched his friend leave the office, then pressed his lips together and faced his sister again.

"What is it that bothers you most? That you aren't going to be best man, that you don't get to be involved and have a say in the wedding plans, or that you didn't see this coming?" Meredith crossed her legs and clasped her hands around her knee, her expression betraying smugness and amusement.

What bothered him most was that over the past seven or eight months, Meredith had slowly been pulling away from the family. Ever since she'd bought that house against his—and their parents'—advice, she'd started keeping secrets, spending less time with them. As the oldest, it was his responsibility to keep his seven brothers and sisters in line, to watch out for and protect them, and to guide them in making their decisions. Mom and Dad had laid that burden on him early in life, and he'd gladly carried it. But how could he express that to Meredith without coming across sounding like a little boy who hadn't gotten his way?

"I'm not bothered, just surprised. You're the last person in the family I'd expect to do something without planning it out well in advance." He gave her his most charming grin. "It is what you do for a living, after all."

She responded with a half smile. "And thus the reason for eloping. Between the busiest event-load we've ever had, the Warehouse Row project, and Major getting ready for the groundbreaking on the restaurant, we were just tired of schedules and checklists and menus and seating charts. Now Marci won't feel like her wedding is being overshadowed by her oldest sister's, since she decided to plan a Christmas wedding and we didn't want to wait that long."

He could see her point, but. . . "Don't you feel like you've cheated yourself out of the wedding you always wanted? Growing up, you and Anne used to talk about your dream weddings."

Meredith shrugged. "Anne always had the ideas. I guess that's why she's been such a great success as a wedding planner—every week she had bigger and grander ideas. Whenever I really thought about it, I couldn't imagine myself in the big dress, my hair all done up, standing there in front of that many people. I guess I never dreamed about a wedding—I just dreamed about falling in love and being married."

Come to think about it, Forbes couldn't picture his jeans-and-T-shirt sister in a fluffy white gown, either. He ran his finger along the edge of the desk blotter.

"And look at the bright side: Now you don't have to find a date for the wedding."

He released a derisive sound in the back of his throat. "Yes, since that worked out so well at Anne's wedding—for my date, anyway."

"How do you always manage to find these women who're just trying to make their boyfriends jealous?"

He shrugged.

"You know, I know someone I think would be perfect for you, if you'd like me to see if she'd be agreeable to being set up on a blind date with you."

His insides quivered at the idea. "Thank you kindly, but I'll have to pass and just leave it up to chance. As I told George Laurence a long time ago; When God's ready for me to fall in love, He'll throw the right woman into my path."

"Uh, did you think that maybe your sisters' and cousins' attempts to set you up on dates might be God's way of throwing the right woman in your path?"

"Not unless He's shared something with you He hasn't told me." Forbes rounded the desk and held out his hand to his sister. She rose, and he pulled her into a hug. "Congratulations, Sis. I'm confident that you and Major will be happier together than you can even imagine."

"I know we will be."

"I'll walk you out."

Halfway down the stairs, he paused. "What about a honeymoon? Don't tell me you're going to just drop everything and take a two-week vacation that hasn't been on the schedule for the past six months."

"No. Since the events next week can be handled by our assistants, we're leaving next Wednesday for a long weekend in Colorado. Amazing how this managed to coincide with the Aspen Food and Wine Classic that Major's always wanted to go to, huh?" But from the smile on her face, he could tell she didn't begrudge indulging Major's wishes in the least.

Heading back to his office after seeing his sister and *brother-in-law* off—would he ever get used to that?—Forbes feigned harriedness to keep anyone from trying to stop him for a chat.

"Samantha, no calls for the next half hour, please," he told his secretary on his way past her desk.

"Yes, Mr. Guidry."

He leaned against his door after closing it. His office, with its walls of built-in, dark wood cabinets and bookcases, seemed to press in around him.

What he'd told Meredith was true; he was absolutely certain that she and Major would have a happy marriage. Both of them were easygoing, almost too eager to give up what they wanted to make someone else happy. Forbes had learned a long time ago that he didn't have the right personality to get married. Every girl he'd dated in high school or college had wanted to go out with him because of his looks. And every one of them had eventually broken up with him for one of two reasons: Either she thought he was selfish and didn't pay enough attention to her, or she thought he was too controlling and tried to smother her.

He'd completely given up on dating after his ten-year high school class reunion, at which he'd overheard two of his ex-girlfriends having a laugh about how it was no surprise to them that he wasn't married yet.

He crossed to the window behind his desk and leaned against the frame, staring down at the visitor parking lot. His twenty-year reunion was coming up in the fall. And while he'd love to find some ravishing beauty to take to it to shut up all those exes, he didn't want the hassle of expectations that came from taking someone out on a date.

When the thirty minutes he'd given himself to brood expired, he opened the office door and asked Samantha to come in to review his schedule for the remainder of the day.

He made several notes in his PDA while she reviewed the afternoon's appointments and meetings. When she finished and closed her planner, she hesitated, biting her lips.

"What is it?" He leaned back in his chair, curious. She'd never acted in the least intimidated or scared of him before. She'd worked for him a little less than a year, but she was the first secretary he'd had who didn't seem to mind a boss others had called a micromanager—had even stood up to him a time or two.

"Someone from *Bonneterre Lifestyles* called a little while ago. It seems you didn't RSVP for the dinner tonight."

Forbes groaned. Ever since he'd assisted in partner Tess Folse's run for city council five years ago—during which he'd given many speeches, appeared on all the local channels' news broadcasts, and had his photo in the paper multiple times—he'd been a fixture on the magazine's beefcake list, having garnered enough votes to win and get his face on the front cover twice.

"I suppose it's black tie?"

Samantha nodded. "That's what the gal said."

"Seven o'clock?"

"They offered a car—a limo—for you, if you want."

He pressed his thumb and forefinger to the bridge of his nose. The three other partners—all women—were thrilled every year when he told them of his inclusion on the list. The articles enumerating his accomplishments were good exposure for the firm, they'd say. Up until now, he'd found some excuse or another to avoid the dinner. This year, Tess, Sandra, and Esther had strongly suggested he make an appearance at the magazine's big publicity event at which the magazine's cover would be revealed and the top five bachelors named and recognized with awards.

He glanced over Samantha's head at the three plaques and two glass trophies on a display shelf. Maybe they needed to give him a new award—Bonneterre's Most *Perpetual* Bachelor. He hoped this year he wasn't again the oldest man on the list.

"Call them back and tell them I'd be delighted to attend, but I'll drive myself."

"Will do, boss." Samantha scooped up her planner and the folders Forbes had given her to refile and crossed to the door. "And Mr. Guidry?"

"Yes, Samantha?"

"Do try to have fun tonight, okay?"

"Uh-huh. As fun as jumping into a pool full of thumbtacks."

Samantha's laughter followed her out of the room.

His gaze flickered back to the emblems of his perpetual singleness. He'd heard the magazine always invited the year's Most Eligible Bachelorettes to the dinner—possibly hoping to set up a relationship and eventual wedding they could report in their pages. Maybe he could find someone there to take to the reunion—so long as she understood there were no strings attached.

Alaine Delacroix scrubbed off her on-air makeup. "Matt, have you seen Pricilla since I went off air? I need to talk to her about the event tonight."

The intern frowned. "I thought you were a guest at the thing, not covering it."

"Who else is going to cover something like that other than me? I'm the only reporter at this station who covers the social scene." Not that she wanted to anymore. But until the news director actually looked at the hard-news pieces she'd been doing on her own time, she'd be stuck covering the fluff stories as she had for the past decade of her life.

"If I see her, I'll tell her you need to talk to her." The college student waved and left the small prep room.

Alaine turned to check her appearance in the large mirror to make sure she didn't have mascara smeared down her cheeks. She made the inspection as quick as possible, hating to see her own reflection with no makeup. Even with her shoulder-length black hair still styled from her noon broadcast, with no makeup on, all she saw in the mirror were flaws—dark circles under her eyes, freckles scattered across her nose and cheeks, and the bumps on her forehead that never seemed to go away.

She applied concealer under her eyes, powder all over her face, and a touch of eye makeup, blush, and lip gloss before returning to her desk in the newsroom. Once upon a time, Alaine Delacroix would have thought nothing of walking around with no makeup on. But that had been a very long time ago; she'd been a different person then.

An envelope with the station's logo and return address in the top left corner sat on her chair when she got back to her cubicle, bearing her name in handwriting she didn't recognize. She opened it—and smiled. She'd hoped the marketing director would be able to come through for her.

She picked up her phone and dialed a number from memory.

"Boudreaux-Guidry Enterprises, Events and Facilities, this is Meredith."

"Hey, girl. It's Alaine."

"Oh—hi." Meredith sounded funny. "What's up?"

Alaine laughed. "I can't believe you're going to pretend you don't know why I'm calling you."

"You—how did you find out?"

All traces of amusement evaporated, her reporter's instincts kicking in. Meredith sounded like someone who had a secret. "You know a journalist can't reveal her sources. So? Spill it. I want details."

"I haven't told most of my family yet. If I give you details, you have to promise you won't say anything to anyone until after Sunday. We're telling the family at dinner after church."

"Strictly off the record." Alaine picked up a pen and steno pad, but forced herself to put them down again and rotate in her chair so that her back was to the desk.

"We had the chaplain at Beausoleil Pointe Center marry us yesterday afternoon. We surprised our parents."

All the air in Alaine's lungs froze solid. Meredith Guidry and Major O'Hara had eloped? "But I thought you were having your cousin Anne plan a big wedding for you. I was hoping to cover it, since Major has become quite the celebrity, what with his cooking segments on my show."

"We decided we were just too busy to try to plan a big wedding. And we've already wasted eight years. Why put it off any longer?"

A flash-fire of jealousy forced the air out of Alaine's lungs. Meredith had been one of her few friends who was still unmarried—and the only true friend Alaine had had in years. She hated being single; even more than becoming a serious journalist, getting married was the one thing she wanted most in life. Yet at thirty-two years old, she was starting to worry that the chances of either dream coming true were not just slipping, but sprinting, away.

Alaine had to swallow past the huge lump in her throat to make her voice work. "Congratulations, Mere. I'm really happy for you." She glanced down at the envelope crumpled in her fist. "Oh, I got the passes for the Art without Limits exhibit preview and fund-raiser at the Beausoleil Fine Arts Center, if you're still interested in going."

"Of course I am. And since Major's catering it, I won't have to feel guilty about going off and leaving him home alone. Thanks again for thinking of me."

"I don't know anyone else who likes art, and I hate going to those things by myself." She twisted the spiral cord around her finger tightly, trying to see if the slight pain would help squeeze out her envy.

"Same here—oh, my other line just lit up. I'll talk to you later."

"Okay. Bye." Alaine turned around to hang up the receiver, then put her head down on her folded arms atop the desk. *God, why is everyone I know married or engaged? Am I the last old maid left in Bonneterre?*

She knew the answer to that, of course. Twenty-four other

"eligible bachelorettes" would be at the *Bonneterre Lifestyles* dinner along with her, if they all showed up. And who wouldn't, when they'd have VIP access to the handsomest, wealthiest, highest-profile single men in town for the evening?

Mother's constant harping on her to get married—and soon—was starting to make Alaine feel like something was wrong with her for still being single at her age. The facts that Joe and his wife couldn't have kids and that Tony, at age twenty-six, wasn't anywhere near ready to settle down put all the pressure of producing grandchildren anytime soon on Alaine. And she wasn't even sure she wanted kids.

She sat up and tried to run her fingers through her hair—before remembering it was still shellacked with hair spray.

Maybe tonight she'd give those bachelors more than just a professional glance. Maybe it was time to get a little arm candy to show her parents—and anyone else who might be looking—that she was at least trying. And she never knew: Mr. Right could be Bachelor Number One, Two, or Twenty-Five.

CHAPTER 2

Alaine stared into the camera lens as if she were talking directly to a person instead of a machine. "The publicist for *Bonneterre Lifestyles* reported that participation in voting for this year's Most Eligible Bachelors was up more than 200 percent over last year. And they expect the July issue, which hits newsstands Monday, will be the top-selling edition in the magazine's thirty-five-year history."

Much more so than the June issue, on which Alaine's photo appeared as the number one old maid in town.

"Tonight at ten o'clock, I'll reveal the winner and give you a preview of the magazine's cover, which will be announced after the dinner feting the twenty-five nominees. Live from the Plantation House restaurant, this is Alaine Delacroix for Channel Six News." She stood still, smiling, until receiving an all clear.

Instead of mingling and making small talk with everyone gathered in the exclusive second-floor dining room of the most expensive restaurant in town, Alaine walked around followed by her cameraman and stuck her microphone in people's faces, asking them silly questions so she could file a story that no one would remember three days from now.

A frisson of excited whispers in the group near the entrance caught her attention. She turned to find the source, and her jaw almost unhinged. In walked one of the most gorgeous men she'd ever seen—and he looked vaguely familiar. His hair was a cross between brown and auburn, and he looked better in a tuxedo than Fred Astaire ever had. But could he dance like the silver-screen legend?

"That's Forbes Guidry."

"I can't believe he actually came."

"He's been on the list for five years in a row."

"I heard he drives a Jaguar and lives in one of those fancy town houses in Old Towne."

Alaine focused on the last whispered comment from the women behind her. One of those town houses in Old Towne? Of course! That's where she recognized him from. They lived in the same community, and she'd seen him out running almost every morning on her way to work.

While she'd toyed with the idea of trying to meet him, she'd never followed through, assuming someone that good-looking must be married. She couldn't believe she hadn't connected her eye-candy jogger with the infamous Forbes Guidry. He was what her mother would call a confirmed bachelor—or in other words, a hopeless case other women had long since given up on trying to make settle down.

Which meant he was definitely not the man for her. But to tide her mother over until Mr. Right came along? It was worth a shot.

Alaine turned to motion Nelson over—but he wasn't behind her. She scanned the room and saw him chatting up the woman who'd been second behind Alaine on the old-maid list. She started toward him, but before she got there, the microphone on the dais at the far end of the room squawked, drawing everyone's attention.

"Ladies and gentlemen, bachelors and bachelorettes, if you would find your seats, dinner service will begin in just a few minutes."

Alaine had arranged a seat and meal for Nelson ahead of time, so she sent him to go eat and went to find her name on one of the tables.

Paying more attention to the place cards than anything else, she gasped and jumped when she stepped on someone's foot.

"I beg your..." Though her four-inch heels brought her up to five foot six, the close proximity to the man forced her to crane her neck to see his face—his gorgeous face—and grayish-blue eyes looking into hers with such intensity, her whole head grew hot.

"No apology necessary, Ms. Delacroix. I believe this is your seat." Forbes Guidry pulled out the chair he stood behind.

"Thank you." She sat, hoping he would walk away with no further conversation so she could compose herself before she had to speak with him again.

He pulled out the chair to her left and sat in it. "I'm Forbes Guidry."

"Yes, I know. I mean. . . ." She ripped her gaze away from his, and her eyes fell on the place card. She nodded toward it. One thing she'd learned over the past ten or twelve years: Men as good-looking as this guy had big egos and loved it when women knew who they were before they were introduced. Even if he was wearing the faintest trace of her favorite cologne—which nearly made her eyes cross with giddiness every time she took a breath—she wasn't about to give him the satisfaction.

Once everyone else settled around the large, round table, they each introduced themselves, coming to Alaine last.

After her turn, one of the bachelors across from her said, "Congratulations on being named Bachelorette of the Year, Alaine." He followed the statement with a wink.

Forbes Guidry's brows formed a straight line that hooded his eyes. "How long have you been at Channel Six, Ms. Delacroix?" Though he addressed her, his intimidating expression stayed focused on the other side of the table; and it worked, as the winking bachelor turned to engage the woman on his right in conversation.

Alaine hid her amusement. "I've been with WCAN twelve years—two as a college intern and ten full-time. And please, call me Alaine." She wracked her brain to find a way to bring up the fact they lived in the same complex without coming across like either a stalker or a fangirl.

"You live in one of the older row houses on the south side of the complex, don't you?" Forbes asked.

"I, uh, yes." Her surprise must have shown, because Forbes smiled apologetically.

"I usually see you in the mornings when I'm out running. Black Mazda RX-8, right?"

He'd noticed her? She nodded. "Right."

"Is yours in the row that overlooks the old Moreaux Paper warehouses?"

"Don't remind me. My house probably declined 10 percent in value as soon as I closed on it a few years ago." She sighed. "Can you imagine that description in a real-estate ad? 'Great view of the highway and a bunch of decrepit, abandoned warehouses.'" She leaned to the side to allow the server access to put her salad on the charger in front of her.

"But once that area's developed, it should increase your property value." Forbes pushed the lettuce leaves around on his plate, looking under them as if checking to make sure no surprises lurked, waiting to jump out at him.

Alaine took a bite. Not the best raspberry vinaigrette dressing she'd ever had, but it would do. "I was told when I bought it a few years ago that some investment company or another was going to go in and revitalize that area, but nothing's ever come of it."

Forbes picked out the three cherry tomato halves and ate them, then put his fork down. "I've heard that it's pretty close to being a done deal."

"It would be nice to have some retail stores closer than having to drive all the way across town to the mall area. Don't get me wrong, I love the boutiques and shops on Town Square, but sometimes a girl just needs to shop at a big chain store."

The handsome lawyer assiduously avoided her gaze. She could almost smell the scoop. "Any word on how soon this deal might be closed?"

The corner of his mouth quirked, and he turned those piercing eyes on her again. "Digging for a story, Ms. Delacroix?"

"Avoiding the question, Mr. Guidry?"

A smile slowly overtook his lips. Alaine almost forgot what they'd been talking about.

"Hey, Guidry, don't monopolize her attention all night."

Forbes held her gaze a moment longer before looking away. Alaine blinked and turned toward the man who'd interrupted them.

Forbes slowed his breathing to try to get his heart rate back down to normal. He'd been around his fair share of beautiful women in his life, but never before had one so discombobulated him that he'd almost revealed confidential information without a second thought.

If he'd blabbed to a journalist about his parents' involvement in the development of the Moreaux Mills area and she'd gone public with it, he would be in all kinds of trouble. If the deal fell through, as it had for the other five or six national and international developers who'd tried to do the same thing over the years, they didn't want the Boudreaux-Guidry Enterprises name held up for derision and judgment in the media.

They also wanted to keep it quiet to try to eliminate any competitors from coming in and buying adjacent land out from under them.

For the remainder of the meal, he participated in conversations around the table, but observed Alaine Delacroix closely. She seemed unflappable, deflecting with aplomb the puppyish attempts at flirting she received from several of the younger men at the table.

The publicist from the magazine came around shortly after the main course was served—Forbes had ordered the chateaubriand the restaurant was famous for and enjoyed every bite.

"I can see y'all have taken the time to get to know each other." She gave a salesperson's fake smile, which faded when she took a second look around the table. Her gaze fell on Forbes and Alaine.

He raised his brows, daring her to comment on the fact that he'd done a little rearranging of the place cards.

She shrugged, but a sly look entered her expression. "Well, if y'all need anything, I'm more than happy to be of assistance." She moved on to the next table.

Forbes allowed the server to take his empty plate. Alaine had eaten only half her meal but insisted she was finished. Well, she was a little thing, so maybe she didn't have much room for more food than that.

"Alaine, I believe you know my sister Meredith." He rested his hands in his lap, trying to set an example for some of their uncouth dinner companions who now leaned their elbows on the table.

"Yes. In fact, I spoke with her earlier today and was shocked to hear she and Major eloped yesterday."

Forbes tore his attention away from the way a few ringlets of Alaine's black hair had either escaped or been left loose from the halo of curls atop her head and caressed her long neck. "Meredith told you about her elopement? I thought she was keeping mum about it until she told the family Sunday."

"I pried it out of her." Instead of looking guilty, though, her expression was more disgruntled than anything else. "I think it's wonderful—very romantic. I don't blame them for not wanting to wait."

Forbes opened his mouth to speak, but the server interrupted them to deliver their desserts—chocolate-cherry bread pudding. Never having been a fan of bread pudding, as it was one of his mother's least successful attempts at baking eons ago, Forbes waved his off.

"Is there something else I can bring you, sir?" the server asked.

"Is it possible to get a fruit plate?"

"Yes, sir. We have a berry salad that has strawberries, blueberries, raspberries, and pomegranate seeds with a citrus-mint dressing."

The idea of combining citrus and mint didn't appeal. "If I could get it without the dressing, that would be great—maybe with a drizzle of chocolate instead?"

The server nodded. "I'll let the chef know immediately and

should have that to you shortly."

Forbes nodded his thanks, and as he did so, caught sight of Alaine quickly turning away an amused smile. He leaned toward her. "Yes, I know," he said in a low voice. "I'm high maintenance."

She laughed. "Tell me, Forbes, are you accustomed to getting your way like that everywhere you go?"

"Not everywhere, no. But you have to figure that an establishment like this doesn't garner rave reviews and a James Beard award unless they're willing to accommodate their customers' wishes." He shrugged. "And it never hurts to ask. The worst they can say is no."

Alaine shook her head, looking at him as if he were some strange science experiment. "I have a feeling that there are very few people in this world who have ever said no to you, Forbes Guidry."

He could get lost in the dark brown pools of her eyes. "Want to put that to the test?"

"How?"

"By seeing if someone says no to me when I ask them to do something." He masked his amusement with a serious expression.

Her perfectly arched brows raised. "Okay."

"Go out with me tomorrow night."

She blinked a couple of times; then a smile parted her full lips. "That sounded more like a command than a question to me."

He inclined his head—she had him there. "Alaine Delacroix, will you go to dinner with me tomorrow night?"

"No." She pressed her lips together; he tried not to stare at her mouth but was having a hard time.

"Now you're toying with me. You want to say yes, but you said no just to prove a point." He looked up and leaned away from Alaine when the server arrived with his plate of chocolate-dressed berries.

"No. I actually mean no. No dinner with you tomorrow night."

He scooted his chair a little closer to hers so he didn't have to lean so far to hear her hushed voice. "No because you can't, or no because you don't want to?"

Alaine's olive complexion darkened. "No. . .because I can't." Her shoulders drooped slightly, and she turned narrowed—but amused—eyes on him. "I so want to be able to say no to you. That's not a fair test."

"Because you do want to go out with me?" What was he doing? This was headed for disaster. But he just couldn't help himself. It'd been a long time since he'd fallen so completely under a beautiful woman's spell.

Before Alaine could answer, the publicist returned and knelt beside her chair. "We're getting ready to start the program, Ms. Delacroix."

"Oh—thanks." Alaine dabbed her mouth with her napkin and placed it on the table beside her half-finished dessert. She turned back to Forbes. "I've got to get back to work. If you're serious about dinner, your sister has my phone number."

He watched her walk across the room, her burgundy gown hugging her curves in a way that made him wonder how she could possibly still be unmarried.

Ignoring the glares of the other men at the table, he turned his attention to his dessert, tuning out most of what the people at the microphone said as bachelors number twenty-five through six were named. Every so often, he glanced Alaine's direction, fascinated to watch the intensity with which she applied herself to her job.

"And now, the moment we've all been waiting for." The publicist had taken over at the microphone. "Will our top five bachelors please rise?"

Since his name hadn't already been called, Forbes wiped his mouth, tossed the napkin on the table, and stood—along with the other four men at his table. He smirked, having assumed that's why they'd had assigned seats.

"This year's Most Eligible Bachelor is someone who's no stranger to the title. Born and raised right here in Bonneterre, he graduated valedictorian from Acadiana High School and summa cum laude from the University of Louisiana–Bonneterre."

Forbes sighed. Looking around at the other four men, he was

pretty sure he was the only one with those honors.

"He graduated top of his class from Loyola Law in New Orleans, where he practiced for three years before returning to Bonneterre to join one of the most prestigious law firms in the state, and he became the youngest partner in the firm's history."

Once again, the other men at the table turned to glare at him. Once again, he ignored them.

"In addition to his work, this bachelor sings in a quartet and works tirelessly with his family to raise funds for the Warner Foundation, the organization that supports research and helps cover the cost of care for patients at the cardiac care unit at University Hospital. Ladies and gentlemen, for the third time, Bonneterre's Most Eligible Bachelor, Forbes Guidry."

Forbes acknowledged the applause with a wave as he made his way to the dais. He suddenly had a vision of himself ten or fifteen years from now, coming to this dinner and being named the nine- or twelve- or even fifteen-time winner of the top spot on the list. A cold chill washed over him.

He accepted the glass trophy from the publicist and waited for her to adjust the microphone stand's height before speaking.

"I don't know if I should be flattered or take this as a hint that I need to get on the ball and try to find a wife. I guess this'll help." He motioned toward the poster-sized front cover with his photo on it. The laughter his remark garnered was about as tepid as the joke itself. "What else can I say but thank you to *Bonneterre Lifestyles* and everyone who took the time to vote. I'm truly humbled that so many people in my beloved hometown think so highly of me to bestow any kind of award on me."

He raised the trophy. "Thank you."

If he'd been on the Academy Awards, they would have had to scramble to start playing his exit music, so short was his speech.

Apparently the announcement and his speech were the signal that the event was over because, before he could get back to his table, bachelors and bachelorettes were standing, shrugging into discarded tux jackets or grabbing purses, and heading for the door. Though from the sounds of it, many of them were leaving here to go down to one of the clubs on Riverwalk. No one bothered to invite him, though, and that was fine. He got his fill of those places whenever he had to entertain the firm's out-of-town clients.

He glanced around for Alaine—well, for the cameraman, since the petite reporter would be hard to spot—and just caught sight of the two of them exiting the dining room.

A few women stopped him on his way out. He applied the polite evasion he'd learned over the years and escaped as quickly as he could. At his car, he divested himself of his jacket and tie and climbed in.

Alaine Delacroix. She was something else. He'd had his DVR set to record her noontime show for the last two years—and not because he had any interest in Bonneterre's social scene. Ever since his next-door neighbor had pointed her out over at the mailboxes one afternoon as they'd jogged by, Forbes had been knocked back to his teen years when he could plaster posters of the female celebrities he found attractive on his locker door and pretend that, someday, he would meet one of them and she would fall madly in love with him.

He pulled out of the parking lot and headed the short distance home.

"Okay, God. It's time You let me in on whatever plan it is You have for my dating life. I have a feeling I made a big mistake tonight asking Alaine out, but I also feel like there's a reason why You chose tonight, of all nights, to throw her in my path. If she's the one, I guess You're about to prove that it's never too late to teach an old dog new tricks."

Chapter 3

"That was the lamest acceptance speech I've ever heard."

Forbes grabbed Jonathan in a headlock. "Yeah? When you win next year, you can show me up."

"Right. Like I'd ever do anything to become that high profile."

"Anyone can be nominated. Get the girls to write you a killer nomination essay, be sure to have them mention you're my little brother, and I'm sure whoever puts together the final list of fifty will include you—and Kevin and Rafe, too. I think they might just love the idea of featuring the four devastatingly handsome Guidry brothers on their front cover. Imagine how many magazines they'd sell." He released his brother.

"Well, don't count on us all still being eligible for the contest next year." Jonathan swept his fingers through his reddish-brown hair and looked around the emptying church parking lot, probably checking that no one had seen his big brother overpower him so easily.

"What do you mean?" Forbes strained to see if the minivan parked beside his car at the back end of the lot was really as close to his baby as it appeared.

"Rafe. He's getting pretty serious about that Tonya girl."

"It'll never happen. Rafe may not realize it right now, but he wants a girl with aspirations, with drive. He won't be happy with someone who's just biding her time working as a receptionist until she can hook some wealthy man who'll support her shopping habit."

"Dude, that's cold. Even for you." Jonathan shook his head. "And how do you know? Have you ever met her?"

"I've seen her when I go down to B-G for Dad's prayer breakfast. When I found out Rafe was dating her, I started observing her. She's a very nice young lady. But she's not for Rafe."

The minivan had parked close enough that Forbes had to edge in sideways between the two vehicles. In all places, he'd assumed his beloved Jaguar would be safe from encroachment in the church lot. He inspected the paint as best he could for door dings.

"Hey, you going to unlock the door or are we going to stand out in the heat all afternoon?" Jonathan slapped the top of the car.

"You damage it, you pay to have it repaired." Forbes continued his inspection, but used the remote to unlock the doors. He didn't see any scratches or dings from this angle; he'd have to remember to check again when he got home. He'd worked too hard to keep the three-year-old sedan in just-off-the-showroom-floor condition to just let a door-ding slip by unnoticed.

As soon as Forbes squeezed in and turned on the ignition, Jonathan began fiddling with the satellite radio. Forbes had figured out a long time ago the reason why Jonathan usually rode to church with one of his roommates and then bummed a ride with him over to Uncle Errol and Aunt Maggie's for Sunday dinner instead of with anyone else in the family: Forbes let him play with the high-tech radio.

"Did you get everything straightened out with the registrar's office to graduate in December?" Forbes slid the sleek sedan into the light traffic on University Avenue.

"Yeah. My advisor hadn't signed off on my internship from last summer, so they hadn't counted the hours." Jonathan settled on a station that labeled itself as "Christian Alternative."

Forbes, who usually kept it set on talk or news radio—or greatest hits of the '80s when assured no one else would hear it—adjusted the volume down from the controls on the steering wheel. "So they're letting you count your work with Anne last summer as an internship?"

"No, the job I had working with Meredith in the Facilities Management Department at B-G—I helped her out with a lot of the OSHA stuff: made sure that safety rules were being enforced, that appropriate signage was posted, and stuff like that."

"I forgot you'd done that. If you're serious about going into business law, that's a good foundation to have." He'd only recently convinced Jonathan that law school was the next logical step after attaining a degree in human resources—and to insure he had more options than just going to work at Boudreaux-Guidry Enterprises.

"Yeah. You know, in talking with my advisor, I'm actually thinking that I might pursue a master's degree in HR, instead. The university has a program where I can work full-time and take classes on weekends and in the evenings." Jonathan flipped down the sun visor and looked at himself in the mirror. "And Dad and I have been talking about a position in B-G's Human Resources Department, if one comes open. If not, I think Meredith might could use me."

"Could. Not *might could*; it's redundant." Forbes couldn't help but vent his frustration by correcting his brother's grammar. "Are you sure you're not just looking at doing that because it's the easiest option?"

The sun visor flipped back up with a pop that made Forbes look to make sure it hadn't broken. Jonathan's lips formed a straight, thin line, and he stared through the windshield. "Nothing says I have to go to graduate school immediately after I finish my bachelor's. I've been in school for a long time now, and I'd like to take some time off, just work for a while, make some money, enjoy not having to study and write papers every night."

"But if you want to be successful in your field—"

"I'll be working in my field, which is more than I can say for a lot of people who've gone to law school or graduate school immediately after college. I'd rather work for a couple of years and figure out what direction I want to go, instead of locking myself into a path right now, investing a couple of years in it, and *then* figuring out I wanted the other thing."

Though he didn't say it in so many words, Jonathan's tone clearly said, *lay off*. For now, Forbes would have to concede the point. "You're right. You have to do what you feel is best. I just don't want you to miss out on any opportunities because you didn't think of them."

He pulled up and parked on the street behind a white Volvo SUV, out of which Meredith and Major exited.

Jonathan hopped out as soon as the Jag's wheels stopped turning. "Hey, y'all! Didn't see you at church this morning."

Forbes caught Meredith's eye and smiled at her as he climbed out of the car. His *married* sister. The first of the eight siblings to get married. The thought twinged. Up until their younger sister Marci had gotten engaged on New Year's Day, Forbes had always been the first at everything among the eight of them. The first to get his driver's license; the first to graduate—high school, college, law school; the first to have a job; the first to not work for Mom and Dad's company. The first to not get married.

Did he really want that distinction? The outlook on spending the rest of his life alone was bleak, especially once all his peer-group siblings and cousins got married and had children and started pulling away from their closely bonded group.

"What's wrong?" Meredith asked when he drew up beside her.

He shook himself from his dismal thoughts. "Nothing." He started to give her a hug in greeting, but she'd been so touchy about that the last six months that he backed off a step. He walked around the vehicle with her to join Major and Jonathan, who'd already devolved into talking about sports.

"I ran into an acquaintance of yours Friday night, Mere." Forbes fell into step with his sister across Maggie and Errol's front yard.

"Oh, yeah? Who?" Meredith, whose high heels sank into the grass, slipped her hand through Forbes's arm for support.

He crooked his arm and slowed his pace. "Alaine Delacroix. She said you told her." He inclined his head toward Major.

Meredith shook her head, a wry smile on her face. "I'd be a horrible secret agent. She called me to tell me she had tickets to an art exhibit we'd been talking about, but the way she opened the conversation, I was sure she'd found out about the—about what happened." She glanced at Jonathan, who paid no attention to her. "So I told her because I didn't want to lie about it. It was only after I got off the phone that I realized I was ten times a fool—that it was my own guilty conscience that made me assume she knew."

Forbes chuckled and squeezed Meredith's hand. "That was how Mom could always get you to confess when we were kids: pretend she already knew, and you spilled the whole thing. Of course, you weren't usually the one who'd done anything wrong, so you never really had a reason to learn how to keep secrets."

"Yeah, well, don't forget that I'm the one who spilled the beans about the surprise party on her fiftieth birthday. She's always known how to push all my buttons."

"But things do seem better between the two of you since you had that talk with them a few months ago."

"After *someone* told them I was feeling taken for granted." She swerved into him, causing him to momentarily lose his balance.

"Only because I knew if I didn't tell them, you never would. You're the least assertive person in this family when it comes to them, and I've never been able to understand why."

"It's just the way I am, I guess." As soon as they reached the wide, wraparound front porch, Meredith squeezed his arm, then let go of him. She laughed when she looked up at him. "Forbes, I know you'll never understand why anyone would have a hard time trying to control every single situation she's involved in. Just accept that we have polar-opposite personalities and let it go at that."

He caught the edge of the storm door as it started to close behind Jonathan and Major.

"So, what did you think of Alaine?" Meredith asked over her shoulder, passing him into the entry hall.

"She's more beautiful in person than on TV. She's little, though. I always assumed she was your height."

Meredith's smile morphed into an exasperated expression. "Other than her looks, what did you think?"

Forbes made sure the glass door latched, schooling his expression before he turned to walk toward the back of the house with his sister. "She's nice."

"Just nice?"

"Yeah. She's a nice person."

Disappointment filled Meredith's light brown eyes. "So you wouldn't be interested in going out with her?"

"Why?" Realization dawned. "Is she the one you wanted to set me up with?"

"Yeah—"

He grabbed her shoulders and kissed her forehead. "Remind me in the future to take you up on your blind-date offers."

"What?"

"Alaine and I sat together at dinner Friday night. By the time dessert came, I asked her out."

Meredith beamed at him. "You did?"

Heat climbed his throat toward his face. "I did. We haven't set it up yet." Because he had to figure out how to get her number from his sister without telling her Alaine hadn't been forthcoming with that information.

"Hey, are you two coming?" Major reappeared in the hall that connected to the kitchen.

Meredith joined her husband. "Guess what. Forbes asked Alaine out."

Major's eyes widened in surprise. "Alaine Delacroix?"

Forbes nodded, wishing they wouldn't make this a big deal.

"Congrats, man." Major grinned shamelessly. "She's a great gal." He looked down at Meredith. "Speaking of great gals, you ready to face your family?"

A hollow feeling that had nothing to do with the fact he'd skipped breakfast this morning filled Forbes at the look that passed between Meredith and Major.

He didn't want to be Bonneterre's Most Eligible Bachelor anymore.

A Case for Love

Alaine kept her sunglasses on after entering the restaurant, despite the dim interior. One of the many things she'd learned from her sorority sisters when they'd made her over was to emit an aura of mystery. If people couldn't see her eyes, it created mystery, right?

Well, even if it didn't, it kept her from having to make eye contact with the burgeoning, Sunday-lunch crowd at Market Street Grill, Daddy's favorite restaurant. Even though she would usually feel comfortable in her black capris and black-and-white, graphic-print halter top in the casual bistro, the fact almost everyone surrounding her had just come from church made her feel underdressed. And if they recognized her, they'd judge her: *Alaine Delacroix doesn't go to church!*

Holding her head higher, Alaine crossed the main dining room, her low-heeled sandals clipping with authority as she headed toward the glassed-in porch in the rear. She went to church—to the Saturday night service that most of the other young professionals attended. Which left her free to sleep in on Sunday mornings. And to dress casually to meet the family for lunch—though usually at her parents' home.

Her brother Joe waved from the round table in the far corner when Alaine stepped down through the doorway. She slid her glasses on top of her head, pushing her bushy hair back from her face. Curly hair and humidity. *Thanks, God.*

When she got to the table, she leaned over to give Joe a squeeze around the shoulders. "Hey, Joe." She edged behind his wheelchair to hug her sister-in-law. "Hey, Nikki."

"Hey, Alaine." Even though the creamy-skinned redhead had been around since Alaine's early teens, Alaine never failed to have a momentary feeling of being a child when next to the woman with the Amazonian stature. "Did you have fun with all those bachelors Friday night?" Nikki's blue eyes twinkled.

Alaine groaned and slid into the chair beside her.

"I see that blush, Al." Joe waved a roll dripping butter at her. "Tell."

"Only if you promise not to call me *Al* any more."

"What? You don't-a like-a being part of the three Italians—Joe, Al, and Tony?" Joe did a horrible Italian accent.

"Considering that we're half Cajun and half Portuguese? No, I don't particularly want people to think I'm a mafioso from Jersey." She melted into a smile when Joe ducked his chin and raised his brows at her. When they were kids, she could yell and scream at him and hold a grudge forever. But since he'd come home from Iraq six years ago with a severed spine, she'd made it her purpose in life to indulge him. Even if it did drive Nikki crazy. "Okay, fine. Whatever. Call me Al."

"You'd better tell us before Mother and Daddy and Tony get here, if you want to save yourself the full-family embarrassment." His triumphant look did still grate on her after all these years.

"Yes, I had a good time Friday night at the dinner. I met several very handsome, very eligible bachelors. With most of them, it's quite easy to understand why they're still bachelors. I got hit on quite a bit. And Forbes Guidry asked me out." She grabbed her water glass and took a huge gulp.

Nikki grabbed her left wrist. "What did you just say? Forbes Guidry—*the* Forbes Guidry? The Bachelor of the Year? Asked you out?"

Flames ignited in Alaine's face. "Why? Is it such a shock I should get asked out?" She forced herself to look at her sister-in-law—who'd known her since before her extreme makeover in college.

"No—just that you'd get asked out by Forbes Guidry and wouldn't be crowing it to the world. He's hot."

"Excuse me?" Joe gaped at his wife.

"I'm married, not dead, Joe." Nikki turned her back on her husband. "So, when are you going out with him?"

"I said no." She cocked her head and tried to recreate Joe's triumphant expression.

"You did *what*? Even if he was a complete jerk, just being seen out on a date with him would rate you a photo on the front of the 'Style' section of the paper."

"And maybe even a mention on my show, huh? Or even take a camera crew along with us." Her viewers would love that, actually. She could see the caption under the newspaper photo now: "Most Eligible Bachelor Has Pity on Number-One Old Maid and Takes Her Out for Dinner."

She wasn't too gentle putting her glass down.

"Why did you say no, Alaine?" Joe started slathering butter on a second roll.

"Because he wanted to go out last night."

"And you couldn't get up and go to church on a Sunday morning to accommodate going out on a date Saturday night with someone like him?" Nikki pressed her hand to her chest as if her heart were failing.

How desperate for a date did everyone think she was, anyway? "I'm not going to rearrange my life just because some guy I've only met once asks me out with less than twenty-four hours' notice."

"Who asked you out?" Tony flopped into the chair on Alaine's right.

She glared at her younger brother—and resisted the urge to push his tousled hair back from his face. He'd had it highlighted again this week, but with blond this time instead of red or purple or green.

"Forbes Guidry," Joe muttered around a mouthful of bread.

"Oh. Who's that?" Tony followed his brother's example and grabbed one of the two remaining rolls and an unused ramekin of butter. He tore off a chunk of the bread and dipped it into the butter before stuffing it into his mouth.

"He's a successful lawyer—who happens to be the most eligible bachelor of the year, according to *Bonneterre Lifestyles*." Nikki turned her head and closed her eyes at the display of macho bread eating surrounding them.

"Oh." Tony shrugged. "Good catch if you can reel him in, Al."

Alaine sighed. God would never have to teach her humility. Her brothers took care of that just fine.

"Wait . . . Guidry—is he part of that family that owns everything in town?" Tony flicked crumbs from his navy polo shirt.

To keep from adjusting Tony's askew collar, which he hated, Alaine picked up her utensil set, unrolled the napkin, and draped it across her lap. "He is."

Joe and Nikki exchanged a look that made the hairs stand up on Alaine's neck. Neither of them ever looked that serious about anything these days. When Nikki turned back toward Alaine, her smile seemed forced.

"You're certain he's part of *that* Guidry family? There are a lot of Guidrys in Bonneterre."

Alaine looked from Nikki to Joe and back. "Yes, I'm sure. I worked with his sister Meredith when I covered the charity event for the hospital back in the spring. Why? What's wrong with his being part of that family?"

Nikki and Joe exchanged another look.

"Nothing." Joe stabbed at the remaining half of his roll with his butter knife.

"Hey, kids, sorry we're late!"

Alaine tore her gaze away from her brother and sister-in-law to greet her parents. "Daddy, you shaved your beard."

Already divested of the coat and tie she knew he'd worn to church, he rubbed his jaw. "A full face of fur is just too hot during the summer. Besides, don't I look younger without it?"

With a full head of silver hair and wrinkles to mark his age? "Of course you do."

Mother, whose dark Mediterranean features Alaine had inherited in abundance, muttered something under her breath—which sounded like Portuguese—as she lowered herself into her seat with the grace only a former beauty queen could possess.

Both of them looked tired. Maybe it was time to talk to Joe and Tony again and see if this was the year to try to convince them to retire. Working the nursery and flower shop in this kind of heat and humidity couldn't be good for two people their ages.

After ordering lunch, each of them gave a short recap of the week and what each had coming up. Alaine couldn't help noticing the looks that passed between Joe, Nikki, and their parents.

Finally, halfway through her quiche lorraine, Alaine shoved the plate back and slapped her fork down on the table. "What is going on?"

Five pairs of startled eyes turned toward her.

"Alaine Desideria Delacroix." Mother rolled the names off her tongue the way only she could. "I raised you to have better table manners than this."

She refused to be cowed. "I'm sorry, Mother, but I know something is going on. I can tell by the way the four of you are acting."

Daddy's shoulders drooped in a defeated way. "I suppose there's no sense in keeping it from you two any longer." He looked at Tony, then back at Alaine. "There's a possibility we could lose the business."

"What?" Tony sputtered around a mouthful.

"How?" Cold clamminess slithered over Alaine's skin.

"Well, you know that a lot of the people who bought up properties in our area to try to flip them have gone into foreclosure. And a bunch of home businesses, like ours, are really struggling and wanting to get out if they can." Daddy took a deep breath, and Mother laid her hand atop his. "At the Moreaux Mills Business Owners' Association meeting Thursday evening, we were informed that a local corporation has been quietly buying up all of those foreclosed properties, and now they're offering a buyout package to about two dozen homeowners and businesses in our section of the Mills so they can tear down all of the old houses and businesses and build luxury condos and apartment buildings and bring in national, retail chain stores to replace us. It's all part of the Warehouse Row development project we've been hearing rumors about." Daddy's whole face drooped.

"Without our knowledge," Joe added, "the president—well,

former president now—of the association met with the city council and agreed on what they call 'fair market value' for all of our properties. If the figures weren't so insulting, they'd be laughable. But so many people want to take the money and run it's going to be hard for the rest of us to stand our ground."

"We did not say anything to you, Alaine, because we believed you might try to do something with the information that might jeopardize your job." Mother suddenly looked much older than her sixty-five years.

"Wait—you said a *local* corporation. You don't mean—" She looked at Nikki and Joe. "It's not Boudreaux-Guidry Enterprises, is it?"

The four exchanged another look.

Nikki pushed a long lock of fiery hair behind her ear. "It is."

The weight of the revelation pressed against Alaine's chest until she could hardly breathe. She couldn't let this happen. If Mother and Daddy lost the business, they lost everything—because it wasn't just a nursery and florist shop, it was their home. . .her home. And Joe's business—and house—just a block away would be gone, too.

With a shaking hand, she raised her iced tea to take a sip, then returned the glass to the table with cool deliberation. "Well, I guess it is a good thing I told Forbes Guidry I wouldn't go out on a date with him, after all."

CHAPTER 4

Alaine trudged up the steps from the garage, the heaviness of her parents' and brother's situation dragging at her feet. She dropped her purse and keys on the dryer in the combination laundry room and pantry, then entered the kitchen to stow her box of leftover quiche in the fridge.

She grabbed a bottle of sparkling water before the door swung shut and took a swig as she turned around. A package wrapped in brown paper on the dining table caught her eye. She swallowed hard and walked over to open it.

While the frame she'd chosen wasn't overly expensive, it was attractive. What it contained, though, brought instant tears to Alaine's eyes. It had taken her weeks to track down the artist whose art deco–inspired work she'd heard Meredith exclaim over. Alaine had been pleasantly surprised that the man hadn't charged her more than she wanted to pay for the commissioned piece—a piece that looked like it was original to Meredith's favorite art era, a chef superimposed over a structure that resembled the Chrysler Building in New York, with era-appropriate lettering across the top and bottom announcing CAFÉ O'HARA. Her wedding present for Meredith and Major.

When it had arrived last week, she couldn't wait to get it framed and figure out a time to present it to her friend. Now she wasn't sure if she could face the daughter of the people trying to force her own parents out of their home and business.

Turning the frame facedown and heading for the stairs, she tried not to think about losing her friend. She was halfway up to her bedroom when her phone started playing the Portuguese national anthem. She ran back to the pantry and dug it out of her purse.

"Mother?"

"Are you about ready?"

Alaine frowned. "Ready for what?"

"The grocery shopping. I told you last week I'd have to do it today because it's going to be a busy week at the shop."

"Right. I forgot. I'll be ready to go when you get here."

"Good. Because I'm turning onto Spring Street now."

Alaine stifled a groan. "Okay. See you in a few minutes." She tossed the cell phone back into her bag, pulled off her sandals, and sprinted upstairs, where she peeled herself out of her capris and slipped into walking shorts and canvas sneakers. Since her hair had decided to completely bush out, she sprayed it with some antifrizz stuff and tried to get it into some semblance of curls with her fingers.

When her mother let herself in through the garage entrance a few minutes later, Alaine was in the pantry pretending she knew what she was doing in making a grocery list.

Mother looked over her shoulder and sighed. "How did I raise such a daughter? Give that to me." She snatched the steno pad and pen from Alaine's hands. "You should get that handsome cook from your program to come over and give you cooking lessons, since you won't learn from me."

"It wouldn't help. Besides, he got married a couple of days ago, so you can quit hinting." *And he works for the enemy.*

The good thing about Major O'Hara's segments for her program: She didn't have to deal with them. They were handled by a production assistant. So she didn't have to worry about what to say or do around him in the foreseeable future.

"Too bad. You need to marry a man who can cook."

The image of Forbes Guidry clattering around her kitchen bloomed unbidden. She forced it aside. As long as this thing with his parents hung over them, she couldn't allow herself to entertain any kind of daydreams about the gorgeous lawyer.

"Maybe you should try some of those Internet dating sites." The end of her mother's statement was muffled as her head disappeared behind the refrigerator door.

"What? You can't be serious!" Try an online dating service? Only dorks, dweebs, geeks, and losers who couldn't meet people to date in real life used those.

Wait. *She* couldn't meet anyone to date in real life. Guess that made her a dork, dweeb, geek, and loser all rolled into one.

"Or a matchmaker service." Mother continued rummaging in the fridge and writing things on the list. "I had been married ten years by the time I was your age."

How many times a month would Alaine have to hear that? "Yes. And you and Daddy only knew each other a week before you got married. If I followed your example there, you'd disown me."

Her mother straightened and closed the fridge. "Not so long as he's as wonderful as your father."

Alaine leaned against one of the chairs across the large island from her. "I'll make you a deal. I'll make more of an effort to meet someone—and I won't take twenty years to get around to marrying him, like Joe and Nikki—if you promise to ease up on the pressure. Deal?"

Mother smiled. "Deal."

Forbes tried to think of an excuse to run past Alaine's town house one more time. He'd made the circuit of the neighborhood five times already—almost three miles—and the heat and humidity were getting unbearable. He wasn't sure if he'd be able to make it all the way around again.

Half an hour ago when he'd rounded the corner onto the street he knew she lived on, her black Mazda coupe had pulled into the garage of the town house in the middle with the sand-colored brick facade and the bay window. He'd never taken the time to notice just how much smaller and less-expensive looking the structures in this part of the neighborhood were until now, even though he knew they went for less than half the price of the all-brick duplex-style town houses in his section.

The next two times he passed her place, an older model, burgundy Lincoln Town Car had been parked in her driveway; but the fourth time he made it around, the visitor was gone. It was the kind of car a parent would drive—maybe her mother?—not a boyfriend. He hoped so, anyway. But she *had* turned him down for a date.

He was pretty sure one of the requirements of eligibility for the magazine's lists was that the person nominated wasn't involved in a committed relationship. That thought helped to quicken his step back home.

When he reached the entrance to the cul-de-sac, he slowed to a walk to start cooling down. He mustered the energy to wave when a blue Porsche Cayman rolled past him and pulled into the garage of the house attached to his. His chest twinged with envy, the way it did every time he saw the luxury sports car. If only he didn't have to occasionally drive clients around, he could have gotten the two-door Jaguar instead of the more stodgy sedan.

A tall, slender African American man came out of the garage, shading his eyes against the glaring sun even though he wore designer sunglasses. "Man, do you have a death wish? What are you thinking, running in this heat?"

Forbes powered off his iPod and used the hem of his soaked T-shirt to swipe at the sweat streaming down his face. "I know. I just had some excess energy I needed to burn off since we didn't run this morning."

"You found out where that chick lives, didn't you?" Shon loosened his tie and unbuttoned his collar.

"What 'chick'?" Forbes started stretching before his muscles froze up—and to have an excuse not to look his neighbor—and client—in the eye.

"The girl from that talk show on Channel Six."

"It's not a talk show—no studio audience. It's a news magazine." At least that's how the on-screen digital cable guide classified it, which he'd seen when he set his DVR to record it every day.

Shon snorted. "Whatever. Look, I've been telling you for years that I can set you up with some of the most attractive women in this city. You'd be amazed at the quality of our clientele."

Even though Forbes had represented LeShon Murphy's business for almost five years, the idea of personally making use of Let's Do Coffee's matchmaking services never entered his mind. "Thanks, but I think I'll stick with the old-fashioned way of doing things."

"That's right—she was at the dinner Friday night, wasn't she? So did you ask her out?"

Sometimes, living next door to someone who'd made his first million by age twenty-five from setting people up on blind dates wasn't ideal. "Not that it's any of your business, but yes, I did ask her out."

Forbes stopped midstretch when Shon didn't respond immediately.

A huge grin broke over Shon's dark face. "She said no."

Since the man was an important client and someone he considered a friend, Forbes bit back a sharp retort. "She already had plans for the night I wanted to go out. She didn't close the door for good, though."

"Right." Shon unknotted his tie and pulled it off. "Do me a favor and just remember what the Bible says: 'It is not good for man to be alone.'"

First his mother, sisters, aunts, and cousins, now his client. "Will do. We back on schedule tomorrow?"

"I'll be out here at 5:00 a.m., ready to go, old man."

"We'll see about that." He raised his hand in a dismissive wave as his friend disappeared into his garage.

Forbes dragged himself up the front steps and was met with a blast of chilled air when he opened the door. He stood in the entry hall, leaning over a floor vent for a few minutes until the drying perspiration on his face, neck, and chest began to itch.

After a quick shower and change of clothes, he sat down to check his e-mail at the desk in the bedroom he'd converted to an office. He replied to a couple of notes from high school friends about their upcoming twenty-year reunion, then turned off the computer.

He wandered downstairs, looking for something to do. In the study, he ran his fingers across the spines of the leather-bound editions of the complete works of Charles Dickens. He stopped at *Bleak House*. He'd read the massive tome at least once a year since he'd been assigned to read it in college. It had been only six months since he'd last cracked the covers. But beginning it would be a good way to fill a long, empty evening.

From a drawer in the cabinet below the bookshelves, he pulled out a small bottle of leather conditioner and the cloth he kept with it. Having paid quite a bit for his collection, he wanted to keep them as pristine as the day he received each one.

Settling into the Queen Anne–style wing chair, he opened the cover, breathing deeply to take in the aroma of the leather, the paper and ink, and the faint scent of dust that accompanied reading his favorite author's books. But today, instead of being transported to the foggy, muddy, raw November day in early Victorian England, Forbes's mind wandered.

A year ago when he'd met the man who would become his cousin Anne's husband, Forbes had known a thrill of excitement at the possibility of discussing Dickens's work with an actual Englishman. . . until he found out that George had never been able to make it all the way through *A Christmas Carol* and had never attempted any of the longer works.

He shook his head and tried once again to focus on the words: the beautiful, magical prose that never failed to carry him away to cold, dreary London.

Had Alaine ever read any of Dickens's work?

An image of her curled up in the chair beside him with one of the other leather-bound books in her lap, twirling an ebony curl around one finger while she read was so palpable, he almost reached over to touch her hand.

Okay. He was losing it. He shifted position and once again turned his attention to the first page of his favorite book. The "ten-thousand stages of endless causes." The "slippery precedents." The Chancery Court of 1840s England. The case of Jarndyce and Jarndyce. The legal system and the fictional court case on which he'd written his senior thesis as an undergraduate student.

As points from his thesis emerged from the mists of memory, Forbes finally cleared his mind of all distractions and lost himself in the familiar imagery and language.

Only when his stomach started growling did he emerge again. He needed to eat dinner. He leaned his head back against the chair's high back and stared at the ceiling. This was the first Sunday evening in a long time he didn't have anything to do: no evening church activities during the summer, no out-of-town clients to entertain, no family get-together, no homeowners' association events. . .nothing.

He picked up his Blackberry from the end table. Scrolling through his contacts, he dismissed Meredith—no way only three-days married she'd be interested in getting together; Jenn would be busy down at her restaurant; Rafe was piloting a late charter back from New York; and the four remaining younger siblings most likely all had plans tonight as well, none of which included hanging out with their decrepit oldest brother.

He tossed the phone on the table and rubbed his eyes. He could always go down to Riverwalk, get dinner, and listen to music over at the new jazz club. He almost always ran into someone he knew when he was out.

Anything would be better than sitting here alone all night.

Shoving himself out of the chair, he started upstairs to change into something more appropriate than shorts and a T-shirt.

Halfway up, his cell phone trilled. He jogged back to the study. Meredith's picture flashed on the PDA's touch screen. "Hey, Sis. What's up?"

"Hey. Major's cooking, which means there's about to be a lot more food here than either of us can eat. I thought if you don't already have plans you might like to come over."

"Yeah—that sounds great. Casual, I assume?"

"Did you hear me say this is at *my* house?"

He laughed. "Right. Fancy food. Ultracasual dress."

"So you're coming?"

"I'll be there in about twenty minutes. Can I bring anything?"

"Just a hearty appetite. Oh, wait—bring that classic-movie trivia game you have. I'm calling Anne and George, too."

"Will do. See you in a few minutes."

"Bye."

He tucked the phone in his pocket, then ran upstairs to put some shoes on. He could wear the new leather loafers—but this was Meredith. He grabbed his oldest, most comfortable pair of Top-Siders and slipped them on.

It was nice to know that some things would never change.

Chapter 5

"Are you going to talk to her?" Meredith sidled up beside Forbes at the kitchen island.

He continued layering the thinly sliced prime rib onto the sourdough roll. "I'm waiting until tomorrow to call her."

Meredith frowned. "Who are you talking about?"

He paused. "Who are *you* talking about?"

"Evelyn," Meredith whispered, leaning around him to look through the kitchen door. "You've done a pretty good job of ignoring her since you walked in the door."

"Oh, right." The annoyance he'd felt when he walked in and saw a stranger seated in Meredith's living room resurfaced. "Sorry. I didn't mean to ignore her. Tell me what she's doing at B-G again."

"She's an executive with the development company Mom and Dad are working with on the Warehouse Row project. She doesn't know anyone here, and when we had lunch earlier this week, she mentioned how lonely she gets when she has these temporary assignments she has to relocate for. . . ." Meredith's voice drifted off. Forbes glanced at her, then followed her smiling gaze to the door to see Major walking into the kitchen.

Forbes sighed. By no means unhappy that his sister had married one of his closest friends, he simply had not accustomed himself to how the dynamics of his own relationship with Meredith would change.

Quickly putting his sandwich together, he carried his plate into the living room, leaving Meredith and Major alone in the kitchen. He crossed to the Stickley club chair near the fireplace—and closest to where Evelyn Mackenzie sat on the sofa.

He gave her a few examining glances as he settled into the chair—shoulder-length dark hair, dark eyes, and legs that went on for miles, modestly displayed by the knee-length shorts she wore. She graced him with a smile, then returned her attention to George's story of how he and Anne had met and fallen in love.

Evelyn set her plate on the coffee table. "Wait. Let me get this straight. Anne, you didn't know that George was filling in for his boss? And George, you didn't know that Anne had once been engaged to your boss?"

"Precisely. But there was one person, who happens to be in this very room, who knew the truth about everyone—and chose not to reveal it to us." George's clipped accent poked at Forbes's conscience.

He smiled at his cousin's husband. "Just as you were bound by the contract you signed, George, I was bound by attorney-client privilege." He really hoped they wouldn't decide to air family laundry in front of a total stranger.

Anne *humphed*, but left it alone and continued the story. Forbes ate his sandwich in peace. Though used to being blamed by his younger siblings—and Anne—of trying to control their lives, they all eventually realized it was for their own good. After all, things had turned out more than all right for Anne and George.

Major and Meredith rejoined them, sitting a respectable distance from each other on the love seat across from Forbes.

"You know so much about all of us now"—Anne shifted her still-full plate on her lap—"why don't you tell us a little about yourself, Evelyn?"

Forbes's eyes snapped to Evelyn's legs as she shifted position. He quickly glanced away, berating himself for such a juvenile reaction.

"Well, I'm originally from Boston, but we lived all over as my father built his business. I went to Columbia for my undergraduate work, then to Harvard Law." She tilted her head and slew her coppery brown gaze at Forbes.

He nodded in acknowledgment at the prestigious pedigree.

"Since then, I've been working for my father's company."

"And what do you do?" Forbes set his empty plate on the table and relaxed into the buttery leather chair.

"I'm the retail development director. Whenever Mackenzie and Son partners with a local company to develop an area, as we have with Boudreaux-Guidry Enterprises, I come in to handle all the details—from the broad legal questions to finalizing the acquisition of the real estate to the day-to-day tasks, such as working with contractors, surveyors, materials wholesalers, and all those sort that the investors don't need to be bothered with."

Frowning, Forbes leaned forward, propping his elbows on his knees. "Mackenzie and *Son*? You're not a named partner in the firm?"

Though Evelyn laughed, a slight tenseness showed around her eyes. "It's not like a law firm where it's named after the partners. When my father incorporated the company, my brother and I were just kids. He assumed that my brother would enter the family business and I would pursue something else—like marriage and a family, or teaching, like my mother did before she got married. I guess he just didn't realize that things would be a lot different for women in the new millennium."

Forbes opened his mouth to remind her that her father could easily file an amendment to his business license to change the name—but a wide-eyed look of warning from Meredith stopped him. He resumed his former, relaxed posture in the chair. He'd taken up for Meredith with their parents a few months ago when she'd admitted to him that she felt like their parents didn't respect her position as an executive director in charge of two of B-G's largest departments—facilities and events—but her unspoken reminder that it wasn't his business to get involved in how Evelyn's father ran his company was correct.

"Evelyn, how do you feel about old movies?" Meredith asked. Major took that as a cue to clear everyone's empty plates from the coffee table.

"Are we talking stuff from the '80s or what?"

"Oh, no. We're talking old. Black-and-white." Meredith skirted the table and grabbed the game box off the top of the built-in cabinet behind Forbes.

George rubbed his hands together. "Brilliant. I love this game."

"That's because you've seen every old movie known to man," Forbes groused. Over the last year, he'd become more familiar with Anne's and Meredith's—and their husbands'—favorite kinds of movies, mostly because either that's what they watched whenever they all got together or because they now loved to play this game, which he'd bought in self-defense to keep from having to actually *watch* the old movies.

"Uh. . .I think I have a classic movie channel in my digital cable package, but I'm never home long enough to watch any of them."

"Oh, it'll be fun. I think you'll be surprised at how many you probably know and just don't realize it. Isn't that right, Forbes?" Meredith dug her knuckle into his shoulder.

"Sure."

"Tell you what. Evelyn, why don't you team up with Anne. Forbes, you can partner with George. And Major and I'll be a team."

Like there would be any thought of splitting up the newlyweds. "Sounds fair." He moved onto the sofa beside George while Anne went around to sit with Evelyn.

As the game progressed, Forbes heard many of his own sardonic remarks about some of the questions and the corresponding film clips on the DVD-based game coming out of Evelyn's mouth at the same time. For the first time, he started to enjoy playing this game because, for once, he finally had someone else in the room who felt the same way he did about old movies—better off forgotten.

He did get a couple of answers no one else did. Though they came as no shock to his relatives, Evelyn gave him a quizzical look.

He shrugged. "I've tried to see every film version ever made of my favorite author's work."

"Your favorite author?"

"Charles Dickens."

She scrunched up her face. "Dickens? Dickens is your favorite author? How did that happen? You don't strike me as the dusty-books-in-library type."

No. He kept his complete Dickens collection well dusted. "I minored in English in college. Rhetoric, but I had to take several literature classes. We read excerpts of *Bleak House* in one of them, and I was hooked. Had to read the whole book—which was not an easy task the first time, I'll tell you. But he had so much to say about the legal system in England in the mid-nineteenth century. I ended up writing my senior thesis on it."

Anne, Meredith, and Major stared at him.

"You never told me that." Meredith looked hurt. "I knew he was your favorite, but I just figured it was for the same reason that John Wayne movies are my favorite. Just because."

He clapped his hands to his knees. "Well, now you know. Shall we continue with the game? I believe George and I just moved into the lead."

"Alaine, come on. You've got promos to do." Pricilla stood in the doorway of Alaine's cubicle Monday morning, tapping her foot.

"Hold on just a second." Alaine bookmarked the Web page on class-action lawsuits in real-estate and eminent-domain cases. "Okay. I'm coming." She shrugged into the cropped red blazer the sponsoring clothing shop had dropped off last week. It pulled a bit in the shoulders, but she only had to wear it for ninety minutes.

As soon as she hit the studio, she got wired up with her lapel microphone, then hooked her interruptible feedback box onto the back of her waistband, turned it on, and plugged in her earpiece just in case someone from the control room needed her. The printout of the show rundown was on her chair on the set.

"Hey, Lainey!" Brent Douglas, the daytime meteorologist, gave her his standard, cocky grin when he entered the studio a few seconds later.

Not only did she hate that nickname, but now every time she looked at him, she couldn't help but remember Meredith Guidry's confession that she'd been in love with him in college, he knew it, and he'd dated and then married her roommate. "Hey, Brent."

"Alaine, fifteen second promo in six. . .five. . .four. . ."

She pasted on a smile and looked into the glass in front of the camera lens that reflected the teleprompter feed. "Tomorrow on Inside Bonneterre, go green with energy saving ideas for the home from a local contractor. Veterinarian Andrew Blakeley will be here to take your calls and answer questions about keeping your pets healthy in this heat. Plus, LeShon Murphy, founder of Let's Do Coffee, will be here to talk about relationships and dating. See you at noon."

After recording a five-second spot and a "Today on Inside Bonneterre" spot that would run the next morning, Alaine went around behind the backdrop and gave her hair, makeup, and wardrobe one final check in the full-length mirror.

Pricilla entered the studio with two interns on her heels. "Guests are all here, and the remote that Jeff did for us this morning just came out of editing and is ready to roll after the third break."

"I think we need to start doing a regular legal-advice segment. We already have a pediatrician and a veterinarian coming in regularly."

"Because they're married to people who work here."

"That's beside the point." Alaine applied a little more lipstick, then checked her teeth to make sure none had transferred. "I would imagine someone here is related or married to a lawyer who could come in and take calls." Forbes Guidry would send her viewers into a frenzy. But she couldn't allow herself to think about him; she had a show to do and couldn't afford the distraction.

An hour later, Alaine fought frustration at the near-flubs and minor mistakes she'd made all through the program because her concentration kept lapsing. A virus named Forbes Guidry had infected her brain.

When she tossed to the news anchor for a quick update at five minutes till one o'clock, Alaine took several deep breaths to try to compose herself before giving the tease for the next day's show and the bye-bye.

As soon as she was clear, she closed her eyes and shook her head. "I'm sorry, everyone. I don't know where my brain is today." She looked around at the three cameramen, Rebekka Blakeley, and Brent, knowing everyone in the control room could hear her as well. "I promise I'll be back on form tomorrow."

Bekka shrugged and gave her an understanding smile. "It's a Monday. We all have those kinds of days." She crossed the small studio, carefully avoiding tripping over the thick cables snaking all over the floor, and perched on the edge of the chair beside Alaine's. "Is everything okay? Anything I can do?"

Alaine could have hugged the newscaster. Bekka Blakeley had been one of the sports reporters when Alaine first started at the station. In fact, watching Bekka rise from reporter to weekend sports anchor to morning news anchor to her current position as the sole anchor of the noon news updates and the five o'clock news hour encouraged Alaine's dreams to move into real news reporting, too.

And Bekka was the only person at the station who was shorter than Alaine. . .by a whole inch. That thought brought her a genuine smile for the first time in twenty-four hours. "Like you said—it's just one of those days." She stood and removed her microphone and IFB box and earpiece. "Bekka, since you were kind enough to let us use your husband for the veterinarian Q&A segment, you don't happen to have a relative who's a lawyer, do you?"

"I do—a cousin—but she lives in Tennessee. I'll ask around for you, if you want me to."

"No, I need to work out the idea for the segment before I start looking for someone, I guess."

"Okay, just let me know if—" Her eyes went vague for a second, a sure indication someone was talking to her from the control room. "Oops, they're calling me to do my teasers." She scurried back over to the main news desk.

Alaine sat and watched the woman only five or six years older than herself record her first promo spot. Bekka—petite with looks that could still pass for a teenager when she didn't have her makeup on and hair done—had managed to climb the ladder due, in part, to her connections but also in large part because she was good at her job. Alaine still struggled to figure out how to get the executives to realize that she, too, had the potential to become an anchor.

She let the whine reverberate in her head as a prayer, begging God to make them give her a chance to prove herself.

Back at her desk, though tempted to get online again and do more research on legal recourse for her parents, Alaine applied herself to her work. First order of business: calling tomorrow's guests, confirming their arrival time, and answering any last-minute questions.

The call to Bekka's husband was quick. He'd done his segment once a month for the past two years. The contractor wanted to know what kinds of things he could bring in for demos, so she invited him to come half an hour early to see what would work and what wouldn't. She saved the call to LeShon Murphy until last.

When she'd booked the twenty-nine-year-old entrepreneur a month ago, she'd done so grudgingly. She'd read his interview in *Bonneterre Lifestyles* and seen the response it had generated from readers from their comments online.

Her conversation with Mother yesterday came back and made Alaine more than a little curious about his service. She pulled up the contact entry for him on the computer and dialed his number.

"This is Shon." The few times she'd talked to him, he'd always sounded breezy and casual. No difference today.

"Mr. Murphy, it's Alaine Delacroix from Channel Six. I hope I've caught you at a good time." She leaned her elbows on her desk and supported her forehead on her free palm, her back starting to ache between her shoulders.

"Yes, Alaine. Please, call me Shon. Are we still on for tomorrow?"

"We are. Do you need directions to the studio?"

"No, no. Our offices are just a few buildings down from y'all." Amusement laced his deep voice.

She could have kicked herself. Right there on the computer screen was the address. Now that she thought about it, the last time she'd talked to him, they'd discussed his proximity to the studio and the fact that he could just walk over.

"Right. Do you have any other questions?"

"Nope. Think I'm good."

"Great. I'll see you tomorrow around eleven thirty, then." They exchanged farewells, and Alaine hung up, feeling like a complete idiot.

Before she made a total fool of herself tomorrow, she opened her Internet browser and went to Let's Do Coffee's Web site to find out how the program worked. She took notes and wrote questions to ask Shon tomorrow on air. The more she read about how his system operated, the more intrigued she became.

"Alaine, are you ready to meet about the remotes for next week—what are you doing?"

Alaine quickly minimized the screen to hide the personality profile she'd been filling out as part of the membership application process. "Just research for tomorrow's guest. I'm ready for the meeting."

She hid her grin until Pricilla turned to precede her to the small conference room. Yes, Alaine Delacroix was ready for a meeting: meeting the man of her dreams.

Chapter 6

"I'm sorry, sir, she's in a meeting right now. May I take a message or put you through to her voice mail?"

He'd left her a voice mail message yesterday, after trying for more than an hour to get past the dragon guarding the switchboard. But now that Forbes had actually reached a real, live person in the newsroom, he wasn't going to let this opportunity slip by. "Before you transfer me to voice mail, please give me her direct phone number in case we get disconnected."

"Hold on a sec, and let me look it up. I'm just an intern and don't have everyone's numbers memorized. Oh, here it is. Three-six-nine-four. Hold on, and I'll transfer you."

Well, her extension number was better than nothing. Not wanting to leave another message in less than twenty-four hours, he hung up and programmed Alaine's extension into her information in his Blackberry. Now when he called, he could get to her straight from the automated answering system on the main line.

He took some files he was finished with out to Samantha's desk.

The secretary looked up from her computer when he dropped the heavy folders into her in-box. "I suspected your chipper mood yesterday wouldn't last all week." She leaned over and looked at the files. "Ah. I see why. The case that just won't go away."

"My own personal Jarndyce and Jarndyce."

Samantha frowned and thumbed through the folders. "I don't see that one in here—and I haven't run across that name. Is it new?"

Forbes smiled for the first time today. "No. It's a fictional case in my favorite book. It went on for many, many years and financially ruined at least three generations of the Jarndyce family."

Samantha returned to her computer. "Sounds boring."

"There's a romance story in it, too." He picked up the stack of unopened mail and flipped through it. He never saw it at this stage—and never this much of it.

"Whatever. You're supposed to be over at the courthouse in thirty minutes. The Pichon injunction."

"Right. Thanks. Oh, file—" He looked up from the mail to see Samantha holding the thick folder toward him.

"Here you go, Mr. Bonneterre."

"Thanks, Ms. Impertinence." He took the folder.

"You're welcome, Dudley Do-Right."

Forbes laughed, glad to have a secretary with a sense of humor who could give as good as she got. In his office, he jammed the file into his attaché case, shrugged into his jacket, and headed out for the parish courthouse.

After going through the metal detector, he checked his courtroom assignment and went to the bank of elevators. One opened immediately and disgorged a bunch of people before he could step in. Some of the judges must be getting their earliest cases on the docket cleared quickly. He hoped his case didn't get called early.

The elevator doors were nearly closed when a hand jutted between them and they reopened. "Sorry. Didn't want to miss this one—oh hey, Forbes."

The doors slid shut behind Russell LeBlanc, a high-school classmate who had turned his back on a fast-track position at a law firm to start a community legal aid office, where most of his cases were pro bono.

"Hey, Russ. So, we're squaring off again today."

"Yep." The other lawyer grinned. "Don't you ever get tired of defending all these businesses that are only out to protect their bottom lines?"

"Not when the cases brought against them are trivial nonsense."

"We'll see what Judge Duplessis has to say about that, won't we?"

"Yes, we will." Forbes tried to keep a stern expression but had never been able to resist Russell's constant good humor. "How's Carrie?"

"Home on bed rest."

"So she's okay?"

"Fine. We've gotten to twenty-eight weeks. We're shooting for thirty-four. But with quads, you just never know."

The doors slid open on the fifth floor. Forbes motioned Russell to exit ahead of him. "Quadruplets. I still can't get my head around it. You with four kids all in law school at the same time."

"Eh. You never know. One might go over to the dark side and decide to become a doctor or a teacher—or even worse, a social worker like their mom." Russ cocked his head and laughed. "See you in court."

Forbes waved and headed the opposite direction. He filled his small water bottle at the drinking fountain, then looked for his client.

Mr. Pichon paced the hallway near the main doors to the assigned courtroom. Forbes straightened his tie, adjusted his jacket, and approached.

"There you are." Mr. Pichon plucked at the knot of his tie as if it was too tight. "I was starting to wonder. . .no matter. Let's get this done today. I'm tired of this property hanging around my neck like an abalone."

"Albatross," Forbes corrected under his breath.

"What?"

"Never mind. Mr. Pichon, again, my recommendation is that you not contest the injunction and that you look at the proposal from the community group."

"I've looked at their numbers. I have six bidders coming in at twice what that group of yahoos wants to pay for my land."

Forbes kept his expression neutral, his voice level. "Yes, but they have e-mails proving that three years ago you promised them that if they developed the lot into a park, you wouldn't sell it without giving the community association the opportunity to purchase it for fair market value. That's going to be a big sticking point for Duplessis."

"But why should I sell it to them when I can make twice the money? Look, Guidry, you're my lawyer, and you're going to do this the way I want. I don't care what's done with the property so long as I get what's coming to me."

Sometimes Forbes did wish he'd taken Russell's path in the legal field. "You know I'll work to get you the outcome you want, Mr. Pichon. That's what I'm here for."

An hour and a half later, walking out of the courtroom, Forbes sent up a silent prayer of thanks that Judge Duplessis had been assigned this case. Duplessis, like Russ, had worked most of his career in legal aid centers and tended to rule in favor of the underdog, so long as there was any legal justification for it. Still, Forbes had made his arguments dance and twirl and spin—like that guy, Fred or Frank or whoever, in the old movies—until he'd had Duplessis in the palm of his hand. Then Russ had reminded the judge of the e-mails with the promises given by Pichon to the community group.

"Mediation. Mediation!" Pichon pulled at his thinning, steel gray hair and let out a string of curses. "I want to sell that blasted lot now, while the buyers are hot for it, not sit down across a table from these idiots and pretend like I'm the least interested in anything they have to say. It's not my fault those people spent too much money building paths and gazebos and other idiotic things that they had no right to build on my property."

Forbes didn't want to reiterate what Russ had brought up in argument: that if the community had not pooled their resources together to rehabilitate the lot which Mr. Pichon had allowed to become a weed-choked dumping ground for trash and old appliances, no one in his right mind would be interested in buying it now.

"Mr. Pichon, I know you want to move on this, but we have to do whatever the judge orders." From the corner of his eye, he saw Russ parting company with his clients. "If you'll excuse me, I need to speak with opposing counsel."

"Yeah. You do that, Guidry." Mr. Pichon stormed off, still muttering obscenities under his breath.

Forbes waited for Russ to get off the phone.

"That was Carrie. She says hi."

"Everything okay?"

"Oh, yeah. She just gets bored and so calls me every hour or so." Russ smirked. "I guess I should be thankful, since I know we'll have little enough time together after the babies come, but it's really starting to. . ." He shrugged. "What's up, old man?"

Forbes cocked a brow at the man only a few months his junior. "I wanted to volunteer for some pro bono work. I'm well short of where I need to be to get my fifty hours this year, and I know y'all are probably overwhelmed with cases. Just keep in mind—"

"I know—nothing going up against any of your firm's clients. That severely restricts what I could be able to send you." His friend grinned. "But I'll keep you in mind. With Carrie likely to pop any day now, I'll be needing the extra help. See you in mediation."

"Right. Later." Forbes reached for his Blackberry when it started vibrating against his belt. After clearing up the notes he'd written in a file for Samantha, he headed back to the parking garage.

The overwhelming workload that Russ carried must be inordinately stressful, yet every time Forbes saw him, Russ looked like he was having the time of his life. Though Forbes enjoyed most of his cases, certain clients gave him cases that made him feel like the Big, Bad Wolf in court. He hated looking across at the plaintiffs and seeing regular people—people who couldn't afford a lawyer's fee many times—and knowing that because of the legal dance he was about to do, they would lose their case. Meaning they would lose the time they'd taken off work to be there, lose money, lose their homes, lose the court costs they'd be required to pay. And when they won, he hated the fact that his clients blamed it on him instead of their own, usually unethical or at least unfair, business practices.

There was a certain glory in the job Russ did. He went to bat for the little guys. He made sure they got their date in court if their case warranted it. He helped them make their voices heard against corporate bigwigs with teams of lawyers on retainer and money to burn.

Forbes took the stack of files Samantha held out toward him without even speaking as he walked back into his office. He paused just inside the door and took in his surroundings.

Of course, there was nothing glorious about the dingy little office where Russ worked, with the secondhand, mismatched furniture and the strong smell of cat urine from the Siamese rescue center that used to be located in the converted house before Russ bought it for an office.

Though his work was sometimes unpalatable, Forbes would take partnership in a prestigious firm over legal aid any day.

Alaine tapped her thumbnail against her front teeth—but stopped when she realized what she was doing. She tried to turn her attention back to the staff meeting, but changes to the content on the Web site didn't interest her much.

How could she have been so stupid? The least she could have done was wait until after the interview. But no. She'd had to jump the gun and activate her Let's Do Coffee account last night. What if LeShon Murphy knew she'd signed up for an active matchmaking account? After all, he only had twenty employees. Surely whichever one of the data entry people saw her name pop up on a new account this morning would have told Shon. In their preliminary phone chat, he'd told her that he personally handled their high-profile clients. She qualified as that, didn't she?

She'd just tell him it was for research purposes—that she hadn't meant to activate the account. . .or input her credit card info for the membership fee. . .or click on the boxes to say she agreed to the morality clause and the terms of service and that she was seriously interested in meeting a variety of men they would choose for her based on the extensive personal profile and personality-type quiz she'd filled out.

He'd never believe her. Besides, the truth was that she did, in fact, want to make use of his company's service.

She should have asked him to bring his wife—or girlfriend, whichever one he had. Getting the story on how they met would make a nice addition to the piece. She grabbed her pen from behind her ear and made herself a note to follow up with him about that. After all, if she was going to trust him with her love life, it would be nice to be sure he was happy and successful in his own relationship.

"Alaine. Alaine!"

Alaine looked up when Bekka Blakeley elbowed her and nodded toward the head of the table, where the news director glowered at her.

"Yes?"

"I'm sorry, are we boring you?"

She could do without the sarcasm. "Just making notes for the interview I'm doing in less than two hours. Was there another question you wanted to ask me?" From the corner of her eye, she could see Bekka shaking her head in exasperation. Antagonizing the very person who could help her move to the news desk—probably not a great idea.

"The Web site. Any special requests from your viewers you'd like to pass along?"

"Just to get the recipes up sooner than Sunday or Monday. Since Chef O'Hara provides those for us when he films on Tuesdays, I don't see why they're not going up as soon as his segment airs on Fridays."

"We'll pass that along." The head honcho of the newsroom smirked at her and moved on to Bekka. He always did that to her—made her feel like a high-school intern who'd accidentally walked into a place she shouldn't be and wasn't welcome. Well, her program had higher ratings than the ten o'clock news, so he could take his condescension and shove it where—

"Hey, are you okay?"

At Bekka's whispered question, Alaine looked around. Everyone was getting up from the conference table.

"Yeah, just thinking. . .about the interview I'm doing with LeShon Murphy today."

"Just checking. You really zoned out there for a while."

Alaine stood and tucked her steno pad under her arm, pen behind her ear. "These staff meetings are a waste of my time. No one ever says something that effects my show, and they're not interested in anything I have to say anyway, so what's the point?"

"The point is"—Bekka followed her out of the room—"if you want to move into main news, you're going to have to start acting like you're interested in what's going on in the rest of the newsroom. And you have to make yourself heard—but not by alienating the one person with the most sway around here."

Alaine shook her head, shoulders drooping. "I know. I knew as soon as I heard the words coming out of my mouth it was a stupid thing to say. I just get so tired of his constantly sniping at me. It's like he doesn't want me to be there."

"Well, my suggestion—and it's just my opinion—is that you do whatever it takes to impress him. To show him you not only deserve to be at that table, but that you also deserve to be moved up the ranks."

Bekka stopped Alaine with a hand on her arm. "Alaine, you've been here for ten years. Granted, when you took over the noon show six years ago, that was a pretty big coup for someone so young. But for someone who's been saying you wanted to be at the big desk for as long as you've been saying it to not have made it one step closer, you really need to stop and take stock of what might be holding you back."

Alaine snorted. "What's holding me back is all the upper-ups who take one look at me and can't get past my exterior to see that I could handle breaking news stories or an evening news anchor position. You didn't have to worry about it the way I did. Your dad was the news director here for twenty-some-odd years, not to mention a silent partner in the ownership of this station and Cannon Broadcasting. Of course you were going to get promoted." Alaine pressed her lips together to stop herself from saying anything else. What was wrong with her, just letting stuff slip out with no apparent ability to censor herself today?

A hurt, resigned expression entered Bekka's brown eyes. "As I said, it's only my opinion. You can take the suggestion or not, as you choose."

"Bekka, I'm sorry. I didn't mean. . .I'm just frustrated. I know you had to work hard to get a job here and to get the promotions you've gotten. The truth of the matter is that I'm jealous that you managed to find a path to do it that I haven't seemed to figure out yet."

Bekka cocked her head. "Did I ever tell you that I didn't want to be in main news?"

Alaine jerked her head in surprise. "What?"

"That's right. I was perfectly content being a sports reporter. It's all I ever wanted to do since I was six years old. Once I became the weekend sports anchor, I was very happy to stay there until John decided to move on to Cannon Sports News so I could take over the sports director position. But John, of course, isn't going anywhere. And once I got married to someone whose career is here in Bonneterre, I didn't want to leave, either. Then, because the marketing department had created so much of an image for me, they started having me cover non-sports stories. When the morning show co-anchor position opened up, I gave it a lot of prayer—just ask my husband; I kept him up plenty of nights because I couldn't sleep. Finally, I decided to take that step. And I've never regretted it."

"But do you miss reporting sports?"

"Every day. But I'm content doing what I'm doing because I know it's where God wants me. So you have to ask yourself this: Do you want to move into main news because you feel like it's where *God* wants you, or do you want it because *Alaine* wants it?" Bekka shrugged. "Until you figure that out, you probably aren't going to be happy no matter what happens." Her cell phone buzzed. "Gotta go. See you in the studio."

"Thanks, Bekka."

Alaine trudged back to her cubicle and tossed the steno pad on top of the papers scattered across her desk. She sank into her chair, slumped over the desk, and dropped her head into her hands, rubbing her temples.

Pray about it? She'd done nothing *but* pray about moving into main news for years. But for some reason Bekka's words continued to niggle at her. Was becoming a news anchor what God wanted for her, or something she desired on her own? Wait. Wasn't there a verse in the Bible somewhere that said something about how if she loved God, He would give her the desires of her heart?

The phone rang, and she picked it up without looking at the caller ID window. "Alaine Delacroix."

"Alaine? This is Forbes Guidry. Are you okay? You sound upset."

How could someone she'd met only once be able to sense her turmoil through just the way she said her name when she answered the phone? "I think I just hurt a very good friend of mine here at the office—one of my few good friends, in fact."

"What happened?"

"Oh, I seem to have lost my internal editor and spouted off at the mouth about something I had no business saying to her that was coming from a need to vent my personal frustrations on someone else." Hey, wait a minute. Speaking of personal frustrations, what was she doing talking to Forbes Guidry—the *enemy*! "Look, now isn't a good time to talk."

"Okay. When would be a good time?"

She sighed. "Forbes, listen, I have a lot going on in my life right now, and. . ."

"And you're just not that into me. I get it. But you can't blame a guy for trying, right?"

Something inside of her broke in half—one side of it crying for her to recant and go out with the handsome lawyer, the other half screaming to get off the phone immediately and have no more contact with the man whose parents were trying to put hers out of home and business.

"Right." Her voice croaked; she cleared her throat. "I really have to finish up some stuff for my program."

"I'm not going to give up. But I'll let you go for now. Bye."

"Bye." She held the receiver to her ear until the dial tone sounded, then slowly lowered it to the cradle.

She wanted to burst into tears. Wanted to bury her head in her arms and just sob like she hadn't done since she was eighteen and Bobby Ponnier broke her heart when he laughed at her invitation to be her date to the Chi Omega Sadie Hawkins dance.

Why was everything in her life falling apart all at the same time?

Chapter 7

"Mr. Murphy. It's nice to finally meet you face-to-face." Alaine walked forward, right hand extended toward the young, African American man.

Even as he clasped her hand in his, LeShon Murphy cocked his head and gave her a remonstrative look.

"Sorry. . ." She grinned at him. "Shon."

"Alaine. I'm thrilled to be here." He flashed a neon-white smile at her. He was much better looking in person than in his press photos—and he was plenty good-looking enough in those.

"Did they get you wired up with a microphone?" She motioned him toward stage three—the dais to the right of the news desk featuring two dark-brown Naugahyde armchairs.

"I'm all wired up and ready to go." Shon sat in the chair adjacent to hers, eyes darting around at the hulking cameras, the flat-panel TV monitors on thick metal poles in strategic locations around the room, the cords snaking across the floor, and probably the giant green-screen in the weather center on the opposite side of the studio from them.

"It's a lot smaller than I pictured it." Shon settled into his chair, his dark eyes fixed on Alaine. "And I by no means intend to be out of line here, but the camera doesn't do you justice."

It wasn't the words that created instant heat in Alaine's cheeks—she'd heard them often enough before. No, it was the way he looked at her, as if appreciating a painting by one of the masters.

"Thank you." She glanced down at her steno pad. Right. Focus. "Once you come out, I'll introduce you and then ask you to tell the viewers about your business. From there, we'll just have a conversation. I won't even have this"—she touched the notebook—"with me."

"You said something about me giving some tips and advice about dating?"

"Yes. I'll eventually lead the conversation in that direction. But don't worry—my job is to make you feel comfortable and look good." Not that he needed any help with the latter.

One of the interns came in with the rundown pages.

"Is that your script?" Shon leaned forward.

"Just for the few parts that are scripted, in case the teleprompter goes out. Most of the segments are extemporaneous. I want the viewers to feel like I'm sitting in their living room—or lunchroom or restaurant—with them, just having a chat about what's going on around town in culture and entertainment." How many times had she given that spiel at speaking events? Yet she managed to conjure a real smile to go along with the serving of dreck.

She waved one of the interns over. "I'm going to have Matt show you around while I record some promotional spots for tomorrow's show. I'll see you in a little while."

Well, at least he hadn't said anything about her account. Alaine blew out a deep breath and reviewed the script for the fifteen-second promo.

Most men flirted with her—but something about Shon made her think he might be interested in her. Strange. She was pretty sure she remembered reading in the article that he was involved in a long-term, serious relationship. Whoever the girl was, she must not have a jealous bone in her body if he was like this with every pretty girl he met.

"Alaine, promo."

"Right." She sat up straight and arranged her face into her on-air smile—the one that looked real but didn't squinch up the skin around her eyes to make it look like she had wrinkles.

At the 12:32 p.m. commercial break, Matt brought Shon to the stage and departed for the control room again.

Alaine smiled at the camera as Nelson counted down "six…five… four…three…" then the hand signals.

"Welcome back to *Inside Bonneterre*. With me right now is LeShon Murphy, founder and president of Let's Do Coffee, a matchmaking service he started here in Bonneterre that has proven so successful, he's expanded into six major cities." She turned to face him. "Welcome, Shon."

"Thanks for having me, Alaine." He flashed that high-wattage smile at her again.

"You know. Shon, it's impressive that someone as young as you were started a business like this that not only survived, but became a runaway success. What is it about Let's Do Coffee that makes it stand out in the market of online dating sites and forums and chat rooms?"

"You've actually nailed it on the head, Alaine. Our clients' first communication with each other is when they meet face-to-face the first time."

"For coffee." Alaine tried to control her expression but couldn't help showing true pleasure over talking with Shon.

He'd probably been voted Biggest Flirt his senior year of high school. "For coffee. Or lunch. Or a jog in the park. Something casual and nonthreatening. Not a big, fancy dinner date."

Alaine asked him a few more questions about how his system worked. Shon was accommodating, vague where necessary. Alaine kept a quarter of her attention on feedback from the control room coming through her earpiece, but the rest of it focused on the wire of electricity that seemed to be growing stronger between her and Shon with each passing moment.

Finally, at the two-minute warning, she turned the conversation. "In this day and age, when people are so busy they don't have time to search for that special someone, what are some tips you could give to help make it a little easier?"

Shon rested his elbows on the arms of the chair and templed his fingers. All he needed was a pair of glasses, a pipe, and a cravat to look like some Harvard professor relaxing in his library. "Well, naturally my first suggestion is to sign up for Let's Do Coffee and let us do the looking for you." He cocked a grin at her. "But other than that, it's all a matter of priorities. We make time for what's important in our lives. But don't waste it hanging out at bars or in clubs. Get involved in the community or your church. Volunteer to work at the food bank a couple of weekends a month. If you're politically active, call the office of a local politician you like and see if they need volunteers. Work with the youth group at your church or a teen crisis center. No matter where your interests lie, you can find some way to turn it into an opportunity to do some good for others—and also meet other singles who share the same interests."

Alaine got the bye-bye signal in her earpiece. "Those are wonderful suggestions, Shon. Thank you so much for coming in to talk to us today."

"Thanks for having me."

Alaine turned to face the camera. "When we come back, veterinarian Andrew Blakeley will be taking your calls."

Once clear, Alaine shook hands with Shon, even as Bekka's husband came up to take his place. Then she observed while every female in the studio—with the exception of Bekka—watched Shon walk out of the room.

As soon as the program wrapped, Alaine got unwired and left the studio—only to find Shon standing just beyond the door, waiting.

"Hey." He beamed. "I hoped you might have a few minutes to chat."

"Uh. . .sure."

He asked her about what went into planning each day's show as she led him upstairs. The small conference room near her cubicle was unoccupied at the moment, so she waved him in. He waited to sit until she'd settled into one of the old office chairs at the beat-up table.

"What can I do for you?" Alaine clasped her hands atop the table.

"It's more of what I can do for you. Your file landed on my desk this morning." He raised his brows. "I wouldn't have thought you'd need a service like ours, but I'm thrilled you signed up."

Mortification blazed across her face. Was that why he'd been flirting with her downstairs? Because he knew she was single and desperate?

"Don't worry. Lots of folks get embarrassed when they realize that someone personally handles their information. But everything remains confidential until you agree to meet another client. No names exchanged until the meeting—and definitely no photos exchanged. Neither party knows more than a general description of the other until you meet. That way, there's no prejudgment based on what someone looks like in a picture."

"O–o–okay. So what's the next step?"

Shon grinned. "The next step is that I take some of these ideas running around in my head about who I want to set you up with, and we start getting you out on some coffee dates."

"What if I don't like coffee?" Alaine kept a straight face.

"You can have tea or cola." Shon leaned his elbows on the table. "You see? There's always a choice out there that's the right one for you."

She hoped so. She really did.

"Mr. Guidry, Ms. Landreneau's assistant just called. She'd like to see you in her office pronto." Samantha leaned through the door, hanging onto the frame like a kid hanging on a garden gate.

Forbes held his groan in. Getting called into the managing partner's office meant one of two things: either a high-profile client with a new case none of the other partners wanted to deal with, or a top client visiting from out of town who needed to be entertained—neither of which he was particularly interested in today.

"Thanks, Samantha. Let her know I'll be there momentarily."

"I'll let her know you're thrilled." Samantha winked and disappeared.

He rolled his sleeves down, straightened his tie, and shrugged into his suit coat before leaving his office. Must keep up the image of a partner—even if he was relegated to an office one floor down from the executive suites, down where all the senior associates slaved away, hoping to be in his position someday.

He paused a moment outside the door to Sandra Landreneau's suite to collect himself. Squaring his shoulders and trying his best to affect indifference—a lawyer's best choice of facial expression—he entered the antechamber.

The secretary, an older woman whose attitude was as frosty as her hair, cocked her left brow at him as if he were an unwelcome intruder.

"Good afternoon, Mary. She asked to see me." He kept his tone light and friendly—not going to let the old battleax join in the ruining of the rest of his day.

Mary's icy expression melted into a smile that almost reached her eyes. She nodded her head toward the door to the inner sanctum. "Go on in. She's expecting you."

He rewarded her with his most winning smile, then entered Sandra Landreneau's office.

A tall woman with shoulder-length dark hair sat in one of the guest chairs across from the still-beautiful sixtyish lawyer at the enormous desk.

"Oh, good, Forbes. Come in. I want you to meet Evelyn Mackenzie of Mackenzie and Son."

Forbes smiled as Evelyn stood and turned to face him.

"I've already had the pleasure of meeting Ms. Mackenzie." He crossed the room and shook her extended hand. He hadn't realized just how tall she was. In heels, she was only a couple of inches shorter than his six foot three. "But it is wonderful to see you again so soon."

"Likewise. I knew you were a lawyer, but not that you were on the legal team for Boudreaux-Guidry Enterprises." Evelyn resumed her seat, crossing her mile-long legs.

Forbes pinned his eyes assiduously to her face, chastising himself for remembering what those limbs had looked like in a pair of shorts instead of black trousers.

"I have recused myself from handling any of B-G's legal affairs," Forbes took the chair beside her. "Ms. Landreneau handles it, as she has since long before I joined the firm."

"Oh, I see." The way Evelyn's eyes crinkled up at the corners when she smiled led Forbes to consider that she might be older than the midthirties he'd originally guessed.

"Forbes, I know this is short notice," Sandra said, drawing his and Evelyn's attention, "because it totally slipped my mind that she was coming in today. But I know how much our other clients rave about their evenings when you entertain them. So would you be available this evening to show Evelyn around town?"

He inclined his head toward his boss. "It would be my honor."

"Wonderful. Oh, and I volunteered your secretary to help Evelyn find a more permanent place to stay than the Bonneterre Oaks Executive Suites, since she'll be with us for a few months."

Samantha would be so pleased to know that. "I have a few ideas that I can get Samantha to look into." Like the town house a couple of streets over from his that the owners were trying to lease out while they traveled around Europe for the next six months.

"Very good then."

He took that as his cue to leave. Standing, he fished out one of his business cards from his inside coat pocket. Evelyn leaned down to pull one out of her briefcase. They exchanged the cards and shook hands again.

"Shall I pick you up at Bonneterre Oaks around six thirty?"

Evelyn's half-hooded eyes sent a bolt of warmth through Forbes. "I look forward to it."

"Ladies." He half bowed and measured his pace out of the office. He stopped in the hallway to catch his breath and let his heart rate return to normal. He hadn't had a reaction like that to a woman in ages—well, actually since he'd met Alaine Delacroix face-to-face a few days ago. But before that, it had been a very long time.

Between thoughts of Evelyn—and the inevitable comparisons to Alaine—interrupting his concentration, the rest of the day proved a test of his perseverance. He eventually managed to lose himself in dictating some motions for Samantha to type. When he surfaced, he glanced at the clock—six twenty! Why hadn't Samantha come in before she left? He threw random files into his attaché, flung his coat over his shoulder, and ran out to the car. He pushed the speed limit and squeezed through a couple of yellow lights to arrive at Bonneterre Oaks right at six thirty.

Evelyn waved and rose from the lounge chair on the wide front porch of the extended-stay hotel. He got out and opened the passenger door just as she reached the car.

"You know, you really didn't need to do this, Forbes. I'm used to finding my way around new cities."

"I wasn't lying when I told Sandra it would be my pleasure to show you around town. Believe me, this is the first time I'm actually looking forward to spending my evening entertaining an important client." He motioned toward the door he still held open.

She sparkled—eyes, teeth—when she smiled at him before getting in. She'd changed from her pantsuit into a sundress. . .that showed quite a bit of those magnificent legs, and more than hinted at the rest of her assets.

Forbes closed his eyes and shut the door. Aside from the fact he'd given up on dating, he had to keep this professional. Not only did he represent Folse, Landreneau, Maier & Guidry, he also represented his parents and, by extension, their company.

He got in and started the engine. "What part of Bonneterre would you like to see first?"

"Warehouse Row. Since that's what I'm here to change, let's start there."

Forbes pointed the Jag toward the southeast side of town. He asked her about her travels, and she spent the next ten minutes telling stories about her last few business trips.

He pointed out Town Square as they drove behind the western side of it, along with several of the more prominent shops and businesses in the restored Victorian buildings lining Spring Street.

"I can see why they call this area Old Towne." Evelyn bobbed her head side to side, taking in the sights. "I'll bet those town houses back there are pretty exclusive."

"The newer section that borders Old Towne is. The older section that's adjacent to the highway is more economical, though still high-end." Especially if they all had kitchens like Alaine's. Forbes had seen it only the one time on TV when Major had shot his first cooking segment there, but it had been a far cry from what he'd expected. "And what you're here to do will only increase their value."

"Is that. . .?" Evelyn stared straight across the intersection where they now sat at a red light.

"That's Warehouse Row."

"It's right across the highway from Old Towne."

"Now you see why my parents have been trying to develop it for years." He drove carefully through the potholed parking lots running throughout the complex of warehouses, empty since the second-largest paper mill in the state went out of business.

"How long ago did your parents acquire the property?"

"The warehouse complex, about five years ago. It's only been in the last six or seven months that they've started buying up all of the foreclosed or high-risk properties in Moreaux Mills—the mixed-use area adjacent."

Calculation entered Evelyn's brown eyes as they raked over the buildings. "This is a wonderful structure. The whole industrial-loft look is quite the cutting edge in retail space design." She folded her hands in her lap, and the motion once more drew Forbes's attention to her legs.

He cleared his throat and averted his gaze again. She either knew the effect she had on him, or she was just one of those creatures out of whom sensuality oozed with no conscious effort. Kind of like Alaine Delacroix.

"So, let's see the rest of the area. I want to know just how run-down it is or if there's any hope in saving any of it."

"Your wish is my command." Forbes drove out into the subdivision. "Before the paper mill closed, a large majority of these houses were owned by the mill workers—and those who worked in the warehouses. That's why the subdivision is called Moreaux Mills. Twenty-five years ago when it shut down and the workers left—either selling or being foreclosed on—the area became mixed-use, with people conducting business out of their homes or buying the vacant home next door to convert into a business."

He'd only driven through this part of town once or twice—and then back in high school to attend youth group activities at someone's home. He slowed when he approached Azalea Lane and decided to turn left, just to see what was there.

The houses were a far cry from the minimansions in his parents' neighborhood, but they weren't the run-down shacks the local news had been making them out to be in recent months. Most of them—the ones that appeared occupied, anyway—were well-kept Cape Cod or ranch-style houses with good curb appeal. While they didn't have the visual impact of the Craftsman bungalows or Victorians in Plantation Grove where Meredith and Anne lived, the mid-twentieth-century neighborhood had its charm.

Many of them also had signs out front for their businesses. He slowed again when he recognized one. "That's the company that cleans the carpets at the law firm. I had no idea they were based down here."

The road curved, then straightened out and opened into a broad cul-de-sac. But instead of a continuous line of houses, the half-circle at the top of the street featured one house in the midst of what looked like the Garden of Eden. He pulled up to the curb to read the sign in the deepening twilight: Delacroix Gardens, Nursery & Florist.

"What an eyesore." Evelyn's sneer reminded him of her presence. "Overgrown and unkempt."

Forbes loved it. It reminded him dually of Jamaica and Spain—his two favorite vacation spots.

"*Dee-la-croy*. Looking like this, they can't possibly be doing great business."

Forbes looked at the sign again. "*Del-ah-qua*," he corrected without thinking. Delacroix. Could Alaine be connected with this business?

"Well, it doesn't matter how it's pronounced, because they'll be gone soon enough. Out with the old and dilapidated, in with the new and luxurious." Evelyn sighed. "I've seen enough. Shall we go to dinner?"

Forbes turned the car around, his mouth tightening. He hadn't allowed himself to think about what would happen to the people who lived and worked down here when his parents took it all over and razed the existing structures to build luxury town houses and condos and create a completely new retail district with major national retailers they hoped would lease the spaces in the old warehouses.

He glanced at Evelyn from the corner of his eye as she rambled on about her ideas for the development. Suddenly, the sight of her long legs had only the effect on him of imagining her grinding these people into the ground with her expensive, spike-heeled sandals. He didn't like that image at all.

"They drove off. Guess they didn't realize we close at six." Alaine's father returned to the table. When most people looked at the Delacroix Gardens building from the street, they had no idea that it housed its owners on the second floor addition, nor that the home had a commanding view of the cul-de-sac and street from their dining room and living room.

"Hopefully they will come back tomorrow." Mother passed the dish of paella to Alaine. "Eat. You are wasting away."

Alaine took another small serving of the rice and seafood dish grudgingly. She couldn't afford to put on weight. The cameras already did a good job of that.

"Whoever it was, I hope they do come back. Fancy Jaguar like that—bound to have lots of money to spend." Daddy shoveled a heaping scoop of paella into his mouth.

Jaguar. . .Forbes Guidry supposedly drove one of those. Probably not the only person in town who did. But still, what were the chances. . . ?

"Alaine, what is the matter with you? Didn't you hear your mother?"

"What?" She shook her head to clear the unproductive thoughts. "No. Sorry. What did you say?"

"I asked if there was a reason you dropped in for supper. Not that we aren't always happy to see you."

"Yes, actually. I wanted to talk to you about this whole thing with the buyout."

Her parents exchanged a look that lit a fire of dread in Alaine's stomach. "What?"

Daddy cleared his throat and put his fork down. "We received notice today that a private investor has bought our mortgage from the bank. They're calling in the loan."

Alaine lost all muscle control in her jaw. She tried to form words, but all that came out was loud sputtering.

"Alaine, please, modulate your voice," Mother reprimanded.

Alaine softened her tone. "How can they do that?"

"Apparently it's the acquiring institution's prerogative to acquire loans and then call them in."

"How long do you have?"

"Ninety days."

Alaine wanted to cry. . .scream. . .yell. . .kick the table. . .something to break her parents' all-fired calm. How could they just sit there like that?

"You have to get a lawyer. You have to stop this. It can't be right."

"Oh, Alaine, you know we can't afford a lawyer." Her father picked up his fork and pushed his rice around on his plate. "We're operating in the black, but just barely. We're still trying to get caught up with the loan payments we missed last winter. According to the letter we got, that's why they're calling in the loan. Because it's more than five months in arrears."

"I'll pay for a lawyer. I'll report what's happening on my show. Surely when a lawyer of conscience hears about what's happening, they'll—"

"No." Mother brought her palms down hard on the table. "You cannot talk about this on your show. You cannot be involved."

"But I have to do something! I can't just sit by and watch y'all lose what you've worked all your lives to build. If I find a lawyer—quietly—who'll take the case without charging you too much, would you agree to meet them?"

Daddy mulled over her question for a while. "You know we're not the only ones in this situation. Joe and Nikki are, too. A dozen others that we know well, and who knows how many that we haven't met. The lawyer would have to be able to help all of us."

"Of course. I wouldn't imagine leaving out anyone who wants to try to stand up for what's right."

Daddy pushed his plate back. "But you have to promise us one thing, Alley Cat."

She actually smiled over the endearment from her childhood. "What's that?"

"You cannot be seen to be publicly involved in this. If this becomes more public than it already is, you have to step back from it. We don't want to endanger your career. You've worked too long and hard to get where you are to ruin it by marching out in front of everyone, carrying the flag of protest."

Alaine pictured herself as a majorette high-stepping in front of a marching band. She laughed, then instantly sobered. "But what if my position as someone with the ear of the public can have some influence on getting this settled quickly and quietly?"

"No. Unless you agree, there's no deal with the lawyer or trying to pursue this any further."

To see her always-happy father so stern, so serious, broke Alaine's heart. "All right. I agree. But I'm going to do whatever I can behind the scenes to make sure you don't lose this place."

Chapter 8

"Congratulations. You have now successfully licensed a Chicago branch of Let's Do Coffee." Forbes reached across the corner of the table and shook Shon's hand.

"Thanks, man. I wasn't sure this one was ever going to go through. As always, couldn't have done it without you."

"Now," Forbes shuffled the folders in front of him, looking for one in particular, "there's just one more thing we need to talk about."

Shon gestured with his hand, open and palm facing Forbes, in a circular motion. "I don't like this facial expression. This can't be good."

Forbes forced a frown. "It has come to my attention"—he opened the red file folder and rifled through a few pieces of paper before finding the one he wanted—"that you appeared on Alaine Delacroix's show on Tuesday."

Shon looked down at the printout of the newspaper article Forbes slid across the shiny wood surface toward him. "Dude, don't do that to me. I thought you were talking about something serious." Shon flipped the page back toward Forbes. "She's a lot better looking in person than on TV—and I didn't think that was possible. Why're you passing up this prime opportunity to hook such a *fine* specimen?"

"What makes you think I'm passing her up?" Forbes feigned

interest in the news clippings still in the red folder.

Shon shrugged. "You haven't gotten her to agree to go on a date yet, have you? Have you even talked to her?"

"Yes, I talked to her Tuesday morning as a matter of fact." Forbes leaned against the back of his chair and crossed his arms.

"And. . .?"

"And. . .she's too busy right now to commit to making plans."

Shon narrowed his eyes speculatively. "Right. Too busy." He shook his head. "Classic evade."

Forbes thought back to their brief conversation. She'd been upset over something she'd said to a co-worker, which, he was certain, tinged their whole interchange. "No, I really believe she meant what she said. She sounded stressed out and like she was being pulled in five directions at once."

"Okay. If that's what you want to believe."

"It's what I know to be true."

Shon held his hands up in surrender. "Fine. But look. . .if you're reentering the dating scene, let me handle everything for you. No, listen," he said forcefully when Forbes tried to interrupt. "I know you don't like giving up control of things, but this is actually a way for you to gain control over the whole thing—meet only a select group of women already prescreened, by me, to make sure that their interests and lifestyles mesh with yours. I'd like to give you a three-month VIP membership for you as a thank-you for all of the extra hours you put in on the Chicago deal that I know you didn't bill me for. I'll handle everything. No one else in the company will ever see your file."

"Let you set me up on blind dates?" A week ago, Forbes would have laughed and said no immediately. Now, however, with his twenty-year reunion coming up, along with the rekindled ember of wanting to share his life with someone—someone like Alaine—the offer didn't sound quite so ludicrous.

What did he have to lose? "All right. Ninety days. I'll meet whoever you feel would be a good match for me."

Shon grinned. "You won't regret this. I promise."

"Yeah, and you won't regret being able to claim Bonneterre's Bachelor of the Year as a client, either."

"You said it, not me."

After Shon left, Forbes slumped in his chair and turned to stare out the window at the tops of the trees lining the opposite bank of the river. The wild tangle of greenery reminded him of Delacroix Gardens. There must be other people in town with that name—he'd gone to school with several Delacroixes both here at the local branch of the University of Louisiana as well as at Loyola Law School in New Orleans. But could Alaine be related to the owners?

He sat up. She'd sounded stressed on the phone. She'd said she couldn't go out with him. Could it be because relatives of hers faced losing their business to his parents' redevelopment plans?

He jumped when the intercom on the phone beeped.

"Mr. Guidry, opposing counsel in the Pichon case is in the first-floor conference room to discuss the schedule for mediation."

He turned and pressed the intercom button. "Thank you, Samantha."

Mediation. If his parents ran someone Alaine cared for out of business, Forbes would need mediation with her if she was ever going to agree to go out with him.

"All right. Thank you, anyway. If you know of anyone. . ."

The line went dead. Alaine crossed the second-to-last name off her list and flipped the phone closed. Finding local lawyers who specialized in real estate law on Google probably hadn't been the best way to find the right person, but so far, her fears over getting hoodwinked by some smooth-talking ambulance-chaser hadn't materialized.

She headed back inside, having already taken five minutes longer than the fifteen she'd allowed herself for this personal break.

One thing was certain: If she wanted to get one of them to meet with her to find out more about the case, she needed to leave out the fact that the potential law suit was against Boudreaux-Guidry Enterprises; because as soon as that name came up, each lawyer hastily made some excuse or another to get off the phone.

She left a message for the last one on her way back to her desk and then tried to put the matter out of her head by finishing tomorrow's post for the Bonneterre Insider blog. Fortunately, her series on local artists to promote the upcoming Artisan Festival—of which the station was a major sponsor—interested her, making it easy to switch her train of thought.

She saved the post, and her cell phone rang. She grabbed it and flipped it open, not recognizing the number that flashed on her screen. "Alaine Delacroix."

"Yes, hello. This is Hank Biddle. You left a message that you wanted to talk to me about a case."

"Yes, Mr. Biddle, thank you for returning my call." Alaine stood up, looked around over the top of her cubicle walls, and, seeing no one at any of the nearby desks, she stayed at her desk instead of going back out into the intolerable heat and humidity. "I'm looking for someone familiar with real-estate cases—specifically with taking on the cause of a group of homeowners who are being forced out when a. . .large company wants to come in and force them out."

"And you're probably looking for someone who could take it on pro bono?"

"Well, we wouldn't have much money to spend, no."

"With as much as I'd like to take on a worthy cause, my current caseload is too full."

Alaine wanted something hard to bang her head against. "I understand. And I appreciate your calling me back."

"You might want to call the LeBlanc Legal Aid Center. This is the kind of case they specialize in."

She sat up straighter and grabbed for a pen, which she had to chase across the desk with her fingers. "LeBlanc Legal Aid, you said?"

"Yeah. Hang on, I have the number here somewhere. . . ."

Alaine scribbled the number in the top margin of her steno pad.

"Thank you so much. You have no idea how much I appreciate this."

"No problem. Good luck."

Alaine closed the phone and squeezed it tightly in her hand. Looking down the notepad page, she reviewed her day's to-do list. The few remaining things she needed to do, she could do at home tonight.

She left a note for Pricilla, out filming a story for tomorrow, to let her know she'd scheduled the blog entry for tomorrow. Packing up everything she'd need to work from home, Alaine hustled out to her car. She dumped everything in the passenger seat, climbed in, then dialed the number for the legal aid center and pulled out of the parking lot.

Someone who identified herself as a volunteer answered the phone and asked Alaine a battery of questions about her case. She assiduously avoided mentioning Boudreaux-Guidry Enterprises but did mention her parents' business and several others in the area by name.

"I will pass your information along to Mr. LeBlanc, and he will give you a call back soon."

"How soon?"

"I'm not sure, ma'am. But he always returns every call he receives, so you can be certain to hear from him."

Her surge of excitement faded. "Okay. Thank you."

Once home, she dropped her bag and purse on the coffee table and collapsed facedown on the sofa, kicking her shoes off. She'd thought finding a lawyer who'd relish the chance to take down a big company like this—to argue a high-profile case—would be a lot easier. The Guidrys had more clout in this town than she'd originally imagined.

After moping on the sofa for a while, Alaine forced herself up and went into the kitchen to see what she had to eat. She opened the fridge and read the tape labels on the stacks of plastic containers lining the shelves. The seafood paella from last night that Mother had made her bring home. *Cozido* stew—too heavy. *Bife*—no, she didn't need the calories in the pan-fried beef in sauce with seasoned rice. *Iscas com elas*—she hadn't had liver in a while, and she loved the flavor it lent to the potatoes Mother sautéed with it. *Feijoada*—no, it was too hot for the bean stew. *Alheira*—Mother's homemade duck sausage also with pan-fried potatoes. Was everything in her fridge meant to make her gain five pounds?

She pulled the half-gallon of skim milk out of the door and set it on the counter, then stepped into the pantry and grabbed a box of frosted flakes. She'd just poured the cereal into a large bowl when her cell phone started chirping. She nearly tripped on the edge of the living-room rug in her haste to get to her purse.

"This is Alaine."

"Alaine—girl, where are you? We were supposed to all meet up at six for supper."

"We—?" Alaine slapped her forehead and returned the milk to the fridge. "I completely forgot that was tonight. Give me"—she looked down at her crumpled blouse and pants—"half an hour, and I'll be there."

"Want us to order you a drink? The bartender seems kinda slow tonight."

Alaine shook her head and dashed up the stairs. "You know I don't drink anymore." Not that she had ever done much drinking in college. But there had been those couple of times. . . "Tell everyone I'm sorry I'm late, but that I'll be there as soon as I can get there."

"Okay. See ya in a little while."

"Bye." Alaine tossed the phone onto the bathroom cabinet and ducked into her closet to change clothes. The enormous walk-in held more clothes than some small boutiques. Yet she still couldn't find anything she wanted to wear for dinner with her sorority sisters.

Finally, she settled for a sleeveless, silky, royal purple blouse, a pair of close-fitting, dark-wash jeans, and strappy, wedge-heel sandals.

She touched up her makeup, trying extra hard to conceal the dark circles under her eyes. Oh well. If they noticed, she'd just tell them she was putting in long hours these days. With all of them being "corporate babes" themselves, they'd completely understand. Besides, there wasn't time to take off all her makeup, put some hemorrhoid ointment on the dark circles, wait for it to reduce the puffiness, and then reapply her makeup.

Halfway out of the complex, she remembered she'd left her phone on the bathroom counter. She rounded a block and, leaving the car running in the driveway, ran back into the town house, wishing she had some legitimate excuse to call them back and cancel. But she couldn't. They only did this once a month, and a couple of the girls had to take off half a day from work to drive in from Shreveport or Baton Rouge to attend.

The drive to the restaurant in midtown took about ten minutes, but the parking lot was packed, and she had to circle it twice before someone vacated a parking space. She zipped her purse closed before getting out of the car—with the way her day was going, if she didn't, she'd drop it and everything would go skittering under all the cars nearby—then climbed out, rolling her neck and trying to rid herself of the black cloud of annoyance and frustration that had dogged her all day.

She had no trouble locating the Chi Omega table as soon as she entered the restaurant. Her five sorority sisters laughed and talked loudly enough to be heard over the din of the full restaurant.

Alaine sighed. So much for a relaxing evening. Not that the girls from Chi-O had ever been accused of being shy and retiring—at least not in their suite, and not once they'd broken Alaine out of her nerdy, quiet, art-major-wannabe shell.

Shrill greetings went up around the table, and Alaine had to make the circuit to greet each one with an air kiss before she could take her seat.

Bethenny, her former roommate, pulled Alaine into a side-hug as soon as she sat down. "It's so good to see you. In person, I mean. I see you on TV all the time."

"Yeah, every time I see you on that screen, all I can think is *I created that*!" Dover grinned at her across the table and passed the plate of fried mushrooms Alaine's direction.

"No you didn't!" Bethenny glared at the tall redhead. "*I'm* the one who had the idea to give 'Laine a makeover."

Alaine bit the sides of her tongue in an effort to keep from frowning and wrinkled her nose in an effort to look amused. Did they have to go through this every time they got together—reminding Alaine of what a dork she'd been up until her sophomore year of college?

" 'Laine, you look stressed. You need a drink." Crystal waved a jewel-encrusted hand to flag down their server. She had always been the heaviest drinker of the suitemates and the one who still tended to lead the rest of them into temptation.

"No—Crystal. I don't drink anymore."

"Yeah, don't forget she went all religious on us after college." Mallory gave Crystal a look dripping with condescension.

"Right." Crystal rolled blue eyes framed by lashes much longer and thicker than they'd been at their last get-together. Obviously she had followed through and gotten the lash extensions.

When the waitress arrived at the table, Crystal ordered herself another mixed drink, and Alaine ordered sweet tea and the biggest platter of fried seafood the place had. If the first ten minutes was any indication of how the evening would go, she would at least soothe herself by eating really bad-for-her food. That was their one and only rule for these get-togethers: No one was allowed to be on a diet or talk about calories or fat grams or going to the gym.

Jessica leaned her elbows on the edge of the table, cradling her super-sized frozen margarita in both hands. "So, 'Laine, tell us all about the Most Eligible Bachelors' dinner. Did you get to meet him?"

"Him?" Alaine smiled at the waitress and reached for the glass of iced tea.

"Forbes Guidry! Who did you think I meant?"

Alaine sprinkled salt on her cocktail napkin to keep it from sticking to the sweating tea glass. "Yes. I sat next to him at dinner, in fact." She looked around the table. Five pairs of eyes ogled her, expressions dripping with envy. She shrugged and allowed only one side of her mouth to curve up. "He asked me out."

The shrill shrieks that went up from her suitemates nearly deafened her and drew remonstrative glances from the diners around them.

Alaine told the story about meeting Forbes, lingering over describing what he looked like in his tuxedo, the reddish tint to his dark hair, the almost periwinkle color of his eyes, the fact that he wore her favorite cologne.

Smugness settled into her chest over the fact that she finally had something to make these girls jealous of her. She hadn't had that since she'd gotten to interview Cliff Ballantine last year after his engagement party. And since someone from each of the local stations had gotten to meet with the megastar actor for a five minute one-on-one, even that hadn't drawn the kind of looks she was getting from the girls now.

Of course, she couldn't tell them that Forbes's family's company was trying to steal her parents' home and business. Nor that she would never stoop to going out with him.

As soon as the girls had drawn all the details about Forbes out of her—the ones she was willing to tell them, anyway—talk turned to the latest celebrity scandals. Alaine drowned herself in greasy fried shrimp and clams and calamari and fish, savoring the french fries dipped in the spicy tartar sauce. She washed it all down with a huge chocolate dessert.

Yet no matter how satisfying the junk food was, she still couldn't get past the pain that came from realizing she had the shallowest friends in the world. While the focus of their monthly dinners was to get together and have fun, if she got to a point where she needed someone to talk to about something serious, she would never consider calling a single one of them. She would never confide anything to any of them—knowing it would not only get around to all of the others, but that they might use it as a source of amusement at a future get-together.

Regret formed a tight ball in the back of her throat. For years, these had been her only friends. When she'd met Meredith Guidry a few months ago, she'd thought she'd finally found a true friend—someone she could turn to, trust with anything. But now she had no one to turn to. No one to talk to about Mother and Daddy's situation. No one to trust.

Why did Forbes have to be a Guidry?

Chapter 9

"Please, Forbes? Go with me. I can't do this by myself."

Forbes stared at Jenn. His sister had asked a lot of him over the years—not the least of which was providing most of the start-up capital for the restaurant in which they now sat. "Ballroom dancing lessons?"

"Yeah. It'll be fun. I've always wanted to learn. Anne and George are going to do it." She inclined her head at them across the noisy table. "Meredith and Major wanted to, but some of the dates interfere with their work events. So will you sign up with me so that I don't have to worry about whether or not there'll be someone there for me to dance with?"

"What about one of the guys you're seeing? Why not ask one of them?"

Jenn shrugged, setting her strawberry blond ponytail to swinging. "Because I don't want to give Clay or Danny or Ward the wrong idea."

"And what would that be?" He probably didn't really want to know the answer to that question.

"That I'm serious enough about any of them to want to spend that kind of one-on-one time with them."

"Why not just split the time evenly between them?"

"Because you have to purchase a package. Plus, according to the Web site, it's very important to be there for the entire series, because many of the steps build off of each other."

Forbes leaned back and crossed his arms. "What about the restaurant?" Even though she'd bought him out fully more than two years ago, he still liked to keep up with the goings-on around here.

"I hired a restaurant manager—didn't I tell you?" Jenn's expression was a little *too* innocent.

"No, you didn't, oddly enough. I trust this person has good credentials?" Maybe, if he got her talking about the restaurant, she'd drop the dancing thing.

"Yeah—well, Major was one of his references."

Interesting. Too bad Major and Meredith were currently in Colorado on their mini-honeymoon. "Well, if Major vouched for him. . ."

"So anyway"—Jenn sounded annoyed—"the lessons are on Monday evenings, which is my new day off. And I'd like for you to go with me."

Should he remind her now that his "Most Likely to Succeed" title his senior year of high school had come with an asterisk: **except in dancing*? His lack of physical coordination had kept him from success in sports and led to girls thinking he was arrogant for refusing to go out on the dance floor at homecoming or prom except for a couple of obligatory numbers. Even then, he picked slow songs so he could do his Fonz-style dance: hold the girl close and turn slowly in a circle.

"Please, Forbes?"

The word *yes* tripped out to the end of his tongue, but he caught it before it escaped. "Let me think about it."

"Don't think too long. The next session starts Monday."

"As in four-days-away Monday?"

"That would be the one." Jenn bounced up from her chair, kissed the top of his head, and flittered off to visit with other patrons in the nearly full restaurant.

Jenn wanted him to go dancing; Shon wanted him to reenter the dating scene. Forbes glanced up at the ceiling, half expecting God to peek around the pirogue hanging there and laugh at him. Just when he had everything under control. . .

"Come on." George nudged his shoulder. "Jennifer is playing our song."

Singing "Me and My Shadow" with George to kick off the Thursday night family friendly karaoke at Jenn's restaurant had become something of a tradition over the past few months. When Major was here, all three of them got up and sang it together.

Forbes could just make out Jenn's lithe figure darting around, working the room beyond thc halo of the stage lights. Maybe he should push her a little more toward Clay Huntoon, the bass in their quartet. With Major and George officially members of the family now, adding Clay seemed like the next logical step.

Forbes and George surrendered the stage to a ten-year-old who started belting out "My Favorite Things" before they got back to the table. As usual, everyone had changed seats; Forbes took the empty chair beside his brother Rafe, who sat slumped over the table, cheek and eye distorted by the pressure of leaning his face against his fist.

"What's wrong?" Forbes stood to lean over and retrieve his tea from his original spot. He sat again and stretched his legs out under the table, crossing his ankles.

"Remember Tonya, the girl at B-G I was seeing?"

Forbes liked the sound of the past tense verb. "Yeah."

"Well, I found out she's been dating someone else all along. Apparently, he works for another company there in the building." Rafe stared morosely at the basket of now-cold hush puppies in the middle of the table.

"And. . . ?"

"And it turns out she was just playing me. She thought that since I'm a Guidry, I had some kind of huge trust fund or something. She flat out asked me how much money I have. I told her I'm saving to buy a plane, that I'd paid cash for the 'Vette, and I have equity in my condo because I did a big down payment. That's when she told me about this real-estate investment guy who apparently makes seven figures a year. It's like she was saying, 'Beat that—I dare you.'"

Forbes tightened his jaw to keep his joy from showing, happy that he hadn't had to figure out how to start convincing Rafe this girl wasn't worth his time and attention. "Sounds to me like it's a good thing you found this out now instead of when things got more serious."

Rafe groaned. "That's the problem. I thought things already were serious. I asked her to marry me. That's when she asked me about the money."

Forbes took in a deep breath, held it a few seconds, then released it slowly. "Had you already bought a ring?"

"No, thank goodness. I was going to take her shopping and let her pick it out herself." He blinked a few times, then sat up straight and turned to face Forbes. "Hey—the guy who lives next door to you. He owns that dating service, doesn't he?"

"Let's Do Coffee. Yes, that's my next-door neighbor."

"What do you know about it? Think it might work for me?"

Only if Forbes got a part-time job there so he could screen the candidates. Well, he'd agreed to trust Shon to find someone for him; maybe he could trust him to find someone for his brother. "It might be worth looking into a three- or six-month membership."

Alaine groaned when the phone on her desk trilled yet again. Didn't people know it was rude to call at four o'clock on a Friday afternoon? If they didn't let her alone soon, she'd never get everything wrapped up before she had to be out in the field covering the concert tonight. She grabbed the receiver on the third ring. "Alaine Delacroix."

"Alaine, Russell LeBlanc here. I looked over the information you gave our volunteer, and I'm calling to set up a time for us to meet so we can discus the case in more detail."

She pumped her fist in the air, then glanced over her shoulder to make sure no one had walked past the opening into her cubicle and seen the gesture. "When would you like to meet?"

"Would you be available for lunch. . .next Wednesday?"

Impatience momentarily overrode her excitement at finally finding a lawyer who might be willing to work with them. She pulled up her calendar on the computer. Wednesday afternoon looked open. "It would have to be after two o'clock. I can't get away from the studio any earlier than that."

"That's great. I usually take a late lunch. Would it be better if I meet you somewhere near your office?"

Even though Alaine didn't have any set office hours—she could come and go as needed—she tried to stick to regular hours; so a nearby restaurant would allow her more time to talk to Russell LeBlanc. But what if someone else from the studio ended up at the same restaurant and realized she was meeting with a lawyer? "Where are you located?"

"In the Moreaux Mills area."

"Perfect! How about. . .Pappas's on Hyacinth Place?" Alaine clicked her pen with nervous repetition.

"The Greek place? Great choice. I didn't know anyone outside this neighborhood knew about it. Want to say two fifteen, since you'll have to drive all the way out here?"

"Two fifteen it is. See you then." Alaine closed her cell phone and typed a cryptic note into her calendar program and set a reminder to pop up that morning. She didn't think she'd forget, but with the way things got around here sometimes. . .

"Hot lunch date next week?"

Alaine whipped around. Pricilla, the production assistant, entered the large cubicle and perched on the edge of Alaine's desktop.

"Sometimes you forget just how thin these partitions are." The plain but hardworking younger woman tapped one of the walls. It wobbled to prove her point.

Alaine hadn't said anything that would clue anyone in to what she was doing. But still. . .she had to be careful. "A potential story. Won't really know until after I meet with him." That should work.

Alaine, Pricilla, and Garnet, their show's producer, were forever chasing down stories that didn't pan out; and none of them wasted the others' time with details of a no-go piece.

Plus, there was the idea that even if he decided not to take on her case, Russell LeBlanc might be interested in doing a Q&A segment once a month like Andrew Blakely and the make-your-life-more-green guy did. So in essence, she'd told the truth.

"Big plans for the weekend?" Pricilla twirled a lock of dishwater-blond hair around her finger.

Alaine looked away to try to hide her annoyance at Pricilla's unconscious habit. "Live remote from the big gospel music concert tonight, and tomorrow I'll be taking Noah down to Riverfront to cover the christening of the *Bonneterre Beauty* paddleboat."

"Oh, I forgot that was Saturday afternoon. Are you doing the dinner cruise that night?"

"Noah's wife is going to meet him down there. Noah's going to cover it as a photo essay. I figured it was only fair. Since he's covering for Nelson, he should at least get to treat his wife to a free evening out, even if he is technically working." Alaine surreptitiously glanced around her desk to make sure that she hadn't left anything lying about that might indicate what her appointment next week was really about. She'd promised Mother and Daddy that she wouldn't turn this into a big news story; and if she wasn't going to break and cover the biggest business scandal in Bonneterre history, she wouldn't let anyone else here get a whiff of it from her.

"I thought I might go out to the dog agility competition at the park tomorrow afternoon, if it isn't raining. I'll take a camera if I do." Pricilla stopped twirling her hair and picked at the already chipped dark brown polish on her thumbnail.

Alaine cringed and looked away again. She kept her nails buffed because she couldn't stomach the idea that each time a piece of polish flaked off, it took a layer of nail with it. "Well, you know if Brent's the one forecasting rain tomorrow, it'll probably be bright and sunny."

"Why do you give him such a hard time?"

"Because I can. Because he hurt a really good friend of mine when they were in college." Alaine swallowed hard. Despite everything going on, she still longed to claim Meredith as a really good friend.

Pricilla shrugged. "To each his own. Oh, hey, you've always said you wanted to learn ballroom dancing, right?"

"I've thought about lessons. Why?" She picked up her pen and twirled it in her fingers. Hardly anyone knew she'd minored in dance her first year of college, and ever since dropping it when she switched her major to journalism, she'd longed to go back to it.

"One of the interns took a call today from someone at that new dance studio that just opened down in Comeaux. Apparently, they're going to be having a six-week ballroom dancing class, starting this Monday. They were hoping we might be interested in covering it for *Inside Bonneterre*. I thought since you already have an interest in the subject, you might want to take it on."

She'd rather be *in* the class than covering it for the show; however, she took the slip of paper from the assistant producer with a trickle of excitement. Maybe now was the time to start dancing again if the package wasn't too expensive. "Thanks, Priss. I'll look into it."

"Well, I'm done with everything. I fixed those links on the blog post and put it up." Pricilla stood and brushed the flakes of nail polish off her shirt and slacks. "Oh, and someone from Systems called. They wanted to know why we can't just post the recipes on the blog instead of on a static page on the Web site."

Alaine should have known that one would come back to bite her. "I'll talk to them about it next week. Have a good weekend."

"You staying much longer?"

"I'll just return this call to the dance studio and then call it a day." She waved the little piece of paper.

"Okay. See you Monday, then."

Alaine waited until all of the rustling from the adjacent cubicle stopped and the sound of Pricilla's footsteps faded away before picking up the phone.

"Arcenault Dance Studio. How may I help you?"

"Hi, this is Alaine Delacroix from *Inside Bonneterre*. I received a message from. . .Ruth about your ballroom dancing class. I'd like to speak with her to see about covering your opening night on the program."

A high-pitched squeak came through the line. Alaine smiled.

"That's so awesome. Ruth is going to spaz out. This has been her lifelong dream, to open a dance studio, and it all just kind of fell into her lap, so she hasn't had a lot of time for promotion or to contact the media. But your show was the one she definitely wanted to get on."

"Wonderful. May I speak with her?"

"Oh—well, she's rehearsing right now for an exhibition at the Savoy tonight. Should I. . . ?" The girl hesitated.

"No. Tell you what, I'll give you my cell phone number. Have her call me whenever she's free this weekend to talk about Monday." Alaine recited her number twice and made the girl repeat it back to her to make sure she hadn't transposed any of the numbers, which she had.

"I'll be sure to get this message to her as soon as she finishes up."

"Thanks." Alaine hung up, threw what she'd need at the remotes tonight and tomorrow into her bag, and left. She still had two hours before she was scheduled to meet Nelson at the football stadium at ULB, where the concert was to be held—so long as the rain held off—so she took a detour leaving downtown and, after a few minutes, pulled into the parking lot of her favorite shoe store—a warehouselike place that carried expensive brands at discount prices.

The clerk straightening the display of handbags near the front door greeted her by name. She waved in greeting but wasn't going to let herself be distracted by purses today. She wended her way through the aisles of hundreds of shoes. In a small alcove in the back of the store lay the siren that had lured her in. . .dance shoes of all makes, models, and sizes. Ballet slippers; tap shoes in a variety of colors, designs, and heel heights; jazz shoes; and on the end, the shoes she sought: the T-strap and X-strap pumps worn by ballroom dancers. Open toed for Latin dances. Closed toed for standard dances.

Lovingly, she picked up a silver shoe. Flexible at the ball of the foot, but, according to the shoe box, with a steel shank for stability. Suede sole. Slightly flared, two-inch heel—much lower than what she usually wore.

The mark of someone who danced.

"Finding everything okay?"

"Yes, thanks." She didn't even bother to tear her eyes away from the shoes she'd wanted since seeing her first Fred Astaire–Ginger Rogers movie at age six. Why she'd ever chosen art lessons over dance lessons, she couldn't remember right now.

When she'd taken her first two dance classes in college, the first had focused on popular ballroom steps, like the waltz and foxtrot and tango. Much of the second semester had been dedicated to the instructor's favorite areas of jazz and modern dance—and much of the routine they'd had to do for their final exam looked a lot like the routine the school's dance squad performed in the pregame show at every home football game. If every class had been ballroom, she might not have dropped the minor.

Gingerly, she replaced the shoe on top of its box and pulled her hand away with great reluctance. Even if she did end up taking lessons, she couldn't justify the expense of shoes she'd never wear anywhere else. Especially since she had two utility bills at home she was waiting to put in the mail until her next paycheck hit the bank.

She was almost back to her car when her cell phone rang. "Alaine Delacroix."

"Ms. Delacroix, this is Ruth Arcenault of Arcenault Dance Studio!"

Alaine pulled the phone away from her ear to keep her eardrum from bursting at the woman's excitement. "Thank you for calling me back." She climbed into her car and pulled her day planner out of her bag. "I wanted to see if you would have time to meet with me for an interview before your ballroom dance class starts Monday evening. Maybe about thirty or forty-five minutes beforehand?"

"Yeah, of course. Whenever you want to come is fine with me.

The class starts at six thirty."

"Will people who don't come on Monday still be able to sign up for the class?"

"Definitely. This first session will be just a basic overview of what the six-week program will include to give people a better idea of whether or not they really want to commit to it. That was why I've been doing a major promotional push this week, trying to get the word out to all the major media outlets in town, so that just in case people don't hear about it till next week, they still have time to sign up."

Alaine made a few notes in her planner. "Okay, that'll help me in determining the direction of the piece."

"I'm super excited that you're coming. You know how to find us?"

"All I have here is that you're located in Comeaux."

"We're three buildings down—south, I think—from The Fishin' Shack restaurant. In the old karate studio."

Alaine's mouth instantly started watering at the thought of the crawfish bisque she'd had the one and only time she'd visited The Fishin' Shack—when she featured it on her show right after it first opened. Maybe it was time to go back and do a feature on them again, since it had been at least five or six years. Something about the owner of the restaurant niggled the back of her mind, but she couldn't put her finger on it.

"Okay. I'll be there between five thirty and six on Monday evening. If you have any information you'd like to send me to review between now and then, you can e-mail it to my address on the TV station's Web site."

After exchanging good-byes, Alaine started the car and headed toward the university campus. A huge raindrop spattered her windshield. Great. Now everything would be in an uproar as they moved the concert into the basketball arena. Hopefully the featured groups would still have time for the preconcert interviews she'd been promised.

The one benefit of being the social-scene reporter: backstage access to every big-name concert that came to town. Not that she listened to much but Christian indie-rock. But it got her face on the evening news broadcasts.

Weariness blanketed her as traffic slowed to a crawl in the now-pouring rain. Sometimes, all the time and energy she put into dreaming and desiring a move to main news didn't seem worth the effort.

She blinked a couple of times. Effort. What had Bekka had said about making an effort to prove herself to the uppity-ups at the station?

Her mind whirled. She had a good video camera at home, and the bookcases in her third bedroom–turned office would make a great backdrop. She'd promised her parents she wouldn't *broadcast* anything about the case. She'd never said anything about not recording an audition tape to show the news director that she could not only report hard news but could do the investigative work behind it as well. And if it happened to create a stir and help stop the Guidry family from ruining Moreaux Mills, all the better.

Chapter 10

As soon as Alaine saw the Fishin' Shack restaurant Monday evening, her memory kicked in. The owner was a Guidry. One of Meredith's younger sisters, if she remembered correctly. She made a mental note to add a sidebar investigation into just how many properties and businesses that family owned in Beausoleil Parish for her reel.

Nelson slowed the van, and Alaine shook herself out of her thoughts. "There it is, on the corner." She pointed to a stand-alone building a few doors down from the restaurant. A hastily printed vinyl sign draping the existing one announced: Arcenault Dance Studio Now Open.

"Pull up on the side of the building—that way the van can still be seen from the street, but we're not blocking the main strip of parking spaces." As soon as the van stopped, Alaine climbed out and opened the side door to get her large, overstuffed canvas briefcase as well as the tripod for the camera so Nelson didn't have to hold it while she interviewed Ruth Arcenault.

What Alaine had learned of the woman's story in her initial research fascinated her—good thing, as it would make a good story for the program instead of coming across as Alaine giving in to a local business's desire for self-promotion.

A young woman so rail thin she couldn't possibly have eaten anything in the last three years jogged out from behind the reception desk to hold open the door for Alaine and Nelson. "We're so glad y'all're here. Come in. Come in."

Music faintly wafted out into the lobby—a jazzy, instrumental recording of what sounded like "Cheek to Cheek." Alaine's heart quickened. Finally, after so many years of regret, she was going to be the closest she'd ever been to actually stepping back out on the dance floor.

"Ruth and Ian are warming up right now, but she said for y'all to come on in once you arrive and she'll give you a tour before the interview."

Alaine nodded and extended her hand. "I'm sorry, I didn't catch your name."

The girl turned redder than her cayenne-colored hair. "Sorry. Talia."

Alaine cocked her head and pulled out her steno pad and pen. "You're gonna have to spell that one for me."

Talia complied, while Nelson shouldered his camera and began shooting footage of the decor of the reception area.

"I'm going to go get some exteriors." The string of bells hanging from the door clanked against the camera as he went outside.

Alaine asked Talia a few questions—the girl had been a ballet dancer trying to make it in New York when she met Ruth and Ian and they offered her room and board and to train her in ballroom, modern, and jazz dance as part of her salary if she moved down here to work as their receptionist.

As soon as she could break away from her, Alaine moved down the long, narrow reception room that overlooked the parking lot to the archway at the far end that led into the studio itself.

The music switched to another jazzy trumpet interpretation of "I've Grown Accustomed to Her Face." Alaine stopped in the arched doorway and let herself be transported. On the other side of the large room, a tall, dark-haired couple glided across the shiny hardwood as effortlessly as clouds through the sky.

Before the song ended, Nelson had joined her, shooting film of the reigning International Dance Grand Prix champions. As soon as the music stopped, the couple seemed to transform from unbelievably elegant to so tall and gangly they looked like they'd been stretched lengthwise.

Dressed in a formfitting, one-shoulder, asymmetrical-hem dress that showed off just how toned she was, the owner of Arcenault Dance Studio approached. "I'm Ruth Arcenault." She held out her hand. "Thank you so much for coming."

"It's nice to meet you." Alaine had never felt as short as she did right now. She shook hands with Ruth, who towered over her by almost a foot. In what looked like almost two-inch heels, Ruth was even a little taller than her dance partner. "How tall are you?"

What idiot would let that just blurt out?

Ruth laughed. "I get that all the time. Without shoes, I'm six-foot-two. Ian is six-three. He usually wears shoes with a little lift in them for competitions so that we're at least the same height. Oh, sorry, this is my husband and dance partner, Ian Birtwistle."

Alaine greeted him as well. She always made an effort to not notice when a married man was extremely good-looking, but in this case, she couldn't help but be affected by his dark good looks. He'd been created to ooze sex appeal without even trying. The British accent didn't help matters much, either.

"Is there a place where we can sit to do the interview?" Alaine bent to hoist the tripod from where she'd set it on the floor.

"Yes, of course. Our office." Ruth motioned for them to return the way they'd come. Over her shoulder, she said to Ian, "Can you run over to the restaurant to see about the refreshments?"

"Yes, love." He kissed her cheek and returned to the studio.

"I don't know what I would do without him." Ruth smiled. Alaine returned it, trying to push jealousy aside, and followed her through the door on the other side of the reception desk.

After getting set up, she began the interview. . .and got so involved in learning everything she could about the world of competitive ballroom dancing that Ian had to interrupt them to let Ruth know clients were arriving.

Alaine quickly conferred with Nelson about getting some on the spot interviews with the customers before the lesson started, and moments later, he followed her out of the office, camera on shoulder, floodlight beaming.

"Neither of you have dark soles on your shoes, do you?" Ruth asked when they reached the studio.

Alaine lifted her foot to look at the bottom of her black pumps. "No. Tan."

Nelson's athletic shoes had white soles. Ruth waved them in.

Across the dance floor, Alaine immediately spotted the person she wanted to talk to first. Tall—but not quite as tall as Ruth Arcenault—and full-figured, Anne Hawthorne Laurence stood in a small group, conversing animatedly while her husband stood off to the side, speaking with Ian Birtwistle, no doubt talking about their home country of England.

Nelson hung back while Alaine approached the group. "Excuse me, Mrs. Laurence?"

Anne's smile glowed when she turned around. "Yes? Oh, you're Alaine Delacroix." She extended her right hand. "It's so nice to finally meet you in person. I've heard a lot about you."

Alaine couldn't stop a genuine smile, Anne's warmth proving contagious. "I hoped I could ask you a few questions for a piece I'll be doing on the studio."

"Of course." Anne turned back to the others. "If you'll excuse me."

Alaine motioned her over to where Nelson stood. She positioned Anne, then took her place beside the cameraman. She started out with a few general questions about what kind of dancing most people did at wedding receptions these days and let Anne talk about the subject from the point of view of someone who actually had experience helping couples choose places to learn classic dance steps.

"A few of my clients are here, if you'd like to speak with them as well." Anne motioned to the two couples she'd been talking with.

"Yes, that would be great." Alaine motioned Nelson to follow her over to get some more sound bites. Anne stood by, looking like a proud parent ready to offer any assistance necessary to the twenty-somethings.

As the two young women answered Alaine's final question, she glanced around to find her next interview—and her breath caught in her chest. In an open-collared, cobalt blue dress shirt and dark gray pants, Forbes Guidry strode across the floor toward them.

Nelson cleared his throat. Alaine snapped her attention back to the people in front of her. "Thank you all, very much, for your input. Nelson, I think we're done here."

"Didn't you want to get some footage of everyone dancing?" he asked.

Why'd he have to remember that? "Yeah. I did." And they couldn't start soon enough.

Forbes waited until Alaine lowered her microphone and turned to her cameraman before approaching. Her being here, at the very last place in the world he wanted to be tonight, must be a sign. The cameraman walked away, apparently getting shots of the studio's interior.

Forbes had to detour slightly to put himself in Alaine's path to stop her from walking away. "Ms. Delacroix, I do believe you've been avoiding me."

Alaine's dark eyes narrowed coolly. "Mr. Guidry. I thought I'd explained sufficiently over the phone. Things in my life are complicated right now and I can't. . ." She shrugged and shook her head, dropping her gaze from his.

Not the reaction he'd hoped for—it seemed to confirm his suspicion that she was connected with Delacroix Gardens and knew his parents were trying to buy up all the property in Moreaux Mills. Surely she couldn't blame *him* for that.

"Alaine, I—"

Forbes broke off when Anne joined them. "Where's Jenn?"

He looked around the studio for the first time. "She's not here yet?"

"Do you think something came up at the restaurant to keep her from leaving?"

"She wasn't supposed to be working today."

Alaine backed away from them. "If y'all will excuse me, I need to get back to work."

"Of course," Anne said graciously.

Forbes wanted to argue, but right now he had a bigger concern. "I'll call her and find out where she is. She's probably just running late as usual."

He stepped out into the front room that ran the length of the dance studio and overlooked the parking lot and street and hit the speed dial button for Jenn's cell phone number.

It rang four times before he heard a click.

"What do you want, Forbes?"

He frowned at her harassed tone of voice. "Jenn, where are you?"

She groaned. "Oh, don't ask. But I'm not going to be able to make it tonight."

Warning bells sounded in his mind. "What's going on?"

"You'll just get mad if I tell you."

He was already getting mad because he could tell from the background noise that she was, indeed, at the restaurant. "Tell me anyway."

"Okay, fine. Wait, hang on. . ." She hollered a couple of commands to her staff over the din of the kitchen. "He lied about his credentials."

"Who?"

"The restaurant manager I hired. *Don't* say, 'I told you so.'"

"I thought you checked him out with Major." Forbes paced the length of the lobby. He had a mind to march out the door and down the block and have this conversation face-to-face.

"Well. . .he listed Major as a reference. I never actually called. I mean, why would he list my brother-in-law as a reference if it weren't true? Come to find out, though, he did work as a *commis* a few times at large B-G events a long time ago, but Major didn't even remember him."

"Two questions. . .what's a *commis*, and I thought you said you hadn't checked with Major."

"A *commis* is an apprentice—basically someone who comes in and does prep work to learn the ropes in a kitchen from more experienced chefs. And I talked to Major today after. . .after it happened."

He sank into one of the molded plastic chairs. "After what happened?"

"He seemed to be fine when I worked with him Saturday and Sunday. Nice guy. Seemed to know what he was doing in the kitchen and in front of house, which is a rare find these days." Jenn paused to yell something else at one of her staff. "Anyway, I figured he'd be okay handling things by himself today. But then my head waitress called me during lunch service to tell me she'd seen him making photocopies of people's credit cards."

Now it was Forbes's turn to groan. "And?"

"And so I came in and confronted him. Things got a little hairy—"

"Jennifer!" Forbes sprang from the chair and jogged toward the door.

"Cool off! The sheriff and three of his deputies were here for lunch so they sorted everything out. Ended up arresting him for disorderly conduct. But now, until I find another restaurant manager, I'll be here every day for the foreseeable future. Sorry about the dance lessons."

"I'm coming over. I'll be there in a minute."

"No!"

While he'd heard her use that tone with her employees occasionally, he'd never heard it directed toward himself. He stopped just outside the dance studio doors. "What do you mean, no?"

"I mean, I'm at the beginning of what looks like it's going to be a very busy dinner service, and I don't need you underfoot, getting all up in my business when I don't have time to deal with you right now. It's handled; there's nothing you can do here except get in my way. Now, I have to get back to work, and if I'm not mistaken, that dance lesson should be starting any minute now."

Consternated by Jenn's sudden show of self-reliance, Forbes couldn't decide what to do. She needed him. He knew she did. But as Meredith had been continually saying for the past several months, Jenn was thirty-two years old. It was time for her to stand on her own two feet.

He turned and went back into the lobby. "Okay. I won't come over. I won't even ask you any more questions about it. But if you decide you want me for any reason, you know I'm just a phone call away."

"Thanks. I appreciate that."

He bade her good night, closed the phone, and set the alert to vibrate-only. Inside the studio, everyone was just taking seats in the chairs lining the mirrored walls of the large room. While the owners gave a brief introduction of themselves and talked about all their international dancing awards, Forbes quickly gave Anne the rundown on what Jenn had told him.

Then there was nothing for him to do but watch as the championship dancers took the floor and exhibited a grace of movement Forbes would never be able to achieve. Dancing with his sisters and cousins at wedding receptions was one thing; gliding across the floor with arms at weird angles and faces angled away from each other was just strange.

His gaze drifted over the others in the studio. Half were silver-haired; he, Anne and George, and the two young couples Anne had brought with her. . .and Alaine Delacroix, whose feet moved in rhythm with the music and whose eyes never left the dancers, made up the other half.

Forbes flexed his jaw to hide his grin. Jenn might not be able to do this with him, but it looked like he might not be partnerless after all.

The music ended, and a smattering of applause forced Forbes to look away from the gorgeous newscaster.

"Now, though we're not officially beginning the lessons in the package until next week, we thought this week we could begin teaching you one of the most simple dances, the waltz." Ruth Arcenault turned slowly as she spoke to make sure she looked at everyone scattered around the room. "So if everyone would line up—men over here, your partners facing you over here—we'll get started."

"Forbes, what are you going to do with no partner?" Anne asked.

"Don't worry about me." He winked at his cousin and passed her in the opposite direction from where all the men were lining up.

Alaine was looking down, writing something on a steno pad, when he stopped in front of her. Her cameraman noticed him and looked away from his eyepiece before Alaine looked up. Surprise, pleasure, and an attempt at aloofness rushed through her expressive chocolate eyes.

Forbes half bowed and extended his hand. "May I have this dance?"

"No—I—" Alaine looked at her cameraman and then back at Forbes. "I can't. I haven't paid for a lesson. I'm working."

"My sister isn't going to be able to make it, and I need a partner." Forbes removed the notepad and pen from her and took her hands in his. "And as you can see, you are the only other person here to dance with." He glanced at her cameraman. "No offense."

The guy grunted what might have been a chuckle. "None taken."

Forbes started backing away. After a moment's initial resistance, Alaine rolled her eyes and followed him, the hint of a smile playing about her enticing mouth.

They had to practice the steps for a good ten minutes standing three feet apart, not touching. Finally, though, Ruth and Ian demonstrated what they called a *standard hold* and told everyone to try it.

Forbes's arms tingled, and as soon as he had his right hand on her back—just below her shoulder blade—he had to grit his teeth to keep from sighing with pleasure. Her hand was so small in his, and he hadn't realized just how short she was until he looked down at her from such close proximity.

She, on the other hand, stared straight ahead, at his chest. Color had risen in her cheeks, and she pressed her lips together as if trying to suppress an unwanted emotion.

A touch on his shoulder brought him out of his admiration for her. He looked around and found Ruth Arcenault standing beside them—throwing Alaine's petite stature into even starker relief, since Ruth was slightly taller than Forbes in her high-heeled dance shoes.

"Find the rhythm in the music and start whenever you feel comfortable. Remember, gentlemen, lead off with the right foot forward and just make a box. You won't be traveling around the room for at least a week." She wandered over to Anne and George, who, of course, performed the steps perfectly.

"Ready?"

Alaine looked up at him. He could lose himself in those endless dark eyes. "Ready."

He tuned in to the classical music playing through the speakers in the ceiling and, under his breath, began counting the rhythm. "One, two, three. One, two, three. One, two, three. . ."

Alaine giggled. "You go on the one," she whispered.

"I know." Heat tweaked his cheeks, and he suddenly remembered just how bad a dancer he was. Now Alaine was about to find out, too. What had he been thinking? *One, two, three. One, two, three. Now, two, three. Go, two, three. Fool, two, three.*

He lifted his foot to start. Alaine anticipated and began to step back, but Forbes hesitated—and threw both of them off balance. Alaine's momentum pulled her backward, and he stumbled forward, stomping on her tiny foot.

She winced. "Ow."

"Sorry. I'm so sorry." He dropped the dance hold and grabbed her shoulders. "Are you okay?"

"I'm fine." She pushed his hands away from her shoulders and put her arms back into the standard-hold positions. When he hesitated, she grinned at him. "Why, Forbes Guidry. I do believe we've finally found something at which you aren't 100 percent confident. In fact, I think you're completely and utterly out of your element."

He narrowed his eyes at her, mortified at having been called out. He had to regain control of this situation. "But that's why I needed you as a partner. Because I am confident that I won't learn this nearly as well with anyone else."

"Will it help if I lead?"

He'd never live it down. "No. I've got this." He started counting again, under his breath. He closed his eyes and visualized his feet moving to the rhythm of the music. "Ready?"

"As I'll ever be."

He didn't have to open his eyes to know her eyes sparkled with silent laughter. He took a deep breath and stepped. *One, two, three. One, two, three. One, two, three. One, two, three. I'm doing it. I'm actually dancing.*

Taking a risk, he opened his eyes. Alaine's eyes bored into his with barely suppressed amusement. "Yes, you are doing it. You are actually dancing."

Ruth came over and observed them for a few moments. "Very good, Ms. Delacroix. I like the way you're staying on the balls of your feet. Mr. Guidry, too stiff—and don't hold your breath. Try bringing your heels up off the floor—and bend your knees a little more on each step. No Frankenstein's monsters allowed here."

He probably could have lived his entire life without learning to dance—and given the choice between that and being called *Frankenstein's monster* in front of Alaine Delacroix, he would have found it preferable. He had to hand it to Alaine, though. She didn't laugh at him. At least, not out loud.

Ruth and Ian stopped the class and demonstrated what they saw most of the students doing and then how they wanted it done. Forbes watched Ian carefully, determined not to draw any criticism this time. Heels up. On the tiptoes for the *two* and *three* counts. Sliding the ball of the foot to the next position instead of lifting the foot and putting it down. He could master this.

He would master this, even if he had to take private lessons. Because when he married the woman standing beside him, he wanted to dance like that Fred-guy from the movies at their wedding reception.

Chapter 11

Alaine slid her sunglasses to the top of her head and pulled open the door of Delacroix Rentals.

"Hey, Sis. What're you doing here?" Joe wheeled out from behind a display of candelabra.

"Do I need a reason to stop by and see my big brother?" She leaned her hip against the front counter.

"No. It's just that you don't usually drop by on a random Tuesday night unless something's up. So what's up?" He parked himself directly in front of her.

"Well, I was hoping to talk to you."

"Just me or me and Nikki?"

She shrugged. "Either way."

"Tell you what. Let's you and me go for a walk." He turned to look over his shoulder. "Hey, Nik!"

Her sister-in-law appeared from the back room. "Yeah? Oh hey, Alaine."

Alaine raised her hand in greeting "Hey, yourself."

"Al and I are going for a walk if you don't mind keeping an eye on things here."

Nikki glanced around the otherwise vacant showroom. "I'll try to keep the crowd under control."

"Thanks, dollface." Joe whipped his wheelchair around and headed for the door. "We'll be back in a bit."

Alaine rushed ahead of him to hold the door, then took her place behind him, not pushing, but touching the bar across the top of the seat back, just in case.

Joe cleared his throat. "Alaine, it's been seven years. I'd hope by now you'd remember that I don't need or want to be pushed, and I'd much prefer it if you'd walk beside me so I can see you when I'm talking to you."

Alaine released her hold and moved up beside him. "Sorry. I just can't help it."

He stopped where the walkway joined with the small, paved parking area in front of the store. "I may have lost the use of my legs, but I'm not helpless. I know you feel like you have to protect me from the world, but you don't. I was an Army Ranger, remember? Even now, you could drop me anywhere in the world, and I'd not only survive, I'd be able to find my way home."

"That's not because you were a Ranger. That's because ever since you were fifteen years old, you've had this weird homing signal that can take you wherever Nikki is."

He grinned. "Too right. Come on. Let's walk up and see what Mother's making for supper." Joe set a quick pace toward the only other house on the cove that had survived the Great Moreaux Mills Fire twenty-five years ago. "Are you going to tell me what's up?"

"I'm meeting with a lawyer tomorrow."

"Having a will drawn up? I can't wait to find out if I get the shoe collection or the treadmill." He made a face.

She punched him in the arm. "No. I talked at length with Mother and Daddy. . .about the business situation. I'm meeting with a lawyer who might be interested in taking on the case."

Joe slowed. "What do you mean 'the case'?"

"If the guy thinks we have a chance, he'll put together a lawsuit of some kind to stop the Guidrys from forcing everyone out of the Mills."

"You're serious?" He stopped, bracing the wheels to keep from rolling backward down the slight incline.

"Yeah. But of even more concern is. . .did Mother and Daddy tell you that their mortgage was bought by an investment firm that's going to foreclose in ninety days if they don't pay what's left on their mortgage in full?"

Joe's normally deep complexion paled. "Them, too?"

Her stomach roiled. "What—you mean you and Nikki are in the same situation?"

"Business has really slacked off in the last few months—especially business from B-G Enterprises. No surprise there, since they're wanting to run us out of business. But I'd never have suspected it of Meredith."

Alaine didn't want to think ill of her new friend, either, but facts were facts.

"Anyway, we've fallen behind in our payments the last couple of months. With our loan coming through a locally owned bank, they were working with us on a plan to get caught up. Three weeks ago, we go in to talk to them about signing the paperwork for the final arrangements, and there's all new people at the bank and they tell us that it was bought out by this investment firm that is in the process of reviewing all accounts and loans. Then last week, we get served with the foreclosure paperwork. More than ninety days in arrears."

Alaine nearly crumpled. "You got that far behind? I wish you'd said something to me. I could have helped."

"How? Mother and Daddy are in the same situation, and we all know that you tend to live paycheck to paycheck because you have a huge mortgage and car payment of your own."

Not to mention the money she spent on clothes and shoes every month. Guilt wrung at her heart. If she'd been a better steward of her finances, if she hadn't had to have the *right* address and the *right* clothes and the *right* shoes, she could have been in a position to keep her family out of this situation.

"Anyway, it wasn't your responsibility to bail us out. We have to face it. The economy tanked. Frankly, with more than half of the business in the Mills closing over the past six months, it's a miracle we're still here." Joe's dark eyes clouded further; he closed them and dropped his head.

"What? There's something else you aren't telling me."

"Nikki and I were finally at the top of the list for a baby, and when the adoption agency found out we'd been served foreclosure papers, they dropped us. All that money and all the time we spent waiting—hoping, praying we'd finally have a child of our own—and we get kicked to the curb just like that."

Moisture welled in Alaine's eyes, followed by bitterness in the back of her throat. How could the Guidrys do this to her family? "Just one more thing I'll be telling the lawyer tomorrow."

Thick, black clouds boiled on the horizon. Forbes stepped on the gas, determined to make it to Comeaux before the thunderstorm did. Twenty-four hours should be all Jenn needed to realize that she wanted him there to help her get through this fiasco and back on track.

Huge raindrops splatted against the windshield as he pulled into the parking lot. Grabbing his umbrella—for the deluge that would surely be happening when he left—Forbes dashed into his sister's restaurant. For six o'clock on a Tuesday evening, she had a pretty good-sized crowd. Of course, given that he'd found her a piece of prime real estate—right on the main highway between Comeaux and Bonneterre—she would have had to try really hard to fail in this venture.

Several of the servers greeted him, including the head waitress, the one who'd discovered the short-term manager's criminal activity. He stopped, returning her greeting.

"You here to talk to her about what happened yesterday?" Lynne asked.

He nodded. "Where is she?"

"Where else?"

"In the kitchen. Thanks." He headed toward the rear of the building and let himself into the kitchen through the Employees Only door. He cringed as soon as he entered. He'd been more than happy to go into the restaurant business with Jenn when she'd decided this was what she wanted to do with her life—because it had been under the express agreement that he'd never have to set foot in the kitchen.

Chaos surrounded him—cooks, servers, porters, dishwashers all hollering at each other over the din of equipment, fans, machines, and the clanking of pots and pans.

"Chef, someone here to see you!" The white-clad yeller hardly even looked up from his task of shucking oysters.

Forbes's mouth watered at the sight of the succulent, juicy mollusks just waiting for a splash of lemon juice and hot sauce and ready to slide across his tongue with a velvety sweet saltiness like nothing else in the world. Maybe he'd have a plate of them before leaving.

Jenn came around the end of the stainless steel island where the shucker worked. As soon as she spotted him, her eyes narrowed and one hand went to her hip. "What do you want, Forbes?"

He worked hard to keep his surprise from showing. "I figured you'd want to talk about what happened yesterday."

She cocked her head to the side, ponytail swinging. "I don't remember calling you and begging you to come down here to take care of me. Don't Marci or Tiffani need you to come rescue them from some crisis?"

Meredith's recent bid for independence from the family was having a bad effect on the rest of their siblings. "I'm not here to try to rescue you from a crisis. I'm here as your legal counsel to talk to you about the consequences and ramifications of what happened yesterday—because I need to hear it firsthand from you and see all of the paperwork."

Jenn blinked a couple of times, then her expression cleared. "Oh.

Okay. Have you had supper yet?"

Fortunately, the kitchen was loud enough that she couldn't hear his stomach growling. "Not yet." He nodded his head toward the oysters. "Those any good today?"

Jenn walked over and leaned down to smell those already on a platter. "Yep. Fresh as can be. Delivery just came in an hour ago. Decker, plate of twelve for my brother."

The prep cook nodded. "Yes, Chef. Plate of twelve."

"Forbes, go on and get a table. I'll get the paperwork and then bring the food out to you."

Even though the dining room would have its own set of distractions, Forbes was grateful that his sister didn't want to do this in her office—a cramped little room that, while well organized, still reminded him of the chaos just beyond the doorway. He waited for two servers and a busboy to exit ahead of him, then went out into the restaurant.

He fixed himself a glass of iced tea at the waitress station, then chose a booth in the corner farthest from the kitchen where there would be fewer interruptions, as members of the staff wouldn't be walking past them every few seconds.

Just when he was about to return to the kitchen to find out if Jenn had gotten distracted by something, she came around the corner, followed by a waiter balancing a tray on his hand and shoulder. She directed the placement of the platter of oysters, the basket of hush puppies, and the bowls of side dishes before taking a seat opposite him.

The first oyster went down like nectar of the gods—the perfect hint of clean salty seawater followed by the sweetness of the meat and the sting of the lemon juice and hot sauce. Forbes barely suppressed a shiver of pleasure.

When six empty shells lined his side of the plate, and three on Jenn's, he finally leaned back, ready to talk.

Jenn grinned at him and bit into a hush puppy. "I'm starting to wonder if you really came to talk to me or if you really wanted an excuse to come down for the oysters."

"Ones that size are hard to come by this time of year. But I did really come to talk to you. Tell me what happened yesterday."

Forbes guided his sister through the story with a series of questions while he sated himself on the greens, macaroni and cheese, and beet salad. . .and the remaining three oysters for dessert.

"So do you really think there are going to be legal ramifications for me—like the people whose information he was trying to copy, could they sue me or something?" Jenn swirled a straw in her tea.

"No, because nothing actually happened to their information."

"I dunno. The sheriff's department confiscated all the photocopies as evidence when they arrested him. While I'd like to have faith that everyone who works at the sheriff's department is trustworthy and ethical, you never know."

"If anything happens now, it'll fall on them, not on you. But if it'll make you feel better, I'll pay them a visit tomorrow just to make sure those copies will be destroyed once they're finished with them."

"Thanks."

"Now, are all of your employees' files up-to-date? Has everyone signed the ethics policy?"

"Do you realize I'm probably the only restaurant that requires everyone to sign one of those things?"

"Do you realize that it gives you the legal recourse to fire someone like that manager when they break it? You're just covering all your bases by doing it. Speaking of ethics policies. . ." He caught himself just before a big, stupid grin broke out on his face as he reached for his wallet. He pulled out a twenty and handed it to his sister.

"What's this for?" She eyed the bill but didn't reach for it.

"It's from Alaine Delacroix. She took your place as my partner last night, but since she was there covering the studio's opening for her TV show, she couldn't accept anything for free. So she asked me to reimburse you for her participation in the lesson."

Jenn's gray blue eyes twinkled. She took the money and pocketed it. "Alaine Delacroix, huh? She's kinda cute."

He shrugged and hoped his face didn't reveal more than he wanted it to. "I guess so." If one liked short, gorgeous women with a Mediterranean look about them. Which he'd recently discovered he did. "She's a great dancer already. Looked like she's already taken some ballroom dancing lessons."

"Sounds like she's the perfect person for you to partner with, then, because she can help you out when the instructors are paying attention to the other students. Goodness knows you'll need all the help you can get." She dodged the straw paper he threw at her. "Hey now, don't go trashing my restaurant!"

Forbes looked up and thanked the server who refilled their tea glasses, then returned his attention to Jenn. "Have you talked to Meredith today?"

"Got an e-mail from her about catering some event in a couple of months. I didn't even know they were back yet."

"They flew back yesterday. I had lunch with Major today to finalize the paperwork for his restaurant."

"That's finally going through, huh? I thought there was some problem with the building permits or something." Jenn's eyes wandered around her own restaurant, taking in everything her staff and customers were doing.

"Well, Mom and Dad—and the consultant they've brought in—are working to get everything squared away with the city and the few property owners who haven't decided to sell yet."

"There're a lot of good restaurants over in Moreaux Mills—at least, there used to be. I've heard a bunch of them have closed down over the past few months. It's a rough time to be a business owner." She heaved a dramatic sigh.

"Yeah, especially for you." He made a face at her.

"No, seriously. It hasn't been easy here, either. My revenues have been down almost 10 percent. I had a waitress quit a few weeks ago, and I decided not to replace her because the workload just wasn't there."

"What kind of marketing are you doing right now?"

She shrugged. "Same kind of stuff as usual: newspaper ads highlighting family-friendly karaoke four nights a week, radio spots on the top tier of stations, TV commercials during the news hours and primetime on local channels, and scattered day parts on cable. Sponsorships—I'm a sponsor, and the caterer, for the fishing tournament down on the lake in October. Trade-out agreements with other businesses in Comeaux—like supplying the beverages and finger foods for the grand opening of the dance studio last night. You saw my banner, didn't you?"

"Looked good. The food was good, too. And Alaine interviewed someone standing in front of it, so that will give you free promotion on her show, too."

"You know, she interviewed me when we opened. I ought to see if I can get her back out here for something. Free coverage by the news—for something positive anyway—is always a good thing." She waved a server over. "Tell Ruiz to bus six, twelve, and fifteen. Cara has customers waiting to be seated."

Forbes leaned around to survey the restaurant. How Jenn had noticed those tables and customers—when they were all almost directly behind her—was beyond him. Of course, that's what had made her such a success.

"So did Meredith and Major have a good time in Colorado?"

"Apparently. Major said he filled a couple of notebooks at the festival with ideas and recipes for the restaurant. Said Meredith came back with almost as much information she wanted to put into use in the events division. He was talking about it like it's going to become an annual trip for them. Maybe next year they'll let you tag along."

"If I can ever get away from this place." Jenn grimaced, then quickly replaced it with a smile. "Not that I don't love doing this. But it would be nice to take a vacation every now and again."

Aha. The perfect opening. "That reminds me." Forbes picked up his suit coat and pulled something from the inside pocket. "Major sent this for you."

"Ooh, what is it?" Jenn's whole face lit up.

He handed her the slip of paper.

As soon as she unfolded it, her expression darkened. She looked up at him with narrowed eyes. "What is this?" She waved the slip of paper at him.

"A list of people Major suggested as potential restaurant managers for you. He already has someone in line to interview for his place—if it ever comes into being—and these are some of the other people he considered or talked to. Most of them he's known for years and trusts implicitly."

A color to rival Jenn's famous beet salad rose in her face. "You told Major?"

Only years of practice kept him from reacting to the venom in his sister's voice. "Yes, I told Major. If anyone would understand, he would; and he's the best person we know to suggest someone who won't do to you what this last guy did."

Jenn slammed the paper down on the table and shot out of the booth. Then, gripping the edge of the table and the back of his seat, she leaned in close. "Forbes, when are you going to stop interfering in my business? I told you I didn't need any help."

He raised his chin—and his left brow—blindsided but unwilling to relinquish his position. "I was only trying to do you a favor by getting a list of names for you instead of having to watch you kill yourself to try to run the restaurant, review résumés, check references, and conduct interviews."

"I don't need you to do me any favors. It's my business. Mine. While I will be forever grateful that you loaned me the capital to get it started, I bought you out more than two years ago. I don't need my big brother swooping in and trying to bail me out every time you think I'm in over my head. I know what I'm doing."

She wadded up the list and tossed it at him.

"I think you're making a mistake if you don't give them serious consideration."

Her fingers contracted into claws. "When I am ready to start thinking about hiring another restaurant manager, I will go and talk to Major myself. But until that time, I'll appreciate it if you'll keep your nose out of my business."

He opened his mouth to speak, but she held up a hand to stop him.

"I know. You're my lawyer. So be my lawyer. You wouldn't have talked to me about another client's problems with her business, so why are you going around behind my back talking to Major about my problems? Where was your high-and-mighty attorney-client privilege?"

Her words took him aback. He hadn't thought about it in that light. "I'm sorry, Jenn. It won't happen again."

His apology seemed as blindsiding to her as her anger had been to him. "You're. . .sorry? Well, I. . .I. . .fine. Thank you. Apology accepted." She straightened and dropped her hands to her sides—after picking up the wadded list and sticking it in her pocket. "Look. I know it's a hard concept for you to grasp, but you can't go around controlling the lives of everyone you love. You have to let us make our own decisions—and our own mistakes. 'Kay?"

"Okay."

One of the servers approached. "Jennifer, I have a customer who'd like to speak with the manager."

"I'll be there in a second." She nodded at the waitress and waited until the girl walked away before turning back to Forbes. "Are we squared away?"

"Yes, Chef. We're squared away as long as you make me a deal."

Curious trepidation entered her eyes. "What's that?"

"If you'll agree to keeping your meddling old brother informed as to what's going on here, I'll agree to stop trying to control it." He stood and extended his right hand. "Deal?"

She narrowed her eyes as if contemplating it, then shook his hand. "Deal. I'll inform; you won't control. Now if you're finished, sir, we need to bus this table so we can seat *paying* customers."

He dropped twice as much cash on the table as the meal cost, then kissed Jenn's cheek in farewell. "Thanks for dinner."

"Get outta here, you control freak, you." She laughed and waved him away, then went to speak to her customers.

Even with his umbrella, Forbes was nearly soaked when he got back to his car. He put the key in the ignition—but didn't turn it. He wrapped his arms around the steering wheel and rested his forehead on his wrist. Jenn was right. He didn't know why he thought he could—or should—control what his siblings were doing in their lives. After all, how could he when he could barely control his own?

Chapter 12

Alaine held her wrist to her ear to make sure her watch hadn't died. Staff meeting had never dragged like this before. She reached for her pen—then remembered Bekka had confiscated it a few minutes ago to stop her from tapping it on the arm of her chair. Instead, she pulled a lock of hair over her shoulder and twirled it around her finger. Only four more hours until her meeting with Russell LeBlanc.

"What have we heard about the Warehouse District and Moreaux Mills development project?" Rodney Milton looked at the chief investigative reporter.

Alaine stilled, interested in the meeting for the first time since she'd been employed by WCAN.

"It's no secret that Boudreaux-Guidry Enterprises bought the paper-mill warehouses and that they've run into a couple of zoning problems that delayed ground breaking on the project about six or eight months. I'm currently tracking down rumors that they're quietly buying up foreclosed properties in the Moreaux Mills subdivision, but so far, all I'm finding is that all trails lead to a development firm called Mackenzie and Son out of Boston."

"So nothing we can run with?"

"Not yet."

Alaine elbowed Bekka and pantomimed writing. Bekka gave the

pen back—along with a warning look. Alaine pulled her steno pad onto her lap and started making a list of everything she already knew about the situation that the chief investigative reporter obviously didn't. She also wrote *Mackenzie & Son* down, planning to research it after the show. . .after the meeting with Russell LeBlanc.

And tonight, she'd start piecing the story together. The sooner she got it on tape—her face, her voice—the sooner she could show it to the producers and the sooner she'd be promoted to main news.

She was still scribbling notes as quickly as she could when the meeting broke up.

"Delacroix—a word, please."

Her stomach twisted at the news director's voice. Surely he couldn't be on to her. No way could he know she knew anything about the Moreaux Mills situation. She flipped a few pages in the notebook so he couldn't see her notes, and set the pad and pen on the table.

As soon as the room cleared, Rodney closed the door and sat in the chair opposite her. "I'm glad to see you're finally starting to take these meetings more seriously." He nodded toward the pad and pen. "It's been hard for us to nip in the bud the cocky attitudes of some of the younger up-and-coming reporters when they see someone with her own show flouting authority openly."

Alaine pressed her lips together, all of Bekka's warnings ringing in her head. Besides, she hadn't meant to cop an attitude with him. He just always seemed to go out of his way to point out she was the person in charge of the *fluff* pieces. . .in front of everyone else. . .in such a way as it seemed calculated to embarrass her. But she didn't want to be known as a diva. That was definitely one way to ensure she never made it into main news.

Rodney cleared his throat and leaned forward. "I understand that you're related to the people who own Delacroix Gardens and Delacroix Rentals over in the Mills area."

Aha. "That's right." She leaned back and crossed her arms.

He cleared his throat again. She enjoyed watching him squirm.

"Do you think. . .I would imagine that they're being affected by this apparent scheme to buy up all the properties in that neighborhood and redevelop it. Do you think they might be willing to give an interview?"

"I don't know. If there is something like that going on, they might not be able to talk about it." And she was going to make sure to ask the lawyer if they could tell everyone who got involved in the lawsuit not to talk to any reporters—except her.

"So you don't know of anything already pending?"

She shrugged. "What am I supposed to know?"

He gave her a tight smile in return. "Well, if you do hear of anything, you'll be sure to say something, right?"

"I'll do what I can." Oh, yeah. She'd share what she knew—just as soon as the Gulf of Mexico froze over.

"Hey, you busy?"

Forbes looked up from the stack of paperwork on his desk to see Evelyn Mackenzie's lithe figure framed in his doorway. He stood, embarrassed to be caught sans jacket, tie loosened, and sleeves rolled up.

He stood. "Always. But do, please, come in."

Evelyn sauntered into his office, none too subtle in her visual appraisal of the space. He motioned to one of the chairs opposite his desk and waited until she sank into the chair before regaining his seat. Somehow those mile-long legs didn't have the same effect on him today as they'd had in their previous encounters.

"I was just upstairs going over some paperwork with Sandra and your parents, and they suggested I come down and invite you to go to lunch with us." When she leaned forward, the lapels of her suit jacket gapped a bit and revealed a V-neck blouse that showed an extraordinary amount of cleavage.

Somehow, Forbes couldn't imagine Alaine Delacroix doing something quite so inappropriate. No, the top she'd worn under her suit Monday had featured a modest crewneck. And none of the skirts he'd seen her wear on TV had ever ridden up to midthigh when she sat down, the way Evelyn's did now.

"Forbes?"

He pushed the image of Alaine aside and returned to the present. "Sorry." He turned to his computer and pulled up his schedule. "Looks like. . .looks like I'll have to take a pass on lunch. I have a deposition at one o'clock."

Evelyn's expression of disappointment seemed calculated. Or maybe Forbes read too much into it since he found himself not trusting her as much as he was sure he should.

"Well, then, you'll just have to make it up by meeting me for drinks after work. The group playing the Savoy tonight is supposed to be excellent."

He should feel much worse about turning down a gorgeous woman's invitation. "Alas, tonight is out as well. I have a couple of meetings at church tonight I can't miss." One of which was quartet practice. If he canceled again, George, Major, and Clay would hunt him down and personally see to tarring and feathering him.

"Church in the middle of the week?" She cocked her head. "I knew you attended regularly on Sundays, but I hadn't pegged you for the middle-of-the-week type."

He wasn't sure he wanted to know what *type* she'd had him pegged as. Her type, possibly, though he could be flattering himself; her interest might be born solely out of boredom and not knowing anyone else in town. "Oh, yes, I've been called to lead in many different areas of ministry—from music to serving on several committees to chairing the board of trustees."

Though she was a pro at showing only what others wanted to see, Forbes detected a moderate amount of surprise and skepticism in Evelyn's eyes. "That's wonderful. It's always great to hear of people in the community who are successful giving back in such tangible ways."

Or in such visible ways, maybe. Okay, he had to stop second-guessing everything this woman said simply because she'd shown no mercy toward the people who could possibly be losing their homes and businesses. "I do what I can."

His phone rang. He looked down at the console and recognized the number. "If you'll excuse me, I really need to take this call."

"Of course." Her smile seemed much more forced than when she'd come in. "I'll talk to you later."

The phone only rang twice, as he knew it would. No sooner had the door closed behind Evelyn Mackenzie than his intercom buzzed.

"Russell LeBlanc on line one for you, Mr. Guidry."

He pressed the intercom button. "Thanks, Samantha." He pressed the button for the correct line as he raised the receiver to his ear. "Russ, what can I do for you today?"

"It's happening—I'm heading to the hospital—emergency C-section—"

Forbes sprang out of his chair. "Whoa, hold on there. Take a deep breath. What's happening?"

On the other end of the connection, Russ gulped air. "Carrie started having contractions half an hour ago, and her water broke. They just called me from the emergency room. She's in labor, but they're going to have to do an emergency C-section or else might none of them survive."

Forbes paced behind his desk. "That's unbelievable. I'll be praying for all of you. But what else can I do?"

"I'm supposed to be meeting with a potential client—can't remember her name. Left the office without my planner. But I was supposed to meet her at Pappas's Greek Restaurant on Hyacinth in Moreaux Mills at two fifteen this afternoon. You said you were wanting a pro bono case, and this looks like it'll probably be one. Could you take it for me?"

"Of course." He dropped into his chair and wrote down the meeting location and time. "You just get to the hospital safely and don't worry about anything but naming those babies when they finally make their appearance in this world."

"Thanks."

"No problem." Forbes repeated Russ's farewell and hung up, then pressed the intercom again. "Samantha, come in for a moment please."

"Coming." A moment later, she sat across the desk from him.

"Russ LeBlanc's wife just went into labor, so he's asked me to meet with a client in a potential pro bono case at two fifteen this afternoon. I'm supervising that deposition at one, but the associates can handle it if I step out early." He turned his computer monitor so they could both see it. "What's this meeting here?" He pointed to a block of *busy* time that started at two thirty.

"That was the time you asked me to block off for you to work on the Pichon case."

"Right. Great. That means you won't have to reschedule anything for me. I'll need to leave here by about one forty-five if I'm going to get down to Moreaux Mills by a quarter after two. If you don't see me coming out of the conference room by then, stick your head in and remind me."

"Will do, boss."

"Thanks. That's all, then." He nodded his dismissal.

"I'll go ahead and take my lunch now so I'm back by then, if that's okay with you."

"Go ahead." He returned the computer monitor to its original angle.

"Want me to pick up something for you?" She paused in the door.

"No. I'm meeting the new client at a restaurant, so I'll just eat there."

"Okay. I'll see you in a bit." She turned and headed for the door.

"Oh, Samantha?"

"Yes, boss?"

"That woman who was here earlier—Evelyn Mackenzie?"

Samantha raised her brows. "Yes?"

"Next time you see her coming, could you give me a little forewarning? I'm not real fond of surprises, you know."

"Sorry about that. I won't let it happen again." Samantha had the good grace to look sheepish. "She was past my desk and standing in your doorway before I knew what was happening."

He could see Evelyn being stealthy like that. "Don't worry about it. Enjoy your lunch." He waved her out of the room.

Alaine bolted from the office as soon as the meeting about tomorrow's show wrapped. It would put her at the restaurant far too early, but she wouldn't be able to concentrate on work anyway.

The last of the lunch rush was just finishing up when Alaine walked into Pappas's.

"Alaine!" Voula Pappas bustled forward and hugged her. "We haven't seen you around in forever. Why don't you come by more often?"

"Oh, you know how it goes, Mrs. Voula—busy, busy, busy."

"But you are here for lunch?" Voula grabbed a menu.

"I am. But I'm meeting someone else—he won't be here for another fifteen or twenty minutes. His name is Russell LeBlanc."

The middle-aged woman grinned. "Oh, yes, we know Russ quite well." She grabbed two laminated menus.

"I wonder if we could have the table in the back corner overlooking the park. I have. . .a sensitive matter I need to talk to him about and don't want to be overheard."

Voula nodded. "I understand. This way."

Alaine took the chair with her back to the window, eliminating the distraction of watching the squirrels and birds outside in the old, drooping oak tree.

"I'll bring you an iced tea."

"Thanks, Mrs. Voula." Alaine pulled out her steno pad and pen. The dark pink gerbera daisy in a bud vase in the center of the table caught her eye. Every morning, her mother stopped by to get a box of pastries for the flower shop's customers in trade for the flowers for the tables. Yet another argument for why this area and these businesses needed to survive: to remind people how businesses should be run.

Voula brought the tea, and Alaine doctored it with sugar until sweet enough. She flipped open her notepad to a clean page and started an outline for the Moreaux Mills story. She would start it with a soft feature on the businesses in the Mills—the Gardens, the rental center, this restaurant. . .and she could use her small video camera at the Fourth of July street fair to get footage to include in the soft open.

Oh—and she could probably find some archive footage of the Guidrys and possibly some questionable sound bites to use. Not to mention contrasting the footage of the lavish Valentine's Day charity dinner she herself had covered with the current conditions in the Mills. And then she could—

A clearing throat broke into her flow of ideas. Though annoyed by the interruption, Alaine affixed a smile and looked up to greet Russell LeBlanc.

"Uh. . .hi."

Her insides froze at the sight of none other than Forbes Guidry towering over her. She shoved back from the table and shot to her feet. "What are you doing here?" She wanted to cover herself with her hands, so exposed and naked did she feel in his presence.

"My friend Russ LeBlanc called me a couple of hours ago and asked me to come in his place."

"Why? So you can exert your charm over me and convince me to give this up?" Fury shrouded her like smoke, hot and suffocating. She should have known better than to trust any lawyer in this city.

An upside-down Y formed between Forbes's well-groomed brows. "What are you talking about? Russ called me because his wife went into early labor and he knew I was looking for a pro bono case to take on. So he asked me to come."

"I don't believe you." She planted her fists on her hips and fought boiling hot tears pressing the corners of her eyes. She would *not* give him the satisfaction of breaking down in front of him.

Forbes glanced around, then returned his steel blue gaze to her. "Obviously there's some miscommunication going on here. Why don't we sit down, have lunch, and talk about your case?"

"Why would I want to talk to you about it?" She wished she'd sounded more authoritative and less like a howler monkey.

Forbes puffed up slightly. "Because I'm one of the top lawyers in this state, and I rarely lose. So no matter what your case is about, I can probably get you a desirable outcome."

Cold suspicion doused the heat of her anger. "You're going to stand there and act like you don't even know what this is about?"

He held both hands up, palms out. "All I know is that my friend called and asked a favor of me."

Could he be serious? Could he really not know why he was here? The chances were astronomical that of all substitute lawyers Russell LeBlanc could call, it would be the son of the people she wanted to sue. She dropped into her chair and frowned at Forbes as he lowered himself into the seat opposite her. She'd worry about giving herself frown lines later. Right now, she wanted to be sure he understood just how displeased his presence made her.

Forbes took a deep breath and gave her a look she could only describe as lawyerly. "Since we're both here, why don't you tell me what your case is regarding, and we'll see what we can do about it."

"You think you're always going to get what you want, don't you?" Alaine crossed her arms and continued to glare at him.

"When it comes to you? No." He high-beamed a smile at her.

She had to look away, perturbed at the way his smile got to her every single time. Only now it reminded her of the way her skin had tingled at the touch of his hand to her back, of her hand clasped in his, of the light tang of his cologne when they'd danced Monday evening.

She steeled her will and looked at him again. The flirtatious expression faded from his eyes.

"Look, I can tell something is wrong, and apparently you need legal help with it. I promise you: Anything you tell me is strictly confidential, and there will be no personal bias in any advice or legal aid I render to you."

She tapped her front teeth together. No personal bias, huh? She'd just see about that.

Chapter 13

"Okay. But I'm holding you to your promise: No personal bias on your part."

Curiosity bubbled in Forbes's chest, but he kept his posture relaxed, his face neutral. "I wouldn't have said it if I hadn't meant it." What kind of trouble could she possibly be in that would elicit this kind of anger—toward him? "So what can I help you with?"

"Let's order first." She nodded over his shoulder, and he turned to see the middle-aged woman who'd pointed him to Alaine's table.

He grabbed up the cheap, plastic-covered menu. "I've never had Greek food before." He flashed a smile at the hostess. "What do you recommend?"

"For a white boy like you, I'd start you off with *spanakopita* or *pastitsio*."

"I'll take the first one you said." He handed her the menu.

"I'll have *horiatiki salata* and *tiropeta*, and I'll finish with baklava."

For someone who'd eaten like a bird at the bachelors' banquet, that sounded like an awful lot of food.

"I'll be back with more iced tea." The woman bustled off.

"So, do you come here often?"

Alaine quirked her head to the side, as if confused by his subject-changing tactic. "All the time. Ms. Voula and my mother are good friends." Her expression closed again at the words *my mother*.

Forbes cringed inwardly. So. . .his suspicions had been on the right track. This did have something to do with Delacroix Gardens. "Your parents are here in Bonneterre?"

"They're *here* in the Mills. Didn't you know that? I know you've seen their business—Delacroix Gardens Florist and Nursery."

Yep. He was right. No wonder she'd been rebuffing him since they'd met.

"Or you've at least heard of Delacroix Rentals—your cousin Anne does a lot of business with my brother Joe. Your sister used to, but for some reason that's petered off in recent months. No need to wonder why." The acidity in her tone could burn through steel.

He rocked back, shocked. "Wait—I thought you and Meredith were friends."

"*Were* being the operative word. How can I be friends with someone when her parents—whom she works for—are trying to run my family out of their businesses and homes?"

And by extension, how could she go out on a date with the son of said parents? Her complete one-eighty attitude change since the night of the dinner now made sense. "You think my parents' company is trying to put your parents out of business?"

She pressed her lips together, raised her eyebrows, and nodded. "And you only needed one guess."

Once realization began to dawn, it burst immediately into fullness. "You mean this—you were going to be meeting with Russ to talk to him about. . .what? Suing my parents?"

She shrugged as if going around suing people's parents was something she did every day. "Their company, anyway."

"For buying up foreclosed properties and revitalizing the area?" He couldn't keep the shock out of his voice.

She snorted. "If that's all they were doing—on properties that were *legally* foreclosed upon—then there wouldn't be a problem. But there's more than that going on. A lot more. As in, they've gotten another company that calls itself an 'investment firm' to come in, buy up loans from local banks, and call them in—and then when the mortgage holders can't pay ten or twenty years' worth of their mortgage in one lump sum, they receive foreclosure notices. Or even when the original bank had worked something out with the mortgage holder so they could get caught up with their payments when business picked up, those loans have been bought out and are now being foreclosed on. It's not right, and I'm going to see that it's stopped before a lot of good people end up losing everything they've worked their whole lives for."

Forbes tried to process what she was saying. He was pretty sure he got it, but emotion had sped her words to the point where they nearly ran together. "So you're saying that what you've seen is something you consider to be unfair or unethical business practices on the part of an investment firm that has come in and bought up the mortgages of property owners in Moreaux Mills." He pulled his Waterford pen out of his inside jacket pocket, flipped open his leather portfolio, and started taking notes.

"Not just any investment firm. A company called Mackenzie and Son. I just discovered the name today so I haven't had time to do any research; however, I think I'll find that once I start digging into their past business dealings, I'm going to learn that they do this all over the country."

A cold dread settled in Forbes's stomach. "Do what?"

Alaine flapped her hands in an irritated manner. "Swoop in when a developer is trying to force a few people out of an area the developer wants to tear down and rebuild as something else. Force them out by shady business deals and questionable accounting and making them feel like there's nothing else they can do but accept a price for their property that's not only much lower than the property's really worth, but definitely not enough for those people to be able to start over somewhere else."

The way her eyes flashed with passion for her topic mesmerized Forbes to the point where he almost forgot what she was talking about. He looked down at the legal pad. The last line he'd written was a scrawl of gibberish. He angled it toward him against the edge of the table so she couldn't see it.

"It's my understanding that the city council decided on fair market value for the homes and businesses in the Mills. Are you saying that they're now being offered a buyout package that's lower than the official assessments?"

She cocked her head again and looked at him as if a rosebush had just sprouted from his nose. "The city council. The *city council*? The city council voted on the property values. The city council that is chaired by Tess Folse—partner emeritus of Folse, Maier, Landreneau, and Guidry, Attorneys at Law. The law firm that—oh, let me think—boasts as its most lucrative client Boudreaux-Guidry Enterprises, the same company that wants to buy up all of the property in Moreaux Mills dirt cheap, plow it under, and then build a planned condo community that they can turn around and sell for fifty times what they originally paid for the property. That city council? No conflict of interest there."

Forbes shifted in his seat and couldn't look up from the legal pad. That was the way development companies worked. Buy low; tear down; rebuild; sell high. But the way Alaine described it shed a new, somewhat seedy light on the whole process. And it tainted Forbes by association—with not just his parents' corporation but the law firm as well.

No wonder she hated him. But Mom and Dad wouldn't be involved in something so underhanded. They loved Bonneterre and all its diverse and unique neighborhoods. And they were huge supporters of local enterprise.

This had to be coming from Mackenzie and Son. Evelyn's voice rang in his head. *"Out with the old and dilapidated, in with the new and luxurious."*

He took a deep breath and looked up, letting the air out in a controlled stream. "Alaine, I promise you that if there is something like this going on, my parents don't know anything about it. They're the most ethical people I know."

A slight raise of her brows and flattening of her mouth indicated her disbelief.

Before he could say more, the restaurant owner returned with their food. She set a Greek salad and something that looked like cheese melted between layers of pastry before Alaine, and something similar to her second dish in front of Forbes—except it also had green stuff between the layers of pastry.

"What is this?" He tried to keep his voice light.

"Spanakopita—phyllo layered with feta, spinach, and herbs."

Should have asked before he ordered. He hated spinach. On principle. Anything that got slimy and stringy when exposed to hot water wasn't worth eating. But he couldn't very well send it back now. "Oh. Okay. Thanks."

Across the table, Alaine ate the olives from her salad first, not raising her gaze from her food. Forbes cut off a small corner of one of the three triangular pieces of spanikopita and lifted it to his mouth, trying not to breathe in through his nose as he did so.

The flaky, buttery phyllo pastry melted on his tongue. The creamy saltiness of the cheese coated his mouth, and the spinach. . . what spinach? Mixed with whatever herbs were in it, the spinach was unobtrusive. He'd have to get Major to come out here and tell him exactly what was in it—and see if he could re-create it.

He followed Alaine's lead and didn't speak while they ate. He tried to pace himself so he didn't finish before she did—and just as he scraped up the last few crumbs and drippings of green-flecked cheese, the woman Alaine had referred to as Ms. Voula reappeared with a plate of baklava—with two forks. Alaine pushed her half-finished salad and cheese pastry aside and picked up one of the forks from the dessert plate. She used it to wave at the other.

"Have one." She cut into one of the sticky-looking pastries.

He'd always heard of this dish but had never tried it. "What's in it?"

"Um. . ." Alaine lifted the top layer of phyllo. "Walnuts, cinnamon, sugar, probably other spices. Oh, and honey over the top."

That, he could do. He cut into the small square on his side of the plate. The warm, spicy, sweet smell of it made his mouth water. And when he bit into it. . .

Baklava was his new favorite dessert—even if it did make his teeth hurt from the combination of honey on the outside and sugar on the inside. Even though the piece was small, he couldn't finish the whole thing, already feeling like he'd need to add a few hours' running tomorrow just to work off his entrée.

He waited until Alaine put her fork down and ordered coffee before broaching the subject of this meeting again—and prayed her anger had abated. "I know it's going to be hard for you to believe me, because in your mind I'm part of the problem, but I want to help you find a solution. I'm certain that with a little digging and possibly bringing together the information from all parties involved, we can discover where the breakdown in communication has happened and get it straightened out." He rested his hands flat on the table. "I'd like to take your case."

She shook her head. "I don't want you as our lawyer. No one would ever trust that you're truly working for us and not to get the best outcome for your parents' company."

Alaine wished she could recall the words as soon as they left her mouth. She couldn't remember everything she'd said to him in the past forty-five minutes, but that last one had been uncalled for—and intentionally hurtful.

And he'd obviously never had someone tell him to his face that he was untrustworthy. Though he'd worn an emotionless mask since she'd started berating him for something he might not have any part in, his too-handsome-for-her-peace-of-mind face now expressed betrayal, disbelief, and a profound pain.

"I'm sorry. What I mean to say is that we need to find a lawyer who doesn't have a personal vested interest in the opposing side of the issue. Who isn't going to be torn or influenced by emotional—and familial—involvement with the defendants. From my preliminary conversations with a few business owners, we're ready to take this all the way—a big, public court case, which, even if we lose, could cause irreparable damage to Boudreaux-Guidry Enterprises' reputation in Bonneterre."

Forbes nodded, stared at the flower in the center of the table for a few seconds, then raised guarded, gray blue eyes to hers once more. "You keep saying *we*, but I know for a fact you don't live in the district. And you don't work here, either. So other than being related to people who are affected by this, what's your involvement in it?"

"My involvement?" She tried not to let him see how his question flustered her.

"Yes. Plaintiffs in a case like this need to be those who are directly affected by the wrongs they're accusing the defendant of. I understand that as a reporter, you have an interest in the public side of it—in arguing the case in the court of public opinion. But do you truly have a stake in the case, or are you just the public face of it to bring more attention and quicker action?"

Her conversation with her parents replayed in her head. She'd made a promise. "No, I'm not the 'public face,' as you put it. I'm the... liaison. Think of me as the agent for the actual plaintiffs. I'll get all the pertinent information, and then I'll gather everyone together and share it with them." She nodded for emphasis.

His right brow quirked slightly. "You realize that if this does go to court, I—your lawyer will take over that role? Are you going to be okay with turning everything over to me—him?"

"Or her. Yes, if I feel that person is trustworthy and isn't out to appease his parents." She clamped her lips shut. She was behaving just like Meg Ryan in *You've Got Mail*—unable to stop herself from piling up the hurtful remarks.

Of course, Meg Ryan and Tom Hanks ended up together at the end of that movie.

No. She couldn't think that way—not about Forbes Guidry, no matter how handsome he was and how her insides melted like a chocolate bar left in the car in August whenever she was around him.

"Have you spoken with any other lawyers about this case?" Forbes reached for his leather portfolio and pen.

She thought about the list in her steno pad of all the crossed-out lawyer names. "I tried."

"What did they have to say about it?"

She might as well give him the truth. "As soon as I mentioned Boudreaux-Guidry Enterprises, they pretty much hung up on me."

"So Russ LeBlanc was your last hope?"

Chewing the inside of her bottom lip, she nodded. "Yes, but I hadn't told him whom the case was against." She regarded Forbes for a long moment. Not a single dark hair out of place. Thick, perfectly groomed eyebrows. Long, dark lashes framing eyes that sometimes looked blue and sometimes dark gray. And no reason to distrust him other than the fact he was one of the best-looking men she'd ever encountered. "Do you really think you'd be able to be objective about this?"

Forbes pushed his plate aside and folded his hands atop his pad on the table. "I have to be honest and say that I don't believe my parents are involved in any wrongdoing. But you've definitely raised some questions about the legalities of things that are going on in the Mills. If you can trust me enough to act on your—well, the plaintiffs'—behalf, then I can promise you that any legal advice I give will be as objective as I possibly can be. Though you may have a hard time believing it, I hold personal and professional integrity at the highest level—not just for me, but for everyone I work with as well as every member of my family. If I discover anything that isn't completely aboveboard, I'll do whatever it takes to make it right."

She wanted to believe him—whether it was because she was attracted to him or not was something she'd deal with at another time. This was just one of those step-out-on-faith moments the pastor always talked about, she supposed.

"Okay. Fine. If you can do this for us, I'll set up a time for you to come meet with everyone who's interested in participating in the case." She bit her bottom lip and swallowed hard. Of course, now she had to rely on her family and their neighbors taking Forbes *and* her at their word that he was on their side.

His forehead relaxed and his perfect teeth showed, even though he wasn't actually smiling. "Great. That's all I ask for—to be given a chance."

"The others might not be as understanding as I am about your involvement."

The booming laugh he emitted wasn't the reaction she expected. "If this is an example of your being understanding, I definitely have my work cut out for me, don't I?"

A sharp retort tripped out to the end of her tongue but stopped when his laughter made her realize the idiocy of her statement. She let out a chuckle and rolled her eyes. "Okay, so I haven't been all that understanding. And I apologize for saying anything that might have been out of line. But just know you'll be facing that from a lot of folks once they find out who you are."

"I'll be prepared; don't worry." He cocked his head to the side and gazed at her with hooded eyes. "I convinced you, didn't I?"

She ran her tongue over her teeth to try to hide the fact that she wanted to devolve into a thirteen-year-old schoolgirl when he looked at her like that. "Only because I know how difficult it will be to find another lawyer who'll take our case."

Her phone beeped with an incoming text message, interrupting Forbes, who'd taken a breath to make a reply. She looked down at it—shocked to see that nearly an hour and a half had passed. "It's the studio."

"I've got to get back to work as well." He picked up his portfolio and slid his pen into his inside coat pocket. "I'll call you later to discuss the meeting with the clients—and we need to set up a time to review all the preliminary research you've done. I'll need your notes to see what you've discovered so far and what avenues you haven't yet explored."

"Okay. . .but I should tell you, I did promise my parents that

I would keep this out of the public eye as much as I can. It'll get suspicious if I start coming to your office." She stuffed her steno pad and pen into her briefcase, then stood and slung the strap over her shoulder.

Forbes rose and motioned her to exit ahead of him. "We already have the perfect cover for getting together at least once a week."

She stopped and turned, and found herself tilting her head far back to look up into those mesmerizing eyes. "We do?"

"We do. That is, if you'll agree to be my partner for ballroom dancing lessons for the next six weeks."

She wasn't sure if he leaned closer to her or if she leaned closer to him. . .but she jerked herself out of the trance and took a step back.

"Dance lessons? You want me to be your partner for dance lessons?" The soles of her feet tingled with the memory of sliding across the parquet floor at Arcenault's. Not to mention the heady feeling from breathing in Forbes's spicy cologne from such a close proximity—like now.

He shrugged. "My sister Jennifer talked me into doing it with her, but now she's had to back out because of. . .personnel issues at her restaurant. I had a good time dancing with you Monday night. And if I'm not mistaken, you were having a pretty good time yourself. You're a good dancer already—I need someone who's better than me to help me figure it out."

Alaine crossed her arms to protect herself from the barrage of charm Forbes lobbed her way. "I insist on paying for my portion of the package."

"Okay."

"And I'm only agreeing to this because, as you said, it gives us a good excuse to see each other regularly to discuss the case."

"Right."

She turned and started for the door again, then stopped and turned so fast, Forbes nearly ran into her. She poked her finger into his chest—his solid, muscular chest. She tingled. "And if anyone asks, we are *not* dating."

"If you insist."

She did insist. Why, she wasn't certain. But for her own sanity, that was the way it had to be.

Chapter 14

Forbes slammed on the brakes to keep from running a red light. He wanted to believe Alaine, but all his instincts screamed she was wrong—or at least misled.

The one thing he knew beyond a doubt: His parents would never do something like that. When they'd taken over Grandfather Boudreaux's commercial real-estate venture thirty-odd years ago, they'd not only championed small businesses, they'd started the Bonneterre Small Business Owners' Association. Eventually, they'd had to leave it based on the guidelines they themselves had written. But they still supported it by donating the office space in Boudreaux Tower as well as conference-room space in the building for the association's monthly meetings. The president of the BSBOA came to Dad's prayer breakfast every week, for crying out loud.

Except. . .Forbes wracked his brain. Come to think of it, the guy hadn't been there for the past few months. But people came and went, turning up some weeks and then not being seen for a few months, then showing up again as if they'd never been gone.

At the next light, he pulled out his phone and called his sister.

"Facilities and Events, this is Meredith." She sounded harried.

"Mere, it's Forbes. You got a minute?"

"Just. What's up?"

"I'm wondering—why did you stop using Delacroix Rentals as a supplier?"

She paused a long time. "Where'd you hear that?"

"Oh. . .I had lunch today with an acquaintance who knows the owners and mentioned they hadn't gotten a lot of business from you recently."

"Really? I hadn't noticed. These things go in cycles, you know. Sometimes a supplier will have what we need, and sometimes we'll have a spate of events that we use other suppliers for. Why the sudden interest in the running of B-G? Doesn't that give you hives or something?"

"Just curious, I guess."

"Well, Mr. Suddenly Curious, I just had eight people walk into my office for a meeting I'm supposed to be leading, so I hope I sufficiently answered your question."

"Yeah. Thanks." He bade her farewell and hung up.

He'd deal with his family members after he looked into whether or not there was any breach of ethics or actual lawbreaking going on—by Boudreaux-Guidry or by Mackenzie and Son.

He groaned when he walked into his office and saw the stack of files in his in-box. Samantha followed him in, reciting a list of things she needed from him before she had to leave—"And I can only stay until five thirty tonight. I have class at six, and we're having a test tonight, so I can't skip. And you can't stay much later than that, because you asked me to remind you that you have a committee meeting at church tonight at six thirty."

He rubbed his neck, trying to stop the tightness from forming into a knot at the base of his skull. "I'll do my best."

He dived into the work, forcing himself to keep on task, not allowing himself to turn to the computer to search though B-G's files to see what they'd been up to, legally speaking, in the last six or eight months. He was down to the last file when Samantha reentered his office at 5:25.

"Well?" She leaned against the doorframe and crossed her arms.

"I still need about twenty minutes on this one."

She closed her eyes and appeared to wilt before his eyes.

"You go on to class. I'll make the necessary copies and put everything on your desk before I leave. Where's your logbook?"

She giggled. "It's all on the computer now, boss. But don't worry about it. I still have to number them, so I'll input them into the log tomorrow morning before I hand the copies over to the courier service for delivery."

"Thanks. Now go on, get out of here. Don't want you to miss your test."

She gave him a jaunty wave and disappeared.

Though most of the associates, interns, clerks, and assistants were still hard at work, the silence in Forbes's office grew oppressive soon after Samantha's departure. Not even the '80s music playing softly through his computer from the Internet radio station helped.

At 6:15, he laid the copies of the last file on Samantha's desk and returned to his office. He glared at the clock. He wanted to stay here and delve into his parents' company's files to start answering some of his questions. But he'd already asked the nominating committee to reschedule twice. He couldn't ask them to do it again—especially not at the last minute.

Frustrated, he turned off the lights and locked the office door behind him. Peeking into files that he hadn't had any part in by choice would have to wait until tomorrow.

An accident left traffic snarled getting out of downtown on North Street, turning a ten-minute drive into twenty-five and making Forbes late for his meeting. The other six members of the committee showed a mixture of relief and annoyance when he sailed into the room.

"Sorry I'm late. Traffic." He flung his suit coat over the back of the only empty chair at the table and rolled up his shirt sleeves before digging the legal pad out of the expanding folder marked *Personnel Committee*.

He closed his eyes and sent up a quick prayer for calmness. "Why don't y'all go ahead and get started on. . .workers for Extended Session. I've got to run back out to the car and get the correct file."

The committee secretary launched into the list of names she'd compiled before he got to the door. Of course, she'd never seemed to understand why everyone else on the committee had elected him chairperson over her. Today, he could clearly see it from her point of view. He had to pull himself together and regain control over his thoughts and actions.

He swapped the personnel committee file for the thicker nominating committee file from the brown file box in the trunk of the car and returned to the small Sunday school classroom—just in time to see Jean rise from her seat and lean over the table.

"Just because people aren't married doesn't mean that they're disposable."

"That isn't what I said, Jean, and you know it. You're too sensitive about it. What I said is that we shouldn't require parents to work in the nursery just because they're parents. It's discrimination."

"Discrimination? To ask people who're creating the work to do the work? Why should single people be required to work in the nursery when they don't have kids?"

"But parents come and put their kids in the nursery so they can attend services. The least those without kids can do is to work in the nursery to afford them that opportunity."

"So people without kids don't come so *they* can attend services?"

"Whoa, hold on a minute." Forbes placed his hand on Jean's shoulder and, with firm but gentle pressure, guided her back into her chair. He set his folder on the table, then settled one hand on his waist, using the other to rub his forehead. "We've discussed this before. We can't require *anyone* to work in the nursery. They have to volunteer, and they have to be approved by the Children's Department director. Now, if we can talk about this calmly?" He looked pointedly at Jean and her adversary. Both nodded. "Good."

Forbes sat and led the discussion into safer paths. He finally ended up assigning Jean and another committee member to approach the people on their newly formulated list to ask them about working in the nursery.

Sunday school teacher appointments were easier to agree upon—usually because there was only one volunteer for each slot, and almost always it was the person who already taught that class. When they got through the list, he looked at his watch and, to his profound relief, discovered they'd only run a few minutes over their hour. "That'll be all for this week. I'll present these names"—he tapped his legal pad—"at next week's business meeting. Frank, will you close us in prayer?"

Jean's adversary nodded, and said a quick, perfunctory prayer. Forbes's mind whirled. Alaine. His parents. Meredith. Nominating committee. Evelyn Mackenzie. Work. Personnel committee. His younger siblings who still needed their big brother. Board of trustees. . .

The knot at the base of his skull grew worse. Great. Now all this stress was going to add getting back in to see the chiropractor to his growing to-do list.

After chatting with a few of the committee members, he stepped out of the classroom into the flow of people coming out of the choir room down the hall. He could go back to the office and spend a few hours looking through B-G's case files—

"Hey, Forbes!"

He turned and searched the crowd for the owner of the booming voice.

Almost head and shoulders above everyone else, the Polynesian man raised his hand to motion Forbes toward him. Forbes excused his way past the dozen or so people still lingering in the foyer.

"Hey, Clay. What's up?"

Clay Huntoon gave him a quizzical look. "Uh. . .rehearsal. Did you forget?"

Quartet rehearsal. They were singing Sunday and hadn't practiced in more than a month. "I just need to go put this out in the car and get my music."

"Oh. Okay. I'll tell the guys."

The heat of the day hadn't dissipated at all, and the humidity seemed to condense on Forbes's skin as soon as he stepped out of the over-air-conditioned building. He returned the committee file to the box in the trunk and pulled his music folder out.

As he slammed the trunk, his phone beeped a new text message. He pulled out the PDA and turned it sideways to read the new message:

3 grls 1 boy
Carrie Doing gr8
Russ

Forbes tapped back a congratulatory message, though he didn't necessarily feel the happiness for his friend he would have if this had happened twenty-four hours later. Forbes glanced up at the still-bright evening sky.

"God, you have a sick sense of timing."

If Carrie LeBlanc had waited one more day to go into labor, Russ would have been the one to meet with Alaine, and Forbes would still be blissfully unaware she had any grievance against his parents' company. And he wouldn't be stressing over it.

Before walking into the choir room, he took a deep breath and composed himself very much the same way he did before walking into a courtroom. He needed to get through the next hour or so, and then he could go home and start putting things into perspective by making a list of actionable items to follow up on.

He strode through the door, trying to give the best appearance of someone with no concerns in the world. Major stood beside the piano, warming up the top of his range while George played scales. Clay paced the opposite end of the large chamber talking on the phone—a sports reporter's work was never finished.

And Anne and Meredith sat in the front row, talking. They looked up when he approached.

"Hey, Forbes. . .you look tired." Meredith's forehead crinkled with her expression of concern. "Are you feeling okay?"

He waved his hand in a dismissive gesture. "Just have a lot on my mind."

His sister's eyes narrowed slightly; then she shrugged. "If there's anything I can do. . ."

A list of questions scrolled through his mind. But now wasn't the right time. "I'll let you know." He walked over to the piano. "So what are we singing Sunday?"

"We were thinking about the a cappella version of 'God of Our Fathers.'" George flipped through several pieces of music on the music rack in front of him. "We know it best."

"And Sunday is Father's Day," Major added.

"Sounds good to me." Forbes flipped through his folder and pulled out the sheet music George and Clay had arranged and written down for them. The main thing he loved about singing second tenor, even though it strained his voice, was that he usually had the melody—as he did in this piece.

George wasn't the best pianist in the world—he admitted it himself—but he could at least play the four parts along with them as they practiced, which none of the rest of them could do. Forbes observed the other three men as they sang, each concentrating hard on learning his part so they could sing it without accompaniment.

He needed someone to talk to, someone he could vent his frustrations to, someone who wasn't involved in family business. With George and Major both married into the family, that excused them from the role of confidante. And while he liked Clay and considered him a friend, Clay was one of the guys Jenn dated regularly—that and Forbes didn't feel comfortable bringing someone he knew as casually as Clay into such extreme confidence.

Anne and Meredith—and everyone else in the family—he excluded for obvious reasons. He needed an outsider, someone who could be objective but also keep everything he said in confidence.

His voice broke on a high note when the reality hit him. He didn't have friends outside of his family circle. He steadied his voice and resisted taking a look at Meredith over his shoulder. Was this the realization she'd come to that had led her to start distancing herself from the family over the past few months?

After they practiced enough so that they could sing the piece all the way through a few times without accompaniment and stay on key, they called it a night.

"We're going to grab dinner," Meredith said to Forbes, joining her husband at the piano. "Want to go with us?"

His stomach had been rumbling the past half hour. "No. I think I'll pick something up on my way home. I've still got some work to do before I can turn in tonight." He edged toward the door and his escape.

"Okay. We'll see you tomorrow night, then."

"I'll try to make it, but I'll let you know if I won't be there." In the few years he and Anne and Meredith and the rest of their siblings and cousins around their ages had been meeting for dinner on Thursday nights at Jenn's restaurant, he'd only missed attending a couple of times.

He slipped out the door as they started to discuss where they were going to eat. In the car, he turned off the radio and let the silence enfold him. He wanted to pray. . .yet he couldn't find the energy or focus to do so.

At the town house, while waiting for the garage door to open, movement next door caught his eye. Shon stepped out of his front door and acknowledged Forbes with a lifting of his chin.

Shon. The weight that had pressed down on Forbes's shoulders all afternoon suddenly lightened. If anyone could keep his confidence, it would be his next-door neighbor.

He stepped out of the garage and met Shon at the bottom of his neighbor's front steps.

" 'Sup, man? We running in the morning?" Shon returned Forbes's handshake.

"Yes. Definitely."

"Good. I've got a couple of prospects for you."

"Prospects?"

"For dates. Remember? Your ninety-day membership."

"Right. I'll make you a deal."

"Huh-uh." Shon shook his head. "You already made me one deal on this."

"But I really need this favor."

Shon crossed his arms and leaned against the banister. "Let's have it."

"I'll go out with anyone you want to set me up with, sight unseen, if you'll let me use you as a sounding board for some stuff I have going on in my life right now."

"Dude, you know you can tell me anything." His grin flashed in the gathering twilight.

"This is big stuff, Shon. Stuff I can't talk to anyone else about because if it ever went public, it could create a lot of chaos for people I care a lot about."

Shon sobered. "You're serious. Whatever you need, man, I'm here for you. And you know me: Everything you tell me will be held in strictest confidence, no matter what. You know, that whole lawyer-client confidentiality thing."

Forbes laughed for the first time all day. "That only applies to me as your lawyer."

"Whatever. I promise to listen to what you have to say and not repeat it to anyone."

"Thanks. I appreciate it."

"No problem." Shon's grin reappeared.

"What?"

"I'm just thinking about all those ladies I'd like to introduce you to."

Forbes groaned.

Chapter 15

Alaine refilled the two glasses of iced tea and handed the second glass to her coworker. "I'm really glad you could come over for dinner tonight."

Bekka Blakeley accepted the glass and followed Alaine from the dining table into the living room. "I'm glad you asked. One of my grandfather's horses is foaling tonight, so Andrew's probably going to be out there all night."

"After working all day?"

"He loves it. He worked full-time for my grandfather for a few years—started just before we got married. But then when Grandpa decided to go into semiretirement, stop breeding, and sell off most of the stock, Andrew went back to the animal hospital. I don't know if he misses working with Grandpa every day or being a full-time equine vet more."

"Is that how you met? Because he worked for your grandfather?" Alaine curled up in the opposite corner of the sofa from the newscaster.

"No. He was still at the hospital when we met. I had an emergency with my horse, and he came out to take care of it for me."

"And it was love at first sight, I'll bet." Alaine teased.

A wry smile spread over Bekka's face. "No. Actually, we didn't start off well. He asked to speak to one of my parents."

Considering it had been more than ten years ago and Bekka could still pass for a teenager when she had on no makeup and was dressed in jeans and a T-shirt—like now—Alaine could understand Andrew's mistake.

"I was dating someone else at the time. You're a bit younger than me, so you may not remember when I was in the news instead of just reporting it. Tim, the man I'd been seeing, had been arrested, and some accusations were made regarding me and whether or not I'd bribed someone to get him out of jail. It was right after I'd gotten the weekend sports anchor position."

"Oh, yeah—he went on Channel Three, on Teri Jones's show, and tried to discredit you, and then she brought out a surprise guest who ended up discrediting him. We watched all of that as it happened in one of my J-school classes. I'd forgotten it was you."

"I haven't."

"So it was after all that when you and Andrew started dating?" Alaine swirled her glass to mix the melting ice into the tea.

"We never really dated. We were always just together. I went to Iowa with him at New Year's to see his parents, whom he hadn't spoken to in years. We were really close after that, but it wasn't until he proposed to me Memorial Day weekend that I knew exactly how he felt about me." Bekka sipped her tea. "Why the questions about how I met my husband?"

Alaine shrugged.

"Have you met someone?"

She shrugged again. "I thought so. Then I found out who he is, and it'll never work."

"I can see this is eating you up. Spill it, girl."

Alaine didn't need a second invitation. It took nearly an hour for her to explain everything; and several times, she questioned the wisdom of telling another reporter all of the details of what could become a huge story, if not one of the biggest scandals in Bonneterre's history. But she trusted Bekka implicitly, especially after having just been reminded of the integrity with which Bekka'd handled her own public scandal years ago.

When Alaine finished speaking, Bekka just stared at her for a moment.

"Do you realize if Rodney knew you were involved in this, he'd flip his toupee?"

"He's already tried to pump me for information because he knows I have family connections in the Mills. Which is why you can't say anything to anyone about it. I promised my parents I'd keep quiet about it—that I wouldn't make a stink about it on my show, as I'd really like to." Though it felt good to have spoken everything aloud, anxiety started chewing at Alaine's insides over bringing an outsider into the situation.

"Don't worry. I'll keep it to myself. But what are you going to do if this does become a lawsuit? Once that happens, it's public knowledge, and Rodney is bound to find out you knew about it." Bekka slipped off her sneakers and tucked her feet up under herself.

"I'll just have to deal with that if and when it happens." Alaine couldn't meet her friend's eye. If Bekka didn't know Alaine was planning to film her own story and turn it in just before anything went public, Bekka wouldn't have to lie to protect her.

"What about this Forbes Guidry? Didn't he ask you out a couple of weeks ago?"

Heat flooded Alaine's cheeks. "He did. But that was right about the time I learned what was going on. Of course I said no. At that time, it was a major conflict of interest."

"At that time? But not now?"

"It doesn't matter. It would be a conflict of interest."

"But you like him?"

Alaine sighed and put her dripping glass of now watered-down tea on the table. "I do. But—"

"I know. 'It doesn't matter.' What are you going to do?"

"About?"

"About trying to make the fact you're attracted to him not matter?"

"I signed up for a membership to Let's Do Coffee. Shon Murphy is even now supposed to be finding matches to set me up on dates with."

"You know, I have a cousin your age who isn't married." Bekka's brown eyes twinkled.

Alaine made a cross with her forefingers as if warding off a vampire. "If I had a dollar for every time someone told me they have an unmarried relative." She giggled. "Is he cute?"

"I think so. I'm sure you've heard of him: Clark d'Arcement."

Alaine sat up straighter. "Clark. . .one of the twins who made a couple million dollars when they were in college because of that Web site they started and then sold?"

Bekka nodded. "Yep. They're partners in a Web site designing company now. I could give him your number. I know he knows who you are."

Alaine chewed the inside of her bottom lip. Was cuteness and wealth a good enough reason to go out with someone? Oh, heck yeah. "Okay. But you can't tell him it's my idea."

"Of course not. Because no man's ego needs the boost it gets from knowing a beautiful woman is interested in him."

Very true. Alaine led the conversation into more casual, less personal topics, but Bekka's statement kept whirring in her mind, bringing the vision of Forbes at the bachelors' banquet to mind. No, his ego hadn't needed the boost it had gotten from the interest she'd unwillingly shown. And no matter how much she protested that her attraction to him didn't matter, she couldn't help but tingle with the anticipation of dancing with him again Monday night.

"Um, boss?"

Forbes looked up from the paperwork in front of him. "Yes, Samantha?"

"That e-mail you sent with the list of files you want copied. . .you know those are in the partners-only file room?" His secretary twisted her long necklace around her fingers.

"Oh, right." He opened his top drawer and pulled out a key, which he held toward her. "Here. That should get you in."

She crossed the office but hesitated before taking the key. "If someone else asks me why I'm pulling the files, what case should I tell them it's for?"

Forbes's insides squirmed. "It's background research for a real-estate development case I'm looking at taking. I need to see if there's any precedent in any of those files that can help me decide if the case if viable or not."

Samantha's anxious posture eased. "Oh. Okay. I just wasn't sure what to say if Mary—I mean, if someone decides I'm not supposed to be up there."

He tried to give her a reassuring smile. "If she—someone happens to ask you what you're doing in the partners-only file room, you can simply remind her that I'm a partner and tell her I asked you to copy some files for me. She doesn't need to know anything beyond that."

His voice oozed confidence but guilt burned through his stomach. While he had every right to access the room containing files of clients handled by the partners—because he *was* a partner, as he'd just reminded his secretary—pulling B-G's files to see what kind of information he could find about their legal dealings with acquiring the property in the Warehouse District and Moreaux Mills wasn't necessarily on the up-and-up. He could go through proper channels and request them through the court system, but that could take weeks, if not months.

He had to know now. And he couldn't tell much from the briefs he found in the electronic files on the server. He needed to read the transcripts, to see the paperwork, to find out exactly what kinds of legal action they'd been pursuing to gain those properties.

He rubbed the bridge of his nose and tried to concentrate on the Pichon file. . .but it was no use. He reached for the large ceramic mug with the Delta Chi fraternity logo on it. Empty.

He moaned and made his way down the hall to the break room.

The extra-large coffee carafe was more than half-full, meaning it had only been made a few minutes ago, as it never lasted very long. He poured the mug three-quarters full, topped it off with skim milk, and sweetened it with two packs of artificial sweetener.

"Oh, good morning, Mr. Guidry." One of the paralegals came in bearing a pink mug with Princess in purple scripty letters across the front.

"Good morning, Geoff. Nice cup."

"Thanks. My daughter's. Only clean one in the house this morning. And if I forget to take it home by tomorrow, I'll never hear the end of it—this is my weekend to have the kids."

Forbes clamped his teeth together to keep from asking when Geoff had gotten a divorce. He needed to get out of his office more often and mingle with his co-workers. He didn't want to be one of those kinds of partners who knew nothing about the people in the ranks who worked longer and harder hours trying to gain what Forbes had already accomplished.

"How old are they now?" He leaned against the counter and unbuttoned his coat.

"Twelve, nine, and five. What about you? You got kids?" Geoff poured his coffee to the rim of his mug and took a slurp before turning to the granite-topped cabinet to doctor it with powdered creamer.

"No. I'm not married."

Geoff chuckled. "Yeah, knew that from the whole Bachelor of the Year thing. But marriage isn't required for someone to have kids."

"For me, it is."

"Nice to hear someone still has some old-fashioned values these days. I mean, my wife comes to me a year ago and tells me she wants us to have an 'open' marriage—because she's met someone else but doesn't want to go through the trouble of a divorce. And she gets majority custody of the kids because I was the one who asked for the divorce, so it looks like I'm in the wrong. Does that seem right to you?"

Okay. Maybe he really didn't need to spend more time with the staff.

"Just because I'd mentioned wanting to go back to school to work on my law degree and asked if she'd be able to make sure she had the kids the nights I had class. And when I had to work late. . ."

Forbes edged toward the door, trying to figure out a tactful way to extricate himself from the conversation.

The administrative coordinator's appearance gave him just the out he needed. "Good morning, Mr. Guidry. Geoff."

"Good morning, Cheryl. Well, I've got to get back to it." Forbes raised his hand in a farewell wave and made a hasty exit. Geoff resumed complaining about his ex-wife before Cheryl got two words out.

Forbes sank into his chair, grateful to have escaped without having to pass judgment on the outcome of the paralegal's divorce and custody. The guy was a few years younger than Forbes, and his life was already a mess.

He turned and stared out the window, across the parking lot to the slice of river he could see through the trees lining it. He'd abandoned the idea of dating years ago because no woman he'd dated had ever been satisfied with him. Had he chosen the wrong ones, or was he really not marriage material? While he'd never been as attracted to anyone he'd dated as he was to Alaine Delacroix, would it turn out the same way with her? Would she end up walking away from him either because she felt like he was too controlling or that he didn't take enough of an interest in her, as he'd been accused in the past?

He'd rather never marry than to go through the pain of a divorce, especially if there were children involved.

Is that what You're trying to teach me, Lord? That I'm not cut out to be married? That if I did, I'd end up like Geoff with my wife wanting out to be with someone else?

Shaking his head, he turned back to his desk and ran the dictating machine back to listen to where he'd left off. This motion had to be filed today, which meant he needed to be finished dictating it so

Samantha could type it before he went down to the courthouse after lunch.

He was almost finished when the phone rang. With Samantha still upstairs making the copies for him, he couldn't let it go unanswered.

"Forbes Guidry."

"Hey, it's Anne."

"Why are you calling me on my office phone?"

"Wasn't sure if you'd be in court or a meeting or something—you usually are. I figured I'd just leave you a message to call me when you had a minute."

"What's up?" He marked his place in his notes and leaned back, propping his right foot on the corner of his partially open bottom desk drawer.

"I just wanted to know if you're going to make it for supper tonight."

The knot started forming at the base of his skull again. "I hadn't gotten that far yet." Really, what he wanted to do was to take the copies of the files home and start reading through them. And maybe order a pizza or something. Or maybe even see if Shon wanted to grab dinner so they could talk—since their run had been rained out this morning. "Why? Is there something going on tonight I'm unaware of?"

"Well, I couldn't say anything in front of them last night, but George and I got to talking and figured that since Meredith and Major are going to put off having any kind of formal reception indefinitely—as in, Meredith has decided she doesn't want one but doesn't know how to break it to the family—we thought it would be fun to have a little informal reception for them tonight. Jenn is decorating the Shack's back room in a wedding theme, Aunt Maggie made a little wedding cake, and George and I are handling everything else."

Why hadn't he thought of that? Oh, yeah. Because he wasn't the professional wedding planner. "Who all's going to be there?"

"Just us—the regulars. If anyone else in the family wants to do something more formal for them, they can. We wanted to celebrate with them before it gets too far down the road and they start to feel like none of us cared enough to recognize their momentous occasion."

When she put it like that, how could he not go? "I'll be there. Are y'all going to be giving them your gifts tonight?"

"I think Jenn said something about a gift table, yeah."

"Okay. I'll have to run home and get mine on the way then."

"But we can count on your being there?"

"I'll be there. Just make sure there's plenty of room on that gift table. I have two boxes and they're somewhat large." For the first time in days, an emotion other than anxiety started stealing over him. Meredith would love the gifts he'd gotten her. At least she'd better, with all the trouble he'd gone through to find them.

"Going to show us all up, huh?"

"That's my goal in life." He grinned. If he couldn't be best man in their wedding, at least he could give them a gift that would make them feel guilty that he never got the chance.

"Okay. We'll see you tonight, then."

As soon as he got off the phone, Forbes finished his dictation and wrapped up a few other small projects he needed to clear off his desk before his meeting in judge's chambers with opposing counsel on his longest-running case. He was tempted to ask the clients if he could request to fast-track the case, just so they could get a court date set and end the barrage of motions and continuances from the other side. But with what his clients paid for Forbes's retainer, in addition to billable hours, the other partners wouldn't be happy if he tried to push for a hasty conclusion to the case just because he was tired of dealing with it.

Samantha returned just before he needed to leave, pushing a rolling cart stacked with hundreds of photocopies. His heart sank. He'd known he'd asked for a lot of information; he just hadn't realized how much it would be.

"Stack those on my conference table." He moved out of the way so she could push the cart in through his office door. "The Pichon motion is ready to be typed. Have a courier bring it to me at Judge Aucoin's office when it's ready, and I'll file it while I'm down there."

"Yes, boss."

"How'd your test go last night?"

"I think I aced it."

"What class is it?"

"Pharmacology."

Forbes shuddered and crossed to help her unload the copies from the cart. While he'd done well in the required math and science classes he'd had to take in college, the idea of purposely majoring in a science-based field gave him the heebie-jeebies. "Are you sure you want to leave all this and become a nurse?"

"Nurse practitioner. Big difference. Once I finish all of my schooling, I'll be able to see patients on my own and write prescriptions." She grunted as she heaved a stack of papers onto the table.

"But people throw up on nurses."

Samantha mumbled something under her breath.

"I didn't quite catch that." He covered the two remaining stacks of copies on the cart when she would have just kept moving them.

"I said, I'd rather have people throw up on me occasionally than to be making copies and taking dictation the rest of my life. No offense, Forbes, but this isn't the most intellectually challenging job in the world."

He leaned over the cart, rested his elbows on the papers, and propped his chin on his fist. "No offense taken. But why nursing? Why not become a lawyer or a literature professor or an artist? If you think working for a lawyer is a thankless job, wait until you work for a doctor." He waggled his eyebrows at her.

She laughed, as he'd hoped, and waved him off the cart. He stood and picked up the few remaining copies and stacked them on the table. His fingers itched to start flipping through them and see what lay in their murky depths, but it would have to wait. Again.

He followed her out of the office. "I won't be coming back

tonight, so go ahead and lock up my office when you leave. And once you finish the Pichon motion—and type up those couple of other things I put in your box, go ahead and leave. You can use the extra time to study all that nasty science stuff."

"Gee, thanks." She pushed the cart to the side of her desk and went back into his office for the dictating machine. "Aren't you supposed to be on your way to Judge Aucoin's right now?"

"Yeah. I am. If you need me—"

"I've got your number."

He had to return to his office twice—once for a secondary file he'd left behind, and the next time for his large, red and black University of Louisiana–Bonneterre umbrella. He made it to the courthouse with bare minutes to spare—but ran into opposing counsel in the line waiting to get through the metal detectors, so let his anxiety ease. They weren't sitting up there, waiting on him.

Two hours later, his expanding files stretched well beyond their original capacity with multiple new motions he would have to write responses to in the next week, Forbes left the judge's chambers. The secretary handed him a courier envelope. He thanked the woman and took the paperwork out of the envelope to look over while walking toward the court clerks' office. For as much as Samantha didn't want to be a lawyer's secretary the rest of her life, she was very good at it.

He filed the motion, stopped and chatted with a few colleagues on his way out, and finally left the courthouse with just enough time to go home and pick up the gifts. He pulled into the garage, leaving everything in the car, and jogged up the three flights of stairs to his bedroom. In the large, walk-in closet sat the boxes wrapped in silver paper and decorated with dark blue velvet ribbons—a rather impressive wrapping job, if he did say so himself.

He carried each one gingerly down the stairs. Not only were they heavy and somewhat bulky, if he broke anything, there were no returns.

Driving with them in the car made him nervous, and he drew nasty looks from fellow drivers in a hurry to get home from work as they whipped around him on Highway 77 when northbound traffic in the opposite lane eased enough that they could safely pass him.

Though he usually tried to park far away from the restaurant to keep anyone from parking too near his baby, tonight, he pulled into the closest space he could find. He leaned in to get the first box.

"Hey, there. Need a hand?"

He hit his head on the top of the doorframe in his surprise. Leaving the box, he stood and turned, rubbing the back of his head.

Evelyn Mackenzie would turn every head in the place tonight in her sleeveless black dress that accentuated every curve the woman had.

Wait. What was she doing here? "Hey, Evelyn. No, I've got it, thanks."

"Well, at least let me get the door for you, huh?"

"Sure." He carried the first box in. "Did Anne invite you?"

"No, Meredith did." Evelyn nodded at the box. "Someone's birthday?"

"We're celebrating Meredith and Major's wedding tonight."

"I wish I'd known. I'd have picked something up for them." Evelyn held open the glass-and-chrome door into the Fishin' Shack.

"Thanks. I just found out about it a couple of hours ago myself." He wound through the buzzing restaurant. He wasn't sure if heads were turning at the sight of the gift he carried or because of Evelyn, but both of them drew the attention of pretty much every customer.

"Hey, you made it early." Anne's eyes widened at the size of the gift in Forbes's arms. "Wow. You really are going to show us up."

He arched his brow at her. "There's another one just like this out in the car."

"Put it here." Anne pointed to a place on the long table covered with a dark blue tablecloth broken up by a silver runner down the middle.

"Anne, you remember Evelyn Mackenzie."

"Yes, of course. Meredith mentioned she'd invited you to come. I'm sorry I didn't know how to get in touch with you to forewarn you we're having a little wedding reception for them tonight."

"Oh, that's quite all right. I just hope I'm not intruding on family time."

"Not at all. We're thrilled to have you and glad we can include you in some of our family activities since you're so far from your own."

After a second trip—with Evelyn insisting she hold the door for him, which, for some reason, included walking back out to his car with him—Forbes collapsed into a chair at the large, round table in the semiprivate room, relieved he'd gotten the gifts here without incident. Transporting them safely back to Bonneterre was now up to Meredith and Major.

"Wow. Looks like the owner went all out for you guys."

He chuckled. "Given that the owner was supposed to be Meredith's maid of honor and just happens to be our sister, yes, she went all out."

Pink, blue, and brown streamers draped over everything stationary enough to hold it—from the fishing paraphernalia tacked to the walls to the pirogue hanging from the ceiling. The pink was Jenn's contribution to the color scheme—back when planning the wedding-that-wasn't, Meredith had insisted she only wanted to use her favorite color, brown, and Major's favorite color, blue, in the wedding decor.

"Is that lace on the cake?" Evelyn leaned over to look closer at what looked like airy, florally brown lace around the base of the three tiers of the white cake dripping with blue and white frosting flowers. "My word. I never knew someone could pipe icing that fine."

"Our aunt, my mother's sister, is a professional pastry chef. She's famous in Bonneterre for her cakes."

Forbes saw to introducing Evelyn to his younger siblings and cousins as they arrived, each expressing his or her displeasure over the size of Forbes's gifts in comparison to his or her own.

"Just remember," Anne said, arranging the gifts in an artful presentation, "it's not the size of the gift that matters, but the intention with which it's given." No one agreed with her.

When Meredith and Major arrived—having been purposely delayed by Mom, according to Anne—both exhibited genuine surprise. . .tempered by the claim that they'd suspected Anne would have planned something like this tonight.

Hearing all about their trip to Colorado took up most of the conversation over dinner. Anne made a production of having them cut the cake, just as if it were a real wedding reception—with George taking plenty of pictures.

"Gifts!" Jenn squeaked like a schoolgirl as soon as the cake was sliced and served. "Mine first."

Anne sat beside them and wrote down each gift and who'd given it. While his family members had given them nice things—mostly items for their house that they'd listed on their registry wish list, Forbes grew more and more confident that nothing anyone else gave them would compare with his gift. He leaned forward with eager anticipation when his two boxes were the only ones remaining to be opened.

"Wow, these are heavy."

Forbes stood to stop Jenn from picking the box up and potentially dropping it. "They'll probably need to open those over at the table instead of putting them on the floor."

Meredith and Major came over, as did Anne and George with the list and camera.

"Should we open them at the same time?" Meredith asked.

"You can."

She nodded at Major, and both started tearing away paper and ribbons. Forbes tried to keep the smug look from his face.

"Oh. . ." Meredith breathed. "Where did you find them? Oh, Forbes, they're beautiful!" She turned and threw her arms around his neck. It was the first hug she'd given him in a while. That reaction made all his trouble in finding the two arts-and-crafts era antique lamps worthwhile.

"You're welcome. I knew you wanted something like those for your living room but couldn't afford the real thing and didn't want to settle for cheap imitations."

She finally stepped away and wiped a couple of tears from her cheeks. "Are they really. . . ?" She returned to the box to examine them. "This one's a. . .Bradley and Hubbard."

"And this one's a Handel." Major carefully extracted the ivory, slag glass shade from the mounds of paper it had been packed in.

"They're not identical, obviously, but they're as close as I could find. Both are supposed to be cast iron bases, and the scrollwork on the shades is brass."

"They're perfect, Forbes. You shouldn't have done something this extravagant, but I'm so glad you did." Meredith hugged him again. "I can't wait to get them home and plug them in."

He returned to the table to the good-natured jeers and ribbing of his relatives and indulged in a slice of Aunt Maggie's cake.

Evelyn pressed her shoulder into his and leaned her head close to his. "You're going to make some woman very happy some day, Forbes Guidry."

He hoped so. . .and that Alaine's tastes ran to lamps that were easier to find than these.

Chapter 16

Alaine stood at the rear of the sanctuary. Most of the people who came to this Saturday night service were young—and dressed to go out afterward. Would they leave here to go hit the bars and clubs in midtown, feeling as if they'd had their dose of church for the week so it was okay to go get plastered afterward?

Her sorority sisters had lived that way—and so had she, even for a few years after college. It was so much easier to maintain good church attendance when one could go *before* getting smashed instead of dealing with the hangover while trying to look properly worshipful on Sunday morning.

"Alaine? Alaine Delacroix, it is you."

She turned at the masculine voice. Her heart gave a little lurch at the sight of Shon Murphy. She could rack it up to his dark good looks, but in all honesty, running into him embarrassed her more than excited her. Seeing him reminded her of her current status as one of his company's clients. . .and the several e-mails from him she hadn't yet responded to.

"I didn't know you went to church here." *Wow. Great opener, girl.*

"This is my first time to come to the Saturday service. Tomorrow's my mama's birthday, and I promised to go to church with them over in Pineville." He looked around the sanctuary. "Looks like we'd better find seats. Mind if I join you?"

"Please do." She took a few deep breaths when she turned to start down the central aisle, trying to keep the heat climbing her throat from progressing into her face. She stepped into a pew in the middle of the large room and edged her way down to the center of it.

Shon sat beside her and flipped open his order of service. Alaine did likewise but didn't take in anything on the page. While she hated attending church alone—and *alone* was how she'd always felt in the regular services on Sunday morning, looking around at all the couples and families—the idea of sitting with the guy she'd paid to set her up on blind dates was a bit weird and uncomfortable.

"Did you have a good week?" Shon's soft voice startled her.

"I did. But really busy. And you?"

"Same here. I saw your piece on the dance studio opening down in Comeaux. Looks like you had a really good time. Was that Forbes Guidry you were dancing with?"

Heat burst full force into her cheeks. "It was. I. . .I met him at the *Bonneterre Lifestyles* bachelors' dinner, and since there was an uneven number of people at the dance studio, he asked me if I'd partner him."

"You looked like a natural. That wasn't your first dance lesson, was it?"

"Thanks." She curled the corner of the bulletin, rolling it between her thumb and forefinger. "My mother thought that my brothers and I should at least know a couple of basic ballroom dance steps, so she taught us at home. It came in handy more for the boys than for me come prom time. I didn't have the advantage of being asked by a boy whose mother thought he should know how to waltz and foxtrot."

Shon cocked his head and gave her a quizzical look. "Did they actually play music conducive to dancing like that at your school?"

She laughed, then cringed when it carried, drawing the admonishing glances of several people sitting nearby. She thought about sticking her tongue out at them but knew that would only draw more glares. "No. But it has come in handy at wedding receptions when older men have asked me to dance. Or my brothers. I tried teaching my sorority sisters, but that wasn't the kind of dance moves they were interested in learning. By then, the lambada was all the rage."

"That. . .or just two people writhing with their bodies pressed indecently close to each other." Shon sighed. "That's when I stopped going to the interfraternity dances. I didn't want any woman getting that close to me but my wife, and since I hadn't met her then, there was no point in going."

"When did you get married?"

"Oh, I'm not—" Shon suddenly became interested in finding the scripture reference for the sermon in his burgundy leather Bible.

"You're not married?" She narrowed her eyes. "But surely you have a girlfriend."

His jaw tightened; his full lips pressed together.

"Let me get this straight." She lowered her voice and leaned closer. "You run a matchmaking agency that's so successful you've opened offices in six or seven major metropolitan areas. . .and you haven't found someone for yourself?"

He shrugged. "What can I say? I'm the pickiest client I have."

She chuckled and shook her head. "You are so lucky I forgot to ask that question when I had you on my show. My, my. What would people say if they knew Mr. Matchmaker himself couldn't get a date."

"Hey, now. I date. Occasionally. Okay, rarely, and usually with the niece or daughter of someone my mom teaches with at Louisiana College, just because I can't get out of it. But I'll have you know that we have a very high success rate of long-term relationships out of the matches we make at Let's Do Coffee."

She held her hands up and stifled her laughter better this time. "No need to sell me on it, I'm already a client, remember?"

"Are you? I was sure you were having second thoughts since you haven't responded to any of the e-mails I sent you this week. I've got at least three clients I'd like to set up meetings for you. . .with." He frowned and shook his head. "With who I'd like to set up for you. . . . You know what I mean. But I can't do it if you don't communicate with me. Remember, you are a paying client. What have you got to lose to give these guys thirty minutes to an hour of your time? If you don't like them, you don't have to see them ever again."

The praise band started playing a soft but fast-paced introduction. "Fine. I'll look at the e-mails as soon as I get home tonight, and I'll let you know Monday if I want to meet any of them. Okay?"

People around them got to their feet when the praise leader stepped to the microphone and started singing.

Shon stood. "Okay. Seems like I'm making a lot of deals outside the parameters of the service recently."

Alaine's forehead barely reached his shoulder, and she craned her neck to look up at his profile. "What's that?"

"Huh—oh, nothing. I just have another client who's giving me a little difficulty when it comes to agreeing to go out on dates, and he also offered me a deal just the other day."

"Isn't that part of the 'package customization' we VIPs get?" She winked at him.

"Careful now. I made you a VIP. I can very easily make you *not* a VIP." He held his index finger up to his lips. "Shush. It's time to sing now."

With a wry grin, she turned her attention to the giant screens at the front of the auditorium and started singing the familiar chorus. She'd never admit to Shon that she hadn't gotten back to him because of Forbes Guidry.

Forbes would never need to stoop to using a matchmaking service. No, he most likely had women throwing themselves at him all day long. But she wasn't going to be one of them.

Forbes rubbed his eyes and checked his watch again. If he was going to make it in time for the seven o'clock game, he needed to go. He changed into linen shorts and a dark red silk T-shirt and slipped into a pair of Top-Siders. Though sandals would be cooler, he hated walking across the dirt parking lot—littered with who knew what—and ending up with filthy feet.

In the car, he let his mind wander back over everything he'd read today. Spending his Saturday reading case files on his parents' company's legal proceedings hadn't been the most fun way to start his weekend—nor the most productive. So far, none of the files revealed anything pertinent to Alaine's allegations of wrongdoing.

The one thread of information that led him to believe there might still be a case was the mention of Mackenzie and Son in the files dealing with the acquisition of the Moreaux Paper Company warehouses—Warehouse Row—which had been legally purchased from the bank that had acquired the property when the previous development company went belly-up before they could get around to developing the site. The information he needed a copy of, but couldn't get to because it was active and therefore still in Sandra's office, was the file containing the negotiations, formal agreements, and contracts between Boudreaux-Guidry Enterprises and Mackenzie and Son. He needed to know what his parents had authorized Evelyn—and her father's company—to do in their name and on their behalf.

As soon as he got out of the car, the heavy, humid air enveloped him with the sticky tang of cotton candy and perspiration. The clanks of bats hitting balls and the jeers and cheers of the spectators surrounded him—along with an immediate swarm of mosquitoes. He locked the Jag with his remote and crossed the dirt lot toward the rickety concession stand—the old wooden shack that had served junk food, sodas, and frozen slushes to players and fans of church league softball every summer since Forbes could remember—to check the schedule and find out on which field the men's team from Bonneterre Chapel would be playing.

He slapped at the sting of a bite on his neck and hurried over to diamond three, hoping Meredith's game was already over. A couple dozen members of University Chapel sat on the first-baseline side of the diamond, so he angled that direction. Most sat in their own lawn chairs instead of on the splintery, old wooden bleachers.

Stopping near a group of people from the singles Sunday school class, he greeted everyone and checked up on their weeks. The shout of "Two minutes!" from the field stirred Forbes to action.

"See y'all later." He jogged over to the bleachers to join the girl in a pink Bonneterre Chapel Women's Softball T-shirt and a ball cap with a ponytail of strawberry blond hair sticking out the hole in the back of it.

Meredith glanced up at him when he leaped up the bleachers and plopped down beside her. "You're late. I thought you were going to try to come for the first game."

"I was working."

"Figures. Here. I know you didn't bring any."

"Thanks." He took the can of bug repellent she held toward him and sprayed every exposed surface of his legs and arms—carefully avoiding getting any on his shirt and shorts lest he stain them. "Your shirt isn't all sweaty. What happened?"

"The other team almost had to forfeit because they were one player short." Meredith looked away from him to watch their team running in from the field.

"Almost had to?"

"Yeah. . .I volunteered to switch over and play for them." She kicked the duffel bag on the board beside her feet. "So the sweaty one's in there, since someone on that team brought an extra. I told her I'd take it home and wash it and bring it back to her next weekend."

"Oh. How'd that go?" A mixture of pride and incredulity filled him. Only Meredith would do something like that.

"Close game. But Chapel managed to pull it out in the end, by one run. I almost had her, too. Look." She held her arm out in front of her and twisted it so he could see the underside of her forearm. A large scrape was already starting to turn a magnificent shade of purple. "I wasn't sure either of us was getting up from that one. But her foot slid over the plate just as I dived for the ball to tag her. It was exciting. You should have been here."

Unable to resist, he wrapped his arm around her neck, pulled her close, and kissed her cheek. "Good job, Mere. Way to take one for the team. Even if it wasn't your team."

She dug her knuckles into his side, right into his most ticklish spot, and he released her and scooted away. But her laughter showed she was getting better on the whole being-touched issue. "I'll be wearing long sleeves to work for a few weeks until that bruise goes away. Mom'll have a cow if she sees it—but only because she wouldn't want any of our clients to see it. Sometimes I have a hard time believing she played basketball all four years in college. She's so anti anything physical or sweat-producing nowadays."

"Whereas you can't get enough of it."

"I'm not real hip on the sweat-producing part of it, but it does feel good to get out of the suits and formal dresses and makeup and get dirty—whether it's sawdust or ball-field dirt." She looked him up and down. "You, on the other hand, are more like Mom and Dad. You'll sweat when it's 'exercise,' but heaven forbid you do anything fun that would raise a bead of perspiration on your brow or get your clothes mussed."

He hoped he was like his parents in more than just that way. His high sense of morals and ethics came from them. . .he prayed that they still held them as dear. He opened his mouth to continue the subject of their parents when Meredith stood—along with everyone else around them. Both teams lined up along the first- and third-baselines, caps in hands.

Forbes stood and bowed his head for the prayer—which he couldn't hear—and asked God to help him find the right questions to ask Meredith to get some usable information.

"Play ball!"

Meredith pressed her fingers to the corners of her mouth and let out a shrill whistle. On the field, Major and their three brothers all waved before taking their positions: Major, Rafe, and Kevin in the outfield and Jonathan as pitcher.

"Here." Meredith reached into her small cooler and handed him a dripping can of diet cola once they were seated again. She held her can away from her when she opened it, then leaned over to slurp the frothing foam that threatened to spill over the edge.

Forbes tapped the top of his can and pointed it well away from his silk and linen garments to open it. He licked the drippage off his thumb—and regretted it as soon as he tasted the bitterness of the bug spray. He took a big swig of the soda to wash the nasty flavor from his mouth, then set the can on the bleacher beside him.

"So what do you know about this Evelyn Mackenzie girl?" His voice had been suitably nonchalant, hadn't it?

"She's a hard nut to crack." Meredith cupped her hands to her mouth. "Straight in there, Jonathan. One more, and you've got him!"

"What do you mean?" He leaned back, propping his elbows on the edge of the bench behind them.

"She's perfectly nice. Seems to be a sweet person, yet she doesn't say much about herself. She's very closed off." A sharp clank from the field. "Foul ball," Meredith muttered under her breath—and sure enough, a millisecond later, the ball landed outside the third-base foul line. "That's okay, Jon, he just got a piece of it. Put him out on the next one."

Forbes didn't bother hiding his smile. While Meredith wasn't aggressively competitive when it came to playing, as a spectator, she was a lot of fun to watch.

"So you don't really feel like you've gotten to know her very well?" He persisted.

"Great strikeout, Jonathan. Two more to go." Meredith took a swig of her cola. "She doesn't talk about herself or her family much. She'll talk about all the different places she's been, about the restaurants she ate in, and her favorite sites, but there isn't really anything personal in any of it. I've seen her around the office for three or four weeks and had lunch with her a few times, but I still don't feel like I know her any better than I did that first night she came over to the house."

"So she's working out of the corporate offices?" Forbes kept his gaze trained on the ball field. Jonathan pitched low and outside to the batter.

"Yeah. Out of the office Rafe used when he was the company pilot." When Jonathan threw another ball, Meredith turned her golden brown eyes on Forbes. "Why? Are you. . .you're not interested in her are you?"

"No."

Maybe he shouldn't have been so quick with his denial. Feigning a romantic interest in Evelyn might have been a good way to get Meredith to try to garner some information on the woman. "What I mean is, I'm not sure. I've only seen her a couple of times and she was. . .well, you said it: closed off. I couldn't get a good read on her, which is unusual for me."

A clank from the field drew their attention. The ball sailed toward right field.

"Come on, baby, catch it!" Meredith stood and continued yelling at her husband as if that would help him catch the ball sailing in his direction.

Major must have misjudged exactly where the ball was, because he ended up having to dive for it, bounced it with the edge of his glove a couple of times, and finally got it to fall in for a catch.

Meredith pounded Forbes's shoulder. "That's my man." She grinned and dropped back onto the bench. The entire set of bleachers wobbled. "Of course, I've been badgering him for weeks to go get his eyes checked. He's having trouble with his depth perception, and I think it's because he needs glasses. He thinks I'm just saying it to tease him because he's almost forty."

"He's not almost forty! He's only two months older than me, and we both just turned thirty-eight."

Meredith stuck her tongue out at him. "In my book, that's almost forty."

"Yeah, well at thirty-five, you're not that far away from it yourself, missy." Forbes couldn't remember the last time he'd been able to just sit and joke around with his next-oldest sibling. They'd both been too busy—and she'd been spending all of her free time in the last six or so months working on her house or with Major, or both.

After Jonathan retired the batters from the other church—giving up only one hit—Meredith picked up their previous topic. "So you're definitely not interested in Evelyn Mackenzie?"

He thought about fudging, then looked into Meredith's eyes. He couldn't. "No. Definitely not."

"That's a relief."

He straightened. "Why?"

"Because I thought you were interested in. . .someone else." Her cheeks looked pinker than usual. But she had been out in the sun all afternoon.

"Someone else?"

She lolled her head to the side. "Alaine Delacroix. Major and I were talking the other day about how well we think the two of you would get along with each other."

"And what prompted that conversation?" He tried to regain his casual air by once again leaning back on the bleacher behind them and stretching his legs out on the one below, crossing his ankles.

"Seeing the two of you dancing together on her show. I was impressed. I've never seen you dance so well."

"That's because I was taking a *lesson*."

Alaine had aired the piece on Wednesday's show. He'd only watched it four. . .maybe six times since then.

"I thought Jenn was going to do that with you."

Without going into the detail of Jenn's trouble, he explained why he'd ended up dancing with Alaine instead. "Since Jenn had to back out, I convinced Alaine to be my partner for the remainder of the lessons."

Meredith jumped to her feet and cheered as Kevin's pop fly hit the grass between the center and left fielders, and he ran to first base. She sank back onto the seat, and the three people who'd been sitting down below them on the first bench got up and moved their blanket to the grass.

Forbes didn't blame them. If Meredith got any more enthusiastic about the game, the whole contraption might just collapse.

"Did you know she minored in dance for a year in college?"

"Alaine?"

"Yeah. Before she changed her major to journalism in her sophomore year, she was majoring in art history and minoring in dance."

A totally new image of Alaine Delacroix started to form in his mind—and a strange one, at that: Alaine, in a long, flowing gown—like the ones they always wore in the movies—swirling around with a paintbrush in one hand, a painter's palette in the other, her hair up in a cascade of curls the way it had been at the magazine dinner, a smudge of paint on her cheek. He chuckled to himself.

"What's so funny?"

"Huh? Oh, nothing. Just picturing Alaine as a dancing artist." He shook his head to clear it. "What do Mom and Dad think of Evelyn? Do they seem to like her?"

"Woo-hoo, good hit, Jon!" Meredith once again leaped to her feet as their brother's hit sent Kevin to third and landed Jonathan on second. Rafe stepped up to the plate next, and for the moment, Forbes gave up on trying to pump his sister for more information.

Forbes frowned, observing his brother. "Isn't Rafe on the wrong side of the plate?"

"How have you never noticed this?" Meredith shook her head. "His high school baseball coach trained him to be a switch-hitter because most pitchers are right-handed and tend to throw fewer strikes against lefty batters."

The depth of his sister's baseball knowledge never ceased to amaze him. Of course, the only times he watched anything close to resembling baseball were the several times a year he came here to watch his family members play fast-pitch softball.

Sure enough, the pitcher walked Rafe; and Major entered the batter's box with the bases loaded—with his own kinfolk, which did not go unnoticed by their entire fan base. A chant of "Guidry grand slam" went up all around them.

"When did Major change his last name to Guidry?" Forbes drawled, hoping to raise his sister's ire.

"Oh, shut up." She whistled again, nearly piercing his eardrum.

"Come on, sweetheart! Bring the boys home."

Major swung and missed the first pitch, then the next two hit the dirt in front of the plate. The opposing pitcher looked unnerved by the constant chatter from the three Guidry brothers on base behind him and by the Chapel crowd and their rhythmic chanting and clapping.

Even Forbes could tell that the fourth pitch would be perfect. Major swung. . .and sent the ball over the fence behind left field. Meredith and the rest of the crowd yelled their approval. She jumped down off the end of the bleachers and ran around the end of the fence behind the players' bench, where she threw herself into her husband's arms as soon as he got back from running the bases. The kiss she gave him drew wolf whistles from the rest of the team.

If Alaine were as enthusiastic a softball fan as Meredith, Forbes might just consider taking up the sport.

CHAPTER 17

Forbes checked his reflection in the visor mirror one last time. He smoothed his thumb over his eyebrows and checked his teeth—and the corners of his mouth to make sure he'd washed off all the toothpaste residue. He hadn't been this anxious since the first time he stood up to give an opening argument before a jury.

A black Buick LaCrosse pulled into a parking space, leaving an empty slot beside the Jag. Forbes climbed out as if he'd just arrived and greeted Anne with a hug—which kept two other cars from pulling into the empty space next to his baby.

"So, did we miss anything important at lunch yesterday?" Anne slipped her arm through Forbes's. They joined George on the sidewalk that ran the length of the dance studio building.

"Nothing at all. How'd the Father's Day wedding go?"

"Went off without a hitch—once everyone in the bridal party showed up." Anne twisted to exchange a look with George. They both laughed, and she turned her attention back to Forbes. "I didn't see your folks at church yesterday morning. Did I just miss them?"

"Meredith said they decided they needed a weekend getaway, so they flew up to Boston."

"Really? On Father's Day?"

"Apparently Dad thought the best Father's Day gift he could

receive would be to get away from all of his kids. But it's not like they don't see us every week, anyway."

"I wish I'd known they were going."

"To Boston? Why?" Forbes opened the front door.

Anne dropped her arm from his and proceeded inside. Forbes motioned George to go in ahead of him, too.

"Because that's where my father was from originally, remember?"

George joined Anne and took hold of her hand. "As soon as we have a free weekend, we shall follow Lawson and Mairee's example and take a weekend trip up there. It's especially nice in the autumn." He lifted Anne's hand and kissed the backs of her fingers.

Anne's forehead knit in a worried frown. "I don't know. It's an awfully long flight."

"You did fine from here to London and back."

Her worry lines melted into a wry smile. "That's exactly what I wanted you to think." She gave him a quick kiss when he looked like he wanted to say more. "Besides, you know my rule. I won't agree to fly anywhere until we go for three weeks without hearing about a plane crash somewhere in the world on the news."

George looked to Forbes, who just shrugged. The fact that Anne had conquered her fear of flying enough to go to England for their honeymoon was a greater accomplishment than he'd ever hoped for his cousin.

Anne turned the subject. "Is Jenn coming after all? When she didn't show last week, I thought you might be off the hook."

"Jenn isn't going to be able to do the lessons. She lost her restaurant manager, so she has to be there until she hires another one." Which, since she had accepted Major's offer to co-interview applicants for his restaurant with him, would hopefully be soon.

"But you're supposed to have a partner for these lessons, so they could make sure everyone had someone to dance with at all times."

"I know. I'll have a partner, don't worry." He glanced around at the dozen or so people already in the lobby filling out paperwork—which they'd done last week. Alaine's story must have drawn in a bunch of new customers. The petite newscaster wasn't among them. Maybe she was already in the studio. He trailed Anne and George halfway down the lobby, then left them when Anne stopped to speak to her clients who'd come last week.

Only one of the older couples who'd been here last week was in the studio—along with Ruth and Ian. No Alaine. He looked at his watch. She still had almost ten minutes to get here.

He turned when a commotion from the lobby caught his attention. He lost all muscle control in his jaw. In walked Alaine in a snug, black top that displayed her strong, tanned arms, and a black skirt that accentuated the curve—and sway—of her hips and ended in a swirl at midcalf. She wore high heels again, making him wish the skirt showed just a bit more leg.

Stopping that line of thinking, he clamped his teeth shut and considered cutting through the crowded lobby to greet her. But something held him back. Several women fluttered around her, acting as if she were a famous movie star descended among them. And she was coming to him. Maybe not at this very moment, but she was here to be his partner; and everyone would see her come to him, take his hand, and give him her undivided attention for the next two hours.

The chirps of "Miss Delacroix, Miss Delacroix!" quickly faded when Ruth Arcenault stepped into the foyer and announced time for class to start.

So he didn't block the doorway, Forbes stepped into the studio to wait for Alaine to come to him. He stepped forward when she entered. The flutter of young women—their sullen and bored-looking partners trailing behind—parted, eyes widening, whispering Forbes's name and coming to the apparently obvious and surprising conclusion that *Bonneterre Lifestyle*'s Bachelor and Bachelorette of the Year were dating. He turned his amusement into a smile of greeting for Alaine, extended his hand, and, once she'd taken it, led her away from the tittering crowd.

"Anne, George, you remember Alaine."

Anne's eyes widened slightly at Forbes's reintroduction. He kept his amusement in check. Unless he was sadly mistaken, the rumor that he and Alaine were dating would be making the rounds in Bonneterre—and his family—by week's end. And other than serve as a boon to his ego, their fair city's love of gossip about its highest-profile citizens would give Forbes and Alaine exactly the right amount of cover he needed while he figured out if her parents and their neighbors had a case or not.

Alaine shook hands with Anne and George. Her movement brought a hint of her fragrance to his attention—something both flowery and spicy. Alaine's scent seemed to whisper, to beckon him to move closer to try to get another whiff. So different from the trumpet blast of Evelyn Mackenzie's perfume, which announced her arrival before she could be seen, created a distracting noise while she was near, and left a lasting echo reverberating around the room long after she left.

Forbes clasped his hands behind his back to keep from either taking hold of Alaine's hand again or putting his arm around her, a restraint he'd learned long ago from far too many female acquaintances who got the wrong idea of his feelings and intentions toward them because of his tactile nature.

Ruth Arcenault went through her spiel once again. Good thing Forbes had listened last time, as the occasional enticing whiff of Alaine's perfume drove him to distraction.

When Ruth called for the couples to take their positions in two parallel lines, Forbes grabbed Alaine's hand and led her out on the floor before anyone else could move. The sooner they got past this in-line stuff, the sooner he could hold Alaine in his arms again and surround himself with that magical scent—er, the sooner they could discuss any developments since their lunch last Wednesday.

The music started. Forbes counted in his head as Ruth counted aloud and demonstrated the steps.

"Now, you all try it."

Forbes immediately and confidently stepped forward with his right foot. One. Slid the left out to the side. Two. Brought his right foot over to join it. Three. Back, one. Out, two. Together, three. Front, out, together. He wasn't even frowning in concentration—okay, not much. He eased his expression with a slight smile. And instead of looking at his feet, he could actually look at his partner without losing the rhythm.

Alaine's brows arched. "You've been practicing."

He shrugged. . .two. . .three. "Not really." Only every morning and evening in front of the mirror. . .three. One. . .two. . . And whenever a three-quarter meter song played on whatever Internet or satellite station he happened to be listening to when in private. . .two. . .three. One. . .

"Well, I'm impressed, nonetheless."

He gave her his most charming smile. . .and lost the beat. Alaine's nose wrinkled when she smiled big enough to show all her teeth. Could she get any more adorable?

Though he'd hoped that the intimacy afforded by dancing together would allow them to talk, Forbes found himself having to concentrate more on his footwork—and keeping his arms up and stiff and in the right positions—which stopped him from being able to keep up a conversation with Alaine.

Finally, though, their taskmasters called for a break. "There are snacks and beverages in the lobby courtesy of the Fishin' Shack restaurant just up the road."

"Annie, can you bring us a couple bottles of water?" Forbes held Alaine back from following everyone else into the foyer.

"Sure." With her grin all lopsided like that, it meant she was thinking something that wasn't necessarily true, but Forbes didn't correct her impression.

Alaine followed Forbes to a row of chairs against the end wall of the studio. She tried to write off her shortness of breath to the fact they'd been waltzing nonstop for the past forty-five minutes. Yet it hadn't really started until she found herself alone with Forbes.

He waited to sit until she lowered herself into one of the molded-plastic chairs. "Have you had a chance to set up a meeting with the Mills residents and business owners yet?"

"My parents are still working on getting something scheduled. They're thinking it'll be toward the end of the week—I hope you don't mind its being last minute like this."

He shook his head. "No, that's fine."

"What have you found out since we last talked?"

"I looked over the last six months' worth of my parents legal files. There isn't anything in them that leads me to believe they've done anything wrong or unethical. However"—he held his hand up to keep Alaine from interrupting—"I didn't get a chance to speak to them this weekend as I'd hoped, because they decided to go out of town. My next step is to look into Mackenzie and Son a little further."

Alaine sat a little straighter. "I did a little digging on them."

"How?"

"Internet." Where else would she have started? "They keep a pretty low profile. Other than their own Web site, which didn't tell me anything, I found a few links to corporate reports where their names were mentioned—but most of them are password protected beyond just a brief, one-paragraph summary of what's contained in the report. There are scant few mentions of them in any news outlet, either. And I called a contact at the newspaper in Boston to see what he might know about them, and he only knew of the company because he's seen the name on a floor directory in the downtown office building that his wife works in." She sighed and slouched in her chair. "I hoped I'd find some message boards somewhere with people posting nasty messages about how horrible they are and how they made a habit of running people out of their homes."

Forbes leaned forward and braced his elbows on his knees. "I could have told you it wouldn't be that easy." He stared at the parquet floor for a long moment.

She'd never noticed before that his hair had a bit of curl to it. Her hand spasmed with her unwilling desire to touch it to see if it was soft or wiry.

"No company that does business on such a large scale could keep *that* low a profile. What about the companies whose corporate reports Mac and Son were mentioned in? Did you look up any of them?"

Why hadn't she thought of following through on those leads? "No. I didn't think. . .I didn't have time to think about looking at them to see if I could find anything showing that they do this with every company they act as consultants for."

He looked at her around his shoulder. "With your work schedule, when do you have time to do all this research?"

When she wasn't in the film archive trying to find footage on his parents that would put them in a bad light for her story. "In the evenings, mostly. I spent a lot of time on it this weekend—when I wasn't helping out in the flower shop, that is."

"What flower shop?" Forbes sat up and turned slightly toward her in his chair.

"My parents' flower shop. They had to let go of their last part-time employee, and since Mom had a couple of events she had to get flowers to, I helped out by working the shop while she made all her deliveries."

"Do you arrange flowers?" The corners of his eyes crinkled up in a very nice way when he grinned like that.

She took a deep breath and clenched her teeth to keep from shivering at the tingle that ran up her spine. "I do some arranging. I did grow up there, you know. I spent every summer since I was fourteen working in the shop or the greenhouses."

"What's your favorite flower?"

"Lavender. It's the national flower of Portugal."

"Portugal?" The little upside-down Y appeared between his brows.

"That's where my mom's from. And it's one of my favorite places to visit."

The sound of a throat clearing snapped Alaine out from under

Forbes's enchantment. Anne Hawthorne Laurence stood over them, grinning, two bottles of water extended toward them.

"Thanks, Annie." Forbes took them and handed one to Alaine. She was rather surprised he didn't open it for her.

To cover her embarrassment at Anne's knowing gaze, Alaine took a huge swig of the icy water—and inhaled half of it. She wheezed and coughed, throat burning, eyes tearing, and cheeks flaming from complete mortification.

"Take it easy there, girl." Forbes patted her between the shoulder blades. It didn't help, but the gentleness with which he did it brought the tingles back. She took a few gulping breaths and finally started feeling normal again.

That was, until Forbes stopped patting and started rubbing his hand in a circular motion on her back. "You okay?"

She pushed out of her chair at Ruth Arcenault's entrance. "Looks like it's time to get started again." She tried to clear the raspiness from her throat with another drink of water. She went back to where she and Forbes had been stationed before, as the two lines formed again.

"To make sure both partners are really learning the steps and one isn't just relying on the other. . ." Ruth walked down to the end of the line and laid her hand on Alaine's shoulder. "Miss Delacroix, I'd like for you to go to the other end of the line, and the ladies will shift up to dance with the gentleman standing to her original partner's left—your right."

For the next thirty minutes, Alaine tried to occupy herself by thinking of all the possible avenues of research she might have missed in the Internet search she'd done yesterday. She should have spent more time working on that and less time in the film archives at the studio looking for sound bites from Lawson or Mairee Guidry about their company or about the community that could be construed as negative.

She'd found a couple that, taken completely out of context, could be seen as Lawson Guidry saying Moreaux Mills on the whole was an eyesore and should be demolished. But only after she edited off enough of the beginning of the sentence to take out the part that proved he was actually talking about the old paper mill being the eyesore that should go.

She glanced across the room at Forbes, looking at his feet again, and guilt pressed in. He was so sure his parents were innocent. Was she letting her own emotional involvement get in the way of being objective about the facts? Or was he?

"Sorry." Again.

Her toes were going to be black and blue after this. "That's okay." She stiffened her arms more to try to put more distance between herself and her stranger-partner. Even though Forbes occasionally lost count and got off rhythm, at least he didn't step on her toe almost every downbeat.

"And return to your original partners."

Thank goodness. She gave Mr. Stompy Toes a tight smile, then hustled back down the line to rejoin Forbes. She never thought she'd be so glad to see him.

They fit better. Even though Ruth had said something about dancing being easier for partners closer in height, the fact that even in her heels Forbes was almost a foot taller than Alaine didn't seem to matter.

"How'd your guy do?" Forbes cast a glare down the line.

"My toes hurt. How'd you do?"

"I've danced with Anne before—at her wedding a few months ago, as a matter of fact. She tries to lead. She can't help it."

Alaine giggled and turned her attention to the couple to her left. Anne and George glided together with almost as much poise and ease as Ruth and Ian.

"Now we're going to work on moving around the room in a circle."

"Oh, boy."

Alaine bit her bottom lip and wrinkled her nose in a grin at Forbes. His tongue stuck out slightly between his teeth and everything around his eyes and forehead had tightened. Could he be any cuter?

No, no. She wasn't supposed to be thinking that way about him. Until he proved otherwise, his status of enemy hadn't changed.

In another half hour, when the lesson ended, Alaine's sides hurt—from holding in her laughter as much as she could at Forbes's formidable frown. For a man used to having things go his way, trying not only to remember the one-two-three but also the quarter-turns and extra steps that moving around the room in a circle required had been an exercise in frustration for him. And the more frustrated he got, the cuter he became.

"We'll work on that more next lesson—which will be in two weeks. Don't forget the studio is closed next Monday for the Fourth of July."

Alaine dropped into the chair she'd sat in earlier and downed what remained of her water. "Do you have plans for the Fourth, Forbes?"

"What? Oh, we do a family barbecue at Schuyler Park and watch the fireworks there."

"Is that an all day thing or just in the evening?"

"Just the evening. Why?"

"I thought maybe, if you didn't have plans already, you might want to come out to the Mills that afternoon for the street festival. It is the most culturally diverse area of town. There's tons of food and lots of different stuff going on. It would give you a good idea of what it's really like over there." And it would mean she wouldn't have to go a full two weeks without seeing him again if her father couldn't get the meeting set up for this week.

Forbes's exasperated expression vanished. "What time and where should I meet you?"

Her heart did a little twirl. "I'll e-mail you the details." Her phone beeped. She picked it up to read the new message. "It's from Daddy. They've gotten the meeting scheduled: Thursday evening at eight o'clock." She looked up at Forbes. "Does that work for you?"

He glanced at his cousin, talking with a few potential customers several feet away, before looking at Alaine. "Yeah. That should work. Come on, I'll walk you to your car."

Alaine oscillated between euphoria and consternation walking out to her car. She wanted to skip, wanted to tell all the young women who'd come because they'd seen the segment on her show and who were now whispering about her that yes, she was here *with* Forbes. But she wasn't here *with* Forbes. It was just a convenient cover for them. Right?

Then why had the thought that she might not see him for two weeks struck her like a bucket of ice? Unbidden, a Bible verse floated through her mind: *Love thy enemy*.

Chapter 18

Forbes swiped at the sweat pouring down the sides of his face. "I can't go tonight."

"Dude, you made me a deal. I'd be your sounding board, and you'd go out with the women I set you up with." Shon bent over, hands braced on his knees.

"It's not that I'm backing out on the deal—it's that I already have plans tonight. A business meeting."

"Okay. Brunch Saturday morning. I won't take no for an answer."

"Fine. Send me the details."

Shon pulled his phone out of his pocket and tapped on the screen a couple of times. Forbes's phone vibrated in his pocket.

"Thanks. I'll let you know how it goes."

"I look forward to it."

Forbes raised his hand and waved off his client. "Later."

"Later." Still full of the youthful energy of twenty-nine, Shon jogged up the stairs to the front door. Forbes went in through the garage, preferring to climb to the main level in the air-conditioning.

In the shower, while getting dressed, and in the car on the way to work, Forbes rehearsed what he wanted to say to the Moreaux Mills Business Owners' Association tonight. Alaine had finally texted him the details on the meeting yesterday—he'd been in the middle of presenting the nominating committee's report during the business meeting and, fortunately, had remembered to silence his phone before getting up to speak.

He sent Meredith an e-mail as soon as he got into the office, telling her he'd had a meeting come up and wouldn't make it to the Fishin' Shack for dinner. He could have mentioned it to her or to Anne at church, but he preferred doing it by e-mail in such a way that it looked like this was an urgent, last-minute meeting so they wouldn't question him further. They usually didn't, when it came to his job, but he didn't want to risk it.

He groaned when Samantha went over the day's schedule with him. Meetings all day, with barely enough time between each to return to his office to get the files for the next one. Maybe it would help to stay busy—to keep his mind occupied with all of these other cases instead of having time to make himself overanxious about tonight.

Rubbing his eyes, he stifled a yawn.

"You look tired, boss."

"Haven't been sleeping well the last couple of nights." He waved his hand over the stack of files on his desk. "Lots on my mind."

She glanced at the paper cup with the Beignets S'il Vous Plait logo on the outside. "Need me to bring you more coffee?"

"I'll get it. You just work on those briefs we discussed."

"Will do."

He followed her out of his office and headed down the hall to the break room. Four people stood staring at the coffeepot, which dripped the black stuff about as fast as an icicle melted at the North Pole in January.

Though he didn't usually make use of the executive kitchen, today called for desperate measures. He left the employee break room without disrupting the other caffeine zombies and took the stairs up to the fourth floor, bypassing the large conference room and partners'-only file room to the walnut-paneled executive dining room and into the kitchen beyond.

Mary looked over her shoulder, then turned to stare at him in surprise. "What're you doing up here?"

"I am a partner, and I do have the privilege of making use of the executive areas—even if my office isn't up here." He waved his coffee cup. "Besides, there's a line for the java downstairs."

The executive secretary's expression said as clearly as words, *I hope you don't plan to make a habit of this*, but she shuffled out of his way, two mugs of coffee clutched in her claws. "Have at it. But if you empty it, you'll have to start a new pot. Or send that secretary up here to make one, if she knows how."

"Samantha is a very capable assistant. And she makes great coffee." He toasted Mary with his mug and turned his back on her to remedy its empty state.

He drank more than half of what he fixed standing there in the kitchen. Once he'd topped it off, he returned to his office to face the first meeting of the day.

By late afternoon, his record for being able to get most of his cases resolved without having to result to courtroom litigation had stayed intact. He passed the files and paperwork off to Samantha and prepared for his last meeting of the day, down at the courthouse.

"I won't be coming back afterward." He signed several documents Samantha handed him. "Just leave everything else in my box. You're off tomorrow?"

"Unless you think you're going to need me. A temp from the pool will be filling in for me. I've left notes on everything she'll need to do to keep you operating at peak efficiency."

"You make me sound like a robot."

"Well. . ." She grinned and shrugged.

"I know. Don't get you started. Your fiancé is coming in town this weekend?"

"Boyfriend, not fiancé."

Forbes steepled his fingers and rocked in his tall-back leather chair. "Mark my words, he'll be your fiancé before he heads back to Denver Sunday night."

Samantha's face contorted as if she was trying to look skeptical instead of giddy. "You've never even met him. You hardly know anything about him. As a matter of fact, you probably don't even know his name."

"Jared. He's a computer geek, and you met him at your best friend's wedding. He was one of the groomsmen, and you were the maid of honor." Pride—and a touch of indignity—struck him at Samantha's incredulous look. "You see, I do listen to you when you talk about your life outside the office. You just have a tendency to keep most of it to yourself."

"But still. . .it's just wild speculation on your part that he'll propose to me. I'm not sure we're to that point in our relationship, since it's only been six months and this'll be the first time we've seen each other since then."

Forbes arched his left brow. "If you insist. But I have a feeling. . . ." He looked at his watch. "I've got to go if I'm not going to be late. It's taking longer and longer to go through security every time I go down to the courthouse."

"Okay. Have a great weekend, Forbes."

"You, too." He packed up his files and left the building. On the way to the courthouse, he called his favorite florist to see if they could deliver an arrangement to Samantha before the end of the day. Even though she'd never know it, teasing her had been just the distraction he'd needed to clear his head from his previous meetings and allow him to refocus on his next two meetings—the official one and the unofficial one.

Maybe he should have called Delacroix Gardens—but if they were so short staffed that Alaine had to help out on the weekends, they probably couldn't do a one-hour turnaround on an order for him.

He arrived at Judge Duplessis's chambers with about five minutes to spare. Russ LeBlanc sat waiting in the secretary's outer office.

"Hey, Forbes." He stood and extended his hand.

Forbes grabbed it, then pulled Russ forward to clasp him around the shoulders in a back-pounding hybrid handshake-hug.

"You know," Forbes stepped back, "you could have asked for a continuance. I'm sure Plessy would have been more than happy to give you a few more weeks."

"Are you kidding me? My mom, Carrie's mom, and Carrie's sister are all at our house. I couldn't wait to get away. Besides, I have four more mouths to feed—not to mention a bunch of medical bills to pay."

Forbes nodded and infused his frown with as much sympathy as he could muster. Next week once all members had a chance to donate, the president of the Bonneterre Bar Association would be presenting Russ and Carrie with a check that would not only cover their medical expenses—Forbes had seen to that with the donations he'd drummed up—but also be substantial seed money for college funds for all four children.

"Well, it's good to see you, even if we are about to go head-to-head in there."

"Hey, that reminds me—did anything come of that case I sent your way?"

"I'm meeting with a group of potential clients tonight." In a way, it was a good thing Russ hadn't been able to meet with Alaine. This case had the potential to become something that could destroy a legal aid lawyer without the money to pour into it.

"Hope it works out well for you."

Judge Duplessis opened his office door. "LeBlanc—you better have brought pictures, young man, or I'm ruling in Guidry's favor on everything today."

Forbes and Russ exchanged smiles, even as Russ reached into his pocket. "Of course, your honor."

Alaine paced the lobby of the community center, watching the parking lot through the windows as she passed them. She'd told Forbes to be here at six thirty so he could meet her family before everything got crazy.

She jumped at a loud squeal of feedback through the PA system in the auditorium, followed by a few choice expletives—at least, she assumed that's what they were, since they were in what sounded like Farsi.

"Joe, you shouldn't use language like that," she called and stopped in the door at the back of the auditorium. Nikki, up on stage, checked the wired microphone attached to the podium, while Joe wheeled around, checking the wireless mikes on stands in each of the three aisles.

"Y'all are sure people are actually going to show up for this?" Alaine leaned against the doorframe.

"Everyone's been chattering about it on the association's e-mail loop. Quite a few have confirmed they're coming."

The squeak of the front door caught Alaine's attention. Mother and Daddy entered, each carrying a pot containing a fully bloomed azalea bush.

"What're those for?" Alaine asked.

"This place is so old and worn down, I wanted something to look nice for your little friend."

Alaine tapped her back teeth together a couple of times. "He's not my friend, Mother; he's a lawyer."

"Eh." Mother swept past her into the auditorium. Daddy just shrugged and followed her.

"Mother, Voula Pappas told me to let you know she's in the kitchen and could use your help, because everyone else is still at the restaurant and won't be here until later."

"Okay." She set her azalea to the left of the podium and showed her husband where to put his, then exited stage right toward the kitchen and reception hall.

"Have I missed anything?"

Alaine shivered at the sound of Forbes's voice, at the tickle of his breath on the side of her neck.

"I didn't hear you come in."

"I can be sneaky like that—like a tiger in stealth mode."

Yes. Sneaky. She had to remember—she couldn't fall for him.

She couldn't trust him. Not until he'd proven himself worthy of her trust and affection.

More feedback—more swearing from Joe, only this time it sounded like it might have been Russian or Polish or something.

"Joe!" Nikki snapped upright, her fists popping onto her hips so fast it looked like it hurt.

Alaine's brother muttered something under his breath in another language—which could have been Greek or Latin for all Alaine could tell—and turned his chair so he was facing away from his wife.

Seeing Forbes's gaze fall upon Joe, she hurried to explain. "Joe was a linguistics specialist for the Army for almost fifteen years—until his convoy in Iraq was hit by an IED. He prides himself on being able to swear in twenty languages."

"Twenty-eight, Al. If you're going to apologize for me, make sure you get your facts straight."

Forbes's gray blue eyes twinkled, and he mouthed, *Al?*

"You *so* do not have permission to call me that." She poked him in the middle of his expensive silk tie.

"You need a nickname. Everyone should have one."

She crossed her arms and cocked her head. "Oh yeah? What's yours?"

He had the good grace to look sheepish. "Does Control Freak count as a nickname?"

She'd have to remember to call him that to his face sometime. "In your case, yes." She tried to make her eyes twinkle like his. Not that she had the first clue how to make it happen.

The moment stretched, and Alaine leaned closer, then cleared her throat and broke eye contact. The enemy, remember?

Love thy enemy.

No. She had to stay objective because if he ended up betraying them to support his parents, she didn't want to be hurt. She'd managed to live almost thirty-two years without suffering a broken heart—sure, bruised a couple of times—and she didn't intend on letting Forbes Guidry be the one to break it.

"I'll be at the podium?" Forbes walked past her down the aisle toward the front.

"Yes. And Joe's setting up the mikes out here so everyone can hear during the question-and-answer part."

"You'll be on stage with me?"

She shook her head. "My father's going to introduce you. I'm supposed to be keeping a low profile, remember?"

"But you're staying, right?"

Was that a touch of vulnerability in Forbes's voice? "Of course. I may not be a claimant in the case, but I'm still concerned about what's going on in the Mills."

"Okay." He joined her midway up the center aisle—just in time for her to hear his stomach growl.

"Why don't I take you back to the kitchen so you can meet my parents before everyone else shows up?" Without waiting for a response, she led him out the same way Mother and Daddy had gone.

As soon as she stepped through the side stage door, a delicious aroma overwhelmed her.

Forbes inhaled deeply. "That smells like. . .like the Greek restaurant we ate at the other day."

"You have good scent memory. Mrs. Pappas is catering the refreshments for after the meeting." She stopped and leaned closer when he halted beside her, as if telling him a secret. "I'm hoping to go ahead and grab a snack. I'm starving." She wasn't really. She'd eaten supper less than two hours ago. Why she felt the need to spare his ego, she wasn't certain. But his smile made it worthwhile.

Mother's eyes widened when she looked up at Alaine and Forbes's entry into the kitchen. Alaine grabbed a Danish wedding cookie from a tray and popped it in her mouth—taking a brief moment to close her eyes and enjoy the sheer bliss of the way the confectioners' sugar and the crumbly cookie mingled together as they melted on her tongue.

When her mother's expression turned from surprised to questioning, Alaine quickly chewed the cookie and swallowed it.

"Mother, this is Forbes. Forbes, my mom, Solange Delacroix."

Forbes took her mother's proffered hand in both of his. "Mrs. Delacroix, it's wonderful to meet you."

"And you, Mr. . . .Forbes." Mother cast a sidelong glance at her friend.

Alaine let out her breath, thankful Mother had remembered to not mention Forbes's last name. Having people figure out who he was when Daddy introduced him would be soon enough.

"And you remember Mrs. Voula Pappas from the restaurant."

"I'd shake your hand, but. . ." Mrs. Pappas held up sticky fingers.

"Quite all right." Forbes gave her the smile Alaine hadn't been able to resist at the bachelors' banquet. "It's nice to see you again."

"We're hungry." Alaine crossed to look over her mother's shoulder at what she was stirring in a large metal bowl. "Any chance of getting a sneak peek at the pickings tonight?"

"Sure—if you'll put all those trays out—those there, the ones covered with plastic wrap." Voula motioned toward several trays sitting in the serving window between the kitchen and the hall.

Alaine snagged another cookie on her way past. Forbes didn't. Several minutes later when all the prepared trays had been moved, she hadn't seen him touch a morsel of food for himself. The longer they stayed in the kitchen, the more certain she became that Forbes Guidry, Mr. Calm-Cool-and-Confident, was so nervous he'd made himself queasy.

"Where's Daddy?" She needed to get Forbes out of here before he ruined all their appetites.

"He went back out to help Joe and Nikki finish with the setup." Mother pulled a tray of spanakopita from the oven. Alaine really wanted a piece of the cheesy, spinachy goodness, but it would be too hot to eat right now. And besides, she'd gained five pounds in the past few weeks already. She didn't need any more.

And Forbes was definitely turning a pretty good shade of chartreuse. She hid her amusement and led him back down the hall to the auditorium. A dozen or so people milled about, greeting each other and finding seats. She prayed a lot more would show up. If they could get almost all of the two dozen or so people involved in the buyout here, that would be great.

"Excuse me, can I borrow my dad for a minute?" Alaine pulled her father away from the guys who owned the bicycle repair shop a few blocks over from her parents' place. "Daddy, I wanted to introduce you to Forbes."

Though not as green as just a minute ago, Forbes still looked pale when he shook her father's hand. "Mr. Delacroix, it's great to meet you, sir."

"Please, it's JD. We're happy to have you here."

Alaine scrutinized her father's face. Though he'd agreed to invite Forbes to come and to hear what Forbes had to say, the guarded expression in his eyes clearly indicated he still didn't consider this a good idea.

Around them, the noise level grew. Alaine estimated the crowd had at least doubled just in the past thirty seconds or so, with more people still flowing in from the lobby.

"Alaine, dear, if you'll excuse us, there are a couple of people I need to introduce Forbes to before we get started."

"Okay." She joined Nikki and Joe on the front row, where his soundboard was set up, but kept Daddy and Forbes in view.

By the time Daddy'd found the third person to introduce Forbes to, she understood. He didn't want the other members of the board to be blindsided by Forbes's identity.

Alaine twisted the hem of her blouse and chewed the inside corner of her bottom lip. Maybe Daddy was right. Maybe this wasn't such a good idea after all. More and more people entered the hall, far more than she'd hoped for. Just how many people did this thing involve?

Her father led Forbes up the two steps onto the stage and to the podium. Joe gave him a thumbs-up.

"We're going to get started, so please find your seats."

While the crowd—which had to number at least a hundred by

now—jostled into the old, wooden, theater-style seats, Daddy pulled Forbes a few steps away from the live microphone to talk to him. Alaine strained to try to hear, but too much noise filled the echoing room now.

As soon as JD Delacroix, recently elected president of the Moreaux Mills Business Owners' Association, stepped back to the podium, the room quieted.

"I'd like to thank everyone for making the effort to come out tonight on such short notice. I know a lot of you even closed your businesses early so you could be here. I pray you'll feel like your effort is rewarded. As you read in the e-mails that went out this week, this meeting is so you can hear what a lawyer has to say about the threat the Mills is under. Then we'll have a question-and-answer session. We'll get to as many people as we can. If we can't get to you tonight, we'll make sure you get an answer by e-mail soon." He looked over his shoulder. Forbes nodded and joined him at the podium.

Alaine's stomach lurched. Moment of truth.

"So, since you didn't come to listen to me yammer, I'll turn the meeting over to Forbes Guidry, the lawyer who's going to try to figure out how to help us."

A frisson of whispers jolted the stillness of the room. Her father left the stage and took the seat beside her, just as Mother and Voula Pappas entered through the side door.

Forbes cleared his throat and rested his hands on either side of the podium. Though he smiled, from this distance, the grimness in his eyes couldn't be plainer. "Thank you, Mr. Delacroix. Good evening, ladies and gentlemen. I'd like to begin by talking about the elephant in the room. You heard Mr. Delacroix correctly. My name is Forbes Guidry. Yes, I am the son of Lawson and Mairee Guidry, who own Boudreaux-Guidry Enterprises."

The trickle of whispers turned into a shower.

Alaine tried to beam encouragement and enthusiasm at him with her smile when he caught her eye.

"I am not here on behalf of my parents nor of their company. I have never worked for B-G Enterprises in any capacity and have acted as legal counsel for my parents only in personal business matters."

Her heart squeezed. He hadn't told her that before.

"But you're a partner in the law firm that represents them," a man called from somewhere in the middle of the small auditorium. "You're here to make us back down, to make us sell out."

"I know it might seem like I'm the most unlikely candidate for someone to help you oppose B-G Enterprises if it's found they've done anything illegal—"

"D'ya hear that?" A woman shouted from the back of the room. "*If!* He's already trying to whitewash Mommy and Daddy's dirty deeds."

"No, ma'am. I'm telling you what any reputable lawyer would tell you: No matter how injured you feel you've been, we'll have to prove the other side has actually done something wrong—broken laws or contracts or conducted business in ways that violate the charters of this city, parish, or state—before any formal legal action can be taken. That means"—Forbes had to raise his voice another notch to make himself heard over the tempest now—"that I'll need to meet with each of you individually to see if you have a claim that is actionable."

"Why should we trust you?"

"Don't listen to him. He's not here to help us!"

"This is a travesty. Delacroix, what are you doing to us?"

With a sigh, Alaine's father returned to the podium. Forbes stepped aside for him, his expression apologetic.

"Quiet please." As soon as a semblance of quiet had been reached, her father adjusted the microphone lower. "I asked Mr. Guidry to come here in good faith. He has promised that he will set aside any personal prejudices and look only at the facts. If he discovers that B-G Enterprises—or any company they're doing business with—has done anything illegal, he's sworn he'll act only on our behalf. Now please, listen to what he has to say."

"Listen to him?" a woman shrieked. "Listen to him? Can y'all believe this? They brought the enemy right into our community—

practically into our homes."

"Look at him in his fancy suit, standing in our community center that probably isn't worth as much as that fancy car of his."

"How much money are you going to make when they tear down all our homes and businesses?"

"Yeah, how much of the Mills are you going to own once we're all kicked out?"

Why wouldn't he stand up for himself? The desire to use one of Joe's favorite foreign words or phrases propelled Alaine out of her seat. Her feet didn't even touch the two steps up to the stage. She bumped her father—who was trying to calm down the frenzy—out of the way and grabbed the microphone from its holder, since she could barely see over the tall podium.

"Everybody sit down and be quiet!" She didn't have to raise her voice much; too many years of live remotes from concerts, club openings, and festivals had taught her how to make herself heard over a lot of background noise. And Joe had probably dialed the volume all the way up on the microphone. She stared at the twenty or so hecklers still on their feet. Slowly they each sat down.

"Thank you." Recomposing her expression from stern to professional took only an instant. She tucked her hair behind her ear. "Most of you in this room know me—if you don't know me in person you've seen me on television. I grew up in the Mills. All of my family still live in the Mills."

Well, that wasn't exactly true. Tony lived in an apartment over in University Heights. "My parents—whom you all know—and my brother and sister-in-law work side by side with everyone here to make a living. So trust me when I say that securing the future of Moreaux Mills is my highest priority."

She scanned the room, keying in on faces she recognized, making eye contact. "*I* asked Forbes Guidry to come here to talk to you tonight. *I* am the one who talked to him about what Boudreaux-Guidry Enterprises is doing in the Mills. And you know why I talked about this with someone who's related to the owners of that company? Because there isn't another lawyer in this city who's willing to take on a case against them. Not a single one would even agree to meet with me. But he did."

Of course, he hadn't known why or even whom he was meeting. "I know you've got your doubts. I did in the beginning, as well. All I can ask you to do is set them aside just for a little while and listen to what he has to say. Let's engage in some civilized discourse and see what we can do to save the Mills."

"But why should we trust him?" one of the original hecklers called.

She licked her lips, heart hammering. "I can't make you trust him. All I can do is tell you that I trust this man with my entire being."

And her entire being included her heart.

Chapter 19

All Forbes's nervousness vanished at Alaine's proclamation. Heretofore, the nearly paralyzing anxiety had been inexplicable. Now he knew: He'd been afraid of disappointing her.

The microphone trembled in her hand as she stood watching her parents' friends and neighbors discuss her words quietly among themselves. He moved closer and rested his hand on her shoulder, trying to express his gratitude wordlessly when she looked up at him, her eyes wide as if she'd just witnessed a horrible accident.

He reached for the microphone, which she seemed only too happy to relinquish. She backed away, then returned to her seat with surprising haste.

Forbes looked over the crowd as he would a group of people considered for jury duty. Very few wore suits. Even Alaine's father wore his button-down oxford with the collar open and no jacket. Appearances could go a long way in a situation like this. He laid the mike on the podium, took his coat off and hung it from the corner of the stand, loosened his tie, and rolled up his sleeves.

The hall quieted again. Rather than stand behind the podium, he picked up the microphone and moved to stand beside it.

"If, as Miss Delacroix suggested, you'll give me a chance, I promise I will do whatever I can to make sure justice is served for the residents and business owners of Moreaux Mills."

As no one seemed inclined to argue this time, he forged ahead, giving a bit of his professional background, then beginning to explain what he'd learned so far—couching everything in generalisms so that nothing he said could be deemed as firm statements of accusation, but so that they understood to what extent he would investigate and fight for them.

The longer he talked, the more the attitude of his listeners changed toward him. Alaine, however, looked as if she'd rather be anywhere than here. He purposely avoided looking at her often. And he could imagine how embarrassed she must be for having made a public spectacle of herself after she'd been determined to honor her promise to her parents not to be seen as the public face of the issue. His trepidation for what she might hear from her parents after this magnified his own over how his parents would react when he told them of his involvement in it.

During the question-and-answer time, though there were still a few folks obviously intent on giving him a hard time, he got the feeling that most of the people were willing to give him a chance, and that most of them were not under imminent threat of losing their property—they were concerned that if development moved forward, they would be run out in a second or third phase of building. Forbes had represented too many people like Mr. Pichon in his career to deny the legitimacy of their fears.

Finally, JD called an end to the meeting. "Thank you all again for coming out tonight. There are refreshments in the fellowship hall, thanks to Voula and Spiro Pappas. Mr. Guidry has graciously agreed to stay for about an hour to try to answer more questions. If you've already had a chance to ask a question in here, please allow those who did not get a chance to talk with Mr. Guidry first. And of course, let's show him the kind of hospitality we pride ourselves on in the Mills."

The sound of the old wooden seats flopping closed almost drowned out the immediate drone of voices.

Forbes needed to get to Alaine, to try to let her know how much he appreciated her standing up for him, but her father waylaid him before he could leave the stage to join her.

"I'd like to apologize to you, son, for the things that were said earlier. I—"

"No, don't." Forbes held up his hand. "You're not responsible for anything anyone said here tonight. When sentiment runs high, people will say things they'd never even think under normal circumstances."

JD's shoulders sagged, and he appeared much older, world-weary, than just seconds before. "No, I need to apologize. Because when you first stood up here, I felt the same way they did. I didn't want to trust you, didn't believe you had any interest other than to defend your—to defend the corporations on the other side."

"You *felt* that way then? But now?"

"I trust Alaine; she's a good judge of character. If she says you can be trusted, I'm willing to take that leap of faith."

The warmth in the older man's eyes succeeded in driving away the remainder of Forbes's anxiety. "Thank you. I will do my best not to squander nor betray that belief."

With a handshake accompanied by a shoulder-squeeze from Alaine's father, Forbes contemplated what he'd just done. Though no paperwork had been drawn up or signed, he was their lawyer, by conscience if not by contract, committed to the cause, to the community, to the case.

"We should join everyone else in the hall." JD motioned him toward a side door.

Forbes looked around at the mostly empty auditorium. Alaine hadn't waited for him. He'd just have to wait until after the reception to try to have a private word with her. He followed JD into the fellowship hall, the crowd parting for them. Some people still looked skeptical, a few downright hostile, but most smiled and nodded in greeting when he made eye contact with them.

JD motioned him through to the kitchen where Solange handed Forbes a plate of what looked like a full serving of each of the hors d'oeuvres Mrs. Pappas had prepared. He ate as much as he could, but even after not being able to eat anything since his early lunch, his riotous stomach wouldn't handle much.

"Where is Alaine?" Solange asked her husband, her accent making her daughter's name come out as *Ah-la-ee-na*.

"I figured she'd come in here with you." JD served a plate for himself and leaned against the counter beside Forbes to eat.

"I have not seen her since the meeting ended. She said she would assist in the kitchen."

The door swung open with a bump and a scrape, and the guy in the wheelchair and the tall redhead who'd set up the sound system entered the kitchen. Alaine had introduced them before, but Forbes's nerves had kept him from taking in their names.

"Ah." JD wiped his mouth with a paper napkin and set his half-full plate aside. "Forbes, this is our oldest, Joe, and his wife, Nikki."

Forbes met Joe halfway across the kitchen and greeted him and his wife with handshakes. "I've heard a lot about you. It's nice to put faces with the names."

The husband and wife exchanged a telling glance—the same kind Anne and George had been giving him and each other at the ballroom lessons the other night.

When Joe turned back around, Forbes got a flash of recognition. "Wait—you were in the Latin Club at Moreaux High School. You were a couple of grades behind me, but you competed on our level my senior year."

"I almost beat you at the All-State Competition, too." Joe grinned. "But they said my accent needed work. My accent, in a nonspoken language."

With a twinkle in her eyes, Nikki poured herself a soda. "So you were a language geek in high school, too, Forbes?"

"My parents wanted each of their children to be competitive in something, and since I wasn't cut out for sports and found Latin easy, it seemed like the best option to make them happy." Okay. Maybe not the best anecdote, given present company.

Nikki laughed. "Sounds like what I would have done."

"Don't let her fool you. She came to almost all of the Latin fairs, exhibitions, and competitions. It's why she fell in love with me." Joe rolled over to her and took the cup out of her hands. She swiped it right back from him. He made a doleful face, and with a sigh, she poured him his own drink. "Thanks, babe." He rotated so he faced Forbes again. "Did you take any other languages?"

"No. Just Latin. I knew before I started high school that I wanted to be a lawyer, so really Latin was my first and only choice. And as I said, I found it easy, so what was the point in switching to something else?"

"I know what you mean. We all grew up speaking Portuguese as easily as English. So Spanish, Italian, and Latin were all simple. French is a pain—because of the pronunciation." Joe went on to talk about the ease or difficulty with which he'd learned his first six languages.

Forbes wanted to hear Alaine speak Portuguese. He already loved the way she spoke English, so he could only imagine hearing the Romance language rolling off her tongue would be symphonic.

When he returned his attention to the conversation, Nikki and Joe were bickering good-naturedly, and Solange and JD were across the kitchen speaking in tones too low to carry.

"I should probably go out and start answering some more questions." Forbes tossed his plate into a nearby trash can before anyone could see how little progress he'd made in the pile of food—food that was at least as good as Aunt Maggie's gourmet offerings and perhaps even better in their ethnic rusticity.

"I'll join you out there in a moment," JD called across the room.

Forbes waved but was glad he'd be on his own, even if just for a few minutes. People would speak more freely and honestly without someone else standing there waiting to censor or stop them if he felt like they were crossing a line.

And frankly, he hoped to be able to speak with Alaine sooner rather than later.

Though at least fifty people milled about the hall, it took only seconds for Forbes to realize Alaine wasn't among them. Had she been so afraid of her parents' reaction that she couldn't face them in a public setting? Or perhaps she sought to minimize the damage by avoiding more attention with her presence at the reception.

Either way, no matter how harsh her parents were on her—though he couldn't imagine it could possibly be too bad, given what he'd observed in JD and Solange—he would do his best to make up for it by showing her just how much her defense of him meant.

Alaine dug through the pile of notebooks and printed research piled on her desk one more time. It had to be here.

She still couldn't believe that she'd practically come right out and said, "I love you" on stage. Had he seen it in her eyes? Had she betrayed her feelings without meaning to?

A stack of papers slid onto the floor.

"Oh, for heaven's sake!"

Instead of picking it up, she pulled the shredder and recycling bin over and started sorting through the avalanche. Most of it was trash—articles and blog entries she'd printed out from various Web sites, including her blog at the station, containing any mention of the Guidrys or Mackenzie and Son. Junk mail. Magazines she'd been meaning to get to for a few months. Notes she'd pulled from her interviews with Mairee and Meredith before the HEARTS to Hearts banquet back in February—those needed to be re-filed.

She shoved the pages back into the green folder and picked it up to set in the seat of her chair—and suddenly found herself being stared at by Forbes Guidry. She'd found it. She grabbed the July issue of *Bonneterre Lifestyles* and threw it into the recycle bin. The blue box slid across the wood floor, coming to a stop when it bumped the base of her credenza.

A heartbeat later, she jumped up and ran to the crate to rescue the magazine. She flipped the magazine open—it automatically parted on the first two pages of Forbes's six-page spread. While most of the men featured in the bachelor-of-the-year edition of the magazine looked like they'd been posing for high school senior portraits or college fraternity "party pix," even with the professional photographers giving direction at the photo shoots, Forbes looked like a professional model in all his shots. Her favorite was halfway through the feature. In dark jeans, a bulky gray sweater, and barefoot, Forbes sat on a red sofa—she remembered it from the lobby of the magazine's offices—laughing. She hadn't seen that side of him often but wanted to.

She glanced down at the article below the photo. The interviewer had asked Forbes who his hero was.

> *"My parents," Guidry responds without a moment's hesitation. "They proved that one can be successful in career and family, building Boudreaux-Guidry Enterprises into what it is today while also raising eight children, making sure we had plenty of love and plenty of discipline. They can do no wrong, in my book."*

Alaine flung the magazine back into the recycle bin, not caring that three subscription cards went flying to different corners of the converted-bedroom office.

Uncertainty tore at her heart—the heart with which she'd believed she trusted him; the heart he could so easily break if she let him.

But not if she didn't give him the chance. She pushed the chair back to the desk and sat—on the folder—and opened her e-mail program. There they were—the e-mails from Shon Murphy this morning. When she'd responded to the first one that she couldn't meet someone tonight, he'd almost immediately sent back the alternate time of nine thirty Saturday morning. She hadn't responded.

She pulled it up and hit REPLY. Hopefully it wasn't too late already.

> *Saturday, 9:30, Beignets on Spring Street is fine. Tell him I'll*

be wearing a black-and-white polka-dot shirt and black capris.

She sent it and closed down the computer, ignoring the several new e-mails at the top of the list. Fatigued from the day's emotional turmoil, she went to bed, silencing her cell phone when it started ringing just after ten o'clock. If it was an emergency, family and work had her landline number. She stared at the cordless phone on the nightstand, waiting to hear it ring, but it didn't.

She rolled over and closed her eyes.

Sleep didn't come.

At midnight, more exhausted than she remembered being in a very long time, she got up and took some p.m. painkiller for her headache and to, hopefully, help her fall asleep.

An hour later, she still lay on her back, staring at the ceiling.

If she prayed, would it do more than bounce off the ceiling? She took a deep breath and let it out slowly. "Okay, Lord. Obviously, I don't know what's going on here, but it seems like You're going way out of Your way to make sure there's nothing I *can* do but try to step out on faith and trust You in this."

Her rash decision to jump up on stage to defend Forbes flickered through her mind. She rolled onto her side, pulled her knees up, and wrapped her arms around her legs. "Why'd You let me make such a fool of myself? Please don't let Mother and Daddy be too angry with me."

She lay there for quite a while, trying to find peace within, silently praying for sleep to come. When it didn't, she stretched out on her back again, staring at the patch of moonlight on the ceiling.

"Please show me how to trust You; show me what You want me to do. And help me to leave this situation in Your hands and not try to run out ahead of You and do things on my own. Because I can't handle it on my own. I can't figure it out for myself." Her eyes grew heavy, and she yawned. "And I'll never understand Forbes Guidry without Your help."

Sleep came. But when the alarm went off at six o'clock, her head throbbed and she did not look forward to the day to come.

For the first time in more than ten years, she paid as little attention as necessary to her appearance—she'd worry about what her face and hair looked like closer to airtime.

At the office, she went straight to her cubicle, speaking as little as necessary to the co-workers she passed in the hallways, and dug into finishing a few stories for the broadcast.

"Hey, Alaine—whoa, are you feeling okay?" Bekka swung back into Alaine's cubicle.

"I'm just tired." Tired of keeping up appearances. Tired of trying to figure out how to get a promotion. Tired of trying to be the person everyone else thought she should be. Tired of wondering about Forbes. Tired of longing to fall in love and get married. Tired of everything. *God, help me turn it all over to You.*

Bekka, who always showed up for work with little makeup and her hair overflowing the top of a clip at the back of her head, raised her eyebrows in an encouraging gesture. "How'd the meeting go last night?"

Tempted to tell her everything, Alaine had to stop herself. Never knew who might be listening around this place. "We'll have to get together for coffee some time next week, and I'll tell you about it."

"And *him*?"

"Seems like he managed to win just about everyone over. Including my dad." Closing her eyes, she could clearly see her father with his hand on Forbes's shoulder—a sure sign JD Delacroix had accepted Forbes.

"That's a good thing, though, isn't it?" Confusion edged Bekka's soft voice.

"Yeah. That's a good thing."

"You're still not sure how you feel about him, though."

Alaine clicked her pen with increasing rapidity. "I'm still trying to work that out. I trust him—I want to trust him. I want him to be everything he says he is, that he's not just showing us one face and is a totally different person in reality."

Bekka leaned against the edge of Alaine's desktop. "Has he given you any reason to believe he's deceiving you?"

Alaine told her about the magazine article in a whisper. "If he believes his parents can do no wrong, then how could he do what we're asking him to do?"

"But Alaine, you have to think—those interviews were done months ago. Didn't you do yours back in February?" She uncrossed her arms when Alaine nodded. "He didn't know back then that they might be involved in something like this—you said yourself he didn't know until you told him. And not only that, he was talking about them as a child about his parents for a magazine which is all about image. If you'd read that about him without this—thing going on, wouldn't you have found it endearing he'd feel that way about his folks?"

The magazine was all about image. Just like her program. Just like *her*. When had she become such a sellout? Stopped looking for what people were deep down instead of just on the surface? She'd become like all of those people who thought they knew something about art but who looked no further than the initial impression they got by gazing at a piece. They didn't examine the hues, the brush strokes, the textures, the use of shadow and light—they didn't even know how to look for it.

"Yeah, I would have found it charming." Just like Forbes. "Thanks for the reminder."

"See you in twenty for the briefing." Bekka patted Alaine's arm and left.

"See ya." Alaine's computer chimed, and she turned to see what reminder had just popped up. Art Gallery Show Opening With Meredith, 7 pm.

In her freshman year of college, she'd read a book by one of her professors about how everything he knew about life and relationships had come from his love of art. She'd taken the lessons to heart, learning to look beyond the "frame" and the "image" to the details of what made something—or someone—a masterpiece. She could blame it on her sorority sisters, who couldn't accept her until they'd remade her in their own image. But culpability for losing herself, for losing the person who'd accepted everyone and not cared at all about someone's social status, or appearance or success, rested squarely on her own shoulders.

She ached to have friends again—the real kind, the kind she'd turned her back on at age nineteen when she decided to become someone she wasn't sure she liked anymore. And tonight, she'd try to rectify that by attending the art gallery opening with Meredith and trying to remember who Alaine Delacroix really was.

Chapter 20

Alaine opened the conference room door at the insistent knocking. She glowered at the intern who stood on the other side. "We're in a prep meeting for the noon broadcast. What is it?"

"Mr. Milton wants to see you. Says it's urgent."

Dread fizzled through Alaine's veins. "Please let him know that I'll be happy to meet with him after the broadcast, but for the next two hours, I'm tied up."

"I'll tell him." But his expression said he didn't think the boss would go for it.

Alaine returned to her coworkers and the meeting continued—until the knocking started up again several minutes later.

"Yes?" Her heart rattled in her chest.

"He said okay, but you're to go straight to his office as soon as you sign off."

"Thank him for understanding and let him know I'll be there immediately after airing." She closed the door and returned to the small conference table.

"What is that all about?" Pricilla asked.

"No clue. Now, where were we?" Getting her two producers to focus on the program notes was easier than returning her own focus to it. What had she done now to deserve to be called into the boss's office? Whatever it was, she would apologize and show him she was turning over a new leaf. Gone was the full-of-herself diva. She just hoped he'd give her a chance to prove it instead of firing her on the spot. Not that he would. Would he?

The inside corner of her bottom lip was raw by the time she got to the set. She had to stop chewing on it when she was nervous, a bad habit she'd started when she forced herself to stop chewing the ends of her pens.

The program went smoothly—thank goodness Major O'Hara's pretaped cooking segment took up more than a quarter of the show. With a few other taped segments, Alaine only had to focus on a couple of transitions, banter with Bekka and Brent before and after the news headlines and weather forecasts at the top and bottom of the hour, and hold an in-studio interview with one of the curators at the Bonneterre Fine Arts Center about the new exhibition, which opened to the public tomorrow.

As soon as she got the clear signal, Alaine unwired herself, took a deep breath, and headed upstairs to the news director's office. The door stood open, but she still knocked to get his attention.

"Close the door and sit down."

Oh, dear. That couldn't be a good sign. She did as bade, clasping her hands tightly together in her lap. "You asked to see me?"

"Yes. What is this?" He flung a quarter-folded section of newspaper at her.

"Um. . ." Not a good time to be flippant. She closed her mouth and looked down at the portion of the page facing her. It was the news-briefs page—the page with snippets of information either too trivial for an article or learned too late for a full article to be written before press time. She was about to ask him what he wanted her to look at when she saw it:

Moreaux Mills Residents Fight Back

Thursday evening, more than one hundred residents and

business owners in Moreaux Mills gathered at the community center to protest the planned redevelopment of the area by Boudreaux-Guidry Enterprises. Moreaux Mills Business Owners' Association president J. D. Delacroix introduced lawyer Forbes Guidry as the man who will be "making inquiries" into the merits of a lawsuit against the local corporation and a development firm they have brought in. Guidry is the son of B-G's owners. Also taking the stage was Channel Six reporter Alaine Delacroix, daughter of the business association president. Continue reading the Reserve *for further details.*

She might throw up. Trembling, she set the paper gingerly on the desk. Of course someone had informed a reporter about the meeting—whether he was there or someone just gave him the information. With that many people, even though they'd all been asked to keep it confidential, word was bound to leak.

"I thought you said you didn't have any involvement in what's going on in the Mills." Rodney leaned his elbows on the desk and steepled his fingers.

"I don't—not directly. My parents, as you saw, are involved, as are my brother and sister-in-law. My only involvement was to find a lawyer who'd be willing to take a case like this against B-G." She couldn't get fired over this. He couldn't be that petty.

"Need I remind you that you have a duty to this station that if you know of something newsworthy you're to bring it to our attention?"

"I couldn't. I was bound by a promise of confidentiality."

"We could have treated you as an unnamed source. No one would have known you were passing us the information."

"I would have known. I know my duty to the station, but I also know my duty to my family, as well as to myself and my own conscience. I could not break my word." The DVD sitting on her desk at home with the finished piece about B-G and the Guidrys weighed on her mind.

"Well, now the news has been broken, your promise of confidence is null and void. I want you to be the primary on this story. It doesn't mean a promotion yet, but if you do as good a job with this—and I want some heavy-duty investigative reporting—as you've been telling me you'd do if I moved you to main news, I'll consider moving you over."

Funny, yesterday she would have given everything for this chance. "No."

"You'll start with something for the six o'clock news today—excuse me?"

"No, I won't report this story. I'm too closely involved in it to be objective. Not only that, but you already have an investigative reporter who's been working on the story and who'll do a much better job with it than I would." And her parents would hold to their promise of dropping out of the lawsuit if she took the assignment.

He rocked back in his chair as if avoiding something she'd thrown at him. "You can't be serious."

"I'm completely serious." She leaned forward. "Listen, Rodney. I need to apologize to you. I know I haven't been the most cooperative employee for the past few years—that I've been the thorn in your side with my mania to get promoted, to do hard news. But I've come to a decision." She swallowed hard. "I want to stay with *Inside Bonneterre* for as long as you'll let me. I have some ideas I'm working on for how I can make it even better, get more involved in the community. If I'm going to start implementing those changes, I'll need all my focus there, not on trying to do the program and investigate what could be one of the biggest stories Bonneterre's ever seen. So while I appreciate your vote of confidence in me, my answer is no."

Rodney's jaw hung slack.

She laughed. "I know. *Invasion of the Body Snatchers*, right? But trust me on this. You want a better reporter than me to handle this story. And I'd like my name to be kept out of it as much as possible. I know I've already put myself into the middle of it by being there last night, but my family has asked me to keep a low profile, to not add my name and image to the media circus that it might become. They don't want me tainted by association if things go badly, I think."

Recovering his wits, Rodney ran his hands over his face. "Well, since B-G is one of the biggest sponsors of your show, I suppose it's better to keep you away from the story as much as we can. I'd—I know you have creative control over your program, but I'd be interested in seeing your ideas for the new segments you have. We need more community involvement, so I'd like to see if we can take your ideas and create some station-wide initiatives stemming from what you do on your show."

"I'd love to talk to you about it." But not yet. "I'll send you an e-mail with the details once I get them fleshed out a little better. I'll go now so you can get someone else in here and brief them on the Mills story." She dismissed herself and stood to leave.

"Yes. Oh, send my secretary in here on your way past her desk."

"Will do." Though she'd never dreamed it possible, Alaine walked out of Rodney Milton's office with no promotion and feeling better than she had in—in longer than she could remember.

Back at her desk, she checked messages on her work phone and her cell phone. Meredith Guidry. . .O'Hara—Alaine grinned when Meredith had to quickly remember to tack on her new last name—had left a message for Alaine to call her to confirm plans for tonight. And she had a text message from Shon Murphy: U r on at 930 Saturday.

Not getting her date's name until he showed up at the agreed-upon time and location worried her a bit. She couldn't help but wish it was Forbes and not a complete stranger. But what would people think if her name became romantically linked with Forbes's now? It was no longer just a case of the bachelor and bachelorette of the year becoming a couple. If this became a lawsuit, a relationship between her and Forbes could become a problem for others involved in the case—always wondering if her parents were getting more attention, better representation, than they were because the lawyer was dating their daughter.

Professional distance was what she needed. If she was to be seen out and about on dates with others, it would help put an end to any rumors that might hinder or damage the case.

"So I see you're not packing up your desk." Bekka leaned against the edge of the wall at the opening into Alaine's cubicle. "Pricilla told me why you vanished so quickly after the program."

"Right. Well, he offered me a promotion."

Bekka's brown eyes widened. "Really? Why? I mean, you know how much I respect your journalistic skills, but he's not your biggest fan."

"I know. But I'm mentioned in the newspaper as having been at the meeting in Moreaux Mills last night. He wanted me to cover the story—in addition to continuing with *Inside*."

"And you said yes, of course."

"I said no."

Bekka must have put more of her weight onto the divider than before, because it wobbled, throwing her off balance. She grabbed it to right herself. "You said. . .no?"

Alaine explained her reasons to Bekka—not just about the issue of her integrity in keeping her word to her parents, but about the underlying cause. "I need to find that person I used to be, the one I used to like. I wasn't raised to be a diva. I wasn't raised to smart mouth my boss. I was raised to work hard for what I want, but to be able to stop and recognize when I've been blessed with what I need, even if it's not what I thought I wanted. If I'm going to keep faith with my parents' expectations of me—and God's—I have to do it in all aspects of my career, not just keeping the promise to not get involved in the story. Does that make any sense?"

Pushing her chestnut hair over her shoulder, Bekka gave her a smile like the one Alaine's mother had worn for weeks after Alaine landed the job as sole host and creative director of *Inside Bonneterre* six years ago.

A vast sense of accomplishment welled up in Alaine. She'd prayed about everything else in her life last night. Figured God would answer the prayer she *didn't* pray.

"I know this'll sound patronizing, but I'm proud of you."

"Thanks. I hope to make everyone feel that way about me from now on."

Bekka stayed only a few minutes to chat, then left Alaine so they could both get their work done—Alaine so she would have time to get ready for the black-tie event, and Bekka so she could prepare for the five o'clock newscast.

Alaine dialed Meredith's office number.

"Boudreaux-Guidry Enterprises, Facilities and Events, this is Corie," Meredith's assistant answered.

"Hi, this is Alaine Delacroix. I'd hoped to speak with our Mrs. O'Hara."

Corie laughed. "Mrs. O'Hara has gone upstairs to speak with Mr. O'Hara. Shall I put you through to her cell phone?"

"Oh, no. Just have her call me when she returns to her office—on my cell." Alaine gave the assistant the number, even though she knew Meredith had it.

Half an hour later, her cell phone buzzed. *Forbes Guidry* scrolled across the caller-ID window. She hit the silencer button and returned to the e-mail she was writing for Rodney to explain the ideas she had for incorporating more community outreach elements to her show. She couldn't talk to Forbes right now. He'd get under her defenses and probably get her to admit her true feelings for him.

The phone buzzed again. Meredith this time. She flipped it open and tucked it between ear and shoulder. "Hey, girl."

"Hey, yourself. I haven't heard from you in ages—since we first arranged this. I was starting to wonder if we were still on or not."

"We are most definitely still on. Art, fine food—at least I'm assuming it is since your husband's preparing it—and a fund-raising auction. Who else would I possibly want to go with but the person who's an expert in these types of gala events?"

"You float through those social waters pretty well yourself. I've seen you in action."

"Yes, but tonight, I'll have no camera, no notepad, no pen."

"And I'll have no clipboard, no earpiece, no wondering if everyone's having a good time."

"Just you and me and the art."

"And a hundred or so other people."

"Right." Alaine mentally kicked herself for depriving herself of Meredith's open, honest, and warm friendship for the past month. "Shall we meet on the steps by the Fontainebleau sculpture at seven thirty?"

"Sounds good. Hey, are you wearing floor-length or knee-length?"

"I'd planned on knee-length. The invite said black tie, but it also mentioned cocktails."

"Oh, okay. You're right. Knee-length, then. I brought both with me, just in case."

"You took two dresses to work with you? Why not just change when you go home?"

Meredith let out a wry laugh. "Dear heart, you've yet to realize that I rarely leave here before six on nights when I don't have anything going on in my department—and when I do. . . I may not be working this event, but my catering division is, which means I need to be here just in case some last-minute crisis pops up so that Major doesn't have to take time away from what he needs to get done to handle it."

"Well, at least you get to see your husband when you stay late like that. But I can imagine he's been telling you to go home, that he can handle everything."

A pause on the other end spoke louder than a yes. "We've been having that argument for years; but now he feels like since he's my husband, I'll automatically do what he says instead of doing what I've always done." She sighed. "In some ways, even though I'll hardly ever see him, it'll be a good thing once we break ground on the restaurant. It'll keep him out of my hair here."

Ah, yes. The restaurant Major was opening with Meredith's parents as his investment partners. Not an official B-G business venture but still tied with the development they wanted to do in the Mills—

New leaf. No more negative thoughts about the elder Guidrys. "I can't wait to hear all about it tonight. But if I'm going to make it home to change clothes—since I didn't have the foresight to bring mine to work with me—I've got to get some work done."

"See you tonight."

"Looking forward to it." And she was.

She got the rest of her work wrapped up and the e-mail sent off to Rodney, wished everyone a good weekend, and left work, appreciating the place far more than she had when she had walked in eight hours ago.

Stomach growling when she walked in the house, she fixed a bowl of cereal and ate it sitting on the counter at the kitchen island, bare feet swinging like a kid's. She'd be hungry again before she got to the gallery, but all the better for truly enjoying Major O'Hara's excellent food.

Oh, that reminded her. . .she slipped off the counter, dropped the empty bowl into the sink with a clank, and jogged upstairs to the guest bedroom. On the floor of the closet, in the back, her wedding gift for Meredith and Major leaned against the wall. She wrapped it and carried it downstairs and set it on the kitchen counter, under her keys, so she wouldn't forget to take it with her.

Humming, she went back upstairs to get ready. With the off-and-on drizzle outside, trying to straighten her hair would be pointless; so she plugged in the curling irons and got out the box of bobby pins. After a quick shower to rinse away the day's gunk and wash her face so she could start afresh with her makeup, Alaine wrapped herself in her favorite Turkish bathrobe—the one she'd actually gotten in Turkey.

At six forty-five, her hair in a cascade of curls at the crown of her head, looking pretty good if she did say so herself, in the knee-length, sleeveless black satin dress with the faux-wrap top and the wide, V-neck shawl collar that showed the definition of her collarbones, Alaine grabbed the gift and her keys and headed out the door. Then went back inside and upstairs to her office for the admission passes.

As Alaine had assumed, Meredith waited for her by the chickenlike modern art sculpture in front of the museum, even though Alaine was almost ten minutes early. She handed her keys to the valet and tucked the ticket into her little black purse.

Meredith looked like a 1940s-era movie star, dressed in a chocolate-brown silk sheath dress with a matching three-quarter sleeve bolero jacket and round-toed heels that completed the retro-vibe. What kept her from looking like she wore a costume though, was the modern, smooth, french twist her hair swept up to in the back, with the front side parted and swept behind her ears.

Alaine must look like a child playing dress-up beside Meredith's stately elegance.

To her surprise, Meredith drew her into a hug in greeting. "It's so good to see you. It's been far too long."

"I know. I'm sorry about that. I've been. . .going through some things that made me keep to myself there for a while." Alaine stepped back and tried to make herself taller. But Meredith had at least four inches on her.

"Believe me, I understand. I hope everything worked out okay."

"Not yet, but it's getting there." She motioned toward the front doors, and Meredith fell in step with her. "Before we leave, remind me to give you your wedding present. It's in my car."

"Thank you so much. You didn't have to do that."

"I know I didn't. I hope you like it."

"I'm sure we will."

The atrium-style lobby of the art museum reverberated with voices and music. Alaine handed the admission passes to the concierge. Both Alaine and Meredith were instantly recognized by other attendees and exchanged apologetic looks before being drawn into separate conversations.

At eight o'clock, someone announced that the exhibit was now open for viewing. Alaine broke away from several older ladies and found Meredith, who'd managed to make her way over to the food tables.

Alaine grabbed a canapé and paused for a moment to let the tangy creaminess of the cheese and the herby sweetness of marinated artichoke mingle and dance across her tongue.

Meredith handed her a crystal flute. "Fruit tea."

"Thanks." She grabbed a napkin to wipe away the crumbs from her fingers and mouth.

"Alaine, good to see you. I feel like you've been avoiding me the last few times I've been down to the studio to do my voiceovers." Major O'Hara, dapper in a black chef's jacket edged with silver piping, shook Alaine's hand, then put his arm around Meredith's waist and kissed her temple.

"Chef O'Hara." Alaine grinned at him. "You know how it goes—busy, busy, busy."

"Yeah, especially when your boss is a task-mistress who micro-manages everything you do." He scooted away from Meredith's elbow to his side.

In the company of other acquaintances, Alaine would have been extremely jealous over the display of affection between the couple. With Major and Meredith, she basked in the radiance of their happiness. "Congratulations on getting married. Of course, I'm crushed that you eloped. I was planning on coming out with a full crew to cover it for the show."

"Why do you think we did it?" Meredith winked at her.

"Because Forbes was trying to make you do it his way?" She cringed as soon as the words left her mouth.

But Meredith burst into laughter. "Obviously you know my brother better than either of you have let on." She exchanged a quick glance with Major, who just shook his head. She shrugged and hooked her arm through Alaine's. "Come on. Let's go look at some art."

Most of the other guests had left the atrium. Alaine picked up one of the souvenir booklets explaining the purpose of the Art Without Limits Exhibit and the fund-raiser for the Beausoleil Artists with Disabilities Foundation. Out of the corner of her eye, she caught the bright light of a live, remote camera. Yep. There was the cub reporter who'd been assigned to cover the event for the ten o'clock broadcast. Nope. Not even a twinge of envy. She smiled to herself.

She and Meredith discussed the pieces in soft voices as they moved through the gallery—discovering they both had similar tastes and noticed much of the same aspects of the workmanship.

They rounded a corner, and Alaine released a small gasp. The large, framed painting portrayed a dancing couple who looked quite a bit like Fred Astaire and Ginger Rogers. The artist had obviously studied Monet's techniques because it looked like something that could have been done by the great impressionist.

Beside her, Meredith exclaimed over the excellence of the work, but Alaine was lost for words. She wanted it. The painting represented the two things she enjoyed most in life: art and ballroom dance.

She glanced down at the card under it which gave the artist's name and the name of the piece. A red dot had been affixed to the corner. This piece would be part of the fund-raising auction. She flipped open her little purse—and then remembered she hadn't put a pen in it. Instead, she opened the booklet and located the page the piece was on, which she dog-eared. Surely it wouldn't go for more than what she could afford to pay, would it?

"Excuse me, I want to go make a bid on this one."

"I'll go with you. I saw one I want to bid on, too."

They found the table where the sheets for the silent auction were laid out. Not too many people buzzed around them—but the night was still young. Alaine found the sheet for her painting. . .and groaned in disappointment. Someone had already placed an opening bid of one thousand dollars—far too expensive for Alaine's meager art budget.

Oh, well. It wasn't meant to be.

The camera light caught her attention again, and she turned toward it, only to find it practically in her face. But the person standing to the side of the cameraman wasn't the cub reporter from Channel Six.

"Teri Jones." Alaine gave the woman who was her direct competitor a tight smile.

"Alaine Delacroix. I'm surprised you're not working tonight.

What, did they decide this story was too important for the social-scene reporter?"

"That's rich, coming from you." Before she could wave her off, Meredith joined her.

"And Meredith Guidry." Teri's eyes narrowed as she looked between them. "That's right, B-G is one of your show's biggest sponsors. Should have guessed."

"Well, you guessed wrong. Meredith and I are friends."

"And it's Meredith *O'Hara* now, thank you." The chill in Meredith's voice surprised Alaine, but she didn't want to break eye contact with the vulture for a moment, not sure when the attack would come.

Teri snapped at her cameraman, and he started filming. Alaine adjusted her expression to try to ensure she looked pleasant and happy to be interviewed by the woman who made Jerry Springer look like a social worker—the woman who'd tried to ruin Bekka Blakeley's career so many years ago.

Teri raised her microphone and turned to face the camera. "I'm here with Alaine Delacroix, of Channel Six news, and Meredith Guidry O'Hara, of Boudreaux-Guidry Enterprises. Mrs. O'Hara"—she turned and thrust the microphone in Meredith's face—"what do you think of the exhibit?"

Meredith began to give a glowing review of what they'd seen so far. Teri cut her off midstream.

"Ms. Delacroix, I find it very interesting you're here with an executive director of Boudreaux-Guidry Enterprises tonight. After all, weren't you one of the main organizers of the meeting in Moreaux Mills last night protesting B-G's development plans?"

She'd guessed as much. "I am not involved in the situation. I was there merely as an observer, out of care and concern for my family, who live and work in the Mills."

"It's my understanding you gave a very. . .*passionate* introduction of the lawyer who came out to speak to them—Forbes Guidry, if I'm not mistaken."

Alaine's stomach twisted around that canapé she'd eaten. "Are you going somewhere with this? If so, I'd appreciate you getting to your point so that I can go back to enjoying my evening."

"Touchy." Teri's smile became predatory. "My sources tell me that Mr. Guidry has taken on this case pro bono."

Alaine shrugged. "As I'm aware of no case being filed, I can neither confirm nor deny that statement."

"It's common knowledge that you have a personal relationship with Mr. Guidry—after all, it was on your own, um, show that you aired tape of the two of you taking dancing lessons together."

Alaine raised her eyebrows and shifted her weight in annoyance.

"It stands to reason, then, that if he isn't getting paid for his legal services by the people in Moreaux Mills, he's being remunerated in a completely nonmonetary manner. After all, what wouldn't a girl do to make sure Mommy and Daddy got the best lawyer money—or whatever—can buy?"

All Alaine could do was gape at her. The nasty insinuation hung in the air between them; but before Alaine could recover, Meredith stepped between them.

"If you air that—or any other filth like it—on your show, you will be sued. And I can't imagine your bosses will be happy with you for generating yet *another* slander suit from my family against you and the station."

Teri smirked. "Come on," she nudged the cameraman. "I've got what I need out of these two."

"Meredith, I'm sorry. You shouldn't have involved yourself in that."

Meredith pulled her aside to a quiet corner. "What was she talking about? What case?"

The last thing she wanted was for that to come between them. "I can't talk about it. I've given my word."

"Okay. I won't ask any more about it."

Alaine's stomach hurt. "And I don't want you thinking that I've behaved improperly toward your brother, either. We've spent some time together, and he agreed to do a favor for me—for my family and their neighbors. But there is nothing between us beyond that."

Kindness beamed from Meredith's light-brown eyes. "I never suspected there was." She hooked her arm through Alaine's again and led her back toward the gallery. "But I'm still holding out hope."

Chapter 21

"Fat-free, sugar-free, mocha latte." Forbes handed over his Coffee Club card for his twenty-five-cent discount.

"I guess it's not even worth asking you if you want an order of beignets to go with that, Mr. Guidry?" The perky cashier batted her eyes at him.

"As always, the answer is no thank you, Kristi." And as always, he refrained from reminding her that he was almost old enough to be her father. "Just coffee." He paid her for it, then scoped out the large café.

He didn't like this no-name, no-picture deal of Shon's. Petite brunette wearing black-and-white wasn't that much to go on. But right now, no one fitting that description sat by herself at a table or in the armchairs over by the greenery-filled fireplace or out on the deck overlooking the river.

Instead of committing himself to a table before his date arrived, Forbes stood at the coffee bar, feeling very much like a cowboy in one of those old westerns Meredith and Major liked watching so much.

The front door swung open. Forbes straightened. Though backlit, the silhouette entering was definitely female—a petite female. She paused, probably letting her eyes adjust to the dim interior. He checked his watch—9:21. Not just punctual, but early. Nice.

She moved toward the cashier. Forbes's knees went weak. Alaine Delacroix pushed her sunglasses up on top of her head and placed her order.

Alaine? Could Shon have possibly—but if he had, why hadn't he said anything? Forbes pulled out the copy of the e-mail with the description Shon had sent. Petite. Check. Brunette. Well, Forbes would have called her hair black, but it could work as a description. Wearing a black-and-white top. He glanced back up at Alaine, making sure to keep himself partially hidden behind the coffee-making station. She was wearing a black-and-white polka-dot jacket. Three strikes—er, three hits—okay, so the baseball metaphor didn't work.

He waited for her to make her way down the long counter to the corner where she'd pick up her coffee, and from whence she'd be able to see him.

Their eyes met. Hers widened, and her full lips formed a small *O*. "What. . .what are you doing here?"

"Good morning to you, too." He saluted her with his coffee. "Are you meeting someone here?"

"I. . .uh. . .yes, I'm supposed to be meeting someone here."

"Devastatingly handsome and wearing blue?"

Her face went from ghostly pale to flushed in a split second. "Tall, dark hair, and wearing. . .red." She frowned and pulled a folded piece of paper from her purse. "It definitely says red, not blue. Wait—arc you here for. . .are you meeting someone here from Let's Do Coffee?"

His face went hot. "I am. Petite, brunette, wearing a black-and-white top. If that isn't you. . ." He scanned the room again, just to make sure he hadn't missed someone else fitting the description.

"Extra large café au lait," the barista called.

Alaine stepped over to grab the tall, ceramic mug. She poured what looked like half the sugar shaker into it, tasted, and added a bit more sugar. He shuddered. It had to be sludgelike by now.

"So if I'm not meeting you," she said, returning to stand at the bar beside him, "and you're not meeting me, maybe we shouldn't be standing here talking to each other when they do come in, or else they might not realize we're the ones."

"Are you trying to avoid me?" He sipped his latte, enjoying how the strong flavor of the espresso picked up the subtle hint of the skim milk and the light sweetness and chocolate of the sugar-free mocha flavoring, trying not to let himself be disappointed that Alaine wasn't here for him.

"Avoid you?"

"You haven't returned my phone calls."

She traced her finger around the handle of her mug. "I wasn't sure what to say to you."

Setting his cup down, he leaned forward. "I only wanted to thank you. To try to tell you how much what you did meant to me. And to say that I hope your folks didn't give you a hard time for it."

Her gaze dropped to his mouth, but then just as quickly, she closed her eyes and turned her head away. Heat coursed through his body. He'd been wanting to kiss her since the first moment they met—actually a long time before that. Unless his eyes deceived him, she'd just told him she'd thought about it, too.

He took a step back for safety. "I saw your name made the newspaper blurb. That didn't make things worse, did it?"

"My parents understood why I did what I did. My boss offered me a promotion to cover the story." She turned her profile to him and leaned back against the edge of the bar's top, cradling her mug in both hands.

"Congratulations."

"I didn't take it. I have a wonderful job—better than most midmarket TV journalists can boast—and I'd be an idiot to give it up to work longer, harder hours under someone else's direction instead of having the virtual autonomy I have on my show." She took a sip of coffee, and finally looked at him again, her dark eyes sparkling like onyx. "Besides, that kind of journalism demands objectivity, and there's no way I could stay objective about this story."

This time, her eyes stayed locked on his, but he found himself once again leaning toward her, toward those enticing, full lips.

They both startled when the bell on the front door jangled. A tall man—a very tall man—with hair almost as dark as Alaine's and wearing a bright red University of Louisiana–Bonneterre T-shirt entered the café and stood inside the door, scanning the interior.

Alaine looked like she might tuck tail and run. Forbes might aid her, if it came to that.

The man's gaze came to rest on Alaine. Forbes's guard rose immediately at the smile that split the guy's face. He approached them. Alaine grew more stiff, and Forbes couldn't help but be impressed by the guy's height. He had to be at least six foot eight, if not taller.

"I think I'm here to meet you. Petite, black hair, black-and-white polka-dot top and black capris."

Alaine nodded, a silent, forced smile on her face, her shoulders practically flat on the bar from leaning back to look up at her date.

"Alaine Delacroix," the man breathed. "They told me I might recognize you once I saw you, but I had no idea I'd be this lucky. I'm Riley."

Forbes was surprised he couldn't hear Alaine's teeth rattle with the force of Riley's handshake.

"Can I get you something—but you already have something." The lumbering giant at long last noticed Forbes. "You two know each other?"

"Riley, this is a business acquaintance of mine, Forbes Guidry."

Forbes's own teeth knocked together when he shook Riley's hand. "Nice to meet you." No. No it wasn't. He should grab Alaine by the arm and sweep her out of here. Wait—a *business acquaintance?* He turned to stare at her.

"I'll go place my order. Don't go anywhere now, Alaine Delacroix."

As soon as Too-Tall was out of earshot, Forbes confronted her. "A *business acquaintance?* I thought we were well beyond that—friends, at least."

Alaine looked over her shoulder, then pushed him back a few steps, her hand burning like a branding iron on his chest. "What was I supposed to say?" she whispered. "I'm here in good faith to have coffee with this guy. He's paid for the privilege of being set up on a blind date with someone—who just happens to be *Alaine Delacroix*." She imitated the way Riley drawled her name. "I need to afford him the same courtesy I would expect to receive if he'd already been here talking to a woman he knows and spends a lot of time with."

Yeah, except Forbes wanted to stake his claim, to let the behemoth know Alaine was spoken for, whether she knew it or not.

The front door chimed again. Forbes didn't want to look, but he did. And instantly regretted it. In walked a woman who could only be classified as *on the prowl*. And she was wearing a black-and-white top—a skin-tight, zebra-striped halter top to be exact.

Alaine's eyes danced with barely suppressed amusement when she looked up at him. "I believe your petite brunette in a black-and-white top just walked in." She picked up her mug from the bar. "Have fun."

"So glad you find this funny." Forbes narrowed his eyes at her.

Alaine laughed. The only thing that could have made the woman any less suitable for him would be if she were wearing leather motorcycle chaps instead of shorts so short they were almost indecent. Alaine had been a little worried when she realized Forbes was here for a date—and not with her—that he might meet someone he'd like more than her. Though Alaine hated passing judgment based on a first appearance, she was pretty good at figuring people out by how they dressed.

This woman defined *cougar*—an older woman out to snag a good-looking, younger man. Alaine hadn't thought Shon would handle that type; but she supposed as long as the money was green enough, he'd take on just about any client.

Alaine's date, Mr. I-Don't-Know-How-to-Dress-for-a-Coffee-

Date, returned to them. With a sigh, Forbes excused himself and went over to speak to Ms. Zebra Stripe.

"Shall we get a table?" Alaine swept her arm to the side to indicate the half-full dining room.

"Yeah. You get a table, Alaine Delacroix, and I'll join you as soon as I get my stuff."

Only with extreme effort did she stop herself from telling him not to call her by her full name. The next half hour would be the longest of her life.

By design, more likely than by chance, Forbes chose a table not too far away and sat so he faced Alaine. As Riley went on about himself, Alaine watched Forbes and his date out of the corner of her eye.

At first, the woman leaned forward, touching her face, her chest, her throat. All signs she found Forbes quite attractive. As time progressed, her hands became more occupied with her coffee cup, then dropped to her lap.

Alaine stifled a grin when the woman crossed her arms, sitting as far back in her chair as she could. Whatever she and Forbes were discussing, the woman didn't like it.

Yep. There she went. Forbes stood and shook her hand, then watched the woman walk out. But instead of leave, he went over and grabbed a newspaper off the rack and returned to his table to read it.

Alaine tried to focus on Riley. But now he was talking about the college baseball game he planned to attend today. And if he said *Alaine Delacroix* one more time—

"You know, Riley," she interrupted, "I really don't follow baseball. Do you like art? I went to the opening of a wonderful exhibit down at the Bonneterre Fine Arts Center last night."

Confusion filled Riley's mossy-green eyes. "Art?"

"Yes. I'm a painter, too. Well, I don't get to do it very often anymore. But I started out as an art major in college." She talked about some of her favorite artists for a few minutes until Riley completely glazed over. Yeah, turnabout's not always fair play. He'd want to leave soon.

"Do you like ballet?" Now she'd make sure he didn't ask for another date with *Alaine Delacroix*. "The new season of the Bonneterre Ballet Company starts in a few weeks, and I'm thinking about getting season tickets." Not that she would—she couldn't afford the expense. But he didn't need to know that.

"B–ballet?" He glanced over his shoulder toward the door.

"Yes. Oh, and the new opera season starts soon as well." Of course, she hated opera.

"Wow. We really don't have anything in common." He glanced at his watch. "Look at that. If I'm going to make it to the ballpark before the first pitch, I'd better go."

"Oh, really? So soon?"

"Yeah—yes. It was great to meet you." He held out his hand.

"You, too." Alaine didn't want to have her brains scrambled again. She barely touched her fingertips to his. *Don't let the door hit you in the fanny on the way out.*

He hurried away. She thought about calling him back to nag him about putting his coffee mug in the dish tray beside the trash can, but that would probably be overkill. With a laugh, she disposed of his cup, then took hers to the counter for a refill.

While waiting, she turned around to see what Forbes was up to. He still sat reading the newspaper and sipping his coffee—at her table. Typical. Yet extremely gratifying.

With her coffee fortified with sugar, she returned to the table, sat, and pulled the "Style" section out of the stack of newspaper he wasn't currently reading. She pretended to read it for a few moments.

Finally, Forbes lowered the *A* section. "So?"

"So, what?"

"How did you like dear Riley?"

"Oh, he's a lovely man—I'm sure Shon will find the right woman for him soon."

"But. . . ?" Forbes couldn't hide the hint of vulnerability in his eyes.

She thought about stringing him along, but what would be the point? He already knew the answer. "But it isn't me."

He snapped the paper upright and disappeared behind it. "I could have told you that."

"And what about Ms. Zebra Stripe?" Alaine didn't look up from her section.

"Not for me."

"Looked like things didn't go so well." She flexed her jaw to straighten her expression, just in case he dropped the paper again. "Looked like she got kind of mad at you."

The paper rustled, then crumpled when he dropped his hands to the table. "If you must know, I mentioned her age, that I wasn't really looking to date someone significantly older than me."

Alaine cringed. "Oh, that poor woman. That was a horrible thing to say."

"No kidding. Especially since she then told me that we graduated from high school together—and she had skipped a grade a few years before."

"So she's a year *younger* than you?"

He grimaced—and even wearing that sour expression was utterly adorable. "Yeah. Talk about foot-in-mouth. She said when she realized who I was that she'd hoped maybe we could attend our reunion together in the fall. Guess it'll just give all the women there something more to use to gossip about me."

"The girls from your high school class like to gossip about you?" Oh to be a fly on the wall at that reunion.

"Yeah—about how horrible a boyfriend I was or how I haven't been able to have a long-term relationship, ever." He smoothed out his section of the paper and refolded it.

Alaine's heart gave a trill like a piccolo. "They don't know what they're missing."

His eyes, almost as dark blue as his shirt, snapped to hers. She couldn't believe she'd said that aloud. She couldn't do this, could she? Yet if she walked away, would she be giving up the only chance she might have for falling in love? She held his gaze, not caring if her indecision showed.

"You know"—Forbes leaned forward and lowered his voice—"falling for your parents' lawyer isn't the worst thing you can do. No matter what that woman from Channel Three said to you last night."

"How did you—"

"Meredith called me last night to ask me what was going on. I didn't tell her much. Just that we're friends, and that I'm doing a favor for your parents. She doesn't need to be dragged into the middle of this."

"I agree. But Forbes, did she tell you how truly vulgar Teri's insinuations were? Other people are bound to wonder the same thing."

"Let them wonder." He reached across the table and took her hand in his.

Her pulse pounded through her head in dizzying waves. "You don't understand. As a representative of the TV station, and especially because of the nature of my show and my primary viewers being stay-at-home moms and senior citizens, I have to protect my reputation as much as I can. If a rumor like that were to sprout legs, it could create a scandal, and the last thing we need is negative public attention on what we're doing."

His thumb made slow, soft circles on her palm. "You worry too much about what other people think. What do you *feel*, Alaine Delacroix?"

All she could feel right now was the way her body tingled in response to his rubbing her palm. "I. . ."

Before she could think, before she could react, Forbes leaned across the table and kissed her. Soft, gentle, undemanding, and too quickly ended. Her hand spasmed in his.

"Need more time to think?"

She pulled her hand out of his and reached for the section of newspaper in front of her, folded it in half, and started fanning herself with it. Feel? The only time she ever gave herself over to her feelings was when she was drawing or painting. Which she hadn't done regularly since college. Did she still know how to feel?

"If you hadn't found out about this whole development thing our parents are involved in right after the banquet, would you have gone out with me?" He took the paper out of her hand and recaptured it.

"Yes, but—"

"And do you think that if we'd gone out on a date, with no family feud looming on the horizon, you might have enjoyed it?"

"I do, but—"

"And if you'd enjoyed that date, would you have gone out with me again?"

"I probably would have, but—"

"And if we'd started seeing each other regularly, don't you think you'd have fallen in love with me as much as you have while you've been trying to avoid me the past month?"

Lawyers. "I've never said I'm in love with you."

He grinned at her. "But you are. Why else would you have flung yourself in front of me to save me from the verbal arrows those people were shooting at me Thursday night? You risked your parents' ire—as well as this reputation of yours that you're now concerned about—without a moment's hesitation. Not to mention the fact that you sat here not twenty minutes ago and ran off our dear friend Riley just so you could spend more time with me. Really now—opera? ballet?"

"Arrrggghhh." She tossed her head back. "Do you always have to get your way?"

Grinning, he leaned over and kissed her again. Her entire skeleton melted into a puddle of wax, and she could barely focus on him when the kiss ended mere seconds—or millennia—later.

He traced her cheek and jaw with his free hand. "Yes, I always get my way."

Chapter 22

Meredith leaned into Forbes's one-armed squeeze. "You look like the mouse who found the cheese."

"It's a beautiful day." He should have asked Alaine to come to church with him this morning. Yesterday had clinched it for him: Alaine fit into his life quite nicely. And while he wasn't ready to take any kind of drastic steps, he wanted everyone to know she was his.

"Really?" Meredith glanced out the bank of windows behind her—on the other side of them, a heavy downpour obscured everything beyond about three feet. "This unusually chipper mood doesn't have anything to do with your attending a certain meeting in a certain area of town with a certain TV news reporter, does it?"

"Maybe."

Instead of breaking into a smile, Meredith's frown increased. "Forbes, weren't you listening when I told you what Teri Jones—"

"You know you can't believe a thing that woman says. How many times have Mom and Dad sued her and that station already?"

"That's beside the point. She will spread the rumor that you're taking payment for handling the Moreaux Mills case in form of. . . well, intimate favors from Alaine." Meredith's voice dropped so low, he barely heard the last part of her statement.

He could tell his shrug frustrated his sister further. "Let people think what they want. In the end, the truth always manages to trump the rumors."

Meredith touched his arm. "Mom and Dad were very hurt when they saw the newspaper article. They don't understand how you could even consider taking on clients who want to sue them."

"Not to sue them. To sue their company. There's a huge difference." He smiled and nodded at several acquaintances passing by in the crowded foyer. Everyone waited for the rain to ease before leaving. They might be here for a while.

"Don't try to argue semantics. B-G is us: It's Mom and Dad, and Major and me. It's the people we work closely with every day." Her volume increased with her intensity. She glanced around.

"No one's listening to us, Mere." He looked around, too, just to be sure. "But you haven't talked to the people who're about to lose their businesses, their homes, everything they've worked for their whole lives, just because Mom and Dad—or B-G or however you want to think about it—want to buy up all of their property as cheap as they can so they can tear it all to the ground and rebuild Warehouse Row and Moreaux Mills in their own image."

"They're only buying foreclosures and from people who want to sell. Some of those people will never make as much as they'll get by selling their property to B-G."

"Not at the scandalously low rate the city council's inspectors set the property values at. Most of them, if they sell, won't even be able to cover the full amount of their mortgages and small-business loans."

Meredith pressed her fingertips to the back of her neck and rolled her head as if to ease tight muscles. "I don't want to fight with you about it. Actually, I don't want to know about it." She inhaled and released a deep breath. "I thought you were planning to attend the art exhibit opening Friday night."

"Oh, you know me and art."

"Yeah, I know. Paint-by-numbers or Elvis on black velvet."

He reached toward her, about to put her in a headlock to make her take that back, but stopped. Not only would it bother Meredith, it would look ridiculous. "You forgot anything made with macaroni and glue."

Major joined them. "Looks like it's letting up a little bit. I'll go pull the car up so you don't have to get soaked."

"That's not necess—"

Major pressed his finger to his wife's lips and stared her down.

She took his hand in both of hers and pulled it away. "Thank you, dear. I would greatly appreciate you for doing that."

"I'll see you over at Errol and Maggie's." Forbes unfurled his umbrella so it was ready to open as soon as he walked out the door.

"At Errol and Maggie's?" Meredith shook her head.

"Yeah. . .for lunch. Like every week after church."

"You mean, you're going?" She took a step forward, utter confusion twisting her features.

Her confusion proved to be contagious. "Of course I'm going. I go every week, just like you do."

"But you know Mom and Dad are going to be there."

He nodded. "Just like they are every week—well, except when they fly off to Boston at the last minute."

"They're going to want to talk to you about this case, Forbes."

Ah, so that's what had her worried—controversy over the dinner table. She'd always had a delicate stomach, easily upset by the least bit of conflict. "They're not going to have it out with me at the table in front of the rest of the family. And if I were to skip out, it would look like I'm ashamed of what I've done or afraid of them, and I'm neither." He pulled his sister into a hug. "I'm a big boy. I can handle Mom and Dad's being a little miffed at me."

"But they're not just miffed—"

"Enough, Mere." He took her by the shoulders and held her at arms' length. "I *can* handle this. Everything's going to be okay. Once I've explained everything to them, I think they'll not only realize I have a point but they'll see things from my point of view and help me work to change what's happening."

Meredith still looked skeptical, but someone called to her that Major had just pulled up. "Come on, we'll drive you over to your car so you don't have to get quite so soaked."

"Thanks, Sis."

But even with his umbrella, his shoes and pants' legs were drenched just from the few feet he had to dash to get from Meredith's SUV to the Jag. Whether it was her intention to keep Major completely out of the controversy or if she'd actually decided to believe Forbes when he said he could handle facing their parents, she hadn't mentioned it again in the brief, shared car ride.

Driving in rain so heavy made claws of anxiety dig into his shoulders—not because of worrying about his own driving ability, but because of everyone else on the road. By the time he arrived at Uncle Errol and Aunt Maggie's house, the muscles across his upper back were tight to the point of snapping. He remained in the car a moment, doing some deep breathing to try to relax before he walked into what could be an adversarial environment. For all he'd told Meredith that Mom and Dad wouldn't make a scene in front of the extended family, if they were angry enough, no telling what they might do.

He joined his thirtysomething siblings and cousins in the florida room at the rear of the house.

"Forbes!"

"Hey, Forbes!"

"You made it!"

Everyone's greetings were bright, cheery—a little *too* bright and cheery. And who was that with Anne? He took another deep breath and slapped on a smile as the tall, curvaceous brunette slinked over to him.

"Evelyn. What a surprise." He took her proffered hands, but did not move in toward her when it looked like she wanted to exchange a kiss on the cheek.

"I was rather surprised when your parents invited me Friday. I guess they realized how homesick I've been the last few weeks. I usually hit a point after about a month where I go through that. But never before have my clients invited me into the bosom of their family to help me feel better about being so far from my own."

Right. Knowing his parents, they'd invited her for some reason of their own, probably because of his involvement with the Mills case. "I'm sorry to hear you've been down."

A melancholy realization struck Forbes, the same feeling as when he'd been told at age eight that Santa Claus wasn't real. In questioning his parents' motives behind inviting a lonely woman they worked with on a daily basis to come to Sunday dinner, he'd taken a giant leap away from the person he'd been not long ago who believed everything his parents said and never second-guessed any decisions they made. He'd lost the last remaining vestige of childhood idealism.

His younger brothers and male cousins seemed eager to recapture Evelyn's attention. Forbes excused himself and ducked out of the room as Major and Meredith's entrance drew attention away from him.

He wandered aimlessly down the hall. He didn't want to go into the living room, family room, or kitchen, where the remainder of the family would be. Being honest with himself, his intestines twisted in knots at the prospect of facing his parents—that they might not hold on to the reserve for which everyone in the family admired them. But would they really do it in front of Evelyn?

The clanging of Maggie's handheld bell echoed through the house. In just a few short moments, he'd find out exactly how his parents were going to react. Steeling himself, he headed for the dining room. He ignored Meredith's doleful expression when he took his seat beside her.

During Papere's blessing, Forbes prayed for wisdom—as well as patience—for the confrontation he was sure would be coming, from the assiduous manner in which his mother avoided making eye contact with him.

Once platters and bowls started going around the table, Forbes got an idea of why his parents might have invited Evelyn on this of all Sundays. She became the center of attention—in which she seemed to revel.

Mom glowed like a proud, well, mother. "Evelyn has done so much in the few short weeks she's been here to further the Warehouse Row project. It's amazing how she's managed to clear some roadblocks that have been hanging us up for months and months."

Evelyn preened under his mother's compliments. "Now, Mairee, don't make it sound like more than it was. I'm just doing my job. It's easier to make something seem simple if one has experience in it."

"I'm only telling the truth, dear. We've been wanting to move on this development project for at least six months, and it's your dedication that's made it happen."

Forbes pushed a wad of chicken and rice casserole around on his plate. He should have listened to Meredith. Fast food from a drive-through eaten at home alone would have been much preferable than listening to his mother fawn over the person who was probably more culpable for the inequities even now bearing down on the good people in the Mills than he could currently prove.

"So is there a groundbreaking date yet?" Major asked. "Jennifer and I have teamed up to do some interviews recently, so I'm eager to know when I might be able to start hiring." He cast a grin at his sister-in-law across the table from them. "After all, I can't let Jenn have all the good candidates simply because she can put them to work immediately."

"For Warehouse Row, yes, we should be breaking ground by Labor Day. That is, of course, as long as we know we're going to be able to go ahead with the rest of the Mills development project."

Forbes tightly controlled his expression when he met his mother's glare. The crowded dining room became chillingly silent.

"After all, what we're doing is best for Bonneterre."

Forbes wiped his mouth and dropped his napkin on the table. Meredith grabbed his forearm and squeezed. With gentle but firm pressure, he disengaged from his sister's silent expression of concern without breaking eye contact with his mother.

" 'Best for Bonneterre'? Don't you mean best for Boudreaux-Guidry Enterprises' bottom line? Because from what I've seen and heard from talking to the people who already live in Moreaux Mills, what's happening is definitely not best for them."

"You can't believe what those people say. They're a drain on our city's resources—always applying for hardship loans and trying to talk their way out of paying their taxes, all the while reneging on their financial responsibilities. We're offering them a helping hand by buying them out."

"After using your considerable influence with the city council to get their property values dropped and their property taxes raised." He shook his head and stood. "I would never have believed my own parents would do something so underhanded—would exploit other people just to make more money."

Near the end of the table, his father shot out of his chair so fast it fell backward with a bang on the floor. "You will apologize for making such an accusation."

"No, sir, I will not apologize. Now more than ever, I believe what you are doing is wrong, and I will do whatever it takes to help the people whose homes and businesses you're intent on ruining." He glanced around the room. No one would look at him.

"Lawson, Forbes." Papere stood as well. "Surely this is a discussion best saved for *private.*"

"Papere, Mamere," Forbes inclined his head toward his grandparents at either end of the enormous table, "my apologies for disrupting dinner. And you're right, this is a discussion best saved for another time and another place—when *all* parties are present, including their legal counsel."

Meredith gave a little gasp. He touched her shoulder and pushed his chair out of the way. "Until such a time, I will consider myself excused from all family gatherings." With a final half bow, he walked out of the dining room.

No one called his name—no one came after him. Just as well. At least it let him know where the entire family stood on the matter: not with him.

By the time he made it to his car, his lungs hurt from pressure worse than what he'd experienced the first time he'd been scuba diving and had gone too deep.

But he could handle this. He could. He'd handled everything else that had come his way in life. He could handle this. Except no matter what he'd faced in his life before now, he could always count on his family to be there for him.

Not this time.

The pressure increased tenfold. He pointed the car east and drove, not caring where he went so long as he was moving. The conversation he'd had with Major just a few months ago about honoring one's parents replayed with the vividness of surround sound in his head.

Taking a stand had been the right thing to do. Wasn't part of honoring one's parents helping them see when they were doing something that hurt others? Accepting what they were doing without raising a question as to the ethics behind their actions would be dishonoring himself.

He pulled the Jag to a stop—in front of Delacroix Gardens. Though the rain had slackened to a steady drizzle, the cloud-darkened sky made it possible for him to see movement in the lighted, second-floor dormer windows of the building that looked like a cottage out of a fairy tale. He pulled into the small gravel parking lot at the side of the dual-purpose house. Unsure of where the entrance to their home would be, Forbes approached through the pergola that stood over the sidewalk leading to the shop's front door, not bothering with his umbrella.

A sign hung over what looked like a doorbell button. After Hours Deliveries Press Here. He pressed it; a chime like church bells echoed distantly. In the shelter of the porch, he wiped the worst of the rain from his face and waited.

The door swung open. "We're closed on Sund—Forbes." JD looked as shocked to see him as Forbes was himself at being here. "Come in, get in out of the rain."

"Thanks. I'm sorry for dropping in on you like this."

"Not at all. Our door is always open to you." JD ushered him in and closed and locked the door behind him. "Come on upstairs where you can dry off a bit."

A cacophony of scents slammed Forbes in the nose—sweet and earthy and spicy. . .and utterly homey. He followed Alaine's father through the flower shop's back room—weirdly shadowy and sparkly at the same time, lined with shelves filled with glass vases in every color imaginable—to a staircase at the back.

"Watch out for the lift chair." JD skirted around the seat attached to a beam that ran up the right-hand side of the staircase. "You just missed seeing Joe, Nikki, Alaine, and our youngest son, Tony. Solange and I were just settling down for our coffee and newspaper."

Forbes stopped. "I hadn't considered—I really don't want to interrupt your day."

"Of course you can." JD came down until he was two steps above Forbes and laid his hands on Forbes's shoulders. "And I can tell by your demeanor that you're having a rough day. You've obviously come here because something is bothering you. From what Alaine's told us, I imagine it has to do with your parents' reaction to finding out you're helping us. So let us do what we can to make you feel better."

Forbes tried to clear the cement from his throat. "Thank you, Mr. Delacroix. That means a lot to me."

"Please, I've asked you to call me JD. Come on, now. The coffee should be ready, and Solange has some baklava hidden in the kitchen that Voula Pappas sent over from the restaurant for the store yesterday."

The stairs came up into a hallway, and a warm light at the end beckoned them forward. Forbes entered a kitchen that looked like it was straight out of the 1950s—the happiness and innocence of the decor imbuing him with a sliver of optimism that, somehow, everything would be okay.

"Joseph, who—" Mrs. Delacroix came into the kitchen through the attached, very informal dining area. "Forbes, welcome to our home." She narrowed her eyes in an intense study of him. "You go sit in the living room. I will bring you coffee and baklava." She winked at her husband.

"Best do what she says, son." JD grinned and waved Forbes on through the kitchen.

If the kitchen had been 1950s kitsch, the living room was definitely Mediterranean, from the soft, seaside colors to the terra-cotta floor tiles to the Portuguese decorative touches around the room. The pressure in his chest eased even more from the warm, welcoming embrace the room wrapped him in.

Moments later, Solange entered with an enormous coffee mug and a plate of pastries, both of which she set on the low table in front of Forbes. He opened his mouth to ask for milk—and to see if they had any artificial sweetener—then realized that Solange had already taken the liberty of doctoring his coffee. It probably would be full fat milk and too much sugar. He'd drink enough to be polite.

As soon as the coffee hit his tongue, he wondered that Alaine would be able to drink coffee made by anyone else. The smooth creaminess coated his tongue—so it was half-and-half, not milk—and she'd added just enough sugar for a hint of sweetness, but not too much.

The muscles in his shoulders started to ease.

JD and Solange let him drink coffee and eat the sticky Greek pastries in peace, allowing his mind and thoughts to settle.

Finally, he took one more swallow of the coffee, set it on the table, and leaned forward, resting his elbows on his knees. "I just walked out on my family's Sunday dinner. I accused my parents of being—" What exactly had he said? "I accused them of being underhanded and of exploiting the people in the Mills. In front of our entire extended family."

"And you're feeling like a bad son." JD swayed back and forth slowly in his plush rocking chair. "If I may take a wild guess, as the oldest son, you've always felt it was your responsibility to step up and fill in for your parents whenever they couldn't be there. You're basically the third parent in your immediate family. Am I right?"

Forbes nodded.

"When anything goes wrong, you see it as a challenge that you can and will overcome."

That went without saying. He nodded again.

"When one of your brothers or sisters disobeyed or openly defied your parents, you took it personally and didn't understand why your parents were sometimes lax in enforcing their own rules with your younger siblings."

Consternated but intrigued, Forbes propped his chin in his hand.

JD continued his slow, contemplative rocking. "But you decided not to go to work for your parents when you finished college because. . .why?"

"Because. . ." He thought back twenty years. "Because I was afraid that if I went into the family business, I'd never be my own man. I'd never see if I could make something of myself without constantly taking from my parents."

"And how do you feel about the man you've become?"

Forbes couldn't answer right away. He had a good life—made an enviable salary, lived in a luxurious home in an exclusive community, drove a high-end vehicle, knew all the "right" people. And he lived alone and ate dinner by himself most nights. "There are some things I'd like to change about myself. Some things I'm working on already. Others I probably need to spend more time studying to see how I can improve."

"Do you think you're a better man than your father?"

"No. I'm a different man than my father."

JD's head bobbed slightly in what could have been a nod. "That's a good attitude to have. I wish I'd realized that before my father passed away. Forbes, you are a good man. You have high morals and ethics. And if I'm not mistaken, you're a man of faith as well."

"Yes, sir." He could visualize everything JD mentioned as if they were boxes of different shapes and sizes. Forbes wasn't sure just how they all stacked together.

"Because I know those things about you, I know that your parents are, deep down, good people. They may have just forgotten it as other influences, such as wealth and prestige, have drawn the curtains over the qualities that they found important enough to instill in their son. The best way you can honor them is to help them remember those greater qualities, help them remember that they're good people."

Air rushed into Forbes's lungs, filling every cell in his body with hope. All of JD's boxes made sense, stacked together quite neatly. "Thank you. That's what I needed to hear. Because the next time I see my parents will most likely be across a conference table with their lawyer—the managing partner in my law firm."

"You have to know that we don't want this to go to court if it doesn't have to. We're praying for an amicable negotiation because we don't want you estranged from your parents, from your family. It might make things awkward."

Forbes could understand how not being welcome at his own family's functions could be awkward for him, but. . . "I'm not sure what you mean by awkward."

JD exchanged a look with his wife—a look replete with mysterious smiles. "Because when you marry our daughter, we want your family to be there to celebrate along with us."

Chapter 23

Alaine tucked the phone receiver between shoulder and ear and continued writing copy. "Alaine Delacroix."

"Good morning." Forbes's smooth, mellow voice oozed out of the phone to wrap Alaine in warmth.

"Good morning to you, too." Caterpillars of excitement crawled up and down her skin at the thought of seeing him this afternoon. "You sound like you're feeling better today than you were last night."

"It's a new day. The sun is shining. And it's a holiday."

"Rub it in, thanks." She sent the finished copy to the printer so she could read through and make any revisions quickly before she went in to film the studio segments of today's broadcast.

"Since I'm off the hook from going to my family's cookout tonight, I'm all yours today." While he hadn't gone into great detail over the phone last night, her heart still ached knowing that she'd caused a rift between Forbes and his close-knit family by involving him in the case.

"I'll be heading out there in about an hour. I've got to roll some tape and edit together a piece before noon so I can run it during my live segment. So you'll probably want to wait until after one o'clock before meeting me."

"I'd rather come and watch you work."

"I'd rather you didn't. No offense, but I have a really tight schedule with this, and I don't need any distractions." Nor the jittery feeling she got whenever he was around.

"I distract you?" The low growl in his voice very nearly pushed her out of her chair and onto the floor in a swoon.

"Incessantly and unforgivably."

"Well, on that note, I won't tell you what else I talked about with your parents yesterday."

Finding out Forbes had been at her parents' house for almost three hours yesterday afternoon had come as quite a surprise; and when he'd told her they'd talked about his confrontation with his own parents, she'd been truly shocked. He didn't even go into all the details with her.

"I'm not taking the bait. I've got to go. I'll see you a little after one at my parents' place. Don't forget to display your parking permit, or you'll have to park in public parking over by the old mill."

"Yes, ma'am."

Alaine turned around at a rustling sound from behind her. Bekka stood in the cubicle's doorway—if only it had a door—tapping her watch.

"I've got to go. I'll see you in a few hours." As soon as she got Forbes to say good-bye and hang up, she grabbed her copy off the printer along with her steno pad and pen. "Sorry. I know, I'm running a few minutes behind."

"We're okay. We still have a few minutes. How was your weekend?"

Self-consciousness flamed in Alaine's face.

Bekka stopped her and pulled her to the side of the wide hallway. "Tell."

Alaine gave her a quick rundown of the incident at the coffee shop Saturday morning. Her heart raced and cheeks ached with the effort to control her expression as she got to the end of the story. "And then he leaned across the table and kissed me."

"He—what?" Bekka's eyes grew big—as did her smile. "He *kissed* you? On the lips?"

Alaine's laugh echoed down the tiled corridor. "Yes," she whispered, "on the *lips*. Twice."

Bekka pulled her into a quick, bone-crushing hug. "I'm so happy for you. It seems like everything is finally working out for you, as I knew it would eventually."

Alaine pulled her along—they needed to be in the studio. "I hope so. We haven't really talked about what it meant, though he did call me last night and we were on the phone for almost four hours."

"If you didn't talk about your relationship, what did you talk about?"

"Everything—nothing. I found out that his favorite author is Charles Dickens. Something about how Dickens wrote several novels that were scathing criticisms of the legal system in Victorian England and he wrote papers about it as an undergrad. Most of it went way over my head. So I paid him back by talking about art for a few minutes. His sister told me that he's not really a fan."

As soon as they stepped into the frigid studio, they separated: Bekka going to the news desk and Alaine going to her comfy arm chair on stage three to record her studio segments for the show. She pulled her jacket—a lightweight broadcloth in navy blue, with three-quarter sleeves ending in a little ruffle detail—on over her sleeveless red-and-white abstract patterned blouse. She thanked the fire marshal for coming in early and explained the process to him.

An hour later, she pulled her little black Mazda into the gravel lot beside Delacroix Gardens and walked the half mile to the community center where the TV station's van was setting up to broadcast. She left her jacket on the front seat of the van, did a quick sound and picture test with Nelson, and then headed into the crowds already starting to form around the dozens of tents lining the streets in all directions—all displaying DELACROIX RENTALS logos on them—containing merchandise and goods from Mills retailers, food of every imaginable ethnicity from every restaurant in the Mills, and carnival style games that filled the air with what Alaine thought of as the sound of Independence Day.

She went to her parents' booth first and chatted with them while Nelson got some footage of the flowers and potted plants they had for sale.

"Seems busier this early than it was last year." Alaine looked around at the visitors milling about.

"It is. And you know what they say—all publicity is good publicity." Her father rearranged the small pots of sweet peas to fill in holes where someone had obviously bought a few. "I know it's not great for Forbes, but I think everyone will be in the black this month due to the increased traffic we'll see today because the news stories have brought thc Mills back to Bonneterre's attention. We've already scheduled appointments to meet with two different landscapers to bid some projects for them in the upcoming weeks."

"That's great. I hope it works out. . . ."

Nelson indicated his readiness, and Alaine switched from daughter playing catch-up to reporter getting sound bites for her piece. After getting quotes from both parents, she sought out some of the more eclectic restaurants' and merchants' displays to make sure that she showed off the cultural diversity of the area to its best extent.

Stepping under the canopy at the tent for Abu Dhabi Restaurant, she bumped into a tall, broad-chested man. "I'll beg your—oh, hey, Major."

Major O'Hara turned. "Alaine, good to see you again."

"I should have known you'd be out here examining all the different cuisine." She turned and motioned for Nelson to start rolling. At his thumbs-up, she held the microphone up in front of herself. "Chef Major O'Hara of Boudreaux-Guidry Enterprises." She paused. "Chef O'Hara, what brings you out to the Moreaux Mills Independence Day Street Festival?"

"As anyone in any profession knows, expanding your knowledge of your profession is vital if you want to keep improving your own skills, so I come out here every year to study—and to taste—the best in multicultural cuisines." He'd come a long way since his first couple of segments for her show, now with a smooth yet casual delivery—

and no *um*s or *uh*s and steady eye contact with her.

Next year she'd have him do a segment where he went around from booth to booth and featured some of his favorite food finds—if the Mills still existed this time next year. "You worked in New York City for several years. How does the spectrum of ethnic foods represented at the festival compare with what you found there?"

"I don't know that any city would be able to compete with New York for the range of cuisines available, but those that we do have here are amongst the best I've ever had."

She asked him a few more questions, then wrapped it up. "Thanks, Major. Have a great day."

"Meredith is around here somewhere. Looking for stuff for the house."

"I'll look for her." She did a quick interview with the owners of Abu Dhabi, then moved on to try to talk to another dozen or so people as quickly as she could. By the time she got back to the van to try to edit her story together, she had so many good sound bites that she wasn't sure which ones to choose.

Finally, she got it cut together in a piece she was happy with—just in time to slip back into her jacket, even though she really didn't want to. She decided to stand in the middle of the community center's parking lot—since today it was a no-parking lot—where the building, the kids' pony ride, the inflated air-bounce thingy, and the large banner hanging from the side of the center could be seen in frame behind her. She positioned her two live-interview guests to either side of her so that Nelson had only to zoom out slightly and pan to the right or left for each one. She turned the volume on her earpiece up so she could hear the broadcast.

And then she made the mistake of looking past Nelson when she noticed someone walking toward them.

Forbes grimaced, then raised his hand in an apologetic wave at Alaine. He'd hoped he'd be able to stay unseen, but the guy in the clown getup had to walk right in front of the shady bench Forbes had found where he was close enough to see her, but not necessarily to hear her.

She rolled her eyes and shook her head and looked back at her cameraman, but not before that cute, deep grin stole over her face. He breathed deeply, enjoying the fragrance of the small sprig of lavender he'd picked up from Solange on his way over here. It would look perfect peeking out from the cluster of dark curls at the back of Alaine's head.

He wished he could have found a place where he could hear her. She seemed to put her two guests quite at ease as she talked to them—they visibly relaxed while she held the microphone in front of each one. Of course, he'd be able to watch the recording of it tonight.

Grinning, he crossed his legs and stretched his arms out across the top of the bench's back. Alaine had laughed harder than he'd ever heard from her when he'd admitted last night he'd been recording her show for years. He'd been surprised when she then admitted that she couldn't stand seeing or hearing herself on camera.

She finished up at ten minutes till one and, after helping her cameraman pack up his equipment, she tossed her jacket over her shoulder and sauntered over to the shade of the oak tree and sat down beside him.

"So what did you think of the horse-and-pony show?"

He wrapped his arm around her in a squeeze but let her go quickly as he could feel the heat radiating from her. "I'll let you know after I watch the final thing tonight." He pulled the sprig of lavender out of his shirt pocket and carefully stuck it into the clip holding up most of her hair. He let his hand drift down to lift one of the stray tendrils and placed a kiss on her neck where it had lain.

She shivered, as if with a sudden cold chill, and goose bumps pebbled her skin. "Forbes, I—"

"Hey, you two!" The wheels of Joe Delacroix's chair whispered across the pavement toward them.

"Joe, your timing leaves a bit to be desired."

Forbes couldn't decide if Alaine was cuter when she was frustrated or disgruntled. Right now, disgruntled was winning.

Joe grinned shamelessly at his sister. "Mother sent me to find you two to find out if you wanted to join the family for lunch. We're going to pick something up for them and take it over to their tent."

"What about your tent?" Alaine repositioned the lavender in her hair, stood, and started walking toward her brother—then stopped, turned, and extended her hand to Forbes.

His heart bounced like the kids in the inflatable castle fifty feet away. He twined his fingers through hers and joined her and her brother, not caring where they went, wanting only to know everyone around them understood he'd won her heart—and she'd won his.

Though Alaine tried to convince him to try Ethiopian, Thai, Egyptian, and Mongolian food, he wanted nothing but Greek food—which was to be found in one of the largest pavilions he'd seen so far. From all appearances, he guessed that the entire Pappas clan was there helping out—and every single one of them greeted him by name.

Voula loaded them up with food—and wouldn't let Forbes pay for any of it. Before she let them leave, she whispered something in Alaine's ear, then kissed her on both cheeks.

They each needed both hands—both arms—to carry all the food.

"What was that all about?" Forbes asked once they cleared the Pappases' marquee.

"What?"

"What she whispered in your ear." His stomach rumbled at the rich, meaty, spicy aromas wafting around them from the bags and boxes they carried.

"I have no idea. Whatever she said was in Greek. But I think she was telling me how lucky she thinks you are."

"Lucky?"

Alaine wrinkled her nose at him. "To be with me, of course."

He wanted to kiss her, but the armload of food made it impossible. "She's wrong."

Alaine's eyebrows shot up. "Oh, really?"

"Really. Because it's not luck. God knew I needed you in my life, and I firmly believe He brought us together." Okay, forget the bags. He moved around in front of her and leaned over their respective burdens. His lips almost touched hers—

"Hey, Alaine Delacroix! Forbes Guidry!"

With a groan of frustration, he straightened. Alaine's frustrated look wasn't quite as cute as the disgruntled one.

He turned to see someone he'd never met before in his life coming toward them, followed by. . .he groaned and moved back to Alaine's side. He'd managed to avoid both Major and Meredith earlier, and he'd hoped to avoid any attention from reporters who might recognize him and want to ask him about Mom and Dad and the case. Obviously, he'd hoped in vain.

"Forbes Guidry, what can you tell us about the Moreaux Mills case?"

"I have nothing to tell you about it." The box tucked under his left arm started dripping something down his elbow.

"Is it true that you're going to be suing your parents' company for the residents of Moreaux Mills against the wishes of your own law firm?"

Ah, so he hadn't been wrong in figuring the reason he'd received three phone calls from Sandra Landreneau this morning—which he hadn't answered—had something to do with this case. "I still have no comment."

"Has your involvement with this case created any tension between you and your parents?"

Now the sauce dripping down Forbes's elbow was the least troublesome thing happening at the moment. "No comment."

Fortunately, the reporter soon grew frustrated with his "no comment" answers; and when Alaine was no more forthcoming with information, he gave up and went away.

"What took y'all so long?" Joe asked when they made it back to the Delacroix Gardens tent.

Forbes glanced at Alaine. She skirted around her brother to the large plastic folding table behind the wood-and-glass display tables and cases and set her bags and boxes down. "We ran into a reporter who questioned us about the case and didn't want to take 'no comment' for an answer."

"Ah, Forbes, let me—" Solange took his cargo and held his arm away from his body in her strong, calloused hand. She led him over to the ice chest at the back of the tent, dunked a paper towel into the pool formed by the melting ice, and wiped the sticky brown liquid off his arm. The frigid cloth against his skin was a welcome relief from the heat of the sun and of the food he'd been toting.

He leaned over and kissed her cheek. "*Muito obrigado.*"

"*De nada.*" She blushed and waved him away. "You go sit, eat."

Nikki and Tony returned with a large bucket of boiled crawfish, a big brown grocery bag from the Ethiopian restaurant, and something that smelled like pickles and beer in a brown bag inside of a white plastic bag.

"No kimchi?" JD poked through all the bags and boxes on the table.

"We figured since you're the only one who can stand it," Nikki said, sliding a bag onto the table under her father-in-law's arm, "that you could go over to the Lees' tent and enjoy it over there. But we did bring this." She opened the double bagged offering.

He stuck his head practically inside the bag. "Bratwurst and sauerkraut!"

Out of respect for the Delacroixes and their neighbors, Forbes tried some of almost everything on the table—most of which he'd never even heard of before, and all of which he enjoyed. He thought about what his family would be eating tonight to celebrate the anniversary of the country's independence: grilled hamburgers and hot dogs, chips, lemonade and sodas, and cake and ice cream made by Aunt Maggie. What he'd always thought of as an all-American meal.

Looking around at the half-dozen or so cultures represented on the table—which didn't include this family's Portuguese heritage—

he thanked God for giving him a glimpse of what constituted a real all-American meal.

"You're quiet all of a sudden." Alaine looped her arm over his shoulder and leaned in close, her whisper tickling his ear.

He craned his neck and kissed her cheek. "Just counting my blessings."

"Yeah, well, if you're done counting," Tony laughed, "could you pass the Pad Thai? Blessings aren't making my stomach stop growling." He ducked the flurry of napkins Nikki flung at him.

Melancholy lodged like a chicken bone in Forbes's throat at the immediate and unavoidable comparison of his own siblings to Alaine's. They, too, enjoyed teasing another sibling's or cousin's new beau—and pretended to disapprove of each other for doing it.

Alaine squeezed his arm and glopped a spoonful of something on his Styrofoam plate. Sorrowful understanding filled her dark eyes, and she mouthed, *I'm sorry*.

He closed his eyes and leaned over to touch his forehead to hers in silent gratitude.

Joe commented on a possible new contract from someone who'd stopped by his booth earlier, and the focus of conversation changed, allowing Forbes a few minutes to compose himself and rejoin the lighthearted banter around the table.

Soon, Joe and Nikki decided they'd been away from their display tent long enough. Tony volunteered to man Solange and JD's tent so they could go have some fun. And Alaine took Forbes by the hand and led him back out into the afternoon sun, away from the fans that had been keeping the nearly unbearable heat at bay inside the tent.

"Come on. I want you to see everything."

Alaine seemed to know everyone and introduced Forbes to the owners of each business. He remembered some of them from the meeting and did his best to recall their names—which the signs on each tent helped, since most of the businesses bore their surnames.

A couple of times, she ducked into a tent with no warning. The second time she did it, he caught a glimpse of a reporter trailed by a cameraman coming toward them.

By the time they'd visited every single booth, tent, trailer, or table under a tree where people sold their wares, cooked, or exhibited displays describing the services they provided, Forbes couldn't hold back his awe.

"How could I have never known any of this existed down here?"

Alaine half-smiled, head cocked to the side. "Because you were raised to believe that 'down here' was a place filled with poor people who're a drain on Bonneterre's resources."

He blanched at hearing her say almost verbatim what his mother had said at lunch yesterday. "You're right. We grew up thinking that anyone from the Mills was from the wrong side of the tracks." He gave her a sardonic grin. "If the railroad tracks around here didn't run north and south along the river."

She gave him a wrinkled-up-nose grin. "Wrong side of the highway, then. One of my suitemates at the sorority admitted to me a few years ago that she voted against me during rush week because I was from the Mills and she didn't think I'd be the right kind of person." She sighed. "Now I wonder if she was right."

"What do you mean?" He let go of her hand and put his arm around her shoulders to pull her in close, then kissed the top of her head. "Of course you're the right kind of person. You're the perfect kind of person."

"But I wasn't when I met them. Forbes, what you see now is a persona I've carefully cultivated over the last decade. Before I got into that sorority and those girls decided to give me a complete makeover, I didn't care about clothes or shoes or handbags or makeup or anything like that. All I cared about was dancing and my art."

He didn't say anything for a moment, letting the sound of the crowd, the distant carnival games, and the '40s-style big band currently playing in the community center and being broadcast through the PA system wash over him.

Finally, he moved to stand in front of her, put her left hand on his shoulder, took her right hand in his, and placed his other hand around her back, and as if he'd been born doing it, Forbes started waltzing with Alaine. Staring down into her chocolate brown eyes, he didn't have to think about the rhythm; it pulsed through him like a second heartbeat, until it was the only thing in the world besides him and Alaine.

"I don't see a persona—I don't see *Alaine Delacroix*." He returned her amused smile at his imitation of Riley's intonation of her name. "All I see is the woman who fills the emptiness in me I didn't even know was there until I met you. All I see is you. And that's all I'll ever want to see."

Thc song ended. The rosy glow of the setting sun reflected in the unshed tears welling in Alaine's eyes. He placed her other hand on his shoulder and wrapped his arms around her waist, pulling her close. "Promise me you'll always be you, that you'll never hold back and pretend to be or feel something that isn't totally, 100 percent you."

She nodded, her throat working visibly when she swallowed. "I promise," she whispered.

He kissed her tenderly. . .and ever so thoroughly.

Chapter 24

Forbes looked up at the knock on his office door. "Samantha, good. I've been wondering where you were. I need you to clear some time on my schedule over the next few weeks. I have a group of claimants in a new case I'm taking on. I'll need a couple of associates, as well, to assist with research and depositions. Make sure they know it's pro bono."

His secretary didn't stir. He glanced up again. Concern blossomed at the fear on Samantha's face. "What's wrong?"

"I was just in Mrs. Landreneau's office. She. . .she asked me about the files I copied for you from the partners' file room."

His mouth went dry. "What did she ask?" The calls he'd avoided from Sandra Landreneau yesterday—obviously she'd decided to try another tactic. But the terms of his partnership gave him the right to take on "cases of conscience."

"She just asked me why I'd been copying B-G files—asked too if you'd told me why you wanted them. I told her what you told me: You were looking for precedent for a case you're researching."

"And what did she say to that?" He stood and put his suit coat back on.

"That I'm not to copy any more B-G files for you." Samantha entered the office and leaned on the back of one of the guest chairs, gripping the back tightly. "What's going on? I heard a couple girls in the restroom whispering that you're going to be suing B-G for a group of business owners in Moreaux Mills."

"Only if I can build a case. I'm still fact-finding." The phone rang. Forbes straightened his tie. He didn't need to look at the caller-ID window to know who it was. "Tell her I'm on my way up." He walked past his assistant, then paused and turned. "I'm sorry you got dragged into this."

Wide-eyed, Samantha nodded and returned to her desk to answer the phone.

Forbes didn't make eye contact with anyone in the halls or stairs. So they were all gossiping about him, were they? Ah, well. That was the least of his troubles.

Mary glared at him over the rim of her glasses. He gave her a tight smile but didn't stop.

For the first time in a very long time, Sandra Landreneau didn't smile at him when he entered her office. "Close the door, please."

Forbes reminded himself of his position of partner, of his name on the masthead. Yet the sensation wouldn't go away of being eight years old and about to be punished by his mother for cutting off all of five-year-old Meredith's hair. The fact that Meredith had handed him the scissors with which to do it hadn't carried any weight with Mom.

He unbuttoned his coat and sat in one of the guest chairs, giving the best performance of being at ease that he could muster.

"I assume I don't need to show you the newspaper articles? Nor point out that while I was trying to get in touch with you yesterday, you were out gallivanting with Alaine Delacroix in Moreaux Mills." Sandra tossed the "Style" section from today's paper across the desk. A large color photo of Forbes and Alaine dancing together under the fireworks was featured above the fold on the "Seen About Town" page.

He stopped himself from grinning and made a mental note to contact the paper to see if he could get a digital copy of that photo. "No, ma'am. I am aware of it."

Sandra pulled off her reading glasses, letting them hang by the beaded chain around her neck. "As a partner, you are not required to have your clients or your cases vetted by the rest of us."

"No."

"*Unless* such a client or case would be directly contrary to the good name of the firm."

"I have not done anything that endangers the reputation of the firm. On the contrary, what better light can be shed on FLM&G than the publicity that can come from taking on the plight of a dozen or so Bonneterrans who are about to lose their homes and businesses to suburban sprawl and retail development?"

"Pretty speech. Save it for a jury." The lines around Sandra's mouth deepened. Must be time for another collagen injection. "Aside from the fact it would have been nice to have some forewarning before phone calls from all the media outlets in town started coming in looking for an official statement, before you agreed to meet with anyone in this matter—publicly or privately—you should have given some thought to the fact that Boudreaux-Guidry Enterprises is our most important client. Taking a case against them is against the best interest of the firm."

He waited for her to make a point, but she sat there, looking expectant. He raised his eyebrows. "And?"

"And—it should be obvious. The partnership agreement of this firm—which you signed when you became an equity, name partner—clearly states that no partner is to take on a case that is in direct conflict to the current work or clients of the law firm. I caucused the other partners, and we are all in agreement: Drop the Moreaux Mills case."

He couldn't let her see the panic that chewed through his nerves. "I respectfully submit that this case falls under the 'case of conscience' clause in the agreement. I will not drop it."

"Forbes, you're not thinking this through. If you insist on taking this case, it could be grounds for demotion to nonequity partner—if not termination. Take tonight to think about it, and give us your answer tomorrow."

Everything he'd worked for since he'd decided at seventeen years old that he wanted to become a lawyer teetered on the edge of this decision. In the fourteen years since he'd finished law school, he'd been on the fast-track: from the prestigious law firm in New Orleans where he'd worked right out of law school to coming home in triumph as the youngest senior associate ever to work at Folse, Landreneau & Maier law firm at age twenty-eight, only to become the youngest name partner of equity status at age thirty-one.

If he took the Moreaux Mills case, he could lose all of it. The prestige of having his name joined with some of the most respected legal minds in the state. The weight his name carried on legal documents because of his position here.

If he didn't take the case, he would be betraying JD and Solange, Joe and Nikki. . .and Alaine. He would be smothering his own ethics. And worst of all, he would be refusing to follow through on the feeling deep within that God had led him to this case, that God was calling him to take a stand here and now.

"I don't need to think about it overnight. My answer will be the same. If there has been wrongdoing by Boudreaux-Guidry Enterprises—or any entity they're doing business with or have influence over—it is my duty to help those who have been wronged seek justice." He stood. "If that's all? I have some depositions to schedule and motions to certify class to file."

"Not in these offices and not making use of any employees or associates of FLM&G. This case is not sanctioned; and if you insist on taking it, you will not utilize company resources in the handling of it until the partners vote on whether or not your taking it violates the partnership agreement."

Forbes nodded. "Just let me know when that meeting will be, and in the meantime, I'll get back to work. Is that all?"

She nodded back. "For now. You'll want to get your book of business ready for evaluation, based on the outcome of the vote."

"I understand. Enjoy what's left of the morning." That the other partners would be upset by his decision to take this case, he'd expected. But that they'd try to say it violated the partnership agreement floored him. Could they truly be so frightened of how Mom and Dad would react that they'd force Forbes out just to avoid that scenario? Or could it be that the other partners were privy to certain information that proved Boudreaux-Guidry Enterprises had acted in harmful ways that circumvented or broke the law?

And how would he ever be able to handle a full-blown, class-action lawsuit by himself without the assistance of associates and paralegals?

By the time he'd made it back down to his office, he'd started formulating a plan. "Samantha, clear as much of my schedule as you can. If you can get me a couple of hours this afternoon, I'm going to see if Russ LeBlanc can fit in a meeting with me."

"I assume you're talking about the Moreaux Mills case and not the Pichon case?"

"Yeah."

"She just called me and told me I'm not to help you in any way for that case, that you're not allowed to use anyone here to help you with it." Samantha reached around to the credenza behind her desk and pulled several sheets of paper off her printer. "So I took the liberty of printing you a list of some part-time people you can use for help, if you're willing to pay them yourself."

"Samantha, I think I love you."

"Yeah, well. . ." She held up her left hand, displaying a sparkling engagement ring. "I'm already taken."

"And you waited this long to tell me?"

"It's not like I've actually seen you before now." She canted her gaze toward the ceiling and back down with an arched brow. "When was I supposed to tell you, with both of us being called into the principal's office this morning? Besides, hearing you say, 'I told you so' is one of my least favorite parts of this job." She grinned at him.

"But I did tell you so." He took the printout from her. "Speaking of the Pichon case, I need you to type up the response to the latest motion from the plaintiff—it has to be submitted today."

"Will do, boss."

Forbes kept the smile on his face until his office door clicked shut. He made it to his desk before doubling over in almost physical pain. He dropped into his chair, arms wrapped around his stomach.

"God, I'm confident I did what I was supposed to do—what You've been telling me to do—with this case. I believe in it. I believe it's right. So why do I feel so wrong about it?"

Alaine typically didn't have to drive home in rush-hour traffic, but working late today had been worth it for the glorious afternoon and evening she'd had yesterday. Her heart pounded again at the memory of Forbes's arms around her, of his kisses under the star-strewn sky, of dancing together to the big-band music under the Mills' own small fireworks display.

She laughed aloud. Forbes had obviously been practicing his dance steps. And even though he wanted to waltz to every song, she had to hand it to him—she'd never seen him so light on his feet.

With a sigh of relief, she turned off Spring Street into the condo complex. Several cars blocked the mailboxes; she'd walk over later—maybe even see if Forbes might want to meet her and go for a walk around the neighborhood with her.

She drove around to the Cheapside portion of the neighborhood... and slowed before she reached her driveway. With the westward angle of the sun casting long shadows over the fronts of the row of town houses, she couldn't be sure—

She stopped. Someone was sitting on her front steps. Taking her foot off the brake, she figured she could ease past and just keep going if the person looked like he might mean to harm her.

Two driveways from her own, she relaxed—and then smiled. Forbes, in a loose T-shirt, knit shorts, and trainers, sat with his forehead cupped in one hand, twirling a leaf by its stem with the other. He startled and looked up when the garage door started to open.

Alaine tried to calm her riotous insides at the sight of him. She'd never seen him dressed so casually—even yesterday, his red T-shirt had been a silk blend and his navy shorts, chinos with a crease down the front.

He entered the garage before she could get her work bag out of the trunk of the small sports car. "I'd kiss you, but I'm all sweaty."

Her pulse exploded like a racehorse out of the gate at the Kentucky Derby. "I don't mind."

His blue gray eyes twinkled—and yet seemed to hold a measure of sadness—and he leaned closer and gave her a perfunctory peck on the lips. "Hi."

"Hi, yourself. What brings you over this evening—and in such a state?"

"I was out jogging and figured you had to be home soon, so I decided I'd wait for you to see if you might care to take a walk with me." His expression sobered, and the hint of sadness she thought she'd seen turned into a palpable aura of disconsolation.

Her throat tightened with the desire to say something that would ease his burden—and the knowledge that she probably couldn't. "Come inside and get some water while I change clothes."

She left him in her kitchen and jogged upstairs to her room. Not caring that half the contents of her bag spilled out onto the bed where she tossed it, she stepped into her closet and stripped out of her suit—carefully separating the pieces that were hers and the pieces that needed to go back to the store that sent clothing over that she had to wear because of the agreement the station's sales staff had worked out. The yellow boucle tweed jacket had looked horrible on her in the mirror—she could only imagine what it did to her under the floodlights in the studio.

Biting her bottom lip, she allowed a tinge of amusement to crack through her concern for Forbes. Maybe she'd suggest they stop at his place so she could watch his recording of today's program just to see how bad the jacket looked.

She slipped into a pair of gray yoga capris and a pale pink

tank top, and carried her pink and gray athletic shoes out into her bedroom. She sat on her hope chest to pull her socks on.

Just from the short time she'd known Forbes, she'd learned that he didn't show any emotion he didn't want people to see. For his control to have cracked so hard she'd been able to see his pain, he must have heard something bad at work today.

Forbes. Oh, Forbes. The idea that had been plaguing her for the past several days came back with a cold reality: Forbes had sacrificed his time, his dignity, and his family for this case.

She stopped in the motion of tying her right shoe and rested her forehead against her up-bent knee. "Lord, thank You so much for bringing Forbes to us—to me. I don't deserve him. None of us deserves the sacrifices he's making for us. Help me—help me and Forbes—to figure out some solution to bring justice to the people of the Mills without Forbes having to make more sacrifices. I don't want him to lose his family, God. Show me what I can do to help."

Downstairs, she found Forbes on a bar chair in very much the same position he'd been in on the front steps, despondency oozing out of him. She took a few moments to stretch, her concern growing.

"Ready?" She tried to sound chipper.

"Yep. Got you a bottle of water, too." He handed it to her.

She took the bottle and grabbed the extra garage-door opener and mailbox key out of the kitchen junk drawer. She clipped the remote to her waistband and slipped the key ring onto her left pinkie finger. "Let's go."

They walked in silence the first several minutes—and at no leisurely strolling pace, either. By the time they'd made it up the gentle hill leading into the heart of the community—toward Forbes's more exclusive section—Alaine almost had to jog to keep up with his long, quick strides. And since she hadn't walked regularly since the beginning of summer—which meant sometime around the end of April—every muscle in her legs and every air sac in her lungs protested painfully.

After fifteen minutes of this, she stopped and leaned down, bracing her hands on her knees, to catch her breath—hard to do when the evening air clung to her like a sweaty gym sock in a steam room. "Forbes—if you want to run some more, why don't you take a few laps and then come back and get me when you're ready to slow it down."

He stopped and looked around as if surprised to discover she no longer bobbed along beside him. The fierceness in his eyes vanished when he saw her. "I'm sorry. I guess I still have more frustration to work off. I thought I'd worn myself out before you got home." He walked back to rejoin her.

Holding her water bottle between her knees, Alaine straightened and pulled her hair band out, combed the escaped curls back up off her forehead, face, and neck into a ponytail near the top of her head, and wrapped it up with the band again, keeping it all folded up together instead of letting it swing free. She then took a huge swig of the water.

Forbes reached over and touched a curl she'd missed behind her ear. "The managing partner at the firm threatened to terminate me if I don't drop the case."

Alaine staggered back, the uncertainty in her knees in direct proportion to the blow to her soul. "That settles it. You have to drop the case. We'll find another lawyer—your friend, Russ LeBlanc. Surely he'd be willing to take on the case. I've already made you lose your family; I couldn't bear it if you lost your job, too."

He actually smiled at her. "Hold on, now. I've reviewed the partnership agreement we all signed, and they have no grounds on which to terminate me. But. . ." He reached for her hand and started back up the hill, much slower this time.

Alaine matched his pace. "But?"

"You know I've spent a lot of time in prayer about this case, about what taking it might do to me and to every relationship in my life."

"Yes. I've been praying, too."

"I am certain God is telling me to continue on with the case, that He'll take care of everything else—my family, the law firm, everything."

Alaine glanced up at his stoic profile. His dark hair curled around his temples, forehead, and neck where he was sweaty. And even though perspiration rolled down his face—as it was about to do on hers—she didn't find his very masculine, very sporty aroma the least offensive.

Shaking her head, she looked away from him so she could concentrate on the subject at hand, not on all his attractions. "It's good you have that confidence. I just wish we could see where this is all headed—if it's going to go to trial or if your parents will see the light and decide to change their plans and help the people in the Mills instead of trying to run them out."

"See, here's the thing. I met with Russ LeBlanc this afternoon. Because my partners are going to be pains about the case and not let me use any resources at the firm, I needed to find some help. And the more I talked to Russ, the more I realized just how much I envy him."

"What do you mean, envy him?" Alaine tripped over a rough spot in the pavement, but with her hand firmly held in Forbes's, she didn't lose balance and recovered before he could react.

"I mean he's so happy, so fulfilled with what he does at the community legal aid center. He hardly makes any money—I have no idea how he is going to make ends meet with four brand-new babies."

Alaine gasped. "He had quads?"

"His wife did, yes. Three girls and a boy. And Carrie's going to have to go back to work as a social worker in less than five weeks because Russ barely scrapes a living from that center. But I've never met two happier, more contented people than the LeBlancs. And I can't help comparing my own sorry excuse for a life with his. He's done something, made his mark on the community. He may not have material possessions, but he has something more. He has dignity and honor and the title of 'neighbor' as Jesus defined it in the parable of the good Samaritan. And you want to know the sad thing?" He pulled her into a grassy area under an enormous oak tree.

"What?" Her throat ached in sympathy for the pain and longing in Forbes's voice.

"Even with as much as I envy what Russ has and wish I could be that kind of lawyer, the idea of giving up my share of the law firm's profits, of losing my extremely high hourly billing rate, of foregoing the incentives and bonuses we dole out to ourselves every year, of not being able to afford the luxurious life to which I'm accustomed—the idea of losing all of those things, those material things and more, terrifies me."

Alaine rested her hands on the sides of his waist. *Let Your words flow through me, God, because I don't know what to say to him.* She breathed in and opened her mouth. "I don't think it's giving up the material things that is what you're really afraid of."

He raised his eyebrows.

"I think it's the sense of control that having all those material possessions gives you the illusion of. With your money and power and prestige, you can fix any problem, keep any situation from getting out of control. And if you can't personally do it, someone in your Rolodex can." Shocked at herself, Alaine tried to stop the harsh sounding words. "But if you think about it, your friend Russ is the one who's really in control. He's in control because he's given up control—to God. He isn't controlled by the need for money or luxury or power or prestige. Sure, he doesn't control who his clients are and how much they can pay him, but he controls his own happiness. You'll never know what it is to have true control of your life until you realize you have to let it go and let God have control of every aspect of your life—including where your next paycheck is coming from."

Forbes stared at her. Alaine started to apologize several times for what she'd said, but the words wouldn't come. After a long time, his expression eased and a smile slowly overtook his eyes and lips.

"So are you saying that you wouldn't care if I went to work with Russ LeBlanc and didn't have a steady income and couldn't afford things like Jaguars and the most expensive town house in Bonneterre?"

She swallowed hard and thought about what her sorority sisters would say—which was exactly the opposite of what was right. "I wouldn't mind. Because I didn't fall in love with your income or your car or your house. I fell in love with who you are, what you stand for."

His eyes flickered in the reddening sunlight as they darted back and forth, searching hers. "Say that again," he whispered.

"I love you, Forbes Guidry. I don't care if you have to sell the town house and buy a cheaper car. What I care about is that you're happy and that you do what God is calling you to do so that you can be proud of your work every day."

He cupped her face with his large, soft hands and kissed her until her eyes—and toes—crossed. "I don't deserve you, Alaine." He pressed his forehead to hers with a mischievous smile. "But you don't have to worry about me losing the town house and the Jag. They're paid off."

Chapter 25

The next weeks passed in a blur for Forbes. He hadn't worked such long hours since his first few years as an associate at the firm in New Orleans. Though he'd convinced the other three partners that they couldn't terminate him—his argument for its being a case of conscience worked—they still refused to allow him to use company resources for it. And with the threat of a review of his book of business pending—the record of all of his clients and the money he was bringing in with each one—he not only had to keep up with all of his current clients but still work on bringing in new business.

The flurry from the media over the case died down after his initial filings for injunctions to keep all of the claimants in the suit from being foreclosed upon, but it flared up again the second week in August when Forbes officially filed the class-action lawsuit.

His one attempt to try to reconcile with his parents and see if they could resolve this without the legal action—by dropping by their home on a Sunday evening and being unceremoniously turned away—had resulted in his receiving a phone call from Sandra Landreneau, legal counsel for Boudreaux-Guidry Enterprises, telling him to cease and desist from trying to contact her clients directly.

To try to make things easier for the rest of the family, especially Meredith and Major, he stopped going to all family functions, including the Thursday night cousins-and-siblings dinner. But at least in that, he had some consolation: Thursday night became his regular date night with Alaine—a welcome relief in what had become a routine of sixteen- to eighteen-hour days, at least six days a week.

Russ LeBlanc had made a small room in his converted-house law office available for Forbes to use for working on the Mills case, but most of the time, Forbes worked on it at home. He'd filled the formerly vacant large guest suite on the fourth floor of his town house with long folding tables and plenty of boxes to hold the sheaves of paperwork the case generated—on both sides. But he had Sandra Landreneau address everything to him at Russ's address.

Before Russ had left the courtroom one afternoon, he informed Forbes a package had been dropped off for him at the legal aid center from FLM—Forbes had long since stopped thinking of his initial as part of the firm's name in this case—no doubt yet another round of motions to dismiss to which Forbes would have to spend all night writing responses.

Mr. Pichon pumped his hand again. "Thanks, Forbes. I really appreciate your work on all of this. I don't even care that we have to share the court costs with them. I'm just glad we won."

"You're welcome. I'll be in touch about when and how to make that payment early next week." Instead of euphoria over winning the case, all he could think about was how much that neighborhood would change now that Mr. Pichon could sell his lot to anyone willing to pay the price he'd ask. He dawdled in the hallway until his client disappeared into an elevator rather than share one with him.

The halls of the courthouse echoed with emptiness. Forbes checked his watch—and drew in his breath between clenched teeth. With an elevator all to himself, he called Alaine.

She picked up on the second ring. "Hey. I'll be ready in about fifteen minutes."

"Hey to you, too. And don't rush. I hate to do this to you again, but I'm going to have to push our date back about an hour. And would you mind if we didn't go see that movie? I've got to go by Russ's and pick up some paperwork on my way home—motions and briefs I'll need to read through tonight." He exited the elevator and waved at the security guards who buzzed the main doors so he could get out.

"Do you. . .do you want to just cancel tonight?" Alaine's voice went reedy.

Guilt—tinged with resentment—pierced him. If it weren't for having met Alaine, this case wouldn't be taking up most of his life. But if it weren't for this case, he might never have fallen in love with her. "No, I still want to see you tonight."

"Oh, okay." Her voice returned to a more mellow, happier tone. "Because if you need to cancel and spend all evening working, I'd understand."

"I'll pick you up at seven thirty. Are you still thinking favorable thoughts toward Italian food?"

"So long as it's at Palermo's, yes."

"That's what I thought. I'll call and see if they can move our reservation back."

She let out a dry laugh. "They will."

"How do you know?" He climbed into the Jag.

"Because everyone always does what you ask them to."

He snorted, thinking about the paperwork facing him tonight. "Not anymore."

"Okay, everyone outside of your family and the law firm."

A drop of rain with the volume of a fire bucket doused the windshield when Forbes pulled out of the parking garage. "I'd better get off the phone. It's starting to rain, and there's still a lot of traffic in downtown. I wouldn't want to have to cancel permanently."

"See you in a little while."

"Bye." He dropped the phone into a cup holder and pointed the car south, toward Moreaux Mills and Russ's legal aid center. As Alaine had predicted, the hostess who answered the phone at Palermo's Italian Grill was only too happy to change their reservation to seven forty-five.

Lights still blazed through most of the windows of the center when Forbes pulled up. Even with his large umbrella and a short few feet to the door, his back and legs got a pretty good soaking from the diagonal rain. The front door was locked and he'd left the key in his briefcase in the car, so he rang the bell.

The glow of the interior backlit Russ when he opened the door. "I was wondering where you were."

Forbes shook off the umbrella before crossing the threshold. "Did the paralegal I hired come by with something for me, too?"

"Yeah, while we were in court, apparently. My secretary put both of them in your office."

Forbes smirked at him. Both of them had gotten quite comfortable with the idea of Forbes having his own office space here. But all things considered, having watched what Russ did on a daily basis, Forbes had to admit he wasn't cut out to provide community legal aid. He much preferred paying clients. He just wasn't sure he'd be able to go back to FLM&G after this. If he didn't need his income from his partnership there to finance the Mills case, he'd have already separated from them and hung out his own shingle—over that vacant Victorian row house office building on Town Square, right next door to Anne's wedding planning business—and a ten-minute walk from his home.

He greeted Russ's assistant and paralegal—hard at work in the kitchen with paperwork spread out all over the lunch table—and went down the hall to the small former bedroom serving as his office. Atop the thrift-store desk sat two thick, yellow envelopes. He scooped them up, gave the shabby room one more look, and turned off the light.

At Russ's office door—which had been the house's master bedroom—Forbes stopped and leaned against the jamb. "How's Carrie holding up?"

"Fourth day back at work. Called me at least a dozen times before noon in tears wanting to quit her job and stay home with them." Russ sighed and rubbed the back of his neck. "I can't help thinking that if I'd gone your way—if I'd taken that job with Folse, Landreneau & Maier as a senior associate when you were promoted to partner—

she'd be able to stay home with the babies and we wouldn't have to worry about how we're going to balance paying all the bills with making sure the kids have more than just the crucial essentials for survival."

"And if you had taken that job, you would have had money, yes, but your soul would have died. You would have hated being on that side of the courtroom, defending the big business owners and trying to squash the little people. I'm finding it harder and harder to stomach these days." Forbes's head felt suddenly heavy, and he leaned it against the door facing.

Russ gave Forbes a sympathetic look, even though Russ had been the lawyer for the losing side in the Pichon case. "Yeah, can't wait to see what the papers have to say about that tomorrow—that you stuck it to one community while trying to stick up for another."

Forbes groaned. "Oh, that's poetic. Why don't you call the editor and give them that line?"

"Sarcasm doesn't suit you, Forbes." Russ wagged his index finger at him in an admonitory gesture. "Besides, their prose is purple enough without my help. They should be paying you a bonus for all of the news you've generated for them this year."

"Yeah, well, between the society pages and the front page, I can't tell if they love me or hate me. They love showing pictures of Alaine and me at any public event we attend—which is just about every event she covers and drags me along to. And they love digging up every last sordid detail of how this case has created a wedge between me and my family, how I'm the black sheep."

"Or the white sheep, depending on who's writing the article." Russ's desk phone rang, and he glanced down at it. "It's a client. I've got to answer."

"I'll see you tomorrow."

Russ waved and picked up the receiver.

As if Forbes weren't already stressed enough, the pounding rain and limited visibility wound the cords of his muscles even tighter. He smiled. Maybe he could convince Alaine to give him another one of her miraculous shoulder massages before they went to dinner. He glanced down at the clock. A quarter to seven. Maybe not. He'd be cutting it close just to get home and change clothes before time to pick her up.

When he turned into the cul-de-sac, the Jag's headlights flashed on a dark object in his driveway—a car he didn't recognize. Waiting for the garage door to open, he glanced up at the front door. A shadowy figure stood at the top of the steps. He pulled the Jag into the garage.

Before he could get around to the end of his car, the mysterious person hurried into the shelter the garage provided.

Evelyn Mackenzie lowered her blazer, which she'd been using as an umbrella with no effect. Her dark hair lay plastered to her head. He averted his eyes from the way her now-transparent white blouse clung to her torso.

"What are you doing here?" He hadn't meant to sound that gruff.

"I need to talk to you." Evelyn stepped forward, her feet making squishing noises in her spike-heeled sandals.

"Without your counsel present, that's not a good idea." He turned to retrieve the packages and his overstuffed briefcase from the car.

"This is off the record—just between you and me." She grabbed his arm. "Please, Forbes, it's important."

"I have to leave here at seven thirty, so it had better be quick." He risked another glance at her, and her trembling and bedraggled appearance gave him a little twinge. "Come inside and dry off and get warm."

"Thanks."

He led her up one flight to the main level. He was about to point out the powder room near the kitchen, but that wouldn't do. He only had hand towels in there. "Come on upstairs."

The guest bathroom on the third floor opened directly off the landing—the door adjacent to his bedroom door. The proximity couldn't be helped. He reached in and turned on the light.

"Towels are there"—he pointed to the plush green ones hanging on the bar beside the tub—"and there's a hair dryer in the linen closet. And if you'll hold on just a second, I'll loan you a dry shirt." Because if they were going to talk, he was going to have to look at her.

In his closet, he grabbed the first T-shirt off the top of the stack he usually wore when running—the one he'd gotten for participating in the charity 10K run last weekend for the Warner Foundation to raise money for the cardiac care unit at University Hospital. Though his parents had helped start the foundation and were the biggest supporters and donors, he'd signed up to participate way back in the spring. And he never broke his promises.

He waved at Evelyn in the bathroom mirror. She turned off the hair dryer.

"Here." He thrust the shirt at her. "It's never been worn."

"Thanks."

He nodded and escaped back to his room. Closing the door of the closet behind him, he quickly changed out of his damp suit into dark-wash, slightly distressed jeans and a light blue, silk T-shirt, then grabbed his olive brown sport coat. The hair dryer stopped. He carried his shoes and socks out into his bedroom, just as Evelyn knocked on the open door.

"Forbes?" Her gaze swept his room, and she took a few steps across the dark hardwood to the area rug, putting her within five feet of him. She'd knotted the T-shirt in the back in such a way that what should have been a very unprovocative tent on her slender frame now had an almost indecently snug fit.

His insides foamed. "Let's go downstairs to my study." He checked his watch. "I can give you about ten minutes.

"Okay." She preceded him down the stairs, her blouse and jacket bundled under her arm, her sandals dangling by the heel straps from her fingers. At the bottom of the stairs, she halted, and he took over the lead, turning immediately left into the study that occupied the front corner of the main floor.

"Wow. This is some room." Evelyn trailed her fingers over the back of one of the leather club chairs as her eyes scraped across the spines of all the books lining the built-in cherry cabinets.

Forbes draped his jacket across the back of his Queen Anne–style armchair and sat to put his socks and shoes on. "What did you want to talk to me about?"

"Hmm?"

He glanced up and almost bolted out of his chair to slap her hand away from Dickens. She ran her fingertips across the leather binding and gold lettering on the spines of the treasured volumes.

Gritting his teeth, he returned his attention to getting his feet encased in the dark brown socks and leather dress shoes. "Why are you here, Evelyn?"

"What—oh, yes." She finished her slow circuit of the room and came back around to perch on the edge of the club chair nearest him. "It's about your parents, Forbes."

His heart and lungs froze solid. "What about my parents? Are they okay?"

She reached over and laid her hand on his knee. "Physically, yes, they're fine. I'm talking about their emotional state. They miss their son—they miss *you*. They're trying very hard to understand why you felt like you needed to take this stand against them, but they're ready for you to come back home, to make a gesture of reconciliation."

Forbes finished tying his shoe, then dropped his foot back to the floor, dislodging Evelyn's hand from his knee. He leaned against the high back of the chair, rested his elbows on the armrests, and clasped his hands in front of him. "They have a funny way of showing it. Last time I tried to contact them, tried to see if we could reconcile this, they had their lawyer call me back and demand I cease trying to contact them."

"About the case, yes. But they're still your parents, Forbes. If you went to them as their son, not as the lawyer for the other side, things would be different." Evelyn crossed her legs, and her skirt, too short to begin with, rode up even higher.

Forbes cleared his throat and ignored the way the surface of his skin tingled at the flash of thigh he caught before he averted his gaze.

"I find it interesting that you, who has what could be described at best an adversarial relationship with your father, are here advising me in parental matters."

"It's because I have such a bad relationship with my father that I'm here, Forbes. I don't want to see happen to you what's happened to me—I don't want to see this case come between you and your parents. I'll admit it straight out: I'm insanely jealous of the relationship that you—and your sister—have with your parents. It amazes me that Meredith can work so closely with them every single day and still have a close enough relationship with them that the three of them have lunch together, alone, at least once a week."

Forbes let out a small huff. Those lunches had been his idea—a time for Meredith to be able to share her concerns and problems with her parental bosses instead of bottling it all up inside and putting up with their running roughshod over her and her department. "Things are not always as they appear."

"No, but that's true in your situation as well. They're not mad at you, Forbes. They understand you felt like your conscience was telling you to take this case. I think they respect that about you. Now they want to reestablish their relationship with their son." She leaned forward, clasping her hands around her knee. Had she intentionally pressed her upper arms close into her sides?

He surged out of the chair and paced the perimeter of the room, coming to a stop at the window that overlooked the cul-de-sac in front of the house. "If they're so eager to reestablish our relationship, why haven't they contacted me? They know how to get in touch with me. They know where I live—obviously, because they told you how to get here."

"Actually, that was Meredith." Frustration laced Evelyn's voice. "They haven't contacted you directly because they aren't sure if you would accept a direct line of contact from them. Why do you think I'm here?"

He turned, crossed his arms, and leaned his hip against the windowsill. "You want me to believe that my parents sent you here as their emissary? You—an outsider? Someone who knows next to nothing about our family, about how we relate with each other?"

"Who better than a neutral party?"

Answering a question with a question. His guard rose even higher. "Did my parents send you?"

"Forbes, why else would I be here?" She pushed herself out of the chair and stalked toward him.

He stopped her with the look he usually reserved for hostile—or otherwise uncooperative—witnesses "Yes or no. Did my parents ask you to come to my house and talk to me about a reconciliation?"

The sweet seductiveness left Evelyn's expression. "Not exactly, no." She closed the space between them until she stood almost toe-to-toe with him. She ran her index finger down his sternum. "I came because I'm worried about you, Forbes, because in the time we spent together earlier this summer, I came to. . .care for you."

Forbes tried to take a step back, but he'd made the mistake of allowing her to trap him in the corner. "Don't do this."

She ran her hands up his arms to his shoulders and leaned forward until her body pressed up against his. "We all want you to come back. Your family needs you. And you need them."

He took hold of her upper arms to try to push her away as gently as he could. Last thing he needed was for Evelyn to bring an assault charge against him.

Stronger than she appeared, she hooked one hand behind his head. With neck and shoulder muscles already sore, he found it hard to resist the pressure of her hand.

Suddenly, her lips crushed against his.

He pushed harder against her upper arms and finally broke the kiss.

The rasp of a throat clearing blasted across the quiet room. Evelyn jumped back; Forbes wiped his mouth on the back of his hand.

Alaine stood in the doorway, her expression inscrutable. "The garage door was open, so I let myself in."

Chapter 26

Alaine willed her knees to stay solid beneath her. When Forbes hadn't shown up by seven thirty, she'd figured she'd save him the hassle of picking her up by meeting him here. But at least now she knew the truth behind why he'd wanted to push their date back an hour.

Past experience with boyfriends who'd cheated on her screamed for her to leave the house—slamming every door behind her as she went—and never speak to Forbes again. But she stood her ground. When she first walked in, Forbes and Evelyn—*Evelyn Mackenzie* of all people—appeared to be entwined in a passionate embrace. But when Evelyn showed herself to be the aggressor and kissed Forbes, the reasonable part of Alaine's brain kicked in and told her not to believe what she thought she saw.

Alaine raised her eyebrows and looked at Forbes, trying to keep every trace of accusation out of her expression. "Don't we have dinner reservations?"

Forbes's posture went limp for a split second; then he composed himself. "Yes. Seven forty-five, which means we'd better go or we're going to be late." He walked past Evelyn and joined Alaine at the door. His blue gray eyes decidedly worried, he leaned over and kissed her cheek. "This wasn't what it looked like." His breath tickled her ear.

"You can explain over crawfish-stuffed fried ravioli."

"I guess I should be going then." Evelyn grabbed a bundle of clothes and a pair of hideous stiletto sandals from the floor beside the chair Alaine usually occupied in this room—that would change as of now.

Alaine gave her a tight-lipped smile. "Yes, that would be a good idea." *And never come back!* she wanted to scream. With pressure from her shoulder, Alaine positioned Forbes so she was between him and the hussy when Evelyn passed them to exit. "Be careful driving in the rain."

Evelyn stopped by the stairs. "Oh, Forbes, your shirt." She reached behind her back and started undoing the wad of fabric, as if she was going to take it off right then and there in front of God and everybody.

He closed his eyes and held up a hand. "Keep it. I was never going to wear it."

Alaine trailed the woman and stood at the top of the half flight of stairs leading down to the front door. Evelyn turned around and looked before opening the door. Alaine smiled and waved. "Nice to see you again. B'bye."

Okay, so maybe catty wasn't the most Christian way to go. But she couldn't help herself. She'd barely started to turn around when Forbes pulled her into an overwhelming hug.

"Thank you so much for showing up when you did." His voice sounded muffled in her hair.

"Yeah, well, I'm hungry, and I was tired of waiting. So"—after a few seconds' struggle, she succeeded in pulling away—"let's go. I had to park behind you because the other side of the driveway was occupied, so I'll drive." She softened slightly at his hangdog expression. "Anyway, I know how much you hate driving in the rain."

She made a mad dash to the Mazda while Forbes, with his giant umbrella, closed the garage door using the security keypad outside. As always, once he got into the car, he fought with stowing the oversized umbrella without sprinkling them both with water.

Alaine pulled out of the driveway. "So. . .Evelyn Mackenzie paid you a visit tonight."

Forbes rubbed the right side of his neck. She softened a little bit more—but no, he had a ways to go to get out of this doghouse. "She was standing at the front door when I got home from Russ's. Said she needed to talk to me. I told her I only had a few minutes."

"And the T-shirt?" Alaine rolled to a stop at the light leading out of the complex and cast him a sidelong glance.

"It was either give her something to change into or try not to look at her sitting there in a soaked white silk blouse. You'd think she'd have learned to carry an umbrella with her by now."

The light turned green. "Uh-huh. So what was it she wanted to talk to you about?"

"My parents."

"Your—" She stole a look at him, alarmed. "Are they okay?"

He nodded, and she turned her attention back to the road.

"That was my first reaction as well. She came under the pretense of telling me that my parents miss me and they want to reconcile with me. That she's worried about them and what this estrangement is doing to them."

"That's ironic, coming from her—at least what you've told me about her." Alaine checked her mirrors, then looked over her shoulder before changing lanes.

"I said that to her, too. That's when she tried the. . .*other* tactic."

"The old 'if you can't beat 'em, seduce 'em' tactic? The hussy." If Alaine didn't think spitting were disgusting, she'd spit. "Coming on to my man like that."

He squeezed her shoulder. "So. . .you believe me, then? That it was all her? That I didn't want to have anything to do with it?"

"Forbes, one thing I've learned in almost two months of dating you is that if you wanted to kiss her, she wouldn't have had to practically strangle you to make it happen." She pulled into the parking lot at Palermo's. "Ooh, look, someone saved us the best parking space." She whipped into the space just a few feet from the covered walkway leading to the restaurant's front door.

Though utterly silly, she sat in the car and waited until Forbes came around and opened the door for her. Sometimes, she enjoyed his old-fashioned ways. Other times, they made her feel ridiculous. But that was something she could deal with for now.

He didn't let go of her hand once she exited the car, but kissed it several times over. "Have I told you recently how crazy I am about you?"

"Or just plain crazy." She laughed, but deep down, the fact that, after all this time, he still hadn't used the *L*-word bothered her. They were going to the same church; he had Sunday dinner with her family every week; he even called her his girlfriend in front of other people. So why couldn't he bring himself to declare his love?

"Well, well, well. If it isn't the supercouple of Bonneterre."

Alaine and Forbes both turned at the familiar voice. "Hey, Shon." Alaine hugged Forbes's neighbor and client. "What brings you out tonight? Don't tell me you have a date!" She winked at him.

He glowered back at her. "No, as a matter of fact I'm working. Let's Do Coffee is hosting a mixer tonight—it's something new I'm trying. I've invited a select group of clients to come in for an informal meet and greet. Afterward, each one will fill out comment cards, and I'll match them up for coffee dates from there." He moved past them and opened the door. "I'd ask y'all to join us, but since you're both off the market, it would defeat the purpose. Although. . ." He eyed them. "I could bring you in as an LDC success story."

Forbes let out a barking laugh. "Yes, but would that be truth in advertising? I mean, seeing as how you set us up with Riley and Zebra Woman, not with each other."

Shon's dark eyes glittered, reflecting the multiple bulbs in the chandelier above them. "*Au contraire,* monsieur. I may have sent other people to the coffee shop at the same time you were there and implied those were the people I wanted you to meet, but I knew they weren't right for you." He pulled them aside so other customers entering could get to the hostess stand unimpeded. "Forbes, why do you think I gave you a free, three-month membership?"

Forbes glanced at Alaine. She shrugged, and both looked back at Shon.

He sighed. "Because Alaine had just signed up for a membership. And I knew from the first time I met her that even if you hadn't had an eighth-grade-level crush on her for a couple of years, she was the right woman for you. But when I took her registration money, I was committed to setting her up with someone I felt was a good fit for her."

"Thanks for refunding that money, by the way." Alaine squeezed Shon's wrist.

Shon ducked his head. "Well. . .after your 'dates,' even though it did get the two of you together as I'd hoped, I felt guilty about how I'd set you up." He turned on his heel and marched over to the hostess stand.

"Yes, Mr. Murphy, we have you set up in the Milan Room in the back." The hostess called someone over her headset, then looked up questioningly at Forbes.

"We'll be with you momentarily," he told the girl, then pulled Shon away with what looked like a painful grip on the upper arm. "What do you mean, how you set us up?"

Shon cleared his throat and glanced around as if to make sure no one could hear him. "Riley and Zebra Lady aren't actually LDC clients. They. . .well, Zebra Lady, as you call her, is one of our coordinators—her name is Laura. And I play basketball with Riley twice a week down at the YMCA. Oh, and Forbes—Laura told me about the whole age thing."

Now it was Forbes's turn to duck his head in embarrassment. "Yeah, tell her again how sorry I am."

"She got a huge laugh out of it. We threw a surprise party at work last week for her fiftieth birthday."

Forbes didn't have the energy to look at the caller ID on the phone when it rang. A few seconds later, the intercom buzzed. "Forbes, she wants you upstairs."

Suppressing the desire to sleep for a week, he hit the button.

"Thanks, Sam." Feeling like one of the living dead, he trudged to the elevator.

While he'd enjoyed the two hours he'd lingered over dinner with Alaine last night, it had meant staying up until two o'clock in the morning, reading all the new motions and briefs. Then he'd woken up at five o'clock with stabbing pain in his shoulder and neck. Since none of the over-the-counter pain relievers he had at home seemed to be doing any good, he got up, got dressed, and came into the office to get some work for his other clients out of the way so he could get out of here early this afternoon and try to get in to see his doctor.

Straightening his tie and jacket—but he couldn't do anything about the dark circles under his eyes—he stalked past Mary's vacant desk and into Sandra's office.

He drew up short just inside the door. At the conference table under the bank of windows, sat managing partner Sandra Landreneau, partner emeritus—and city councilwoman—Tess Folse, and partner Hayden Maier. Mary watched him owlishly from the opposite end of the long table, a stenographer's notebook in front of her. His bowels twisted into a knot.

"Come in and shut the door, Forbes."

He was getting really sick of hearing Sandra say that. He took the seat directly across from her—beside Hayden—and took a slow, deep breath.

"Mary, please start taking notes," Sandra directed. "This is an emergency meeting of the partners of Folse, Landreneau, Maier, and Guidry, Attorneys at Law, LLC. It has become increasingly apparent that an amendment to the partnership agreement is needed." She handed a piece of paper to each of them to read. "In short, the amendment states that no partner shall take a case against an existing client of the firm; to knowingly do so will be grounds for demotion or separation. This amendment is retroactive."

Forbes's skin went clammy. Amendments to the agreement only needed a majority, not a unanimous, vote. Stepping outside of his own situation, he could see the merit of the amendment in protecting the partners and the firm from accusations of conflict of interest.

"The floor is open for discussion."

"It seems very well laid out to me," Tess looked over her reading glasses. "No questions or comments. Hayden?"

The youngest of the three women—only seven years older than Forbes—looked up from her copy. "It's in the best interest of the firm. Forbes?"

God, why is this happening to me, now? Hearing that the other three were in favor of the change—probably discussed and drafted between the three of them without his input—what would be the point in arguing? "No comments or questions."

They all gaped at him for a long moment. Sandra shook herself out of it first. "Very well, then. All in favor of amending the partnership agreement thusly, raise your right hand."

Sandra, Tess, and Hayden all raised their hands. Big surprise there.

"Opposed, by same sign."

Forbes raised his right hand.

"Amendment is approved and goes into effect immediately." Sandra reached for another folder, which she opened, then turned and laid in front of Forbes. "Pursuant to Amendment 16, paragraph (c), as you are the signatory counsel for the case of *Moreaux Mills v. Boudreaux-Guidry Enterprises*, this is your one-week notice. You have seven days from today to decide between leaving the firm or resigning from the Mills case. If you decide to leave the firm, you will have fourteen days from the date of your decision to contact your book of business to inform them you're leaving. If you resign from the Mills case, no further action will be taken against you nor will this situation reflect negatively on you.

"Your answer must be made to the other three partners in writing by"—she looked at her watch—"nine o'clock next Friday morning." She pulled the folder to her and wrote the date and time in the appropriate blanks, then slid it back toward him. "Please sign and date at the bottom indicating that you understand the reason you've been given this letter and that you will abide by it."

He did so—surprised that blue ink instead of blood flowed out of his pen.

"Do you have any questions?" Sandra's reading glasses swung on their beaded chain as she retrieved the folder.

"No, ma'am." He pushed his chair back a little. "Now, if that's all, I have a very busy day today."

"Mary will make a copy of this for you." Sandra held up the file. The gray-haired secretary scuttled over and snatched the folder.

Forbes stood and gave a little half bow. "Good morning, ladies." He followed Mary from the office but hung back when she went to the photocopier. No sense in getting too near the bear in her den.

"Here." She thrust the copies at him, then craned her neck to look around him toward Sandra's door. "And off the record"—she lowered her voice—"I think it's horrible that they're doing this to you. I think it's a right noble thing you're doing for the people down in the Mills. I grew up down there, you know. My daddy was a foreman in the lumberyard before the paper mill shut down."

Forbes could have sat down in the middle of the floor and laughed—or cried. He settled for kissing the irascible woman's cheek instead. "Thanks, Mary. And your secret is safe with me."

The crisis—the panic—didn't set in until Forbes made it back down to his office. "Hold all calls please, Samantha." He blew by her desk, not even looking at her because if she had the least sympathy or concern in her eyes, he might lose it.

After closing the door, he couldn't get his coat and tie off fast enough—pulling off one of the buttons in the process, which skittered across the wood floor. He flung the coat and tie onto the small conference table, not caring about the paperwork they scattered.

"Why now, God? I had everything under control. I was handling everything."

Well, maybe the situation with the family wasn't controlled or handled as much as compartmentalized and not thought about. And attending a different church to avoid the uncomfortable encounters with his family wasn't controlling or handling the situation, but running away. And while he was handling working eighteen-hour days, six days a week, he'd long since lost the feeling that his life was in any way, shape, or form under his control.

Excruciating pain shot down the side of his neck and across the top of his right shoulder. He stabbed his finger on the intercom button on the phone. "Samantha, cancel the rest of my day. I'm going to the doctor, and then I'm going home."

"Y–yes, boss."

He looked around his office. Typically, he'd take most of the paperwork now scattered across the table and floor home with him to work on over the weekend. But not today. He retrieved his coat and tie—and the button that had rolled behind the ficus tree—grabbed his nearly empty briefcase, and walked out, locking the door behind him.

Snarled traffic and pain every time he moved his head didn't improve Forbes's mood. "What do you want from me, God? All my life, You've put me in situations where I've had to take control. I don't understand what I'm supposed to do."

When no audible answer came, Forbes turned the radio on and switched it from the news station to the next preset. He'd caught it just as a new song started. The twangy guitars and old-fashioned organ music sounded familiar. Yep—this was one he'd listened to with the guys as a possibility for the quartet. He sang the opening line along with the Southern gospel group on the radio.

" 'All to Jesus I surrender, all to Him I freely give.'" His throat nearly closed at the impact of the words.

Control or surrender?

He pulled into the parking garage at the medical center and turned off the engine. Silence filled the car—but a silence different than any he'd ever experienced. He tried to bow his head, but pain stopped him. He closed his eyes and found a comfortable position.

"Lord, I don't know how to surrender. I only know how to control. But I feel like You're telling me it's time to let go and let You handle everything. I can't promise I'll never try to control anything again. All I can do is promise to try to surrender my will to You and ask for Your help in learning to do it."

He sat a little while longer, enjoying the moments filled with nothing to control, then got out of the car feeling, for the first time in weeks, that things might work out okay, after all.

Following a three-hour wait and a diagnosis of stress-triggered muscle spasms, Forbes picked up the prescription muscle relaxers and painkillers on his way home. Deciding he deserved an indulgence, he stopped at Maxi's Diner in midtown and ordered a deluxe cheeseburger with onion rings *and* french fries to take home for lunch.

He changed into running shorts and a TV-station-logoed T-shirt he'd gotten at one of Alaine's live remote events, then carried his food and a bottle of sparkling water upstairs to the fourth-floor media room to watch the recording of Alaine's program on the big-screen plasma television, which he usually didn't use unless he had people over to watch movies. He fast-forwarded through the first ten minutes of headlines and weather—even though he really liked Bekka Blakeley the few times he and Alaine had gone out with the newscaster and her veterinarian husband. He wasn't watching this for news.

As soon as Alaine's face appeared, larger than life, the pain in his shoulder eased—though it had been almost half an hour since he'd taken those pills. He devoured the junk food while watching the love of his life on TV doing her thing.

Soon, though, he slowed, then stopped eating altogether. Keeping his eyes open seemed to be his most important task at the moment. Giving in to the fatigue, he stretched out on the sofa—on his left side—and promptly fell asleep.

An incessant buzzing sound woke him. He caught the phone just as it vibrated itself off the coffee table. "Hello?" His voice sounded like he'd eaten lava rocks for lunch instead of a burger.

"Forbes?"

He cleared his throat. "Yeah, Mere, it's me."

"Oh—you aren't sick are you?" The concern in her voice warmed his heart.

"No. Just taking a nap."

"Taking a—you aren't *sick* are you?"

He laughed—and it felt good. "I have muscle spasms in my shoulder and neck. The drugs the doc gave me knocked me out." He blinked the bleariness out of his eyes and squinted to focus on the small clock on a shelf of the built-ins. Almost five o'clock. That had been a long nap. "What's up?"

"Major and I were wondering if you and Alaine would be interested in meeting us at Magdalena's for supper tonight. He did that guest segment with the head chef from there that aired today, and they invited us to come to the restaurant for dinner tonight at six—and told us to bring guests. So I thought of you and Alaine, since we haven't seen you in several weeks."

"Please tell me that Evelyn Mackenzie isn't going to be there."

"No. Why?"

He launched into the story as he gathered up the remnants of his lunch, now soggy and unappetizing to look at, and carried the detritus all the way down to the garage to put straight into the trash bin.

"And she told you that I gave her your address?" Meredith sounded not just appalled but outraged.

"That's what she said." He rolled his head, then his shoulder, testing the muscles. Still painful, but nowhere near as bad as before.

"The liar. I'm so glad she left today."

Forbes tripped on the stairs going back up to the main floor. "What?"

"She didn't tell you last night that she was going back to Boston today?"

He sank onto the steps and rubbed his stubbed toe. "No. Why'd she leave? And when is she coming back so I'll know when to start worrying about her showing up at my house again?"

"She's not coming back. Mom came in and told me this morning that they'd come to a mutual agreement that Evelyn had done everything she needed to do here and until. . .until the case is settled, there isn't anything else Mackenzie and Son can do for us."

The doorbell echoed from upstairs. "Hey, Sis, someone's here. I'll call Alaine and get back to you about dinner tonight. You said six o'clock, right?" He jogged up the remainder of the stairs to the front hall.

"Yeah. But if y'all need extra time, we'll wait for you."

He finished the conversation with his sister and tucked the phone in his pocket before opening the door.

Alaine stood on the other side of it, her fine brows pinched together. "Are you okay?"

He stepped back so she could enter. "Yeah, I'm fine. Why?"

"I called your office before I left work, and your secretary told me you'd left this morning and said you were going to the doctor and then coming home. What's wrong?" She planted her fists on her hips.

Laughing, he pulled her into a hug. When her arms went around his waist and tightened, he almost forgot his pain. He told her about the doctor visit and the diagnosis.

She tilted her head back, mischief twinkling in her dark eyes. "So it's official? You really are a pain in the neck?"

He leaned down to kiss her, ignoring the way his neck twinged at that angle. He ended the kiss quickly, for his own safety, and tucked her back into his arms, resting his cheek on the top of her head. "I was on the phone with my sister Meredith when you arrived."

"Really?"

"Yeah. She called to see if we'd like to meet her and Major for supper at that Spanish restaurant—Magdaline's?"

"Magdalena's. Oh, they've got great food. But"—she pushed against his chest, and he allowed her to move back a little—"how do you feel about meeting them for dinner? I know you've been trying to limit your contact with them to try to protect them."

"No, I've been avoiding them to try to protect myself." The words came out of his mouth before he'd even thought them through. "But that's over. I'd really like to go if you want to."

"I'd like to. I've missed Meredith."

"You don't talk to her anymore?"

"I figured you knew that, seeing as how we never talk about her."

"No. I thought you probably just weren't telling me when you'd talked to her or seen her."

"Out of respect for you, I've also been limiting my contact with her and Major, though it's slightly harder with him since he does come into the studio at least one day every week for a voice-over session."

He kissed her forehead. "Thank you for that. But I don't want you giving up your friends just because of me."

She smiled and shook her head.

"So, how fancy is this restaurant?" He looped his arm around her neck and escorted her up to the main floor.

"Shirt and tie, chinos or khakis. Not overly fancy. What time are we supposed to meet them?"

Instead of turning right at the landing and going into the living room, he turned left and led her into the study—but then, as soon as his eyes swept over the corner, he looked down at her, regretting his decision.

But Alaine was already moving away from him. She walked over to sit in the club chair nearer the fireplace instead of the one she usually sat in—the one where Evelyn had perched last night.

"Forbes?"

"Huh? Oh, we're supposed to meet them there at six."

Alaine looked at the antique clock on the mantel, then checked the time on her cell phone. "Forty-five minutes." She bounced back out of the chair again. "I'll run home and change clothes and pick you up at five thirty."

"Pick me up?"

"You told me you've taken prescription painkillers and muscle relaxers and slept at least three hours this afternoon. I'd rather not have you fall asleep behind the wheel, even though we aren't going far." She raised up on tiptoe and kissed his cheek. "I'll see you in a little bit."

He grabbed her hand before she got past him and pulled her

back for a real kiss. "Have I told you recently how much I love you?" He'd meant to save it for a special occasion, but now was as special a time as he needed.

Alaine's face paled, but her eyes glowed. "No, as a matter of fact you haven't."

"How remiss of me." He cupped her face in his hands. "I love you"—he kissed her forehead—"very"—the bridge of her nose—"very"—the tip of her nose—"very"—her left cheek—"very"—her right cheek—"very much." He pressed his lips to hers and lost himself in the wonder and joy that came from finding the one thing in life he could easily surrender to: love.

Chapter 27

Alaine still hadn't stopped tingling by the time she pulled into the restaurant parking lot. He'd said it. He'd actually said it.

She cut the engine and popped out of the car—only to come face-to-face with a disappointed-looking Forbes.

"Oh, fine." She unlocked the car and climbed back in just so he could open the door and assist her out. "You're so weird."

"Nah, he's just a control freak." Meredith and Major joined them. Alaine stood back while Forbes and Meredith hugged, holding on to each other for a long time, seeming to try to catch up on two months' worth of missed communication in hushed tones.

Alaine chatted with Major, who had some ideas for upcoming segments to feature executive chefs at other restaurants in town, which Alaine was all in favor of, especially when he mentioned several restaurants in the Mills.

Finally, Meredith and Forbes finished their whispered conversation. Meredith hugged Alaine in greeting, and the foursome entered the restaurant. The hostess showed them to a table in the back of the restaurant—a table for six. Forbes balked, and Alaine had to stop with him, since he had hold of her hand.

"Who else is coming?"

"What?" Meredith looked at the table. "Oh, we asked Anne and

George to come as well, but they had a wedding rehearsal tonight so couldn't." She looked at Major, who gave a slight nod. "We thought about asking Mom and Dad to come but didn't want to cause any trouble."

Major rubbed his hand in a circle on his wife's back. "And I wanted Meredith to be able to actually eat and enjoy the food tonight."

The executive chef came out; and as soon as he saw Alaine, he turned incoherent—in English or in Spanish. She even tried Portuguese, which only sent him further into raptures. Listening carefully, she managed to get the gist of what he was saying—that just since the show aired that afternoon, their phone had been ringing constantly for bookings.

Within minutes of their arrivals, plates of tapas appeared on the table. Each dish held a measure of familiarity for Alaine, being from the same part of the world as her own ethnic cuisine, which Mother made so well and so often. And yet the chef's signature shone through in each presentation. She'd have to bring Mother and Daddy here—maybe get Joe and Tony to pitch in and bring them for their anniversary or something.

After tapas came six or seven main courses, which were set in the middle of the table so they could try some of each. Forbes reached for the dish closest to him but put it down and reached for his Blackberry.

His expression clouded as he read whatever message he'd received that was urgent enough to look at during dinner. But he clipped the device back to his belt and squeezed her hand before going back to serving himself.

"So, anyway," Alaine said, returning to her conversation with Meredith and Major, "I played softball on the girls' team at church during the summer a few years. I hated it. But it was either that or soccer, and I disliked soccer more. Too much running around. In softball, they stuck me in the outfield, and at eight or nine years old, most girls aren't going to hit it past the bases. And those who were serious about playing the game—you know, who wanted to go on to play in high school or college—played in the city league anyway."

"But what about watching it?" Meredith asked. "We're usually out there on Friday nights playing, but the citywide interchurch pastors' conference is this weekend, and since so many of the teams have their pastors on their teams, they gave us a bye weekend. You ought to come out next Friday to watch us play. As a matter of fact, I think my team might be playing the ladies' team from your church."

"Are the stands air-conditioned?"

Meredith and Major both laughed. "You're right, Forbes, she is perfect for you."

Forbes sat silent, contemplating the food on the plate in front of him, not reacting in the slightest to his sister's comment. Alaine exchanged a concerned look with Meredith, then turned and touched Forbes's shoulder.

He startled and snapped his attention away from his untouched main courses. "I'm sorry. What was the question?"

"It wasn't a question, we were just worried because we lost you there for a minute." She rubbed her hand lightly along his shoulder. "Is it bothering you again?"

"No, it's not that." His jaw took on a hard set. "It's nothing. Let's just enjoy dinner."

"We can't enjoy it if you aren't." Meredith put her fork down. Alaine and Major followed suit.

"Was it the message you received a few minutes ago?" Alaine nodded toward the phone.

"Partially." He sighed, wiped his mouth, and tossed the napkin on the table beside his plate. "Something happened at work today. I—the other partners called a meeting to vote on an amendment to the partnership agreement. . .which is basically the contract we all signed when we became equity partners in the firm that states how profits are to be divided, how we're to conduct business, and what, if any, actions can lead to separation—getting fired."

Alaine's heart sank. "So they finally did it?"

His lips pressed together in a grim line. "I have one week to decide if I'm going to leave the firm or if I'm going to resign as lead counsel for the plaintiffs in the Mills case."

More like *only* counsel than *lead* counsel, but she wasn't going to quibble.

"Then, a few minutes ago, I got an e-mail from B-G's lawyer—who is the managing partner of the firm that's just given me an ultimatum—saying that B-G wants to meet with counsel for the class, me, to discuss another offer."

Alaine frowned. "But we're—they're not asking for a monetary settlement. What are they talking about?"

"What it means is that they're going to change the amount they're offering to buy everyone out. They just don't *get it*." Forbes's hands, which had been braced flat against the table now balled into fists. "Why can't they see what they're doing is wrong? Haven't I staked everything on that assertion?"

Alaine laid her hand atop the closest fist. "You just have to have faith that God is going to show you how to get through to them. You have to let go of the idea that if you just work hard enough or sacrifice enough, they'll see the light and change over to your perspective. It was never going to be as easy as asking for a different dessert than the other sixty people at the banquet receive." She ducked her chin and gazed up at him.

He dislodged his hand from hers and bumped it gently under her chin before leaning over to kiss the tip of her nose. "You're correct, of course. But that still leaves the decision about the job. I believe in the merits and principles of this case so much so that I have already staked my career on it just by taking it. But I have to be sure I'm not making the decision to choose the case over the firm for reasons that are less than. . .objective."

Alaine interpreted his significant look at her. "You're afraid that our relationship might cloud your judgment because my family is involved. Would it make any difference if I told you that I'd still love you no matter what you choose? Because that's the truth. I want you to be happy, Forbes. I don't want you to ruin your career on a case you don't believe in just because we're dating. Nor would I want you to ruin your soul by staying in a job that's become increasingly unsatisfactory for you in the past couple of months. I mean, come on, think about how often I've heard you complain about the Pichon case. About how if you had your choice, you'd have been sitting in Russ's position in that argument."

Forbes didn't say anything for a long time but put his napkin back down on his lap and started eating again, for which Alaine was grateful. The tapas had been tasty, but not filling. She could almost hear Forbes praying about his decision, and she interceded on his behalf the entire time.

After several minutes, Meredith returned to the innocuous topic of softball. Alaine kept half her attention on Forbes, though.

A few minutes later, a "eureka, I've found it" smile overtook Forbes's handsome face.

"What?" Alaine asked.

"Tomorrow, I'm going to find out who's the real-estate agent for that vacant office space next door to Anne's on Town Square." He shoveled a huge spoonful of paella into his mouth.

A chunk of beef from Alaine's *cocido Madrileño* slipped off her spoon and plopped back into the bowl. "You mean. . .you're going to start. . ."

"My own law firm. I have several clients who'll follow me over if I hang out a shingle, and there are a lot of good people out there who need more help than what a community legal aid center can provide—but can't afford a billable rate of five hundred dollars per hour or more. I can run things the way I want to, take on only the clients I want to."

Alaine could hardly stay in her seat from wanting to dance around the table in joy. "Sounds like a plan."

"Of course, it's going to take a while to get it up and going, and even longer before I start to see a steady income." He raised his eyebrows and cocked his head.

"Good thing you already own your town house and car outright." She winked at him. "I'm sure you have savings you can live on for a few months. Some things are worth working and waiting for."

The office space had seemed much larger than this when Forbes had done the final walk-through last week before signing the closing papers. The large, open room that comprised the first floor of the converted Victorian row house smelled of fresh paint and sawdust from the newly laid wood floors. The furniture he'd rented—from Joe Delacroix—to suffice until he could afford to buy all new stuff hadn't filled the space by any means, but now, with the dozen claimants included in the class action for the lawsuit seated in every available chair—including the four he'd borrowed from Anne next door—the room felt tight and overcrowded.

His nerves fought to get the better of him. This would be his first official action as the sole lawyer at the Forbes Guidry, Attorney at Law, law firm, without the prestige of being a name partner in the most successful law firm in town.

JD and Joe Delacroix, bless them, had worn themselves out helping Forbes get everything set up so that they could meet with Sandra Landreneau and Forbes's parents here instead of in the more intimidating executive conference room at Folse, Landreneau & Maier.

Alaine finished her phone conversation with someone from her work and came to stand in front of him. She made a fuss over the position of his tie's knot, then smoothed her hands down his lapels. "I'll be praying for you the whole time."

"Thanks. I'll need it." He kissed her cheek. As Mom and Dad and Sandra had not yet arrived, Forbes needed to use this time wisely. He went to the middle of the room and asked for quiet.

"I'm not certain exactly what they're going to come in here and offer." He looked around and tried to make eye contact with everyone. "But no matter what they say, don't react—positively or negatively. This is like haggling at a bazaar. If you show the least sign of vulnerability or emotion, the other side has you where they want you.

"What's most likely to happen is that they're going to come in, make their offer, and then give us time to discuss it so we can decide if we want to respond immediately or take longer. No matter what they offer, I intend to ask for at least a week to respond; that way we can come up with a counterproposal."

Rustling sounds behind him quickened his pulse. "Does everyone agree?" Nods and murmured agreement surrounded him. "Good."

The front door swung open, and Sandra Landreneau processed in like a queen—with Evelyn Mackenzie following her like a spoiled princess, and Mom and Dad like supplicants waiting to perform their lieges' bidding. Forbes's heart sank. Evelyn's reappearance spelled doom for a reasonable settlement offer.

"I'll go now." Alaine touched Forbes's arm. "Don't forget, I'm praying."

He caressed her cheek. "I love you."

"Love you, too." She wrinkled her nose at him and went outside, past the large front window toward Anne's office.

"Ms. Landreneau, are you ready to proceed?" Forbes asked, motioning for them to sit at the long table, where JD and the other business association board members sat waiting.

"We are."

Forbes took his seat, then signaled for Sandra to begin. He took copious notes during her twenty-minute opening statement—none of which represented much more than her legal double-talk that basically said that her clients had done no wrong and therefore the residents of Moreaux Mills represented in this case should consider it an honor to receive an increased settlement offer from the defendants.

Through continuous covert glances, Forbes tried to gauge what his parents were thinking during all of this. His father looked grim, his face set in that infuriatingly unreadable expression he'd developed for hiding his emotions. Mom's mouth grew thinner and thinner the longer Sandra talked. Evelyn smiled slightly but looked only at Sandra.

". . .and it is therefore the privilege of the plaintiff to receive—"

"Ms. Landreneau," Forbes interrupted with a sigh, "it's almost three thirty. Most of these people have taken time away from their jobs—time for which, unlike you, they are not getting paid. Can we dispense with the posturing and get on to the settlement offer? Some of us would like to get out of here sooner rather than later."

Outrage flashing in her eyes, Sandra inclined her head. "If you insist."

Forbes flipped to a clean page of his legal pad, steeling himself to show no outward reaction no matter what he heard.

Sandra finished rustling through her notes. "The defendant, Boudreaux-Guidry Enterprises, under advisement from myself and their partner firm, Mackenzie and Son, have agreed to offer an additional 20 percent of the value of each property represented in the class; and if the terms are accepted, the plaintiffs represented in the class cannot solicit bids or buyers for—"

A hand slammed down, open palmed, on the table. Forbes—and everyone else in the room—jumped.

"That is *not* what we agreed to." Mom stood, one hand on her hip, the other pointing at Evelyn and Sandra. "I want to go back to the original settlement offer. Original—"

"Don't say anything else!" Sandra jumped to her feet. Forbes wouldn't have been surprised if the lawyer had clapped her hand over Mom's mouth to keep her from saying anything else.

He kept his startled amusement under lock and key. "Do you need a few minutes to sort this out with your clients?"

"No—"

"Yes, we do," Mom answered.

"Fine." Forbes stood as well and looked around at all of his clients. "I would imagine y'all want a break as much as I do. There's a coffee shop just a few doors down that has a public restroom if you need it. Let's give Ms. Landreneau and her clients fifteen minutes, shall we?"

Forbes caught JD by the arm to have a private word with him at the back of the group crowding out through the front door, and by the time Forbes made it out onto the wide, shady sidewalk, he had only one goal in mind.

Everyone crowded around him once the front door shut behind him, wanting to know what just happened and how it would affect the case. He tried to set their minds at ease, while edging toward Anne's office. Finally appeased, everyone moved down the covered sidewalk toward the Beignets S'il Vous Plait coffee shop.

His hand barely touched the doorknob on Anne's front door when Alaine came out, holding her cell phone toward him. "Mother wants to talk to you."

He pressed the small phone to his ear and listened in complete silence to what Solange had to say, thanked her when she finished, then handed the phone back to Alaine.

"What was that all about?"

"I'll tell you later." He placed her hand in the crook of his elbow and led her to the bench against the wall between his and Anne's offices. He waited for Alaine to sit first, then sat beside her and took her hand in both of his. "Do you realize, if I lose this case, or don't get a favorable settlement or ruling for the people in the Mills, it could ruin my little fledgling law firm?"

"Even with other clients, this case is that big a deal?"

He cocked his head and tapped her forehead with his finger. "Uh...it's why I was forced out of my previous law firm."

"But I mean, big enough to be something that if you lose, you'll never work in this town again kind of thing?" She waved his hand away and leaned into his side, resting her head on his shoulder.

"Potentially."

"I've already told you I love you no matter what happens. And I know that God has your future in His hands, and He's not going to lead you down a dead-end street."

"I know. I just wish...." He leaned his cheek against her soft hair.

"You just wish you had God's omniscience so you could see everything that was coming so you could control it."

"No. I just wish the future wasn't quite so uncertain."

"But without uncertainty, there'd be no need for faith."

"There are some things about the future we can control, you

know." He turned her hand over and made lazy circles on the palm with his thumb.

A shudder wracked Alaine's body; he smiled. He liked knowing he had such an effect on her. "Like what?" Her voice came out strained.

"Oh, like making wise decisions—decisions based on godly principles, not worldly advice. Living each day with our eyes open for the opportunities God is putting in front of us. And most importantly, realizing when waiting for a more opportune moment to do something is stupid." Keeping hold of her left hand, Forbes turned and went from bench to one knee on the sidewalk in a flash.

Alaine jumped and let out a little gasp—as did several people around them who'd returned from the coffee shop. JD stood out of his daughter's line of sight, a big grin splitting his face.

Forbes kissed Alaine's hand. "I was planning to wait until tonight while we were out dancing, because I wanted this to be connected with one of your favorite things in the world. But I find myself unable to wait any longer." He pulled the small velvet pouch out of the inside pocket of his suit coat and shook its contents into his other hand.

Though wracked with nervousness just half an hour ago waiting to find out what would happen with his parents, nothing in the world had ever felt more right, more comfortable, than this moment in time as he slipped the platinum band with the large marquis diamond onto Alaine's finger.

He clasped her hand in both of his. "I love you more than anything in the world, and I cannot live without you in my life. Will you marry me?"

Two huge tears rolled down her cheeks, but he'd never seen her smile grow so wide or beam so brightly. "Yes, yes, yes, yes, yes, yes, yes, *yes*!" She flung her arms around his neck.

With a whoop, Forbes jumped up, hoisting Alaine in his arms, jubilating in her response and the cheers of the crowd around them.

He lowered her feet to the ground and leaned down and kissed her right and proper, drawing more cheers and wolf whistles from the crowd.

JD came over to hug his daughter. Anne's office door swung open, and she and George joined them. Forbes could hardly wait until JD and Anne finished hugging Alaine to pull her back into his arms again.

The door of his office burst open.

"No!" Mom's voice echoed under the canopy covering the sidewalk. "I don't care what Mackenzie and Son recommends—they're the ones who got us into this mess in the first place. I want to know what *my son* recommends." Forbes's mother halted abruptly—Dad had to swerve to keep from running into her from behind. The small crowd parted for them.

Forbes wouldn't let Alaine step away from him. He wanted his parents to be able to figure out what had just happened here.

"I am warning you, Mairee, Lawson, if you fire me and cancel the Mackenzie contract, you're taking your business down the road to ruin."

Forbes had never seen Sandra Landreneau so red in the face. And from Evelyn's narrowed eyes, he could tell she instantly recognized the tableau outside for what it was.

Sandra seemed to be the only one oblivious to what she'd walked into. "This is not a case about sentimentality or hometown values or whatever the other nonsense was you were talking about in there. This is a case about profits—about what's profitable for us and for the city."

A beatific smile transformed Mairee Guidry's face from that of a tired, middle-aged woman to a woman in her prime. She turned on her former sorority sister. "You're wrong, Sandra, which is why we're firing you. This is not a case about money. This is a case about *love*. And if Lawson and I hadn't been so blinded by the pursuit of money, we would have recognized it all along. But that's a mistake we still have time to rectify."

"Sentimental dreamer. You always were, Mairee." Sandra wagged an accusatory finger in Mom's face. "You mark my words, though. One of these days, it'll come back to bite you."

Mom shook her head. "Never in a million years. We could lose Boudreaux-Guidry Enterprises tomorrow, and you know what? I think I'd consider it a blessing. It's because we were more focused on business that we almost lost our dignity and our integrity. But even worse than that, we almost let ourselves lose our son, whose good opinion of us is not, I hope, forever lost, and whose forgiveness I pray we can one day deserve." With those words, she turned to face Forbes. "Because I would really like to be invited to the wedding."

Disentangling himself from Alaine, Forbes met his mother halfway and hugged her, then his father. "I love you both. You know that. And forgiveness is needed on both sides for things that have been said—or unsaid—over the past several months. But we have all the time in the world for that."

"And we would like to sit down with you and everyone here," Lawson made a sweeping gesture of the couple dozen people crowded around, "to discuss our new plans for revitalizing Moreaux Mills and assisting the current homeowners and business owners there in any way we can to save the Mills."

A chant of "Save the Mills" went through the little crowd.

Alaine joined Forbes and was instantly pulled into a jubilant hug by Mom and was then sandwiched when Dad encircled both of them in a hug. She emerged laughing.

"Anne," Mom called over Alaine's head, "we'll need to call Meredith—and Alaine's mother—and get on both of your calendars to start discussing the wedding plans. I'm thinking spring, in the gardens at Lafitte's Landing."

"Mom!" Forbes covered Alaine's ears with his hands. "Don't say things like that to her. I'm thinking we might pull a page out of Meredith's book and elope."

Alaine pulled his hands away and turned around to stand between his mom and Anne. "Not on your life. We're going to have the biggest most elaborate wedding Anne can give us—and I'm going to cover it for my program." She poked her finger into his chest. "And the only answer you're allowed to give about anything is 'yes, dear.' Because if there is one thing that is definitely *not* under your control, my love, it's me when it comes to the wedding I've been dreaming of since I was eleven years old."

Mairee laughed and pulled her into another swaying hug. "Oh, I'm going to like having you for a daughter-in-law. And we have a couple of months' lost time to make up for."

"But not today." Forbes caught Alaine's hands and drew her close again. "Tonight, I'm taking my fiancée dancing because it's what she loves to do."

"You—dancing?" Dad hooted.

"Oh, Mr. Guidry, he's a wonderful dancer."

"Yeah, Dad, I am. But it's because I have a wonderful dance partner."

"Okay, okay, it's getting a little thick out here." Mom laughed, then kissed them both on the cheek. "We'll expect you at our house for dinner Saturday night. And Forbes, we'll call your office tomorrow to set up the first Save the Mills meeting."

The Mills crowd followed his parents down the sidewalk, clamoring to have their ideas heard for how to revitalize the area.

JD kissed his daughter's cheeks and shook Forbes's hand. "Will we see you Sunday for dinner? Or maybe this week you should go to your family, since you haven't seen them for so long."

Forbes reached out and clasped his future father-in-law's shoulder. "You are my family, and we'll be there for dinner Sunday."

JD snuffled and dashed the back of his hand across his eyes. "Alaine, you'd best call your mother soon. I'll be home in about twenty minutes, and you know how she'll react if she hears all the details from me."

Alaine looked at her father, then at Forbes, then back at her father. "Wait a minute. Did you—Forbes, did you tell him. . . ? Was that why Mother wanted to talk to you?" She laughed. "I'm not just marrying a control freak, but a gentleman control freak."

They said good-bye to her father, and Forbes pulled Alaine back into his quiet, empty office. After a long kiss, Forbes went around to sit behind his desk—or at least the one he was using until he hired a secretary who'd need it, and until he got the air-conditioning vents upstairs working.

"Hey, I've thought of a slogan for your Web site." Alaine perched on the edge of his desk.

Forbes still couldn't get over the fact that he'd asked Alaine Delacroix to marry him, Forbes Guidry, the perpetual bachelor of the year. He wondered how many anniversaries they'd have to celebrate before he truly realized how blessed he truly was. "Oh, yeah? What's that? The most devastatingly handsome lawyer in Bonneterre?"

She leaned over and kissed his forehead. "No. Forbes Guidry, the lawyer who made a case for love."

Discussion Questions

1. What expectations did you have when you began reading the book? Were your expectations met? What did you like best? Were you disappointed with anything in the story?

2. Alaine Delacroix and Forbes Guidry are both "beautiful people"—the kind that are usually featured in romance novels. Was there anything about them that set them apart—that made them different that the other "beautiful people" one usually reads about in novels?

3. Forbes is a self-proclaimed control freak. Why do you think he tries to control everything going on around him? What drives him to want to be involved in the lives of his siblings to such a level they feel like he's trying to manage or dictate their lives or even their businesses?

4. Alaine feels like she gets no respect at work. How did her attitude toward the news director affect the level of respect she receives?

5. Did Alaine deserve to be considered for promotion to a news anchor position? What brought about the change in Alaine's attitude toward her position as host of Inside Bonneterre?

6. Alaine wants to use her clout with the public, as a popular TV personality, to bring attention to the situation in Moreaux Mills, but her parents refuse to let her do anything that would bring media attention to the situation. Why do you think they did that? What do you think would have happened if Alaine had turned in the story she was putting together on Boudreaux-Guidry Enterprises?

7. In *Menu for Romance*, Forbes counsels Major O'Hara to obey the command to honor his mother (by not keeping her or her condition a secret from Meredith any longer). In this book, however, Forbes seems to do just the opposite by taking a legal case against his parents and their corporation. Was Forbes breaking the fifth commandment ("Honor your father and your mother" Exodus 20:12 NASB)?

8. Both Alaine and Forbes refuse to do something their employers ask of them: Alaine refuses to give any information about the lawsuit once it becomes public, and Forbes refuses to give up the Mills case. Can you think of anything you'd be willing to stand up for against an authority figure in your life? How important would something have to be for you to risk losing your job over it?

9. Throughout the course of the story, God slowly whittles away everything that Forbes thought he had control over. When Forbes receives the ultimatum from the other partners in the law firm, he is faced with the realization that not only is he barely handling things, he has definitely lost control of most things in his life. Why was it important for God to bring Forbes to this kind of a crisis point? Has there ever been a time in your life when it seemed like God was stripping everything away from you, only to find out He wanted to give you an even greater blessing?

10. Near the end, Forbes complains to Alaine about his dislike for the uncertainty of the future. Alaine responds, "But without uncertainty, there'd be no need for faith." Do you agree with her statement? Have you ever been in a situation filled with uncertainty in which you had to rely on faith to get you through? What did you learn from that situation? What effect, if any, did it have on your relationship with God?

Kaye Dacus holds a Master of Arts in Writing Popular Fiction from Seton Hill University and is a former Vice President and longtime member of American Christian Fiction Writers. A Louisiana native, she now calls Nashville, Tennessee, home. To learn more about Kaye, visit her online at kayedacus.com.

Other Books by Kaye Dacus:

The Matchmakers series

Love Remains

The Art of Romance

Turnabout's Fair Play (coming November 2011)